FRAGMENTS OF
LIGHT

THE SPECTRUM OF MAGIC – BOOK 1

BETH HODGSON

FRAGMENTS OF LIGHT

Copyright © 2018 by Beth Hodgson

Fragments of Light is a work of fiction. Names, organizations, places and incidents portrayed in this novel are either products of the author's imagination or are used fictitiously. Any resemblance to actual, events, locales, or persons is purely coincidental.

Interior character portraits and cover art by Mansik Yang
Interior map and character illustrations by Beth Hodgson
Map cartography by Doug Turner

Edited by Crystal Watanabe

www.thespectrumofmagic.com

First edition: November 2018
ISBN: 978-1-7327130-0-0
Printed in the United States of America

In loving memory of my dear sister Karis Mae Heapy-Hughes.
(1974–2009)
May you live on in the spectrum as light orange.

ARCADIA
2384 M.E.
(MILLENNIUM ERA)

UNIMARK
BUILDING

CATHEDRAL
OF LIGHT

WESTERN
SECTOR

STAR TIDE
OCEAN

NORTHERN
SECTOR

EASTERN
SECTOR

PALACE

CITY
GATES

TO
WESTERN
WASTELANDS

THE
CORPORATION
(LAB 34)

CITY
BORDER

SOUTHERN
SECTOR

ART: BETH HODGSON
CARTOGRAPHY: D.TURNER

THE TWIN
KINGDOMS

OLYMPIA

THE
UNITED
KINGDOMS
2384 M.E.
(MILLENNIUM ERA)

ILLUMINA

WESTERN
WASTELANDS

STAR TIDE
OCEAN

ARCADIA

WORLD SECTORS 1-6
4402 P.A.
(POST APOCALYPSE)

RUINS OF W.S. 1

LANDS OF
DESOLATION

TOXIC CURRENTS

SAFELAND
HIDEOUTS

W.S. 2

MINES
OF W.S. 2

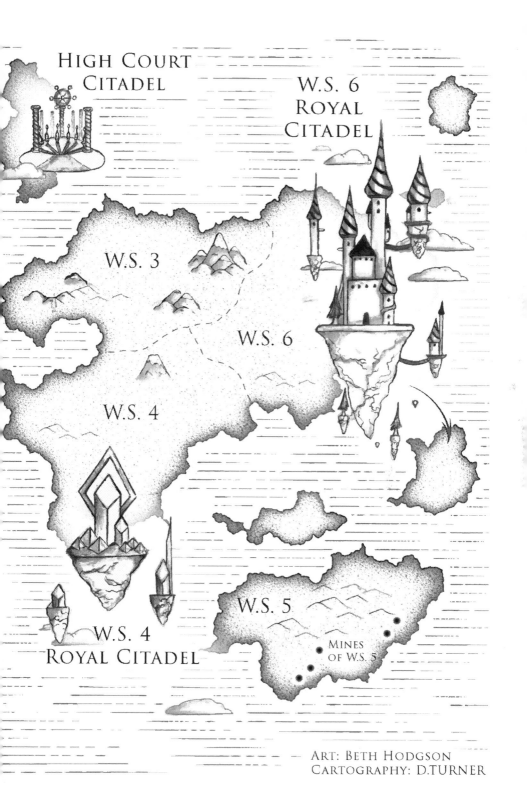

HIGH COURT
CITADEL

W.S. 6
ROYAL
CITADEL

W.S. 3

W.S. 6

W.S. 4

W.S. 4
ROYAL CITADEL

W.S. 5

MINES
OF W.S. 5

ART: BETH HODGSON
CARTOGRAPHY: D.TURNER

PROLOGUE

Geeta, where are you? What era did you run off to?

A multitude of stars and galaxies encompassed Suresh as he stood studying the countless time portals that hung in the starry sky like floating mirrors. The glowing, swirling whirlpools rippled with blue magic, mesmerizing Suresh with their magnetic power.

His green eyes wandered, taking in the beauty of the glowing paths in the space-time continuum. They were like bright pebbled tracks, scattering colored stars throughout the galaxy. No matter how much he traveled, it never got old.

Some trails were much more vibrant compared to the older ones, which had faded over time. All were colored in violets, greens, or blues. The purple and green tracks were obvious—those were his and Geeta's. But whose were the blue ones?

He didn't know how long he had been searching for Geeta throughout the flow of time, but he was sure it had been at least eight years, perhaps even nine. His straight, forest-green hair was starting to get longer than his liking, over three inches or so. The bland gray tunic he wore was now torn and in desperate need of mending, but he hadn't bothered to fix it. He had to find Geeta.

Suresh had always been one step behind Geeta, their paths never crossing. He kept up the pace, but every time he gained on her—or so he thought— Geeta happened to skip to another time or place. And now, he felt completely lost. Every path at that moment intersected and intertwined, and he could no longer tell which violet path was the most recent.

Frustrated, Suresh sat down among the paths, examining them intently. Rolling up a sleeve of his tunic, he massaged his distorted arm, pitted with scars that resembled a wild animal bite. Even though he'd healed it with his green magic years ago, he wasn't fully able to restore the broken flesh to its original state. Every so often, it burned with a tingling sensation.

Memories of that day flooded him. He never liked thinking about that day, but it was the day that he made a paramount decision, one that he'd questioned every day for the last eight years. He had consumed another gifted's blood in an attempt to aid Geeta in finding her "Ghost Man." Blue-gifted blood. And now he was cursed by the gods, as he had done the one thing that was forbidden by them.

Geeta's image on that fateful day remained crystal clear to Suresh, as clear as the day it had happened, the moment she walked into the temple that set everything in motion. Her long, cascading violet hair falling to her sides as she moved, with a red scarf gracing her head. Her golden tikka glittering in her hairline, capturing the light's essence. Her violet eyes shimmering brightly.

That image contrasted very much with the memory he had from when she unleashed her violet magic—hair wild, dress ripped, her jewelry matted in her hair, and all the while her body writhing on the temple floor from the effects of the new magic settling in her body. And her ferocious deep-violet eyes… so unforgiving. There was no one that could read Geeta's expression like Suresh could, not even her husband. And on that day, her face was masked with pure hatred, something Suresh had *never* seen in Geeta before.

Whatever vision Geeta had about the Ghost Man, Suresh knew that she wouldn't have fought with her husband, Vihaan, unless she was wholly convinced that the dream came from the gods themselves. Suresh doubted this, but he never doubted Geeta's faith in the gods.

I will never forgive you… Those had been her sharp words to her husband, the words she spoke before she consumed his blood.

Suresh shuddered at the thought, not wanting to spend any more time dwelling on the past. No sense in it.

In the corner of his eye, something caught his attention. A sudden burst of energy. A white twinkling comet streaking across the sky. It burned Suresh's retinas, causing him to squint. In the comet's illuminating tail, a new path burned with white energy, beautiful as a shooting star.

Suresh glanced at where the path ended and saw more portals far across the space-time continuum. The new set of portals caught his attention, appearing like larger stars, only these rippled with magic instead of light.

I should be looking for Geeta and her Ghost Man, he thought. But there was something different about this path. The magic within him stirred, and Suresh couldn't help himself; his curiosity got the best of him.

Following the path for some time, Suresh finally came upon the new batch of blue glowing portals. One in particular was smaller than the others, and a much lighter blue.

It appeared that the portal had been activated by someone recently. Was it Geeta? There were no violet tracks…

Pausing for a moment, Suresh studied the portal, calculating his next move. Making a decision, he boldly took a deep breath, then stepped through the magical gateway.

Galaxies dissolved, the star-speckled space melted, and a blur of bright blue magic surrounded him. The blue magic pulsated as Suresh fell through an endless glowing blue eternity. The magic flowed faster around him, swirling with a white-hot tint to the azure magic, until everything was one solid blur.

When he was about to pass out from the drop, the blue energy began to ripple and form all around him like a tidal wave over his whole body. As the magic pulled away, it started making shapes through its power. Details of a bedchamber appeared around Suresh, forming into familiar shapes, colors, and patterns. White walls came into his vision, and gold crown molding outlined the room while white-marbled floors with golden flecks appeared under his feet, capturing the brightness of day.

Suresh gathered his senses, leaning against one of the walls for support. Time travel always disagreed with him, and it always made him feel slightly woozy. He wasn't meant to travel. He was green-gifted; he was meant to bring forth life, restoring and renewing one's body. Only the blue-gifted were meant to travel, as they were masters of the time and space dimensions.

Something caught his eye, causing him to gasp in amazement. It wasn't the ornate details of the room; they were wondrous enough. No, it came from outside the window.

Peering out from the oversized glass, Suresh took in a massive city with imposing buildings that rose to the heavens, thrusting into the clouds. The city was built with machinelike metal, and glowing images scattered its skyline. Machines dotted the skies, flying to and from the buildings. Suresh had traveled into the future before, but not this far. It was truly awe-inspiring, and at the same time, terrifying.

Breaking the silence, Suresh heard a woman's soft cries from within the room.

Glancing around, Suresh immediately noticed a marbled platform, with stairs leading up to it. A huge canopy bed sat at the center of the platform. Sheer lilac curtains surrounding it wisped delicately back and forth.

Agonizing cries of pain came from behind the curtains.

Slowly, Suresh made his way up the stairs to investigate. He could see outlines behind the sheer curtains.

There lay a pregnant woman, appearing to be in her last month. She had long wavy hair the color of snow that rested delicately on the pillow, framing her pale dainty face. Her swollen belly seemed unfitting for her thin body, which was dressed in a silver silk gown.

The woman scrunched her face, crying again as tears flowed from her shut eyelids.

Suresh took a clumsy step and made a loud scuffling sound against the marbled stairs.

Startled, the woman glanced through the transparent curtains, then gracefully pulled the curtains back to have a look. She gasped, then desperately grabbed her blanket as if it were a barrier of protection between them. Her white eyes immediately focused on his, then she turned to gaze at his hair. She smiled weakly as she put down the blanket, recognizing who he truly was—gifted. She held out her hand, offering it to him.

He accepted, embracing it. As he did so, she squeezed it desperately, clearly hoping that his touch would offer some comfort. He felt the flow of magic throughout her body, like a gentle summertime wind.

"You are like me," she whispered as tears streamed down her face.

Good, he could understand her dialect. The more Suresh traveled throughout time, the more languages and dialects he began to master, but it seemed this language had become popularized over time.

Suresh nodded, inspecting her. She was gifted, just like him. But she was unlike anything he had ever seen.

She had the gift of the white.

Suresh never knew that the gift of the white existed. If anyone would know about the gift of the white, it would be him, Geeta, and the others from his era. The gods of the Spectrum bestowed gifts of color to mankind from the birth of the world, when time began on Earth. Only a few select peoples of Earth were born with the gift. The gods chose inhabitants of Earth to bless them with their powers, to be their champions.

Red, representing the elements: earth, wind, fire, and water. Orange, the gift of illusion and transmutation. Yellow, prophecy and protection. Green, the gift of restoration, renewal, life, and rebirth. Blue, space and time. And violet… Geeta's color. Force and control over mind and objects. But the gift of the white, what was that? There was no god or goddess of the white. Was it a complete accident?

The gods don't make mistakes, he told himself.

Removing himself from the woman's grip, Suresh laid his hands upon her belly. Her womb stirred as the baby inside thrived, kicking and turning. However, the woman was dying.

Gazing into the endless whites of her eyes, she told him silently what he already knew.

Holding his gaze steady on her face, Suresh focused on the life deep within his soul. His fears flooded him, haunting him as he called forth his magic. Fears of not finding Geeta, fears of this poor woman dying from complications due to the baby. Fears that the future of Earth would fade away, and it would be no more without finding the Ghost Man.

The power fed on his fear and began to surge through his body, jolting through his veins. A warm green glow appeared within his hands as he summoned the magic. His power swelled at his fingertips as he gently laid his hands on her body once more. The magic transferred to the woman's body, enrapturing her as he released the magic from his hands. His vision went dark for a moment, then an intense sweat formed over his body, causing him to shiver.

When he regained his sight, Suresh was stunned. The woman no longer had her icy hair or her pale eyes. They had both turned green, matching the vibrancy of an emerald gemstone. Suresh gasped, taking a step back. She'd somehow absorbed Suresh's magic, giving it to herself. The woman's face was revitalized, and she appeared to have no pain.

She sat up in her bed, taking notice of her newly green locks of hair, then began to weep.

"I never knew what my gift was until now," she breathed, tears filling her eyes. Wiping them away, she asked hesitantly, "Have you come to take me home?"

"Home?" Suresh looked confused, shaking his head.

With hard realization, she began to sob. "They told me they would come back for me. They promised me," she wept, wiping her tears. Locks of green hair fell in her face. Noticing the color again, her eyes expressed sheer panic. "I can't let him find out. I just can't!"

Her face hardened as she closed her eyes, and her muscles tensed along her limbs.

With a loud cry, she threw back her head, almost as if she was going to birth the child, but instead, Suresh saw all the green magic leave the woman, gathering at her belly. Then suddenly, with a white flash, the green magic was gone, and the woman's white features returned to her.

Afraid for the life of the child, Suresh urgently placed his hand on the woman's belly. The baby's heartbeat was still strong and healthy, and its blood radiated with life magic. The woman had somehow transferred the green magic to the baby.

There was a knock at the door, and the woman looked at him with alarm.

"Please, hand me that golden case over there on that nightstand," she requested, pointing to a small box.

Suresh retrieved it, then handed it over to her quickly.

"Queen Elyathi, are you quite well?" a voice called out from behind the door. "I heard a noise…"

The Queen sat up in the bed, opening the golden box. She grabbed a small pale-blue clear circle, then placed it on her right eye, then did the same to her left eye. She gazed at Suresh with the fake blue eyes.

"Please, you must leave," she begged. "The King has become obsessive with the Spectrum of Magic. He has had delusional visions, ones that should not be taken into action. And if he were to find out about you, he would surely find out about me and make those delusions reality. I can't let that happen, especially since there are those greater than he who seek my power." Elyathi waved Suresh away urgently.

"Are you going to be all right?" Suresh asked sadly, aware of her circumstances. It pained him to leave her, as it was apparent she was entangled in a great many things.

Elyathi's false blue eyes sparkled with tears. "Yes, quite sure," she said softly. "I have handled myself for many years alone, I can continue to do so."

Suresh bowed to her, then stepped away. "Goodbye..."

"Elyathi."

Suresh gave her a sad smile, then bowed to her, closing his eyes. He summoned the melancholy feeling that the Queen radiated, the emotion needed to call forth time. A deep greenish-blue flow of energy surged from his body and surrounded him, flashing with brilliance.

"Please, tell them that I am still waiting for their return," Elyathi said, her voice trembling, mixing in with the sounds of pounding on the door and muffled yells.

"My Queen, the door is locked! Please, open up!" a woman's voice yelled from behind the door.

"Who's *them*?" Suresh called out from the enrapturing green-blue magic that jolted with bright flashes of energy streaks.

"The future." Elyathi's voice echoed in his ears as the room melted away.

"...And the God of Light hurled the brilliant light of his right hand to the earth, shattering it amongst the peoples. For no person, nor any being besides the God of Light himself, should possess the Spectrum of Magic.
And thus it was so. The fragmented light split into the colors of the world. Each color chose an inhabitant of the earth, transforming them into The Gifted."
—excerpt from *The Spectrum*
Recorded by Piountus Aventus, 483 M.E.

"The creation of light is through complements, for each color yearns for its other half. For the two colors opposite can eradicate all shades of darkness."
—Indradhanush Granthon, *The Rainbow Mantras*
Recorded by Brihaspati Kaartikeya, 3182 B.E.

CHAPTER 1

Arcadia. The most technologically advanced city-kingdom in the entire region. The crowning jewel of the west.

Prince Derek held his breath, marveling as he peered out the window from inside his air transport. Far below the flying vehicle lay a vast sea of towering skyscrapers, shimmering in all their glory. The clouds that clung to the building tops drank in the colors of the city, illuminating the twilight sky in hues of blues and violets. The heart of the city held Arcadia's royal palace, the very place where Derek was heading. The glowing green gothic glass structure loomed over the city, making the other skyscrapers appear like toys. Its long turrets impaled the clouds, reaching for the evening sky. One turret was especially higher than the others, its shadowy figure rising against the full moon.

Derek's palms broke out in a cold sweat just thinking about Princess Emerald, the one who occupied that turret. The last he saw the princess was when he was twenty-one years old. Seven years had passed since then. And every day for seven years, Emerald's image burned within his mind.

What would Emerald say when she saw him? Would she be as friendly with him now as she had been in her youth?

Derek nervously toyed with his jet-black crown of loose curls, then closed one of the clasps of his cobalt tunic. It had been opened by his neck to cool him during the long transport ride, allowing him a bit of comfort. The blue brought out the color of his icy eyes in contrast to his black hair and pale skin. Since he was traveling, he didn't want to wear his large ruff collar along with his back spikes, the grand fashion he was known for.

As his transport landed, the city below slowly grew dark as the sun set off in the horizon and was replaced with an expanse of flashing neon lights in all colors of the spectrum. Stepping out of the vehicle, Derek's long black cape caught a strong gust of wind, exposing his tall stature and muscular form. The high levels of Arcadia, or any city for that matter, had strong wind currents, unlike the mid and lower levels.

The lower levels… the underbelly of the city. Thank God he never had to step foot down *there*.

Derek's eyes wandered again to the tallest turret, wondering if the princess had seen his arrival. His eyes lingered a few moments longer, then he turned his attention to the palace guards approaching him. With them was King Damaris's advisor, Councilor Emerys.

Emerys bowed, meeting Derek's entourage. "Your Highness."

"Councilor Emerys," Derek said, nodding his head in greeting.

"We were not expecting you so soon. I was told you would be visiting these parts later in the season," the advisor said, his dark eyes weary. Emerys took a small handkerchief from his embroidered gray robes, patting the sweat from his brow. Derek noticed a silver streak across the councilor's receding hairline and dark bags under his eyes. It appeared that the stress of advising Arcadia was taking a toll on Emerys's body. Derek couldn't blame the councilor—if anyone had to advise King Damaris, they would age quickly too.

"Forgive me, Councilor, that was the original plan," Derek said. "But some time opened up in my schedule to visit sooner. I hope I am not imposing. I know it didn't give you much time to prepare for my arrival."

I would have been here years ago if it weren't for my father and Damaris's falling out, Derek thought.

"Not at all," Emerys said with a small smile. "We all had thought that you would never grace our presence again, considering… the circumstances…" His voice trailed off, then he cleared his throat, leading him into the palace with Derek's entourage following suit. "However, when word came that you were to pay us a visit, many excited whispers began circulating within Arcadia's court."

"Indeed. It took much convincing of my father to make such a visit." Derek sighed flatly under his breath, disappointed Emerys didn't say more on the matter. To this day, Derek still had no idea what had happened between his father and Damaris years ago. No one seemed to know, or else if they did, no one said anything regarding the matter.

"How is His Majesty of York as of late? I have been told of many infrastructure improvements within York, along with the markets rising every day," Emerys said.

"My father is extremely well. York is in the best state it has been in during the twenty years that my father has reigned."

"Truly wonderful. And you? No wife?" Emerys inquired slyly, hinting a smile.

Derek felt his nerves trying to take over, but he pushed them aside. "Not yet, Councilor, although I do hope not to remain eligible forever," Derek joked mildly, running his fingers through his short curls.

Emerys gave a knowing look, grinning. "Rightfully so. Well, there are plenty of eligible ladies within the houses of Arcadia. Most will be in attendance this evening. The lords will be grateful to see you again as well, along with the Arcadia press, I am sure."

"What's the occasion?"

"You are fortunate to have arrived on a good night, as the King decided to throw quite a large party with the houses of Arcadia. Don't ask me why, he just happened to be in one of his rare pleasant moods the last couple of weeks. Also in attendance will be the lords from the other territories, such as Prince Xirxi of the Twin Kingdoms, Lord Varian from Olympia, and a few barons from the Second Kingdom."

"Well, I shall be happy to see familiar faces," Derek stated, flashing a nervous smile.

"Your family is much missed in this kingdom," Emerys said, pausing to glance at Derek. "It would be a great thing to reestablish the old alliance between our kingdoms."

"I, for one, would like to see that as well, Councilor," Derek said, nodding in agreement. "I hope to mend the tensions and past transgressions that took place between Arcadia and York."

Whatever transgression that is, Derek thought, annoyed.

"I know several on the Inner Council who would like to see that as well, Your Highness."

As they walked through the palace, many people recognized him and bowed as he passed by. Courtesans, lords and ladies, barons, and many of the serving staff all stood in awe of his arrival. There were gasps of excitement, thrilled whispers, and a few joyous, secretive finger points. Derek flashed the courtesans a nervous smile as he walked by, already anxious for the evening's event.

Emerys stopped at the bottom of a grand black marble staircase that curved off to the left, with multiple glass lifts framed in silver on the other side of the hall.

"Just up those stairs are the Sapphire Quarters. I think they will suit you," the councilor said with a bow. "Take all the time you need to freshen up before dinner. There are some guests that have already arrived, but the party doesn't start for another hour. Do not worry about showing up late. It will be quite the surprise for many of those attending who haven't heard the gossip about your unexpected arrival."

"Thank you, Councilor," Derek said, heading up the stairs with his personal entourage of servants and guards.

"By the way, I am sure that the princess of Arcadia will be delighted to see you. She has been quite a bit… lonely these last few years," Emerys called out. "I do hope you get a chance to converse with her." The councilor flashed him a knowing smile, then bowed, motioning for the guards to be on their way.

Turning, Derek headed up the rest of the staircase. As he was ascending, he gave himself a private smile. *Perfect*, he thought.

His personal guards led him to the Sapphire Quarters, opening the double doors and revealing the interior of the sitting room. Its walls were in deep shades of blue, with black-and-white checkered marble floors, black furniture, and silver polished accents throughout. Derek was notorious for wearing mostly blues, and he wondered if Emerys knew that fact, as it seemed highly coincidental he was being housed in this particular wing of the palace.

Walking past the sitting room, Derek entered the master bedroom. In it was a large bed adorned with azure silk sheets and twisted black posts that reached to the ceiling. It was stationed near a grand window with a sliding glass door that led to a private balcony, where there was a small garden dotted with blue and white flowers, hanging vines, and an iron-rod table and chairs.

His servants began unpacking his belongings, laying out his outfit for the evening. Derek nodded in approval at their choice, then began to undress. His servant Silas had selected a deep-blue doublet with a black fur collar and large puff sleeves accented with black stripes and silver details. For his bottom half, they chose snug black pants along with black leather boots.

"Is the jewelry still packed?" Derek asked.

"Yes, Your Highness. It will be brought up with the next set of guards." Silas bowed.

"And my back spikes? Where are those?" Derek eyed the room, starting to get impatient for the evening. "I presume that they are with the jewelry."

Silas bowed. "They are, Your Highness."

"Please send communication to the guards on the platform. I want them brought up as soon as possible. I want the back spikes and the sapphire jewelry set."

Silas bowed, then went to the next room to call for the guards. Other servants were still bringing in his belongings, setting up the room for use.

As he began to remove his traveling tunic, he unzipped the inside pocket. He reached inside, and his hands emerged with a small, velvet box. Upon opening it, his heart beat quickly as he gazed upon a large emerald ring with a platinum setting, fashioned with swirled scrollwork.

The ring was ornate and delicate, just like the princess herself. Derek gazed into the jewel's depths, its surface refracting his face on the shiny surface. Mesmerized, memories of the princess came flooding into his mind of the last day he saw her.

"*Derek…*" Emerald's voice reverberated from within. He recalled her praying in the palace chapel, surrounded by countless glimmering candles. Her bright-green eyes were smiling, inviting him to come sit with her. He'd wanted to tell her right then…

He *should* have told her. It was his chance. The perfect opportunity. All those years prior, he had been working up to that moment.

But he never did. And that was the last he saw of her. Seven years ago. Their evening had been interrupted, and he was forced to leave Arcadia in haste with his father.

Derek took one last look at the jewel as he caressed the deep-green stone with his thumb, pushing back his memories. Snapping the box shut, he turned away to get ready for the evening.

CHAPTER 2

⸎—◇————————————◇—⸎

GREEN

Life comes in all forms, and in it the lifestream flows. Deep within the depths of its green tide lies healing, restoration, rebirth, and death. For even death can give birth to new life.

—excerpt from "Chapter of the Green," *The Spectrum*
Recorded by Gaius Secundius, 2041 B.E.

Princess Emerald quickly put down her paintbrush, interrupted by the noise coming from outside her balcony. Paint splattered on her forearm as the paintbrush rolled off her art table.

Was it evening already?

Rushing out to her balcony, Emerald watched excitedly as many private air transports began to dock at the palace receiving platform, one by one. Below, she saw the outlines of the party attendees as they emerged from their transports. Lords and ladies had traveled from all over to attend tonight's feast. Emerald always loved these occasions, and she looked forward to each time her father declared such an event, as the palace hardly ever hosted such festivities.

Taking in a deep breath of the cool air, Emerald smiled, daydreaming at the thought of mingling at the party while dancing through the night and into the early hours of the morning. The wind tickled her neck while her long, wavy emerald-green hair softly flowed in the gentle breeze. She lazily rested her chin in her hands, smudging a fresh blob of paint on her dainty face. Realizing what she had done, she quickly released her pose, not wanting to get any more defiled than she already had.

From her tower, her gaze wandered from the palace platform to the city itself, teeming with life as the sun set far off in the horizon, giving the ocean nearby a deep glimmer. The citizens looked like little ants, scurrying from one building to another through the city skyways, bustling with energy. Each platform and balcony was lit up in different bright color combinations while advertisements of the city gleamed with luster. Through a parting of the cloudy atmosphere, Emerald caught a glimpse of the mid-levels. Sounds of the city could be heard, even from her balcony far above. Sounds of laughter, music, air transports, and even the occasional authorities' sirens.

What would it be like to go down there? Emerald wondered, entranced by the colors. She would give anything to have a moment away from the palace, joining in with all the citizens of Arcadia with their nightly activities. Everyone appeared so free, and she was so *not*. But it was no use lingering on the thought; her father would never allow such a thing.

Glancing at the city below one last time, Princess Emerald turned away from her balcony, retreating into her chambers.

Near the glass patio door sat her small art table with tubes of acrylic paints. Some tubes were neatly put away in color order while others were left out from her current use. The easel held her current painting, still unfinished. Emerald plopped back down in front of the orange painting, determined to finish the picture. Something about it didn't sit right with Emerald, but she couldn't figure out what it was exactly.

What is wrong with you? Emerald silently asked the painting, studying it intently. She picked up her paintbrush, then dabbed at the orange paint, layering its pigment onto the canvas.

All day Emerald had been painting a woman she'd found in one of her new magazines. The woman was fierce, with wild hair, dressed in fashions that Emerald had not seen before. The magazine picture intrigued Emerald, which made her determined to paint the woman. Everyone had a color about them, which reflected the soul of the person. By painting these pictures, Emerald explored people's personalities without meeting or having a single conversation with the person. It was like reading a book about that individual, a book that they didn't know had been written. Emerald wasn't sure if it was a natural talent or the power from her gift that enabled her to somehow figure out a person's color.

Gifted. That's what the people born of magic were called. That's what she was. Born with the power of green magic, the gift of life. Only a handful of people knew of her power: her father, her dead mother, the Inner Council, and a few servants in the palace. No one had ever seen a gifted before, not in at least a thousand years, according to ancient writings. The gifted of centuries past had all died out, and belief in the God of Light and his gifted was now no more than a myth.

People were not ready to believe in magic, she recalled her father saying. In these modern times, who would believe in such power of the God of Light? Religion was for the ancients, surely not for the present time. No, mankind put their faith in the power of science and what was tangible, not in myths or magic, and certainly not in the holy book, *The Spectrum.*

And if the world *were* to discover her true power, there would be countless attempts from the other kingdoms to capture her for the use of her magic. And for that reason alone, her father had ordered Emerald to remain in the palace, heavily guarded from the world outside, only to meet other lords, ladies, and royals that visited. Emerald could count on her fingers how many times she had been outside the palace. Four. And during those four times, her father had a swarm of guards hounding her, and they never gave her any space.

"Guess who's here?" Emerald's bedroom door swung open wildly, startling her from her painting. Glacia, Emerald's first handmaiden, burst through the door with a bright smile. She hurried over to Emerald and gave her an ecstatic shake. "You're still painting?" she asked, aghast.

"Calm down, I'm almost done." Emerald chuckled politely, waving her free hand in a dismissive gesture as she continued painting. "Who's here?"

"Prince Derek." Glacia's hazel eyes sparkled with intensity.

"Derek?" Emerald answered slowly. She paused for a moment, meeting Glacia's eyes nervously.

"Yes, Prince Derek. You know, the most handsome man ever to walk this earth? *That* Prince Derek," Glacia teased. "Now forget your picture and get ready! You have paint all over yourself!"

"Glacia, I thought Derek was supposed to visit several months from now," Emerald said, cleaning her paintbrush in a glass of water. The water swirled with orange pigment, releasing its color. Her stomach felt jumbled, knotting up as she watched the water twirl in the water jar.

"Princess, no one knows why he decided to make an early arrival." Glacia laughed. "Honestly, who cares? Now is your chance."

"Perhaps he is betrothed to another woman," Emerald stated flatly.

Glacia bent over to whisper in Emerald's ear. "Actually, the word around the palace is that he is still single." She nudged her, giving Emerald a warm, giddy smile, then flipped her soft brown hair back.

"I think I feel sick," Emerald muttered, slumping her face into her hands.

"Oh, you'll be fine."

Emerald felt suddenly nervous, and her hands started to shake. She couldn't have said it better herself. Prince Derek *was* single-handedly the most handsome man Emerald had ever known. No, he was no man, more like a sculpted statue of a god, perfect in every way. Not only was he beyond perfection, he was well mannered, charming, good natured, and slightly humorous at times. Just thinking of Derek, Emerald felt her old feelings of attraction start to resurface.

"By the way, I picked up these while I was out," Glacia stated, tossing a shopping bag on her bed.

Emerald wiped her hands free of paint, then walked over to the bag. She pulled out a couple of fashion magazines, two music albums, and hair accessories that she needed for the evening's event.

Emerald held out the albums curiously. "What's this music? Never heard of these bands."

Glacia chuckled, wiping Emerald's arm and face free of paint with a hot towel. "They are the hottest rage in the mid-levels. Even the upper levels are catching on. Just listen to them. You might actually like them."

"If you say so," Emerald answered, slipping the albums back into the bag. The thought of Derek returned to her, and instantly her nerves took over.

After Emerald finished getting cleaned up, she hastily sat down at her vanity, applying her evening makeup to her pale complexion. As she applied her eyeliner, the light freckle under her eye caught her attention. It was the only freckle she had, and it always seemed to show itself, even through her makeup. How she hated that freckle; it always seemed to get the best of her. It made her feel so self-conscious.

As Emerald powdered her face, she caught a glance of her painting in the mirror's reflection, demanding all of Emerald's focus. *Why are you so wrong?* she asked the painting in the reflection, still vexed by it. Emerald kept staring at the lines of her brushstrokes, wondering if they were the issue.

Glacia returned with a gown, breaking Emerald's concentration on the picture. She slipped on a long purple dress with puff sleeves, then adorned herself with magenta jewelry. The handmaiden combed Emerald's long wavy tresses, leaving her hair down for the evening.

Emerald glanced in the full-length mirror, inspecting herself one last time.

"There. You look perfect, Princess," Glacia declared, giving Emerald a once-over. Glacia smoothed a piece of Emerald's hair that was out of place and fixed a twisted earring. "Now, how about you manage to make the Duke of Gefroy jealous tonight by giving Prince Derek a giant smooch." Glacia laughed.

Emerald's eyes popped open widely. "Glacia!" She gave her a playful shove, then rolled her eyes. "That's not going to happen! And just so you know, I was trying to forget about the duke. He's so... *mundane.*"

"But you two looked like you were getting along *so well* at the last party," Glacia teased.

"More like I was trying to escape him," Emerald retorted.

Emerald saw a flutter of white dresses. The other handmaidens had arrived, waiting to escort her to the feast.

"Did I miss something?" Celeste, the second handmaiden, asked as she appeared.

"We were just recapping her encounter with the Duke of Gefroy," Glacia joked. The other handmaidens chuckled.

Emerald's cheeks burned. "Enough about him," she said, clearly annoyed. "Come, let's get going. I will already be late, and you all know how my father is."

Glacia bowed. "Yes, Princess, indeed I do."

"Yes, Princess," the others murmured, then turned to lead the princess out of her chambers.

For a moment, Emerald paused, looking back at the painting.

She realized her mistake. She'd used the wrong color.

The fierce woman needed to be painted in yellow. One would think she was happy and free by the looks of the picture, which would align with the color orange. But Emerald had been fooled. A gentle, quiet devotion had been hidden inside of this strong woman.

She radiated love and faithfulness.

Breathing a sigh of relief, she knew she could finally enjoy the party without giving another thought to the painting.

CHAPTER 3

"The *fuck* is wrong with you?" the tattoo artist grunted. "If you keep moving, it will look like I smeared shit all over you."

Gripping the cigarette with his mouth, Kyle took a long drag, then exhaled a stream of smoke. "Sorry, man."

He tried to review the artist's work on his right bicep through the corner of his eye, but between the amount of alcohol in his bloodstream, the smoke, and the artist's needle, Kyle couldn't see shit. Instead, all he saw was the cigarette in his mouth, the rings on his fingers at his side, the dark red walls with pitted holes, and his friend Diego, all simultaneously blurred together.

"It was about time you got that shitty yellow out of your hair," Diego commented, inspecting his freshly bleached white hair. "It looked like a dog took a piss on you."

"Thanks, asshole," Kyle remarked, taking another drag. "It doesn't fucking help with everything being so damn expensive with this new tax shit. Plus, I don't have Sonja around to bleach it anymore. She was pro at getting it white, and best of all, free."

It was about the only thing she was good at, he thought, trying to sneak another peek at the tattoo. *I dodged a bullet with that chick.*

"What are you doing after this?" Diego asked.

"Nothing, why?"

"Let's get lit at my place. I'll get the other guys to come over. It will take your mind off that crazy ass bitch." Diego took a swig of his flask, then slammed it into his hip pocket.

"I *was* trying to forget about her." Kyle sighed. He continued to puff his cigarette periodically while the tattoo needle hammered into his bicep. He was somewhat numb throughout his body, all thanks to the alcohol, and the needle felt like nothing more than someone poking him with their finger.

"Well, you were the one to bring her up."

"Whatever."

"Just fucking forget about it and get shit-faced at my place. We'll swing by the corner store and get a few forties. I'll even pay this time," Diego said.

"Naw, dude," Kyle answered as he exhaled a sizable puff of smoke, "I think I'm gonna go home. I don't feel up to it tonight. Besides, I need to practice."

"You can go home and jack off whenever you want. You haven't hung out with us in a while outside of practice and our shows. Just come over."

Kyle scowled, glaring at Diego through the smoke. "Fuck you. Can't a guy go home and be alone? I didn't know I had to service you."

"Do you fucking mind?" the artist snapped.

Kyle realized he moved.

"Won't happen again," Kyle said to the artist. Turning to Diego, Kyle pointed his free hand to him. "And no, I'm not going out tonight. I need to practice. Plus, I'm tired as shit. If it will make your ass happy, I'll come out another night."

"Fine. But if you don't come out with us in the next few nights, I'm dragging your ass out." Diego snickered, guzzling his flask.

The artist paused, turning off the tattoo machine. "See what you think."

Kyle took another drag of his cigarette, exhaling quickly. His fingerless black leather glove snatched the cigarette butt from his mouth, putting it out in the ashtray next to him. He stumbled out of the chair, looking in the dirty mirror on the adjacent wall. It looked like someone had snotted all over it, then rubbed it around for good measure. Through the dingy reflection, Kyle saw the line work was clean and precise, or so he thought; it was hard to tell for sure through his drunken eyes. The fresh black ink shot out in contrast with the complexion of his muscular arm. The skin around the newly inlaid design was deep red and slightly puffy, with the ink seeping out of the skin.

It was about time Kyle added to his tattoo; it had been a while. His black tattoo consisted of sharp, angled lines plastered on his right bicep. He had started this tattoo back when he left his home in the wastelands and came to Arcadia. Every time something major affected his life, he would add another thick black line, angled in a new direction, like a giant life maze. Big events called for long lines; small events were shorter. Kyle had always told himself once the tattoo reached his hand, he should be dead, because what fun would it be to be an old ass and unable to get around in life? As of right now, his tattoo reached two inches above his elbow. The last line he added was meeting his ex, Sonja. The line before that was from his first gig with the band. The one before was word of his mother passing away. And on and on until the beginning. This new line was because of his split with Sonja.

Damn, I'm gonna die before I hit thirty at this rate, he told himself.

He flexed his bicep, then gave himself a small, satisfying grin at the sight of his muscles protruding from his sleeveless black leather vest. His dark eyes moved to his angled chin, then to his spiky hair. His silvery-white hair was almost as light as he was, standing out against his dark eyebrows. Damn, it was a good thing he'd rebleached his hair like Diego said. He had been looking like major shit as of late.

"Looks good, man," Kyle said with a nod of approval. His attention turned to his ears, each lobe stretched with a curved black spike earplug. *Not today,* he told himself, thinking how he wanted to stretch his lobes bigger. Pulling out a few crumpled-up bills from his black leather pants, he paid the tattoo artist.

The two of them staggered out of the tattoo parlor, which was a few levels up from the street level. It was nearing dusk, and all of the street lights were already on. Kyle hopped onto a metal staircase railing, sliding down faster than he expected to. Diego followed him, both of them chuckling. The metal studs in their clothing rubbed against the railing, making a slight screeching sound. As they slid past them on their way to the bottom, passersby holding giant protest signs shot them a look of annoyance. Kyle and Diego reached the ground level, hopping off onto the sidewalk.

The street was packed with rioters. The citizens of Arcadia had gathered much earlier today, compared to the last few days. Who could blame them? The royals were taxing the fuck out of its citizens with their new tax laws, and people were pissed. Street fires were ablaze while the rioters threw bottles, trash, and other objects at the buildings, then looted them. Others were more daring, throwing objects at the Arcadia police, who blocked it all with their shields. Kyle turned his attention to a large ground vehicle on fire, its plumes of smoke blanketing the crowd.

"Damn, I forgot about the protests," Diego said, lighting another cigarette.

"Yeah, me too. Let's get to our bikes and get the hell out of here. I am gonna be really pissed if I see it on fire."

"Same here. You sure you don't wanna hang?" Diego asked as they both squeezed their way in and out of the inflamed crowds.

"Yeah, I'm sure," Kyle replied. They both made a fist, then tapped them together.

"See ya tomorrow, bro. Don't be fucking late like last time," Diego yelled at him through all of the street noise, hopping onto his motorcycle. "We want to keep our gigs with this place lined up."

"You're starting to sound like Remy."

"Asshole."

"Don't worry, I'll be there on time. Later."

Turning to his bike, Kyle climbed onto it, then started his engine. They both took off in the narrow back alley, leaving the riots to fend for themselves. Riding away from that sector's protests, they approached the next city sector. Diego turned onto a different route, leaving Kyle to ride alone. Ahead, massive gridlock of ground transports crammed the roadway, but the traffic never slowed him down. He simply wove in between the vehicles, leaving them behind to wallow in the street trash and the rank sewage stench.

Within the street puddles, Kyle could see the reflected neon signs from the shops and local strip clubs. Fog steamed from the sewers, capturing the city lights, casting the street level in a thick haze in all sorts of colors. Occasionally, Kyle's eyes would dart up at the glowing skyways above him, seeing shadows of people crossing between the buildings. The crowds of people on the sidewalks, the other biker gangs, the shitty ground transports, shitloads of trash, and the smell of piss and vomit—all worked in harmony to make the lower levels of Arcadia what they were.

This was what freedom was like. The winds beating his face while he drove through the city, free of everything. He didn't have to think, he just drove, emptying his mind of everything that pissed him off. The city itself tried to confine and keep people controlled. But not him. His motorcycle liberated him. That and his guitar.

Reaching his apartment building, Kyle turned into the underground entrance and parked his motorcycle. Pressing the parking elevator's button, Kyle lit up a cigarette while he waited. When the elevator opened, he continued to puff on his cigarette, then pushed for the thirty-sixth floor, the highest of the lower levels before one needed to pay the tax with an Arcadia Transportation-issued keycard. Fuck the tax. He didn't need to go to the damn mid-levels anyway. Those people had sticks up their asses.

When the elevator opened on his level, Kyle dropped his cigarette to the elevator's floor, rubbing the butt into the ground. Walking down the hall, he stopped at his apartment, pulling out his keys. The door across the hall opened.

Rosie…

Rosie appeared from behind her door, taking small steps that exasperated her in her old age, making it seem like she was about to crumble at any moment. Her pet rat was perched on her shoulder with its nose twitching. The thing was like a damn parrot to her, always attached to her body whenever he saw her.

Shifting his eyes to her doormat in the hallway, Kyle noticed a new celebrity gossip magazine that had been delivered. With her shriveled hand shaking to reach the tabloid, Kyle shook his head, grabbed it, and handed it to her.

"I can't believe you read this shit," Kyle stated, making sure that Rosie had a secure hold on it before he released his grip. "What's up, Zaphod?" he said to the rat, stroking its fur with one of his fingers.

"That girlfriend of yours was here earlier," she said, her voice wobbling. "She was screamin' and poundin' right outside your door. I think she had one too many drinks. I got several complaints from the other floor tenants, so I threatened to call the authorities."

God, Sonja just won't give up. She's fucking crazy. "Did you?" he asked.

The woman smiled and nodded, petting her rat, who moved to her hand. "That convinced her to take a hike. I told her that if I saw her face again, I wouldn't even give her warning."

"Sorry about that, Rosie. I don't want to see her any more than you do, believe me," Kyle said, fidgeting with the lock on his door. "I don't even have a phone anymore thanks to that woman." He continued to fuss with the lock, kicking the door while turning the key.

Rosie watched him struggle. "Do you want me to have someone fix that?"

"Don't bother. I need to give it a good kick every once in a while," Kyle muttered under his breath, finally prying the door open.

"If you say so." Turning to her magazine, Rosie giggled like a small child. "Prince Derek, rumored to be in Arcadia…" She shuffled into her apartment, closing the door behind her.

Rosie and her magazines. Who gives a crap about some damn prince? he thought as he entered his apartment and closed the door behind him.

CHAPTER 4

YELLOW

I called upon my dreams, and the gods came to me. I saw a barrier of protection, shielding me from a darkness that was on the verge of overcoming me. I cried out to the gods, afraid that I could no longer see their embrace. They did not show me their faces, but instead basked me in their pure yellow light. Within its golden rays, they whispered, "Do not be afraid, for we will protect you from all harm, and in the night, show you indescribable things that will come to pass."
—excerpt from *Akachukwu's Lost Prophecies*, 1435 M.E.

Auron took one last look of the sun's rays peering through the sky citadel window, then turned his attention to the court. There were fearful whispers all throughout the audience hall, principally among the gifted, while everyone waited anxiously for Emperor Cyrus and Empress Ayera to appear. Auron knew exactly what they were saying without hearing a single word. The mysterious magical illness had claimed another gifted's life. The second death attributed to this plague.

How many had lost their magic over the years from this epidemic? Hundreds within World Sector Six. For those who contracted the plague, all but two gifted had survived their sickness, but they had lost their gifts. There were a little over eighty or so gifted left in World Sector Six, mostly in high positions within court. All entirely made up of reds, oranges, and yellows, except one blue, Lord Kohren, and one violet, the Sorceress Ikaria.

Anxiously clutching his staff, Auron fumbled with it in his ebony hands while a warm perspiration glistened within his stubby golden hair. He was nervous for the moment, wondering what the Empress would ask of him. He didn't have an answer for her, nor had he had some god-inspired vision explaining the source of the illness. And for that, he knew there would be much disappointment within the court, particularly from the Emperor and Empress themselves, as they were desperate to rid the land of the plague that was ravaging their people. And no one would be more disappointed than himself. What kind of High Court Priest was he if the God of Light didn't grant him a vision or a prophecy regarding the magical plague and how to stop it?

Auron's golden eyes shifted to the only one in the room who didn't seem worried: the Empress's sister, the Sorceress Ikaria. If she was, she was hiding it extremely well. Violet eyes within her narrow slits remained lifeless, and it appeared her thoughts were somewhere else. Auron noticed that her violet hair wasn't done up within her headpiece like it usually was. Instead, it flowed down her back all the way to the floor like a bolt of unraveled silk, with her bangs sharply cut above her brows, making her high cheekbones, long neck, and angled jawline appear more menacing than usual. Her tall, imposing hourglass figure was squeezed into a silver outfit that was much more revealing than the last set of garments she'd worn during court. Didn't she have any sense of decency? A woman nearing forty should know better.

Auron had never trusted the sorceress. She wasn't even a true sorceress; she'd only had the title bestowed upon her by the Empress herself. Ikaria was the only one born with the gift of the violet in all of time, as there had been no accounts of any other violet in history, but she had no idea how to tap into her magic, no matter how much she studied the subject. It had been whispered that Ikaria had a secret love for evil ancient technology while outright opposing the God of Light's established High Court at every turn. And no wonder she couldn't wield her violet magic, even if she tried. It was the God of Light's retribution; he was simply not allowing such a vile person to wield his great power.

"His Majesty, High Ruler of World Sector Six, Emperor Cyrus. Her Majesty, Second Ruler of World Sector Six, Empress Ayera," the court herald announced, and all eyes turned to the hall entrance. The doors opened, and the whole court audience bowed as the royal couple appeared.

Emperor Cyrus came first. He donned a long, flowing white robe trimmed with gold and a thick golden belt fastened around his waist. Atop his soft brown curly hair sat a golden circlet with pearls.

Walking behind her husband, the Empress Ayera came into view. She was very much like a younger version of Ikaria, but a much softer, smaller, and shorter version. She was dressed in fashions from the sisters' homeland: a white kimono embroidered with golden flowers along the hemline and around her neck. Her obi was made of gold satin, just like her husband's belt, but instead of being plain like Cyrus's, hers was heavily beaded. On top of her delicate head rested three triangle hair combs fashioned into a crown. Attached to the back of her head was a golden ring, which encircled her head like in one of the ancient celestial paintings. The Emperor and Empress each carried a golden scepter, signaling their position of authority.

As the two walked down the center aisle to assume their thrones, Ayera's midnight-black hair trailed behind her, flowing like a river as it kissed the floors. Her bangs were not cut like her sister Ikaria's, but one could argue for either sister on who had the longer hair. Her dark, narrow eyes had a hint of worry behind them as they passed by.

They seated themselves on their thrones, then the Emperor waved his scepter in greeting. Court was now in session.

"Duke Sansall, is it true what has been said about Lord Valamir?" the Emperor said sternly. "Did the sweat claim his life? I want a full report on this matter. And why was I not told of this incident sooner?"

The duke came forward, then bowed. "My utmost apologies, Your Majesty. Lord Valamir was discovered this morning by one of the citadel's gardeners."

"*Did* he have the sweating sickness?" the Emperor demanded. "Has the plague now spread to our inner courts?"

The duke nodded, his face grave. "Yes, Your Majesty, it appears so. Upon discovery, Lord Valamir's clothes had been loosened by his neckline, the first indication of the sweat. There are a few witness accounts that confirm that Lord Valamir exited the theater during the performance. They claimed he looked overheated."

"Did anyone else exit the theater?" the Empress interjected. "Perhaps this could be more than the sweat?"

"Unlikely," the duke replied. "No one else left, and there were no indications of foul play, Empress. It appears that Lord Valamir's sweat became intense, as his clothes were completely soaked through, even his doublet. And by all accounts about how we found him, he must have been hallucinating. His body was badly bruised from a fall off one of the garden benches and the... disfiguring of his body... There was blood on his own fingernails." The duke sighed, pausing. "I must say that, just like in Lord Valamir's case, it is almost exactly like the death of the orange-gifted, the Lady Yasmin, from weeks ago." He paused again.

"Well, go on," the Emperor urged.

"Lord Valamir's magic hadn't disappeared, just like in the case of Lady Yasmin. Both Lord Valamir and Lady Yasmin contracted the plague, no doubt, as the sweat was one of the symptoms. And just like the Lady Yasmin, his magic was intact, as we saw the red power of his life force within his eyes. And there's the fact that they both succumbed to death, whereas all the other gifted survived the magic leaving them."

There was silence over the court. Everyone held their breath, including Auron.

"Perhaps this is not an illness at all," Ayera countered. "Perhaps we should view these as suicides. You said yourself Lady Yasmin was quite out of her mind when she contracted the illness. It was known that she begged for her lover within the ramblings of her madness weeks before the disease took her."

"Under normal circumstances, I would agree with you. However, I can tell you in full confidence that Lord Valamir and Lady Yasmin were victims of this plague. It is the same illness, as both of these gifteds' deaths have the same attributes of the magical plague—the sweating, strong signs of hallucinations... It's enough for them to be not in their right minds to inflict terrible pain upon themselves. I have talked with the court priests, and they think the disease has mutated into a darker magic, causing a kind of possession somehow."

Ikaria belted out a loud laugh, and it echoed over the court. "Somehow?" she parroted the duke's words. Every eye in the room went straight to her. She elegantly placed the back of her hand over her mouth softly, then quieted herself with the small sound of clearing her throat.

"Excuse me, Duke Sansall, for questioning you." Ikaria stepped forward, swaying her hips. "But how would you, or the priests, shall I say, even begin to fathom that the disease mutated *somehow*? What supports your claim? A few priests spouting off their manufactured opinions? They don't have the gift of the green, therefore they would not be able to begin to understand any disease, earthly or magical."

The duke turned red, holding back his anger.

"Do they, Duke Sansall?" Ikaria asked pointedly.

Auron was about to step forward to defend his priestly brothers and sisters, but the Empress waved her scepter in a sweeping gesture.

"Enough, Ikaria!" Ayera ordered.

Ikaria whipped around to face her sister and the Emperor. "This is why we need technology," she said strongly, narrowing her eyes on Ayera, then addressing the court. "We need hard science, the science of old! How will speculation help us? We, as a society, have gone too long with just speculation. Look what our ignorance is doing to us! Taking away our power. And now, it is killing us."

Ikaria stared down everyone in the court, then paused at Ayera before continuing. "We still have many artifacts that have not been turned over to the High Court. We could study them before handing them over. Perhaps one of these might have an answer to what we are looking for stored within its data, endless knowledge of medicines or other cures."

There were murmurs in the court hall, some in agreement with the sorceress, others opposing such an idea.

Ayera clenched her armrests, annoyed. Ever since Ikaria had been appointed court sorceress, she had brought up the same argument at *least* once a year. Only each time, she was much more clever going about it than the last.

"What you are suggesting is against the law, and *heresy*," Ayera said sternly. "You, as well as everyone else here, know that we will not break our pact with the High Court in regard to technology. We would have the other five sectors, along with the High Court, at war with us if we chose to do so." Ayera snapped her head in the direction where the other world-sector diplomats were sitting. "Isn't that right, Lady Zara?" she asked, singling the older woman out.

The woman bowed, lowering her eyes. "Quite right, Your Majesty."

Ikaria didn't move, looking directly at her sister. "I don't think you understand. We don't have power of green magic, a magic that can truly heal and restore one's body. Really, what can the power of red elemental magic do against this? Nothing. And the power of orange's illusion and transmutation?

Nothing. Or yellow's prophecy?" she asked, freezing in her spot. Ikaria glanced right at Auron, her eyes seething with hatred for him. "Nothing. Absolutely nothing! And the blue... peering into the past would produce answers, but it is outlawed by the High Court! How is it heresy to better our lives by finding cures with the use of the old technology?"

Wild whispers erupted all around Auron, echoing throughout the court. Many gasped while others whispered the word "heresy." Indeed, what Ikaria had said was heresy.

Emperor Cyrus bolted up, shooting Ikaria an irritated glare. "Silence!" Cyrus boomed.

Instantly, the court went still, and all Auron could hear was the sound of the Emperor's echoes. "By what you are saying, you mock the High Court and every other world sector!"

Ikaria tilted her head upward in pride, unmoved by the Emperor's words. "No, Your Majesty," she said, her violet eyes flashing, "I am not *mocking* the other world sectors or the High Court. I am merely suggesting that we renegotiate our treaty with the other world sectors. Or even ask the High Court to reconsider their position on the ancient ways. If this disease is proving to be fatal, such as it has been reported, we need other means for us to survive." Ikaria gave the Emperor a hard stare with her haughty eyes. "I don't know about you, Your Majesty, but *I*, for one, like living."

Then, in a sarcastic tone, Ikaria hissed, "Oh, I forgot." She raised her hands in a sweeping gesture. "The illness only affects the gifted. You wouldn't know the fear that we are facing."

A half smirk appeared on her face, and Cyrus gritted his teeth. "Oh, but I do, *Sorceress*," Cyrus sneered. "I fear losing my whole damn court. Some of those gifted are our guards, while others are in important positions. Without them, we would have no enchanted objects, or even our citadel. Need I remind you how this is affecting us all? Or perhaps your thinking has already become too muddled with your fancies about ancient technology!"

Ikaria was about to counter the Emperor, but Ayera rose from her seat, interrupting. "I will not renegotiate our treaty with the other sectors like you suggest, sister. And I'm certainly not going to ask the High Court to reconsider their position regarding technology unless I wish to welcome a death wish for myself and the rest of World Sector Six.

"And furthermore, if they had heard you utter such heresy from your lips, they would have had you imprisoned or excommunicated to work the toxic earth below!" Ayera stood on her platform, narrowing her eyes at her sister. "Do you wish to bring calamity to our sector by the use of technology and end up how the ancients did? Because what you are suggesting is just asking for another apocalypse!"

"Sister, you misunderstand me. I am only trying to give sound reason within this court. I would never dream of defying the High Court." Ikaria bowed to her sister. "I am suggesting that we send an envoy to the High Court and the other world sectors to raise arguments against the laws in place, in hopes that new laws could be temporarily written to aid us in these dire times. It is hard to imagine that using small amounts of technology could bring on world destruction."

Cyrus seated himself, slamming his hand into the throne's armrest. "No one asked for your opinion, Sorceress."

Ikaria glared at Cyrus. "It is my duty as court *enchantress* to be studied on all forms of magics. And if it is known that this magic is beyond our ability to control, I am forced to advise an alternative. Forgive me, Your Majesty. I didn't realize my opinion was not needed."

"Most of the time your opinions are not needed," Cyrus reiterated. "I don't seem to recall ever summoning you to speak in front of the Empress." His eyes peered at Ikaria with a smug look upon his face. "I had thought you were appointed to speak on the subject of magic, not about the lost art of science. Perhaps, instead of being so enthralled with ancient science, you should learn to tap into your violet power and be of some use to us!"

His words "use to us" echoed through the halls. Everyone in the court went wide eyed. Cyrus had finally said the unspoken truth. Even Auron couldn't believe it.

Auron saw Ikaria holding back her tongue while her narrow eyes lowered to the floor. Her jaw clenched, but otherwise, she made no other movement. "Yes, Your Majesty," she said, spitting the words out of her mouth as if they were poison. Without losing composure, she gave Cyrus a hard stare, then bowed, taking her place off to the side of the court once again.

"Does anyone feel the same as our court sorceress?" He looked all around at the stunned faces. No one spoke; no one dared to defy the Emperor. The halls remained silent. "That's what I thought." Cyrus looked over at Auron, casting an invisible net over him with his stare. "High Priest Auron, please proceed."

The moment that Auron was dreading had finally come. Cyrus was not in the best of moods, not now that Ikaria had set a sour tone.

"What say you? Do you have insight to this matter?" Cyrus barked at him. He threw himself back into his throne, letting the back of the fabric embrace him.

I have nothing to tell him, Auron thought.

Rubbing his chin with his jeweled fingers, Cyrus continued. "Well?"

"Your Majesty, I have been meditating on the matter daily, praying fervently for an answer," Auron started.

"And?" Cyrus asked eagerly.

Auron bowed. "I am sorry to report, Your Majesty, that I have had no visions regarding the disease. The same is true with the other yellow-gifted."

"So, in other words, nothing. We are losing more of our gifted every day. *Every day.* Pretty soon, we will have no gifted left in our sector."

Cyrus's eyes simmered; Ayera's face was downcast. Ikaria glanced in Auron's direction, giving him a subtle smirk only he could see. Even with her exchange with the Emperor, she had still won the fight against Auron and was gloating in her achievement. She was hellbent on him being miserable. After all, Auron was the one who'd had the vision prophesying who would sit on the throne after their father's reign. Ikaria blamed both him and the High Court for losing her right to be in the line of succession. Who she should be blaming was herself. Maybe if she truly had faith in the God of Light, she would have been placed on the throne.

"Auron, please continue to pray," the Empress said, breaking the awkward silence. "I know that we cannot rush the God of Light. I only hope he answers us before the plague takes all of our gifted's magic, or their lives. Our very survival depends on our magic. Without it, our way of life will be destroyed," she said sadly. Turning to address the court with her head held high, she added, "And the same goes to all of the rest of you. I need any and all reports as quickly as possible when the next person is infected."

The members of the court bowed at her order in unison.

"Empress, might I say one thing?" Auron asked.

All eyes were on him. Whenever he was about to speak, every eye was always on him. They were all afraid if he had a vision that it would prophesy their sins, because most all of the pious peoples were gluttons for worldly desires of the flesh. He had nothing of the sort *this* time.

"You may speak."

"I can say for certainty, as High Priest of the God of Light, that if we even begin to dabble with the use of machines and technology, as the sorceress suggested, it will bring on our destruction, just like it did two thousand years ago in the Millennium Era. The God of Light has *no* room for the proud and arrogant peoples that put their faith in the machines. And as to his testament, he obliterated the most advanced world sector, hurling toxic meteors from his heavens to our earth as punishment. The whole earth had to pay for the sins of one world sector. We cannot break our pact again, otherwise others will have to suffer for our sins."

"I agree with you wholeheartedly, Auron," the Empress said, nodding in acknowledgment. "We must learn from our mistakes." Ayera side-eyed her sister, glaring. "And that is why we must continue to follow in the faith, not in man's ideals."

Ikaria narrowed her eyes at her sister as Auron bowed and returned to his spot.

"Duke Wellington, please come forth," Ayera's voice ordered.

A large graying man stepped in front of the Empress. "Yes, Your Majesty?"

"I need you to assemble our gifted into teams, then rotate them into shifts. When the next word comes around of another infected, I want us to be ready." The man bowed. "First priority is the yellow on that team. The infected need every bit of prayer that they can get. Have them cast as many spells of protection on the infected. Reds, I need you to soothe their pains with your ice and water. As far as the oranges, they need to stay behind in the citadel. Unfortunately, their power cannot help these matters. If we can't stop the sweat from taking their magic, perhaps we can stop them from hurting themselves, or dying at the very least."

Duke Wellington bowed deeply to the Empress. "Yes, Your Majesty. I will notify you immediately when any of our teams are dispatched."

"Thank you, Duke," said the Emperor.

"Lord Kohren," the Empress called out.

A man appeared before Empress Ayera. He had the same facial features as the sisters. His bright blue irises shone through his slits, and his straight, waist-long, water-blue hair was swept to one side of his shoulders. His robe was sky blue, embroidered with silver designs.

"Your Majesty." He bowed. "How can I be of service?"

"I need you to read any and all manuscripts regarding illnesses, notably ones mentioning magical ailments and plagues. There must be some record in Earth's history of what happened in prior centuries. I need to know if you come across anything worth reporting."

Ikaria flashed her sister a look of protest, but her body remained still.

Kohren bowed. "Yes, Your Majesty. Right away."

"If you do happen across something of interest, I will request an audience with the High Court. With enough evidence, they might grant you permission to scry time. There has to be some event that has happened in the past that mirrors our current situation. History often repeats itself."

Lord Kohren bowed, then stepped back into place.

As court was dismissed, Auron headed through the crowded hall, slowly making his way to the exit. Over his shoulder, he saw Ikaria's pale violet eyes staring in his direction.

Then a sneer appeared on her face.

Auron sighed quietly, then shook his head as he turned away. He knew that even at that very moment, Ikaria was calculating her next move against him.

Some people never change.

Even if the God of Light intervened, Auron wasn't sure if Ikaria could change. Her heart was too far gone, consumed and corrupted by the darkness.

CHAPTER 5

GREEN

When Emerald arrived at the main hall with her entourage, the feast was in full swing. The electronic orchestra filled the hall with its upbeat music, while many of Arcadia's lords, ladies, and businesspeople were dancing, socializing, and starting on the first course.

For the event, the black marbled hall was decorated with banners of green and silver, the king's colors. The twisted pillars that lined all sides of the room were streamed with forest-green banners that featured Damaris's house insignia, a sword and staff crossing an emerald in the center. Behind the giant columns were candlelit dinner tables and chairs for the guests to sup. Crystal chandeliers hung from the ceiling in increments throughout the room, with richly embroidered jade fabrics streaming from one to another. White light shone through the crystals of the chandeliers, creating soft prisms throughout the room.

The herald noticed Emerald immediately, bowing to her. He was about to announce her to the guests, but the princess held her hand up, shaking her head.

"Please, there is no need," Emerald said quickly, smiling at him. "I don't want the photographers to come running."

The herald smiled, bowing. "Yes, Princess."

Emerald took a deep breath. "Here goes nothing," she muttered, then submersed herself among the crowd on the main floor, her handmaidens following closely behind.

Emerald skimmed the crowds, hoping to spot Derek amongst them, but the floor was incredibly packed. She saw Prince Xirxi of the Twin Kingdoms, who was engaged in a heated conversation with Lord Ryland of Arcadia's Eastern Sector. Prince Xirxi had been one of the many suitors that had asked for Emerald's hand in marriage, only to be rejected by her father. She had no personal feelings for the prince, but he always seemed like he would make a fine companion in life.

Glacia calmly leaned into Emerald. "I don't see him, Princess," she whispered.

"Who?"

"Prince Derek, of course."

"Why are you so obsessed with finding him?" Emerald asked sharply, still holding a smile for the guests as they walked by.

"Because I know you are looking for him. I was just trying to help," Glacia said nonchalantly, sounding slightly defensive. She bowed as important figures strode by.

Under her breath, Emerald laughed. "Sometimes I hate you because you know exactly what I am thinking."

"How many years have I served you, Princess?"

"Too many," Emerald answered. Lowering her voice, she stated, "Perhaps the prince is toward the back of the hall or still upstairs in his quarters."

"I'll keep my eyes open for him," Glacia whispered, her gaze wandering throughout the crowd.

A server walked by, offering a goblet of wine. She gracefully accepted the glass, drinking the bitter liquid carefully, not wanting to spill it on her dress. She turned to Glacia and her other handmaidens. "Go enjoy the party. I need to make my rounds."

They smiled happily. "Yes, Princess."

The handmaidens bowed, then wandered off to a group of male servants from the palace, all except Glacia, who paused for a second. "Good luck, Princess," Glacia said, giving Emerald a small wink before joining the others. Emerald smiled to herself as she saw Celeste flirting with one of the servants. The servant was seemingly enraptured by her presence.

Good for her, Emerald thought. *At least someone will have a pleasant evening.*

Without warning, Emerald heard the snapping sounds of the photographers' cameras. She let out a small groan, then flashed her best smile, pausing for the cameras. The partygoers, realizing that their princess had arrived, stopped their conversations and bowed, talking amongst themselves. No doubt it was about her ensemble for the evening. They all then resumed their activities as she walked by.

After finishing up a few photos, Emerald observed several of her father's Inner Council talking amongst themselves. Emerys, who was among them, saw her glancing in his direction. He gave a slight nod of his head, then a quick half smile, continuing his conversation with Councilor Lysander. Emerald hinted a smile back, turning away.

"Princess Emerald," an even voice called out from behind.

Startled, Emerald glanced behind her. There he stood, more gorgeous than she remembered.

Towering over her, Derek's muscular build was well suited in a blue regalia, while his ice-blue eyes shimmered in the light, framed by dark lashes. Within his black curls rested a silver and sapphire circlet. He revealed a solid handsome grin, accentuating his angular features.

Emerald's heart stopped.

"Derek?" Emerald exclaimed, more breathlessly than she would have liked to let on. It couldn't be helped; he had caught her completely off guard.

He took her hand and kissed it gently. Emerald's body jittered with nerves, and it took everything to not show it. Derek gave a deep bow, his back spikes thrusting into the air behind him. As he rose upright, his grand black ruff fanned out behind his head, his deep-blue satin cape swept to the floor. Everything about him was tidy and precise, even down to each curl on his head. He was the epitome of perfection itself. The thought made her melt.

"I thought you were going to walk by and not even say hello to an old friend," he said, smiling and leaning into her.

Emerald couldn't help but notice how close Derek was, and it made her blush. "I just might have if you hadn't said something," she managed to say as her heart raced in her chest.

"Well, then, it's a good thing I spoke up." He chuckled.

"I can't believe you are here. I knew you were planning on visiting later in the season, but then I got word that you arrived this evening."

Derek gave her a bright smile. "I *was* to come later," he admitted, "but I was able to get out of this season's engagements a bit early. Besides, my father's court doesn't need me all the time."

He offered his arm, which Emerald happily accepted. His doublet's fabric was soft to the touch, and as she drew closer, she became acutely aware of the prince's light scent of cedar.

"What's your agenda while you are here? Will you be staying awhile?"

Derek led her to the royal table, then pulled out the chair reserved for her. Smiling, Emerald seated herself as he pushed it back in for her. "It all depends if business works out in my favor," he said. A server came by to fill his glass as he sat down next to Emerald. He took a drink of his wine, continuing. "Sometimes it takes longer than planned." His eyes reflected the candlelight from the tables.

"Oh, and what business is this you speak of?" Emerald laughed, biting her lip nervously.

Derek looked at her, smiling. "That, Princess, is a secret. But hopefully it won't stay a secret for too long."

"Secret? You can tell me, Derek. I'll keep it safe," Emerald joked mildly, taking a drink of her wine.

"I know you would," he replied in an amused tone, a small smile forming.

Emerald could tell Derek was not going to say anything further on the matter and decided not to press him. She instantly felt silly for her poor attempt at her bold statement.

Derek raised his chalice to meet hers, then took a drink with his eyes locked on hers. She felt her cheeks flush, unsure of what to say. She tried to act to casual while drinking her wine, but she was doing a poor job of it.

"Well, I hope your visit isn't short. It has been too long since we have seen each other," Emerald said.

"It really has," he agreed. He gave her another smile, then his gaze turned to his glass. "Seven years is far too long. Don't you agree?"

Her heart pounded through her chest, and a gush of nerves mixed with excitement hit her all at once. *Is he visiting because of me?* The happy thought caused her to beam brightly at him.

A server came by, providing them with the evening's main course. Derek didn't start on his dinner but continued drinking his wine.

"So, tell me, Princess, what have you been up to all these years since we last saw each other?" he inquired. "I have seen you in some fashion ads in magazines and online with Arcadia's businesses, but you do your best to stay out of the media's eye for the most part." He leaned into her, lowering his voice slightly. "Or dare I say that it has something to do with your father?" He gave her a knowing look.

Emerald sighed. Derek had always been aware of how irrational her father acted, and it had been an old habit of his years ago to inform her of this awareness during every visit.

"Unfortunately, that has not changed since you last saw me, Derek," she explained. "And as far as the fashion shoots, I am not that good at them. The photographers need to give me a lot of direction, and I just feel... well, uncomfortable being the center of attention."

"From what I have seen, you seem to do a fine job at it."

Emerald laughed, swirling her goblet, then taking a drink. "You are much too kind. If you ever saw me in action, you would understand." Emerald thought for a moment about her last shoot. It had taken twice as long as usual for Haze to get the poses he wanted from her.

"Are you still painting? You were always so good at it."

"Yes, I am. Every day. It is the only true activity that lets my mind escape these walls," Emerald said quietly, letting out a soft sigh. "And you? What is the *Prince of York* up to these days? I have seen online that you have been the subject of all the presses. Much work within your court, I see. Also, you attend almost every gala and party within York's nearby kingdoms."

Derek looked amused. "Princess, the press has embellished my life to the point that nothing they say is true," he said dismissively. "As far as the work within York's court, that is true. But I rarely attend the galas unless my father demands it of me."

"The press does have a way of redecorating the truth."

"More like bending reality." His eyes lit up, then they both laughed.

A server came by and filled their goblets with more wine. He glanced at her in the candlelight intently, drinking her in with his eyes. Embarrassed, Emerald felt her cheeks burn once again, but otherwise she remained calm.

He lifted his glass to her. "Let's toast."

"Okay. What shall we toast to?"

"How about to... rekindling our friendship." He held up his glass, waiting for hers to meet his.

Emerald returned the favor, clinking her goblet to his. "To rekindling our friendship."

They both took a drink and smiled at each other.

Right then, Emerald felt an annoying tap on her shoulder.

Turning her head, Emerald found Haze, the palace photographer, standing over her with his tan skin glowing as his mouth curved into a smile. He looked tamer than usual, but that wasn't saying much. His short silver hair was slicked back, with dark eye makeup and silver lips accenting his face. His silver jacket had large puffed sleeves embellished with black-and-white striped patterns. Yes, this was one of his "dressed down" days.

He held out his hand. "Princess, Princess…" He shook his head. "How dare you not dance with me yet this late into the evening?" His smiling dark eyes told her *shame on you.*

She laughed back at him. "I didn't realize that I had to make my evening all about you," Emerald said playfully, rolling her eyes. "Not feeling so well this evening, Haze?" Emerald eyed his flashy outfit, then gave him a joking smile. Derek raised an eyebrow.

"Believe me, Princess, you don't want to hear about it," Haze commented. "I believe you owe me a dance this evening."

Derek eyed Haze with a hard stare. Emerald wasn't sure if what the prince was thinking was good or bad, but it was definitely about Haze. Emerald turned to Derek. "Will you excuse me for a moment?"

Derek's face held firm, but then he nodded, taking a drink of his wine. "Sure. Don't keep me waiting too long."

Believe me, Derek, that is not the plan.

Emerald and Haze walked to where others were dancing. They bowed to each other, then started dancing with everyone else. Emerald spotted Haze's date off to the side of the onlookers. He gave Emerald a slight nod in approval, then wandered off into the crowd.

"How's Troy?" Emerald asked, referring to Haze's partner.

"He's fine. A bit over the top lately, if you ask me."

"Oh? How so?"

"You know how I am. I like to go out with friends. He doesn't. The usual."

"I see."

"Don't you worry your pretty little head about me," he said, swiftly turning her as they danced. Haze leaned in. "So, tell me how this evening is going? Are you having a smashing time with Prince Derek?"

Emerald followed Haze's lead. "Yes, I am, actually. I haven't seen him in years and am very happy to see him."

"Fabulous. I didn't think you needed to be rescued from his conversation, but I had to find out what is happening between you two. You know, the whole *room* is talking about it." He laughed as he swayed her.

Emerald joined in with his laughter, giggling at this news. "Oh, they are?"

"Well, why wouldn't they? You both are not betrothed and are spending almost the whole entire evening together. It makes for great gossip."

"I suppose it does." Emerald smiled at the thought of everyone talking about them. The image of her and Derek together made her beam stupidly.

"He is watching us," Haze whispered in her ear. Emerald's cheeks began to burn, then as she was about to turn in Derek's direction, Haze warned, "Don't look at him!" He pulled her body back in his direction, laughing. "Then he will know we are talking about him. Besides, it's good to let him stew over there."

"Haze, that's not very nice," Emerald said playfully. "Besides, what if I want to make all the rumors become true? I can't keep him waiting too long."

"Oh, don't worry. He'll wait for you," Haze said.

"How can you tell?" Emerald's heart began to pound in her body.

Haze held her close, finishing the dance between them. "I just can," he said with a wink.

***

Derek stood next to a pillar with his arms folded, watching Emerald with the eccentric man. He had vacated his dinner spot just to see her dance. Her long emerald-green waves flowed against her body as she moved with her dance partner.

Jealousy filled him as he soaked in the visual image of the silvery man dancing close to Emerald. They smiled and exchanged words. What were they talking about, Derek wondered.

Derek began to curse himself for not asking Emerald to dance with him first. *She is loved within the kingdom. I can't expect to take up all of her time at the party,* he thought. *I must ask her to dance before it gets late and she decides to retire.*

After eyeing every movement between Emerald and the man, Derek heard a scuffle of boots next to him. Out of the corner of his eye, Derek saw a deep-jade tunic embellished with silver and glittering with emeralds.

Damaris!

Derek turned quickly to find the King standing in his company, taking a sip of wine. The King didn't bother to glance at him but instead focused on the source of his attention—Emerald.

"Your Majesty," Derek said, immediately bowing. "I apologize for not requesting an audience with you when I arrived, but I was told that you were preoccupied, as the evening engagement had already begun."

Damaris continued to gaze at the dance floor, not giving Derek the attention he had hoped for. His long silky blond hair softly rippled as he drank his wine, and his pale-green eyes continued to stare at his daughter.

"Prince Derek. What brings you to Arcadia after all these years?" He paused, maintaining a smug look on his face. "Wait, there is no need to answer. I presume you are here to woo my daughter," Damaris said indifferently.

Derek was a bit taken aback by the King's statement, trying to think how to best respond. He kept formulating sentences in his head, but the words weren't coming out of his mouth.

"Well, am I correct?"

"Indeed, Your Majesty," he said, fumbling with his words. "If it had been up to me, I would have come sooner to court your daughter. Seven years sooner."

"I am sure your father had good intentions by you not doing so, given what happened between us," the King said. He abruptly turned to Derek, focusing on him with his striking green eyes. "Did you know the friendship between me and your father goes all the way back to our childhood?" There was no movement from Damaris's body; not even the fabric of his cape swayed.

"Yes, Your Majesty. That is why I came in hopes that you would... perhaps think of me as a favorable suitor for your daughter," Derek answered.

"I cannot let Emerald go so easily," Damaris replied. With his body still frozen, he gave a menacing stare, then lifted his wine glass to his lips, taking a long drink.

"Name your price."

Damaris laughed. It was a laugh that made Derek uncomfortable, as if he were the brunt of a joke.

"Did I say something amusing?"

"Yes, quite so. I have known your father a long time. For me to ask for anything, as you stated, he would want something in return. Much more than a bride for you. Correct me if I am wrong."

Derek frowned, looking down into his own glass of wine, nodding. "Yes, you are correct. My father doesn't give his generosity so freely."

"You see, I like ruling. Emerald is worth far more than a normal princess dowry. And if your father would be able to afford such a price, he would insist that Arcadia be his for how much he would pay for my daughter."

It will not be easy to win Damaris over, even if Emerald were smitten, he recalled his father telling him before he left. *Damaris is a hard man. Always has been, always will be. You must make more friends within the council in order to persuade the King, as he has a personal vendetta against York...*

Derek took a deep breath, thinking of Emerald. Emboldened by the King's pushback, Derek took another step closer, lowering his voice. "Your Majesty, forgive me for being so forward, but I thought that I could bring much favor to you and your kingdom. I have heard that your kingdom is in need of more financial help. Much more than it needed seven years ago. Some would say that Arcadia is on the brink of financial ruin. The kingdom of York is willing to level out *all* debts that yours has racked up, restoring the crown's credit. In return, I would only ask for the Princess Emerald's hand in marriage. My father would ask that you continue to govern Arcadia under an alliance between Arcadia and York."

Derek took a drink of his wine and pressed on. "I'd say that is more than a fair offer, considering your kingdom is about to collapse, and on a colossal scale like no other city-kingdom has before."

"Of course, he would grant me comforts during my last days living," the King said with a mocking tone.

"Sire, with your kingdom being on the brink of a financial devastation, would it not be better to restore it and live out your days in glory rather than shame?" Derek asked. "You would still be able to rule Arcadia!"

"The answer is no. You cannot marry my daughter."

"You would ruin a whole kingdom just to spite my family?"

"Indeed, I would." Damaris's words stung him, though the coldness on his face hurt more. "Go back to York, and marry another princess. You cannot *afford* Emerald. Whatever offer you make me, I highly doubt I would accept. Arcadia is *mine*."

Derek's heart sank. He couldn't leave without Emerald. He'd known his trip would be difficult, but not to this extent.

Damn Damaris!

Derek's eyes flared up, but he kept his poise. He bowed, then stated firmly, "That is not an option, Your Majesty. I would do anything for Emerald. *Anything*."

"Anything, you say? The only way I would agree to your marriage is if the kingdom of York graciously restores Arcadia's debt, Arcadia remains mine, and I remain *king*. Your father would have absolutely no ties, nor any control of Arcadia, and there would be no alliance. And even then, after you marry my daughter, she stays here in Arcadia, at the palace."

Derek stood stunned at the King's mockery. Damaris was insane. "You know my father would never agree to that."

"How badly do you want my daughter? You told me you would do anything for her." Damaris's sharp eyes flickered back.

He is serious. No wonder every suitor left Arcadia empty-handed. No kingdom would agree to those terms.

Damaris gave him a smile, knowing exactly what Derek was thinking. He took another drink of his wine.

"I give you one week. If you cannot make an acceptable offer within that time, you will leave and never return to Arcadia ever again."

Derek's stomach dropped. *One week*, Derek thought? He had better make every day count while he was in Arcadia. He bowed to Damaris, his eyes lowered. "Your Majesty, I will be in contact day and night with my kingdom to prepare an offer. One that will hopefully be pleasing to you."

"Good. I look forward to most favorable negotiations that will satisfy Arcadia," the King said. He didn't look at Derek, instead he walked off into the crowd, his guards trailing behind him.

Derek leaned up against the pillar, finishing his wine.

Father will never agree to his demands, he thought. *I must speak to the others in the council as soon as I can. Maybe they can reason with Damaris.*

The server came back, filling his empty glass. He watched Emerald dance. *Tonight is about Emerald. Tomorrow, I will start with the council.*

Finishing his wine in haste, he set his goblet down on a nearby table, then boldly walked out to the dance floor.

***

As the orchestra finished up the next song, Haze bowed to Emerald while she returned the favor with a curtsy. Haze's face gave Emerald a "there is someone behind you" glance. As she peeked over her shoulder, she saw Derek shadowing her. When their eyes met, he gave a polite bow to them both.

"I am so sorry to interrupt you two, but I was hoping to ask the princess for the next dance." Derek smiled at her with his pale eyes, then flashed Haze a forceful stare.

"Certainly, I would be delighted," Emerald replied, exchanging looks with Haze.

A smirk appeared upon Haze's face. Haze bowed to them both, grandly waving his jeweled fingers. "Have fun," he told Emerald, turning away into the crowd.

Derek took Emerald's hand in his as his other hand wrapped firmly around her waist, pulling her close. His intoxicating scent lingered once again, making her blood temperature rise, tickling her senses.

"Should I be jealous?" Derek questioned jokingly as they began to dance.

"Haze?" Emerald asked, blushing. "No, Derek. He's not like that." She faced him again after he spun her slowly, giving him a faint smile. "You have nothing to worry about."

"Good. I don't like competition."

"Oh? Is that so?" Emerald said playfully. "Are you saying that you are competing for my affection?" She realized it was the wine talking and not what she would say truly, but it didn't matter. She wanted to make Derek perfectly aware of her flirtations.

Derek laughed at her suggestion. "Would it bother you if I were?" He tightened his hold around her waist, drawing her close to his face.

The two paused for a moment, looking at each other while the room continued to dance. Her heart leapt through her chest, making it impossible for her to remember to breathe.

In her enraptured state, all Emerald could do was remain breathless. There had been no other man she had ever wanted like Derek. All these years, she had thoughts of him, fantasized about him coming to Arcadia for her. Never did she ever think it would actually happen. It was like she had stepped into one of her dreams, and she never wanted to leave.

Gathering her senses, she smiled shyly at Derek. "No, it wouldn't. In fact... I would quite encourage it," Emerald stated softly.

Derek answered her back with a bright smile, pulling her closer as they continued to dance. Emerald saw from the corner of her eyes photographers taking photos of them, their cameras flashing continuously. By morning, all of Arcadia would know about her dancing with the prince, and no doubt many of the articles would speculate a possible betrothal. And for good reason. The prince and princess dancing together, both still eligible for marriage. That story would fuel the media for quite a while. The flashes continued, and more photographers kept coming.

With each flash, Emerald became more and more dizzy. The wine was hitting her very hard and very suddenly.

Derek noticed, leading Emerald off the floor while shooing away the photographers in the process. "Are you okay?"

"I've had too much wine. I should retire for the evening before I make a fool of myself or possibly black out."

Derek put his arm around her. "There is no possible way that you could make a fool of yourself," he assured her. "Come, let me escort you to your quarters."

"Are you sure? I do have my handmaidens to escort me."

"I was actually just making an excuse to see you just a bit longer before the night was over," he confessed with a smile. "Feel free to play along."

Emerald flushed. She scolded herself in her mind for suggesting she was such a weakling. "Well, then, please, by all means."

Derek led Emerald through the hall, supporting her weight with his arm around her while she tried to focus on each step. The floor began to swirl, and faces became a blur. All the while, she felt Derek's strength leading her out of the main hall and into the depths of the palace. Splotches of white entered her vision, and she felt a tugging at her fabric as Derek picked her up into his arms. Derek's hard body was warm and inviting. And strong. So strong.

Emerald smiled to herself as he continued to carry her through the hall of blurs; the only thing she could see was the pattern on his sleeve. Emerald buried her face in his tunic, letting the moment sink into her memory.

What seemed like only seconds later, they had arrived at her quarters. Derek put her down carefully as a white blur, who only could be one of her handmaidens, retreated inside to prep the room for her, giving Emerald her privacy.

Emerald looked into his intense eyes, the only thing that remained clear in her blurry state. She leaned back against the frame of the door, giving him a wanting look.

"When will I see you again?"

Derek leaned into her. Her body began to throb as he took her hand and kissed it with a hot breath, then placed it against his chest. "Tomorrow morning, if that would please you," he said smoothly, reaching for a lock of her long wavy green hair and lightly brushing it aside. The very touch gave her a warm flutter inside, her heart quickening.

"Yes, it would," Emerald answered, giving him a delicate smile. "Very much so."

A moment of hesitation appeared on Derek's face. His icy eyes shone as he gazed upon hers in silence. Was he going to kiss her? How she hoped that he would.

"Good night, Emerald," he said as he bowed to her.

Her body trembled while she tried to contain her excitement. "Good night, Derek," Emerald murmured dreamily, the smile still on her face.

He kissed her hand one last time. His lips lingered above her hand where he had kissed it, then he gave Emerald a soft smile. After a brief moment, he retreated down the hall, his deep-blue cape swaying gently behind him.

She watched Derek until he had disappeared into the darkness. After he was out of sight, Emerald slid her back down the frame of the doorway, then gently rested her head against the wall with a pleased sigh.

She had no idea how she'd manage to fall asleep.

CHAPTER 6

VIOLET

The heavens shook from the aftershocks of the red and stirred from the sadness of the blues. Out of their depths formed a new color: violet. It was so intense, so beautiful. More beautiful than I had ever seen. The color took a hold of my mind, and I was lost in its intensity. The more I lost my mind, the more I lost my body. I then had no control over my being, and instead, the color consumed my consciousness. I became a slave to the color. It controlled me and made me do things that it wanted.

—excerpt from Saint Helen's writings, 2671 B.E.

Enchantress Ikaria," Suri interrupted gently, nodding her delicate neck ever so slightly. "You have been summoned by the Empress to meet with her in the council chambers."

Ikaria finished her spellbinding enchantment on the metal circlet before her, wafting her violet magic away as the energy slowly diminished. The onyx crown emitted a deep-violet radiance, the jewel glowing a dark radiant purple.

Turning her attention away from the enchanted object, Ikaria eyed her servant. "Do you know if the Emperor will be present?" Ikaria inquired. Her eyes lowered to her fingers, ensuring none of her lacquered amethyst nails had a chip.

Suri shook her head. No movement came from her black hair, only the jingling of her bronze hair ornaments and the rustling of her simple yellow yukata. "No, Enchantress. I believe it will only be the Empress."

"Excellent. I don't feel up to dealing with *His* Majesty today," Ikaria jeered.

Looking back at her newly enchanted object, she cracked a satisfactory smile. Ikaria had experimented with several objects, successfully enchanting them with her newfound orange magic mixed with her existing violet power. To add the power of control into enchanted objects excited her. No one in the history of mankind had ever done such a thing, and she was the first and only one to do so. All thanks to the Lady Yasmin's blood.

"What do you think of this, Suri?" Ikaria asked, holding the circlet up for her servant to see.

"Impressive, Enchantress."

"It is, isn't it?" Ikaria flashed a wicked grin. "There are times that I even impress myself."

Ikaria set down the circlet on the empty throne next to her. It was an ornate chair, designed with swirls that intertwined with silver and a deep-purple velvet padding. She was seated in an identical matching throne, near her enchanted firepit. The chairs were an early engagement gift, courtesy of Cyrus himself. That was when *she* was to ascend the throne, before she lost her place as heir. Whenever Ikaria sat upon the chairs, it made her hate the Emperor and the High Court all the more. But instead of burning them, as she wanted to do every day, she vowed with every living breath that it would be Cyrus's execution chair when she became Empress.

Suri stood frozen in front of her for a moment. Her orange eyes met Ikaria's, giving off a slight twinkle. "Also, Enchantress, there was another… technological artifact found on the surface. I saw one of the commanding officers from the surface workforce deliver it to the citadel's gates about an hour ago." Suri's pink lips hinted a smile, but no other emotion appeared on her face.

Ikaria stretched out her body within the confines of the throne, grinning. "Does the Emperor know about this delivery yet?" She got out of her chair, smoothing her skirt fabrics.

"No. Only the two guards on duty. I believe they were to deliver it to Lord Nyko." Suri's eyes locked onto hers. "I have everything arranged in our favor."

"Thank you, Suri." Ikaria flashed a wicked smile and gingerly brushed her hand against Suri's smooth face. Suri blushed the moment Ikaria's fingertips touched her lips. "You always know how to brighten my day," Ikaria whispered, then waved her hand to dismiss Suri.

"Enchantress." Suri bowed, sucking in her breath. "It is always a pleasure to serve the true and rightful heir. And I have none other than you to thank for my... gift. It is very invigorating."

Ikaria laughed, thinking about her own body, raging with more power and passion now with the addition of the orange and red magic. She was sure Suri's body had felt the same when she drank from the Lady Yasmin. If Ikaria could compare the two colors that she'd consumed, orange was far more sensual and erotic than red.

"My dear Suri, you are so loyal, much more than anyone who has ever served me. I just wanted to show you my gratitude for assisting me with Lady Yasmin and Lord Valamir. I looked rather beautiful that night. Or should I say *you* did?" Ikaria laughed, swiping her hair off her shoulder. "I love illusion magic. And to think that Lord Valamir thought he had everyone fooled at court. What a sorry excuse for a High Court spy. His blood was quite delectable, wouldn't you agree?"

"Yes, quite so, Enchantress."

Ikaria glanced at Suri, revealing a faint smile. "If you continue to be loyal, I can promise you the power of my violet blood. Besides, someone has to fill the enchantress position once I am Empress. Please continue to use your new power with discretion, as we would hate to give away your newfound identity. Especially around the other orange-gifted. We don't want people to start asking questions."

Suri smiled softly, her eyes in reverence of Ikaria. "I will. Thank you, Enchantress," Suri murmured, bowing deeply.

"And Suri, do expect that we will have company in my chambers this evening. I have my eye on that new servant of the Emperor's."

"Yes, Enchantress."

Ikaria gave herself a private smile, delighted at what was to come that evening. How she loved blond men. They looked *nothing* like the Emperor.

Walking over to her full-length mirror, Ikaria checked her lipstick, which had faded from drinking her morning wine. Reapplying her violet cream, she posed for her reflection seductively. *I still look better than most of the court women combined.* She flirted with her reflection one last time with a devious smile, then walked out of her chambers.

When Ikaria arrived at the council chambers, she found Ayera sitting at the small glass table, dressed in a red kimono trimmed with gold. Her hair was fixed up in a large ornate half bun with many hair accessories woven throughout. Ayera's dark eyes fixated on Ikaria as she walked across the room.

Ikaria sensed her sister's thoughts. A knowing feeling came over her, one that told her that her sister did not suspect her involvement in Lord Valamir's demise. Satisfied, Ikaria seated herself at the table.

"What's this all about?" Ikaria said casually. A servant came by, offering Ikaria a drink, which she happily accepted. Ikaria glanced at her sister, noting her glass remained empty. "No drink, sister?"

Ayera ignored her question. "So I hear you have changed your title to court enchantress."

"Sorceress had such a negative connotation, don't you agree? We wouldn't want everyone to get the wrong idea about me."

"They already do, sister."

"Yes, yes. I am the *cursed* gifted. The one who can't use her power. Thank you for reminding me," Ikaria sneered, taking another drink. *How long must I keep up this damn charade?* "Did you really summon me here to chat about my change of title? Because if so, I can think of twenty better things to do with my time."

"I am assigning you to study with Lord Kohren. I have already informed the guards stationed at the citadel's main library to give you access to all necessary documents."

Oh, this is going to get good...

Ikaria smacked her lips, tasting the bitter wine, then relaxed in a comfortable position. "Sister, I was under the impression that my input isn't needed. In fact, I believe, your husband told me so," Ikaria replied in a cynical tone. How she hated him.

"I don't care what he said. We both know that you are known for your studious skills, and in truth, would be better off doing the research instead of Kohren. As much as I like the man, he is taking too much time and coming up with no results." Ayera paused, then eyed her. "Our sector needs you. I cannot afford to lose any more gifted, whether it be their power or their lives."

Sneering behind the drink of her cup, Ikaria shrugged. "Truthfully, sister, why should I help you? I have every reason to hate you."

Ayera's face softened. "It's not my fault, sister. I didn't want to marry him. It was Father's wish."

"You mean the High Court's wish."

"I had no choice," Ayera said, sounding flustered. "Must we continue to fight over this? Can we please put this aside for the good of our sector?"

Ikaria huffed, narrowing her eyes at Ayera. She was such a peacemaker; it made it even harder for Ikaria to hate her. She was right. It wasn't her fault. It was the High Court's fault. Always.

Ikaria swirled her goblet in a circular motion lazily, taking a deep drink of her wine.

A chance to prove how wrong Ayera is about the damn High Court is worth studying with that boorish loser. And the fact that he is blue-gifted... I couldn't have asked for anything more perfect.

From the moment of the first incident of the magical illness reported years ago, Ikaria knew the High Court was somehow behind the magical plague. It was remarkably coincidental that the gifted losing their magic were secretly in favor of technology in their sector, and were her father's old supporters. Now that magic was disappearing at a more rapid pace, it was almost consuming those who had no opinion on the matter. Ikaria suspected that the High Court was removing any and all who would oppose them.

They were plotting to take her magic away. They had to be, seeing as she was the only violet in the world. She'd been a threat to them years ago when she was to assume to the throne, and she was a threat to them now. She had what they couldn't possess. Ikaria could see right through them, and the High Court knew it. They had planted many High Court spies within Ayera's court, and Ikaria was simply weeding them out one by one as retribution for them taking away her throne. Her sister just happened to be an innocent bystander in their whole plot.

It was true, Ikaria was to blame for those two unfortunate gifted—Lady Yasmin and Lord Valamir—losing their lives. But it was justified, as those two were vehemently in support of the High Court's laws and undercover spies. If Ikaria were to crush the High Court after she completed the Spectrum of Magic, it would be on the blood of the High Court's pious champions. Their magical blood contributing to her ultimate power.

After a long moment of silence in the chamber, Ikaria said, "Have it your way, sister. I will help you. Although, when I find out the source of this illness, will you be willing to hear the truth?"

Ayera's eyes narrowed, and she leaned in. "What do you mean?"

"You know damn well what I *mean*," Ikaria said. She stood up, adjusting her top so her breasts fit back in place, then smoothed her hair. Flashing her best smile, she stated, "Now if you will excuse me."

"Do not go down that path, Ikaria," Ayera said. "You will only stir up trouble if you do."

Ikaria turned her head, glancing over her shoulder. "Perhaps. But either way, I promise I will find the cause."

"Please stick strictly to your orders. I know you have much fascination for the ancient ways. We cannot afford to lose any more time."

"I will try not to get sidetracked, sister, but there are no guarantees." Ikaria bowed, heading for the door.

"Three weeks. I want to see results by then," Ayera called out, still seated at the table. "And please, do not disclose this to the Emperor. He would be furious if he found out that I am assigning you to this task."

Ikaria's mouth curved into a frown. "Believe me, sister, I have nothing to say to him."

"Thank you. And do try not to quarrel with Lord Kohren. He is the only blue in our sector."

And soon to be mine.

"Only if he deserves it. You know I cannot tolerate jabs against my... lack of abilities," Ikaria said pointedly.

"I mean it."

"Yes, Your *Majesty.*"

As the doors opened for Ikaria to exit, Auron appeared before her in the doorway. His golden eyes met her violet ones, giving each other a hard stare.

"Sorceress," Auron acknowledged with a nod.

"It's *Enchantress,*" Ikaria snapped. She loathed reminding Auron, as she knew he was among those who made fun of her "lack of power." It was almost like a curse word. Soon they would realize how truly powerful she was. All in good time.

Auron's cumbersome body walked past her, then he turned his head. "The position is court sorceress, as I recall."

"Well, I changed it. I think you must be suffering from some sort of memory failure," Ikaria retorted, walking away from him before he could get another word in. That damn priest always got under her skin. *He will regret being on the wrong side*, she told herself, trying to calm her anger.

Ikaria made her way through the sky citadel's maze of hallways and corridors. From the royal audience chamber, the main library was on the top level of the citadel, somewhat near her quarters. Many staircases and corridors had to be traveled to get to the higher levels. The main level had the court halls, audience chambers, shop quarters, the royal theater, gardens, and housing for some of the commoners who could afford to live within the royal sky citadel. The higher levels were for all of the wealthier citizens, a good portion of the World Sector Six guards, courtesans, lords, ladies, and of course, any and all of World Sector Six's gifted.

It was required that all gifted of the sector be housed within the royal sky citadel, whether they wanted to or not. It was their duty, in case the Emperor needed them for any reason. All other citizens of World Sector Six were housed in other floating citadels scattered throughout the territory. Only prisoners were sent to work on the surface. It was a death sentence, brought on by inhaling the noxious fumes, and it was anything but quick. The only people who knew how to survive the surface were earth-dwellers and prison enforcers, able to live in their structures for months at a time if needed.

Ikaria vowed that someday she would visit Earth's grounds for herself. Throughout her rigorous studies, she was always looking for an answer on how to best restore the earth to its natural state, a dream she'd had since childhood. And the only answer she had ever found was through the gift of the green. A power that was most desired, next to only hers.

Ikaria arrived at the library. The guards on duty opened the door for her, then bowed their heads. "Sorceress," they said.

Ikaria gritted her teeth. As much as she wanted to correct them, she was much more excited to dig through the citadel's historical documents and didn't want to waste her breath on some lowly guards.

Stepping inside, Ikaria took in the scents of the stale books, scrolls, and papers. It had been at least a year or so since she had set foot in the library. Only those with the Emperor or Empress's permission gained access, which forced Ikaria to study in the lesser libraries within the citadel. The documents stored within this library were extremely rare and valuable.

The library gleamed with intense white light, like the inside of a crystal. The white walls rose high above her, shelved with many books, scrolls, and papers, all categorized by eras. The ceiling was pure glass, allowing the sun to shine its rays into the room, lighting it like the daytime sky. There were rows of bookshelves with glass tables down the main center aisle, along with enchanted lamps radiating a warm orange glow. Kohren sat toward the back of the library, the second to the last table, engrossed in a scroll laid out in front of him.

As Ikaria approached Kohren, he made no movement, not aware of her presence. Ikaria plopped down in a chair across from him, sliding the scroll that he was reading away from him, then placed it in front of her.

Kohren flashed her an annoyed glance. "What are you doing here?" he asked, reaching for his scroll.

Ikaria slid the scroll further away from him, fixing her eyes on his elegant visage. "Apparently my sister is impatient. You are taking too long finding the answers she requires."

Kohren's face darkened, but otherwise he made no movement. "What she requests is nearly impossible. There are so many documents within here, it would require at least a team of us to read through this whole room in the time frame she requires."

"I agree. Luckily for you, I am the most learned of the court. I have ideas of where to look." Ikaria put her feet up on the table, crossing one leg over the other. The slits in her skirt opened, baring most of the skin on her legs, causing the fabric to fall to one side. Kohren eyed her naked legs, unaffected, reaching for the scroll in Ikaria's grasp. Leaning back, Ikaria began read the scroll he so much desired.

Kohren's water-blue eyes had disbelief written all over them. "No doubt you are quite skilled in the art of study, but I am reluctant to believe that you have an idea where to look."

"Really? Is that so?" Ikaria said. "What documents have you read from the Millennium Era?"

"None. Why would I? There was no magic during that period."

"I daresay you are quite wrong," Ikaria said.

Kohren narrowed his eyes. "What makes you so sure?"

"Only that if you had read historical documents, ones that the High Court deems inaccurate, you would find when the rebirth of magic surfaced. That, my lord, happened sometime in the Millennium Era. That means there is magic during that time that needs to be studied. Perhaps there is an account of a plague but having the opposite effect."

Kohren shook his head. "So you are going off false accounts? Everyone knows that the birth of magic happened *after* the Apocalypse, not prior. It is a wonder you are still appointed court sorceress."

Inflamed at his dismissive behavior, Ikaria threw the scroll back at him, smacking him in the face. Leaning in to him, Ikaria sneered. "Need I remind you that *you* are failing at your job? I daresay you would be much more brilliant in your thinking if you would read all historical accounts, not just ones that the High Court stamps with their mark of approval. Unless you have personally scried that time and can give me a full account, I will be looking through the Millennium Era documents. Now, are you going to continue to insult me, or are you going to work with me? I have no problem giving a full report to my sister. Which will it be, Lord Kohren?"

Kohren's face remained frozen except for his eyes, which flashed with annoyance. In a smooth voice, he said, "I think it's best not to argue over the details if we are to work together."

"Excellent," Ikaria said, then sat herself back down again. "I quite agree. You may continue to search through the Post-Apocalypse documents, and I will focus on the Millennium Era documents, possibly the Beginning Era."

Pausing for a moment, Kohren nodded, clutching his scroll. "Good plan."

"Thank you. It's about time someone acknowledged my skills," Ikaria said coldly. "Now, let's have some wine and get started." She flashed him a fake smile.

"I don't drink. It clouds my mind."

"I daresay, you should try it, my lord. It makes you much more creative in your thinking," Ikaria said smoothly.

"No, I am fine," Kohren said firmly, sweeping his long blue hair over one shoulder. He immediately shifted his focus to the words of the scroll in front of him.

"If you insist," Ikaria huffed, wandering off down one of the side aisles. "Why is everyone in this sector so dull?" she said loudly enough for Kohren to hear a few tables away.

Deep within her consciousness, Ikaria summoned her violet magic. Her power was a shade darker violet than before—a result of her red blood consumption. The same thing had happened when she consumed Lady Yasmin's orange blood.

Magic seeped out of her mind, reaching out and mildly brushing Kohren's thoughts without leaving any of her mind's fingerprints behind.

A crooked smile appeared on her face as her violet eyes narrowed. *Just what I thought. We have another roach in our sector.*

Ikaria then disappeared into the depths of the bookshelves.

CHAPTER 7

GREEN

The fragrant scent of lilacs filled Emerald's nose as she awoke to the morning dawn. The sun's pale pink light painted a warm glow over her bedroom, replacing the dark mood with a lighter, more hopeful feeling. Everything looked different since her last night with Derek.

Emerald sat up in bed, immediately noticing a bouquet of lilacs sitting on her nightstand. Her heart began to pound in her chest, wondering if it was Prince Derek who had sent them. Smiling, she selected a lilac from the vase, sniffing the soft fragrance of the flower. Purple had always been her favorite color.

"Rise and shine, Princess," Glacia said in a chipper voice as she came in with a pitcher of water, setting it down on her nightstand next to the bouquet. Her eyes looked a bit tired, but with her wild white eyeshadow and deep rouge lips, the handmaiden looked well put together for having so little sleep.

"Glacia, who are these from?" Emerald asked, smelling the lilac one last time before inserting the flower back into the vase.

"Who do you think sent them?" Glacia giggled, wandering off into Emerald's closet and rummaging through the clothing. "How did you sleep?" she called out.

Emerald smiled. "Hardly." An image of Derek entered her mind: the moment he kissed her hand. The image she'd had in her mind all night long. She gazed dreamily at the lilacs Derek had sent her. "When were the flowers sent up? Did you bring them in?"

"They came sometime in the middle of the night. I waited until you were asleep to set them up. Which, by the way, took you *forever*. I was literally up all night, no thanks to you."

Emerald laughed. "It's not my fault that the prince sent me flowers."

"Yes, it is. Completely your fault." Glacia appeared from the closet with several dresses in her hands. She held up each garment one at a time for Emerald. A sea-foam green, a white, and a soft pink. "Which one do you think?" Glacia inquired.

Emerald glanced back at the lilacs, then turned back to Glacia. "I would like to wear something in light purple. Please fetch me what I have in that color."

Glacia beamed and chuckled softly. "Sure." Glacia quickly went back inside the closet and returned, holding a sheer lavender dress. "Princess, you must wear this. It's perfect."

And perfect it was. The lavender dress hugged her from her chest to her hips, then flowed to the floor. The bodice was secured by a silver choker with a large purple stone in the center. There were strings of pearls secured to the front and back of her bodice, which laid the delicate strands of beads across her bare shoulders. Emerald selected a matching silver circlet and earrings, both adorned with purple gems. Glacia combed Emerald's green locks, letting them flow softly down her back when she was finished.

By the time they arrived at the platform that housed the palace gardens, the morning fog over the city had begun to dissipate, allowing Emerald to see the ocean that was distant on the horizon. The morning air was perfect, cool, and refreshing. The gardens had many exotic flowers, trees, and shrubs from all over the world, perfectly manicured, permeating with delightful scents of all kinds. Freestanding stone pillars stood tall and proud with crawling vines decorated with assorted blooms.

She spotted Derek seated at a table at the far end of the patio, drinking what appeared to be his morning coffee. He was dressed in a light-blue jerkin adorned with silver. The image of him looking out into Arcadia's expanse was a picture in and of itself. Everything was at peace. Him, the city, and the gardens all melted in a bask of golden colors from the sun's rays. The transports that streamed across the sky twinkled as their metal reflected the warm light. She noted to herself that this very picture would be her next painting.

As Emerald walked through the gardens on its stone walkways, Derek turned in her direction. His sapphire amulet flashed in the sunlight as he moved, along with his silver rings and an ear cuff fastened on his left ear. The light of the day captured the depths of his icy blue eyes, instantly searching hers, watching her every move. As she approached him, her heart began to race.

Emerald extended her hand, and he bowed, gently touched hers and giving it a soft kiss. Peering with his captivating eyes, he greeted her with a warm smile.

"Good morning, Princess." He took her hand and escorted her to the table, then seated her and himself.

Emerald nodded from her seat, returning his smile. "Good morning, Derek." Nervously, Emerald continued. "I received your flowers this morning. Thank you. They were quite lovely." Her cheeks burned as she smiled at him sheepishly.

"You are welcome. I wanted to be the first thing on your mind this morning," he said, letting out a small laugh. "Did it work?"

Emerald started in on her coffee. "I am not telling."

Amused, he cracked a smile, then took a sip of his own. "I will take that as a yes."

"How did you sleep? I hope your quarters are suitable."

"They are quite remarkable. But as far as sleep, I must admit someone robbed me of it."

Inside Emerald was screaming with excitement, and it took every ounce of her energy not to show it. "You flatter me," Emerald jested, waving at him dismissively.

"That is no flattery," he said, laughing and flashing her a dashing smile. "By the way, I didn't get a chance to compliment you on your hair color. The last time I saw you, you still had your natural color."

"Thank you, Derek. It took my father some convincing, but in the end, he finally approved. I thought it would be fitting for my namesake," Emerald said, swallowing her lie. Derek never knew her secret, nor her true hair color. The last time he saw her she was seventeen, still hiding it under an auburn wig. Emerald had used wigs until her coming of age at eighteen.

"It looks rather beautiful on you. I would even say that it looks more fitting on you than your natural color," Derek said, admiring her locks.

What would Derek think if he knew that she was gifted? The thought always crossed her mind. They had been close growing up, but would he be accepting?

Best not to tell him, Emerald decided. *I don't want him to think I'm out of my mind. He might not even believe me anyway.*

Wanting to avoid any more conversation about her hair color, Emerald changed the subject. "What are your plans today? Business meetings throughout the day?"

He paused for a moment, his eyes piercing hers, then continued. "Emerald, do you know why I came to Arcadia?"

"I don't know, Derek," Emerald answered quietly. "As I recall, you were evading the subject last night."

He held out his hand across the table, waiting for hers to meet his. Emerald eyed his open palm, then slowly rested her small hand in his. Her hand looked so miniature against his with him being so grand in stature. He closed his hand around hers, and she suppressed a tremble of excitement.

"I can't hide under the pretense that I came here on business." Derek paused, taking a deep breath. "I came here for you."

Emerald's blood was pumping hard through her body as her nerves began to get the best of her. "You did?" Emerald asked slowly.

"Does that please you?" he asked, leaning forward in anticipation of what she would say next.

Emerald let out a small laugh in disbelief. She gripped his hand firmly. "Yes, it does."

Derek let out a sigh of relief. He still held his strong posture, but the tension melted away from his face. A smile appeared in its place. "Your words please me, Princess. I have waited for this day for many years." He got up from his seat, then moved toward her, getting on one knee. He reached inside his jerkin, pulling out a small box.

Emerald's heart skipped a beat, her body trembling. She gasped as he opened the box, revealing a beautiful emerald ring, the stone cut into an elegant elongated gem. Emerald gasped, covering her hands over her mouth lightly as tears of disbelief formed in her eyes while her heart stopped.

His blue eyes met hers, as clear as the daytime sky. "I had intended for this to be your engagement ring. However, with the many challenges that I have come to face—your father, mainly—it might not be official for some time yet."

Emerald tried to find words, but nothing came.

"Think of it as a promise ring, leading to our engagement." Derek smiled, grasping her hand. "Emerald, I can't fare through this week of negotiations without knowing how you feel about me."

"Yes." Emerald laughed faintly, repeating her answer. "Yes. There is nothing more that I want than to be with you." She held her breath in, then laughed once again as happy tears began rolling down her cheeks. Seeing Derek's piercing eyes gave her hope for the first time in her life.

Derek took her hand, then slipped the emerald ring on her finger. As soon as he secured it, Emerald leapt out of her chair and into his arms, embracing him. Before she knew it, his lips were locked onto hers in a deep kiss. Melting in his strong arms, Emerald kissed him back fervently. His soft lips felt delightful to hers, causing a stir in her that she had never known.

It was the first time they had ever kissed, let alone shown any sort of affection toward each other. There was a longing that was released within her, a passion ignited that had been holding her back all these years. It was almost surreal; they had grown up together, felt the same for each other for years, and now their feelings were out in the open. She no longer had to be reserved and guard her affections. It felt so good to feel so free.

As their lips parted, Derek squeezed her hand one last time, kissing her newly acquired ring. He smiled at her, helping her back into her seat, then returned to his.

Emerald wore a giddy smile upon her face, as it was impossible to hide her joy. Then her thoughts turned to her father. Derek mentioned her father being an obstacle. A sinking feeling came over her.

"Derek. You spoke to my father regarding our betrothal?"

Derek hesitated for a moment. "We had an… *exchange* last night. He had guessed right away of my true intentions in coming to Arcadia, and I told him of my affections for you, and the prospect of marriage. He proposed unreasonable terms for your hand. Terms that no kingdom would ever agree to." Derek eyed Emerald, then took a sip of his coffee. "Princess, when I said your father was going to be a challenge, that was putting it mildly. It will take intense negotiations on York's behalf for our betrothal."

Derek's words suddenly made her succumb to reality. Her father had rejected every offer of marriage from the other kingdoms, and it seemed this would be no different.

"Derek, if I might ask, what were the terms my father put forth?"

"To pay off your kingdom's outstanding debts. And for us to stay here in Arcadia, living in the palace under him, while Arcadia remains under his ownership. Your father seems to not want to give up his crown, nor ruling, even if it were to his own daughter."

Emerald sat in her seat, stunned. "What debts do you speak of?"

"You don't know?"

Emerald shook her head. She had never heard of any debts the crown owed, no conversations, no whispers from within the palace.

Derek looked at her intently. "Emerald, Arcadia is on the brink of financial collapse. Over the years, Damaris has run up so much debt that your kingdom is billions of dollars in the red. Many other kingdoms, my kingdom included, as well as the world banks, have eased Arcadia's financial grievances with loans. Your father has never paid the world banks back, and the kingdom of York has not seen a cent from your father."

He paused, an uneasy look on his face. "No one knows what he is spending his money on. And now, he is right back in his same predicament, only worse. No bank or kingdom is willing to settle the debts, unless someone buys out Arcadia, allowing Arcadia to have a new ruler. Your father has been so desperate for money that he passed the new tax laws across all levels of Arcadia to squeeze any money he could get from the people. Emerald, people are taking to the streets in rebellion."

Derek's words sunk into her. "Rebellion?"

"Haven't you seen the street levels on the broadcasts?"

"No. I haven't seen a single broadcast on the subject."

Derek frowned, then lowered his voice slightly. "Figures," he muttered. "Damaris must be censoring what is actually happening within the city so as not to frighten the palace."

"Derek, please," Emerald pleaded, lowering her voice to match his. "What is happening to Arcadia?"

"The mid to lower levels are in chaos right now. The last few days, people have been looting, rioting, burning, and destroying the city. Even the upper levels are worried, though they dare not express their opinions to the council or the King. Their money is in the stock markets. Arcadia's trade has plummeted daily, and many have lost a fortune."

"I don't believe this."

"It's true, Princess. This could stop with financial relief from my kingdom. I had hoped your father would allow me to marry you in exchange for leveling all of Arcadia's debts, restoring peace and financial stability within the kingdom." He looked down. "Apparently I was wrong."

Emerald sat there in silence, contemplating. "I must speak with him and convince him to accept your proposal."

"Believe me, I will do everything within my power to win your father over. I would do anything and everything for you, as well as for the people of Arcadia. I contacted my father earlier this morning, and York is working on extreme proposals, several options that your father might take interest in."

"Derek, this is truly concerning. What if my father refuses all options? Then what?"

Derek sighed, offering his hand across the table. "I haven't thought that far yet. But I promise you, I will find a way."

Emerald relaxed her face for a moment, but the worry still hid in the pits of her stomach. "I hope you do. My father is very stubborn."

"That, my princess, is an understatement." He glanced at the ring on her finger. "Please, do not tell your father that I have proposed to you yet. Knowing him, he would take offense to it. It would give him more ammunition to say no to me."

"I swear it. Although I don't know how long I can stay silent on the subject. Arcadia in peril." Emerald sighed in distress. "People turning to violence… And here I am, having breakfast in the palace's gardens! It's terribly frustrating."

Derek finally took a bite of his food. "You shouldn't feel bad. There is nothing you can do to fix it."

"But I *should* be able to do something about it. After all, I am Arcadia's princess," Emerald huffed, taking another sip of her coffee. "You would think that I would have some sort of power or authority to help."

Derek set down his fork, looking at Emerald solemnly. "I know your father shuts you out of all the royal councils, and that he isn't instructing you in the ways of how to govern a city. I can promise you, once we are wed, that will change."

His soothing words took the sour edge off her mood and lightened weight in the pit of her stomach. He believed that they would be married. It gave her confidence, seeing in her mind's eye that she would eventually not be under her father's rule, a privileged prisoner locked within the palace. Hinting a small smile, Emerald said, "Your words encourage me."

Out of the corner of her eye, she saw a glimpse of white. Derek turned his head, and they both saw Glacia enter the gardens, heading over toward them. Glacia remained poised but flashed a knowing smile at Derek as she approached.

Glacia bowed to them. "Forgive me, Prince and Princess." She turned to Emerald and continued. "Princess Emerald, you will be late for your appointment if we don't leave now."

"Appointment? Can it wait?" Derek asked, raising an eyebrow.

Emerald's blood appointment. She had forgotten all about it.

"I apologize, Derek. I do have to go. I cannot miss any of my medical appointments."

"Are you sick?"

"It is to monitor my health. My father requires that I have weekly blood tests. He gets them done as well."

"What for?"

"To monitor for any possible terminal illnesses before it develops, or to catch it in the early stage. That way they can stop the disease before it progresses."

"Sounds like your father is more terrified of becoming ill himself," Derek said flatly. "And this is standard within your kingdom? How long have you been doing this?"

"Since my early teenage years," Emerald said. She placed her hand on his worried face, then caressed it. "Don't fret about it. It is really nothing. I am not sick, and I am not dying."

"I have not heard of anyone doing that, that is all," Derek said reluctantly.

"It is a standard procedure with the royal family. You have not heard of us doing this procedure on your previous visits?"

"No, I can't ever recall."

Emerald smiled at him. "I know my kingdom is a bit more advanced than yours, but not by that much," she teased. Derek relaxed his face somewhat. She couldn't tell if he was persuaded, but he dropped it. "I am so sorry that I have to cut our breakfast short. Believe me, I would sit with you all day out here if I could."

"Are you ready, Princess?" Glacia asked, motioning to Emerald to get up.

"Yes," Emerald said to Glacia. She turned to Derek. "Perhaps we can see each other later. Possibly before dinner?"

Derek rose from his seat and grasped her hand, caressing it playfully. "Let me take you out. To the upper levels."

The thought of leaving the palace gave her heart a jolt. How desperately she wanted to see the outside world and all that it had to offer. But as quick as the thought came, it was replaced with thoughts of her father, knowing what he would say if she dared ask.

"I would love to, but I don't think my father would allow it." Emerald smiled sadly. "Especially if what you said... well, I should say, considering what you told me earlier."

"Let me ask him permission at the very least," Derek said as he continued to touch her hand, moving toward her. The heat of his hand made her heart race, giving her pleasure in each soft stroke of his fingers against her hand.

Coming to her senses, Emerald shook her head. "No, let me do it. It would be better coming from me, especially after your exchange last night. I doubt he would give me permission, but it's worth a try, at least. I, for one, would love to get outside of the palace. It's been far too long since my last outing." Emerald smiled. "I would love to visit the city with such delightful company." She turned to Glacia, nodding to silently to tell her that she was ready to depart.

Derek bowed to her, then kissed her hand. "Send word either way. If Damaris denies your request, I shall see you before dinner."

CHAPTER 8

Ever since Derek had arrived at Arcadia, Damaris was on edge. The very notion of the Prince of York staying at the palace irritated him, reminding Damaris of the pompous twit's infuriating father. He would have rejected the prince's request for him to even visit Arcadia, but it was the perfect setting to ensnare him in his trap. He just had to tolerate the prince a little while more in order to catch his daughter's foolish admirer off guard.

Five councilmen were sitting around a glass table in the Inner Council chambers, with Damaris in the center. The room itself was encircled by glass, with the exception of the entrance. It had a perfect view of the city below, more so than any other room in the palace, though it was not the highest point in the structure itself.

Damaris sat listening to issue after issue that the Inner Council spouted off to him. Riots. Revolts. The financial markets. Large corporations ready to leave Arcadia. His advisors continually hounded him with a plethora of problems. He had developed a headache just by listening to them. The mumblings of the councilmen became background noise, and Damaris didn't care to focus in to hear all of the woes. All he saw when he closed his eyes was the spitting image of King Samir's face in Derek's, minus the blue eyes. The very image of Derek renewed Damaris's loathing for Samir.

Elyathi. The most beautiful, the most *desired* woman in the world. The only one as equally beautiful as him. He had pursued her in the wastelands for many years, for the legends of her beauty had reached all the courts, and all the princes of that time had been in hot pursuit of her. But Damaris got to her first. She was his and his alone. His bride and trophy, for all the world to see. She was the only person for whom he had felt an inkling of the stirring of his heart.

And Damaris had given her everything a woman could want: jewels, fine gowns, and the grandest quarters in the palace. And she'd betrayed him. With none other than his best friend.

Damn that whore, Damaris thought spitefully. *Opening her legs for Samir. She deserved to die.*

Damaris's fist shook, and his wine wobbled in his glass. Steadying his hand, Damaris took a drink, turning his thoughts to his daughter, the one true gift Elyathi gave him in return. A gifted child. A daughter to make him the most powerful king and conqueror on Earth. A daughter with the ability to bestow magical regeneration properties to an army, an army of machines mixed with humans, all with the use of her blood. And for that, he could not afford anyone to find out about her true power. Emerald was staying right where he wanted her, within the palace, never to be married off. Her blood and power was his and his alone. He couldn't let anyone, or any kingdom, steal his power away from him. She was the key to overthrowing all other kingdoms, with him reigning supreme.

Count Jadeth was still blubbering on about some account of the eastern sector being plagued with power issues. Something about how some of the utilities within the city needed to be upgraded, resulting in more spending that Arcadia couldn't afford. He didn't care; all the issues within his kingdom would stop once his army was complete. There would be more than enough money and resources coming in once Arcadia invaded and conquered its first target.

It had amused Damaris seeing the other royals, lords, and dukes from the surrounding kingdoms at last night's celebration, seeing their smiling faces one last time before he crushed their kingdoms. It was a worthy cause for a celebration and gave him much joy just thinking about it.

"Sire, what do you think?" Count Jadeth stared at him, waiting for a reply. All eyes of the council were upon him.

Damaris rose from his seat, taking a drink of wine while casually walking over to view the whole city spread out before him. He felt the eyes of the council watching him patiently for an answer. They were stressed from the recent events, and with good reason.

"Councilor Zane," Damaris called out, still watching the city below him through the window.

"Yes, Your Majesty?" the councilor asked, still seated at the table.

"When will our army be complete? I grow tired of waiting," Damaris said, taking a drink of his wine again. He turned, flashing his green eyes at the councilor. "I was told that the completion date was to be over a month ago. Then two weeks. And then a week… and on and on and on." Damaris snapped his head at Zane. "Where is my army?"

Councilor Zane stood up, then bowed. "Your Majesty, the corporation began running out of… subjects… several months ago. They found what they needed in the wastelands, but it set them back at least a month and a half."

Hearing those words was completely unacceptable to Damaris. With the uprising in the lower levels, he couldn't spare any more time.

"So, you are telling me that they should be ready in two weeks?" Damaris walked over to the councilor and set down his glass, glaring at him. "Because what is happening now is all *your* fault. I gave you this great responsibility to ensure our army is prepared for invasion. From the plans, we were supposed to have a steady flow of resources coming into Arcadia from our first victory, which was supposed to be happening at this moment."

Councilor Zane's face remained still, but a hint of worry came over him. "Your Majesty, we will still have our resources after the invasion. It will just be delayed by two weeks."

"By your account, half of Arcadia will be up in flames in two weeks. You should have been more on top of the corporation. Remind me, how many billions of dollars are we paying for such incompetence?" Damaris briskly walked away from the councilor, seating himself once again.

"Your Majesty, you have my word that the army will be ready in two weeks' time."

"It had better be, otherwise there will be severe repercussions."

The councilor bowed to him, then sat down. Damaris observed the sweat on his brow; the man was obviously nervous about his predicament. *Good,* he thought. *He is lucky I haven't thrown him in the cell blocks. Or had him executed.*

There was the sound of the doors opening, and everyone's eyes turned to the entrance. His daughter appeared with one of her handmaidens. She waved her hand to dismiss the servant, who then bowed and quickly exited the room.

Councilor Emerys gave the princess a slight nod, Count Jadeth scoffed, and the other three remained silent as she approached him. He didn't even have to guess why Emerald came before him.

That damn prince.

She bowed, her eyes firmly meeting his. "Father, please forgive my interruption." She nodded at the men at the table. "Council."

"As you can see, I am busy at the moment," Damaris said, glaring at her sternly. "Whatever it is, it can wait until this evening."

"But by then, it would be too late." Emerald stood determined.

The men at the table sat silently, their faces surprised, which angered him further. Emerald had never interrupted his meetings before. It had to be the prince instructing her to do so. Why else would she do anything so out of character?

"Would you excuse me for a moment, councilors," he said, his voice resonating with annoyance. Damaris grabbed his daughter's arm and dragged her away from where they stood, over to the edge of the room, near the window. She glared at the hand he had latched onto her arm. "What is the meaning of this?" he snarled, keeping his voice low.

Emerald looked alarmed at his tone but pressed on. "Father, Derek wants to take me out this evening. I would very much like to go with him."

"No. Absolutely not."

That name. He did not like that name. It was almost as bad as the name Samir.

"Please, Father," she begged in a soft whisper. "I have never asked anything of you before. Please reconsider."

"The answer is no." He let go of her arm and began to walk away.

"Why *not?*" Emerald raised her voice.

Enraged, Damaris spun around to meet her glare, getting in her face. "Because I don't like him! *Especially* him!" his voice boomed, causing the men at the table to turn their heads slightly in their direction.

Damaris's eyes lowered after a moment, then he saw it. A sizable emerald ring on his daughter's finger. At once, all the feelings of hatred toward Samir were channeled into Derek, just by seeing that ring.

Grabbing her hand, he held it up between their faces, shaking in anger. "Where did you get this?"

Emerald lowered her eyes, not answering him. That was all he needed to know.

Samir must be behind this, undermining me. Who does he think he is, having his son waltz into Arcadia to steal my daughter from me, he thought. *First Elyathi, now Emerald. That bastard!*

He flung Emerald's hand free. "Give it back to him. Regardless of what he thinks, I will not have *my* daughter wed anyone from York, no matter how good they think their offer is. Period."

Gathering her composure, Emerald got in his face. "What do you have against York?"

"*Everything.* Now drop this conversation this very moment and leave, and I will excuse this insolent behavior. The councilors are waiting," Damaris said, shooing his daughter away. He looked over his shoulder, then added, "I forbid you from seeing the prince again. You should forget about him." Damaris returned to his seat, all the men waiting for him to resume their meeting.

Emerald didn't move from her spot. She stood her ground, tears forming in her eyes, holding her gaze at him. "Father, why are you doing this to me? Do you want me to be miserable for the rest of my life?"

Damaris slammed his hands on the table. He sensed everyone at the table would run if they could, but they remained motionless, holding their breath. Marching back to his daughter, he came within an inch of her face, narrowing his eyes. "You will *not* be wed, especially to those who live in the other kingdoms! Ever! You will continue to do your duty and stay in Arcadia. You are too important to be married off. Do I make myself *clear?*"

Emerald stood there stunned in disbelief. She took a step back, shaking her head with renewed tears. "You would hold me hostage in Arcadia for the rest of my life?" Emerald said quietly. "Because that's essentially what you are doing!"

"This conversation is over!" With a sharp, sweeping gesture, he grabbed her hand. Stunned, he saw his daughter's eyes go wide, and she tried to pry herself away from his grasp.

"Father, stop! What are you doing?" Emerald cried, struggling to free herself. "You're hurting me!"

Damaris ignored her, clenching her hand tightly. He yanked the emerald ring off her finger, then held it up in her face. "*This* is what I am doing!" he snarled.

He flung the ring across the room. The gentle pinging sound of the ring falling against the marbled tile was all that could be heard in the chambers, minus his daughter's sobs.

"Guards!" Damaris roared.

The armored men came running in, awaiting their orders.

"Please escort the princess to her quarters, and see that she does not come out until the morning."

Emerald's eyes widened, tears continuing to stream down her face. "What? Father, you can't be serious..."

The guards encircled her, then motioned for her to exit the room.

"Quite serious," Damaris said, gritting his teeth. Several guards grabbed Emerald, surrounding the princess. "Remove her. I have had enough this afternoon."

Emerald's eyes narrowed at him, filled with contempt. They looked exactly like Elyathi's eyes. It was as if she had come back to haunt him.

"I now understand why Mother was so unhappy! There is no reasoning with you!" she yelled as the guards forcefully escorted her out the door.

"Get her *out* of here!" Damaris roared at the guards.

The guards and his daughter disappeared as the doors shut behind them. There was silence once more. Damaris turned to face the council. "Continue, Count Jadeth. What were you saying?"

The count took a drink of water, then cleared his throat with his meaty hands, looking at Damaris hesitantly. Damaris nodded, and the count continued his report on the eastern sector.

Suddenly, Lysander interrupted. "Sire, forgive me for what I am about to say. Perhaps the princess has a point."

Damaris turned sharply to the advisor. "I have had quite enough for one day, Lysander."

"Just hear me out, Your Majesty. Why don't we accept the prince's proposal and take York's money? We need it now."

"Councilor Lysander is right, Your Majesty," the Baron von Aedard interjected. "We are already planning an invasion on York anyway, so what is the issue with taking their money now? Besides, morale is low in the city, and the people love their princess. A wedding could unite Arcadia from within while we execute our plans."

"No. You know as well as everyone else in this room that I loathe Samir," Damaris said, eyeing the baron. "I don't want to give him one ounce of satisfaction, even if it is under false pretenses," he spat. "Do you think for one moment that my daughter could continue to keep her secret to herself while she is engaged to the prince? You can see how infatuated she is with him. If the prince found out, it would cause alarm from within York. It's a horrible idea. The very thought of marrying them."

An image flashed in his mind. Of seven years ago. Samir holding Elyathi in tears. If Damaris hadn't discovered the plot, York would have had so much power within their grasp. To this day, Emerald still had no clue what had truly happened, nor would anyone dare speak of the incident. They knew the consequences. The cell block or death. He preferred death, personally. It always taught a lesson while ensuring compliance.

He turned to Councilor Zane. "Our army better be ready as you said, Councilor. Two weeks, we take over."

"Your Majesty," said Councilor Zane, "what about the prince?"

"What about the prince?" A maniacal smile spread across Damaris's face as he took a drink of his wine. "Samir will be lucky to have his son as Arcadia's prisoner by the time we are through with him."

Damaris held his glass up, cheering himself as he took another drink.

CHAPTER 9

Derek sat in Councilor Lysander's personal sitting room, waiting patiently for his meeting to begin. He absentmindedly stirred a sugar cube in his coffee, wondering what was delaying the councilor.

The councilor was an hour late, and there had been no messages given to Derek or the servants regarding the councilor's whereabouts. One of the palace servants came in the room to fill Derek's cup but noticed that the prince hadn't even taken a sip.

"Would you like a fresh spot of coffee, Your Highness?"

Derek snapped out of his thoughts, noticing the servant. "No, thank you. I'm fine."

The servant bowed, then left Derek alone in the chambers once again.

Sighing, Derek relaxed into the chair, gazing out the window at the city sprawled out before him. He couldn't have asked for a more perfect day, albeit the councilor being late. Princess Emerald, the only one he'd had eyes for all these years, would be his. She said *yes* to him! Nothing made him happier, and he was relieved to know that she was soon to be his. Everything would be perfect. That was, unless Damaris refused to comply.

The thought of Damaris made his heart sink slightly. What was his issue with York anyway? What had happened between him and his father for him to reject Derek so?

Not wanting to dampen his good mood, Derek's thoughts turned back to Emerald. He would see her tonight. He would take her to dinner and the opera house; Emerald would love that. He could see her excitement now, amazed at the city before her. He would be there for her to experience it all. Just the thought of that made him feel important, and also protective of her. After all, it was up to him to show her what Arcadia and the rest of the world was truly like. Her father and mother certainly hadn't. All they had done was shelter her from everything all these years, with the exception of a few times for royal visits.

Emerald. It seemed like a lifetime since he had seen her, but it had only been this morning. His stomach fluttered at the thought of how long it would be before he saw her again.

Derek finally took a sip of his coffee. It had turned cold. Maybe he should have allowed the servant to give him a new cup.

What is taking the councilor so long? Derek thought impatiently. He knew that the councilor had other meetings throughout the day, but this was getting absurd. Perhaps the councilor forgot? Or maybe… the councilor had decided he didn't want to pursue relations with York. Damaris had a way to scare everyone into submission, even the strongest of men. But that wouldn't deter Derek. He was not going to give in to Damaris's scare tactics. Especially with Emerald's hand in marriage at stake.

Derek heard the door open and immediately got to his feet, turning toward the door.

"No need, Your Highness, it's just me," Silas called out, appearing in the room.

Disappointed, Derek flopped back down into the chair. "What is it, Silas?"

"Your Highness, a transmission came in a few minutes ago. Your father," Silas said, bowing before him. "I told him you were in a meeting with one of the councilors and that you would contact him when you were done. I assumed that you would have been finished up by now, but it appears that I was mistaken." Silas glanced around the empty room.

"Indeed, you are." Derek sighed, taking a sip of his coffee. "Did my father mention any new offers?"

"Yes, he mentioned that there are a couple of attractive offers for you to extend, but he didn't go into details."

"Perfect. That's what I like to hear," Derek said, smiling to himself. He pushed aside his coffee, then got up from the table, fixing the collar on his jerkin. "Silas, I will send my father a transmission. I am curious to see what proposals that he is willing to offer. Will you please inform Councilor Lysander's attendant that we will have to reschedule our meeting when the councilor has a more *open* schedule?"

"Yes, Your Highness."

"And what of the princess? Any word from her?"

"None, Your Highness."

Derek frowned slightly. "Well, she must be busy. I'll hear from her soon, I'd wager," he said, smoothing his midnight curls. "If you haven't heard from her handmaidens within the hour, please send word for me."

Derek started for the door while Silas flagged down one of the councilor's attendants. After Derek was out the door and down the hall, Silas caught up with him.

"Your meeting has been rescheduled for tomorrow at one."

"Let's just hope that the councilor shows up."

"Apparently he has been in the same meeting with the King since this morning."

"Is that so?" *I wonder if Damaris is keeping the councilor on purpose...*

Derek and Silas stepped onto the glass lifts, and Silas pressed their floor's button. On the way up to his quarters' floor, Derek got the keen sense that something was wrong.

First the councilor not showing up, then Emerald not sending word.

It seemed Damaris was determined to make Derek fail, one way or another.

CHAPTER 10

GREEN

Emerald was still in disbelief, crying a steady stream of tears as the guards escorted her through the palace halls. She had half a mind to summon the underlying power built up within and unleash it on the guards. But she was better than that, and she didn't want to cause a scene. It wasn't their fault; they were just following orders like everyone else in the palace.

Her ring. The most precious thing she had ever received in her life, and it had been ripped from her, tossed aside with no care. Just like her feelings. Her father didn't care.

She had not always agreed with her father, respecting his decisions because she thought he had her best interests at heart regarding her secret. But she thought that eventually, when she came of age, that she would be married off to some duke or prince. However, it was quite apparent that that was not the case. All her father cared about was himself and her power, not her or her wishes.

Under normal circumstances, Emerald wouldn't have fathomed arguing with her father. After all, it was just a request for an outing. But the more unreasonable he became about his decision, the more it had upset her. And now, learning that her father had absolutely no intentions of accepting any sort of proposal from York regarding a marriage, she had learned something else about him: He was deceitful. To York, to the people of Arcadia, and to her.

When they arrived at her quarters, the guards opened the main door, bowing to her and remaining silent. Just for petty self-satisfaction, Emerald didn't acknowledge them, still furious with her father. Glacia entered behind her, and the door shut. She could hear several of the guards positioning themselves outside her door, the shuffles of their boots and armor clanging.

She crossed her sitting room, then let herself into her bedroom and slumped down onto her vanity bench. A new batch of tears flowed as Glacia calmly approached, kneeling down beside the bench, hugging her.

"Princess… what happened with your father?" she asked in a low voice.

"Everything happened," Emerald said, forcing the words from her trembling lips, wiping away her tears.

Glacia sat motionless as she continued to embrace her. "What did you say to him?" she asked quietly.

Shaking her head, Emerald said in a jittery voice, "All I know is that I will continue to remain in Arcadia… for an indefinite amount of time." She grabbed a handkerchief from her vanity, dabbing her tears.

Glacia's hazel eyes studied her. "Does that mean there will be no engagement?"

"There will never be an engagement. Not with Derek, or anyone else." Emerald wiped her nose with her handkerchief.

Never had Glacia been silent like she was now. She always had something to say. But what could she possibly say?

Emerald shuddered with grief. Glacia touched her shoulder as a comforting gesture and went to retrieve a glass of wine for her. Emerald got up, then walked through her bedroom to her outside balcony. Glacia returned with a glass of red wine, bowed, then retreated inside, giving Emerald time alone to sort her feelings.

A deep despair came over her as she viewed the city bustling with activities. More than anything else, she desperately wanted to marry Derek and be free of her father. Instead she was to be his prisoner, trapped, never to leave the palace walls ever again. Her father had withheld the truth from everyone except a few people about her gift, under the pretenses of "keeping her secret." That was a lie. All he really cared about was her power and controlling everyone else around him. And if it weren't for Derek, she would still be naive to the impending collapse of Arcadia's financial markets. Just another thing her father wasn't forthcoming with.

Her thoughts turned to Derek, about him questioning the blood samples. Derek didn't seem convinced. And now, she wasn't so sure either. Come to think of it, she had never actually been sick before. Was it even possible for her to get sick, with her being born of green magic? A sobering thought came to her: What was her father doing with her blood?

Day melted into night. Emerald watched the transports cross the kingdom's sky, like sailing ships in endless waters, soaring through the colored fog that rose from the depths of the city. What she would give to eternally fall into those colors, to lose herself and her existence.

Emerald thought of her mother. What would she do in her situation? Most likely do as she was told and continue to be unhappy. That was what her mother had done, and look where it got her. Emerald's life was escaping her by the second, trapped within the palace walls in the same unhappiness that her mother had felt. She couldn't relive her mother's footsteps. Otherwise she would meet the same fate.

A thought struck her.

Emerald rose in a hurried fashion, then went inside her bedroom. She turned to the painting of the wild woman, still sitting on her easel.

Give me strength, she confessed to the picture.

Emerald began to rip the lavender dress off her body, running into her closet. At that moment, she heard the door to the sitting room open.

"Princess, this came for you," Glacia said, holding out an envelope. She stopped in her tracks, looking at Emerald curiously as she dug through the closet. "What are you doing?"

Emerald found what she was looking for, yanking it out of the closet as Glacia handed over the small envelope, sealed with no known symbol.

"Who is it from?" Emerald asked, putting down her garment.

"Don't know. It was slipped under your sitting room door."

Emerald ripped open the letter, revealing Derek's engagement ring inside, along with a note.

Thought you might want to have this. —E

Emerys. The only good man on the council. Him, and perhaps Lysander.

"It's Derek's ring..." Glacia said, looking over her shoulder.

Emerald held it close to her heart for a brief moment, then slipped the ring onto her finger. Taking a deep breath, she then shoved a purple corset halter top into Glacia's hands. "Lace me up," she ordered.

Hesitantly, Glacia followed through with Emerald's demand. Emerald pointed at purple leggings that she'd thrown on the closet floor, along with a pair of metallic purple thigh-high boots. Glacia grabbed the garments, then began to dress Emerald.

"Can you at least tell me what's going on?" Glacia asked with confusion in her voice, tugging on the corset strings in the back.

"I can't live my life under my father's rule," Emerald announced. After Glacia secured the back of her top, Emerald finished putting on her leggings and boots.

"Are you leaving?" Glacia asked, raising her eyebrows.

Instead of answering, Emerald grabbed a silver bag from the closet, filling it with a few articles of clothing. Realizing what Emerald was doing, Glacia got in her face. "No, Princess! Don't do this!" Glacia tried to grab her bag, but Emerald dodged her hands, sliding it onto her arms. "Have you even thought this through? You know your father will find out. Then what?"

Emerald turned and faced her. "Glacia, my father made it very clear that all he cares about is himself. I am to stay here, unmarried, in the palace, most likely until he passes away. Do I really want that for my life, living out my days until I grow old, confined?"

Glacia was unusually quiet.

"I cannot do that. I have had enough! No more will I live under my father's rule," Emerald said forcefully. "I never knew what my father was until he showed me his true self today. Despicable. Truly despicable."

Glacia hung her head, lowering her eyes. Emerald knew Glacia agreed with her.

Emerald walked in front of her vanity, looking at her reflection. She hooked a pair of large flashy earrings in her ears, then noticed her hair. Everyone would recognize her by her colored locks.

I can't have that, she thought.

Closing her eyes, Emerald clenched her hands into fists. The powerful force that stirred within surged at her calling, begging to be released. It had been too long since she had touched the life force bubbling within her.

Tapping into the magic, she sucked away the power, moving her life force into her core essence. The magic began to vibrate within, swelling through her blood, burning. Power surged as the life of magic ripped through her, as if a black tidal wave was washing over her life-giving magic. Slowly, she opened her hands, and a black glow with a green halo of magic enveloped them. Like water draining, the green magic from her hair was sucked dry, replaced with a natural, deep-red auburn. It was the hair color that she would have been born with, if it weren't for the magic.

Sweating, she opened her eyes. A look of satisfaction came upon her at the result. She had taught herself that trick early on in her childhood, when no one else was around. It was like hiding her life magic within her body, draining it away and storing it within. Emerald knew she could drain others' life force away if she tried, but it was horrible to even think about such a thing. That was pure evil, and not what the God of Light intended for his power to be used for. If she was in real danger, Emerald had decided that was the only time she would ever use the dark side of her magic.

Hopefully no one will notice me, she thought. *My father will have the whole city looking for me once he realizes that I am gone.*

Emerald heard Glacia gasp behind her, stunned at the sight of her magic. Emerald hardly used her magic in front of others except to heal her father, and even that was rare. Glacia had seen it no more than five times in her service at the palace.

In the corner of her vanity's reflection, she caught a glimpse of the bouquet of lilacs that Derek had sent her. She at least owed him an explanation before everyone discovered that she was gone. Would he approve of her decision, or at least understand? Her heart hurt at the thought of leaving Derek behind, never to be with him. She could very well try and run away with him, but knowing her father, he would start an all-out war with York, and Emerald could not stomach the prince being the scapegoat for her decision to leave. No, she couldn't do that to him. He deserved far better in life.

"Glacia, would you fetch me a pen and paper, please? And I need a necklace chain."

Eyes still glued to Emerald's new hair color, Glacia finally turned away, hurrying off to the sitting room. She came back quickly with the items. Handing the pen and paper to Emerald, Glacia said, "Princess, where are you going to go?" She set a small silver necklace next to her on the vanity.

"I don't know." Emerald snatched the chain and unclasped it. She slipped off Derek's ring, then placed the chain through the ring and secured it around her neck. She then began to write her note to the prince.

"Do you even have any money?"

"Only my card," Emerald replied, continuing with her penmanship, not breaking eye contact with the paper.

"Princess, you cannot use your card! Your father will track you down in no time."

Emerald's hand paused for a moment, looking at her. "You're right, I hadn't thought of that," she stated, returning to her note. "I guess I will have to forgo the money and figure it out once I am out of here."

Glacia sighed loudly, shaking her head. "Hold on," she muttered, retreating to the sitting room. After what seemed like several minutes, she returned with a big rolled-up stack of bills, handing it to Emerald. "Don't spend it all in one place."

Emerald quieted. It was Glacia's savings. Every time she got paid, she pulled out cash to save it for an emergency, as she tended to be reckless with her card spending. Shoving the money back, Emerald shook her head. "Glacia, I cannot accept this. You have been saving this for years."

Glacia forced the money into her hands. "Princess, I still have money on my card. Don't worry, I will be fine. It's *you* that will be without any money."

Emerald faltered, then nodded. "Glacia, thank you."

Underneath the sadness, a smile appeared on Glacia's face. "Anything for you, Princess. What shall I tell the guards when they retrieve you in the morning?"

"Just stay in the sitting room. When they question you, it makes it that much easier to say I must have left while you were asleep." Emerald finished up her letter, then sealed it, handing it to Glacia. "Deliver this to Derek sometime tomorrow. Tell him I am sorry."

Glacia bowed, her lip trembling. "Yes, Princess."

Snatching the bag and throwing it over her shoulders, Emerald headed toward the balcony and onto the fire escape.

Climbing over the railing, she then secured herself on the escape ladder. She had never dreamt of getting on it, nor had any fires ever broke out in her tower. Looking down at the miles of airspace between her balcony and the city made Emerald feel queasy.

She heard Glacia gasp in the wind, crying out, "Oh, Princess, I can't watch you do this!"

"Then don't!" yelled Emerald from the ladder.

Gusts of wind whipped her hair as the sound of the breeze and transport jets filled her ears. The green glow of the palace's glass panels was intense, causing her to squint occasionally.

Closing her eyes, Emerald gathered her strength, then opened them again, focusing on the task ahead of her. She started the descent, one step at a time, ensuring that she had a secure grip on the ladder. With each step downward, she made sure her boot was level on the next bar, ensuring her stability on the contraption while fighting the winds. Her upper arms began to tingle as she continued her descent.

After several minutes, she glanced up to the balcony. The shadowy outline of Glacia loomed above her, silent in the wind. Emerald turned her gaze downward at the bar where her boot rested, seeing the city below her again. Overwhelmed with a sense of dizziness, the city began to twist and turn in the depths below. She looked straight ahead of the palace's green glass panel, where the ladder was secure, and took a deep breath. It made her feel slightly better, but not by much.

Emerald focused again, lowering herself bar by bar, until she had passed a few more levels. Her arms began to burn, weakened from the exertion, and her limbs shook.

I don't know if I have the physical strength to do this, she though. *But I must try... I can't go back!*

She lowered her foot to the next step. Her arms promptly gave out, causing her to miss the bar under her foot. Emerald flung wildly with her arms in a mad dash to grasp the bar, but it was too late.

She was plummeting to the city below.

The rush of wind burned against her face as she screamed long and hard. An explosive green burning light enveloped her body as she shot straight to earth. Hotter and hotter the power became, melting away the red color from her hair and replacing it with her gifted color. The pain was so intense, it felt like her muscles were peeling off her body, exposing her organs to the magical light within. She continued to scream helplessly.

Please! she cried to the God of Light in her mind. *Protect me!* She closed her eyes, waiting for her imminent death.

Just when she thought she was either going to burn up by her own magic or strike the earth like a limp rag doll, the intense magical light was suddenly replaced by a swirling green-yellow glow around her body.

Instantly, the pain subsided.

Opening her eyes, she saw that she was floating in a translucent greenish-yellow bubble. Her long hair floated around inside the barrier weightlessly, while small bright particles swirled around the bubble, creating a protective barrier shell.

Turning her attention down to her limbs to see how much damage the magic had caused, Emerald saw it left no trace. Amazed, she turned her arms, continuing to inspect them.

What if the people of Arcadia saw her magic? She had fallen halfway through the sky. She couldn't be seen. If any word reached her father, he would know that she was gone.

With an instant shift, the greenish-yellow barrier turned a greenish-blue, and she began float downward rapidly; it was as if the bubble knew what she was thinking. There was a connection from her mind to the barrier, as if her mind was controlling the protective magic. Continuing to speak to the magic, she urged it to get her to the ground in haste.

Through the barrier, she saw transports jet by, jerking their vehicles at the sight of her. Several almost hit her. Bodies began to gather in the skyways. They all saw her magic.

Hurry! she cried to the barrier.

Without warning, the magic responded with an intense flash of green-blue energy, then withdrew its power, dropping her bubble like a marble without any friction.

Emerald screamed. The bubble fell, dodging any and all buildings and platforms. It neared a darker part of the city, which was poorly lit.

The magic burst, dropping her ten feet from the ground. All she heard was a loud thud as her head hit the concrete and her vision went black. The feeling of sticky trash fell through her fingers as she crawled a few feet until she felt a brick wall. Clawing her hands against the wall, Emerald attempted to prop herself up.

That was the last thing she remembered.

CHAPTER 11

ORANGE

The God of Orange looked upon the earth. Where he saw darkness, he transmuted the darkness into the light. The darkness tried to assume its original form, but the Orange God did not allow it to do so, but instead illuminated it, manipulating it, ensuring that the darkness would sit in the shadows of the light, transformed by its image.

—Indradhanush Granthon, *The Rainbow Mantras*
Recorded by Arjun Laghari, 3459 B.E.

Daddy! Daddy!"
As soon as he closed his apartment door, his little girl's bright eyes greeted him, and she latched onto his leg. Gwen's fine golden hair shone in the rays of sunlight that streamed from the window while her rosy cheeks greeted him happily. Nothing gave him more joy than to see the sheer delight that radiated from her.

He picked Gwen up, tossing her in the air while she squealed. "You, little one, are getting heavy!" he exclaimed, laughing and kissing her cheek. "Can you tell Daddy how old you are?"

Gwen wrinkled her face, not understanding the question.

"Three, Gwen," a woman's voice said from the hallway. "Can you say three?"

He held up three fingers, then tried to get Gwen to do the same. She fumbled with her gestures, distracted by his glasses, running her hands over the lenses.

"Three…" he said. "Three…"

Voices started talking over his conversation. What they uttered, he did not know.

"Three…" echoed the voices.

Glitch.

"Three…"

Glitch.

Gwen's face faded away into nothingness. Hundreds of voices filled his mind, all talking at once within the same network. Nine hundred and seventy-eight of them to be exact. The garbled voices continued to talk over each other, becoming a steady stream of conversation that was mixed with uncertainty, confusion, and horror. Louder and louder they became, until he could no longer think in the confines of his own mind.

What happened? a voice asked within the network.

They are the masters, answered another. *Always follow the masters' orders.*

Slaves to the humans, cried another in the computerized stream.

I am not human? another voice called out in question.

Program error.

Stop! he commanded himself. *Make them stop!*

His body began to shake. His head throbbed in agony as the voices continued to speak. Was Gwen there?

No more. We are human no more.

Cybernetic implants.

Bionic. We are bionic. Humans mixed with machines.

I am not human? repeated the voice.

STOP!

The circuitry didn't comply with his command. His body jolted hard, vibrating with the voices in his head. A shock ran down his spine, and the metal within him vibrated, shaking his organs.

Malfunction.

There was silence. The voices were gone. In their absence, the sounds of humming machines filled his ears.

He couldn't open his eyelids; a mechanical metal lens obstructed one of his eyes. His right hand felt like a dead weight, like it had been cut off or removed. Struggling with his left hand, he guided it over the foreign metal object that was fused to his right eye.

Another violent jolt shocked his body, causing him to shake. His mind tried to access his data banks. A switch triggered, and he was back online; he had control. The network of voices came back, but this time it was filtered, and it only had permission to enter his network with his approval. He denied their access.

Now having command of his eyes, he cracked them open. The metal around his right eye adjusted as the lens came into focus. Peering into the darkness, he began to take in all the colors and shapes. There were wires and tubing highlighted in cool whites and blues all around him, fuzzy and out of focus.

A processor turned on inside of him, shooting electronic orange data inside his cybernetic eye. Information poured into him, telling him that the room was cylindrical and painted in black.

Black. Was that the absence of color?

Malfunction.

Was it all the colors combined?

Malfunction.

The wires in his brain needed adjusting.

Behind the tangled circuitry, he noticed a small window with bluish-white light pouring from it. Massive amounts of tubing were suspended from the ceiling, with wires coming from all directions of the room, intertwined and tangled amongst themselves. But they all had one destination. Him.

Where was he?

Access denied.

His head scrambled like white noise.

Who was he?

Access denied.

The network switched off again.

He attempted to prop himself up from the cold metal platform, feeling lethargic. As he did so, his heavy right hand made a loud screeching sound, metal against metal. Swinging his right hand in front of his face to inspect it, the bluish-white light filtered onto it, revealing small orange squares glowing on his arm, and long sharp metal fingertips. As he observed the squares, they started to make a pattern, switching between bright orange and white. He was communicating; his eyes and brain were talking to each other. As the light pattern danced back and forth, he saw other patterns infused onto his right hand and all the way up to his shoulder. It was some kind of circuitry woven throughout his skin.

A shadow appeared from behind the glass, keeping the light from filtering into the room. Like a menacing demon in one of his nightmares, it stood there for a moment, watching him. A burning sensation came over him, focused where each of the wires were connected to parts of his body. The burning subsided, replaced with an immense coldness. He became acutely aware of his nakedness. His body shook, then twitched with mechanical glitches.

Where was Gwen? Was she here?

The obscure figure disappeared from the glass. Within seconds, the door opened, and the shadow entered his chamber.

Suddenly the room lit up like the heavens. He jolted; his good eye was not used to this kind of intense lighting. The brilliance of the light sent an exploding pain to his brain. He couldn't see what or who was in front of him. Orange data flashed quickly within his mechanical eye.

"I'm sorry, Drew, I didn't realize that the light would bother you," a woman's soft voice said gently. A moment later, the light turned off. Once more, darkness enveloped the room, except for the bluish-white light from the window. "I saw that the network was interfering with your boot-up, so I unplugged you from the mainframe for a while, only connecting you to the sub network. You will be fully back online again soon, after you recover from the shock."

Drew? That was his name? He tried to recall that name from his memory. *Access denied.*

The woman returned to face him once more, studying him. What his left eye couldn't see, the cybernetic eye filled in with information. Midforties. Honeyed hair cropped to her chin. Black-rimmed glasses covering her light brown eyes. Average weight, medium build. He sat, calculating his thoughts, trying to recall if he knew this woman. The data banks were coming up empty.

With a look of marvel and wonder across her face, she reached out and touched his hand, then moved to his chest, listening to his breathing. Taking out a small flashlight, she held it in front of him.

"Drew, I know your eyes are getting adjusted to light, but I need to do a routine inspection. It will only take a moment."

Without waiting for a response from him, she turned on her flashlight, examining his cybernetic eye. His eye flooded with information, warning him it was too bright. Drew struck the flashlight, hurling it to the ground.

"Sweetie, I know it's a lot for you to take in," the woman stated warmly, "but please, try and remain calm. It will only be another minute or so, then you can rest." She walked over to the flashlight and pulled it out of a tangle of wires. Appearing in front of him again, she held his face and inspected his left eye. Gasping, she took a step back.

"My God... It can't be..." she uttered.

God? Drew glanced around the room. There was no god in here. What was she referring to? Another glitch.

Malfunction.

She continued to check his left eye in disbelief and fascination, until water began to pool in the corner of it. The tears finally released themselves, flowing down his face. Holding his gaze for a moment, she proceeded to inspect the bionic areas of his body, guiding her flashlight away from his face.

Where is Gwen?

His body jolted again, but this time it was a clear reaction to his thought. As if he was not permitted to access those memories.

The blonde woman patted him on the shoulder, then turned off the flashlight. "It's okay. Try not to think too much right now. You are adjusting," she said sympathetically. "It will take you a few days to get back to one hundred percent capacity." She took out a modified pair of glasses—the right side was completely missing, with a hook coming from the bridge of the frames. After screwing the bridge of the altered spectacles to his cybernetic lens, she slid the modified frame's earpiece behind his left ear.

"There. I know that you can now see perfectly with the wiring that we installed, but I thought you should have a little bit of your old self back." She stood, admiring him with glassy eyes, her mouth curled in a small smile. Rubbing her eyes from behind her glasses, she breathed in, composing herself. "I am glad you came back to us."

Came back?

Where is Gwen?

Drew opened his mouth to ask the woman where his daughter was, but nothing came out, just pure air.

Malfunction.

"Oh, Drew, you don't have a voice box. I haven't wired one into you yet." Drew frowned, frustrated. Drew... that was his name.

"Don't worry, you will have one soon," she said as she started typing in code in a nearby machine, hidden within the tubing and wires in the room. "The head director has been breathing down everyone's backs the last few weeks, pushing us to get every cyborg booted up and online. We had to put your voice box on the back burner for the time being."

Head director?

The woman looked over her shoulder. The light from the window highlighted her face. He tried to recall once more if he knew this woman.

Access denied.

The woman turned to walk out of the room. "Get some rest," she called out as she closed the door behind her. "Surviving the initial boot-up takes a toll on your body."

Drew lay down back on the cold platform; his circuits were drowsy. He felt a pinprick within the wires connected to his body. Then another. And another, until his whole body burned with pain. Electricity entered some of the wires while others flowed with blood and saline. It made him realize how cold he was. Shivering, he opened his mouth to yell, but only silence answered him.

As the foreign elements entered his bloodstream, relief came, and a blanket of comfort enveloped him. An old feeling, a feeling that he hadn't felt in a long time, registered in his brain. Euphoria. He no longer burned, no longer felt the wires around him. He no longer sat in a room, caged like an animal.

An orange power surrounded him. Unlike the data that registered in his cybernetic eye, the orange energy embraced him in a world very different from the world he awoke to. Joy filled him, replacing the confusing, confined room with his distant memories.

CHAPTER 12

VIOLET

A warm vibration shuddered from Ikaria's lower body. He felt good, his hard muscle giving her much pleasure. But his flesh paled in comparison to the sensation of when new magic entered her bloodstream. The power of a color was like an aphrodisiac, causing her fleshy desires to burn with lust.

Rolling off the top of Mikko's firm torso, Ikaria slunk in the bed next to him, gathering her senses. Through Mikko's heavy breaths, his glistening tanned body emitted an orange glow, slowly coloring his hair from blond back to his original orange.

Cyrus's new blond servant was indisposed this evening, so Ikaria had to compromise with someone else. After countless hours of studying in the library, Ikaria had needed a mental break from all the dull reading. As much as she loved to read and study old manuscripts, the ones she'd found were all uninteresting. Not only did she not find anything for her sister, nor any connection to the High Court and the disease, she didn't find anything useful about time travel or any recorded incident regarding a green-gifted individual.

In order to confront the High Court and overthrow them, Ikaria needed to complete the Spectrum of Magic. That would give her the unmatched power to annihilate them all. No one would be able to stop her. And to do that, she had to find someone in time with the green gift. And so far, no luck. If she were to consume the blood of the blue and traveled through time searching, it might take her years. And that was unacceptable. She had no time to grow old within different eras, trying to find clues of the green-gifted blood. The High Court needed to be gone *now*.

As Mikko got up to pull on his pants, Ikaria contemplated if she should kill him instead of letting him walk free. During their sexual encounter, Ikaria had felt his mind, and she knew that he was hiding something. Something that had to do with her sister. She couldn't break into his mind fully without him knowing, so that was only an option if she intended to kill him. No, he was not worth the risk.

Of course, Ikaria had to keep up pretenses and continued to not use her magic in front of others. If she did indeed kill Mikko, it would cause alarm within World Sector Six's court, and Cyrus would make sure that the gifted imprisoned her, especially since he had been seen arriving at her quarters. No, she was not ready yet. She needed the other colors. And so Ikaria had to play the powerless fool a bit longer. Best not to alert anyone until she was ready to travel back in time.

Ikaria watched as Mikko finished dressing, rolling over onto her stomach. Reaching over to her nightstand, she took a long drink of wine, then gave him her best smile as he was about to depart.

"Thank you, Enchantress." Mikko smiled with pleasure.

"Let's not make anything more out of this than we have to," Ikaria said casually, drinking more of her wine, eagerly waiting for him to leave. There was still much to study in the library, and she wanted to get a head start this morning.

"Yes, Enchantress." Mikko nodded, exiting her chambers.

After a moment, she heard her outside chambers close as Suri let him out. Jumping up, Ikaria walked out into the sitting chambers, not bothering herself with clothes. Suri bowed to her, then walked into the adjoining room.

"I don't know why you didn't want to join us this morning, Suri," Ikaria called out, taking another sip of wine. "Mikko was tolerable, not like half of the others."

Ikaria knew why, but she knew better than to speak of it.

"I was not in the mood, Enchantress," Suri said from the other room. She appeared before Ikaria, then bowed. "I have something to show you." Suri's bright-orange eyes twinkled as she spoke, her head remaining frozen in place.

"Really? What is it?"

"Please, just follow me."

Suri led Ikaria into the next room, where Ikaria's private collection was housed. It was filled with any ancient technology finds that she could smuggle in without the Emperor, Empress, or the High Court knowing. Anything that was not yet cataloged for departure, Ikaria made sure it came to her.

In the center of her desk sat a large computerized chip. With a sudden burst of excitement, Ikaria dashed to it, running her hands all over it. It was what the ancients stored data on. Knowledge, somehow contained within that metal. If only she could figure out how to access it. This metal chip was one of the many keys to restoring their future.

Laughing with excitement, Ikaria whipped her head in Suri's direction. "How did you get your hands on this without anyone finding out? These things are documented on Earth's surface before they are brought up."

"In one of my discreet outings in court, I heard of an artifact that was going to be smuggled to another lord here within the citadel. Only, I ensured that I obtained it first before the other handler."

"Really? Another collector? Sounds like we may have an ally here within court. Do you know who this lord is?"

"Lord Hiroshi, Enchantress."

"Well done, my dear Suri, well done, indeed."

Suri revealed a small smile, then bowed. "Anything to please you, Enchantress." Then she left the room, returning with a lavender kimono for Ikaria. Ikaria haphazardly put on the robe, returning her focus to the computer chip while Suri left her alone.

Ikaria marveled at the computer chip's beauty, admiring the circuitry. Her fingertips ran over it lightly as she wondered how much information was stored within it. To think the High Court had hundreds of these, all at their disposal. The very thought angered her.

They are going to pay. Every single one of them.

Closing her eyes, Ikaria called forth her violet magic. The power responded gently, rushing like a gentle river through her soul. As she opened her glowing eyes, deep-violet magic began to flow around her. Some of the power grabbed her hairbrush, softly combing and styling her hair, then inserted hair ornaments in her lavish hairstyle in one half of her hair. The other half of her hair flowed to the ground unadorned. Other parts of her violet magic surrounded her kimono, fixing it in place and securing it with an obi. When the magic was finished getting her ready, Ikaria released it, pulling it back into her core.

With a cheerful tone, Ikaria called out to Suri in the next room.

"Suri, I shall be back late this evening. I am feeling quite refreshed, and I plan on spending all my time in the library today."

"Yes, Enchantress."

Ikaria grabbed a carafe of wine and her glass and headed out the door.

***

Ikaria finished reading the last sentence of the ancient tome, then shut the book carefully, ensuring that the paper wouldn't crumble as she did so.

It was noon. Half the day had passed, and still she had read nothing of interest. Most of the books that Ikaria had skimmed through the past week dealt with two gifted brothers and their warring kingdoms. One had been in favor of the establishment of magic worldwide with a court system in place to uphold laws; the other was for technology and the continuance of the smaller kingdoms. Their bitter feud resulted in the worldwide technology ban, a ban that had been upheld for two thousand years, which had continued to this day.

What was unclear from all the scribes' written accounts was whether the brothers and their war fell during the Millennium Era or Post-Apocalypse. Whatever the case was, it didn't matter to Ikaria. As much as she enjoyed studying the past, that information didn't help her in any way, and was just another waste of time.

One thing that perplexed Ikaria was a certain book that she recalled seeing in the library during one of her prior visits—*The Genealogy of Kings*. It was either misplaced or missing.

The book had recorded the gifted from the start of the Post-Apocalypse Era. Ikaria remembered quickly flipping through the pages while deciding if she wanted to study it. It had listed the names of the royals and court positions, and if anyone was gifted within the court, it stated their color and their offspring. Her sister had given her only two days to study that time, so Ikaria didn't get a chance to read it, as she had specific books that Ayera requested she study, though she'd also secretly skimmed books on blood consumption.

But now that particular book was of importance, and it was imperative that she study it. It was the only material within the library that would have a clue on any account of a green-gifted person. Ikaria *needed* that book.

Ikaria had searched the shelves several times all week but couldn't seem to locate it. She had a vague idea of where the book could have gone. She glanced over at the other table where Kohren sat, engrossed in the book he was reading.

Traitor, she thought. *Probably has the damn book in his possession, if he hasn't turned it over to the High Court yet. Knowing them, they are out seeking the green-gifted too. Damn them!*

Her mood darkened as she thought about the missing book. Shaking off her thoughts, Ikaria got up from her spot, arching her back to give it a good stretch, her eyes moving from Kohren's face to his blue mane. The brilliance of his deep-blue hair looked so desirable. How his magic tempted her, seducing her every thought. The azure color flirted with her imagination, almost daring Ikaria to make a move. The very thought stirred her insides, lusting for what was to come. She couldn't wait to taste the blood of the blue.

But now was not the time.

Making her way into the section of the library she had been pulling books from, Ikaria meticulously set the tome she had been reading back on the shelf, then selected a new one. A musty old book with a worn gold binding stuck out on the shelf, mildly piquing her interest.

As she went to grab the book, she saw it was wedged in rather well between two larger tomes. She tugged at it—the book was stuck. Gritting her teeth, Ikaria yanked the book several times. It still held firm.

It would be nice if I could use my magic right now, she thought irritably. *Damn Kohren is around the corner.*

Ikaria turned her attention to one of the larger tomes stuck against the small golden one, forcing it out of the bookshelf. It took a few hard tugs, but the massive tome finally came free, allowing the small one to fall sideways on the bookshelf. One of her nails broke in the process.

She glared at her nail. *Now he really is going to pay for me breaking a nail!*

Checking the damage one last time, Ikaria gritted her teeth and turned her attention back to the shelf. As Ikaria went to retrieve the small golden book, she noticed something behind it, stored in the back of the bookshelf. Curious, Ikaria stuck her hand in and retrieved another small book, this one bound in ivory leather with faded silver decoration. Puzzled, Ikaria wondered why this special book had been shoved behind the others. There was no title on the front cover, and the silver markings on it were rather ordinary. Turning to the spine, Ikaria saw no words printed for the title, either.

Grabbing the book, Ikaria headed back to her spot within the library, seating herself back in the uncomfortable, stiff chair, groaning. What she would give to use her violet magic right about now. She much preferred to seat herself within the air, hovering with the use of her controlling magic on her body rather than sitting on the hardened metal with padding. Air was much easier on the body, and it allowed her to think more clearly.

Slinking into the rigid chair, Ikaria opened the book, flipping to the first page. The title page read:

Jaadoo ke niyam
The Laws of Magic
translated by Oliver Jorgenson

Immediately straightening her posture, Ikaria suddenly became very interested in the book.

"Found something?" Kohren asked, glancing at her for the first time that day.

"No. I just needed to readjust myself in this godforsaken seat. It's killing my back," Ikaria said inadvertently, then turned back to her book, not wanting to call more attention to herself. "Besides, it's just another boring book about the clash between the Kingdom of Arcadia and the Kingdom of York in the old World Sector One," Ikaria lied. "Two idiotic brothers seeping testosterone just to prove who was the better man. So archaic."

"Huh?" Kohren asked, looking confused. "What is testosterone, an old scientific term?"

"Never mind."

"Perhaps you should reconsider reading about another era?" Kohren suggested, turning back to his text.

"Perhaps. But for now I think I will keep going with this era," Ikaria called back, shrugging.

Out of the corner of her eye, Ikaria saw Kohren completely focused on his tome. She turned her attention back to her book, then flipped the title page to the table of contents.

Colors and Properties. Analogous and Adjacent Colors. The Dark Side of the Spectrum. Blood Consumption. This book had everything Ikaria had ever dreamt of knowing about. Throughout her life, she had read bits of scattered information regarding blood consumption. And what she *could* find of it were all theories, untested. Blood consumption had been outlawed by the High Courts throughout time, ever since the first establishment of the High Court itself. She hadn't known what would happen until she tested it herself, and when that happened, it was obvious why such a ban was in place.

It was clever, what they had done. Everyone was too afraid of the God of Light's judgment if they were to consume blood, for the High Court and all the priests told the world that they would end up in the fiery pits of hell. But somehow, since the old holy book *The Spectrum* had been translated by the world's third High Court, Ikaria had no faith, nor any trust, if that was truly what was going to happen. Considering the reward, it was a risk she was willing to take.

Analogous and Adjacent Colors? What is that?

Ikaria thumbed through a quarter of the book that dealt with colors and their properties before arriving back at the Analogous and Adjacent Colors section, then began reading the first page.

> *Analogous colors are a mixture of the gifted's main color, along with the colors that fall next to their color in the Spectrum of Magic. For example, say a gifted's main color is orange. Their analogous colors are orange-red and orange-yellow. The adjacent colors are the true pure color that falls immediately next to the gifted's color in the Spectrum of Magic. For instance, if the gifted's main color is orange, their adjacent colors would be red and yellow. Each gifted has the automatic ability to tap into their analogous colors, which allows the gifted access to limited abilities within their analogous color magic. Some gifted have the unique ability to use the full magical potential of their adjacent colors, but these cases are quite rare. In fact, they are so rare that there are only a few documented cases throughout all of history.*

Ikaria was stunned. She reread the last part of the paragraph just to make sure she had read it correctly. *Each gifted has the automatic ability to tap into their analogous colors.* Every gifted had the ability to *use* their analogous colors. If this was true, why was it that the gifted in her time, including herself, did not seem to possess the ability to use analogous magic? Ikaria was sure that this bit of information was somehow connected to the current gifted losing their magic altogether. Somehow the present-day gifted were not only unable to use their analogous colors, but they were also losing their main color.

Ikaria continued to read.

> *One might note that throughout all studies that have been recorded with the red and blue-gifted, those particular gifted all had trouble accessing their analogous colors: red-violet and blue-violet. There have been no studies on violets being able to use their analogous or adjacent colors, as there have been no recordings in the history of man of a violet-gifted person.*
>
> *Many priests have concluded that if the Spectrum of Magic is observed as a line instead of a circle, that it ends with violet, thus breaking the cycle of moving back into the beginning of the spectrum, starting again with red. On this point, it has been argued among priests that the Spectrum of Magic should indeed be symbolized as a line instead of a circle.*

Ikaria stopped reading, as the chapter was now getting into priestly theories and arguments over their beliefs of the line verses the circle. By today's standards, the Spectrum of Magic took to the circle theory, but it had evolved to a sphere. Priest theories were boring and made her think of Auron, who annoyed her to no end. She thumbed through the rest of the section, but nothing riveting struck her. Ikaria turned the pages to find the chapter on blood consumption properties, then began reading.

> *The art of blood consumption is like the art of gambling. It is not ever consistent and not guaranteed that one would have the same results as another.*
>
> *A non-gifted who chooses to partake in the blood consumption of a gifted is not guaranteed to inherit magic, nor even the color that they consume. For instance, a non-gifted may consume the blood of the yellow. That non-gifted has a great chance of not ever becoming gifted, even by consuming the blood. "The magic chooses the person," as stated in the holy book* The Spectrum. *However, if the magic does indeed choose that person, and they do become gifted, one might not actually receive the yellow magic they had consumed. The consumer has a chance of getting any color in the Spectrum of Magic.*

Ikaria thought back to Suri. When Suri drank the Lady Yasmin's blood, the blood of the orange, she ended up receiving the orange magic, Lady

Yasmin's true color. Suri must have been incredibly lucky to even receive the gift, as well as the exact color she consumed. Ikaria smiled. It was further proof that fate was on her side, approving her quest to rid the land of the corrupt High Court.

Once the gifted is bestowed with their given color, they are able to consume the blood of the other colors and inherit the exact blood and power that they consume. Also, when those gifted with other consumed colors use any form of magic, whether it be from their own color or their consumed colors, the magic will always appear to be their true original color, but a shade darker. The only exception to this rule is that their true analogous and adjacent colors will show as true, as those powers have attributes to their main power.

One might note that when the gifted consume another color, they will not be able to summon the analogous color of the newly consumed color. The gifted are only able to summon their original analogous colors. Furthermore, the gifted might not be able to use the full power of the newly consumed color. It varies per color, and per person.

So far, Ikaria had not had any problems using the full force of the red and the orange, but it could interfere with her plans to time travel. Hopefully there would be no issues when she consumed the blood of the blue.

As stated previously, once the gifted has consumed a new color of blood, their original power appears a shade darker. With every new color consumption that is added to the host, their magic emerges darker each time. It has been written that if one has consumed all the colors of the Spectrum of Magic, a new godlike power is unlocked: the gift of the black.

This theory has never been tested, as there has never been a time when all colors of the gifted were born at the same time or during the same era. However, there have been tests that have been conducted on a few select gifted individuals who consumed multiple blood colors. This test proved the theory of the host's magic deepening in color.

The gift of the black. Unlocking godlike powers. That statement was music to her ears. Ikaria had read once a long time ago that completing the

Spectrum of Magic within one's self could unleash power that increased one's magic by a hundredfold. Whether it was true or not, Ikaria still wanted to have all of the colors of magic, because if she had them all, she could wipe the High Court out of existence. But it seemed that this gift of the black was a real thing. She had noticed her magic getting darker, and even her hair was growing to be a deeper violet. And each time she drank a new color of blood, her magic felt stronger.

To think, not only would she have every ability of the Spectrum of Magic if she completed it, but her power would increase a *hundredfold*. No one would be able to stop her. Not Auron, not her sister and her fool husband's gifted servants, and not the all-powerful High Court. And with that power, she could restore Earth to its former glory and establish a new era. The thought gave Ikaria much pleasure.

Lingering on her daydream a little bit more, she turned her attention back to the text.

> *There have been a few select cases that involved non-gifted subjects who consumed gifted blood who then were granted a tinted color by the magic, not a true color. Through various accounts, these "tinted-gifted" subjects only had a selected ability within that color and not the full power of the color. All "tinted-gifted" that have been recorded were born non-gifted and only became tinted by experimentation of blood consumption.*

Well, that's interesting… Ikaria smirked, thinking about her ex-lover. *That explains everything about him. No wonder he's so defective. He's nothing more than a tint. How nice.* She turned back to the text.

> *Please note that there have not been many studies on blood consumption as a whole, as it had been outlawed by the first High Court in 42 P.A. All tests were done prior to that date and have since then ceased.*

Ikaria looked over at Kohren, who remained silent, reading the text in front of him. She wrinkled her nose in disgust, knowing that another High Court spy was sitting in her midst, gathering information for them. He probably reported to them every night about her findings in the library, using his blue magic to teleport to them.

Kohren could *not* find out about this book. More so, the High Court could not find out about this book.

Ikaria turned her attention to the Colors and Properties section of the book until she came to the color blue, the color that she was most curious about. Anything she could learn about time travel and scrying time would be of use to her.

The Angel of the Blue hindered the gifted's ability to travel through time, for the flow of time would be disrupted with many blue-gifted traveling through the space-time continuum at once. Thus, one's physical body cannot travel through time and have their body withstand that time, for their physical body was not made for that time, and their body would turn to dust in a mere matter of minutes. The Blue Angel made the gifted's mind withstand time, not their body.

All blue-gifted that have been recorded as time travelers have returned to their time with their findings, their bodies severely damaged, and all returned just in time to save their lives. However, it is theorized in the early writings of The Spectrum, *from the Beginning Era, that the Angel of the Blue made a pact with the Angel of the Green, allowing the blue-gifted to withstand another time with the consumption of green blood.*

That in itself created a huge problem for Ikaria. She needed the blood of the green to complete the Spectrum of Magic. Ikaria was willing to travel through all of time to find a green-gifted, despite how trying that would be for her. Ikaria had the will to do it. But with this new information, it put a damper in all her plans. She had to somehow consume green blood in a matter of minutes in order for her remain alive in that time. That meant she had to find the green-gifted from across time and space, and somehow, through time, persuade the green-gifted to give her their blood.

And if and when she did travel, her body would be weakened before consuming the blood, making it hard for her to overpower the green-gifted in that time. If she had to use forceful violet magic, she might not even be able to do it. Even trying to unlock a gifted's mind swiftly would be difficult. Her body would disintegrate if she took too long.

The only real way she had a chance was to try to use her control magic within a past person's mind to convince them otherwise. It was already hard trying to unlock the mind of a gifted. But across time? It seemed impossible.

Now, more than ever, Ikaria needed to find a green-gifted across time. And the book that could aid her was missing.

Ikaria knowingly glanced over at Kohren. *How convenient. That bastard.*

Ikaria had to hide this book somehow. This book had the potential to be dangerous, especially in the wrong hands. Someone else had recognized that this book was dangerous too. Why else would it be hidden behind the other tomes? But who? If the High Court found out that gifted had the ability to use their analogous colors, or even the full potential of their adjacent colors, they would find a way to make laws restricting it.

Or perhaps they already knew this information and had found a way of dealing with it with their mysterious plague. The World Sector Six gifted were more powerful than they realized. Or were. Somehow everyone's ability to tap into their analogous colors had ceased to exist, otherwise surely someone would have discovered they could do so by accident?

Damn the High Court. They had to be the ones who were consuming and removing the magic from all the gifted through their so-called "sweating sickness" so they could become "gods," forcing everyone to become non-gifted, leaving the people unable to defend themselves and rendering them useless. Perhaps they had been aware of the gift of the black this whole time, and that was their intended goal. She hated the High Court all the more. This had their stink all over it.

Ikaria read the entire book from cover to cover, until she had a complete understanding of all the sections regarding magic. Putting down the book, Ikaria glanced over at Kohren. He was still in his seat, reading away at another selection.

Getting up, Ikaria returned to the same spot she had found the *Laws of Magic* book. Luckily the spot was not in view from where Kohren was sitting. As quietly as possible, Ikaria moved the thick tomes, then shoved the mysterious book back against the bookshelf, behind the other books, then precisely placed the thick tomes back into place.

CHAPTER 13

GREEN

Shouts pierced her ears as Emerald slowly opened her eyes. She wasn't sure if she was in Arcadia or in the pits of hell itself.

Shadows surrounded her in the abandoned alley where she leaned against a rough brick wall while the glow of car fires illuminated the main street before her. There were swarms of people crowded in the streets, screaming and yelling at Arcadia's authorities, while more people passed her by to join in on the action. One person even tripped over her, stumbling for a moment, then hastily ran off to wreak havoc with the protesters. Emerald winced at the sounds of glass being smashed and shattered while fiery Molotov cocktails were thrown at the police. Mixed in the noise was the rumbling of powerful engines vibrating down the streets, shooting down the alleyways and into the main road. Turning toward the noise, blackened silhouettes of what appeared to be motorcycles drove past the fires, trying to make their way through the crowds.

Grimacing in pain from the initial hit on the head, Emerald clawed at the brick wall behind her while trying to rise to her feet. Shaking, Emerald stumbled back to the ground, landing in a fresh pile of trash. The smell of urine, feces, and smoke filled her nostrils. Repulsed by the putrid scent, she began to gag, quickly holding her nose while choking on the lingering scent in her nostrils.

Frightened and weak, she was unsure of what to do, so she scooted back against the wall once more, watching the fires flicker as the crowds became more violent. The agitated protesters began to beat several officers, causing the Arcadian authorities to unleash a small but deadly force on the crowd.

The men in this unit were unlike anything Emerald had ever seen. Men that had flesh and bone but were infused with machinery of some kind, glowing an eerie red within the circuitry. Some of the men had grafted weapons on one of their arms, others were more normal but wielded unnatural strength.

Emerald watched in horror as many people tried to set the men on fire by throwing burning bottles at them, but the robotic men were unaffected. They moved in on the crowd systematically, fighting the people into submission with their dominant force. Several of the mechanical men lifted their gun arms, and without a moment's notice, they began shooting into the crowd, raining bullets throughout. Blood from the victims painted the living protesters red as their bodies squirted their lifeblood. Screams pierced the air, people cried for help, and many of them dispersed, trampling on their fellow dead protesters, trying to get away from the domineering machines.

Emerald looked around in a panic. She had to get out of the alley before she got hurt or killed—whether it was at the hands of the crowd or the mechanical men, it didn't matter.

Attempting once more to get up, she tried to rise to her feet, but her legs gave out as her strength failed her. The magic spent saving her from the fall had taken an enormous toll on her body, and she wondered if she had any magic left in her core to at least heal her frail body.

Suddenly a lock of her hair fell in her face. It was green; it had revealed itself through her fall. She couldn't have anyone find out who she was, especially down in the midst of a riot, and especially given who she was. She was in the midst of an aggravated crowd, a crowd who hated the royal family with such passion that they were destroying the very city they lived in.

Looking around, she saw that the passersby were so engrossed in what was happening in the streets that they had not noticed her, and she deemed it was safe enough to attempt to summon her magic, though she'd have to do it quietly.

Laying her hands upon her chest, she closed her eyes, calling forth the remaining healing life force within her. Her magic answered her, like a soft brush of wind flowing inside of her. Feeling her warm magic run through her veins, the green power seeped into her body as it renewed her strength, settling within the aches of her muscles.

After the soft green magic restored her within, she reversed its flow, sending it back into the core of her being. The magic quickly responded, coloring her tresses a deep scarlet color once more.

Opening her eyes, Emerald glanced at her surroundings. No one had seen her.

Thank goodness.

Still in her same position, Emerald watched the crowd in motion, continuing to retreat from the machines. But the mechanical men were pursuing the crowd no more. Instead they were stopped in their tracks, their eyes locked in her direction down the dark alley. Somehow she knew they were acutely aware of her gift.

How did they know that I used my magic? Emerald asked herself, panicking.

Thinking that she imagined it, Emerald paused, seeing if the mechanical men made any movement.

There was none, but their eyes remained fastened on her.

Jumping to her feet, Emerald ran out of the alley and into the rioting crowd. From the corner of her eye, Emerald saw the mechanical men's eyes following her every movement while the authorities were yelling orders at them to continue their suppression of the crowd. The machines returned to their gunfire after she passed them, spraying more bullets through the crowd, causing a massive exodus. A young teenage boy was in the line of fire, and his body slumped to the ground lifeless right in front of Emerald. More of the crowd pushed and pulled their way to escape the scene.

Horrified, Emerald gasped, then quickly skimmed the crammed streets, trying to figure out which way was the fastest escape route. In one direction, motorcycles were weaving through the crowd, heading away from the retreating rioters. That way looked a bit more dangerous, as it neared the authorities for a split second, but the path was much clearer than the fearful crowd.

She hurriedly squeezed her way through the crowd toward the path of the motorcycles, dodging the police by ducking low through the fleeing peoples of Arcadia. In pursuit of the motorcycles, she pushed and shoved through the crowd.

As she sprinted behind the bikes, the crowd began to lessen with each city block. The streets became clear, and the motorcycles began to disperse into the teeming city, driving to their intended destinations. As they peeled off, Emerald found herself in the heart of the sector.

I can't believe all of this is happening in Arcadia. Derek was right! Emerald thought, still shaken by the scene. She absentmindedly clutched her necklace chain, feeling the prince's ring within her hands while she slowed her run to a stroll, taking in the city around her.

The streets were still plenty crowded with the population of Arcadia, but at least she wasn't in the middle of the riot. The maze of the skyways above her glistened in bright yellows, and the city flashed its neon colors throughout Arcadia's buildings and streets. The streets were lined with half-naked women dancing in the windows and homeless sprawled out on the sidewalks, passed out drunk, while others were vomiting in the streets.

Cinching her nose, Emerald looked in disgust at the vileness around her.

At that moment, Emerald felt a pang of regret in leaving the palace. This was no place for her, and she doubted that anywhere in the lower levels would be safe for her to stay. She had to try and make her way to the mid-levels.

Picking up her pace with each step, Emerald continued down the clogged street. The traffic didn't move, though the motorcycles continued to pass by the ground transports.

Several blocks later, she came upon another enormous crowd dressed similar to the magazine ad she had been painting before she escaped the palace. Motorcycles began to gather within the crowds, and riders parked their bikes in the streets and down the side alley of a building. Most of the crowd was drinking out of bottles, smoking cigarettes, or breaking into fights. Loud, harsh music blared from within the doors of the building.

Emerald slowed her pace, watching the scene with curiosity and intrigue, until she came to a complete stop.

A hard tap hit her shoulders. Swinging around, she looked up at a large, heavy-set man in a black T-shirt with leather-strapped jewelry.

"Hey, sweetheart, you in line?" the man asked gruffly.

"Line?" Emerald repeated back to him, confused.

"Yeah, either you get in line or I have to tell you to move on. We need to clear the space in front of the building," he stated.

Promptly agreeing with the man and not wanting to cause trouble, Emerald nodded. He guided her forcefully into a newly formed line on the side of the building. As he did so, Emerald observed other men, who appeared to work at the venue inside, told others to scram, in a not-so-pleasant sort of way.

"You from the mid-levels?" a young woman asked, lighting a cigarette.

Embarrassed, Emerald was unsure how to respond to the woman, who looked to be about her age. "Why do you ask?" Emerald asked in a timid voice.

"No reason." The girl snickered while she took a drag of her cigarette, then blew it in Emerald's face. Her eyes reviewed Emerald's outfit, then turned away to someone behind her. The line progressed to the door as people were let inside. As Emerald approached the door, a man standing by held out his hand, waiting for her to give him money. Reaching for a few bills that Glacia had given her, she handed the man the payment, then he waved her in.

Taking a deep breath, Emerald gathered up whatever courage she had and stepped foot inside.

CHAPTER 14

"Where the fuck have you been, man?" Remy cursed loudly as Kyle pulled up in the alleyway behind the club. "Did you fucking forget that we had a gig at the last minute or what?" Remy grabbed the last of the equipment from the band's run-down transport, slamming the back door down. Remy always had a stick up his ass about one thing or another.

Parking his motorcycle, Kyle killed the engine, then swung off the bike and lit a cigarette. "Dude, I left early, and there was still a shitload of traffic," Kyle said nonchalantly.

"We are about to go on soon, and you haven't even tuned your shit yet." Remy eyed him, clearly pissed. He huffed and stalked off, carrying the equipment to the back door of the venue. "And you better not be fucked up like the last show," Remy called out, nearing the entrance. "We don't need this shit right now."

"Fucking good evening to you, too," Kyle muttered. He doubted Remy heard him. Not like he cared if he did or not. When Remy was in a pissy mood, no one wanted to be around him, including the other band members.

What's up his ass? Kyle thought as he continued to puff the cigarette that clung between his lips. *He's so damn serious all the time.*

As Kyle stepped inside the club, the other band members were finishing hooking up the remaining equipment. Kyle slung his guitar case off his back, then flicked the butt of his cigarette to the ground, rubbing it into the ground with the heel of his boot. Grabbing his guitar, he fussed with it, tuning it until he was satisfied.

Taking a quick peek at the venue from the side of the stage, Kyle saw it was similar to all the other clubs that Disorderly Conduct played at. The place was a shitty hole-in-the-wall joint with graffiti sprayed everywhere, along with walls that were decorated with puke and blood. There were ragged tables back by the bar, which Kyle would bet would soon be overturned when the show started. The bar itself was framed with four big planks posing as pillars, with a neon-blue glow over the whole section. The crowd in the venue was typical— studded black leather-clothes, brightly dyed hair, and completely obnoxious. His favorites. They always made for a better show.

"It's bigger than the last venue, at least," Diego said, standing beside him with his bass guitar. He took one last drink of his flask and tucked it away in his jacket.

"Yeah," Kyle agreed, turning away. He grabbed his own flask, took a long drink, then wiped his mouth with the back of his hand, grunting. As he did so, he heard someone announce their band. The house lights went dark as lighting flooded the stage in a cool white. He could hear the audience cheering from the floor of the venue, filling the place with high energy, the kind he needed to make him feel like he was alive. Truly alive.

Kyle grasped his guitar, starting to play as he came out on stage with the others, except Kamren, who was already playing his drums to the beat of the first number. The crowd began to scream and yell as he started to sing and strum his guitar. Several fights broke out in front of him, one resulting in blood flying. He continued to play and sing through as if nothing was happening. It wasn't like he would let the fighting stop his music. Plus, what was a show without blood flying?

Soaking in the intensity of the crowd, it fed Kyle's spirit with ferocity as he began to sing. Beer began to fly, girls screamed while the guys shouted and slammed into each other. The crazier the crowd became, the more Kyle drew from their electrifying energy, letting that energy fill his voice, throwing it right back at them. The crowd loved him, and he them. The alcohol, the girls, the blood, the vomit, the piss… the craziness of it all. The wildness of the night embraced him like a lover.

This was his life. This was what he lived for.

As the band played into the night, Kyle saw the venue transform into a bloodbath from all the fights, and those without blood were soaked in beer. A haze enveloped them from all the cigarette smoking, which made it hard to see past the first five rows. It didn't matter; he knew they were all having a good-ass time by the amount of noise in the place.

Kyle finished up the last song in the set, then nodded to the other band members. They gestured back to him, then waved to the crowd as they walked off stage.

"Thanks, guys," Kyle said to the wasted crowd, throwing a fist up in the air. "You're fucking great." They answered back by screaming and cheering. Kyle couldn't wait to get shit-faced like the rest of them.

Exiting the stage, he passed by the next band that was going to play as they waited for Disorderly Conduct to tear down their equipment. As soon as the stage went dark, Remy began getting the equipment unhooked, along with Kamren and a couple of stagehands. Kyle joined them by packing away his guitar, then helped Remy and Kamren get their equipment into the ground transport, which was parked out back in the alley.

"Hey, Kyle, we're heading to that new bar down the street. You wanna come?" Diego asked, shaking his blue hair and wiping the sweat off his neck, packing the last of the equipment into the transport.

"Yeah, sounds good. I'm just going to get a drink before I head over," Kyle replied, lighting a cigarette and shutting one of the doors of the transport.

Diego nodded. "See ya in a bit, then." He hopped out of the back of the transport, then got on his motorcycle, riding off behind the band's transport as it pulled onto the main street.

Kyle puffed his cigarette, walking back inside the venue. The nicotine gave him instant gratification. Now all he needed to do was get a damn drink. He could have waited to get over to the other bar, but his flask was empty, and his mouth was watering.

Hugging the back wall, Kyle moved his way past the crowd to get to the bar. As he approached the glowing blue area, he waved to the bartender, trying to get his attention. After several attempts, the bartender finally noticed him.

"Whiskey," Kyle ordered. The bartender nodded, and Kyle retreated back by one of the wooden pillars, leaning against it indifferently, waiting for the bartender to return. As he inhaled another drag of his cigarette, he saw a young woman across the bar. She had extremely long wavy red hair pulled into a ponytail. As she moved her hands to take a drink, the light from the bar illuminated her face, capturing her beauty. The pale softness of her skin, her perfect red heart-shaped lips, the deep-red halo that surrounded her hair.

And her big bright eyes. They were the greenest eyes he had ever seen, framed with long dark lashes. She was, by far, the most gorgeous creature he had ever seen.

There was something about this woman, like a powerful force that demanded his presence. Kyle studied the girl, and he continued to smoke his cigarette. He noted that she was obviously not from the lower levels, and he had a definite feeling that she wasn't from the mid-levels, either. The way she handled herself seemed too… proper, giving him the first clue that she had to be from the upper levels. She was poised with her back straight, which enhanced the curve of her chest within her tiny frame. She held her chin up high, but her eyes contradicted her, as they were wide with trepidation. He almost would have laughed at her for sticking out like a sore thumb in a hellhole like this, but he knew it was no laughing matter. Most everyone in the joint could see her for what she was—one who didn't belong.

Kyle asked himself why the redheaded woman was even here. She didn't seem like the type who liked the kind of music that was playing.

Taking a long inhale of his cigarette, Kyle exhaled gradually, streaming the smoke from his lips. The bartender came back with his drink, giving Kyle a quick nod. Kyle left his wooden pillar and snatched his drink up at the bar, throwing a bill down on the counter. As he did so, he looked out of the corner of his eye, noticing that the woman was staring at him peculiarly. Guzzling the shot, he slammed the empty glass onto the counter, rattling the other empty glasses on the bar. Retreating to the wooden pillar once more, he leaned against it, taking another drag of his cigarette. The woman continued to eye him for a few seconds more, then turned her attention elsewhere in the venue.

After Kyle finished his cigarette, he walked toward the bar, smashing the butt into an ashtray. As he turned around to leave, he saw a large bald man with half of his face tattooed hovering over the redheaded woman. He leaned in far too close for comfort, and her face told him that his advances were unwanted.

Kyle began to take a few steps away from the bar, then paused. At that moment, a nagging feeling came over him. He didn't care to help any upper-class person, as they hadn't done a damn thing to help out the lower levels. But seeing this beautiful woman, he knew that she was helpless, especially against an asshole that size.

"Dammit," he cursed under his breath. *I hope I don't fucking regret this.*

After a moment, he reached for another cigarette and lit it. He swung his body back in the direction of the woman, the stream of smoke trailing behind him.

"R-really, I am fine," the woman stuttered as her face leaned away from the tattooed man. "I am… I am waiting for someone. He should be here any minute…"

Kyle and the tattooed man both knew that she was lying.

"Where is he?" his gruff voice asked, calling out her bullshit. "Why would he leave you by yourself?" His face got in hers, and he rested a hand on her shoulder. Her eyes flinched in disgust.

Continuing to puff smoke from his mouth, Kyle interrupted. "*He* is here. Fucking take a hike," he said sharply, getting in between the woman and the tattooed man. Kyle puffed his cigarette between his lips, exhaling in the man's face.

The man flashed an immediate glare at Kyle, making no other movement than a snarl of his lips. Kyle's eyes trailed to the woman, her face pleading silently at him in fear, her lower lip quivering.

"Fucking asshole," the man roared in Kyle's face, yanking the cigarette from his mouth and flinging it.

Reaching for his pocket knife, Kyle flipped it open, then swung it in the tattooed man's face, lodging it into the bar in front of him. "Get lost, shithead," Kyle said.

The tattooed man jumped up, hurling a barstool to the ground. The moment he jumped up, the redheaded woman edged back to the bar area, hiding in the shadows of the blue lights. The people by the bar instantly began to cheer for another fight.

The tattooed man swung at Kyle, aiming for his chest. Luckily Kyle was smaller than the guy and dodged, quickly landing a solid punch in the man's gut. He was unmoved by Kyle's punch; he'd clearly been in many fights before. The man sneered, then swung back at Kyle. "That all you got?"

Kyle dodged the blow, but he wasn't quick enough. The tattooed man bashed the side of his nose, and a hot shock of pain shot through him, vibrating into his face, causing Kyle to tumble to the ground. He could taste a bit of blood running down his nose and into his mouth. His nose wasn't broken, but it would have been had he not moved. Snarling, Kyle wiped his bloody nose and lips and jumped onto his feet. The man was about to swing again but missed as Kyle rolled to dodge the man. Turning swiftly, Kyle landed a hard punch squarely below the man's chest, causing the man to gasp for air. His eyes bulged out as he tumbled to the ground.

"Hey!" yelled the bartender. "We don't want any shit back by the bar. Take it outside!" A few bouncers came, yanking Kyle away from the man before he could strike again.

"You're a dead man!" shouted the tattooed man, still gasping for breath. He violently pushed the bouncers, all the while swinging wildly to get to Kyle. It was a good thing there were more of them and only one of him.

"Good luck, asshole," Kyle shot back, spitting a gob of blood and phlegm at the man, his nose burning. A surge of adrenaline ran through his veins, overwhelming him with the urge to fight the bouncers and kick the man's ass. Swallowing his pride, he tried to remain calm, not wanting to get kicked out of the place. Remy would never forgive him if Disorderly Conduct got banned from playing at that club.

It took four men to hold the tattooed man back, and he screamed obscenities as they pulled him away from the bar. Kyle watched him disappear into the crowd, knowing that the man would be thrown out onto the street. Others were explaining to the bouncers what happened. Breathing heavily from the rush of the fight, Kyle waited to be released.

When they finally let him go, he nodded to them in thanks and wiped the sweat off his brow and shook his open black leather vest in a sharp jerk, trying to cool off his sweat-soaked body. Eyes were still on him, and he used that to his advantage. With the eyes of the bartender on him, he flagged him over, the silver from the studs on his leather bracelets catching the neon-blue light. The crowd resumed their conversations and drinks. The band onstage started their first number.

"Yeah?" the bartender asked, his voice gruff.

He lit another cigarette, looking in the redheaded girl's direction. She still hadn't moved from the corner, but her eyes were locked on him.

"Two shots of whiskey," Kyle said to the bartender. The bartender looked at him for a moment, then eyed the redheaded woman in the corner. Kyle motioned his head at the woman. "Think that's her poison?"

The bartender bared all his crooked teeth in a rotten smile, laughing hoarsely. "Not a chance in hell."

"Yeah, I didn't think so," Kyle mumbled, burning the cherry of his cigarette as he inhaled. "Get her one anyway."

The bartender returned with two glasses in his hands. He slammed down both in front of Kyle, then poured the liquor in the shot glasses, spilling it onto the counter. Kyle didn't move except to jerk his head at the woman, gesturing for her to come up to him.

Slowly retreating from the corner, she eyed him curiously with her bright-green eyes.

"Here, I think you need this," he offered, sliding one of the glasses toward her. Without saying a word, she nodded. Raising the shot glass, he waited for her to do likewise. After a moment, she caught on, raising her glass to match his. Then they both downed the whiskey at the same time, and he slammed his glass against the counter. She squeezed her eyes shut tightly, setting the glass down gently. Amused, he chuckled, knowing that the alcohol was much too strong for her. But for what it was worth, he could tell she was trying not to show it, and she appeared able to hold her composure.

"Thanks," she said after she cleared her throat, tears in her eyes from the burning alcohol.

"Hopefully it will make your night a little less shitty," Kyle said, inhaling from his cigarette.

The woman smiled at him. "I meant getting that man away from me, but I suppose it can mean the drink too."

"That guy was an asshole. The world needs a lot less of them." Kyle's cigarette continued to stream smoke as he seated himself by her. He hoped to God his face wasn't fucked up or swollen. That would be really shitty, him all fucked up while talking to a beautiful woman.

"Well, thank you. I wasn't sure how I would have gotten out of that situation." Her green eyes looked at him with gratitude.

"You wouldn't have," Kyle told her bluntly. Taking the cigarette between his ringed fingers, he put out his cigarette, then exhaled the last of his smoke. He gestured to the bartender for another round. He lowered his head, dropping his voice. "Word of advice: Don't try to bullshit people in the lower levels. They can smell it a mile away."

"What?" The woman looked stunned at his statement. "Why do you say that?" She straightened herself in the chair with her chin raised. "How do you know that I wasn't waiting for anyone?"

In a hushed voice he stated, "No offense, but you don't look like the type to be just hanging around alone waiting for a guy in a place like this." Kyle fetched his drink from the bartender, guzzling it down. "And your outfit. It's a dead giveaway."

She eyed the people around her, finally seeing what he saw. They knew she didn't belong. She flashed a half convincing smile at the people around her, those who were staring. There was a sudden fear in her eyes. Turning back to Kyle, she blurted, "Am I that obvious?"

"Yeah." With another whiskey in his hand, he pushed the drink toward her. "This isn't the upper levels, where everything is safe. Girls shouldn't be by themselves down here."

The woman's green eyes went wide, sucking in her breath. Leaning in, she whispered with concern, "You can tell I am from the upper levels? Do you think the people in this place know that too?"

Kyle shrugged. "Maybe. Just take another shot and don't think about it."

"I suppose." The woman's eyes lowered to gaze at her full shot glass, her lips slightly trembling.

"Don't worry about it. If you want, I'll stay here until you are ready to leave. I'll even drop you off at the station if you need a ride." Just then, he remembered that his friends were waiting for him at the other bar. *To hell with those guys.*

"I would like that." Her sparkling green eyes met his, and she hinted a smile with her cherry-red lips. "Thanks…" She was searching his face for a name.

"Kyle."

"Thank you, Kyle." She flashed him a bright smile, taking another shot.

"What? I don't get to know your name? What kind of shit is that?"

She paused for a moment, hesitant. Kyle continued to smoke his cigarette, watching her face contort while she battled some kind of internal struggle. He waved his cigarette. "It's fine. You don't have to tell me."

"Em," she said finally. "You can call me Em."

"Em? Never heard that one before. Is it short for Emilia or something?"

"Something like that," she said, her voice faltering. She gave no other details.

"Right," he said, not sounding convinced, but he rolled with it. "So, Em, what great house were you born into? Or is that a secret too?" Kyle opened his pack of cigarettes, taking one while holding it open to offer one to her. Em declined by politely waving her hand.

"I would rather not say." Her eyes met his. "And it doesn't really matter. I am not going back."

"Ah. You ran away?" Kyle lit his cigarette. Now this was interesting. What girl in her right mind would run away from a life of luxury?

She paused for a moment. "Yes. That's exactly what I did." She leaned in. "And I mean it. I never want to go back. Ever."

"I see," Kyle said. This girl was something, that was for sure. "Where are you staying, then? Not down here, I hope. No one volunteers to run away to the shittiest part of Arcadia."

Em's face looked a bit sad. "I don't know where I am staying. I was hoping to rent a room somewhere until I figure it out."

"I know a motel in a better neighborhood. I'll take you there when you want to go."

Em revealed a warm smile, causing his insides to burn. Her beauty was intoxicating, like a wicked poison that was seeping under his skin. God, he hated this shit. It drove him nuts.

"Yes, please. Is it in the mid-levels?" she asked.

Kyle shook his head. "As much as I would love to bring you to the mid-levels, I can't afford the tax. The place is in the lower levels, but it's in a better area. Still, don't expect much. Anywhere in the lower levels is still shitty."

"I see." Em appeared to be thinking it over. He knew that he'd let her down about the mid-levels, but her being some type of highborn, she probably never had to worry about paying for things. Her expression melted away, and she focused on him. "I will take you up on the ride to the... motel, if you don't mind."

"Sure."

The two talked for a while more, until he had about two cigarettes left in his pack and the final band was packing up for the evening. The bartender hollered for last call, and the crowd began filtering out of the venue. Kyle wouldn't have minded sitting there longer, but he had no choice. It was time to go.

Em caught on to the people leaving, giving him a look. "Well, I think we had better be going. Can you still give me a ride?" she asked as she bit her ruby-red lips, tossing her high ponytail aside over her shoulder. "That is, if you are fine to drive."

"Yeah, I'm fine. Come on."

He led her out back to where his motorcycle was parked, and she stopped in her tracks, frozen. "I have to ride on *that?*" Her voice shook with fear.

Kyle laughed, the smoke coughing out of him as he did so. "You scared?"

"Yes, very much." Em's eyes studied the motorcycle.

"It's the only transportation I got, but I'll go slow for you. Get on."

"How… old is it?" she asked hesitantly.

"Yeah, yeah, that seems to be the question when everyone sees it," Kyle said, sighing.

Em's cheeks flushed. "I'm sorry, I didn't mean to insinuate…"

"Don't worry about it. I won't be losing sleep over it any time soon. The guys give me shit daily about it." Kyle shrugged, motioning his head for her to get on his bike.

Em seated herself behind him. Kyle felt the warmth of her body against his back, sending a thrill of pleasure through him. She grabbed hold of his shoulders, bracing for him to take off.

Kyle cleared his throat awkwardly. "Hey, Em, that's not gonna work. You're gonna have to hold on to my waist," he managed to say. "Otherwise you'll fly off the bike. Don't want that to happen."

"Okay," she said, hesitantly slipping her arms around his waist. Kyle felt her grip tighten as his motorcycle engine roared. Her hands felt good.

God help me…

"Hold on tight," he ordered.

Then he took off, and the two of them were soon racing through the neon-blue and violet streets of Arcadia.

CHAPTER 15

GREEN

The city was alive. Truly alive. The streets glistened with a light dew, streaked with reflections from the red and green traffic lights mixed with colorful neon signs. Emerald caught whiffs of sweet meats and steamed vegetables from the local shop carts selling foods to those who needed nourishment at a late hour. Other scents of spicy drinks, aromatic smokes, and the putrid smells of the sewers lingered, the last of them causing Emerald to keep her head close to Kyle's studded jacket. The worn leather had Kyle's scent on it, overpowering the others. A strong, fresh scent.

On one hand, the lower levels frightened Emerald, with its fair share of rough citizens, fights, riots, and the sheer grime that covered everything, casting an overall menacing appearance throughout. But looking past the strangeness of it all, there was a sense of freedom that emerged, giving Emerald a taste of new possibilities that had not been an option before.

"Hey, dickwad, can you go any slower?" a man shouted from behind. A considerably large motorcycle weaved past them, spitting out trash from beneath the peeling tires as the bike drove away.

Kyle ignored the bike and kept driving, but not without revving his engine in response.

Kyle was strange, no doubt about it. From his looks to his mannerisms, he was by far the most bizarre character that Emerald had ever met. But that wasn't saying much, considering she had lived her entire life in the palace and only met citizens from the upper levels.

Emerald glanced out of the corner of her eye, noticing a body lying on the side of a street as they drove by, covered in blood. On the other side of the street, a medical transport drove by, passing the man.

"Why didn't they stop?" Emerald asked loudly.

"Huh?" Kyle called out.

"The medical transport. That man needed help."

"He couldn't afford it, so they don't even bother."

"How do they know that? It didn't stop to find out," Emerald asked.

"They didn't have to. You take one look at a person, and you know who can afford what," Kyle stated.

"But that's so wrong!"

"Welcome to the lower levels," Kyle called out, continuing to drive. "It's complete bullshit and pisses me off. But what the hell can anyone do about it? It's always been like that; always will be like that. You'll get used to it after a while."

"I could never get used to it," Emerald huffed under her breath. *If I was Queen, I would make things different...*

The two of them pulled up to a building in semidecent condition, lit up in pink neons with a flashing yellow sign that read "Vacancy."

Kyle parked his motorcycle and killed the engine.

"Thank you for the ride," Emerald said, getting off the bike. She turned to face Kyle, shuffling her boots. "I guess this is it?"

An amused smile appeared on Kyle's face. "Em, you think I would just dump you out here and take off?"

"I don't know," Emerald said. "Is that not normal?"

"No. That isn't. It would be a dick move if I did. I mean, I'm an asshole, but not like *that*." Kyle nudged her playfully. "I'll at least make sure you get a room and you're safe before I leave."

"Thank you," Emerald said appreciatively.

Kyle cracked a small smile in response. It looked like he was about to say more on the subject, but he didn't, and Emerald kept silent, giving him a smile in return.

As the two started walking toward the entrance, Emerald slowly took in the motel's visuals and gulped. Even with the bright neons of the lights, suspicious characters paid no heed to concealing their fight. Two men near the sidewalk, each with a knife in their hand, were trying to stab one another while shouting obscenities. Sirens wailed, probably being called to the very scene Emerald was witnessing. Emerald tried to not stare in their direction and turned her gaze in Kyle's direction. He seemed unaffected by the heated exchange of words, casually lighting up another cigarette. Within hours of being in the lower levels, Emerald had already witnessed two brawls. Was this what life was like all the time down in the lower levels?

"You said this is one of the better places down here?" Emerald asked quietly as she quickly walked past the argument.

Kyle laughed, then took another drag of his cigarette. "I told you it wasn't much, Em."

Emerald nervously eyed her surroundings. She had never spent a night without guards or servants. And here she was, in the bowels of the lower levels. No guards, no servants. Only accompanied by a strange guy in black leather with erratic hair. The feeling of being alone in Arcadia unnerved her.

"Lemme talk to motel owner," Kyle said before he opened the door. "The less you talk, the better your chance in surviving this place. They might just think you're from the mid-levels if you don't say anything."

"Okay," Emerald agreed, shying away behind him.

The metal door made a loud creak as they entered, slamming hard behind them. Emerald followed behind Kyle closely. Beyond the thick layer of smoke that enveloped the air, there was an empty stained counter, snagged carpets on the floor, two lounge chairs that desperately needed to be replaced, and an elevator with a taped sign that read "Out of order, use stairs." In a corner of the room, Emerald saw a monitor broadcasting the local news.

Kyle exhaled his cigarette causally, dinging a bell that sat on the counter.

"Why isn't it electronic?" Emerald asked Kyle quietly, referring to the bell.

"Down here, everything is a piece of crap. Costs too much for all that fancy shit."

"Oh." Emerald lowered her face, feeling embarrassed for even asking.

"Hello?" Kyle called out, dinging the bell again. He leaned back against the counter, taking another puff of his cigarette.

Emerald watched the broadcast as they waited. Images of the riots appeared on the screen. Protesters burned stuffed representations of her father, King Damaris, lighting them on fire. Images of the strange robotic men, gunning down citizens with grafted arms.

"*Hello?*" Kyle said, raising his voice, slamming the bell over and over. "Anyone fucking here?"

At that moment, Emerald heard a back door open behind the counter.

"I was starting to think the sign out front was full of shit," Kyle stated.

"The wife," a man said as he rolled his eyes, appearing before them. "You know how it is. You leave in the middle of her talking, there is hell to pay." The man took a drink from behind the counter.

"Sorry, dude. I know how that goes." Kyle shrugged, exhaling a waft of smoke into the thick air.

"Don't we all?" The man eyed Kyle, then glanced at Emerald. "How long you need it for? Two hours?"

Two hours? Why would anyone need a room for two hours?

"It's not like that," Kyle said, shifting his eyes and taking another drag. "She needs a room for the night."

Suddenly Emerald felt completely stupid, realizing what the man was insinuating. She turned away, flushed with embarrassment. Did people really rent a room just to do *that*?

"Sure, whatever you say," the man said back. He let out a loud laugh and took another drink. "Need to see her ID."

Emerald's heart quickly leapt out of her chest. She had no ID. She froze in place. The only movement she could make was her hands fumbling nervously on her ponytail.

Kyle's dark eyes met hers and gave her a knowing look. Quickly turning back to the motel owner, Kyle opened up his wallet, sliding his ID across the counter.

"I need hers," the man said, sliding Kyle's ID back to him.

Emerald was about to open her mouth, but Kyle interceded. "She lost it. You don't really need hers, do you?"

"Yes, I do. If she's staying in the room, I do. It's the law."

"Since when?"

"Since recently."

"Listen, just use mine. One ID for one person."

"Can't, buddy. I get audited. I don't need this place closed down on account of some girl off the street," the man said, drinking another glass, eyeing Emerald. "Or should I say, someone from the mid-levels."

He knows I'm not from down here…

"It's fine, Kyle," Emerald whispered quickly. "Thank you anyway, sir." She was about to bow, but then stopped herself from doing so, awkwardly waving instead.

"Yeah, thanks. For *nothing*," Kyle muttered as they exited onto the street.

"I'm sorry for wasting your time. I had no idea that they needed an ID I feel terrible that you drove me all the way here for nothing," Emerald said, lowering her gaze.

"I don't blame you for not wanting to show your ID The authorities would find you immediately if someone reported you missing."

"I don't even have an ID to show."

"No ID?" Kyle glanced at her quizzically. "What are you talking about? Everyone has an ID to get around in this place."

"I've… never had one," Emerald managed.

"Well, that's a first. Don't they have IDs on the upper levels? Or is it only us lower and mid-level scum that they need to subdue?"

"Subdue? What do you mean?"

"Em, you are really strange."

Emerald popped open her eyes. "Strange? You think I am strange?"

"Yeah, you are." Kyle's lips curled, half amused. "Let's get going."

"Where are you taking me? I can't rent a room anywhere…" Emerald began.

"My place," Kyle said, taking the last puff of his cigarette and flicking it on the ground. "That is, unless you wanna squat on the street somewhere. I know a couple of abandoned buildings." He got onto his bike, starting the engine.

Emerald glanced at him, pausing.

He's right. It's much better staying at his place rather than the street, she reasoned.

Deciding she was better off taking her chances, Emerald slid onto the back of motorcycle seat and wrapped her arms around his waist. Her cheeks burned again for being so close to an almost complete stranger.

Though he was a very *interesting* complete stranger.

CHAPTER 16

VIOLET

How Ikaria loathed attending evening court events. Especially the dinners. Watching Cyrus eye the latest court beauty made her blood boil. Little twits half his age laughing at his stupid jokes and shooting him longing stares. And he had no shame engaging in their advances. Everyone pretended he did no such thing, even Ayera, but Ikaria noted each encounter, hoping to eventually turn it into his shame.

How was it that she'd once fallen in love with that fool? And to think she had been engaged to him.

What aggravated Ikaria even more than Cyrus's ridiculous flirting was that the *Laws of Magic* book had gone missing. Every so often, when Kohren was not around, Ikaria would check to see if the book was still in its hiding spot. And this morning, it was gone. Ikaria could safely bet that it was now in the hands of the High Court.

That High Justice bitch Belinda, thought Ikaria. *Anything to hinder me and the world sectors.*

Dressed in her full regalia—long-horned headdress and revealing black-and-violet gown tailored with bell sleeves that swept the floor—Ikaria entered the dining hall with her back arched and head held high, like the Empress she was supposed to be. Most of the court was already seated at the oversized crystal table and had started in on their first course. The courtly gifted came trickling in along with the non-gifted members of the court. A flamboyant red-gifted who loved drama appeared in a ball of fire, then smoldered, his fabrics glistening with embers. An orange-gifted faded out of thin air, staying invisible until he needed to make his presence known. Lord Kohren came flashing in, appearing instantly next to Auron at the table with his space and dimensional magic, the only magic he was allowed to use since the High Court had banned all use of blue time magic.

Hovering magical lamps were casting a warm orange brilliance on the crystallized room, revealing a few glances from the table that came Ikaria's way. Several nodded with respect, acknowledging her, but the majority of the others ignored her, something Ikaria had never gotten used to. As a princess in her youth, people used to kiss the ground she walked on and sang her praises. But that was when she was supposed to be the next Empress of World Sector Six. When Ayera was named as the heir to the throne, everyone abandoned her. Traitors. They were all nothing more than pretenders, and Ikaria loathed pretenders. The very thought of their ersatz loyalty made her grit her teeth.

Arriving in front of her sister, Ikaria bowed. She never gave Cyrus the time of day unless she absolutely had to, and she chose not to bow to him now. It was only fair, as he had never given her anything but scorn and mockery in the many years he had been Emperor. The only satisfaction Ikaria got was that she knew what he truly was and could see it right through the masked illusions.

"Your Majesty," Ikaria said with a nod, then took her seat beside Ayera. Cyrus didn't even glance her way as she approached, appearing to be in a deep conversation with the Duke of Orza. His gaze was glued to one of the orange-gifted servant girls, her beauty and her bust heavily enhanced with her magic. Auron, who was not engaged in any conversation, glanced at Ikaria from across the table. Kohren seemed only interested in his dinner, and Lord Jiao was talking to another red-gifted beside him.

"Sister." Ayera nodded, waving her hand for the nearby servant. One approached, filling Ikaria's glass. "How goes your… assignment so far?" Ayera asked, carefully wording her question in front of Cyrus.

Ikaria glanced at Cyrus, who was being quite loud and obnoxious, his laugh booming as he drank his wine. Their concern seemed unwarranted—the Emperor was paying no attention to Ayera. Ikaria's eyes trailed to Kohren, who continued to pick at his food.

"Quite disconcerting," Ikaria said.

Ayera's face turned serious, leaning in. "What do you mean? Have you found something?"

"No, quite the opposite," Ikaria hinted, thinking of the *Laws of Magic* book. "Something seems to be missing. Several things," Ikaria said, acting distressed and taking a calculated sip of her wine. Kohren had looked up from his food, looking in the direction of the two sisters, seeming mildly interested in what was being said.

Ikaria's glance moved toward Auron. He ate in silence, oblivious to his surroundings. He looked tired. Probably tired of praying, since that was probably all he did as of late. The poor priest who so desperately wanted to stop the magical plague. But little did he know his prayers wouldn't save their sector. No, it would be his worst nightmare that would rescue their sector.

Her.

Ayera set down her glass and pushed her plate away. "What is missing?"

Ikaria twirled her wine, then drank a large gulp, watching Lord Kohren. "Sister, who has had access granted to the library since my last visit? I know that you don't go around granting just anyone permission."

"Only five others. High Justice Oriel, High Justice Perserine, Lord Grayson, Lord Miles, and Lord Kohren. You are now the sixth. Why?" Ayera asked curiously, keeping her voice low.

Lord Grayson had died of natural causes a few months back, and Lord Miles had lost his orange magic due to the plague. Quite interesting. The High Court probably knew that one of those two found out about their analogous colors and took care of them. Ikaria guessed that it was Lord Grayson, considering the High Court wouldn't let someone live with that kind of knowledge of magic. That and the fact that he'd told a few people he had made some revolutionary findings and was writing a journal detailing his discovery. And after his death, no one could find his writings on his discovery. How convenient.

A false look of confusion washed over Ikaria's face. "Well, it seems to me that a few of our tomes from the Millennium Era have gone missing. I have searched all week for those books," Ikaria said in the most innocent voice she could muster. "It is very odd. One of them I had recently read, and I needed to refer back to. The other ones I *know* existed from my last visit, and those are gone as well." Ikaria sat, unmoving, eyeing Kohren. He went back to eating his food, stirring his fork and pretending not to be listening.

Let's see you worm your way out of this one, Lord Kohren. Ikaria narrowed her eyes, taking another drink of wine.

"That's impossible. Our sector records are quite secure," Ayera said under her breath.

"What is secure?" Emperor Cyrus swung his head in their direction, wine glass in hand, his face fully flushed with the effects of the alcohol. He had always been a sloppy drunk, and his chestnut curls fell flat when he drank, making him look woefully pathetic. Cyrus looked at the sisters, waiting for an answer. Ikaria didn't have any desire to converse with the Emperor, but it looked like she had no choice.

Ikaria rolled her eyes at her sister as a private jest, then turned to Cyrus. "That new artifact that was discovered on the surface. Two gifted are en route to the High Court to deliver it as we speak. They should be very pleased with this one," Ikaria said. It was a half lie. What she said was true—it was being delivered, but it was being "delayed" in her chambers until she could properly study it.

"Very good," Cyrus replied, uninterested, and he turned back to continue his conversation with the Duke of Orza while giving the gifted servant girl another big grin.

Ayera paused for a moment, waiting for Cyrus to immerse himself in his conversation with the duke. After a minute, she leaned in to Ikaria. "Sister, are you sure about the documents? Perhaps they were misplaced?"

"Quite sure, sister. You know of my love for the technology of the Millennium Era. I value those documents above anything else in this citadel," Ikaria answered. "Why would I fabricate something like this? It would serve no purpose. I am merely pointing out the fact that we have missing documents, and it's quite interesting that only high justices have visited the library, with exception of the deceased Lord Grayson, Lord Miles, and Lord Kohren."

Ayera leaned in closer, whispering in Ikaria's ear. "Sister, I know what you are doing. You are walking a fine line. I warned you earlier."

"You told me you wanted to see results. How can I do what you ask of me if part of our library seems to be *missing*?" Rage flooded Ikaria's heart, quickening its pace. She grasped her goblet tightly and took a sip of wine, the liquid balling in her throat as her hatred continued to burn. How could she make her sister see what was clear as day?

"Sister, I will advise you one last time: Do not try to *frame* the High Court," Ayera whispered sternly. "It will amount to nothing and will lead to you being imprisoned. If you continue down this path, I cannot save you from their judgment. Do you *want* to be sentenced to the toxic earth below? Is that your desire? Because if that's the case, you are heading in that direction."

Ikaria narrowed her eyes, her hand shaking her glass. She wanted to crush the fragile goblet with her violet magic. But no. That would amount to nothing. Restraining herself, she firmly set the goblet down on the dinner table, her face flashing in anger at Ayera. Leaning in to her sister's ear, she whispered sharply, "I am telling you, someone *stole* those documents. As I recall, you asked for my help, knowing deep down I would hate every moment doing so." Ikaria narrowed her eyes in resentment. "But I swallowed my pride, because you are still my blood. And yet I give you warning about a grave issue, and you doubt my words." Ikaria rose from her seat. Raising her voice, she announced, "Don't come *crawling* to my feet asking for my help ever again."

A few people surrounding them became terribly interested in their food, while others at the far end of the table didn't seem to have noticed the exchange. Cyrus looked in her direction, narrowing his eyes. "What is this all about?" he asked, staring at her with annoyance.

"I am taking my leave, Your *Majesty*. It seems that Her Majesty cares not for my advice. After all, I am just court *sorceress*. What do I know?" Ikaria didn't bother to bow to either one of them. Instead she raised her head high, too proud to give them the respect they were entitled to.

As Ikaria huffed off, she noticed that Kohren's seat was vacant. *That's right, fool. You better hide. Go run and tell the High Court of my discovery*, Ikaria thought.

Angrily, Ikaria marched through the citadel corridors, full of scorn and disgust. For a moment, she paused, trying to collect her thoughts. It seemed it was useless trying to convince her sister of anything. To continue would only amount to more frustration on her part. She was done trying.

No matter, she could just take the situation into her own hands, like she had done with the others. Best to do it now before the book was used by the High Court to destroy more of her power.

Ikaria called upon her violet magic, power tingling within her thoughts as the magic streamed its way through to her target. Through her power, she entered the target's mind, careful not to brush his mind abrasively. There was a plethora of doors inside his core being, guarding his innermost thoughts.

The doors were both large and small in size; all shut. But there was one door that had a minuscule crack, one that would allow her access.

Reaching out with her violet force, Ikaria gently tugged at the door. The door didn't budge. It was stuck.

If she gave it a yank now, the target would know. She needed some time to work on it gradually, so the target wouldn't be aware.

Gifted minds are so damned difficult sometimes, she cursed.

She suddenly felt a shift in her target's mind.

So that's how it is… Ikaria laughed to herself privately.

Changing course, Ikaria summoned the invisible magic from the orange power that now resided in her. She glowed her original violet color, then slowly melted away into thin air, making her body unseen.

Concealed, Ikaria came upon the citadel library, passing the guards on duty outside. Upon entering in secret, Ikaria saw the moonlight shining through the glass ceiling, illuminating the shelves in a blue hue. The orange lamps had not been activated but remained floating in the airspace above the tables.

Keeping her footsteps as quiet as possible, Ikaria walked to the table where Kohren always sat.

With a sudden gust of air around her, the room and everything around Ikaria immediately became colored in a blue hue, and a burst of bright blue magic flashed before her. Kohren appeared out of nowhere, knife in one hand, glass vial in the other. Time began to crawl, eventually coming to a complete stop.

One step ahead of Kohren, Ikaria's violet magic burst out of her outstretched hand, and she reappeared in full form. With a violent swing of her hand, her violet power paralyzed Kohren's body and crippled his mind, causing time to return to its normal pace. Kohren attempted to fight her off, struggling to summon his power to aid him once again. Ikaria squeezed his thoughts, suppressing the control he had over his body and his magic. The doors within his mind finally opened. The only control he had was what Ikaria allowed him to have.

With Kohren's mind and body compromised, the world returned to its original color. Ikaria could feel him struggling internally. He was utterly shocked his body wouldn't cooperate. Loud grunts issued from his mouth.

Removing the knife from his hand, Ikaria caressed it gently, using it to file her nails. Admiring the beauty of the enchanted steel, she turned quickly to face Kohren. "Kohren, Kohren," she said mockingly. "How gracious of you to honor me with your presence." Ikaria strutted around his inert body, his face strained from the invasion of his mind. Taking the vial from his other hand, she sighed loudly, throwing it against the hard tiled floor, the fragments scattering everywhere. "Did you really think you could retrieve my blood? I can't believe the thought even occurred to you."

Her magic surged, forcefully squeezing his mind, causing him to yelp in response.

"Silence!" she hissed. The violet magic obeyed, and his mouth was forced shut. "To think, I was just in the beginning stages of mustering up an elaborate plan for your blood. You have saved me a whole lot of time."

Kohren's face froze in fear.

Ikaria hoped the guards outside the library hadn't heard anything. She was relying heavily on Suri to distract the guards, either with her orange magic or with girlish charms. She was so creative, much more than Ikaria. It made Suri a dependable companion in times such as these. "Now, humor me. Where did you *misplace* those books?" Ikaria shot an explosive bolt of pain through Kohren's body.

He let out a muffled cry, arching his back.

"I will give you one chance to tell me."

He stayed silent, his resolve holding strong.

What an imbecile. With a flash of her finger, Ikaria sent a shockwave of violet magic to him, squeezing his entire body. Crying out once again, his head shook from the pain. His nose started to bleed, pouring down his face.

"I really don't have time for this, Kohren," Ikaria said flatly, looking bored.

He tried saying something.

"I can't hear you. You need to speak more clearly." She held out her hand, cupping it to his face, and released the hold on his ability to speak. Her nail color caught her eye. The lacquer had a chip on it. How she *hated* having a chip on her nails.

"Please, I am just following orders!" he exclaimed breathlessly.

"Now we are getting somewhere!" Ikaria proclaimed. She stood in front of him, petting his long, soft hair. She coiled it around her fingers, smelling it. A fresh floral scent filled her nose. It was too bad he wasn't blond. The thought crossed her mind to play with him, as he was still very attractive. But no, she had no time.

"What are in those missing books that caused the High Court to make a thief out of you?"

"What do you mean?" he asked in a hoarse whisper.

"Oh, I know *all* about you and the High Court. You were sent here by them, years ago. I can smell the high justices' stench all over you. Now tell me, what was in those books, my lord?"

Ikaria forced more energy into his body. More blood ran down Kohren's nose, dripping onto his clothing. The struggle amused her; it was almost pathetic. No magic matched the gift of the violet. Especially now that her magic was growing more powerful with each new color of blood.

With another rush of dark-violet energy forcing its way through the labyrinth of Kohren's mind, she saw it. The thought of green magic came rushing in.

"Green magic. I see." Ikaria hovered over him, then narrowed her eyes. "I *knew* it!" she spat out.

His eyes widened in shock as he cursed himself from within his mind. Green magic, one of the colors that no one had heard of or seen in thousands of years.

"It was in that damn genealogy book, wasn't it?"

Kohren remained silent.

Ikaria shot an immense amount of force into his body, and it shook him violently, sending fresh blood spurting out of his mouth and nose.

"Yes…"

"Where are those tomes now?" Ikaria demanded, getting in his face.

"High… Court… Justice Belinda," he said, struggling.

Ikaria flung out her arms, her limbs flexing hard as violet magic shot through his consciousness. Kohren tried to scream, but the magic held back his voice. Pure hot air came out with no sound.

Just as she thought. Kohren had delivered the most key documents to the High Court. Not only were they somehow sucking away all of the gifted's magic within World Sector Six and suppressing everyone's adjacent and analogous colors, but now they were truly after the gift of the green like she suspected.

They wanted to complete the Spectrum of Magic just like her. Ikaria knew it deep down. Just like how she knew that they were behind the plague. Why else would they be trying to find a green-gifted? And now they had the genealogy of everyone in the history of the earthly courts, documented with their given color, able to pinpoint where a green-gifted was most likely to be. With two high justices sitting on their panel, they had the gift of the blue to scry through time and travel back to find this green-gifted.

It was now a race between her and the High Court. And to hell if they were going to get the green magic first.

Just you wait and see, Belinda, you bitch! I will get that green magic first, even if that means I have to break every single nail in the process to ensure I come out on top!

Ikaria narrowed her eyes at Kohren. "Who has the green magic? What era?" Ikaria surged more magic through his body.

Kohren struggled, remaining silent except for little gasps of air. He continued to fumble with his thoughts, trying not to give away anything.

"Fine, have it your way," Ikaria spat. She squeezed the breath out of him, until his soul was on the brink of leaving him. She released her grasp, and he breathed, rasping for air. Then she did it all over again. And again. Ikaria continued until her magic found what she was looking for.

Kohren's knowledge poured into Ikaria's consciousness like a shiny precious jewel being discovered. Only this jewel was an emerald. Princess Emerald. A gifted from the Millennium Era, a time that was very close to the Apocalypse of the Earth itself, settled within the kingdom of Arcadia. Ikaria gasped with an odd pleasure at Kohren's thoughts and memories—he had been studying the princess before Ikaria had shown up. His orders from the High Court were to find a green-gifted person. That whole time, he had been combing through the library, reading all about Arcadia. No wonder Ikaria had read so much about the warring brothers. Everything prior to them had been removed. The missing books had dealt specifically with the princess.

Turning to Kohren, she frowned dramatically, mocking him. "Thank you, Kohren, for sharing your knowledge with me. It was quite useful." Ikaria narrowed her eyes, straining her hands while her violet magic continued to pour into his mind. "One last question: How is the High Court taking away everyone's magic?"

Kohren shook his head, the blood of his nose continuing to run down his face and onto his delicate clothes. "They aren't."

"Really?"

"I swear it!"

"And the Spectrum of Magic? Is the High Court trying to complete it? *Have* they been consuming magic?"

"What? No!"

"I don't believe you."

"It's true!"

Ikaria forced her energy through his mind, streaming her way through his thoughts. He wasn't lying. What he said was true to him. It wasn't surprising that he was doing their bidding while being left in the dark.

"I have no further use for you. It's a shame to see you end up like this, being that we are good friends and all."

Kohren's eyes bulged, fear painted on his face.

With that, Ikaria sliced his neck open with the knife, his glowing blood spilling to the floor. A hot rush of excitement filled her, knowing she now had access to the gift of the blue. She was one step closer to overthrowing the High Court.

Advancing to his neck, Ikaria reached out with her tongue, licking the blood coming from his jugular, tasting the iron flavor. Ensuring that the power would come fast, she latched on and drank the blood pouring out of his neck, until she felt its magical effects. Vibrations overwhelmed Ikaria as her heart quickened, beating firmly with the magic working its way through her body.

"Suri," Ikaria called out in a raspy voice with her blood-soaked lips, slumping to her knees. "Are you there?"

Her servant appeared with an orange glow, fading out of the shadows, appearing before her. "As always, Enchantress."

Ikaria's breaths became irregular, gasping for air. "Please, clean up this mess," she said, waving around aimlessly. "I won't need help out."

"Yes, Enchantress," Suri murmured, bowing her head. She made her way over to Ikaria, gracefully laying her on the floor and brushing Ikaria's hair out of her face.

Ikaria closed her eyes as the magic pounded its way through her system. It was like the first time she had sex—pain and pleasure all at once.

The pounding became heavier as a deep sadness sunk her soul into despair.

Memories of that lonely moment, the one where everyone had betrayed her. It came raging in, playing with her emotions.

Ikaria screamed in agony. Flashes came before her. Faces of the High Court. Their sneers. Her father's sad face. And Cyrus. Where was he? Missing. Coward.

They would all pay.

As the magic began to subside, time and space swirled around Ikaria, beckoning her to call upon them, consuming every fiber of her being until she did so. Thinking of the Princess Emerald of Arcadia, her mind began to swim through time, like flowing down a river through a galaxy of stars. It came to a stop, giving her a view of a fantastical city, one the likes of which Ikaria had never seen in her lifetime. Within the city came an image of the princess—beautiful long, wavy emerald hair and glowing green eyes, with ivory skin like porcelain. But there was another overshadowing her, one that was somehow the key to her power.

A prince, shrouded in blue. A tall, dark, handsome prince.

And his mind was accessible.

Completely accessible.

CHAPTER 17

GREEN

Swirling portals and galaxies faded away as another era formed around Suresh. Blacks, grays, and crimson reds assimilated into patterns and shapes, slowly melting into recognizable figures.

An ornate room spread out before him, with ruby walls patterned with black designs. Thick crimson velvet curtains draped the windows, and the black floors gleaned with slick polish. Bookshelves lined the room, containing many books, scrolls, and tomes haphazardly shoved on the shelves. On the back wall stood a grand fireplace with a sizable freestanding harp nearby, cast in silver.

What year is this? Suresh wondered.

No one appeared to be in the room, as no sound could be heard except the roaring fire and the thumping of Suresh's heartbeat.

Cautiously glancing in each direction, Suresh decided to approach the fireplace. The space-time continuum had always chilled him to the bone, and the fireplace looked rather inviting.

As he approached, Suresh sensed the fire's magical properties, enchanted with the magics of red and orange. Fascinated, he held his hands toward the fire, warming them. The flames still burned with intensity, but they were transparent and smokeless. He was amazed at how the future gifted had conceptualized the idea of enchanting things with combined magics. Why hadn't the past ever thought of it? It was brilliant.

Out of the silence, a light clanging sound echoed in the room. Suresh's heart stopped, and he glanced out of the corner of his eye. Had someone seen him?

Sharply turning around from the fireplace, all Suresh was met with was a lavish black desk squeezed in between two bookshelves, with papers scattered about. He was in someone's study, or possibly a personal library. There were empty chalices and wine bottles, some dirty, empty, and thrown about, others cleaned and ready for their next use.

The sound clanged again, this time louder.

Suresh paused, still and silent, waiting for it to happen again. A minute went by, and the noise rattled once more. This time, it was ever so softly.

Acutely aware of where the sound was coming from, Suresh turned toward its direction. A wired cage stood in close proximity of the desk, rattling with slight movement. Meeting his gaze was a red parrot perched within, cocking its head curiously at Suresh.

Sighing a breath of relief, Suresh smiled at the bird, laughing inwardly from being startled by such a creature.

"Silly bird," Suresh muttered under his breath.

"What are you doing here?" a voice called from the corner.

Suresh jumped in place, startled at the voice. Whirling around, he glanced at the shadowy corner of the room where the harp sat.

From the depths of the darkness appeared a well-dressed man with chin-length crimson hair pulled back in a stubby ponytail. As he stepped into the light, Suresh saw the man had light skin with flaming red eyes, his body adorned with amulets, rings, and earrings. He was dressed in rich fabrics. The firelight caught the jewels, giving the man a shimmering effect.

There is a Ghost Man with the power of red that needs our help! he recalled Geeta saying. Was this the man?

The man walked across the room and pushed aside the dirty chalices, looking for a clean cup. After he found what he was looking for, he poured himself a glass of wine and sat down in his chair, taking a deep drink.

"It's not every day that a green-gifted appears in my room. Especially when they shouldn't have the power to do so." The man eyed him, inspecting Suresh's clothes.

"I'm sorry, I didn't mean to intrude..."

"Where are you from, time traveler? Or should I say, what era are you from?" the man asked, making himself comfortable in his chair.

"The past."

"'The past' is quite vague."

"The beginning," Suresh answered slowly. "The beginning of time."

The crimson man took another drink, reflecting on Suresh's words. "And what brings you here, time traveler from the past, to my chambers, specifically?"

"I am trying to find someone. Well, two people, actually."

"Really? Do tell."

"Yes. A woman with violet magic. I have been following her for many years. I need to find her."

The man raised his eyebrow, leaning in curiously. "What business do you have with her?"

"She is looking for the Ghost Man."

"Ghost Man? Never heard of him." The man laughed as if Suresh had just told a joke, finished the last drop of his wine, then poured himself another. "But as far as the violet-gifted, if your business is with Ikaria, then we will have some issues, you and I."

"Ikaria?" Suresh gave the man a confused look. "I don't know any Ikaria, sire. I am looking for Geeta."

"Geeta, you say? The only violet-gifted I know of is the newly instated Sorceress Ikaria of World Sector Six." The man put down his wine glass, walking toward the harp. "And this Ghost Man you speak of, I am not familiar with him, and honestly, I don't really care."

The man was about to play his harp but was interrupted by a knock at the door. Unsure of what to do, the redheaded man quickly stretched out his hand, funneling orange magic over Suresh, making him invisible. The fiery man shot Suresh a look, indicating that he should be quiet.

Suresh gasped at the man's magic, taking a step back in awe. This man had the *full* capabilities of his adjacent magic, something that was rare with all gifted throughout time. Through Suresh's green gift of life magic, he could sense the man's life force. The man not only had the full power of the orange gift, but the violet gift as well. But there was... something else.

Maybe he has consumed other colors? Suresh wondered. But he quickly decided against his thought, as the man's hair hadn't turned any shade darker—it was still pure red.

"Get behind one of the curtains. They will still be able to detect you even if you are invisible out in the open," the man said in a sharp whisper.

Obliging the man, Suresh followed through and stashed himself behind the thick velvety curtain.

Another soft knock came from the door.

"Come in," the man called out loudly.

Suresh heard the door creak open, then shut. Light, swift footsteps could be heard.

"High Inquisitor Rubius," a gentle woman's voice said in greeting.

Rubius walked quickly over to the woman. "Not today, Poliente. I'm not in the mood."

"But we had this arranged already… I need the money," the woman said insistently.

"Here." Suresh heard coins jingle. "Five hundred pounds. What we agreed to."

"Are you *sure* you don't want—"

"Yes, I am sure," Rubius said, cutting her off. "Please leave. Perhaps next week we can arrange something."

"Sure," the woman agreed.

Suresh heard the door open, then shut. A minute of silence followed.

"You can come out, stranger," Rubius called out.

Suresh emerged from the curtains, still invisible. Rubius waved his hand, and the magic twinkled orange around Suresh, dissipating around him.

"Sorry about that. As you can see, I have my own problems, and I have little time to be dealing with others." Rubius's eyes took in Suresh's color, then he gave a weak smile. "Sorry to disappoint you on your quest to find those people you are in search for. I am not much help."

"Are you sure you have never heard of the Ghost Man in passing conversation? Not even in myths or legends?"

"Quite sure," Rubius replied. "However, perhaps you can answer me something. Something that has been troubling me for many years." The crimson man took another drink of his wine, then walked over to his harp, strumming it softly.

"You can ask, but I am not sure I have the answers you seek," said Suresh.

Rubius nodded, his eyes glowing with red magic while he played a tune. "There is a woman who has appeared in my dreams for as long as I can remember. She is green-gifted, very beautiful. Delicate pale skin, bright-green eyes, and long wavy green hair the color of an emerald jewel. I see her every time I close my eyes. I feel like a fool for even telling you this, for it all sounds a bit ludicrous." Rubius faltered for a moment, pausing his tune, eyeing Suresh. "Have you come across any woman like that in your travels?"

He awaited with anticipation, not making any movement, nor any sound from his harp. Not even his parrot rattled in its cage.

Suresh thought about Queen Elyathi. She had absorbed his healing magic for a moment, then transferred the green power to the baby inside her womb. He had seen no other green-gifted in the times he had traveled, mostly red- and orange-gifted, as Geeta was in search of the man with the power of the red magic. But what about Elyathi's child? Maybe this man was dreaming about her?

"I haven't seen any green-gifted woman," replied Suresh, then he paused. "Although there was a unique woman I encountered during my travels. Her power absorbed my magic, transferring it to the baby in her womb. I believe she had the gift of the white."

"Gift of the white. Never heard of that one before," Rubius said, sighing in disappointment. He walked over to the parrot's cage, opened the door, and gave the bird inside a soft stroke.

He must not know of Elyathi. Suresh frowned, thinking of the sad queen. He'd wanted to help her but didn't know how.

"And the baby? Was it a girl?"

Suresh snapped out of his thoughts. "I am most certain it was a girl in the woman's womb," he answered. "I felt her life force."

"I see," Rubius said, letting the parrot out of the cage, allowing it to perch on his shoulder. "And where is this woman?"

"Back in the Millennium Era. I don't know the exact year, as I never know most of them precisely, but 2100–2300 M.E., I would gather." Suresh hesitantly sat down on the man's furniture.

Rubius sat down across from Suresh, grabbing his chalice and drinking in silence for many moments. Finally he said, "If you do happen across this green-gifted woman, would you please come back and tell me? I would be forever indebted to you if you did so, time traveler."

"Unfortunately, I cannot at this time," Suresh started. "You see, I have to find the Ghost Man. It is imperative..." Suresh's thoughts raced about the fate of the world. *There will be no green-gifted woman, or anyone else for that matter, if I don't find Geeta or the Ghost Man.*

"I understand," Rubius said, taking another drink. He downed the liquor, tossing the cup aside.

Suresh got up from the couch, then started heading for the door. Violet magic splashed in front of his eyes, pouring over the door, then a clicking sound could be heard as the door locked.

"Oh no, friend. You can't go out there."

Suresh turned slowly to face Rubius. "Why? I told you before, I have to find the Ghost Man."

"Not in this time era, you won't." Rubius turned his attention to Suresh, getting up from the couch. The parrot squawked. "I think it would be best if you go now. You see, if you tarry here any longer, I will be in a bit of a predicament, forced to hand you over to my superiors. It would be a shame for someone like you to get caught up in the politics of this time. My superiors would kill for green-gifted blood. And that, my friend, puts a giant mark on your back."

"If my blood is so desired, why wouldn't you want to turn me in to your superiors?"

Rubius laughed, amused. "Let's just say that I really don't feel like dealing with them right now."

"I guess I should say thank you, then?"

"If you like. Sorry I was not of any help to you. Hopefully you find your Ghost Man."

"I hope so too, for all our sakes," Suresh said. "And I hope you find your green-gifted woman."

"I as well, for my sanity," the man said bleakly. He gestured for Suresh to leave.

Suresh called upon the power of blue magic that burned inside of his life force, focusing on his unnatural consumed color. It surged through his soul, rumbling inside like a force waiting to be unleashed. He felt the world around him turn black, and the red room faded away into nonexistence.

Suddenly a tugging feeling overwhelmed him, a surge of power radiating from the man to him, connecting the two. Through his natural green gift, Suresh saw what was inside the man—green magic, filled with life, radiated from the man's life force, binding his soul together.

"Why is there green magic within you? Does it have to do with the woman you seek?" Suresh called out, his question echoing through the time magic as the room started to disappear around him.

The man went pale and was about to speak, but Suresh's deep greenish-blue magic washed over him, and the man faded away into the void. Familiar galaxies and swirling, glowing portals of magic took the room's place, glowing brightly in the space-time continuum.

Once more, he was at the crossroads of time.

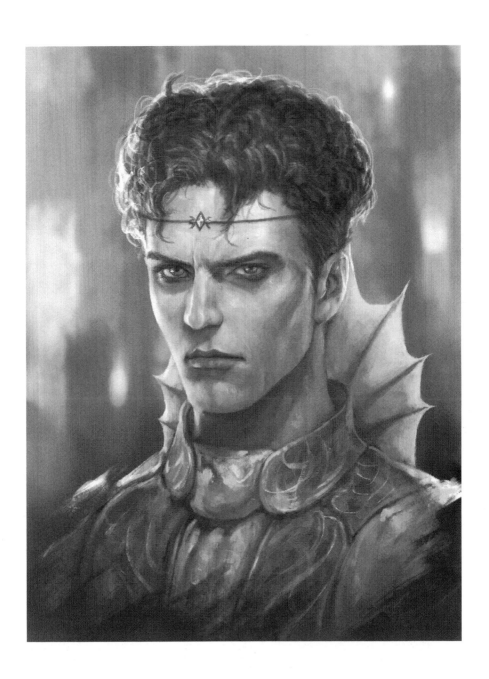

CHAPTER 18

Within the deep azure of the night, warm delicate hands touched Derek's chest softly. He stirred in response, awaking to its touch. The hands glided their way toward his neck, the caress igniting a desire deep within him.

Emerald appeared next to him, kissing his neck with a feral force. Confused but obedient, he let Emerald continue her motions as flowing waves of her emerald-green hair fell lightly on his chest, the tickling sensation arousing him. Her soft kisses upon his neck continued to climb up his body until her lips met his ears, nibbling them playfully. Desperation burned inside, seeping deep down into his lowers.

Responding to her desire, Derek ran his hands down Emerald's body, brushing the tips of his fingers across her sheer clothes, then made his way down to the lower portion of her body. He stopped, hesitating. Was this truly happening?

Emerald smiled at him deviously as her eyes went bright. She returned to kissing his neck, guiding his hand down to her lowers, letting out a small moan. Derek paused, unsure of what to do. Emerald continued to kiss his ear, brushing her lips toward his while grabbing his free hand, guiding it toward her thigh.

"Don't you want me?" she whispered with fierce desire.

"More than anything," Derek said, his voice faltering.

Her lower body began to rub against his, and all at once, his mind exploded in pleasure. His member throbbed; he wanted nothing more than to ravish her at that moment. But something made him waver.

Emerald closed her eyes, entering a state of bliss. The ecstasy of her eroticism made him harder, and he closed his eyes to join her motions. Pulling her into position as she hovered above him, the feeling came back.

Shaking his head, Derek slowly slid his body away from Emerald. A sharp tug clawed at his soul as he did so, and the more he withdrew and edged away, the more painful the tug became. His body was nothing without her. He needed her. She was like an everlasting force that he needed to survive.

Emerald opened her eyes once again, taken back. "What is it?" she breathed.

Those eyes. There was something about her eyes. They were violet, not green.

It was not Emerald.

Shooting up from his bed, Derek saw the pale dawn's rays kissing the walls of his bedchamber. Breathing heavily from the dream—or should he say, nightmare—he tried to calm himself, rubbing his temples with his fingertips. His body was drenched in sweat, and his sleeping pants and sheets were soaked through. His throat felt dry and cracked, and he needed some sort of liquid to replenish it.

"Silas," he called out hoarsely, hoping that his servant heard him.

The door cracked, and Silas's face appeared. "Yes, Your Highness?" The pale manservant bowed and entered the room.

Derek withdrew from his drenched bed, his feet pressed against the cold floor. "Help me get ready for breakfast," Derek said, wiping the sweat from his brow. "Please pick my best morning garments."

The servant bowed and left his bedchambers.

He sat down on his private balcony, waving his hand for another servant to get him some water. His body burned from the inside as he continued to sweat profusely. The morning sun, however cool it was in the morning, was making him feel worse outside on the patio. His servant returned with his water, and Derek drank the whole glass immediately, resting the empty, icy glass against his forehead.

Why was he feeling so terrible? Did he have that dream because he was worried about Emerald? He hadn't seen her the night before. She'd never sent word. Nor had she shown up to dinner. Not a single person had mentioned the princess last night. He had a hunch that Damaris had barred her from attending. Why else wouldn't she have come?

A sudden, stabbing pain strained his heart, making him double over. He dropped the iced glass, and it shattered against the marble tiles of the patio. His knees weakened, making him lose his balance, and he almost collapsed on the glass shards. Derek grabbed the rail, guiding himself to a nearby velvet couch inside his chamber. Plopping carelessly onto the velvety cushions on his stomach, he began to break out in a fresh sweat as the pain in his heart escalated.

Was he dying of heartbreak? Wisps of the dream came back to him, and Derek's heart ached to see Emerald again. Just one glimpse to comfort him, to know that she was okay.

Another sharp pain rocked Derek, causing him to convulse in the softness of the velvet couch. He let out a sharp grunt. He squeezed his eyes shut, trying to block out the pain as much as possible.

Loud footsteps pounded against the floor, transferring its vibrations to his head. "Your Highness, I heard something break!" Silas saw the shattered glass, then saw Derek lying on the sofa. "Are you not well?" Silas ran over to him, turning his body over while placing his hand over his burning forehead, gasping. "I'll fetch the palace physician."

Derek stopped him, waving his hand. "No, that is not necessary. It must be the food from last night's dinner not agreeing with me. I must get ready," he said as his thoughts focused on Emerald. "I need to see the princess."

Silas stood above him for a moment in disbelief. "Are you sure? You don't look well at all—"

"I insist," Derek interrupted. "Now, tell me what garments you chose for me."

"Your Highness, I have selected your light-blue regalia this morning."

"Fine choice. Just let me rest here for a few minutes."

"Yes, Your Highness." Silas bowed. Derek heard his footsteps trailing out the door, then shut the door behind him. Every movement Silas made was bothersome, as if the volume of the noises had been turned up.

Derek closed his eyes again to take the edge off his headache. The light in the room was much too bright for him, causing him to wince. A sudden spasm in his chest twisted his insides, like his heart was collapsing, or worse, failing him.

Get through this, he ordered himself. *Emerald will be there. You must see her!*

Derek continued to lie on the couch, thinking of Emerald. Her bright-green eyes. Her beautiful smile, the one she'd given him the night they danced.

Her delicate touch as he held her close in his arms. With each thought, his mind eased, the pain melting away.

Within the depths of his mind, he heard a subtle laugh.

Wasn't that fun? the voice inside his head asked. *We should play more often.*

Alarmed, he looked around the room. No sounds were heard but the wind coming from the patio. He was alone.

***

The tension was thick as Derek entered the main dining hall. His pale-blue cape swept behind him as he moved across the room in anticipation, hoping to see Emerald. Scanning the hall, he saw with disappointment she wasn't present—only the Inner Council and King Damaris were seated at the grand table. His heart sank.

As he approached the table, Derek became keenly aware of his boots clicking on the marble tile, echoing within the hall. At the table, no one had lifted a single piece of silverware to start in on their meal; they simply sat in silence. The Inner Council's faces were pale in contrast to King Damaris's, which was beet red and flush with anger. No one bothered to greet Derek as he walked up and took a seat. Instead his presence was met with resistance, and he got the distinct impression he was not wanted. Damaris's eyes held fast on Derek, watching his every move.

"Is everything all right?" asked Derek, eyeing the King as he took his seat hesitantly. Every face locked on to his, making Derek regret asking such a question.

Damaris's face darkened, his green eyes seeping with hatred. Without a word, he slid a folded note toward Derek. The seal had already been broken—most likely everyone at the table had already read it.

"What's this?" Derek asked, his heart quickening as the Inner Council continued to stare at him.

"I had hoped that you would tell me," the King snarled, folding his hands on the table. "We found it in the first handmaiden's possession."

Picking up the note, Derek opened it cautiously, his heart pounding in his chest. After a final glance at Damaris, he began to read it.

Derek,

I am sorry that it has come to this. My father made it very clear that we are not to be wed, nor will we ever be. My heart was sincere when I said that I wanted nothing more than for us to be together, but it seems that it is not possible in this lifetime. I hope you find true happiness in someone else.

Emerald

Swelling anger bubbled in Derek's chest, burning with bitterness and resentment toward Damaris. Derek's eyes jolted straight toward the King. Crumpling the note within his fist, he slammed the table, rattling the delicate china. "Tell me, is this true? Was I never to have a fair chance to wed your daughter?" Derek asked, raising his voice. "Was me trying to bend over backward to win the princess just a game to you?"

Without moving from his seat, Damaris's eyes narrowed. "No, you never had a chance. Nor will you ever."

Derek shot up, hovering over the table, clenching his fists. He threw the note back on the table. "Then why give me hope? Why did you tell me that I had a week here in Arcadia?"

Damaris sneered at him. "Because I wanted to see your face when I wore you out and told you no at the end of the week. Haven't you learned, *boy*, I despise your father, which means I despise any rotten spawn of his."

"I don't know what my father did to wrong you, but I am not my father!" Derek turned, peering at the table. The Inner Council didn't bother to jump into the conversation, not wanting to feel Damaris's wrath. "Where is she? Where is the princess? Why isn't she here? What have you done with her?" Derek demanded.

Shooting up from his seat, Damaris roared, "You tell me, Prince Derek!"

Derek froze at the King's words. "I don't understand..." He fumbled the words, not grasping the situation.

A small voice interrupted the moment of silence. "Prince Derek, the princess has gone missing. We cannot locate her anywhere within the palace," Councilor Emerys said gravely. "Did you see her at all yesterday afternoon? Or perhaps in the evening? We must know."

All eyes were on him, as if he knew exactly where Emerald had gone.

Derek couldn't believe that no one in the palace had any idea where Emerald was. Emerald, gone? That was impossible. The King himself had had her on lockdown within the palace for how many years, with handmaidens and guards constantly watching over her like a prized animal. It seemed unfathomable that she had slipped past everyone. But at the same time, her note did have a sense of finality about it.

Worry spread through Derek like wildfire. He was panicked just thinking about Emerald, out somewhere in the midst of Arcadia. The mere thought caused a physical pain to flare up, spasming deep within his chest. His right hand smacked down on the table, propping him up weakly while the pain twisted in his heart. Taking a deep breath, he composed himself.

"The last time I saw the princess was yesterday morning," Derek said mildly, catching his breath from the chest pains. His gaze met Damaris's, their eyes locking on to each other's. "I was under the impression that she wanted to see no one last night, including myself. After all, that was what I was told by everyone at dinner."

"Do not mock me," Damaris snarled, throwing his wine glass to the floor, giving Derek a cold, hard stare. "*Where* is she?"

"I truly have no idea where she is, Your Majesty," Derek said, shaking his head anxiously. "But we must find her. I will do everything I can to help."

"There is no *we*," the King said.

Derek jerked his head to Damaris, moving swiftly toward him. "Whatever differences you have with my family, please, Your Majesty, let me prove myself. Let me find your daughter for you." Derek didn't like begging, but this was his last hope to win Damaris over.

"This is *your* doing!" the King spat. "If it weren't for you, my daughter would still be happily wandering the palace!"

Derek looked at him incredulously, turning wildly around at the room of eyes peering at him. "*My* doing? This has nothing to do with me."

"This has everything to do with you! *EVERYTHING!*" Damaris roared, kicking the dining table. The bulky table moved a good two inches, making a screeching sound against the flooring, rattling the china. "Guards! Arrest him!"

Derek flung back his cape in disbelief as guards came running in, closing in on him in a circle. "On what charge?" Derek spat out.

"For interfering with the royal family's business!"

"Interfering? You mean talking with the princess? Telling her that I care for her?" Derek said, raising his voice and turning around to face each of the guards.

"For meddling in my affairs!"

"Ridiculous. This is utterly ridiculous." Derek fumed as the guards surrounded him. His eyes met Damaris's, his face narrowing into a scowl. "You are making a grave mistake."

"Confine him to his quarters, and purge any and all communication devices from it!"

"Yes, Your Majesty," the guards said in unison.

"Word will reach my father," Derek said loudly. A guard reached for his arm, but Derek yanked it away. He was much more muscular than the guard, and both of them were keenly aware of that fact. "Don't even think about touching me," he snapped to the guard in warning. He turned to Damaris. "My father will know when I don't contact him. He will send troops, that I can assure you."

"Did I just hear a threat?" Damaris laughed mockingly. "Let your father send troops. I *dare* him," he said sharply, waving him away. "Now, remove him from my sight before I start handing out execution orders!"

The guards hurriedly pushed Derek away, leading him out into the palace corridors. He had only been in Arcadia less than forty-eight hours. And within that time frame, he had proposed to the princess and been arrested. Just for making his intentions known. His father had warned him, but Derek had never thought it would come to this. And what of Emerald? The thought of her lost in the city sickened him.

He needed to find Emerald before something happened to her.

CHAPTER 19

GREEN

Emerald awoke in the early hours of the morning. She glanced over the edge of the cot to see Kyle lying on a single ragged blanket sprawled across the floor. He was passed out, oblivious to the world around him. Next to him was his pack of cigarettes, an empty liquor bottle, and an ashtray littered with cigarette butts. One half-smoked cigarette butt was wedged in the holder.

She was still tired from the night before, but her excitement from leaving the palace overruled her need for sleep.

Intrigued by Kyle's apartment, Emerald ran her eyes across the room. It was the smallest living place she had ever seen. The apartment was laid out in a square, with one large window opposite the entrance. Next to the door, Kyle's small bed hugged a half wall. The other side of the wall housed a small kitchenette and space for a table. But Kyle didn't have a table; instead a guitar and amp occupied the spot. There was a used wooden chair near the window, clothes stuffed in a corner, and one door leading to a bathroom. The bathroom itself had enough space for only one person to stand in, unless one was in the shower. The very thought that people lived the way Kyle did gave Emerald a new perspective on the life of Arcadia's citizens.

Emerald thought back to what had happened at the motel. If what Kyle said was true, she needed to somehow get an ID card. Was there a way to acquire one using a false identity? As much as she would feel guilty doing so, she didn't have any other options. She made a mental note to ask Kyle when he woke up. Emerald perceived him to be the kind who knew how to cheat the system, or had friends who did.

Quietly leaning over the cot, Emerald snatched her backpack from the floor. Rummaging through it, she grabbed a clean set of clothes, then tiptoed across the floorboards to the bathroom to change, careful not to make any noise to wake Kyle. She slipped on a shiny purple tube top, along with purple leggings and her tall boots. She brushed her hair up into a high ponytail, then secured it with a flashy purple bow, sliding on an armband, earrings, and the chain that had Derek's ring hanging from it.

Derek. Memories of him flooded her mind. Memories of his lilacs on her nightstand. The moment he confessed his true feelings for her. Her engagement ring in his hand. In her mind's eye, she could see the very position of how he held the ring out toward her with his adoring eyes. Emerald softly touched the ring, grasping the chain in her hand. A sadness came over her, but she shoved it out of her mind.

It was never meant to be, she reminded herself, questioning once again if she had done the right thing. *Father told me so.*

After Emerald used the toilet, she walked back into the room. Kyle was still sound asleep. It amazed Emerald that one could sleep through her making so much noise, as much as she tried to be quiet about it. Amongst the papers on his floor, Emerald found a piece of scrap paper and a pen in the mess. Seating herself on the ground next to the only window in the apartment, she began to sketch random images that came to her. While drawing, Emerald thought about what she should do next. She couldn't stay with Kyle forever. She knew nothing about him, and she was lucky that he was willing to take her in for a night.

Just when Emerald was about to finish her drawing, Kyle stirred from his spot. Emerald watched as he felt around for his pack of cigarettes, not even bothering to open his eyes. Blindly, he found the pack, then lit a new cigarette, still with his eyes closed.

A sudden coughing fit sent his torso upward, and he sat himself up. Reaching for an empty liquor bottle, he hacked up a wad of phlegm and spit it into the bottle. He continued to smoke his cigarette, acting like the coughing attack had never happened.

Charming, Emerald thought.

Kyle grunted, then rubbed his head, still tired from the night before. His sleepy eyes landed on her as he realized someone else was in his apartment.

"You're still here?" he asked, confused, puffing on his cigarette.

"Was I not supposed to be?" Emerald asked.

"I dunno. It's entirely up to you. I would have thought you would be gone by morning. Most women would." He laughed, the smoke forcing its way out of his mouth.

Is he serious?

"I didn't want to wake you. If you want, I can leave now," Emerald said, getting up and reaching for her backpack.

"I'm only fucking with you. You're fine. Really, you don't have to," Kyle said casually, taking another drag, still sleepy. "Unless you have somewhere to be."

Plopping herself back on the floor, Emerald wrapped her arms around her legs, feeling insecure. Reaching for her chain, she rubbed the gem of the ring with her fingers, wishing she could see Derek again. But that was impossible.

"I think it's obvious that I don't have anywhere to go," Emerald confessed sadly. "And honestly, I don't know what I am going to do either." Emerald met Kyle's eyes through the smoke. As the words departed from her lips, her insides began to tremble. What *was* she going to do? She had been so caught up in anger when leaving the palace that she had no true plan. "I would hate to impose on your favors any longer."

"Favors?" Kyle said with an amused look on his face. "Is that what you call it?"

"Yes, favors. The kindness you bestowed on me by letting me stay here for the night. How else would you describe it?"

"I consider favors to be something… very different," Kyle commented, finishing up his cigarette. "You really are one of a kind, Em." He got up, digging through a pile of clothes piled up in the corner of the room. "You can stay here until you figure your shit out." He yanked off his shirt and pulled on a different one from the pile.

Immediately upon seeing his chiseled chest, Emerald looked away, turning her body in the opposite direction. Embarrassed to have seen him in the shirtless state he was in, her cheeks flushed. She heard more rummaging, accompanied by a small chuckle.

"You can look now," he said from behind her. Emerald returned to her original position, still embarrassed and not wanting to meet Kyle's face.

"Sorry…"

"About what?"

"A-about…" Emerald stuttered.

Kyle laughed again. "There you go again, Em. Being strange."

She made a face, looking slightly offended. "What if I were to tell you the same thing?"

Kyle shrugged. "Come on, let's go."

"Go where?"

"To get something to eat," he said, like it was completely obvious. "I'm never up this early, but since I am, damn if I'm not gonna eat some breakfast." Kyle smirked, his cigarette hanging from his lips. "Bet you're hungry too."

She was hungry. Emerald hadn't eaten anything since before she had escaped the palace. "Indeed, I am," she answered, reaching for her backpack on the floor.

"No need for that. Leave it here. The less you carry out there, the less likely you'll be mugged," Kyle said, motioning for her to put her pack down.

"Mugged?"

"Yeah, you know, robbed? Left for dead in a grimy alley."

"Oh."

His eyes snapped to her drawing next to the bag. He leaned over to get a closer look at her sketch, picking it up. "You drew this?" He held out the scrap drawing out.

"Yes," Emerald said shyly, shuffling her foot. "Although I prefer painting to drawing."

Kyle studied the scrap another moment. "It's really good."

"Thank you," Emerald murmured politely.

I suppose I can stay with him for a little while, she thought. *He's not so bad.*

"Is it someone you know?" he asked, referring to the sketch.

"No one in particular," Emerald lied.

Kyle took another glance at it, then set it on top of her backpack. "Looks familiar." He opened his apartment door, holding it open for her. "Let's get going. I'm starving," he said, motioning for her to follow.

Emerald glanced back at the drawing, seeing Derek's face in the doodle. She missed him.

CHAPTER 20

His expression looked so peaceful. Blue light from the cryogenic capsule graced his marred, half-burnt face, frozen in time. His eye, the only one that survived the accident, remained shut in his eternal sleep.

Telly touched the glass that separated her and Drew, pretending she could once again feel his rough visage. Stubble accented his jawline; Drew was always lousy at shaving. She had nagged him so much for not doing a decent enough job when he was living, but now the memories haunted her every time she gazed upon his inert face. So much guilt. She couldn't shake it no matter how much she tried.

She recalled Director Jonathan's words. *We can combine his research with a new technology, unlike anyone has ever seen. A power with the capability to revive and heal. Don't you see the beauty in it? He will be made alive again with his own research!*

Those words echoed in Telly's head as her memories faded away. She was no longer in Drew's cryogenic holding room from years ago. She was back in her lab, staring through the observation window. On the other side of the glass, Drew emitted a strange orange glow and energy from his body, the same color as his left eye. It had changed. It was no longer blue; it was bright orange. The very thought made Telly shudder.

When Telly had approved of Drew being a part of the corporation's experiment, she'd had no idea what kind of power Jonathan was referring to at the time. All she cared about was finding a way to bring back Drew, choosing to freeze him on the brink of death. And with years poured into his research, her funds dwindling to nothing, she had no choice but to accept the corporation's proposal. It was the only way to bring him back to life. But what made it so hard for her to accept was that she had to hand over all of her and Drew's research, and Drew was to be considered company property. Only Director Jonathan knew of her attachment to Drew, and so he had made sure she was positioned to oversee him. Knowing that she could see him alive once again, Telly accepted.

Never had Telly ever dreamt that the variable that would save Drew's life would be magic. The blood sample that was infused into Drew had powerful life-giving properties, and it was the most remarkable and extraordinary thing Telly had ever encountered. The corporation's use of bionics, paired with Telly's expertise and Drew's research, made the impossible possible.

But knowing how fantastical the blood really was and witnessing firsthand the power of the cyborgs, it was still hard for her to swallow reality. Telly had never been one to believe in superstitions, especially in the ancients' *magic*. There had to be a logical explanation for the unusual power within the blood. And for Drew's unique… capabilities. She needed answers.

A large body hovered over her, permeating the air with the scent of coffee and sanitized gel. Telly knew only one person who smelled like that. The director. His obsession with caffeine and germs never ceased to amaze her.

"Yes, Jonathan?" Telly said, not taking her eyes off Drew. His body faded, flashing with orange like a broken monitor that needed adjusting. *It's just the side effects of the blood*, she tried to calmly remind herself. *Just like the other cyborgs when we booted them up.* Although all the other cyborgs didn't emit strange power like Drew.

"I wanted to congratulate you and your team," Director Jonathan said smoothly, positioning himself next to her. He glanced through the window at Drew, then held his breath. "It seems that the magic really took to him."

"It appears so," Telly admitted, her face fixated on Drew. Intense bright-orange light continued to burn from Drew's body, lighting up the experiment capsule so intensely even Telly had to squint through her glasses. His body remained motionless as it fluctuated between a dream and reality. "Why… why is he *different*, Director?"

"You still don't believe, do you?" Jonathan said under his breath.

Telly turned to him as if looking at him for the first time. "Tell me," she said sharply.

"Because the magic chooses. That's why." Jonathan's dark eyes lowered, frowning. Pausing for a moment, Jonathan continued. "Listen, Telly, I am not one to read religious material, but might I suggest you take a look at *The Spectrum*?"

"And why would I do that? It's nothing more than an ancient text littered with stories and outdated laws," Telly scoffed. "What good will that do?"

"Even you, as much as I don't want to admit it, can't deny the fact that Drew now has the gift of the orange."

"Gift of the orange?" Telly repeated, the words foreign on her lips. Telly's head was overwhelmed by the mere thought of old superstitions. She was exhausted. She had worked so much overtime to ensure Drew would be revived successfully. And now the director was talking to her about magic, power, and a religious text. Telly sighed, her breath fogging the glass in front of her. It was all too crazy.

"Thanks for the suggestion, Director, but I think not. I have no use for that kind of reading."

"Just a thought." The director shrugged. "By the way, you better get cleaned up."

"Why?"

"Because I must report Drew's abilities to the head director, which he will then report to Councilor Zane. I am sure that the councilor will be here within a couple of hours to inspect Drew. Perhaps even the King himself will make a special visit."

Telly's heart stopped. "What? You think Damaris will visit our lab? The King, *here*, in our lab? You can't be serious, Jonathan."

"Look at Drew, Telly. Just look!" he insisted. "Why wouldn't the King visit here? He now has another subject for extraction. Instead of one donor, whoever that is, he now has two. Even though he sends Councilor Zane all the time, it's really because Damaris wants to know anything and everything that goes on here. And now that we have a cyborg with *magical* capabilities, we can certainly expect His Majesty to make a special trip."

"What does this all mean for me? Do you think I will still be assigned to Drew?"

"I don't know, honestly." Jonathan put one of his hands on her shoulder. "But I will do my best to ensure that you do. However, it may be that the King will want to keep Drew with him at the palace. He is rather... protective when it comes to anything remotely to do with magical abilities. Councilor

Zane made that very clear to Director Santiago."

"Drew? At the palace?" Telly's voice faltered, taking a step back. "He needs to be here, Director! You know that as much as I do! All the equipment is here…" There was no way that she could allow Drew to be taken away from her. He was hers! She had done so much for him. And for them to take Drew away?

"Calm down, Telly, calm down. Don't get all worked up yet. I just suggested that it *could* happen, not that it's *going* to."

Telly turned away from him, clenching the tablet in her hand. "It had better not, Director. It just *can't.*" Rubbing her eyes under her glass frames, she let out a loud, tired sigh. "Please excuse me. Looks like I need to get to the lab showers. I still have much work to do on Drew."

"Telly, whatever you two had in the past, Drew will never be the same person. He is mostly machine now. Do not get your past feelings involved now that he is back with us."

Telly whirled around, flashing Jonathan an annoyed look. "Why are you telling me this?"

"Because sometimes we need to be reminded," he said with caution. He nodded, walking away.

"I don't want to be reminded," she said quietly to herself. "I just want to be *remembered.*"

Giving Drew one last look, Telly made her way down to the lab's showers.

***

After getting cleaned up, Telly received word from Jonathan that Councilor Zane was indeed en route to the corporation, accompanied by His Majesty himself. She managed to brush her honey-colored chin-cropped hair and dress herself in fresh clothes and a clean lab coat. She carefully wiped the fingered smudges off her black-framed glasses and even applied light makeup, something that she normally was not accustomed to doing.

Telly joined the staff of her level by the elevator lifts, along with several of the directors, including Jonathan. There were nervous whispers amongst the other scientists, making Telly uneasy. Telly had always been confident, and she had never been anxious for any important visits in all her years working in the lab. But today, her insides were a wreck. A complete, nervous wreck.

Just thinking about Drew's near future made her stomach twist.

Just as Telly caught up to the gathering, the elevators chimed, and the symbol on the lift lit up as the doors opened. The King stepped out, dressed in a black royal jerkin trimmed with green and silver. His long silky, pale hair ran down his back, flowing with his icy movements. He gave her a hard stare with his cold face. There was no warmth from that man, nor did it seem he had any emotion. But for as old as he was, he was still incredibly handsome. Councilor Zane came trudging behind the King, also dressed in black but trimmed with reds throughout his garb. He looked as nervous as Telly felt.

Everyone in the lab bowed simultaneously. "Your Majesty," Head Director Santiago said in reverence.

Ignoring the head director, Damaris proceeded further into the lab and began to eye the rows of glowing glass capsules, each intact with a cyborg in different stages of preparation.

"Director Santiago," Damaris said, waving his hand at the man, not acknowledging any other staff. "Thank you for preparing the lab on such short notice. I know everyone is extremely busy, especially since they are now weeks behind the initial deadline that I *ordered.*"

Santiago swallowed but did not change his facial expression to react to Damaris's stinging words. "Yes, Your Majesty. We are almost at completion. Another week and a half at the most. All the cyborgs are now online. There are several that need more tuning, but other than those few, we are ready to go. We released a large number of the cyborgs into the police force to test them out, which was a complete success. With the use of the cyborgs' force, the authorities were able to subdue the crowds in record time. Even with the reported injuries inflicted on the cyborgs, most of the wounds had been regenerated by the time they were returned to us. The rate of their healing capabilities is incredible, faster than what we had thought initially."

"Excellent. That is exactly what I wanted to hear." Damaris turned to Councilor Zane, giving him a cold stare. "At least I am getting some good news finally." Councilor Zane did not reply, but nodded to Damaris. "And what of this new cyborg? This new... gifted? I want to see him now."

The King pushed through the group, waiting for someone to show him the way. Jonathan nudged Telly, then jerked his head slightly, silently telling her to escort Damaris.

"Certainly, Your Majesty," Telly answered in a high shrill voice, shaken with nerves. "Right this way." Telly walked toward the King, gesturing for him to follow.

Damaris turned to the head director, annoyed. "Who is this?" No one said anything in her defense; even Jonathan remained still.

"Telly Hearly, Your Majesty." Telly bowed awkwardly, trying to remain calm with her movements. She had never encountered a royal before, and it was a strange feeling trying to bow to the ruler of Arcadia himself. "I am the lead scientist in Lab 34."

Damaris poised himself with his head held high, looking down at her with a rigid stare. Her heart thumped loudly in her chest, but she continued. "Please, follow me."

The King nodded, following her lead. "It is good to know that there are still people who don't act like lemmings when I ask questions," he said, directing his words at the group.

Damaris walked beside Telly as she led him past the first set of cyborg capsules. She held her breath, unsure whether she should say something to him or hold her tongue. She decided it was best not to say anything.

Telly led the King down the third long row of cyborg capsules, finally coming to another section of the lab—an area with more restrictions. She inserted her security card in the slot, punched in her code, and the door opened with a chime. The group continued to follow Telly through her team's workstations, then to Drew's observation window, where there appeared to be orange flashes from within.

Drew still had not stopped emitting his strange energy.

Damaris watched as Drew's magic flickered, his face in awe. "Truly remarkable," he stated, fixated on the orange power.

Telly bowed to Damaris in agreement, then flipped a switch, powering the main lights inside the encapsulated room for Damaris to get a better view. Inside, Drew jolted, the metal flap of his mechanical eye flipping upward, adjusting as his left orange eye squinted. A warm orange glow vibrated around him. Then his body faded in and out of Telly's vision, like a shimmering star.

With a wide smile, Damaris shook with excitement, his eyes burning bright green with joy. "Open the capsule," he ordered.

Nodding, Telly cleared the hatch door, and the two of them stepped inside while the rest of the lab scientists remained silent behind them.

Damaris carefully walked over the sprawling wires and tubing to stand in front of Drew. Telly could hear Drew's cybernetic eye focusing on the King as he backed away from him, though he had nowhere to go.

"I was told that he was booted up last night, is that correct?" Damaris asked, studying the cyborg.

"Yes, Your Majesty. At nine p.m. precisely," Telly said, bowing before him. *I wish we had the tablet hooked up to him.*

"What kind of abilities does he possess?"

"He has only displayed this power that you see now. Just fading in and out. He doesn't move much, as his body is in a state of much confusion. He needs time to adjust to being alive again."

Drew looked at them both, cocking his head. Damaris studied him, marveling at the power surrounding Drew, the orange glow of his image disappearing and reappearing. Drew inched closer to Damaris, and the wires plugged into him moved with him, like heavy shackles on a prisoner.

"Miss Hearly, how long before he is up and running at full force?" Damaris inquired. Drew shifted his gaze to Telly, as if understanding the conversation.

"He will be ready for deployment along with the others in a week and a half, Your Majesty."

Damaris's face melted into a look of disdain. "I need him sooner than that. Much sooner," he said sharply.

"Sooner? Y-your Majesty..." Telly fumbled with her words. "We only resurrected him just over thirteen hours ago. There are several tests that still need to be conducted—"

"I don't care about those tests," the King snapped. "I need him as soon as possible. Now, what are you going to do about that?"

Telly withheld a flinch from his harsh words, pausing. Did he want to start the extraction process of Drew's blood already?

Disheartened, Telly murmured, "I can have him ready in five days. However, if Your Majesty wishes, we do have other cyborgs in this lab that are ready for deployment."

"Miss Hearly, I do not care for any of the other cyborgs. I want this one. Tell me, it is within this cyborg's capabilities to track the original blood donor, is it not?"

"Correct, Your Highness. All of the cyborgs, including Drew, appear to be drawn to the original donor's blood—it acts like some type of magnet."

"Good." He turned to her, finally acknowledging her presence. "Then this reaffirms my decision. I have found what I need right here: one to overpower the others." Damaris cracked a wicked smile, then narrowed his eyes. "I am glad this little visit wasn't a waste of my time."

"Your Majesty." Telly bowed with a bit more grace but still came off rather clumsy.

"Five days. I *must* have him at my command in *five* days. After that, I want him as a secondary donor. Once-a-week extraction."

Damaris turned away, leaving Telly at a loss of words. Once a week? That was not viable for any human. She was about to open her mouth in protest but hesitated. Who was she to argue with the King?

No, she had to defend Drew, no matter how inhuman he was now.

Just as she was about to speak up, Damaris slipped out of sight. Telly heard the directors and the King walking away in conversation, the group's footsteps fading away, leaving her alone in the room with Drew.

"I am sorry, Drew. So sorry," she said softly, almost as if talking to herself.

Drew cocked his head, his eye focusing on her, glowing orange.

Shuddering, Telly looked up at Drew guiltily, feeling foolish. "I never thought this would happen. Had I known, I never would have signed the corporation's contract," she said, her voice full of sadness. "Never."

Drew didn't flinch. He remained inanimate, listening to her.

"And now I don't know what I am going to do… I just don't know." Telly breathed out heavily, glancing at him. "I don't know if there is anything I *can* do."

Her heart hurt. Why now? Drew had just come back to life, and now he would be taken away from her once again. And the original donor—Drew was going to track this person? If that was the case, the original donor must have similar powers as Drew, which in turn could get extremely dangerous for him. Drew shouldn't be out on some kind of mission for the King. What Drew needed was to be rehabilitated one day at a time, giving him the time he needed to come to terms with his self-awareness.

Telly gave Drew one last look, then lowered her eyes. "You might want to lie down for a bit. You are going to need all the energy you can get."

Drew sparked orange energy in quick, sporadic flashes, complying with her instruction, lying down on his platform.

I'll think of something, Drew, I promise… Telly thought, giving him a sad smile before turning away. *I promise you.*

Emerging from Drew's room, Telly saw her lab alive, everyone at work. Two of her team members were working on what remained of Drew's missing bionics, ones that had not been needed for his boot-up. Others on her team were plugging away at code, monitoring Drew and the other cyborgs on their unit. Telly assumed they'd overheard the King demand Drew within five days and were wasting no time once the entourage left.

Every scientist was crunching toward the King's deadline for the dispatch of the cyborg army.

All except her. All Telly could do was remain motionless in the middle of the lively room.

CHAPTER 21

GREEN

The breakfast would have been considered subpar by palace standards, but Emerald thought it was simply delightful. A bit of eggs, bacon, and sausage were all slopped together, held together by a large flour wrap, doused with a tangy red sauce. The grease from the meat soaked through the wrap, causing it to rip in her hands and the contents to spill all over her serving basket. But she didn't care. She'd never even heard of a "burrito" before, and it was the first time she had ever eaten a meal without silverware. The thought made her spirits rise with an odd sort of naughty delight.

Kyle kept staring at her, giving her a strange look every so often as she ate her burrito. "You're eating it all wrong," he pointed out. He took the remains of her breakfast, then rerolled the burrito wrap, tucking in the bottom, then handed it back to her. "There, eat it like that."

Emerald looked at him teasingly. "I would have never thought there was a right way to eat finger foods…"

"You should try this hot sauce," he said, sliding over a bottle. "That shit burns."

"And tell me why I would want that? It sounds horrible." Emerald eyed the bottle's wrapper, decorated with a skull. It was clearly something that she wouldn't want to try.

"Because it cleans out your sinuses. It helps after a night of drinking," Kyle stated. "I know for me, I get all gunked up and need to get that crap out of my nose and throat."

Emerald stared at him, her face twisted in disgust. "That sounds…

lovely," she remarked. She looked down at her food, then pushed the rest of her meal aside.

Kyle noticed her reaction and gave no sympathy. "Your appetite ruined?"

"Quite so," Emerald said sickly.

Kyle continued to pour on hot sauce, then proceeded to devour his burrito. Emerald studied the way he ate, how he cradled the grease-soaked wrap with his hands, the oil running over his polished silver rings. She would never have suspected that he would be so delicate when it came to holding his food and had guessed he would be somewhat of a sloppy eater, considering how unrefined he was.

Kyle caught her looking at him as he took another bite, his face curious. Embarrassed that she'd been caught staring at him, her cheeks burned, and she took a sip of her coffee to defuse the awkward situation.

After he finished his burrito, Kyle lit a cigarette, the smell of smoke permeating within their booth. The soft gray wispy cloud toyed around them gently, dulling the colors of the restaurant, which was decorated in whites, oranges, and yellows.

After he puffed a few times, he said, "I have to go practice with the band later this afternoon. You should come with me."

"Sure. I would like that," Emerald said. A rush of excitement came over her. More chances to see the city and to experience Arcadia. "When is your next show?"

"Tomorrow evening. I got to pull my shit together for a new song that we've been rehearsing. I pretty much have it, but the other guys seem to be jacking off."

Almost spitting out her coffee at those words, Emerald pressed her lips together, hovering over her cup in case she couldn't keep it in. Kyle watched her struggle with a look of amusement, flicking the ash of his cigarette in the ashtray. Swallowing hard, Emerald raised an eyebrow. "I can't believe you said that."

"What? That they're jacking off?"

"Yes," Emerald whispered, lowering her head into his. "You didn't have to repeat that."

"It's an expression. Don't people have slang in the upper levels?"

"No. We say precisely what we mean."

"I find that hard to believe. I am sure the guys are simply modest around the women, holding back their real language in front of the ladies."

"No one from the upper levels would ever dare speak like how you just did, ever. I can attest to that fact."

"Not likely. The guys are just fooling you. Believe me, if you weren't around, they'd say much more interesting things about you and your manners," Kyle teased.

"I don't believe that."

"Well, think what you like, Em. Stick your head back in the sand and pretend it doesn't happen. But I'm telling you, all guys are like that. The more you realize that is the truth, the longer you'll survive in life. Especially in the lower levels." He finished up his cigarette, then took a drink of his coffee. Black, without any sugar or cream. "And, if you are in any way right, it sounds completely boring if people actually talked and acted that way. I mean, what fun would anyone really have being like that?"

Staring into her cup, Emerald watched the cream in her coffee swirl gently, still in motion from her last sip. Did Derek ever talk like that? She doubted it. Kyle was just different. And of course he thought that. Everyone else around him talked like that, most likely. People were crass within the underbelly of the city. Derek was refined and above all that.

Settling the matter in her mind, Emerald took another sip, confident that Derek had never uttered any sort of obscenities about women, especially about her.

"How far away is your practice? Will it take long to get there?" Emerald asked abruptly. She no longer wanted to think about what Kyle had said.

"Depends on how shitty the traffic is. Without traffic, it will take us about thirty minutes. There shouldn't be any at the time we are taking off. Hopefully."

"Are we riding public transport?"

"Are you kidding? That would be the last resort. Even I wouldn't consider taking that piece of shit unless I had a death wish. Only junkies ride that. The only transportation I would ever consider besides my motorcycle, and the band's ground transport, would be a cab. And transport cabs are expensive as hell."

"Oh," Emerald said. "I see." She was nervous about riding the motorcycle again. It scared her silly.

"What noble house did you say you came from?" Kyle asked.

"What?" Emerald wondered, confused. She didn't recall her slipping in her conversation about where she'd come from. She glanced at his direction; his face held steady. Aware of his ruse, she narrowed her eyes.

"Nice try," she hinted coolly, eyeing him.

"Damn," he uttered, relaxing his face. "You catch on quick." Flattered at his unusual compliment, Emerald smiled. He casually leaned back into the booth. "So, why did you run away, exactly? Life too hard?"

Emerald narrowed her eyes. "What's that supposed to mean? You have something against my kind?"

Kyle leaned in, his face serious. "Did you see the rioters last night? Did you see how angry they were?"

"Yes."

"Well, *your* kind are taxing the shit out of *my* kind. And now, *my* kind can't fucking move a muscle anywhere within Arcadia without paying out the ass. We are stuck in the lower levels. I would call that justified anger."

"I know nothing of the taxes, believe me," Emerald shot back, her eyes burning with rage. "If I did, I would have fought against it. But I was treated like nothing more than a rich… daughter of a wealthy lord. I was shut out of any business that the upper class took part in. You can even say that I was held prisoner, in my own right."

Unaffected by her speech, Kyle took a long inhale of his cigarette, burning the cherry of it. Blowing out the smoke into rings, he said, "I wasn't blaming you personally. Only your kind. Why do you think I felt the need to help you out? You seem clueless to Arcadia, even though you're supposedly from here. And… very different from any other of the upper-class stiffs I've ever encountered." He continued to focus on his smoke rings. "Which isn't many, but you get the point."

Slightly embarrassed at her raging words, Emerald bit her lip, lowering her eyes to her coffee cup, "Sorry, I didn't mean to get angry."

"Don't worry about it. I would have probably done the same," he said nonchalantly. "Besides, you left all that upper-level shit." He paused, glancing at her. "Right? You aren't planning to go back, are you?"

Emerald shook her head. "No. I have no desire to. I was tired of being a prisoner in my own home, having no say in my life." Her ruby lips curled into a smile. "My whole life, I have dreamed of seeing all of Arcadia. The places, the people, the city life. I had always imagined what it would be like."

Kyle smiled back. "Take life by the reins and tell it one giant fuck you. You are in charge. Live your life as if it's the only one you got."

Emerald gave him an odd look. "We only have one life."

"Yes. And how have you lived it so far? How you pictured it?"

"No."

"Then you need to figure out what you need to do to change that," Kyle said, taking one last drag of his cigarette.

"I shall," Emerald agreed confidently. Her eyes met his with resolve. She gave him a bright, excited smile. Kyle managed to withhold his, though he didn't do a good job of it, and it came off as a half smirk.

"What house did you say you were from again?"

Emerald grabbed her napkin, wadded it up, and threw it at him across the table. "Do you think me stupid?" she retorted. Amused, Kyle chuckled, getting up from the table and slapping down a few crumpled-up bills to pay for breakfast.

"Hey, I thought I'd try."

***

Before Kyle and Emerald arrived at his practice, the two of them stopped at a few shops, so that Kyle could grab more liquor and Emerald more suitable clothes, something she'd insisted on acquiring. Every passing hour that she was in the lower levels, it became apparent that she was completely out of place. The clothes she had packed when she ran away were city fashions that came from the mid to upper levels, and she did not want to draw attention to herself any more than she had to. Especially now that her father and half of Arcadia were probably looking for her.

Kyle didn't rush her while she picked out her clothes. He sat there chatting with the owner of the shop, sharing his new bottle of liquor. Before she knew it, the store became more like a hangout, as a few of his street friends happened to pass by and see him. All of them eyed Emerald curiously, which made her more timid with each passing second. She heard the other people ask about her, and Kyle just shrugged, joking to the others, saying he found her on the street. They all laughed, thinking he was just playing with them. However, it wasn't far off from the truth.

After she picked out a few things, she changed into her new clothes—a deep-purple corset top with a denim-studded jacket, black tight pants, and black combat boots. She left her hair up in a ponytail, as it made the length of her hair appear shorter. Not by much, but it did help. No one down in the lower levels had long hair. But it was one thing that she would never do—cut her hair. Another trend she saw within the lower levels that she did like was several piercings in one's ears, unlike the high levels, where people only had one set of holes in their ears or wore ear cuffs.

Emerald paid for her outfit, then packed up her old clothes. She reminded herself to ask Kyle about the piercings. Just another thing to add to the list to ask him. ID, and now, where to pierce her ears.

When they arrived at the warehouse that the band rehearsed in, Emerald was dumbstruck at the upkeep of the building. It had to have been the worst structure that she had ever stepped foot in. If she had to guess, the building was almost at the point of being condemned. Or maybe it already had been, and the band didn't care. The walls were rundown, covered with scribbles and spray paint in all colors. There were thick black marker drawings inked throughout the color, mostly phallic.

"Hey, asshole, what happened last night?" Emerald heard a voice call out from behind the band equipment. "You didn't fucking meet us." A head with blue dyed hair appeared, glancing in Emerald's direction. "Oh, damn," he mumbled, not saying anything further.

Stepping behind Kyle, Emerald instantly felt shy.

"Sorry, I got caught up in some shit last night," Kyle said.

"It would have been nice to get a fucking call, but I forgot, you don't even have a phone," the guy joked.

"Would you like to pay my phone bill?" Kyle didn't bother to wait for a response from the other guys. Instead he set down his guitar case, pulling out the electric guitar and plugging it into an amp that the band had already set up. "By the way, this is Em, everyone. Em, that's Diego, Kamren, and Remy," Kyle said, pointing to each one.

The other guys nodded, continuing to tune their instruments. Emerald waved shyly, meekly blurting out the word "hello." She sat herself down on the only piece of furniture in the place—a shredded red couch with beige insulation foam exploding from the cushions.

"So, Em, I'm surprised that you decided to hang with this asshole," Diego remarked, taking a drink from his liquor flask. He eyed her, then looked over at Kyle, nodding. "He's a dick most of the time. I can hardly stand him."

"He really isn't so bad," Emerald said, laughing sheepishly, turning red. "He just acts tough." She bit her lip, wondering if she'd said too much.

Diego laughed along with the other members of the band, but Kyle shot her a look. "What the hell is that supposed to mean?" Kyle asked, tuning his guitar. "If I didn't know any better, I would say you were being a pain in my ass," he said half amused, half annoyed.

"I'm pretty sure it's the exact opposite," Kamren chimed in from behind his drums, giving Emerald a wink. "I can hardly fucking stand you during practice, either."

"Fuck you," Kyle muttered, strumming his electric guitar loudly. "Are we going to do this, or are you all gonna fuck around all damn day and insult me?"

"So damn sensitive. Is it that time of the month?" Diego said, joining Kyle with the chords.

Emerald tried hard not to show her exasperation at Diego's statement. Either Kyle didn't hear him or just ignored it. The other two guys joined in, and within moments, they began rehearsing one of their songs.

Emerald listened patiently to the band's practice. Several times the guys started cursing at each other; other times they goofed off. But even so, Emerald could tell they had a passion for their music, which showed through their songs.

The shabby couch was starting to get to Emerald's back, causing her some stiffness. She got up, stretched, and started walking through the warehouse, listening to the music while scanning the drawings and graffiti that plastered the walls. She accidentally kicked a thick black marker while coming around a corner, and it scooted across the cement flooring. Emerald walked over to the marker, picked it up, and opened the cap. The marker tip was still intact. Shrugging to herself, she decided to start drawing on the walls. And why not? Everyone else had had their share of the wall at one point or another, and at least it was something to do to keep her occupied. She didn't want to be a distraction from their practice.

Pressing the fresh black ink against the wall, she began scribbling furiously along with the band's music. Glancing over her shoulder, she wondered if the band could see her. Emerald saw she was too far around the corner of the wall where the band was practicing, which set her mind at ease. She didn't like when too many people watched her work. It made her self-conscious.

While she was drawing, a magical-like trance came over her, filling her with power that was similar to hers but with a different feel to the energy. Her vision went black, temporarily blinding her. Emerald began to panic, but the magic soothed her within her mind, comforting her. The tender force guided her hand softly, causing her to draw what it wanted her to draw, while the soft glow of the yellow-green color filled the void of her darkened vision.

She had felt this magic several times in her life, one being when she fell from her balcony, but she had never purposely summoned it. She didn't know how. It came and went as it pleased.

Emerald didn't know how long she was stuck in her state, but when the magic released itself from her, there was no more music playing. The band was done.

Stepping back to see what she had drawn, a frightening image greeted her. There, within the harsh blackness of the lines, her likeness emerged. Her face and body had a mass of wires coming out all over her, intertwined and tangled, floating outward to the corners of the wall. The wires reminded her of her life at the palace, being strangled and imprisoned by loneliness. But Emerald knew that it wasn't the point of the drawing. The magic was trying to give her a message. But what?

Emerald could smell Kyle's cigarette. He was right behind her.

Turning her head, Emerald met Kyle's eyes slowly. He puffed on his cigarette, studying the drawing. There was a moment of silence, and Emerald couldn't muster up the words to even begin to talk. Besides, how could she explain to him that she had been under some type of spell? Had he even seen her use her power? Was it visible? The thought frightened her.

Finding her words at last, Emerald sputtered them out. "I… I decided to add… to your walls."

After what seemed like an eternity of Kyle smoking and staring, he said, "It looks like you are in a deep load of shit."

Nodding, Emerald shuffled one of her combat boots. The rubber tip caught on the cement floor, which made her foot stop mid-action. The other band members came over, liquor bottles in their hand while smoking.

"Whoa, that's kickass," Kamren said. "You should draw the flyers for our band."

Diego took a drink, nodding his head. "What do you think, Em? Can you draw some cool shit like this for us? Remy drew our logo, and look how shitty it is," he said, laughing, pointing to the symbol on the drum set.

"You guys are fucking assholes," Remy said, drinking his liquor. "But Em is pretty good, I'll admit." He looked at her, giving her a small smile. "What do you say? We can even give you some money to do it. I'll make sure we take it out of our gig's earnings tomorrow."

Kyle studied her face through his thick gray clouds of smoke. Unsure of what to do, Emerald searched Kyle's eyes. He nodded to her silently.

Her embarrassment melted away, replaced with the excitement of the others' approval. It also gave her hope that she could start earning some money doing something she knew that she could do.

"Sure, I will," Emerald said, smiling at them. "Just tell me what you want your flyer to look like."

Remy began spouting off ideas, so Emerald gave him her full attention. Black and white. Inked with some color. Drawings of the guys. At one point he was making no sense, and Emerald glanced at Kyle. He was staring at her with a unique smile, one that she had never seen before. She couldn't help but beam back at him. Suddenly aware of her response, he took a drag of his cigarette and hastily turned away.

What was that all about?

Emerald watched as Kyle grabbed his guitar, packing it up while Remy continued to chatter.

CHAPTER 22

The servants around Derek continued to pack up his things within the Sapphire Quarters, for if there was just a moment of opportunity for the prince to escape, he would need to be ready to leave at a moment's notice.

Derek's headache continued to linger throughout the day, and the pains in his body hadn't subsided, which forced him to drink wine, hoping that the alcohol would dull his pain. He was seated outside on the balcony, watching the sun set into the heart of the city. He compared himself to the sun, both he and the sun losing their light as their hearts continued to be weighed down by the gravity of this world. His light being the hope to wed Emerald.

Just the thought of Damaris aggravated him. He had never intended to give Derek a fair chance and had placed him under house arrest. The *nerve* of Damaris. Father had warned him about the ruthlessness of the King, but Derek hadn't wanted to hear it. He had longed for Emerald throughout these years and wanted no one else but her. And now she was out there alone in the midst of Arcadia, and he locked up under Arcadia's guard. The very thought made him well up with anger.

Damn him. This is all Damaris's doing, he cursed under his breath. Derek took another hasty drink, then went inside.

He saw Silas inside the wardrobe, pulling his garments off the closet bar. Silas noticed him from within the closet and came out to check on him.

"Your Highness, everything will be packed up in another hour."

"Excellent. Let's just hope that my father has caught wind of our dilemma. I don't want to be here any longer than I have to, especially with Emerald gone." Derek sat down briskly, having another sip of his wine.

"Agreed, Your Highness. Hopefully His Majesty of York hears of our confinement, and of the missing princess, and sends some of York's troops to come to our aid."

"That he would, Silas. You can count on that." Derek nodded. "My father wouldn't tolerate this one bit."

If there would be anyone, just anyone, on the council to notify my father, it would be Emerys. Let's hope he comes to his senses and does the right thing…

Derek rubbed his temples. The headache had advanced, his mind twisting in pain. Even with Silas's soft noise coming from the wardrobe, each hanger Silas pulled off the rack was a pounding sensation within Derek's mind, like a hammer to a stone, over and over again. His body began to sweat.

"Silas!" Derek called out, rubbing the sweat off his brow.

Silas peeked out of the closet. "Yes?"

"More wine," he ordered. "And please, will you leave me for the time being? I cannot take any more noise."

Silas saw Derek's face and gave him a look that said *you don't look well,* but Derek ignored it. Silas retrieved a full chalice and a carafe to accompany it. Derek dismissed Silas with a wave of his hand, and the servant excused himself to the adjoining sitting room, leaving the prince in peace.

Derek drank the full glass promptly, seeking immediate relief from his pain. The wine was so bitter, but it made him forget about his exploding headache. As he poured himself another glass, he noticed his clothes were completely damp, drenched in sweat. Peeling off the majority of his garments, Derek felt much better, remaining only in his black pants, leaving his jewelry intact as well.

Downing another glass of the dark drink, Derek's eyes shifted to the vanity, where he swore he saw a twinkling flash streak across the mirror. Staring into the reflection to get a good look, he saw the whole room as it was. Shaking his head, he took another drink, blaming it on his splitting headache.

A moment later, another colored blur appeared across the vanity mirror.

Setting down his glass of wine, Derek approached the mirror with caution. He glanced at his reflection, only seeing his pale face, dark circles under his ice-blue eyes. He looked terrible. Even his midnight curls had lost their luster. The strange sickness was taking a toll on his body and his appearance.

For a moment, he chuckled softly at the mirror, shaking his head. Perhaps he was losing his mind.

A cackling sound joined in with his laughter from within his mind. Derek stopped sharply, turning all around within the room. But the strange laughter continued, over and over again, with the pain in his head pulsating in unison.

Derek doubled over in throbbing pain, smacking his head on the cold wood of the vanity in the process. For a moment, the pain dulled and the laughter stopped, releasing him from his bondage. His head rose slowly, his eyes carefully looking in each direction. He expected to find only himself, minus his sanity. But instead his eyes met Emerald's alluring image, standing within the mirror.

Was she in the room with him?

He turned around sharply to see Emerald behind him, but she was not there. Derek slowly looked back into the mirror, and there he met her lovely image once again. He decided that he was indeed going insane. This was all a dream. Or a hallucination.

The image of Emerald gave him a seductive glance, smiling coyly at him with her bright eyes. She walked toward him, swaying her hips as she moved, the slits in her black mesh dress exposing her thighs as she stalked toward him.

His heart pounded hard at the sight of her provocative movements. The blood that pumped through his veins burned and ached, making him aware of his primordial manhood needs, making him feel so alive. He took another drink of his wine, indulging in the tempting image, for if it wasn't her, he could at least enjoy it.

But then Emerald closed in on him and reached through the mirror, pulling him to her lips. Derek passionately responded to her longing, tasting her desire for the first time as her body gently glided out of the mirror and into his arms. His body ached from her soft kisses, the same ache he had felt for her for so many of those long years. Her tongue massaged his, drinking in his every lust while the soft flesh of her hands ran up his firm exposed torso, exploring every part of his body, causing him to burn with an insatiable appetite for her flesh.

This madness was much more appealing and rewarding, he told himself. Why fight it? Within the madness, he finally had her.

Emerald took his hand, ever so gently, guiding it to the swell of her back. She continued to embrace him, squeezing her curves against his hard body, kissing him wildly. Derek couldn't contain himself and answered her cravings by pushing her against the wall. Emerald thrust one of her legs up and around his hip, returning his kisses while running one of her hands down his backside, squeezing.

Then Emerald laughed, the same laugh that had come within from the back of his mind. The laugh was the end of the spell, causing him to snap out of his fantasy, waking him from a pleasant dream.

Startled, Derek stumbled back, seeing the true image of Emerald for the very first time. Only it was not Emerald. More like a violet witch, all in purples and blacks.

"Derek, Derek...." the woman said, thrusting her back against the wall, like a lioness stretching after a long nap. Her large breasts stuck out, barely contained in her outfit, as her hands caressed the wall, as if it were a lover. "Who knew that a man with such strength and such *vitality*, could become so lost within the depths of his mind... all over a single woman. It is too bad you aren't blond. We would have had much more fun," she said, her violet eyes sparkling through her narrow slits. She was rather beautiful, and rather frightening.

Derek stood shocked, unsure what to do. When he finally came to his senses, he yelled, "Guards! Silas!" He kept his eyes locked onto hers while slowly backing away, confused as to whether this woman was a dream or real. "Hurry!" he cried out.

The guards came running into the room, with Silas trailing behind him.

"Oh, Derek, there is no need for that, is there?" said the woman with a laugh. The violet woman lifted her right hand and gave a loud snap of her fingers. Silas and the guards' bodies froze in place, and no movement or breath came from them.

The air around Derek suddenly felt still. The light puff of wind from his balcony was no longer blowing, and the world was tinted in a deep-violet hue, except he and the woman were in full color. Time had stopped.

"Much better. Now we can talk uninterrupted. It is so much more personal this way, don't you think?" the woman said, laying her hands against Derek's naked chest, gliding her fingers across it. She flashed him a charming smile, then turned away, swaying her hips as she moved across the room. She spotted a glass of wine, then sat herself down in midair, as if the air itself was a chair. Her hair began to float around her softly, a soft glow of dark-violet magic lightly swirling around her, playing with her hair and the fabrics of her dress.

She took a drink from the goblet. "Oh, Derek, this wine is simply delightful." She leaned back in the air as if getting comfortable.

Derek continued to move backward until he hit a wall, frightened. "Are you real? How do you know my name?" he asked, his voice shaking with confusion and fear. His headache returned, and he rubbed it to try and ease the pain. "Never mind, please don't answer." Derek closed his eyes. This was all a dream; it was not real. And damned if would he give in to his craziness by answering himself.

"This is no dream, Derek," the woman answered. Derek opened his eyes again, hoping that she was gone. But she was still there, floating in midair with some sort of purple energy flowing around her. "And us... well... that was real too." She smirked, taking another drink. "You should have done to the princess what you did to me to seal the deal. Women like bold men." She smacked her lips, flashing him a knowing smile.

Derek was in utter disbelief, taking in the whole situation before him. Watching the woman and the violet flow of energy around her, he began to inch closer, still proceeding with caution. *This has got to be a dream. No one in the real world can do what she is doing.*

"Oh, Derek, I thought we just went over this. The magic is real, that I can assure you. Just ask your sweet princess," the woman said in a honeyed voice with a layer of sarcasm.

His heart stopped when she mentioned Emerald. What did she mean by that?

"Oh, I am sorry." The woman laughed, her violet eyes burned with intensity. "Didn't your princess ever tell you?"

His eyes widened as he gasped. "How? I don't understand..." Derek said, stunned. Overwhelmed at everything, he attempted to reach out for the carafe, wanting to pour himself a glass of wine. It wasn't real. It had to be a nightmare. She said Emerald had magic. *Magic.* Yes, he was deep in a nightmare. Perhaps if he drank himself cold in his dream, he would wake up, and this shade of a woman would disappear, along with her magic.

Before his hand reached the glass, the chalice and carafe was surrounded by a purple glow, floating from its place on the table. It hovered in midair, the carafe pouring its contents into the chalice until the glass was full. After, the chalice floated toward Derek, hovering right in front of him, waiting for Derek to snatch it.

Derek's eyes shot to the woman, who gave him a smile. She nodded her head, gesturing for him to drink it. Staring at the woman, wondering what to do, he accepted the magical glass, grasping it with his decorated fingers, downing the harsh liquid.

Derek lowered his glass, studying the woman. "Who are you? I might as well entertain this nightmare," Derek said, still unconvinced that the whole situation was real.

"Oh, how rude of me." She made a sweeping gesture. Derek couldn't tell if she was genuine or if she did it out of propriety. "Some address me as Sorceress," she said in a scornful tone, "but you may address me as Enchantress. Enchantress Ikaria."

"And where do you exactly hail from, Enchantress Ikaria?"

Ikaria gave him a half smirk, seeming delighted that he had addressed her properly. "I am from far into the future, my prince. So far in advance that all of this"—the woman waved around—"does not exist." Her eyes darted to the window. "And by the way, this city is truly fascinating. Quite remarkable, really."

Derek eyed her curiously. "What do you mean that it does not exist?"

"Precisely what I mean. This city. Many of the world sectors. The technology. The world is much changed in my time. My world relies on magic, whereas your world depends on technology. Such a shame, really. It would be nice if they could coexist in harmony," she sneered.

"Magic. You are telling me magic is the source of survival in the future? Not technology?" Derek asked, watching her. "Are you sure I am not dreaming?"

"Rest assured, my prince, you are not." She got up from her invisible chair, then spun around slowly midair, as if she were lying on her stomach on a bed, propping herself up with a hand, the other hand holding on to the glass.

Derek saw his chalice fill magically with more wine, as the carafe next to him emptied. "What do you want with me?" Derek asked her curiously.

The woman took a drink, then gave an approving look at her glass. "I didn't come to visit you just so I can have a moment of pleasure, although

I have thoroughly enjoyed myself," Ikaria said nonchalantly as she slammed the rest of her wine, then placed the goblet in midair. It stayed suspended in motion by her deep-violet magic. "There are people in the future, people who are corrupt far beyond anything you can imagine, people who outlaw technology, who have supreme rule over the entire Earth. These people are after your darling princess. Well, her blood, that is."

"Really…" Derek was not convinced.

"You ask what I want? There is nothing I desire more than to seek and destroy the whole lot of them. But to do that, I, too, will need your princess's blood. If I acquire it, I will destroy them, and take back *my* throne. I will rid the planet of supreme authority, restoring the future sectors as they should be, along with the balance of magic and machines."

Derek couldn't believe what he was hearing. Magic and machines? It was all nonsense. "Is what you said earlier true? Does Emerald have magic? Truly?"

"*Green* magic. The most desired color in the future. There hasn't been anyone documented to be born of green magic. That was, until a recent discovery."

Derek frowned. Had Emerald had magic this whole time? She had not once, for as long as he'd known her, ever confided in him. It hurt his pride.

Ikaria saw his downcast face. "It is such a shame that one as special as her did not share her secret, bare her burdens to someone as *loving* as you." The woman smiled. Her words stung him, wounding his ego further.

"That did not help," Derek snapped at her. "And what does this all have to do with me?"

The woman eyed him, her violet irises glowing. "My prince, I have come here to ease your troubles" she said smoothly. "I think we can benefit each other."

Derek scoffed, thinking about Damaris and turning away. "You know nothing of my troubles."

"Oh, come now, of course I do. I have been in your mind the last twenty-four hours, have I not? I know what you need." Ikaria's violet hair wisped in the air softly.

"Oh, really? What's that?" He continued to look away from her.

Ikaria leaned into his back, her fragrant aroma softening the stiff air. "Damaris is such a… nuisance, don't you think?" she suggestively whispered, her hot breath against his ear. "It would be so much easier if he just agreed to your terms, allowing you to marry the princess."

Derek snapped his face in her direction. She did know of his situation. But how? She couldn't really be inside his head.

"Oh, yes, my prince. King Damaris will need much convincing. Especially since you are now his prisoner. And what about that siege that he will lay to your kingdom? I believe it will happen within a fortnight."

Derek ran up to her, face to face. "What siege? I don't believe you. He barely has a functioning military."

"Indeed, he does. And it's more than a military. Man, machine, and magic combined, using your princess's blood. Cyborgs, I believe they are called."

"Cyborgs?"

"They are completely unstoppable. Well, for the most part. And I find them quite a turn-on." She ran a finger across her chest playfully. "Your city-kingdom won't last through their invasion."

"Are you sure? How do you know?"

"Have you not been paying attention? I have seen the future of this city. I have seen what happens to your princess, and I know who she marries. It isn't you, I am sorry to say." Ikaria leaned into his face, giving him a charismatic smile. "But we don't have to follow what has been done before, do we now?"

Derek's heart stopped. Emerald not married to him? That he could not stomach. He was meant for her. No one else could have Emerald but him.

His eyes met Ikaria's, and she looked back at him with a knowing understanding.

"Why me?" he asked. "Why do you want to help me?"

"You have so much to offer." She came over to him, floating in the air as if she were effortlessly swimming, streaming dark-violet magic behind her. "And let's just say I have a soft spot for unrequited love."

Derek scoffed. "You? I highly doubt it." Derek turned away, drinking more wine.

"Oh, come now, my prince. I am human." Ikaria placed one of her hands on his shoulder. She held out the other, as if showing him a secret. Within her palm, an image of a crown appeared in her hand, emitting a dark-purple glow. The crown was the color of onyx, with a shadowy purple jewel in the center.

Derek eyed her hand on his shoulder until Ikaria removed it, then he reached out to the glowing circlet. As his hand met the crown, it ran through the image. It was a hologram.

"What is this?" he asked, curious.

"Part of our little arrangement. I want half of Arcadia's cyborg army and a vial of the princess's blood. In exchange, I will see that you are set free. I will ensure the King agrees to let you wed the princess. And I will also throw in this trinket."

"Why would I want that?" Derek asked, eyeing the glowing circlet.

Ikaria smiled deviously at him. "Well, I can't make Emerald fall in love with you, but this will at least help."

"Nonsense. Emerald already loves me. She has said so herself," Derek said sharply.

Ikaria shrugged, then shook her head. "Whatever you say, my prince. The rest will be attainable once you give me her blood."

"This arrangement sounds much more in your favor." Derek took another drink, then stumbled to a nearby sofa. He'd had much too much wine. "Besides, I cannot bargain for what is not mine. I am not the King, and I have no say in such matters."

"I will ensure you become king," Ikaria said casually. "We'll take care of that first. That shall be a little present from me to you, so you know that I am serious."

"But how will you know if I will fulfill my end of the bargain? I never said yes," Derek said.

Ikaria extended her hand slowly, and glowing violet magic spilled out of her palms, guiding the crown to his vanity. It stopped two inches from the surface, hovering, still in a transparent form. "Because you will be needing this, more than you know, and you cannot have it until I have the blood." Ikaria gently set her feet down on the ground. "The other minor details, dealing with the cyborg army and what not, we can work out after you give me the blood and when my body is in your time."

Derek snapped his head up at Ikaria, as if he truly was looking at her for the first time. "You mean, you aren't really here? Then how... did we..." Derek stumbled on his words, too afraid to finish the sentence.

"The mind can do wondrous things, along with a little help from blue, violet, and orange magic." Ikaria smiled wickedly at him.

"This was all in my head?" Derek asked, confused from the effects of the wine mixed with the image of Ikaria.

"You looked so tense. I just wanted you to have a bit of fun."

For the first time, Derek felt like he was trapped inside of his mind and had no power or control to determine what was real or not. Taking the chalice in his hand, he hurled it at the sorceress as hard as he could.

"You damned witch! Get out of my mind!" he yelled.

The cup flew through her transparent image, smashing into the wall behind her, and the dark liquid splashed all over the walls and floors.

Ikaria eyed the fallen cup, then tsked. "Don't make a mess on my account," she said, then her gaze met his. "When you are ready to give me the princess's blood, call out my name near the circlet. Just one vial should be sufficient."

"Never." Derek ran over to the nightstand, snatching up a lamp and throwing it at the enchantress. "Get out!"

"You can thank me later, once you become king," Ikaria's voice called out as her body began to dissipate before his eyes, proudly sweeping back her hair.

With a sudden violet flash, her image was gone.

"Remember, just one vial of her blood will do…" she said, her voice reverberating through his mind, every word torturing him.

Derek felt her presence in his thoughts, her control deep within him. The pain in his mind was worse. Much, much worse.

Finally, the violet hue disappeared, and the world turned back to full color. Silas and the guards were in motion, running to Derek.

"Your Highness! What is it?" asked Silas in a concerned tone, looking around at the room. He spotted the broken glass and the puddle of wine on the floor. "What has happened?"

"Prince Derek?" asked one of his guards. "Is everything okay?"

Derek sunk into a nearby couch, letting the velvet fabric envelop his naked torso, rubbing his fingers through his sweat-soaked curls.

Everything was not okay.

CHAPTER 23

GREEN

Kyle slowed his motorcycle as he neared the location of the band's next gig, with Emerald clinging tightly behind him. A horde of transports, motorcycles, bikers, punks, gangs, and drunkards stood between them and the building, leaving nowhere for Kyle to park. He came to a complete stop before the crowd. Through the masses, Emerald saw the band's ground transport trying to get through, with Remy yelling and cursing out the driver's side window at a group of people. Whatever was happening, it didn't look good.

Kyle revved his engine, warning those who stood in his way. A few people moved, allowing him to gradually inch his way through the thick crowd, meeting the transport with Remy's half-outstretched body hanging out the window. Kamren had his head sticking out of the passenger side, slinging profanities at the biker gang blocking the way.

"What the hell is going on?" Kyle growled at Remy, annoyed.

"Some asshole named Jaxx wants to be a dick and block the band transport. Apparently he rounded up all these shitheads to do it."

"What in the hell is his problem?"

"Who the hell knows. The guy probably just wants to be a jackass," Remy said.

"Fucking Diego, man," Kamren cursed. "Most likely went on a tirade and pissed off the wrong guy. He always has the habit of making enemies."

"Yeah." Kyle shrugged.

The gang became agitated as Remy honked his horn and yelled more obscenities. Emerald frantically fidgeted with Kyle's guitar case strap slung across her back, making sure it was secure. She was starting to worry if Arcadia's authorities were going to show up. Especially the strange robotic men.

As Emerald scanned the crowd, her eyes locked on one man in particular, rendering her motionless. It was the tattooed man, the same man who had been giving her trouble the other night. He just happened to be the leader of the biker gang. This had to be the Jaxx Remy said was stirring up trouble.

Emerald gripped Kyle's waist tightly as she leaned closer, afraid of what was about to take place. A moment later, Kyle saw Jaxx approaching, and her stomach fell into her gut.

"Fucking *really*?" Kyle muttered, recognizing the tattooed man as well.

"I came here just for *you*. You should feel fucking special." Jaxx laughed while the other gang members joined in, snickering.

"Don't you have anything better to do, like go fuck yourself?" Kyle asked coolly.

"No, I don't," Jaxx spat, the tattoos on his face folded in anger. Jaxx lunged toward Emerald, then firmly grabbed her, yanking her off the bike.

Emerald yelped, reaching an outstretched arm toward Kyle as her body flew off the vehicle, landing right into Jaxx's iron hold. She tried to force her way out, but he pulled her close to him effortlessly while his gang created a barrier around them.

Kyle furiously leapt off his bike in Jaxx's direction, tearing through the gang to get to them.

"Don't you fucking touch her!" Kyle roared. The gang members held him back as Kyle swung wildly, struggling to make his way to her. Kamren and Remy were watching in shock.

"She's mine now, bitch. What are you gonna do about it?" Jaxx said, taunting Kyle.

Emerald grimaced in disgust and fear as he gripped her arm harder. Her eyes met Kyle's from afar. She shifted her attention to his hand, nervously wondering how she was going to get out of this mess.

Kamren and Remy leapt out of the transport to help, but it was no use. They were outnumbered.

"Get your fucking hands off her!" Kyle screamed. "I'm gonna stab the shit out of you!"

"Let's see you try, pussy," Jaxx said, his voice booming with laughter. He turned to Emerald, his mouth right up against her ear. His rancid breath tickled her ear, making her cringe. "Hey, sweetheart," Jaxx grunted. Emerald wriggled in disgust, struggling.

"You are a fucking dickless wonder!" Kyle shouted from across the gang, continuing to swing wildly.

Emerald knew she had no chance to free herself from him, unless she called on her magic. But did she dare release her magic upon Jaxx? Everyone would see it, and her father and the authorities would soon know where she was. But one glance at Jaxx triggered the thought of his hand moving further down her body, and she decided right then to call upon the dark side of her power.

But instead of his hand moving anywhere else on her body, Jaxx yanked the guitar case off Emerald, then released his grip, throwing her to the ground. Jaxx held out the guitar case, then snapped one of his fingers, signaling for one of his gang members to come and take it from him. One of them complied with his demand, taking the guitar case from Jaxx, then disappearing into the gang. Then they kicked Kyle and stepped away.

Kyle dashed toward Emerald, and she ran into his arms. He put his hand around her shoulders, holding her close. Emerald's heart was pounding, but it also pounded with a new sensation. What was that?

Remy met them, and Kyle handed her over to him gently.

"Get her away from here, now," he ordered Remy. "In fact, you might want to leave too, because I'm most likely going to end up in jail after I am done with this asshole."

Remy nodded, guiding Emerald away from Kyle and Jaxx. Emerald turned back to see Kyle through the growing crowd, then yanked away from Remy, pushing her way back toward Kyle. She caught a glimpse of him charging toward Jaxx, attempting to punch him, but he missed.

"You just don't fucking give up, do you? First the girl. Now my damn guitar! What the hell is it with you, asshole?" Kyle roared. He swung another punch at Jaxx, this time clipping his ear. Jaxx threw the guitar case to one of his friends behind him, then got in Kyle's face.

"You fight like a pansy," Jaxx taunted. "Come on, pretty boy, let's see you make an ass out of yourself to your girlfriend," he said, his voice booming with laughter.

Emerald watched as Jaxx swung his hefty fist against Kyle's side. Kyle grimaced, then swung back, landing a punch to Jaxx's side, missing his kidneys. Jaxx shot his face up in pure rage, clenching his jaw and making an audible grunt. He swung a punch in return, but by then, too many onlookers had pushed their way in front of Emerald, making it hard for her to see what was happening, and she could only hear their shouts.

"You want your guitar, asshole? Tell you what, let's have a race. Winner gets the guitar. Loser gets the hell out of here," Jaxx yelled over the crowd.

"You want a fucking race? Fine!" Kyle snarled, reappearing in Emerald's line of sight. He hotly marched over to his bike as the crowd began to cheer. "You better be prepared to have your ass handed to you!"

"Kick his ass!" Diego's voice could be heard from within the crowd. Remy reappeared next to her, along with Kamren.

"You okay?" Kamren asked.

"Yes. But his guitar," Emerald fretted. She suddenly felt guilty about Jaxx taking Kyle's guitar from her.

"Our gig…" Remy groaned. He anxiously smoked a cigarette, trying to relax, but instead became more intense with each puff.

"Fuck the gig! This is way more entertaining. Besides, our man is the shit when it comes to riding," Diego said, coming up to them smiling. He was enjoying himself while drinking a bottle with a brown paper bag wrapped around it.

"And where in the hell have you been? We needed your ass!" Remy scolded.

"I just got here. I wouldn't have been able to do much anyway." Diego shrugged, taking another drink from his bag. "Did you see how many of his gang members there were?"

"Chicken shit." Kamren eyed him, clearly annoyed.

"So what if I am?" Diego said casually. "At least I'm smart about my odds."

The crowd formed on each side of the street, waiting for the race to begin, allowing Emerald to see Kyle once again. By the minute, there were more people joining in the spectacle, the numbers swelling in size. Emerald wouldn't have been surprised if all of the southern sector's lower levels were piled up in the street at that moment.

Kyle and Jaxx got on their bikes, lining up in the street. They sat on their motorcycles, revving their engines as if to compare whose bike was more intimidating. Jaxx's mouth was hurling insults, but what he said, no one could tell over the roars of the engines. Emerald saw the kind of motorcycle that Jaxx was on, then compared it to Kyle's. Though she knew nothing of motorcycles, even she could tell that Jaxx had a much more powerful engine than Kyle's. Kyle's bike seemed like a child's toy compared to the monstrous power of Jaxx's humming engine.

The motors were drowning out the noise of the crowd. Emerald became nervous for Kyle, biting her nails. Emerald saw Jaxx's mouth move again, most likely trying to squeeze in one last insult to Kyle before they took off, but Kyle paid no attention to Jaxx. His face was stone cold, looking directly forward.

Emerald absently clutched on to Diego's arm, shaking with nerves.

Diego nudged her. "Don't worry, Em. Kyle does this kind of shit all the time. He always wins," he said, attempting to reassure her. "Drink?"

I hope so, Emerald thought, then shook her head to Diego. She couldn't drink at a time like this; it would make her a nervous wreck.

The engines roared one last time. A man dressed in studded leather stood in front of the two bikes.

"Go!" he yelled.

In a flash, the men sped off while the crowd roared, screaming for their favorite biker.

Emerald watched Kyle race down the street until he was out of sight, turning a corner. The crowd began to move in anticipation. Small fights broke out, bets were being called, and liquor and drugs were passed around, causing Emerald to be pushed away from Diego and the other two band members. In a panic, Emerald began to push her way back to her original spot, but it was no use, as another fight blocked her way.

A sharp jab hit her shoulder suddenly. Ignoring it, Emerald thought someone had accidentally bumped her. A second passed, then a hard shove pushed her, causing Emerald to slightly stumble.

Whipping around to see who had shoved her, a woman with black chin-length hair and magenta lips gave her a dark smile. She brought a liquor bottle to her lips, guzzling its contents, then hurled it to the ground. As the bottle shattered, the crowd inched away from the woman, leaving room around the two of them.

"You with him?" she asked, hands on her hips.

"Who?"

The woman pushed Emerald again. "Did you come here tonight with *him*?"

"Kyle?" Emerald asked, blinking in confusion. She had not an inkling who this woman was.

"Yeah." She approached Emerald, ready to make another move. "Are you two serious?"

"No, we most certainly are not," Emerald assured her, narrowing her eyes.

"I don't believe you," the woman accused, her drunken eyes burning with jealousy. She closed in on Emerald's face, her liquor breath strong. "I saw his tattoo."

What about his tattoo?

"I have no idea what you are talking about," Emerald shot back. With another glimpse of the woman, Emerald realized this girl had to be a past jilted lover of Kyle's.

The thought of herself and Kyle entered Emerald's mind for a split second, quickening her heart. The thought was new; it had never crossed her mind before until that moment. Secretly, Emerald liked the idea of herself with Kyle, though she couldn't admit it. He was someone who she would never be able to have. She was a princess, and he was… well… Kyle. What could a guy like him see in a girl such as herself, anyway? A dull girl from the upper levels of Arcadia? Kyle was so fierce, so wild, and everything Derek wasn't.

Her mind filling with self-doubt, Emerald reached for her necklace, feeling Derek's jewel against her fingers. *Prince Derek was meant for me*, she told herself. Although in her heart she wasn't sure she believed those words.

"You are mistaken; we have nothing between us," Emerald said quickly. "And even if we did, what is that to you?"

"Bitch!" the woman screamed as she shoved Emerald hard, causing Emerald to slam to the ground. The people around her saw that a fight was starting and formed a circle around them. Angrily, Emerald whipped her ponytail out of her face, rising steadily to her feet. With a hot gush of fury, Emerald's blood burned. This woman aggravated her to no end.

The woman laughed, most of the crowd joining her. Emerald felt all the eyes of the crowd glaring at her, as if they somehow knew she wasn't from the lower levels, jeering and throwing insults and making jokes about her and "her kind." Emerald even heard voices from within the crowd declaring the woman to be the winner before the fight began.

Not if Emerald could help it.

Emerald pounced, quickly entangling the woman within her grasp. The woman clawed at her with her sharp, painted lacquer nails, aiming at Emerald's face. Each time, Emerald was quicker, dodging the woman. Emerald didn't know how to fight, nor had she ever had to do so, but she followed her gut. Within her soul, she felt the magic within her boiling over, begging to be released. The desire to unleash her dark-green magic grew unbearable, but she resisted the urge to let the magic have its way, forcing it back down within her soul.

The two tangled with each other, then the woman pushed herself and Emerald to the ground. She was about to swipe at Emerald's face, but Emerald pushed the woman off with her boot, causing the woman to lose her balance. There was a loud crack when the woman's body hit the concrete, and she fell flat next to her. Emerald heard the woman gasping for breath.

She had knocked the breath out of her by the fall.

Taking that opportune moment, Emerald shot up over the woman, clutching the woman's shirt in her knuckles, forcing her face into the woman's. Emerald's eyes narrowed, glaring. Emerald allowed herself to give a satisfactory smile to the woman, then to the crowd, as if she had proved everyone wrong about their initial assessment of her.

Kyle's colorful words came to her mind.

"Don't fuck with me," Emerald warned, panting for breath.

The woman continued to find her breath, grasping her chest. The crowd that encircled them began to cheer. Realizing that there were still onlookers, Emerald flung the woman to the ground, releasing her grasp on the woman's shirt. There on the ground, the woman finally began breathing, wheezing for air.

With her adrenaline still pumping, her magic began to swell like a balloon inside of her, like she was going to explode. It built up greater and greater, and she began to choke on the magic, trying every moment to hold it back. With every ounce of will she had inside of her, Emerald forced her magic back down inside her core before her dark power took control.

Taking a few more deep breaths, Emerald turned and pushed desperately through the crowd that circled her, making her way back toward the street, anxious for the race's outcome.

***

Kyle ignored everything around him. The jeers of the crowd. The throwing of trash against him. Jaxx's lame insults that he yelled over the roar of the engines. They could all go to hell.

"Nice fucking bike. Did you put it together from the junkyard?" Jaxx laughed.

Kyle didn't even give Jaxx the pleasure of seeing his reaction. Instead, he revved his engine in response.

Jaxx continued to laugh over the booming sound of his own engine. "I bet your dick is as small as your bike. Can't even satisfy your woman."

Kyle had every urge to flip out his pocket knife and stab the shit out of Jaxx, but he clenched his jaw in anger, revving his engine again.

Don't give in to that fucking asshole, Kyle told himself. It took every ounce of his strength to appear as if he wasn't the least bit affected by Jaxx's words, but inside, he was about to explode with fury.

Kyle didn't just want to win the race, he *had* to win. Yes, Kyle was pissed about the damn guitar. But the pile of shit had laid his hands on Em, something that made him utterly rage. Just seeing her body twist in his arms inflamed him.

He was no fucking white knight, but his damn honor was at stake. And to hell if he was going to have that shithead win. There was no fucking way. What would Em think of him if he lost?

Em. His head was spinning. From the moment he met her, he couldn't stop thinking about her. It was pissing him off. So fucking beautiful, and he didn't have a chance in hell with her. And why would he? He was some fucking broke aspiring guitarist trying to make his way through the world. He had nothing to offer to a woman like Em. The thought made him more angry and confused.

Never fucking gonna happen, Kyle, he told himself. *Don't waste your time…*

A man stood in front of Jaxx and Kyle with one of his arms held up, the other looking at a watch. Kyle maintained his focus straight ahead, ignoring every distraction, awaiting any sort of movement from the man's hand.

With a sudden jerk of his hand downward, he yelled through the noise of the engines, "Go!"

Kyle instantly gunned it, his motorcycle peeling away from the crowd. Jaxx's bike could be heard doing the same thing, both engines competing with one another. The noise of the crowd faded, replaced with the rumbling of his engine as he shifted gears, gaining speed.

Jaxx's engine roared next to his, drowning out the sound of his own bike. It was time to settle this shit once and for all. Curling his lip in contempt, Kyle leaned inward, trying to be as aerodynamic as he could with the winds raging against his face.

The winds always favored him somehow. Always.

Kyle pulled in the clutch as he and Jaxx turned a corner, both bikes still neck and neck. Coming out of the turn, he shifted back into gear, gaining momentum once again.

The road ahead was clogged with ground transports, with stop-and-go traffic.

The fuck?

He immediately pulled in the clutch, downshifting to weave through the crowded obstacles. Some people from the sidewalk cheered, others yelled to watch where he was going, while jaywalkers scrambled out of his way. A hovering sound could be heard above him from air transports.

Better not be the damn authorities.

He viciously spun through the traffic, dodging all the transports that blocked his path. Out of corner of his eye, he saw Jaxx do the same, although his bike was much larger than Kyle's, causing him to be slower with the maneuvers, letting Kyle have the upper hand.

Take that, asshole!

Kyle accelerated as the road opened up, giving him a solid lead on Jaxx. He pulled the throttle back all the way, furiously making his way to the corner of the block. He pulled in the clutch once again, letting the bike glide into the turn, then shifted back into gear as he moved into the next block.

It was beautiful. Nothing in the way this time.

Faster and faster, he drove, like a maniac out of the pits of hell. The city lights began to blur, and sewer fog blanketed the street in one giant shape from the velocity of his bike.

From behind him, Kyle could hear the sound of Jaxx's engine. Second by second, Jaxx inched closer to him, until they were even once again. Jaxx leaned in closer to Kyle's right side, leaving almost no gap. Kyle veered to the left, but he was close to the other side of the street, near the middle of the road. He was so damn close to the oncoming transports he could kiss them. Jaxx rode closer again, so close that it was a miracle the bikes weren't touching. Jaxx kicked his left leg out, hitting Kyle's bike.

Kyle's bike fiercely skidded into the other lane, into oncoming traffic. Wild honks and alarms sounded. With a quick maneuver, Kyle weaved out of the transports' way, swerving back into the correct lane.

They both glanced at each other evenly, then Jaxx's facial tattoos twisted into smile that only an asshole would give. Kyle saw Jaxx flip a switch. Suddenly, his engine roared and flamed as if his engine was on steroids.

The motherfucker used nitrous oxide.

"Fucking pussy," Jaxx shouted as he laughed, racing past him.

Angrily, Kyle pulled back the throttle as much as he could to gain speed, but it was useless. There was no way in hell his bike could match against another bike with fuel that mimicked crack.

Kyle leaned into the next corner, pulling in the clutch. Kyle watched in pure frustration as Jaxx, who was now ahead of him by a long shot, blazed down the street. Kyle snarled, trying to catch up, but it was no use. Jaxx was now nearing the next corner and had gained more distance between them.

That piece of shit!

Determined to not let the asshole win, Kyle sped as fast as he could, letting the winds glide against his bike.

As he approached the turn, Kyle saw a miracle drop out of the sky, a literal fucking miracle. Out of nowhere, a ground vehicle collided into something on the other side of the street, and it went swinging right in front of Jaxx. Jaxx veered off sharply to avoid the turn, but he had to slam on his brakes. Kyle was instantly prepared, since he was far behind. He veered off course, missing the transport, then passed Jaxx, leaving him behind in street trash as he turned the final corner.

In the distance ahead, he saw the venue, where the crowd was cheering.

The invisible finish line.

Kyle sped past the man who'd started the race, and the man proclaimed Kyle the winner. The crowd roared with cheers for the most part, although there were some who were booing and throwing their liquor bottles at Kyle, especially from Jaxx's gang.

After thirty seconds, Jaxx came racing past the finish line. Jaxx slammed his brakes, sliding like butter against the concrete, then jumped from his bike, slamming it to the ground like a child having a tantrum. He gave his bike a kick, turning to his buddies.

"Guitar!" he roared, gesturing for the case.

Kyle lit a cigarette, taking a drag. He held out his hands, waiting for Jaxx to return his guitar, eyeing his every movement. The guitar was handed over to Jaxx, who looked at Kyle for a moment.

"What are you waiting for?" Kyle sneered. "I won. Hand it over."

Jaxx opened the guitar case, throwing the case aside. He looked intently at Kyle's guitar, studying it.

"Come on, man," Kyle said coolly, watching his every movement.

"Go to hell, asshole!" Jaxx screamed, smashing the guitar into the ground, then he threw what was left in his hands at Kyle's feet.

"You motherfucking asshole!" Kyle shouted, throwing himself at Jaxx. He slammed his fist into Jaxx's face, then quickly went in for another punch. Jaxx roared, hurling his knuckles hard against Kyle's cheek, just missing his jaw. Kyle latched onto Jaxx, then successfully landed a huge blow to Jaxx's face. Jaxx tumbled to the ground, bringing Kyle down with him. The massive biker got above Kyle, then grabbed Kyle's skull with his meaty hands and slammed it against the concrete.

Kyle's head instantly became fuzzy and his mind delirious, the fight becoming nothing more than a blur. Blood and blows. Over and over again, the two exchanged punches, both men pummeling each other's bodies. Kyle saw Diego's face, with him trying to pull Kyle away from Jaxx, but Kyle was too infuriated, and he swung aimlessly at his buddy. Every successful punch filled Kyle with satisfaction, but at the same time, he kept getting smacked back. After a while, Kyle had no idea if he was giving or receiving the punches. It didn't matter. That asshole deserved it.

Very faintly, Kyle heard sirens. Arcadia's authorities.

Jaxx's gang began to pull their leader away, yelling at him about the authorities coming. The sounds of Em's boots clacked as she ran up to Kyle, shaking his arms.

"Kyle! The authorities are coming! We have to go!" she exclaimed, her blurry face fearful.

"Fuck the authorities," Kyle spat, attempting to get up to resume the fight. He instantly stumbled back to the ground. He was now out of Jaxx's reach, no thanks to his gang. "Fucking bullshit!" Kyle raged. "I won fair and square, and the asshole fucks me anyway!"

Kyle felt a cool hand against his hot flesh, and he became acutely aware that his face was bruised and bloodied. The sirens became louder. Through the blur, flashing colors of the authority lights could be seen.

"Kyle, please listen," Em pleaded with him softly. "We have to go."

Em's hand lingered on his swollen face. Her cooling touch made his face feel better with every passing second. She gently turned his head toward her, and his eyes made contact with hers. Her eyes were so beautiful. Even that freckle under her eye was so damn cute.

"The authorities must not find me," she said quietly but fiercely. "Please, Kyle, please," she begged.

It was her words that subdued his rage, like a spell that broke him from his trance. She really didn't want to be found by the police.

Now that was his type of woman.

"Okay, Em," he said, staring into her vivid green eyes as the sirens grew louder. "For you, I will leave."

God. Why did she have to be so damn beautiful?

CHAPTER 24

The message came right as Emerys was finishing his late supper. Damaris had summoned an emergency Inner Council meeting. Emerys took another bite of food before his personal attendant rushed him out of his quarters.

Damaris had been very irrational lately, but in his defense, the princess was missing, and the kingdom was broke. But Emerys did feel truly sorry for Prince Derek's situation. Had Emerys known before the prince's arrival that the King's intention was to hold Derek hostage, Emerys would have thought of some way to convince Damaris otherwise. Or secretly make it known to Derek. Emerys had always admired the York royal family, and he had no desire to see any harm come to the prince. And what Emerys wouldn't give to have a true and upright ruler like Derek on the throne of Arcadia, and not some hothead who had delusions of grandeur of living forever with his daughter's powerful blood.

Walking in haste through the upper-mid section of the palace corridors, Emerys came to his floor's lift. Noticing that it was in use on another level, Emerys decided to use the stairs. Heaven knew he needed the exercise, as he never got enough of it sitting in those council chairs all day. As he hurriedly skipped down the staircase, he nodded in acknowledgment to others of great importance as he was ascending. He had no time for anyone else, as he knew it would cause further delay, but he did feel a bit sorry for those whose greetings he did not return.

Emerys crossed the encased glass bridge that led to the Inner Council chambers. It was nearing evening, and Emerys could see the night sky below his feet through the glass and the green neon lights of the palace. The bridge had a spectacular panoramic view of the city, one of the best views in the palace, with exception of the King's and princess's quarters. Emerys promptly entered, his eyes met by Damaris's empty gaze.

Upon his arrival, Emerys immediately noted that Damaris did not look well. The King was sitting in the room alone, his face pale with a light sweat on his brow. He seemed disturbed, almost as if he had not slept, with dark rings around his eyes, and his cheekbones were sunken in. Even considering the amount of wine he drank, he did not seem himself; it was more like a zombified version.

For all of the years that he had known and served Damaris, he had never seen the King distressed or disturbed. Well, not like *this*. His Majesty was always composed, had much self-confidence, and had a sharp bite ready for those who opposed him. He did not flinch in times of trouble, except with the stunning revelation of the Queen's affair. That was the only moment Emerys had finally seen the King lose his collectedness. But right now, one could argue that this was worse just by the sheer look of Damaris. Much worse.

As Emerys approached, he bowed to Damaris, then seated himself at the table. The other members of the council began to trickle in one by one, until they all arrived. They sat in silence until Damaris spoke.

"Councilors and lords," Damaris said, addressing them by title, "I have called upon you this evening to discuss with you the future of York." He gazed at them sternly with an awkward movement.

Emerys and the other councilors waited for the King to continue, remaining silent. Damaris took a sip of his wine, then gently set down the glass.

Emerys was confused. Had Damaris just sipped his wine like a lady of the court?

Damaris continued. "I have summoned you here to announce that I will agree to Prince Derek's terms of marriage to my daughter, Princess Emerald."

Everyone around the table looked at each other, each with a stunned expression. Emerys sighed inwardly. *For once, he is not being irrational,* Emerys thought.

"What made you change your stance?" asked Baron von Aedard, quickly nodding in agreement with the King. "Not that I disagree with you, Your

Majesty." He took a deep breath. "But... after your... opposition to the prince this morning, we—"

"I was out of sorts. You will all have to excuse me," Damaris replied.

Emerys raised an eyebrow. King Damaris never asked *anyone* to excuse him.

"This is wonderful news," Councilor Zane interjected. "With the betrothal of the prince to the princess, he can remain a hostage here while we invade York. And if the King of York doesn't surrender to our forces, we will continue to have a powerful pawn in the game, and his money." He smiled crookedly, stroking his beard.

"There will be no invasion of York, Councilor," Damaris snapped. Everyone's faces dropped. Each of the men sucked in their breath, including Emerys. This was not like the King at all. Not that Emerys disagreed with the King's decision, as Emerys had opposed the invasion of York from the start. But this was all out of character.

There was an uncomfortable pause, then Councilor Zane stroked his beard again, continuing nervously. "Well, then, let's prepare Arcadia for a wedding," Councilor Zane said. "After we locate the bride, of course." He forced a half smile, trying to ease the high tension in the room.

"Yes. We need to locate my daughter," Damaris stated coldly, slamming his hand into the table. "The *only* one with green magic, and she's out there, just waiting for someone to snatch her up!"

"Your Majesty, the corporation confirmed with me that the gifted cyborg will be ready on schedule to track the princess," Councilor Zane said.

Damaris's eyes shot to him, and his expression almost seemed like it was the first time the King had ever heard that news, and he paused for a moment. "Well, they *better* have it ready. I need that damned cyborg as soon as possible. The princess must be back in these palace walls soon. Or *else*." His head jerked back into the headboard of the chair. His eyes closed, and his face was strained as he massaged his temples.

"She will, Your Majesty," Zane said nervously.

"Thank you, Councilor." Damaris waved his hand in dismissal at Zane. "Also, I have other news," the King continued, keeping his eyes closed a moment longer before snapping them open. "I want you all to draw up a decree. I will name Prince Derek my heir. He is to inherit the kingdom."

Madness broke out along the table, all of the men talking out of turn, utterly baffled at his statement.

Damaris slammed his hand down on the table. "Silence!" The men stopped, giving him mixed looks.

Emerys was dumbfounded but made no objection whatsoever. He liked where this was going and wanted it to come to pass. Arcadia would *finally* have someone to rule it properly, and perhaps the other members would finally be expelled off the council. None besides Councilor Lysander was worth a damn. The other councilors cared not for Arcadia, only for lining their pockets with wealth and titles. It was in their best interest to eat the scraps that fell from Damaris's hand and not have Derek on the throne.

"Your Majesty?" questioned Count Jadeth. "Are you quite sure? Do you really want the prince privy to Arcadia's secrets? And for you… to give your throne to a foreigner? Pardon me for saying so, but this is ludicrous. What about the princess?"

"You *dare* question me?" Damaris snarled, taking another sip of wine. Count Jadeth shrunk in his chair. "Yes, I am damn sure. I want Derek to marry my daughter, and he will inherit Arcadia. I am so damn sure, in fact, I want you all to draw up a document here, right now, before I force you all to resign."

Emerys bit his lip in amusement, trying to hold back an audible laugh.

Count Jadeth snorted in laughter, thinking it was all a joke. Emerys knew this was no joke. Jadeth's laugh was the only noise in the room. Not one person dared to join in with the count. Jadeth looked around the room while his laugh died out, coming to a complete stop. "You are serious, Your Majesty?"

The King turned sharply to the count. "Yes, I am damn serious! Get me the document drawn up! *Now*! And send for the prince immediately!" Damaris barked. Councilor Lysander nodded, then walked out of the room, most likely to fetch the guard stationed at the door.

The King rose from his seat, taking his glass of wine and pacing the room as the men began to formulate the law. Emerys scribbled furiously while the others gave input to how to word the decree, offering language and wording advice as Emerys wrote.

When the document was complete and the Inner Council had agreed on the decree, Emerys handed over the scroll to the King, placing it in front of him. Emerys watched with satisfaction as the King's vacant eyes shot from left to right, reading the decree, then he picked up his quill and signed it.

Emerys took the decree, then walked over to the law machine.

A new era of Arcadia is dawning, he thought excitedly.

Emerys scanned the document into the machine as Damaris nodded in approval. The document became digitized, its new information uploading to the kingdom's online laws.

After Emerys finished, he turned and saw Derek entering the chambers with many of Arcadia's guard surrounding him. The prince was clearly tired, almost as sickly looking as the King himself, and by the dark looks he gave the councilors, he clearly had no interest in being in the room longer than he had to. Every few seconds, Derek scowled at the guards. Emerys didn't blame him. He'd had a most undeserving welcome, had braved Damaris's outburst, and then endured a short confinement.

"Your Majesty," Derek said, nodding his head, not giving a proper bow to the King. He gritted his teeth. "Have you sent for me to be humiliated once again? To have a pleasant conversation about my time so far as a prisoner?" His voice was laced with bitterness. "Because I can tell you I take no pleasure in it."

Damaris ignored the sarcasm. "I am accepting your original terms to the betrothal of the princess. You are no longer Arcadia's prisoner. Furthermore, you will be named heir to my kingdom."

The prince's puzzled face shot up, then snapped around at the others in the room, asking with his eyes if it was true. The councilors sat silently but nodded in agreement.

"*Really?*" Derek looked at Damaris, clearly combative and suspicious. "And what of this morning? You informed me, in so many ways, of your feelings regarding me." Derek closed in on the King, but Damaris held fast, staring at him. "My lords will have to pardon me, but I don't believe this."

"I have just signed a decree. It is already law," Damaris said pointedly. "As soon as we locate the princess, we will plan for our two houses, our kingdoms, to unite by the marriage between you to my daughter. Arcadia will be yours to rule."

Derek eyed Damaris, still unconvinced.

"It is true, Your Highness," Emerys said. "Would you like me to pull up the decree in the computer?"

"Yes, I would," Derek said firmly.

Emerys quickly went over to the computer, pulling up the law for Derek to read. Derek hastily read the proclamation, scrolling through the screen, then turned around to face Damaris. "I don't understand. Is this some sort of trick?"

"No. Consider it a present for our *arrangement*," the King said effortlessly, revealing a faint smile. "And I expect you to follow through with your end of the bargain."

Derek's face went white, and then he tumbled into a nearby chair, not taking his eyes off the King. He motioned for some wine, and the servants brought it over to him. Without removing his eyes from the King, Derek answered in a slow, cautious voice. "I would be forever in your debt for allowing me to marry the princess, Your *Majesty*."

"As you should be."

CHAPTER 25

GREEN

Emerald lay awake, listening to the night sounds of the city coming from outside Kyle's apartment window. In the dark, she watched as one of the neon lights outside flashed between green and blue, highlighting the walls and ceiling between the two colors.

Several hours passed, but Emerald knew that Kyle wasn't asleep yet by the uneven sounds of his breathing. She heard him light a cigarette, and the smell of the smoke permeated the air, paired with the sloshing of liquor in the bottle he drank from. Kyle had been beaten pretty badly, but he didn't utter one word of complaint about his pain.

It seemed almost a lifetime ago that she had left the palace. Her life, Glacia, and Derek were more like a lost dream rather than a recent reality. Derek was now a shade from her past, disappearing to the back of her mind. The only real proof of his existence was his ring, which still hung around her neck.

Since Emerald had left the palace, she had a whole new perspective about Derek. She had told herself that she was in love with him that night when he arrived at Arcadia. But what did Emerald or Derek truly know about love? Sure, Derek spoke eloquently, always knowing the right words. He was very charming and obviously had the highest respect for her. All of those things were much desired in a suitor.

But the more she thought on it, Derek didn't seem to act on his words or feelings. He had waited nearly a decade to confess his feelings for her. Why hadn't he come for her sooner if he cared for her as much as he declared?

And how was it that he was truly in love with her? Derek hadn't seen her in years. People changed over the years. As far as Emerald knew, Derek could be a completely different person than the Derek she knew growing up. She had only seen him for a couple of days, and their exchanges were quite brief. The thought left her feeling confused and conflicted.

Emerald heard Kyle's steady breathing from the floor. *Good, he's finally asleep.*

She peeked over the edge of the futon and saw that Kyle was out cold. Her gaze tarried, taking in every detail of his face, her heart quickening with each second. Through the blue hues of the night, she saw his face was swollen from the exchanges of punches, and awful bruises colored him. Kyle had washed up the best he could before he retired for the night, but the cold water didn't help with the swelling in the least.

What Kyle had done was unlike anything anyone had ever done for her. He had gotten involved on her account, protecting her twice now from those who troubled her. Kyle had no qualms about throwing a punch at some guy who'd mistreated her, whether it be from words or touching her. It didn't matter. He was her protector, masked as some tough guy who didn't care about anything but his bike and his band.

Emerald found herself comparing Derek to Kyle. Emerald wasn't convinced that Derek would be the kind of guy to be confrontational, willing to physically fight for her if it came down to it. He seemed to be above all of that, most likely resorting to bartering with those who opposed him. Perhaps he would fight, but only with those who carried his same status. There had been a time when she wanted nothing more than for Derek to come rescue her from the confines of her own life, but looking back on it now, she had just been plain desperate, and she'd pegged him as the prince who was her happily ever after. But now her life was beginning for the first time, and between Derek and Kyle, she felt the gap between them. Like she'd known Kyle for years and Derek for a few days, even though it was quite the opposite.

Ever since earlier in the evening, when Kyle's ex-girlfriend insinuated that they were together, Emerald's mind had been stuck on it. She wanted her thoughts to linger on that moment, the moment when she first thought of her and Kyle together. It sparked a fire within her, and there was no putting it out. Emerald felt strangely attracted to everything about Kyle. His wild behavior, his sense of freedom, his carefree spirit. Even his crazy white hair, the bizarre inked designs on his arm, the thick curved spike earrings. He fascinated her, and every day was a new adventure with him.

Emerald observed Kyle for several more minutes, ensuring that he was sound asleep. Her eyes wandered to his lean body, and she watched his chest breathing in and out evenly. What she would give to touch every crevice of his chest, to run her hand along his flesh. Her heart raced, beating loudly, pumping hard at the mere thought. Emerald realized that she had been gazing at him longer than she should have, and her cheeks burned with embarrassment.

She arose slowly off the futon, quietly placing her feet on the floor. Emerald hesitated for a second, afraid that Kyle would wake up and see her hovering over him. She watched him take a few more breaths, then deemed it safe to do what she intended, and kneeled beside him.

Emerald paused for a moment, wondering if she should really go through with what she was about to do. What would Kyle say in the morning? Would he wake up while she was in the midst of healing him? Then what? He would know her secret… What would he think of her then? Would it change everything?

The questions kept coming, but Emerald pushed them aside. She had been born with a great power. What good was it to keep herself from using it to aid others? Especially on Kyle, who didn't even have to think twice about helping her.

Emerald closed her eyes and thought about the healing magic within the Spectrum, the magical life force flowing within her body. She called upon her fears, allowing the magic to stir within her. The magic began to pump through her veins, welling up inside of her. It began to gather itself within one place in her body—the core of her being. Opening her eyes, she summoned the healing magic, beckoning it to gather in the palms of her hands. It answered her call, and her body began to glow green. It came gradually at first, but as the magic continued to gather and intensify, Emerald's color burned a bright greenish-white.

Gentle as a brush of wind, Emerald laid her hands on Kyle's swollen cheek. As soon as her hand met his face, the magic poured over him. Her green glow faded away from her, covering him instead. The power settled within him, then dimmed over time as his flesh began to restore itself to its natural state.

Kyle's eyes cracked opened, glazed over from sleep. Emerald suddenly went still, biting her lip anxiously. Her heart began to beat wildly once again.

It took a moment for him to focus, but he saw her peering down at him. "What are you doing?" he asked, rubbing his head.

Emerald casually got up. "I was trying to get to the restroom when I accidentally bumped you. Sorry. It's so dark in here," she apologized softly.

"Don't worry about it. Even I have a hard time seeing shit in here at night, and I live here," he muttered, half asleep. He turned over on his blanket, falling back asleep.

Breathing a sigh of relief, Emerald played along with her charade, heading toward the bathroom.

CHAPTER 26

ORANGE

There was a knock on the chamber doors. Someone wanted to see Ikaria. Suri hurried to Ikaria's private collection room, peeking her head inside. The Enchantress was burning with violet magic, consumed by her power. She had been like that for hours, transfixed in her state.

Suri heard another knock on the door.

Best not interrupt the Enchantress, Suri thought. *I don't want to interfere with her plans.*

Turning away and closing the door to the private room, Suri called forth the joy she had in serving the Enchantress. How she loved the Enchantress, how the Enchantress was so good to her. The Enchantress entrusted her with many things, including all of her secrets. If the Enchantress succeeded in all of her plans, it would make Suri the happiest servant ever, allowing her to serve such a kind and powerful woman. Perhaps, just maybe, Enchantress Ikaria would see her in a different light...

From her life force, joy flooded her veins, converting the energy to her orange magic, running through her body. Summoning up the power, Suri released it, letting the magic envelop her entire being. Her body burned bright orange, then slowly began to morph itself into the very image of Enchantress Ikaria herself. Suri shot another wave of orange magic through herself, focusing it on her voice box.

Another knock ensued. Glancing in the mirror, Ikaria's image peered back at Suri. It was perfect.

"Coming!" Suri called out in Ikaria's voice.

Hopefully it's not an orange-gifted at the door, Suri thought.

Suri opened the door to find the Ambassador Liliana and breathed a sigh of relief. The non-gifted ambassador was from World Sector Two and had recently arrived in World Sector Six, still very new to ins and outs of the court. The night Suri had assisted Ikaria with Lord Valamir, Ikaria herself had impersonated the ambassador in order to seduce Valamir of the Red.

"May I help you?" Suri asked, smiling and motioning for the ambassador to step inside.

"Enchantress Ikaria," the ambassador began, looking around at Ikaria's chambers as Suri closed the door. "I am surprised to see you answering your own door. I would have thought that you had a chamber servant."

Suri laughed. "You are correct, Ambassador. I normally do have my maid answer the door, but she is unwell at the moment."

"I am sorry to hear that."

"No need to be sorry," Suri said. "What brings you here to my chambers?"

Liliana cleared her throat, then lowered her eyes to the ground for a moment. "You see... there is a certain lord..." The ambassador faltered, sweeping her long, thick hair aside.

Suri continued to study the ambassador, letting the woman stumble on her words. Because that was what the Enchantress would do.

Liliana continued. "Back in World Sector Two, our court sorceress was... knowledgeable in many of the ancients' potions."

"I understand," Suri said. "You are seeking an amatory potion, then?"

Liliana's sparkling green eyes met Suri's, hinting a bit of hope. "Do you have any that I could purchase from you?"

Suri laughed as best as she could in Ikaria's tone. "I am sorry that you thought I would be able to help you out, Ambassador. But you know as much as everyone else at court that the use of potions are banned throughout the sectors."

Clearly embarrassed by the situation, Liliana bowed to Suri, her cheeks reddened. "I... I'm so sorry. Please, do not tell anyone I came here." Her eyes looked instantly worried. "It would be an embarrassment if anyone at court found out... and if the High Court..."

"Don't worry, Ambassador. I will not say anything, you have my word."

Liliana quickly bowed again, relieved. "Thank you, Enchantress. I owe you my gratitude. It seems everyone at court has loose lips, looking for the next rumor to spread."

"That is the truth. But you needn't worry about me."

Liliana smiled, then headed for the door. She turned back for a moment before opening the door. "Will I see you this evening at dinner? I know you were absent yesterday."

Suri shook her head. "Unfortunately, I have quite a bit of studying to do."

Liliana nodded, then let herself out of Ikaria's chambers.

After a few moments, when Suri deemed it safe, she melted her illusion away, revealing her true form once again. She shuffled to Ikaria's private collection room, checking on the Enchantress again. From the doorway, she saw Ikaria was no longer bathed in her violet power. She was stretching out to ease her stiffness from sitting in the same position for hours. Suri lingered for a moment, glancing at Ikaria's form, then darted her eyes away.

"I heard someone in my chambers," Ikaria called out.

"Yes, Enchantress. It was Ambassador Liliana."

"What did that self-righteous bitch want?"

"An amatory potion, Enchantress."

Ikaria suddenly belted out a long laugh, throwing her head back as she did so. Tears of laughter formed in her eyes as she continued. "Really?" she said, chuckling.

"Yes."

"That is too much. Oh, Suri, you always know how to make me laugh." Ikaria wiped her tears carefully, ensuring that none of her eye makeup smeared. "What did you end up telling her?"

"I reminded the ambassador that concocting potions are banned by the High Court," Suri offered.

"You are far too nice to people, my dear Suri," Ikaria said nonchalantly, clearing her throat of laughter. "You should have told that bitch not to make a mockery of my position by asking for ridiculous love potions. I mean, who does she think she is, lecturing our court about certain object enchantments while telling *us* that we are in violation of the High Court's laws. And then to come groveling at my feet for a mere potion? I've seen that twit flirting with the Emperor on more than one occasion. I know the game she's playing." Ikaria got up, snatching up a carafe of wine near her, drinking straight from it. "Looks like we need to pay closer attention to her, Suri."

"Yes, Enchantress. Rightfully so."

"You never know, her sector could have sent her here to break up my sister and Cyrus. Or the High Court, even," Ikaria continued.

"Is that possible, Enchantress?"

Ikaria smirked. "Oh, yes, my dear Suri. It quite well is a possibility. Anything to get at me and my power. And if they got my sister out of the way, there would be no stopping their foolishness." Ikaria took another drink, then gave her a dark smile. "But I won't let it come to that."

"How fares the past, Enchantress?"

"There is a minor setback, but I will have the green blood soon, along with a powerful army. Oh, Suri, if only you could see these things! I haven't encountered one yet, but just seeing them within Damaris's mind…" Ikaria smiled wickedly.

"I look forward to seeing the Enchantress's army. Anything that pleases the Enchantress, pleases me." Suri bowed. "Also, I wanted to remind you that there is a small meeting with the Enchanter's Guild later this afternoon."

"Go in my place. I know for a fact there won't be any orange-gifted present. I have much to do in the past, and I don't have time to listen to those dolts drone on about useless enchantments."

"Yes, Enchantress. I will let you know if there is anything important discussed."

"Thank you, Suri. I'm sure that there won't be, but nonetheless, do fill me in," Ikaria said. "By the way, what are the whispers regarding Lord Kohren? Does anyone suspect anything?"

"Nothing at all. All that has been circulating is that he was overcome by the plague. There have been no other theories."

Ikaria smiled, her violet eyes flashing brightly. "Good. That's what I like to hear. Now please, fetch me a plate of food. I must get back to focusing more of my power and influence in the past. I still have the prince and King on a leash, but I need to make it tighter."

Suri bowed, smiling at Ikaria. "Right away, Enchantress."

"Such a good girl you are." Ikaria's eyes sparkled. "I know I can always count on you."

Suri felt her cheeks burn and her heart quicken. She quickly turned away, exiting Ikaria's chambers.

How she loved the Enchantress.

CHAPTER 27

From his apartment window, Kyle sat smoking his cigarette, watching the city paint itself black as the sky darkened and the neon signs popped their lights on one by one. Kyle studied the murky outlines of Arcadia's citizens strolling through the glowing greenish-yellow skyways, much like Rosie's rat Zaphod running through his cages in one of his tubular mazes. Man, did he ever relate to Zaphod most of the time. He felt so confined within Arcadia. Everything and everyone was up each other's ass. Buildings crammed together, streets clogged with shitloads of vehicles. And him having to put up with being constantly bombarded by assholes. It left Kyle no breathing room. The only source of a bit of freedom was riding his motorcycle.

Impatient, Kyle got up and hovered over Em, who was sitting on the floor across the room, sketching out a design for the band with her new art supplies they'd bought for her earlier in the day.

Kyle cleared his throat. Em was so focused on her picture that she hadn't noticed him standing above her.

"Come on. Let's get out of here," he announced loudly.

Peering up from her drawing, Em gave him a quizzical look. "But I have to finish this. I told Remy that this would be done in the next day or two."

"Fuck Remy. I'm in the band just as much as Remy, even though he pretends that he's in charge. Let's get out of here. Besides, do you really want to sit inside all night, especially after you told me that's all you did before you ran off?"

"But what about last night? What if we run into that gang again?"

"We won't," Kyle said.

He was still trying to understand why his face wasn't all black and blue from the fight with Jaxx. He'd seen the condition of his face before he went to bed. He'd looked like a mangled piece of shit. But when he woke up in the morning, it was like the fight had never happened. His face was completely normal. He must've just thought he was worse off than he really was. Then there was that bottle of whiskey last night before he went to bed.

Em stared at him for a moment, her cheeks reddening almost to the color of her hair. She finally put down her pencil, then closed her pad of paper. "You are right," she said.

"Damn straight I'm right. Let's go for a ride."

Em laughed nervously, getting up off the floor. "Okay, but promise me you will not go crazy? The last time I thought we were going to die."

"I'm always crazy, and I can't promise nothing," he said with a smirk. "But I'll see what I can do to accommodate you."

She punched him playfully, flashing him one of her signature smiles. "Fine. Have it your way. But give me a minute to get ready." She picked up her backpack and headed to the bathroom.

Knowing that Em would take longer than a minute, or in reality more like twenty minutes, Kyle plopped onto his bed and lit a cigarette, watching the smoke curl. He glanced downward, eyeing Em's pad of paper on the floor. Curious, he picked up the pad, thumbing through the paper until he saw her drawing. Each of the band members' torsos were outlined on the paper, Kyle front and center. Em was really damn good at drawing. It looked just like him, but more of a tougher, sexier version of himself. Did Em view him like that? He smiled to himself inwardly as he took another drag.

"You weren't supposed to see that yet!" he heard Em exclaim, closing the bathroom door behind her.

Surprised, Kyle set down the pad of paper. Kyle glanced up at Em across the room. His eyes drifted to her lovely red lips, then lower to her outfit. Her upper torso was half exposed with a red-and-black corset, with black leather riding shorts and black boots. Seeing the skin of her body and the curve of her breasts made his heart begin to pump harder, causing a stir inside of him. Long dangling earrings kissed the sides of her neck, toying with him, as if inviting him to do the same.

Suddenly, his head became a mess all over again. He wanted her.

After an awkward moment, Kyle quickly hopped off the bed, lacing up his boots.

"What is it?" Em asked.

"Nothing."

"You gave me a weird look," she said, peering down at her outfit. "Do I need to change?"

"Not at all," Kyle blurted out. *I'm so fucked*, he thought.

"Then why did you look at me like that?"

He wanted to tell her she was fucking gorgeous, but instead, he told her coolly, "God, let's just get going before I say stupid shit." He put his hand on her back, directing her out the door. Em crossed her arms in protest, letting out a loud sigh.

They rode the escalators down to the basement of the building, where the tenants' ground vehicles were parked, Kyle's motorcycle included.

Kyle got on his bike, and Em slid in right behind him. He felt the warmness of her body as she wrapped her arms around his waist. She gently rested her head on the back of his jacket, giving his insides a rise. Her body shivered as her gentle hands firmly gripped his stomach.

"You okay?" he asked, wondering what that was all about. She probably smelled the street sewage pouring into the garage. It was unbearable at times, and a girl like her would never get used to it.

"Yeah," she answered in his ear, then buried her head once more in his jacket.

Kyle started the engine, then spun out of the parking garage and into the brightly lit streets. Steam emitted from the sewers, catching the lights of the shops on the street, coloring them in mystical blues, violets, and neon greens. The road was somewhat clear, more so than any other night he had recalled in a while. He took advantage of it, shifting to a high gear to give Em a little thrill. He was going fast, but he didn't want to be too reckless with Em behind him. He felt her hands grasp him tighter, and he smiled. Nothing like a thrilling night ride. Besides, Em needed to live a little.

As they flew by other ground transports, the stream of lights from the city became a blur, the speed filling him with a thrilling euphoria. This was what he needed to feel free. It was the only time he ever felt like he was truly free, flying from the entanglements of the fucked-up social structure within

Arcadia, putting distance between him and his wasteland past. It numbed his pain over his mother, her remains buried far off in the wastelands. It gave him a rush of newness, revitalizing him from within. It was like each time he rode he was renewed all over again. It was this very feeling that he channeled into his music.

Kyle came to Arcadia's oceanfront, parking his motorcycle. There were several people by the pier, but it wasn't overly crowded like it was during the daytime.

As he killed the engine, Em hopped off, then peered into the night sky, in awe of the city's neon colors dancing in the waves, which slowly faded away into the blackness of the ocean. The wind was strong, tickling his face with the taste of salt water in the air. His element. He could argue that he had a natural affinity for fire much more than the wind, but it did give him power. And life. They were the pillars of his soul's foundation.

Em's long scarlet hair whipped in her face, waving in every direction. She curled her ponytail into a loose bun, securing it with the rubber band already in her hair. Em's pale face looked heavenly in the darkness. Her glistening red lips, painted the color of blood to match her hair, made her sparkling green eyes stand out all the more, almost as if they had a glow to them. They were ethereal, her eyes. It had to have been how the light was reflecting in them. Em was like a pleasant dream, one that Kyle did not want to wake from.

"It's breathtaking…" Em whispered, kneeling down in the sand, brushing it between her fingers.

Kyle lit a cigarette. It took several tries to do so, as the wind kept extinguishing the flame. "I come here often when I need time to myself," he said, plopping down next to her. "I like it since it makes me feel like I'm not so damn trapped. Arcadia is too big."

Em smiled at him, grabbing a handful and playing with it. "I can see why. It's so peaceful," she said, looking around at a few people walking by the road. She took off her boots, rubbing the sand through her toes. "I always thought the waterfronts were closed at night."

Kyle smiled, then took a drag. "Does that ever stop me?"

Em laughed. "No, I suppose not," she said, turning back to gaze at the rippling ocean waves. "Have you been to other places?"

"Only to Illumina."

Em widened her face in surprise, curious. "Are you from there?"

"Nope," he said. He hoped she wouldn't ask the next question, but it sounded like she was going to.

"Then you are from Arcadia? Did you grow up in the lower levels?"

Kyle took a deep inhale of his cigarette, then exhaled, watching the smoke get whipped into the wind. "I'm from the Western Wastelands."

"Wastelands? Don't you mean the desert? Aren't the people who live out there drifters?" she asked, surprised at the revelation.

"The desert folk call themselves wasteland wanderers. They hate the term drifters."

"Sorry," she whispered.

Kyle smiled at her, slightly amused. "Don't worry about it. None of the wasteland wanderers are fond of the term, but technically they are drifters. Several of them hack banks, businesses, and governments to make a buck, all while moving through the deserts like nomads, not staying put at a camp or dwelling for too long, as they don't want to get caught by the authorities."

Kyle paused for a moment, then took another drag. "Recently they've stayed put a bit longer, as their hacking skills have gotten better, so there hasn't been as much pressure as before to keep moving, but who the hell knows," Kyle said, laughing at the thought of his old friends. As much as he missed his past, he'd never fit in with the others. He didn't give a shit about computers and loved city life, even though half the time he cursed Arcadia for one reason or another.

"It all sounds so fascinating," Em said dreamily. "It must have been nice to live outside the city, to not be worried about all of the troubles that the city brings to a person."

Kyle laughed, seating himself next to her in the sand. "It sounds so damned good and all, but live out in the desert longer than a week, you'd be saying something different. Food and water is hard to come by, and it's rationed within camps. It gets so damn hot in the days, freezing temperatures at night. Not a place for..." He caught himself before he let it slip.

"For someone like me?" Em said slowly, finishing his sentence.

"Yeah." Realizing he had just made himself sound like a complete asshole, he scratched the back of his neck nervously. "Listen, I don't know what you've done in your past because you haven't even really told me much, but most of the upper levels folks have never set foot in the wastelands. It's harsh living, and no one in their right goddamn mind would purposely subject themselves to it unless they had no other option. As much as the lower levels of Arcadia are a giant hellhole, it sure as hell is better than living in the wastelands," he said, meeting her eyes. "That I can promise you."

There was a long pause, causing Kyle to wonder if he should have opened his damned mouth at all.

Breaking the silence, Em said, "I wanted to get married."

The phrase caught Kyle off guard. "What? What are you talking about?" Kyle glanced at her, taking a deep breath. *Married? Oh hell…*

Em gazed at him with her delicate eyes shining in the darkness. "I left home because my father didn't approve of the suitor of my choice."

Kyle sat in silence. That was something he hadn't expected her to say. *Damn it all.*

"There were many suitors, actually. My father turned them all down, because in truth, he didn't want to let me go. Finally, the one suitor I wanted to marry, my father told me he would never in his lifetime approve of that particular match. I was angry, and so I left." Loose hairs fell out of her bun, flowing in the wind, her ruby lips trembling. "My whole life, I did everything I was supposed to. I followed every rule and stayed out of trouble. But after my father said such horrible things about the man I chose, telling me that I would never marry anyone, well, it made me realize my life was passing me by."

"Why are you telling me this?" Kyle said, finally managing to get the words out.

"Because you just said that I have hardly told you anything about my past. I figured I would start with this." She looked at him anxiously.

Kyle's insides twisted, but he managed to not let it show. Acting as casually as he could, he asked, "Do you love him?"

"Who, my father?"

"No. The guy…"

Em's face turned intense. "I… I honestly don't know. I did at one point, years ago. Then time passed, and the feeling faded. Just recently, when he returned to Arcadia, I entertained the idea of us together, and I became infatuated with him again. But… I would not necessarily say that I am in love with him. It had been years since our last visit, and really, I hardly know anything about him since then. As for marriage, I wanted nothing more than to marry him, as I am, or was, convinced that he was the one for me. I thought of him as the one who would save me from my imprisoned life."

Em grabbed the necklace she was wearing, showing him a ring. The gemstone was the biggest damn jewel he had ever seen. In the light, it sparkled a brilliant green, just like her eyes.

"This was to be my engagement ring," she told him.

"Holy shit," Kyle said, his jaw still dropped in amazement of the size of the jewel. "That guy is damned serious. You know, you really shouldn't be wearing that in the lower levels. Shit, I would be shitting bricks if you just left that in my apartment."

Em laughed, shrugging. "What does it matter? I'm not getting married anyway."

Kyle wondered who this other guy was. Instantly, a twang of jealousy shot through him, envious some unknown man who had the resources to give her such a ring.

Trying to take his mind off the suitor, Kyle decided to humor himself. "What house did you say you were from again?" he said innocently. Eventually, he would wear her down and find out.

Em threw a handful of sand toward his legs enthusiastically. "You just won't give up!" she said, giggling.

Surprised at the unexpected shower of sand, Kyle exhaled, then dropped the cigarette in the sand, rubbing it out. "Hey? What was that?" he asked, feigning offense.

Em threw sand at him again, this time hitting his chest, laughing.

"Seriously, what the fuck?" But he laughed with her, grabbing some sand. Before he could throw it at her, she took off, running barefoot down the beach toward the waterfront.

"Hey!" He ran after her, chasing her while she giggled. She stopped ten feet in front of him, grabbing more sand. She was about to hurl it at him, flashing a big smile on her face.

Kyle ran into the waves shin deep. A cold shock went up through his legs, but he didn't care. The icy waters of the ocean were always so damn cold, no matter what time of year it was. She missed him entirely with her sand throw, sending the handful crashing into the waves. He bent over, splashing the freezing water at her. "What are you waiting for?"

Shaking her head and laughing, she ran out of splashing distance. "You're crazy!"

"You're just figuring this out now?" he said, splashing more salt water toward her. Em giggled, getting out of the way, but this time she didn't retreat. Her lips were starting to tremble, and her teeth chattered, as she was not wearing a jacket.

Kyle got out of the water, his boots sopping wet. He took off his jacket, then threw it over her shoulders.

"Thanks," she replied, giving him a bright smile. Her eyes looked so beautiful when she smiled.

Dammit! Not this again…

His head felt like it was heading toward a clusterfuck. It was too damn soon to care about anyone. Especially someone as beautiful and innocent as her.

***

"Oh, please, stop there!" Em yelled from behind Kyle. One of her hands was waving and pointing to the left. Not knowing what Em was pointing at, Kyle found a spot, pulling over the motorcycle on the side of the street.

"What? Where did you want to go?" Kyle glanced around at the glowing neon signs, puzzled .

"That place. I want to go there," Em announced, her finger pointing to a tattoo and piercing shop.

Kyle eyed her. "I never pegged you wanting a tramp stamp."

"What's that?"

"Forget it. You want a tattoo?"

Em shook her head. "Not at all. I want to pierce my ears," Em said, hopping off his bike. "Let's go."

"Fine. Just let me park my bike in the alley." Kyle pulled into alley while Em went inside the shop. Kyle lit a cigarette, trying to take his mind off the numbness of his feet from his cold, wet boots. He just wanted to get to his apartment and put on a pair of dry socks. But fuck, how could he say no to her?

Walking into the shop, Kyle was met with bright-orange walls and yellow neon lights reflecting off the metal counter. Em was already talking to the woman, pointing to the high ridge of her ear. The woman, who had pink cropped hair and a black septum nose ring clinging to her nostrils, nodded at Em's request, then her eyes shifted to Kyle. Her dark eyes smiled deviously, as if she knew the mess he was in for even being with Em. Kyle looked away, trying to not pay too much attention to Em, and instead turned to check out the drawing samples of tattoos displayed on the walls. He then took out his flask, downing most of it.

After browsing the art, Kyle peeked into one of the mirrors and saw Em flinch when the woman punctured the needle in the ridge of her ear. She did it three times, slipping a small curved spike earring in each hole. The woman finished, then turned to Kyle, giving him a smile.

"Cute, huh?" she said, winking at him.

Kyle walked over to Em, seeing her beautiful smile appear on her face as he approached. Quickly moving his eyes to the piercing, he nodded in approval.

"You like it?" Em asked innocently. She turned to look into the hand mirror the woman had set in her lap.

"Doesn't matter if I like it. Do you like it?" Kyle said indifferently, drinking the last of his liquor. He did like it. Very much. It was rather cute on her. But what was he to her? His head was starting to spin just thinking about Em.

In just a matter of a few days, Em had turned his whole life upside down. His thoughts were entirely consumed by her presence, and his life had shifted onto a whole new course, one that he had never expected in his lifetime. Much like the lines that inked his arm.

Fuck it.

Kyle pulled out a wad of money, tossing it over the counter to where the woman was. He plopped himself down in one of the orange vinyl chairs, pointing to his tattoo. "I need some work done. That should be enough to cover her piercings and my work, right?"

The woman counted the bills, then raised her eyebrow. "Depends. This isn't enough for a big job."

Pointing to the heavy black lines on his bicep, he stated, "Just add a line to this. Make it in a different direction than the last one. Completely opposite, in fact."

"Sure."

Em looked at him curiously. Kyle could tell she was wondering what he was doing, but she didn't ask. Before the woman began the work, Kyle pulled out another bill, waving it toward Em to take.

"Do you mind getting a bottle for me at the convenience shop next door? I need more liquor."

"Okay." She nodded, taking the money. Em flashed him a smile, causing him to stare longer than he should. "Be right back," she said, walking out of the shop.

Kyle's glance lingered in her direction. Catching himself in the act, he glanced away promptly.

"How long you been together?" the woman asked as she began to draw the line on his bicep.

God, if only. "We aren't," Kyle said casually, lighting a cigarette.

"Your loss," she muttered under her breath, then began inking his arm. After she started hammering away with the needle, she put a hand on her hip. "What does this mean, anyway?"

"Nothing of importance."

The woman smirked, as if she understood his cryptic response.

"Don't be such an asshole," she chided. Her statement was directed at his behavior toward Em, not his response to her question. "She's too cute for all that bullshit."

"Whatever."

He needed a drink before he thought any further.

CHAPTER 28

YELLOW

With each breath he drew from the pure, crisp air, Auron's tension melted away, though his troubled thoughts still lingered. It was hard to clear all the daily troubles from his mind. The plague continued to ravage his sector. Ikaria with her wicked ways, was trying to influence the court with technology. There was no heir to the throne, and the Empress was without child. Ikaria still had a claim to the throne if anything happened to Ayera and Cyrus, heaven forbid. There were so many troubles, it made Auron sick to think of them all.

Over the last week, two more gifted had lost their magic. Of the two, one of them lost their life: Lord Kohren. It seemed there was no stopping this curse. All Auron could do was pray in earnest that the God of Light would intervene.

Cast your cares unto the God of Light, Auron. Have faith! But even as high priest, Auron felt doubt deep within, not believing in the holy words himself.

Auron turned his thoughts to the cool air that streamed in gently from the entrance of the temple. It was as if the air itself was cleansing him from within, purifying the troubles that had been vexing him. The incense braziers burned with a light, fragrant smell, a smell that Auron imagined was like one of the earth's rare floral fields below. Auron had secretly hoped that he would see them in his lifetime. But the older he got, the more reality set in, and his hope faded. He would probably never see them.

Staring between two of the temple's white marble pillars, Auron gazed at the sunset directly aligned between them. This was the time to commune with the God of Light.

Auron meditated three times a day—at dawn, high sun, and sunset. The evening was when he felt the least in contact with the divine, because it was when the light was snuffed out from the world, bathing it in darkness. And now, more than ever, he was in dire need of a sign from the God of Light, because magic would soon be gone from humankind if the plague wasn't stopped.

Perhaps the God of Light willed it, that magic be wiped off the face of the earth, but Auron did not get that sense. He felt the disappearance of magic was the doing of the Lord of Darkness. It was evident enough that the Dark Lord desired all colors of magic, as it was written in *The Spectrum*, and somehow this wicked being was stealing it from all the gifted. And he was consuming their lives while doing so. Above all else, Auron was convinced that Ikaria was behind it all, hoping to make a fool out of Ayera, causing the court to restore her as rightful heir. Auron had no evidence, nor any vision as corroboration, he just felt it in his soul.

The sun began to melt into the horizon, burning a bright orange before turning a deep ruby red within a rainbow sky. Auron sat quietly, looking into the intense light, asking within his mind for the God of Light to grant him insight on the magical plague. The sun had almost set when Auron's asking turned to pleading, but the sun disappeared from the twilight sky, and nothing had come.

Auron closed his eyes as soon as the sun was gone, focusing his magic and gathering it from within his heart and mind. He could feel the burning devotion and love from inside, the same love he had the day he chose to enter the priesthood. The bright yellow light flared around his body, but he dared not open his eyes. Auron would be blinded, as anyone would be if they dared to gaze upon a gifted priest in mediation or during a vision using their gift.

The smell of the incense tickled his nose lightly, causing him to lose focus.

The scent had never bothered him before, but for some reason it kept making his mind stray from his meditations. An image of the incense smoke appeared in his mind, dulling his thoughts to a bland gray while creating a clouded barrier between him and the God of Light. The more he tried to push the thought aside, the greater it became.

Within his mind's eye, the image of the rising gray smoke became thick as fog as it flowed around him. It gently wafted to the heavens, blocking out all that was good. As the smoke curled in all different directions, each tendril began to take the form of a certain color, until all colors were represented, and the gray was no more.

Auron floated amongst the wisps of colored smoke, amazed by their beauty. The colors separated into their own group of smoke, encircling him, flowing with power.

With sudden sharp movements, each color evaporated into a puff, turning into an intense colored fire, burning brightly. The colored ring of fires looked remarkable, like none Auron had ever seen. Each fire began to slowly turn prismatic, until he could no longer distinguish the colors.

Staring into the sparkly flames, Auron tried to recall which fire was what color, but it was no use. They were all the same. Reaching out to embrace the beauty of one of the blazes, the fire before him snuffed out immediately. He turned to the next fire, trying to touch it, and it too died in front of him. Same with the next. One by one, each fire became extinguished, until one remained, burning brightly and more intensely than the others. Auron noticed that the sky had faded, light had fled, and he was in complete darkness with the exception of the prismatic fire burning in front of him.

The fire shifted, turning black. Deep flames of pure blackness crackled with violet undertones. From within the black fire came the shadow of a beautiful naked woman. She danced within the flames, commanding the fire to be her partner, her lover. Her arms stretched to the heavens, embracing the power of the magic. Her shadowy face turned in Auron's direction, staring right into his soul, piercing his heart with just one glance.

He knew those eyes. Eyes that had hated him for years. Eyes that belonged to none other than the sorceress herself.

Auron became instantly engulfed in the black fire, and it melted away his flesh. Ikaria's narrowed eyes laughed at him; she knew he couldn't stop her. Fear overwhelmed him, and his mind became muddled. He had no coherent thought.

Crying out to his god, Auron felt his yellow magic surge within his soul, asking it desperately to aid him in his time of need. To his dismay, none came. Instead, the shadowy woman continued to drink in his yellow magic, just like a thirsty desert wanderer, as if the image of Ikaria was bone dry of magic.

Auron yelled in agony as the intense flames seared his body. His charred bones jutted out as his flesh began to disappear. The fire continued to grow in size, until the sky could no longer hold the swell of magic. With a giant burst, the black fire exploded into thousands of shards, hurtling to the earth below.

Darkness washed over time and space. Auron's body did not exist anymore; only the breath of his soul remained. The glimmer of the fragments of light died out, and all was lost.

The earth was no more.

Time was lost, the earth was gone, and magic disappeared. Auron cried out to the God of Light, but only the darkness answered.

Then there was a small gleam of color from the earth below. It glowed softly at first, a deep red. As time continued, the glow burned brilliantly with the power of red magic. The red turned white. Pure, bright white light. The white light formed into the transparent figure of a man holding Auron's staff, his spirit searching for his other half of the spectrum—his complement.

The transparent man did not see Auron, but Auron saw him. Rage consumed his eyes, burning with the fires of hell, the same color as his crimson hair. He was going to wreak havoc on the darkness, the black void who held his complement captive. And he was furious. This man…

Ghost Man.

***

Auron hurriedly made his way through the palace, walking with a brisk step, trying not to break into a run. His eyes darted in every direction as he passed other members of the court, who were making their way back from their evening events. Some nodded at him, others bowed, but Auron had no time to acknowledge any of them.

The Emperor and Empress had to be warned. His biggest fear was that he was too late to stop Ikaria.

Auron approached the doors to the main audience hall. The guards standing watch gave him an inquisitive look, raising an eyebrow.

"High Priest Auron," they said, bowing.

"Please summon the Emperor and the Empress. It is of the utmost importance," he said, short of breath.

"I will see if His or Her Majesty will receive anyone this late," said one of the guards.

Auron shoved his face near one of the guards, latching on to the man's breastplate with his large, meaty hands, panting heavily. The sheer size and bulk of Auron intimidated the guard, and the guard's eyes flicked to Auron's hand. "You must get either of them now! It is vital that you do so," Auron urged.

The guard quickly bowed and hurried off to fetch the Emperor and Empress, while the other guard gestured for Auron to enter.

Auron wandered into the empty hall, watching his golden reflection glide across the black marble floors. He shuddered, thinking about his vision, him lost within that darkened world.

Curse that Ikaria, he thought. The vision made it apparent; Ikaria was consuming the other colors of blood. She was trying to become invincible, like the God of Light himself. But little did she realize that she would be consumed herself by a dark force, an evil magic that was granted from the Lord of Darkness. *Black* magic, Auron had read before. What Ikaria was doing was unspeakable. It was against the laws of nature, and of the God of Light himself.

Auron had heard about the ancients' form of healing, how they injected blood into each other to cure sicknesses. The science of old was heresy to the God of Light, as it was apparent from the God of Light's wrath upon the earth. That cataclysmic event had destroyed the old world, with the most advanced sector of that time being decimated into a toxic wasteland. In fact, most of the old world became toxic, and hardly anyone could survive on the ground except a few mining areas that were deemed safe. That was the power of the God of Light's judgment. But now, it seemed that the Lord of Darkness was determined to undermine the God of Light once again. If mankind couldn't be tempted by the Lord of Darkness's deceitful technology, they would fall into despair through the lustful power of magic. Or should Auron say, Ikaria's lust for magic. Dark magic. The whole world was about to be destroyed because of her dark heart.

The doors opened, and footsteps followed. The Empress appeared quickly, dressed in a simple white robe, her long black hair in a split ponytail. The Empress bowed to Auron.

"Auron, what has happened?" she asked, her voice sounding fearful.

"Where is His Majesty?" Auron asked. "Is he coming?"

"I am here," Cyrus called out from behind him. Cyrus came trailing into the room, dressed in a gold satin robe. Auron turned and bowed to the Emperor, waiting for him to seat himself on the throne. "What is the meaning of this?" he demanded.

The Empress eyed her husband, then asked, "Did you have a vision? Please. Tell us."

Auron bowed to them both, his gaze locked on the Empress, then moved to the Emperor. "Our future, the future of Earth, is in peril."

The Empress gasped, and Cyrus turned from sleepy to serious.

Auron's eyes shifted back to the Empress. "Empress, this vision has shown me who is behind the disappearance of magic. I regret to inform you that it is your sister. Ikaria has been consuming the other gifteds' blood."

"Ikaria?" Ayera said in an unbelieving voice, becoming quiet. "No. She wouldn't dare," she whispered.

"Do you think she means to use her power against us? She probably wants to form a coup against the current court!" Cyrus said heatedly. "I *knew* she had it out for us ever since Ayera and I assumed the throne!"

"Perhaps," Ayera said gravely, slightly agreeing with her husband. "But I would think that her ultimate goal would be to confront the High Court. She has always had a vendetta against them. More so than us, Cyrus."

"I cannot say for certain Ikaria's true intent," Auron said, "but what the vision did reveal was that if Ikaria acquires of all of the colors of the magic, the world *will* be destroyed. Earth as we know it will no longer exist." Auron looked up at both of them on their seated platform. "It was never intended by the God of Light for humans to complete the Spectrum of Magic. It is only meant for the God of Light himself. If a human were to consume all the colors of blood… the gift of the black would appear."

"Gift of the black?" Ayera sucked in her breath.

"Yes, Your Majesty. It is speculated among religious texts outside *The Spectrum*, that if one were to consume all of the magics, it would summon black magic into the life force of that individual. It is said that it is a power so great, it would bring calamity to our entire world, shadowing it in darkness."

Ayera's face appeared mortified.

"But what of green magic? There is no way to complete the spectrum without the gift of the green," Cyrus argued. "It simply does not exist."

Auron hesitated, then met Cyrus's eyes. "Correct, it does not exist in this time. But it did in the past."

Cyrus and Ayera's eyes shot at him, like they finally understood what was happening.

"If that is the case, she must not travel back. We must stop her," Cyrus said.

Auron saw the Empress's face was frozen, much like Ikaria when she was deep in thought. He could also see the fear radiating from her eyes. Auron knew it was hard for her to stomach, with Ikaria being her sister. But Ayera was no fool when it came to Ikaria's interests. She always kept her close to keep a watchful eye on her. Even their father, Emperor Ojin, knew of the potential dangers when the transfer of the named heir had gone to Ayera. Ikaria had always been the clever one.

"We must warn the High Court. They must be made aware of Ikaria's plans," Cyrus said, then he turned to Ayera. "You must convene the High Court and ask them for reinforcements from the other sectors. She may not be able to wield her magic yet, but either way, we must be prepared for anything. In the meantime, I will make sure certain gifted are aware and on guard while you are away. We will await the High Court's help."

"Certain gifted?" Auron asked. "Why not all? They are all in danger."

"No. I do not want Ikaria to get wind that we know of her actions. We must be discreet."

Auron bowed. "Yes, Your Majesty."

The Empress Ayera gave a slight nod to her husband and Auron, then began to descend from the throne platform, making haste down the stairs. "Guards! Guards!" she yelled.

The guards entered, bowing as she moved quickly toward them. "Yes, Your Majesty?"

"Prepare one of the airships immediately. We need to be ready within twenty minutes for departure," she barked as she exited.

"Right away, Your Majesty." The guard bowed, following the Empress out of the room.

Cyrus was still seated on the throne, rubbing his chin. He lightly tapped the armrest of his throne in thought.

"What is it, Your Majesty?" Auron asked.

"Auron, do you think Ikaria has figured out how to wield her magic?"

"Which magic, sire? Her violet? Or her new colors?"

"Any of them."

"I do not know. In my vision, she did not use her magic until she completed the spectrum. It is hard to say. But it's best to be prepared in any case," Auron cautioned.

"Yes, yes, of course," Cyrus said casually, still in thought. He waved his hand, dismissing Auron.

Auron began to walk away, but then stopped, turning around quickly. "I forgot to mention one thing while the Empress was present."

"What is it?" Cyrus asked, still distracted.

"The gift of the red. There is someone with the red gift who has the ability to stop Ikaria."

Cyrus's eyes shot to Auron, him leaning in. "Truly?" he asked curiously.

"I don't know who he is, or where he comes from, but he is out there," Auron said. "I only saw him as a ghost of some kind."

"Interesting," Cyrus said. He leaned back in his throne, in thought once again.

Auron gave a bow and was off.

CHAPTER 29

"What the hell is taking you so long?" Kyle muttered impatiently, hovering over Diego's shoulder as the bassist typed on the keyboard of his computer.

"Dude, I'm really shitty at typing okay?" Diego shrugged, taking a drink in between typing letters.

Kyle continued to watch as Diego struggled to find the letters on the keyboard. Homeboy had no clue about computers, almost as much as Kyle did. "Yeah, I can tell. You only use two fingers," Kyle said under his breath.

"Would you like to sit down and type, dickwad?" Diego shot back.

"No, I don't. I hate computers."

"Then you're stuck with me typing. And if I want to type with two fucking fingers, then you will have to fucking deal with it."

Kyle huffed and kicked the computer desk lightly, irritated. "Tell me, why was Remy busy today?" Kyle thought about how much more computer savvy Remy was.

"I dunno. All he said is that he had shit to do. I didn't ask. Maybe if you got a phone, you could call and ask him yourself."

"What makes you think that I can get my phone reconnected when I can't even afford a decent fucking guitar," Kyle said, turning away and lighting a cigarette.

He wanted to pull his hair out watching Diego fuck around with the computer. It had been two days since Jaxx smashed his guitar, and Kyle still hadn't replaced it. He had no savings and just a little money left over from the two gigs prior. And with Jaxx fucking up his guitar, the band had missed their last gig. That screwed Kyle even further, because now he was guitarless *and* broke. It was a vicious cycle. He needed the guitar to make money, but he needed money for a guitar. He was fucked.

Over the last two days, he had spent his free time over at Remy's apartment, searching online for a used piece-of-shit guitar in the classifieds, but they were all over his budget. At least that's what Remy said, as he was the one that did all the searching. But today, for some damn reason, Remy was busy, and Kyle was forced to go over to Diego's place and deal with all his bullshit.

Kyle fought with himself off and on about asking the guys to borrow money. But he was too damn prideful and didn't want to bring it up unless the guys did it first. He was actually waiting for them to offer, considering they needed his ass for their upcoming shows. But they were daft at times and couldn't take a fucking hint. If they didn't offer by the end of the week, he was gonna have to swallow his pride and just ask. Hopefully it wouldn't come to that.

Another thing that was driving him completely nuts was Em. He was going insane. He had every urge to take her in his arms and have his way with her. But Em was not that kind of girl, and he didn't want to risk coming off like a complete asshole. If any other woman stayed around as long as she did, they either wanted a good fuck or were about to pursue some sort of commitment. But Em, somewhat naive to the world around her, seemed fine regardless of her situation, content to hang around with Kyle and the band.

Even though Em had told Kyle that she wasn't in love, she sure seemed to be attached to the man who gave her that ring. Kyle noticed that she never took it off the chain around her neck, and sometimes she would grasp the ring in her hands, almost like she could summon the man's spirit to her just by touching it. Sure, at times she flirted with Kyle, but Kyle chalked it up to her being herself without the barriers of her old life holding her back, and he didn't think it was something special meant for him.

Between Em and his guitar, he just wanted to punch a wall in frustration. And Diego fucking failing at his computer skills just added fuel to the fire.

"Where's Em at today? How come she didn't come?" Diego asked, scrolling through a list of guitars on a secondhand site.

"She said she had to finish the flyer."

"That's a lame excuse."

"Forget about Em," Kyle said impatiently. "Did you find anything? I really need to find something soon, otherwise we're fucked." Thinking about Em made him crazier, and every time he tried not to think of her, he kept getting reminded of her. It was like a damn curse or something.

"Nope. Not yet. It's kinda hard when you don't have any money to spend." Diego took another drink, continuing to scroll. His middle button input device made a grinding sound, worse than normal. Diego took the device, smacking it several times, then returned to scrolling again, giving it a good shake. "Dammit. This thing is going. I need to replace it."

"Wonderful," Kyle said sarcastically, taking a drag of his cigarette.

Diego slammed the device down again, then shook it on his desk, seeing if the cursor showed up on the computer screen. Kyle already knew what was coming.

"Yep. Broken. Damn. Looks like I need to replace it."

"Great. Fucking great. Waste of time."

"Sorry, dude. I'm not like Remy. He's willing to spend his money on a decent machine. This shit is used. I can't help if this shit breaks so easily."

Kyle turned away, grabbing his jacket and throwing it on. "I'm going home," Kyle snarled. He took a long drag, then exhaled, rubbing his cigarette butt hard into the ashtray.

He was pissed. Why did this shit always happen to him?

"Going home to Em, huh? Did you get her to play with your dick yet?" Diego called out, smiling.

Swinging an about-face, Kyle marched right up to Diego, swinging aside an empty chair, lowering his face into his. "Don't ever say that shit to me again!"

"Oh, so you haven't," Diego said, unaffected by Kyle's attitude. "Well, damn, dude. What the hell are you waiting for?"

Angrily, Kyle clenched his fist, wanting to swing at his buddy. But it wasn't worth it. Dude was being a dude.

After a moment's pause, Kyle clenched his mouth shut, forcing every swear word back in his body. He quickly marched toward the door, then kicked it, venting his pent-up frustration. Swinging the door open wildly, Kyle left, slamming the door behind him.

***

Kyle rode all the way home, pissed. God, Diego irritated him sometimes. The fuck was Diego thinking saying shit like that to him? The dipshit didn't use his brain half the time.

Returning to his apartment building, Kyle took the elevator, then walked down his apartment floor's hall, catching a glimpse of Rosie, also walking down to her door, with a basket of laundry.

Rushing to help her, Kyle snatched the basket out of her hands.

"Kyle, I really don't need help. What do I look like? Old?" Rosie joked. She shuffled her feet as they walked, cracking a smile.

"Don't bullshit me, Rosie," Kyle said, following her to her doorstep. While he waited for Rosie to unlock her door, Kyle glanced down at the stack of her mail. Of course, without fail, there were three fresh new gossip magazines in the pile, one on top of the other.

"Thank you," Rosie said as she opened the door.

Kyle followed, entering her apartment. He set down her laundry basket on her couch, then headed back toward the entryway.

"By the way, where is your girlfriend?"

Not this shit again.

"I don't have a girlfriend," Kyle said, trying to hide his irritation.

"You don't? Well, who is that pretty girl staying with you?"

"Just a girl, Rosie. Just a girl."

Rosie smiled and walked over to Zaphod's cage, retrieving him, then setting him on her shoulder. The rat gave her a little nudge with its nose to greet her. "Have I met her before? She looks familiar."

"No. You couldn't have. She's been staying with me only a few days."

"Oh." She gave Zaphod a small pat, and the rat nudged her affectionately in return.

"Well, later, Rosie. I gotta run," Kyle said abruptly. He was in no mood to chat, no matter how sweet Rosie was. He was still irritated about the girlfriend comment.

"See you, Kyle. By the way, next time you run to the store, can you pick me up some milk?" Rosie called out. "I'll give you some money. I would do it myself, but I just picked up groceries a couple days ago, and my body is still recovering from it."

"Sure. I'll let you know."

"Thanks, sweetie."

Kyle left her apartment, shutting the door behind him. He was about to cross the hall to go to his apartment, but he saw that Rosie had forgotten to grab her magazines.

Kyle shoved his cigarette between his lips, then bent over to pick them up. One managed to slip out of his grasp. Cursing at himself for dropping it, he picked up the remaining magazine and set it on top of the others in his hands, then he froze.

Holy motherfucking shit!

Staring at him was Em, right on the cover of the magazine. Not Em, but Emerald. *Princess* Emerald.

Dropping the other two magazines, Kyle frantically flipped through the magazine, searching for the main feature. "Prince of York Pursues Princess Emerald" read the headline across the article.

Kyle stared at the picture of Em, dumbstruck. There she was, Emerald, dancing with the Prince of York. He gazed at the magazine until his cigarette was gone, then immediately lit another. Kyle knew Em was from the upper levels—that fact she had not hidden from him—but this was insane. It was one thing to have the wealthy daughter of some noble lord in his apartment. It was an entirely different thing to have a royal staying with him, let alone the princess of Arcadia. No wonder she was worried about the authorities finding her. The King was probably on everyone's ass to find his daughter.

That must be some dye job on her hair, Kyle thought, looking at Emerald's green hair in the picture. He understood why. Everyone recognized the princess by her green hair.

Kyle finished chain smoking three more cigarettes before he managed to pull himself together. Closing the magazine, he slipped them under Rosie's door and walked across the hall. Behind that door, the princess of Arcadia was in his apartment, drawing a picture of his band. He was suddenly thinking back on all the crude things he'd said in front of her.

He took a deep breath, trying to calm himself before he freaked out. *She is still the same person, dipshit*, he scolded himself.

As Kyle entered his apartment, he saw the princess sitting cross-legged, bent over her painting. Emerald heard him, and her face shot up from the painting she was working on, revealing a big smile.

"Did you have any luck finding a guitar?" she asked, looking achingly hopeful and happy.

"Nope." Kyle cautiously plopped down across from her, smoking his cigarette.

"Well, that's good." She shot up from her spot with a bounce in her step, making her way into the kitchenette.

"Tell me, how is that good?" Kyle called out to her. *Stay calm. It's just Em.*

"Because…" She came back from around the corner, holding a long brown package. She ran over excitedly, then set it in his lap. Stunned, Kyle already knew what it was before he opened it.

"No, no, no." Kyle shook his head in disbelief. "I can't accept this."

"You don't even know what it is. Open it."

Obliging, Kyle opened the brown package, revealing a black guitar case. A beautiful red electric guitar sat within the folds of the plush cushion of the case. It had to be the most expensive damn guitar he had ever seen. It was the best brand of guitars, and one of the nicest models around.

"I know your old guitar was black, but I thought red suited you…" Emerald began to say, fumbling with her words. Nervously, her eyes darted to his. "Do you like it?"

"Fuck yeah, I love it." Kyle peered at her, as if it was the first time he was seeing her for who she really was. He then glanced at the guitar, feeling small. "But you really didn't have to do this for me."

"Yes, I did. If it weren't for me, that Jaxx guy wouldn't have come looking for you in the first place. I felt responsible for your guitar," she said, trying to convince him. "I had hoped to make it up to you." Emerald shifted her head shyly, slightly blushing.

"I did what any normal person would have done," he said, nervously scratching the back of his neck. His eyes soaked in the color of his guitar as he sat admiring the beauty of it. Testing it out, he strummed a few chords. "How did you know what to get? And how the hell did you afford this?"

He cursed the stupidity of his last question as soon as he said it. She was one of the wealthiest people in Arcadia, after all. One might assume that she was carrying a shitload of money on her. But maybe not, since she'd run away.

"When we were over at Remy's the day after the incident, I talked him about it. I gave him the money, and he agreed to buy it for you. But I told him that you should have a red one, whatever he chose. Red is your color. He delivered it today when you were at Diego's."

"Was Diego in on this scheme of yours?"

"Yes. The band all pitched in, but I gave the biggest portion," Emerald said proudly. "Although, I don't have much money left, so hopefully the band is happy with the flyer and is willing to give me more work." Emerald winked, then sat back down in front of her painting. She picked up her brush and proceeded to paint red between the black lines where Kyle's figure was.

He suddenly felt guilty and completely insecure. Never in his life had he felt that way, especially when it came to women. He never had to think twice around them. But damn, Em was the *princess of Arcadia*.

Shifting uncomfortably on the floor, he said, "Em… you didn't have to spend your money on me. Really."

"Nonsense." Emerald waved at him nonchalantly. "I had to. You've given me a place to stay for a while. Consider that rent for a month."

"Ha ha," Kyle joked sarcastically, turning back to strum his guitar. "Red, huh?"

"Everyone is associated with a color."

"They are?"

"Well, yes," Emerald said definitively, as if there was no reason to question it. "It is stated in *The Spectrum*."

"You believe in that?"

Emerald looked at him, confused. "Why, yes, don't you?"

"I suppose there is some great being out there. Never gave it much thought, though." Kyle shrugged, continuing to strum his guitar.

"Don't you ever wonder how the world was created, or what happens to us after we die?"

"Don't really care. All I know is that I hope to die when this"—he nodded his head at his tattoo—"reaches my hand." Kyle puffed on his cigarette through pursed lips. He heard an interworking of a new melody in his head and tried to play it softly through their conversation.

"Doesn't matter if you believe it or not," Emerald said, shrugging. She turned to her picture, painting it while he played. "Your color is red. Get used to it," she said playfully, as if that was the only way to convince him.

"And what's yours? Purple?" he said, picking a random color, as he already knew the answer.

The princess cracked a smile. "Purple is a shade of violet. And no, I am not violet. Just because I like that color, doesn't mean it's my true color."

"What is your true color?" he asked casually.

Let me guess, green.

"Green," she said, continuing to paint her picture.

"How the hell do you know that?"

"Because… I just do," Emerald said simply, not meeting his eyes.

Kyle watched her dab globs of different colors together on a clean section of her palette, mixing them. "What are you doing?" he asked, curious.

"I'm making black."

"Wouldn't it be easier to just use black paint?"

Emerald gave him a smile. "I suppose it would, but I like making mine."

Kyle continued to watch her mix, until the paints uniformly turned dark. "So black is all of the colors mixed together?"

"It is if you are talking about pigments," Emerald explained. "But if you are referring to light, all of the colors combined makes white." She made a few black strokes on her painting, then picked up another brush, dabbing it with red paint.

"Why do you think my color is red?" Kyle asked curiously, setting his guitar down off to the side. He grabbed an ashtray next to him, putting out the cigarette.

"You always seem angry."

Kyle snorted at her answer, slightly amused. "That hurts, Em! Do I really come off as an asshole that much?"

Emerald leaned over her painting, her face hovering two inches in front of his. Kyle's heart began to pound in his chest, unsure of what she was going to do.

There was a long pause between them, both of them unmoving.

Oh God… Kyle thought, staring at her bright eyes. *Oh my fucking God…*

Suddenly, he was startled by a wet brush stroke of paint on the side of his face.

Emerald leaned back to her painting, giggling. "Yes, most of the time," she teased.

"The hell?" Kyle laughed, completely caught off guard at her playfulness.

He grabbed a paintbrush off the floor, then a tube of green paint that was next to it, squirting it on the brush.

The princess was already anticipating his next move. She shot up from her painting, running across the room, laughing.

Kyle dashed after Emerald, cornering her, dabbing her cheek with his wet paintbrush. Emerald fought back, brushing another stroke across his neck rather quickly. Kyle responded by painting a giant green stroke on her arm.

Emerald tackled him, then they both tumbled to the floor, still wrestling back and forth with the paintbrushes. Emerald was starting to become slippery from the paint, and they were both covered in their respective colors. Both of them tried to reach for the paint tubes to recharge their paintbrushes, but with their playful fighting, they both failed. Instead, Emerald continued to wrestle with him until she twisted from his grasp, making her way on top of him with her legs wrapped around his waist.

Acutely aware of her position, Emerald's face froze, awaiting his reaction.

Kyle made no attempt to continue their game and went still as well. He watched Emerald soaking in the visual of his chest rising and falling as he inhaled and exhaled. He breathed steadily in and out, each breath sucking in more hunger for her.

Slowly, she unzipped his leather vest, exposing his chest for her eyes to indulge. Reaching for her paintbrush, she painted a fresh red line from his neck, then guided the paintbrush down until the paint crossed over his pectorals, then further to his abs, then stopped right above his groin. As her paintbrush worked its way down his body, his blood began to boil with an insatiable desire.

God, he wanted her.

Emerald finished the stroke, then set her paintbrush down. She nervously placed her hands on the newly painted stroke, then slowly guided her hands down the painted trail on his body. Her touch stimulated him, causing his lower member to stir with hardness. His hands reached for hers, enclosing his strong hands around her dainty ones. They were soft, softer than any other woman's that he had held. Kyle then guided her delicate hands to his lips, kissing one of them.

"I'm scared," she confessed as her hands trembled in his.

Kyle knew what she meant. She was a virgin. Considering who she was, she had to be.

Not in a million years would Kyle turn away sex with her, but he couldn't be the one to defile her, princess or not. It just didn't seem right. She was innocent, and he was, well… not.

"Em, you don't want to do this. You are too good of a person," Kyle told her in a whisper. "*Don't* waste it on me."

Emerald blushed, then took his hand and rested it against her cheek. "But I want to," she answered with fierce desire.

Kyle's heart quickened.

Before he could respond, Emerald leaned over him with eager eyes, her lips brushing against his. The scent of her lit a fire within him, and his arousal turned feral. Placing one of his hands on the back of her head, he pulled her head to his, and their lips pressed together, and they wildly tasted each other for the first time. She was an aphrodisiac. Nothing tasted as sweet as her lips, and he wanted more of her. He had wanted her the moment he met her, and now that he had tasted her, she was somehow causing him to lose control of himself, sinking into the fleshly desires of his heart.

She moaned softly in between their exchange of passionate kisses. Emerald's hand traveled down his naked chest, resting it where he throbbed uncontrollably. He yanked her closer, his thigh pressing between her legs. He heard a raspy moan, then her lips were kissing his ears, biting them playfully. Responding, he kissed her neck roughly as she moaned with pleasure. Kyle could feel that she was damp with excitement, which made him even harder.

A random, annoying thought instantly flashed in his mind. It wasn't the thought about Emerald being a princess. That thought had come and gone. It was the color yellow.

The fuck was he thinking about color at a time like this? It must have been his conversation with Emerald about colors.

Go away, he said harshly to the thought. *I'm fucking busy. Literally.* But the thought continued to pester him, like a damn annoying fly that one could not swat. Forcing himself to cast the thought out of his mind, it finally left him free of distraction once again.

Then he took Emerald's lips in with full pleasure, working his mouth in a downward direction against the burning flesh of her skin, until it stopped at the top of her breasts. She placed her hands upon his head, guiding him, letting him know she wanted him to continue.

Damn, it was going to be a good night.

CHAPTER 30

Damaris walked madly through the palace to Elyathi's quarters with a quickened pace, hoping to catch the little snake before it was too late. With each step, Damaris felt the urge that he needed to punch something, or someone. Especially if what was told to him was true. There would be hell to pay.

Of all the people to betray him, it had to be his closest friend and ally, Samir. Damaris expected much better of Samir, him being a loyal father and husband to the Queen of York. Never in a hundred years would Damaris have imagined Samir being tangled up in an affair. Especially one with his *wife.*

Damaris, along with ten men from his personal guard, arrived outside the elaborate carved double doors to the queen of Arcadia's chambers. Without a moment to waste, Damaris nodded to one of the guards, giving them the signal. Immediately, the guardsmen began to pry the thick doors open with crowbars, yanking the doors free from its lock.

As soon as the doors flung open, Damaris briskly stepped inside the chambers, first entering Elyathi's sitting room. No one was there, not even her handmaidens. His eyes narrowed. Her servants were not supposed to leave the Queen alone. Ever.

Damaris advanced to the next set of doors, which led to the Queen's bedroom. Sounds could be heard from behind the doors. Elyathi's sobs, and another low voice.

He knew that voice. It was none other than Samir.

Hurling the door open, Damaris charged inside, instantly seeing what he feared most. The King of York was with *his* queen, holding her in his arms as she continued to sob, stroking her hair.

Both Elyathi and Samir's attention shifted immediately to Damaris, alarmed. Elyathi's crystal-blue eyes were puffy from crying, and her long, wavy white hair was wild with fear. Samir's black hair and eyes stood strong, fearless of the situation about to unfold.

"So, it's *true*. My wife and my best friend. The two people that mattered most."

Elyathi shook her head, stepping away from Samir. "It's not what you think."

"And I am supposed to believe that?" Damaris snarled, walking toward Elyathi.

She took another step back, almost in a protective stance. What did she think he was going to do? Hurt her? He would never dream of doing such a thing. Only Samir. He would kill him with his own bare hands.

"She's right." Samir stepped forward, confronting Damaris. "Despite what you think, it's not as it seems."

Damaris came within an inch of Samir, seething hatred from his lips. "How dare you come into Arcadia, march into my wife's personal bedchambers, and try to take her away from me!"

"Think whatever you want. But that is not the truth."

"Let me rephrase. You have come to loan my kingdom money in exchange for making a whore out of my wife in secret!" Damaris's fists began to shake. "Is that more like it?"

Samir clenched his jaw, snarling. "I am *not* making a whore out of Elyathi!"

"He is doing no such thing," Elyathi called out meekly. "I am leaving Arcadia. With Emerald."

Damaris shot his face toward the Queen. "You are *not* leaving! You will *never* leave this place!" he shouted. Damaris swung a fist toward Samir, landing a blow to the chest. Samir stumbled back, slamming against a wall. "No one is going *anywhere*! Not my wife, and not my daughter!" He turned to Samir. "Especially not *you*."

Samir quickly got ahold of himself, then charged toward Damaris, leaping onto him, knocking both of them to the ground. Elyathi cried out while they tumbled back and forth on the ground, throwing punches.

"Elyathi has already made up her mind! She doesn't want to be in Arcadia anymore. You must listen, my friend," Samir yelled as he threw another punch.

Friend. The word was a slap to Damaris. Such hypocrisy.

The image of them paused as time stood still within the confines of his mind.

Damaris released his grasp on Samir, then stood up, hovering over his body. Rage consumed him. No, it *possessed* him.

With the King of York's body frozen in time, Damaris kicked Samir's statuesque body, smashing his boot into the man's face. Samir didn't move or budge, just remained as he was.

Glancing over at his wife, Damaris drank in her beauty. She was the most beautiful when she cried. So beautiful. And yet so deceitful.

"*Why?*" he roared at Elyathi. "The only person I have ever felt something for, and you go and do this! Why? All I wanted was for us to live forever! Why couldn't you see that?"

Elyathi was so adamant about not using Emerald's blood. Did she not see? They could live an extended life, ruling Arcadia for centuries. Arcadia would be the most powerful kingdom on Earth, using Emerald's gift. His dreams had told him so.

Interesting… said a woman's voice from within his mind.

"You again!" Damaris called out aimlessly, spinning around, trying to find the source of the voice. He looked in every direction and saw no one, only hearing his own voice reverberating through the chamber. "Let me have my mind back, whoever you are!"

That would be counterproductive, considering all the groundwork that I have paved for the prince.

"What?" Furious, Damaris clenched his fists, shaking with anger.

The prince will soon be the ruler of Arcadia.

"No! What do you think you are doing? After all the work I have done for you!"

Work?

"Yes! The cyborgs! The vision… You gave me the vision years ago."

Vision? What vision?

"The one that I was to conquer the earth with my army! With the help of my daughter!" Frustrated, Damaris kicked a wall, his foot sinking into the drywall. He removed it, and a large hole was now in place where he had struck. Flakes of white dust covered his expensive shoe, and white powder fluttered about. "Now return me to my body! I still have much work to do."

Then he heard a laugh echoing in the chambers. The walls shook at first, cracking where his boot hit the wall. As the laugh continued, the crack spidered up the wall, splitting the palace into massive pieces. Elyathi and Samir remained still and solid like stone, but the room shook violently as the ground tore apart, rolling them around on the ground like simple chess pieces.

I'm so sorry, my king. But I can't let you return. You are a mere pawn in this game. Your daughter and her blood are mine; *the army of cyborgs are* mine. *You can tell the High Court "checkmate" when they come calling again.* Damaris heard a wicked laugh as the ground shook.

Damaris spun around again, trying to see what direction the voice was coming from. The ground split under him, causing him to stumble. The palace rumbled again, pulling itself apart. In the voided cracks, a deep-violet color flared, endless as space itself. There was another sudden violent earthquake, causing Elyathi and Samir's bodies to roll into the void.

"Who are you?"

Me? I am the High Court's worst nightmare.

"I demand you release me!" Damaris roared, plummeting to the floor. He looked underneath him, seeing the ground tearing itself apart once again.

In due time, my king. Don't worry, we will have fun, I promise you that. But not without ensuring that Derek is Arcadia's king first…

CHAPTER 31

GREEN

The sky had been overcast since morning, masking the city in a gray haze. The glowing advertisements, neon signs, and skyways all looked out of focus from the thick fog.

Emerald held her arms around Kyle's waist firmly as the two of them rode through the city, making their way to Kyle's next show. As much as the wind ripped around their bodies, it couldn't blow away Kyle's warm scent, which made her senses go wild.

All day Emerald had been out of sorts. She still hadn't told him. Since their sexual excursion the previous night, Emerald's gut felt heavy, like she'd swallowed a piece of iron that was slowly working its way through her digestive system. She had to tell Kyle who she really was, but she couldn't find the opportune time to do so. The more she thought about it, the harder it became for her, like a giant obstacle she couldn't overcome. It seemed so easy—all she had to do was utter a few words. But it was the aftermath she was most afraid of. What would Kyle even think of her being a royal? Somehow, Emerald imagined that it wouldn't go over well with him.

They came upon the city's northern sector, where the palace was located. As they drove through the streets, Emerald looked up at the palace looming between the skyscrapers. She had never realized how majestic the palace appeared compared to the neighboring buildings. It burned with intense green lights, casting a halo around the surrounding structures and skyways. The street level near the palace itself looked clean, bright, and enticing, the most it could ever look for the lower levels. Emerald noticed guards stationed on the outskirts of the palace blocks, along with many officers from Arcadia's authorities. There were so many of them.

Ducking into Kyle's studded jacket, she buried her face in his back, ensuring that she wouldn't be seen or noticed by the guards or authorities. She didn't have her green hair, but her wavy locks were still very noticeable, and it was possible the guards had been made aware that she was on the run with red hair. Knowing her father, he and his Inner Council had probably drilled poor Glacia extensively about any and all details the night she left. That would lead to them searching for her with red hair.

After she deemed it safe, Emerald lifted her head out of Kyle's jacket, glancing to the side. They had passed the palace area and were moving into the eastern sector. With each block they passed, the lighting changed to a dimmer tone with neon signs in poor condition, and the streets became lined with trash. Back to the usual appearance of the lower levels.

Coming up on a parking garage, Kyle pulled in and parked. They hopped off the bike and exited, walking into the bustling street.

Kyle pointed to a platform across the street. "That's the platform we need to get to. I think there's an escalator that will take us up to the mid-levels," he stated, looking upward.

"Mid-levels?" Emerald said excitedly. Finally! She would be able to see what the mid-levels were like.

"Yep. First time playing in the mid-levels. I don't know how the hell Remy was able to get a gig there, but he did. It'll cost a shitload of tax, but the venue is paying us extra to cover it."

Emerald froze for a moment, thinking about her paying the tax to cross levels. She would need to provide an ID when paying the tax. Her eyes shot to his, suddenly nervous.

"Don't worry," Kyle said quickly. "I got you an ID. It'll get you through." He gently slid his guitar case off her back, then slung the shoulder strap over his body and across his chest, playfully grabbing her hand.

With a relieved smile, Emerald nudged Kyle, holding their entwined hands up. "I would have never guessed a tough guy like yourself would hold a girl's hand."

Kyle, lighting a cigarette, began to puff it. "Oh? Well, I don't have to," he teased, dropping her hand quickly and walking away.

"Hey! Wait for me!" Emerald ran to him, as he was already a few feet away, then ran in front of him, crossing her arms. "Why did you do that?"

"I thought you were complaining."

"No, I rather liked it," Emerald said, grinning at him.

Seizing the cigarette from his mouth, Emerald then placed it between her lips, taking a deep inhale. Immediately, her lungs burned and itched, her eyes watering simultaneously. With a sudden force, she hacked out a loud, deep, chesty cough.

Kyle laughed, taking the cigarette from her hand and throwing it to the ground, rubbing it in. "Wow, Em, I didn't expect that. You okay?"

In response, Emerald continued to hack, nodding.

"It feels like shit the first ten times you do it," he said, rubbing her back in a circular motion as she bent over, still hacking.

"I wanted to… give it a try. Now that… I have, I have decided that… it is completely and utterly… horrible. How can you *do* that to yourself?" Emerald asked, forcing the words out of her mouth.

"Believe me, it gets better." He stopped patting her back. "It's a lot like fucking. The first several times, you have no idea what the hell you're doing. After that, it gets good."

She stood up straight again, catching her breath. Her breath tasted awful, like burnt dirt on her tongue. "Thanks for that comparison." She continued to cough, giving him a look.

"Yeah, you're right. Probably not the best analogy," he said, giving her a playful grin.

Kyle gestured for her to follow, leading the way through the maze of Arcadia's busy skyways, coming upon a set of escalators. They took the pair high up, reaching the highest level Emerald had ever been since she had left the palace. She glanced below as they stood on the escalators, looking down at the sprawling city below.

The escalators led them to a large platform. It looked like one of the public transport stations, but it was different. Toll signs were posted everywhere, and attendants sat in booths, collecting money from citizens.

Kyle walked up to one of the booths, showing both of their IDs while he slid the toll money to the attendant. The man behind the station scanned the IDs, then took the money, nodding for them to proceed through the station.

"By the way, where did you get that ID?" Emerald whispered to Kyle as they stepped onto the next set of escalators.

"I got friends."

"Diego?"

"Oh, God no," Kyle laughed, lighting a cigarette. "That guy wouldn't even know how to plug in a monitor." Emerald let out a small giggle. "No, my friends from the wastelands."

"How were they able to get you an ID?" Emerald asked, surprised. "They are out in the desert! And that quickly?"

"When I was at Diego's yesterday looking for a guitar, I contacted my friend Garrett online. He uploaded data on an old ID card I picked up from some random dealer while I was out." They continued to rise on the escalators. "Besides, I knew you were gonna need one ever since that ordeal at the motel."

Emerald flushed, a bit embarrassed. "Thank you."

"No need to thank me. You just need to get out more," he joked, putting his arm around her. The heavy leather of his jacket weighed on her bare shoulders, giving her warmth.

The escalator brought them to another platform, this time being settled in the heart of the mid-levels. There were walkways and shops lined up throughout, connecting to the various buildings encompassing them. A multitude of skyways, escalators, and elevators dumped crowds of people into the hub, packing the level with crowds of Arcadians. Large neon advertisements in various screen sizes competed for the crowd's attention while the noise of street musicians, shop music, and laughter filled the hub.

As they walked past the shops, Emerald saw a glimpse of herself: an advertisement that used an image from a photo shoot she had done with Haze before she left the palace. There her image stood, plastered for all the world to see, sitting in a regal fashion with her emerald-green hair flowing to her sides, displaying a perfume in her hand.

Flushing red, she grabbed Kyle's hand, walking quickly. She didn't realize how easy she was to spot, even with red hair. "Come on," she urged, yanking him.

He stopped right in front of the picture, then turned around to face her. He pointed with his thumb back to the advertisement, and smiled. "Hey, Em, she looks just like you," he joked.

Emerald's heart went into shock. It was the perfect time to tell him, but her mind went numb with fear.

Pulling him quickly, she stated, "Not even close."

Kyle managed to keep in step with her fast pace, still being pulled by her grip. "You sure? The face resembles yours," he said casually, taking another drag of his cigarette.

Emerald ignored him. He was obviously teasing her. Did he really suspect something more? Why couldn't she just tell him?

As they made their way through the mid-levels, they came upon a nightclub, all lit up in blue neons. Kyle flashed his ID to the side door, and they were both escorted in, passing a crowd of people outside the club.

"There are so many people," Emerald said in awe, giving the long line of people a once-over.

"Yeah, looks like it."

As they entered, Emerald smiled excitedly at the layout of the venue. It was beautiful, not in terms of traditional architecture, but very modern, decorated with large glass squares on the walls and floors. Every so often, the square would flash an electric blue, then slowly fade away into black as if it had a heartbeat of its own. The bar in the back was lit up in violets and had several water tanks brightly lit up in a neon aqua color, water bubbles rising from the bottom.

Kyle shrugged, looking around for the others. "Must be early." He turned to her. "I'm gonna go backstage to start setting up. The guys are probably back there." He flashed her a charming smile and gave her a quick kiss on the cheek. "Be close, will ya?"

"Of course," Emerald said, smiling at him. "I wouldn't dream of being anywhere else." A sudden twang of guilt came over her.

She had to tell him…

***

It was minutes before the band was about to go onstage, and Emerald had to use the restroom. No matter how hard she tried, she couldn't contain herself any longer. She had to forgo her spot up front and center, reluctantly leaving it for other fans to fight over.

Sorry, Kyle, she thought, cursing herself for not going when they first arrived at the venue.

Squeezing through the excited crowd that was waiting for the show to begin, Emerald pushed her way to the side of the room. She found the signs that pointed upward to the bathrooms, then took the industrial metal staircase upstairs.

A strange feeling came over her, like someone was watching her, causing her to shudder.

Glancing anxiously over the metal bars of the staircase, there was nothing or no one unusual that stuck out to her. Casting the disturbing feeling aside, she turned her gaze away from the crowd.

The top of the stairs was packed full of latecomers to see the show, hoping to get a good view since the floor was crowded. In the far corner, a hot pink glow indicated the women's bathroom, and Emerald headed in that direction.

Inside the lavatory, which was stylishly decorated with vibrant pink and polished chrome, Emerald chose a stall and relieved herself. After, Emerald washed her hands, glancing over to a woman next to her, who was also washing her hands.

It was the woman's eyes that caught her at first, shocked by her deep-purple mohawk. The woman appeared about ten years older than her, with a gaunt face and high cheekbones. She was exotic in appearance, with soft brown skin and cool violet eyes. In the middle of the woman's forehead was a small ornate violet jewel. A hoop ring clung to the woman's sharp nose and one of her ears were pierced from the bottom all the way to the top of her ear, dangling with long silver earrings of different designs. But unlike its mate, the other ear had a single stud in it.

She has violet eyes…

The woman glanced at Emerald for a moment as she washed her hands, then thought nothing more of her as she turned away to dry them. Emerald watched her in the mirror's reflection until the woman exited the bathroom, then grabbed a paper towel.

Muffled music came from outside the bathrooms; Kyle's band had started to play their first song.

Quickly finishing up, Emerald made her way back downstairs to the main floor. There was absolutely no room for her. It was far too crowded. Emerald decided to get a drink at the bar in the back, since that seemed like the only place with room for her to stand.

Shouldering her way along the sides of the wall, that overwhelming feeling of someone watching her returned, and her stomach started to twist.

Glancing over her shoulder, all Emerald saw were screaming fans having a good time. She even caught a far-off glimpse of Kyle, singing with a demanding presence.

Smiling at the sight of Kyle, Emerald turned her attention back to the bar.

Her heart stopped.

A tall, slender older man with a shaved head and thick-rimmed glasses was watching her. His eyes were like a magnet, snapping his face in her direction with a riveting expression. Or with a lack of expression; Emerald couldn't tell. Her heart beat furiously in her chest, and the bad feeling was replaced with dire alarm.

The man cocked his head strangely as Emerald took a step backward. The man continued to stare at her, his gaze fixated on her every move, instilling an immense fear.

In a split second, Emerald fleeted in the opposite direction, shoving her way fearfully through the crowd. People cussed and yelled at her as she did so, pushing her back in the process. Second by second, her fear rose, her heart pounding. She had to get away from that man and get near Kyle. She felt safe around him.

There was an orange flashing glow in the crowd behind Emerald as she caught the light in the corner of her eye.

Oh my God. He has magic, like me!

The man was suddenly twenty feet behind her. He made no movement, only standing there with a lack of emotion across his face. Shaking in disbelief, Emerald rapidly pushed further through the crowd. A few seconds later, the magical orange flash appeared again from behind, but this time closer in proximity.

Emerald screamed, but it was no use. The crowd screamed along with her, but for different reasons. It was like no one else saw the man. Instead they gave Emerald dirty looks and pushed her aside.

Another magical orange spell flared through the crowd, this time across the whole venue. Faces in the crowd finally noticed the magic, turning their heads toward the direction of the magic, confused.

The man appeared right in front of Emerald, his eyes burning with orange power, expressionless, rendering her frozen in denial. He was somehow instantly in front of her, no matter how much distance she put between them. The man's face warped in and out of reality, from smooth skin and thick-rimmed glasses to a half-robotic machine with a mechanic eye.

"Please…" Emerald begged, taking another step back.

The bionic eye focused on her, glowing with intensity. As he fully extended his right arm, warm orange magic swirled around it. Fingers gave way to a machinelike arm, shooting out blades from his fingers, readying himself to attack her.

An orange glow swelled in his hands.

Without a second thought, Emerald bolted.

***

Everyone saw it, Kyle included. A big fucking bright-orange flash.

Eclipsing the orange light was Emerald, hurling herself toward the stage with her arm outstretched. Her mouth formed a scream, but the crowd was too loud for him to hear her cries.

With another sudden orange burst, a bionic man appeared behind Emerald, latching on to her. He yanked the princess back toward him, then the two of them vanished instantly.

The crowd went nuts. The people who were near the magical flare were running like scattered rats, trying to push over others that stood in their way.

Ripping off his guitar in a frenzy, Kyle dove into the crowd where Emerald was a moment earlier. The band continued to play a few seconds then the music slowly died out, the guys clearly confused whether to continue to play or stop.

"Em!" Kyle yelled, jerking his head in each direction, wondering which way to go. It was no use; the crowd was in complete mass hysteria, and she was gone. Kyle fought the crowd as they scurried over each other, pushing him down. Kyle swung wildly to give himself room to get to his feet.

Another bright-orange flash appeared. This time it was by the back emergency exit.

"Em!"

Keeping his eyes fixated in the direction of the burst of light, Kyle pushed his way to the exit, slamming the double doors open. The emergency alarm sounded, stirring more commotion from the crowd.

"Em? Where are you?"

"Hey, you can't be here!" yelled a security guard from behind the door.

"The hell I can't be here!" Kyle roared, turning each way in hopes to spot Emerald down the concrete hallway.

"Oh, wait, sorry about that..." the guard apologized, recognizing Kyle as one of the band members.

"Have you seen a girl with red hair just now?"

"No, I just happened—"

"Forget it," he said, cutting off the guard, turning away from him. "Em?"

He heard her muffled screams in response, coming from down the hall.

Running as fast as he could, Kyle saw an orange flash near the second emergency exit.

Charging down the hall, Kyle felt the air around him shift, the weight of the draft heavier.

Trusting his gut, he jumped into midair, hoping to land on the invisible man. Instead, the wind shifted, and Kyle landed right on his ass.

"Kyle!" Emerald's voice called out. "Behind you!"

Kyle turned around quickly. Materializing out of a gust of orange-red wind, the mechanical man was suddenly before him, the princess in his grasp. His bionic eye glowed orange, focusing its lens on Kyle while his real eye, also orange, stared from behind his odd glasses.

One of the man's arms extended, and intricate circuitry lit up his arm and hand. Long, sharp clawlike needles protruded from his fingers, swinging wildly at Kyle while the other hand held Emerald firmly in place.

Kyle rolled out of the way, barely avoiding contact with the claws.

What the fuck is that thing?

Having no time to try to figure it out, Kyle threw himself toward the cyborg.

The mechanical man's entire body began to pulsate with a bright-orange glow. Right when Kyle was about to make contact, the bionic man and Emerald became a hologram, causing Kyle to aimlessly plow right through their image and slam against the hallway.

A dark-green glow appeared in the air, gathering in one area, its brilliance highlighting a strange halo on Emerald and the mechanical man, revealing their exact location to Kyle. He lunged at the energy, landing on top of solid, firm "air." He was on top of the cyborg. Better yet, Kyle realized he was holding on to the cyborg's neck.

He couldn't have asked for a better position.

Kyle locked his arm around the bionic man's neck, squeezing with all his strength. He knew he couldn't overpower the cyborg, but it was enough to stun him.

With an orange flash, the mechanical man and Emerald appeared in full view, his grip around her weakening. Emerald broke free.

"Get out of here! Go!" Kyle urged her.

"I can't leave you here!" Emerald said. "You have no chance against him."

"Better me than you!"

Emerald hesitated.

Kyle saw the mechanical man glow again for a quick second, then turned to glance back at Emerald. They were fucked and had little time.

"The authorities will be here any second! I will catch up. Promise," Kyle said, waving her away.

Nodding, Emerald was down the hall in a split second, making her way toward the exit. The bionic man jerked, then turned his attention to the princess. The cyborg shot in her direction, almost as if he was flying, with orange winds powering his body from below.

As the cyborg flew by, Kyle lunged at the bionic man, landing a punch in its side. The cyborg whirled to the wall, then shot out his mechanical fingers, summoning orange-red flames within his palms. The mechanical man hurled a fireball toward Kyle, missing. With another quick jolt, the cyborg slashed his clawlike hands at Kyle, determined to get rid of him one way or another.

This time, Kyle was hit. The inferno blades slashed his arms in one solid swipe, puncturing his flesh. Blood squirted out, and he screamed.

"Motherfucker!" Kyle yelled in agony, falling to the floor. Through his scrunched eyes, he saw Emerald running toward him.

"What are you *doing*? Get out of here!" Kyle yelled as he doubled over, afraid that the cyborg would get her.

"I can't leave you, Kyle!"

The cyborg materialized right in front of Emerald within a vast swirling light of orange magic.

Instantly, the most intense lightning Kyle had ever seen flashed in hues of deep purplish-red, striking the mechanical man. It kept coming in waves, stronger, fiercer, and with more voltage and power.

The cyborg began to shake violently from the magic, his circuits sparking wildly. If Kyle had to guess, the damn robot appeared to be going into overload.

Not even a second later, another wave of purple energy funneled down the hall. But instead of electricity, it was a bright violet stream of glowing magic, rushing like rippling water, flowing over Kyle. The power tingled, gathering over his open wound, then repaired his flesh quickly. The strange violet magic *healed* him.

The hell?

Kyle looked in the direction of the healing purple energy but couldn't find the source. The purple healing wave suddenly stopped, and the cyborg was blasted with another round of violet-red electricity.

"Get up!" yelled a woman's voice, echoing down the hall. "What are you waiting for?"

The cyborg's circuitry smoked profusely, causing him to move in a slower fashion. It seemed the cyborg didn't care how hard he was hit with the electrical blast; he kept moving toward Emerald.

"Go!" commanded the woman's voice.

"I agree with whoever the fuck that is. Let's get out of here," Kyle said to Emerald, grabbing her hand and jumping up. Kyle saw flashes of purple light behind them, with oranges blinking intermittently. He knew they weren't in the clear yet.

Kyle and Emerald hurried through the emergency exit, landing on a small platform on the outside of the building. The ground below looked like a drop of death. If they fell, their bodies would be bouncing off the skyways all the way to the ground like a game of *Pong*. The only way off the platform was a metal escape ladder.

The humming sounds of air transports could be heard, and suddenly they were in view.

Arcadia's authorities. They knew that their princess was there.

"Great," Kyle said sarcastically. "Fucking great."

Emerald grasped his hand, her eyes full of fear. "Kyle, they can't take me!"

"I am open to suggestions if you have any," Kyle said sardonically, watching as the air transports hovered at their level. The authorities began to emerge from hanging rope ladders as they neared the platform. "Any thoughts, Princess?" Kyle asked impatiently.

Emerald's face froze, shocked. Her eyes were wide with alarm. "What...? You knew?"

"I'll explain later." Kyle paused, then grabbed her hand. "Besides, it doesn't change a damn thing how I feel about you."

Emerald's face relaxed a bit, then she turned her focus to the authorities. "Kyle, we are going to have to jump," she stated.

Startled, Kyle shot her an alarming look. "You have got to be kidding me. And here I thought I was the crazy one."

"Ready?"

"Ready for what? To jump to our deaths?" Kyle asked, now watching the swarm of air transports hovering. "I'm supposed to die when my tattoo reaches my hand, remember?" he half joked, half shitting himself with fear. Did Emerald really expect to jump and survive? What the hell was she thinking?

Emerald threw her hands around his neck, then pulled him toward her, kissing him swiftly. While locked on to him, Emerald firmly pushed them off the edge with a sudden jerk of her boot.

Kyle's eyes bolted open, watching the world race by. His heart dropped into his stomach, paralyzed with fear. He was really going to die.

"Holy *shit!*"

"Hold on to me and don't let go!" she ordered.

He held her as tight as he could, almost too tight.

Emerald's eyes closed as she shot her hands palms up, swiftly outstretching them. A sudden burst of intense green-yellow light enveloped them, then transformed into a hard circular shell encasing the pair as they plummeted. That very same moment, her hair revealed its true form—emerald green.

Frantic, Kyle jerked his eyes around, stunned at the impossible power that protected them, then turned his gaze back to her hair.

Insane. This is completely fucking insane.

The green magic intensified, shifting to a glowing green-blue color. Quickly but safely, the hardened bubble guided them downward, and all the while, Kyle noticed Emerald was completely focused, her face not moving a muscle.

Orange energy rippled across the city, and the buildings began to glow a soft orange. The structures twisted and warped in several directions, tangling and entwining like a massive hollow ball. It made it completely impossible to tell which way was up or down, or even where the ground was.

Emerald continued to guide them down at a fast rate as her eyes looked around at the maze, confused.

"What the hell is going on?" Kyle asked.

"Magic," Emerald answered.

The air rippled in front of them, and the cyborg emerged from the mysterious power. He flew downward at the same rate but with much more control, using orangish-red winds to guide his body.

They continued to drop at an alarming rate, scaring the hell out of Kyle. Even with the protective shell around them, Kyle wasn't depending on that damn bubble to save his ass.

The cyborg shot out an orangish-red blast of ice, its frosty power glazing over their barrier. It didn't penetrate the shell; instead it just made the barrier hard to see out of.

Determined, Emerald countered by shooting out one of her hands, forming a dark-green cluster of energy. Suddenly, the strange power enveloped the bionic man, creating a magical link between him and Emerald. It ripped through the cyborg, sucking away his life force and flowing into Emerald, draining him.

For a split second, the cyborg jerked, causing the images of the twisted buildings to flash away and reappear how they were supposed to be—standing upright.

It was all just an illusion. The cyborg was creating false images.

Flashing her hands up, Emerald released the drained magic, and the cyborg plummeted to a mid-level platform, stunned. She quickly guided them to the lower levels, leaving the cyborg far behind. As they neared the ground, Emerald released the protective barrier, its greenish-blue magic fading away.

"I hope we are close to your motorcycle," Emerald remarked desperately.

"This way." Kyle grabbed her hand, and the two of them sprinted through the streets. Kyle could hear the authorities talking over their megaphones, but he couldn't make out anything they were saying, and he didn't need to know. They just wanted their princess.

Not on your fucking life, assholes.

Emerald had to be damn lucky, because she had somehow managed to land them about a block away from the parking garage where his bike was parked.

As they made their way into the entrance of the garage, Kyle heard more sirens coming their way.

"Holy fuck, I think we have all of Arcadia on our ass," he said, hopping on his bike. Emerald jumped on after him, and he immediately peeled away.

Kyle burst through the garage exit at full speed. Above, he heard the aerial transports, the authorities continuing to yell through their megaphones. Gripping the throttle, Kyle flew through Arcadia's streets, driving as fast as his motorcycle could go.

An orange flash rippled through the skies above.

Dammit!

Within several feet of his bike, the cyborg materialized, matching their speed as he flew next to them. With a swipe, he reached out to yank Emerald off the bike, but missed as Kyle swerved just in time.

Again, the cyborg lunged at the princess, but this time Emerald shot up her hand. A magical translucent greenish-yellow barrier appeared in front of her and Kyle. The cyborg's mechanical hand swung ferociously at the barrier, causing green sparks to fly on contact, as if he was scraping glass. He struck again and again, each time furiously trying to break the shell. But each time it held.

The cyborg burned a bright orange, then multiplied copies of himself in the distance while the original one continued to bash at their barrier. They were coming from all directions.

Kyle tried to keep his eyes straight ahead of him, but it was hard with all the magical orange and green flashes happening all around him, and now several fucking cyborgs were chasing them.

The mechanical man gave up on the barrier and flew past Kyle's motorcycle, far ahead of them, leaving a trail of orange magical winds flowing behind the machine's path. Ahead, Kyle saw the cyborg begin to glow an intense orange-red. With a sudden jolt, the machine threw his hands out, causing the road in front of them to instantly shake with orange power. The magic burst through the ground, causing the earth to shift and pull apart, creating a large crevice. The earth rumbled once again, and the crevice slid further apart, creating a massive canyon in front of Kyle and Emerald.

And they were heading right toward it at full speed.

"Hey, Em," Kyle called out to her, "if you have any other magic tricks up your sleeve, now's the time to use them. Otherwise we're completely fucked!"

"Keep driving! Don't stop!"

"Right," Kyle answered, gritting his teeth. *Trust her. She's gotten us this far with her magic,* he told himself. Kyle gripped the throttle tightly, keeping it thrusted upward, heading full speed toward the newly created canyon.

The authority transports were behind and above them; the sounds of sirens and yelling filled the air.

Emerald shifted in her seat, then Kyle felt one of her arms release his waist while the other held on to him firmly.

They were coming up on the canyon, and nothing was happening.

Oh God, Em, please do something!

Just as the motorcycle was about to meet the crevice, a bright-green-blue glow burned in Emerald's outstretched hand, pouring all over the motorcycle.

The motorcycle rolled off the last piece of earth, and suddenly there was nothing below the tire.

They were airborne, flying across the canyon.

Green-blue magic continued to funnel into the bike, causing it to be guided by the power. Kyle's stomach jumped in his chest as he saw the bottomless pit underneath his bike, as if he was looking below in slow motion. In a blink of an eye, the green-blue power flashed them across safely, and they landed smoothly on the other side of the canyon, allowing them to continue uninterrupted.

Trying his best not to shit bricks, Kyle furiously drove his way through the city on the other side of the crevice, weaving furiously in and out of anything that got in their way, from pedestrians to ground transports.

They had to make it outside the city. Or at least try.

Kyle heard more ground transports. A spotlight shone on them from the air transports overhead. Within the sea of neon flashing by him, the cyborg appeared again, enveloped in his orange energy. This time, he caught them off guard, giving him a chance to grip Emerald.

She screamed. The motorcycle swerved, spinning in a direction toward the police.

Just as the cyborg was about to yank Emerald off the bike, a violet force of energy hit the cyborg, causing it to fling off course. Kyle swerved the bike back on track, continuing on the road. Up ahead was an exit get outside of Arcadia. They were close, so damn close.

When the edge of the city's gate came into view, Kyle saw Arcadia's police transports blocking the way out, along with more aerial transports flying overhead. There was also a small army of the authorities on standby, waiting to take their princess by force.

Emerald grabbed Kyle, her hands trembling.

"In the name of the King, I order you to stop your vehicle now!" yelled the megaphone overhead. "I repeat, stop your vehicle now!"

The sky rumbled in response. Another violent purple shockwave shot through the skies of Arcadia, hurling the air transports in all different directions. Several transports slammed into the sides of the buildings, causing explosions.

"I think we have a friend," Kyle yelled back to Emerald. He wasn't sure if she heard him or not with all of the wind in their faces and the noises of the crashes above.

More transports were coming, and more ground vehicles from behind.

"Shit, don't these people ever give up?" Kyle yelled.

"Never. My father does not like to lose," Emerald answered loudly.

As they drove toward the barricade of transports, Kyle was about to turn sharply, but something changed their luck. A magical purple force parted the barricade as if the police transports were toys, throwing them aside in both directions, creating a clear path for Kyle. In the middle of the violet magic stood a woman with a purple mohawk. The woman's eyes were locked onto his, glowing bright violet.

Without thinking twice, Kyle gunned it through the path, passing the mysterious violet woman.

She tracked Kyle, her eyes studying him, watching him almost as if he were driving in slow motion. He swore he saw her shake her head in disappointment as she disappeared in a violet mass of magical energy.

Kyle looked away and gunned it, passing through the city-kingdom's border into the wastelands.

CHAPTER 32

Derek's cape flapped wildly in the wind as he exited his personal air transport. Walking briskly through the investigation site, Derek took a mental picture of how much damage had been inflicted on the building. It was half decimated, scorched and cindered from fire. It was a wonder the building was even standing considering how much damage had been inflicted with the impact.

Could this all be from Emerald's magic?

Emerald had been spotted, Derek had been told by Emerys, fleeing from the authorities on the back of some street vehicle. A motorcycle. How absurd was it that the princess of Arcadia was on the run from the authorities? On a *street* vehicle. Derek understood that she never wanted to live with her father again, but this was over the top. They'd been tracking her with Arcadia's newest technology: a cyborg. That is, until it crashed into a building, rendering it useless.

The future sorceress was right about the cyborgs after all; they were truly Damaris's secret weapon, infused with Emerald's blood. The whole blood appointments made sense to Derek, and by now, Emerald had probably figured it out as well. It had to be why Emerald was so determined to not surrender. Derek didn't know if he should be thanking the witch for divulging Damaris's secrets or hiding from her, knowing how powerful she truly was.

But above everything else that had happened, what really infuriated Derek was that Emerald was with *another man*. Based on the only video clip that the aerial transports captured, the man looked like some low-life abomination from the pits of Arcadia. Derek had watched the footage over and over again while en route to the scene of the cyborg accident. With each viewing of the clip, Derek twisted with greater fury seeing the princess's arms wrapped around another man. He needed to find Emerald soon, before this fiasco got out of hand, and before rumors started to circulate about princess outside the palace, or worse, about her being *seen* with a low-level man.

Luckily, the whole incident would be resolved soon. Once they found Emerald, Derek would marry the princess, and they would rule together. End of story. She didn't have to run anymore, nor did she have to be afraid. If only word had reached her that she was going to be safe under his protection.

As Derek walked through the impact site, his chest began to flare with spasms. Shooting pains rocked through his chest, causing his vision to blur. The intense pain swelled so much in and around his heart that he felt he was either going to black out, or worse, die. Sweat ran down his brow and onto his face, and his sight began to darken.

He needed Emerald. More than ever.

Tumbling against one of his guards, they all were suddenly alerted.

"Your Highness!" One of the guards pulled him upward as Derek leaned on him, gasping for breath. The more he breathed in, the more he felt he was losing air.

Derek reflected on Emerald. The very image of her soothed his thoughts. How soft her long locks of hair felt within his fingertips the night they danced. Her bright, big eyes. Her smile.

"Shall we escort you back to the transport?" asked the guard he was leaning on.

"I'm fine. Just fighting a cold," Derek gasped, struggling for breath as he pushed away the guard. He took a deep breath, then forced himself to stand upright, calmly collecting himself. He ran his jeweled fingers through his sweaty curls.

"I want to see the head sergeant. Now!" he snapped.

They led him through a crumbling wall inside the lobby of the building, where the sergeant was standing, talking with his task force. The sergeant glanced over at Derek, then immediately approached him, bowing.

"How could you let her get away?" Derek asked, not even addressing the sergeant formally.

"Your Highness, as much as we appreciate your concern, there really is no need for you to be here. We are working on locating the princess."

"There is every reason for me to be here, *Sergeant*. You had almost the entire task force on her trail, including an overpowered cyborg, and she *still* managed to escape."

"With all due respect, Your Highness, this is a matter for Arcadia and the royals who govern here." The Head Sergeant eyed him, giving him a signal that he took orders from no one besides Damaris.

A hot rush of anger boiled his blood. With being out of sorts with his headaches and sweat, Derek had no time to mind his manners.

Getting in the sergeant's face, Derek stood over him, a full head taller. He narrowed his piercing icy eyes, and a scowl appeared across his face.

"I daresay you are wrong, Head Sergeant." Derek leaned in within an inch of the sergeant, raising his voice. "Have you checked Arcadia's laws lately? In case you haven't, I have been named heir to the kingdom. Meaning, I will be king after Damaris. Princess Emerald is my fiancée, and what happens to her *is* my concern. Do you understand?"

The head sergeant's face remained stiff, then he nodded, quickly understanding the prince's status. "Yes, Your Highness."

"Now, tell me. How did the princess get away?"

The head sergeant paused, hesitating to speak. Derek knew he wanted to speak of her magic but didn't know where to start.

"If it's about the princess's *unique* abilities, I already know."

The sergeant cautiously eyed Derek, then spoke. "The princess used her... abilities to aid her escape. The specialized cyborg that had the ability to track the princess found her at a mid-level club."

"A *club*?" Derek repeated incredulously. What was Emerald doing at a club?

"Yes. The specialized cyborg located her at the venue. He captured her for a short period of time, but she managed to escape."

"What happened?"

"There was another gifted there."

"Gifted?"

"Yes. One with magic, Your Highness. This gifted tracked the cyborg and used a heavy amount of purple lightning on him, causing the cyborg to go into complete overload, crashing off course. And here is where you see the impact from his body's crash." The sergeant waved his hand, indicating the lobby.

Purple lightning? Could this be Ikaria's doing? She wanted the princess's blood. Perhaps she'd decided on a more forward approach to getting the princess's blood rather than relying on him to get it for her...

Derek's thoughts immediately shifted. "Who was the princess with on that motorcycle?"

"Kyle Trancer. We ran his background. A few misdemeanors for possession of drugs. No felonies."

"*Drugs?*"

"Yeah. The charges were from years ago. He currently has a clean record, except for the registration of his vehicle, which we just found out about. Looks like he never reported it. Don't know how he hasn't been caught yet."

"I can't believe this." Derek shook his head. His chest pains were flaring up again.

"His band was playing at the venue when the cyborg first located the princess. Don't know any other connection between the two of them. But our officers are still interviewing other witnesses from the initial scene, including the other band members."

Derek snarled just at the thought of Emerald with that man.

"Thank you, Head Sergeant." Derek curtly nodded, then headed off, getting back to his transport.

As they made their way back, Derek saw a woman with two other men crouched over the remains of the cyborg. Derek couldn't get a good look at it, as most of its body was blocked by the three scientists. For a moment, the woman glanced up at him curiously from under her thick framed glasses, then turned her attention back to the cyborg.

Magic. It had the power to obliterate the strongest buildings and stop technology. He marveled at the way it had sent the cyborg crashing, caused it to overload. The ones that were deployed in the rioting streets were unstoppable, so Derek had heard. To think, this special cyborg had even more abilities. And magic just tore it apart. Maybe not completely, but enough to take it down.

It was all too much. The sorceress. The magic. And now the princess, with a low-life *rocker*, fleeing the authorities. All he wanted to do was find

Emerald, and everything would go back to the way it was supposed to be before this all happened.

Derek and his guards got back into the transport, settling in their seats.

"You are requested for an audience with King Damaris," his driver called out from the front. "Transmission just came in."

Good. He could ask Ikaria if that was her doing with the purple magic.

The witch had been controlling the King's body since the night he signed the decree naming Derek heir. After that night, Ikaria had placed Damaris in a comalike state most of the time, leaving him bedridden unless she needed to use his body to further her plans in some way. The good thing about it was that now he was privy to all of Arcadia's secrets.

I wonder what she wants now, Derek thought, annoyed.

Another thought flooded his gut. What if Ikaria had found a way to journey to this time and decided that she didn't need his help anymore? What if Damaris "woke up" from Ikaria's control and took back what he had decreed in his new law...

His guards were taking too long getting situated in the transport, frustrating Derek.

"Hurry up and get seated! You heard the driver! His Majesty expects me!" Derek snapped at them. They all looked at him with confusion, as he had never been short with them before.

"Yes, Your Highness," they all managed to say, quickly getting into their seats, and the transport was off.

***

Telly had been biting her nails the whole time while in transit. She checked her tablet again, and temporary relief flooded her when she saw that Drew's vitals were still intact. His heart continued to beat, but according to the readings there was no movement in his body. If it weren't for the healing properties of the powerful blood, he wouldn't have survived.

A large crowd, made up of lower-level residents surrounded the scene where Drew had crashed. All of them were trying to get a peek at what the commotion was all about. As Telly emerged from the corporation's transport, she saw the flashing red and blue colors of Arcadia's police sirens. A multitude of bystanders stood behind a line of yellow line tape put up by the authorities.

Two other members of her team, Robert and Michael, followed closely behind her, equipment in their hands, ready to be put to good use.

As she approached the yellow line, Telly flashed her ID to one of the authorities guarding the scene.

"Telly, from Lab 34," she said to the large uniformed man. He inspected her ID for a moment, then scanned the barcode with his scan gun. There was a pleasant beep that came from the device, meaning she was cleared. Robert and Michael handed theirs over next.

"Go on, the robot is right inside that building," the policeman stated, pointing in a direction off to the side.

"*Cyborg*, actually," Telly corrected him sharply, fixing her glasses. How hard was it for people to understand the difference between a cyborg and a robot? It never ceased to amaze her how incompetent people were sometimes. "He is, after all, part *human*."

"Whatever," the policeman said, rolling his eyes, moving aside for her to step through the taped line.

Telly sighed loudly in response. *Some people are so inhuman. And they think the cyborgs lack emotion.*

Biting her tongue, she hurried past the policeman and through the site, with Robert and Michael behind her. As she passed by a group of authorities, she saw shattered glass, strewn building materials, and several collapsed and overturned shop stands. But amongst all the debris, one thing was clear: There was a complete, concise path cutting straight through it all, charred and seared black, leading down the street and ending inside of a building.

"Telly, do you think Drew did this?" asked Michael as he inspected the damage. He was punching code into his tablet as they followed the charred path.

By Drew's readings, there is no possible way he could have done this damage... I think. Unless the data retrieved was inaccurate.

"It could be the magic component," said Robert matter-of-factly. "We don't know what he is truly capable of yet."

"Yes," Telly agreed. The thought worried her. What if Drew had no way to control the magic, considering half his brain was machine?

Their group stepped carefully over a charred wall that had been punched through, leading them inside the lobby of a business building. As they entered, a group of Arcadia's authorities saw her immediately and resumed talking amongst themselves. She could hear them arguing with each other; others were taking notes on their tablets or using their communication devices.

There. Drew's body was stuck to a chrome secretary desk, half his body melted and charred—the side where his circuitry ran through. His eyes were glowing orange, staring at the inert nothingness, not blinking or moving. Half of his wires weren't connected to flesh; instead they hung out limply, sparking with electricity. His body jolted and twisted in intervals.

"Oh God! Drew?"

Telly ran over to him, skidding to her knees, then cradled him in her arms. Tears stung her eyes, lightly fogging her glasses, and her gut ached at the sight of him. Telly couldn't believe how much damage had been inflicted on him.

"Drew… I'm here now," she whispered under her breath. "I am going to get you back to the lab to make you whole again," she told him in a reassuring voice.

Drew's pupils focused on her, then glowed slightly brighter orange through his thick-rimmed glasses, understanding what was happening.

Robert knelt next to her, helping Michael ply Drew's melted circuitry off the desk. They laid Drew down steadily once they freed him, then began to hook him up with the equipment.

"He will be okay, Telly. The tablet shows positive signs that his organs are intact and functioning," Robert reported.

The magical blood saved his life, protecting him somehow, Telly thought. How, she did not know. The blood never made any sense. There were no formulas, no scientific explanation. It just did whatever it wanted to do. It was an uncontrollable variable.

Telly rubbed her teary eyes behind her glasses, then laid her hand on Drew's chest as his body continued to jolt with seizures.

"Geez, Telly, why are you getting so emotional over a piece of equipment?" Michael asked as he plugged a scanner into their equipment to stabilize Drew.

Telly whipped around to face Michael, then narrowed her eyes. "Say that to me again and see if you have a job after that."

Michael chuckled under his breath. "I was only kidding. Lighten up. We'll fix him."

"This is not the time to tell a damn joke," she snapped.

"Always like walking on eggshells around you," muttered Michael under his breath. "Especially when it comes to this guy."

Ignoring his statement, Telly gave Michael a hard look, then turned back to Drew, helping Michael and Robert finish hooking him up. The smell of Drew's flesh reeked of sulfur mixed with melted plastic. Drew looked up at her, his eyes flashing at her.

"Oh, Drew, what happened?" Telly asked under her breath. "Who or what could have done this to you?"

A loud voice rang out within the lobby of the building.

"I have been named heir to Arcadia. Meaning, I will be *king* after Damaris. Princess Emerald is my fiancée, and what happens to her *is* my concern. Do you understand?"

Telly and her team looked over at the commotion for a moment. Standing there was one of the most beautiful men she had ever seen. Deep black curls framed his head, and he wore royal clothing and jewelry set in blues, silvers, and blacks. Adorning his forehead was a circlet, showing his regal status.

Princess Emerald is engaged? Telly thought. *Surely that's Price Derek.*

The prince continued to bark at the head sergeant. Turning away, Telly resumed her efforts on Drew, continuing to work with her team.

"Drew, we need to make sure you are stabilized in order to get you moved," Telly said.

Drew's eyes burned brighter than before, as if answering her. Michael scanned his body as Telly and Robert two began typing code into their tablets. "It appears that all of his circuits went into overload. We need to replace all of the transistors and give him another dose of the sample blood," Michael said.

"Telly, right?" said a deep voice from behind her. Turning her head over her shoulder, Telly saw the head sergeant of Arcadia.

"Yes, that is correct." Telly looked away from her tablet, getting to her feet to meet the sergeant.

"Thank you for responding on such short notice."

"I'm glad that I was near the area. I tried to get here as fast as I could," Telly said. "Did anyone see what happened to him? No one has told my team anything. It seems very unlikely that he would have ended up like this."

"Eye witnesses, including half of the task force, claim that he was struck by some kind of purple-colored lightning." The sergeant gave her a skeptical look, as if he couldn't believe he was saying those words himself.

"Purple lightning?"

"Yes," he confirmed. "The cyborg tracked down the subject. During the chase, he was hit several times by the lightning. Each time, he seemed to recover slightly, allowing him to continue pursuing the suspect. At one point, there was a purple force that struck him while in midair, causing him to crash off course."

"Purple force?"

"Yep. I know it sounds crazy. But considering the subject he was chasing, it's all a little beyond us. That's about all the information that we have at this time. You and your team must get this thing moved before the rest of the squad comes in."

Telly cringed at his use of the word "thing." "We will, thank you, Sergeant."

Several other men from Lab 34 appeared, hauling a stretcher. They carefully loaded Drew onto the bed, strapped him down, then placed a white sheet over him.

Who is the subject? Telly wondered, thinking back to her conversation with the sergeant.

Then it dawned on Telly. The princess. That is why that dark-haired prince, her fiancé, was here. She was the one being tracked.

All of these years, the donor blood that they had been using for their cyborgs flowed from the princess's veins. Princess Emerald's. She... she had magic. Had the princess known how the corporation had been using her blood? Recalling what she knew of Princess Emerald, Telly immediately thought of her green hair and eyes.

She must have green magic! Just like Drew has orange magic!

The princess's blood samples had healing and life-giving properties. That was why the cyborgs were able to regenerate themselves. Well, those who were more human than machine, anyway.

The sergeant said Drew was chasing the subject... Is the princess running away? Is that why the King was impatient for Drew to be readied so quickly? Suddenly, guilt hit Telly in her stomach. From just piecing the King's and the sergeant's words together, she had a sneaking suspicion that the princess had been forced to give her blood unwillingly. And now Telly was tied to this mess.

Telly followed Drew's stretcher outside to where the corporation's transport was waiting for them. Telly looked up and saw the prince's transport, hovering above her and her team for a moment before departing, and she couldn't shake the guilty feeling.

***

As soon as the transport landed on the loading platform, Derek made haste through Arcadia's palace. At night, the corridors seemed lonely, and only the neon colors of the lifts and wall trims lit the empty passageways.

Arcadia's palace was by far the saddest court that he had ever visited in his life. No doubt the structure itself was one of the most beautiful architectural pieces he had seen, with its hallways, stairs, and lifts infused with light and glass embellished with gold and silver.

But without evening activities, parties, or engagements, all the decorations in the world couldn't breathe life into the stale atmosphere. The walls themselves seemed to drown out any joyous conversation, replacing the sounds of life with ghostly whispers and melancholy tones. The night of the ball had truly been an exception, where the palace came to life instantly, as if everyone had been waiting years for an event like that.

Once he was king, Derek would make sure that Arcadia's court would no longer have a dark cloud cast upon it. People needed laughter, and living without it was much too depressing. With even the little time Derek had spent in the palace, he was starting to let the depressing air sink into him.

Derek crossed over the glass bridge that led to the Inner Council room, seeing the expansive glowing city-kingdom dancing below his feet. He glanced in the direction of the edge of Arcadia's borders, hoping that by some miracle he would see a sudden gleam of Emerald's magic, but it was useless. There were nothing but lights glittering as far as the eye could see. Emerald was in that direction, somewhere in the wastelands.

Damn that man! Taking her out there.

As Derek entered the council chambers, he found Damaris sitting alone, enjoying a glass of wine with his legs crossed. Or rather, *Ikaria* was sitting, as it appeared that she was in control of Damaris's body.

"Had fun?" Damaris's empty eyes glimmered.

"No," Derek said, annoyed, slumping down in a vacant chair. He hastily grabbed a chalice and poured himself some wine.

"Well, that's too bad." Damaris took another sip of his glass. How Ikaria got enjoyment out of controlling Damaris like she did, Derek couldn't understand. "You'll never know what intriguing piece of information I found while controlling this body."

Derek leaned back in the chair and closed his eyes, readying himself for another onslaught of a headache. "Should I care?"

"You might not. But I find it rather fascinating."

"What now?"

"Did you know that your father was going to take Queen Elyathi back to York with him in secret?"

Derek's eyes shot open, and he dropped his glass on the floor, stunned by the revelation. It was the first piece of information he had ever heard regarding what happened between his father and Damaris.

"Truly?"

"Yes. The Queen had an elaborate plan to escape with King Samir on his last visit, years ago. It was going to involve Princess Emerald going with them. That is, until Damaris caught your father in her chambers." Ikaria made a *tsk-tsk* sound through Damaris's voice. "You people from York can't seem to get enough royal flesh from Arcadia."

The new information provoked the question. He just had to ask.

"Were they having an affair?"

Ikaria shrugged through Damaris. "Usually that's what people do when they are visiting each other's chambers, my prince. After all, Queen Elyathi did seem quite lovely through the eyes of Damaris. I would do her if I were a man."

Derek let out a loud burst of air in disgust at the response. His father and Queen Elyathi. Derek had a hard time swallowing that one. Was Ikaria lying? But even so, his father had never spoken of what happened. And then there was the fact that they were not invited to the Queen's funeral.

"Are you sure? It seems out of character for my father," Derek said, hesitant to believe it.

"Quite sure."

It made sense, but he didn't want to admit it to himself. His father always seemed so in love with his mother, but he did live a very private life as much as he could.

"All these years of not knowing what happened. I suppose that is why we were never invited back to Arcadia again…" Derek trailed off, completed stupefied by the new information. Derek's gaze shifted to Ikaria, meeting the soul within Damaris's eyes. "Looks like Damaris is 'feeling better.' Finally got his body moving, did you?"

"I can't have the King be a complete vegetable. After all, I do need to ensure that you ascend the throne."

Derek paused. "Why?" Derek eyed Damaris's body suspiciously, curious for her response. "Why do *you* care who ascends Arcadia's throne?"

"I already told you why."

"Yes, but all of this over a vial of blood?"

"Don't forget the army of cyborgs."

"Yes, that too. But why go through all the trouble of making me king?" Derek brushed the back of his neck. "Don't misunderstand me, I do with all of my heart want to marry the princess and see Damaris step aside."

"Well, I do too, lover boy," Damaris stated wryly, cracking a smile. "Let's just say for both of our sakes, you need to ascend Arcadia's throne."

Derek wasn't satisfied with that answer but decided not to press further on the subject. The sorceress was evading his questions, not giving him full answers. Regardless, her objectives benefited him, and who was he to complain? But the other purple-gifted...

Damaris's body turned to Derek, eyeing him with Ikaria's movements. "I feel your mind. What is it? You found something."

"Were you involved with the attempt to capture the princess?"

Ikaria laughed through Damaris's body. "No. Why would you even think that?"

"For one, you want her blood."

"That is why I have you. You are going to get it for me."

"And two, there were reports of a mysterious person on the scene. A *gifted* with purple magic."

Suddenly, Damaris's legs were no longer crossed, and his body was seated at full attention. "Really?"

"Yes. Purple lightning. It fried the cyborg that was tracking Emerald. Do you know anything about that?"

Damaris's face remained frozen in thought. "Interesting. Purple lightning, you say?" Damaris's body got up, walking in thought, then his face turned dark. "Damn the High Court! Just as I was one step ahead of them!"

"You think the court in your time is involved?"

"Of course they are! I told you they are after your princess's blood! The High Court in my time is working probably with this gifted to get the blood for themselves. This violet-gifted has to be from this time, with the abilities to use their adjacent color. Or perhaps…" Damaris's eyes narrowed in the same motion that Derek had seen the sorceress do. "Perhaps this gifted has consumed other gifteds' blood. Damn them all to *hell*! This is much worse than I thought. I must get that blood, and quickly!"

"What if that gifted was helping the princess? I was told the magic overcame the cyborg. If the cyborg was after the princess, what if the gifted interfered, allowing her to escape?" Derek had a feeling it was that, and not what Ikaria thought about the High Court.

"Either way, I can't take any chances. I *need* that blood."

"It's impossible without Emerald," Derek said, stating the obvious.

Suddenly, a twang of guilt came over him. Just the mere thought of him retrieving Emerald's blood for the sorceress made him feel sick. And wrong. But Ikaria had gotten him this far in overcoming Damaris's rejection. What was just a drop of blood in relation to making everything right with Arcadia?

"I'll force the Inner Council to send another deployment of that special cyborg. We need to find her, and soon. For both our sakes."

"I hope so."

"Don't worry, my prince. We will find her. You can count on that."

The man Emerald was with came into Derek's mind once again. With that image came a wave of crushing pain in his chest, causing him to clench his doublet.

Damaris looked at Derek, taking another drink of wine, noticing. "You are bothered."

"Yes, I am damn bothered! Emerald escaped the city with another man."

Ikaria gave Derek a smug look. "I told you that you would be needing the circlet."

"You… you saw him when you saw the future? That man?"

"No. But I did see him through your eyes when you watched the video. Over and over again." Damaris rested his head in the back of the padded throne, kicking up his feet on the table. "A man with white hair. I don't blame her. He has a sort of… *ferocity* to him, don't you agree?" Ikaria laughed, touching Damaris's body coyly.

"Whose side are you on?"

"I'm merely keeping an open mind."

"I'm done with you and this conversation," Derek said, angrily tossing his cape over his shoulder. "Don't you have someone in *your* time that you can harass?"

"Plenty. But you are by far my favorite."

"Wonderful."

Ikaria laughed once again. "Lighten up, my prince. You just need a good hard romp with your princess to relieve some tension. We'll just have to let your balls turn blue a little while longer."

Derek angrily turned to her. "How dare you speak to me in such a manner! What kind of court enchantress are you, anyway? Have you no propriety?"

"None whatsoever."

Annoyed, Derek stormed off, making his way out of the hall. He wanted to completely avoid seeing Ikaria's wicked smile. It was particularly vexing on Damaris's face, combining the two people who annoyed him most.

CHAPTER 33

❖━━━━━━━━━❖

GREEN

Kyle drove in sheer darkness, his headlight piercing through the endless black void, as Emerald held on for dear life. There were no street lights, no buildings, no nothing out in the wastelands. Only the stars to guide them and the white light from the pale crescent moon.

Every so often, Emerald thought she saw an outline of a sand dune or an eroded building eclipsing in the moonlight. She wasn't sure if she imagined it, but one thing was for certain—the scenery never changed. The same endless void of black outlines of rolling hills, shrubs, and decayed structures. It was endless. Emerald had never realized how vast the wastelands were.

So lonely, she thought. *How can anyone live out here?*

Almost two hours had passed since the fateful chase with the authorities. Emerald's body was completely iced from the chilly winds. Her teeth chattered violently, and her weakened arms wobbled, tired from holding on to Kyle's waist. She didn't know how much longer she could manage.

She mustered up what strength she had left and gripped Kyle firmly again, biting her lip while trying to hold back thoughts of how cold she was.

Kyle must have realized that she was getting tired because he yelled out, "Hold on! It's not that much farther!"

"Kyle, please hurry," she said faintly, though she knew he couldn't hear her.

Emerald redoubled her efforts, bracing herself again Kyle. Taking a deep breath, she closed her eyes to block out the burning pain and numbing sensation of her muscles.

The two of them had not stopped since the chase. Emerald had no idea where in the wastelands Kyle was driving to, but she knew they couldn't drive that much farther without more gasoline. Luckily, whoever the woman was who'd unleashed her violet magic on the police stalled the authorities, giving her and Kyle enough of a head start. With the amount of damage that was inflicted, it would take the authorities at least an hour or two to regroup. Most of their vehicles were beyond repair.

Who was that gifted woman? What was she doing at the club? Did she know who I was? Why did she help us? Her thoughts shifted to the bionic man. He was a lot like the cyborgs she'd seen in the lower levels, but this one had orange magic. Questions kept pounding through Emerald's mind, the same questions mixed with new questions.

That cyborg had to somehow be under her father's direction, that she was sure of. Why else would it be after them?

Recalling the orange and violet magic, the feeling that came from it was unlike anything she had ever experienced. Through the magic, she'd sensed the other caster's emotions. A jealous pain seeping from the violet waves, while ecstasy flowed from the orange. It was the first time she had encountered another person's magic. It was almost intrusive and invasive. Emerald contemplated if the other gifted could feel hers as well.

The real question she refused to ask herself was what Kyle thought of her magic. He had somehow figured out that she was the princess of Arcadia, and it didn't seem to bother him. But what of her power?

"We're almost there!" Kyle yelled. "It's right over those hills!"

Emerald opened her eyes, looking out into the vast darkness.

Nothing had changed. It was the same endless outlines of black dunes eclipsed with pale light.

With an abrupt jerk, Kyle turned off the main road. The road became very rocky, and the motorcycle shuddered as it slowed its course on the dirt path.

In the headlight was a large boulder, and Kyle pulled over, parking behind it. Kyle got off the bike, then turned to Emerald, helping her off. She could no longer feel her legs and arms, and her entire body felt weak and light.

Kyle whipped off his jacket and threw it around her shoulders, then held her close to his body.

"Sorry I couldn't get you the jacket earlier," he said. "I didn't want to chance stopping."

Somehow, Emerald managed a smile from her numb face. "There is no need to apologize. I don't know how you managed to drive through all of Arcadia the way you did, and we somehow made it out alive. I must admit, I was frightened the whole way."

"You were scared?"

"Of course I was scared! Weren't you?"

"Only when you pulled that stunt off the building. I really thought I was going to die," he answered, chuckling. Emerald felt Kyle put his hand down the jacket's pocket, rummaging for a cigarette. "You scared me shitless." He found his cigarettes and lit one. The orange spark lit up his face, burning as he took a drag. "After that, I knew we would make it out safe with your magic."

"I'm not sure that we would have made it out of Arcadia without that violet woman's power," Emerald confessed.

"I don't believe that for a second." Kyle leaned in to her, and she saw the outlines of his reassuring expression. "You are just as powerful as that other woman, and much more determined." He took another drag, holding her closely, then softly brushed his ringed fingers against her green hair. He gently turned her head toward hers, his face now fully illuminated in the moonlight. "I put my trust in you and your abilities to get us out of there, regardless of that other woman's influence. I knew you could do it the moment I saw your power." He kissed her, gently stroking her face as the wind tried to intervene. "I think you should do the same," he whispered.

"You… you are okay with my magic? You are not the least bit alarmed by it?"

"Me? Alarmed?" Kyle asked. "I've seen worse." He laughed, pulling her into his chest, holding her for a moment. "Besides, Em, I think it's pretty badass that you have magic."

"You do?"

"Well, yeah. But remind me not to piss you off. I'd hate to be on the receiving end."

Emerald chuckled, nudging Kyle. "That would never happen!"

"I hope not!" Kyle took a drag, lighting up the darkness for a brief second. "All joking aside, it's no wonder why your father never let you leave the palace. With power like that, people would be shitting themselves. Half of Arcadia is being put through the shredder, so between the magic flying and the authorities chasing us, the city probably has one giant crap in their pants. Wonder how they're gonna spin that one on the nightly broadcasts."

"Lovely," Emerald remarked while smiling with relief. She turned very serious, facing him directly. "Kyle, I was so… worried about what you would think about my true self. I wanted to tell you ever since the night we…"

"Fucked?"

"Yes… that."

"You should have. You could have unleashed your power on me. We could have kept going all night…" Kyle paused, looking up at the sky with mock longing. "God, just thinking about that is making me hard."

She punched him lightly. "I'm being serious. Besides, it doesn't work like that."

"Damn. Well, it should. Maybe you could try?"

"Kyle!" Emerald gave him a hard shove.

"You're right." He paused, stopping her for a moment. "I told you earlier that it doesn't change a damn thing about how I feel about you. Princess, magic… hell, you could be a she-demon and I would still feel the same."

"Don't be ridiculous."

Kyle pulled her in, putting both his arms around her shoulders, the tip of his icy nose brushing hers. "Em, now it's my turn to be serious. I've never met anyone like you before. It's like you feel so… *familiar* to me. Like I've known you forever."

Emerald's heart quickened, then a warm feeling came over her. She knew exactly what he meant, because she felt the same.

Kyle paused, waiting to see her reaction. "It's crazy, I know."

"It's not crazy. It's the same feeling I get too," Emerald whispered in the wind, just slightly louder than the air itself. Her heart continued to race through her chest while her mind flooded with excitement.

Kyle tenderly ran his hands down her cheeks, then brushed his lips against hers, kissing her, and she melted in his arms. The way he held her reaffirmed an underlying love for her, stirring her response. She felt connected to him; her soul and life force were linked to his.

After their embrace, he gently put his arm around her waist and began guiding her once again through the endless desert.

"By the way, where are we going?" Emerald asked, trying to make out any recognizable shapes in the night.

"My old home," he said, holding her close.

As they continued to walk down the rocky path, Emerald's muscles shook from the strain of the bike ride and her extreme hunger. She needed food and sleep.

Kyle noticed her shaky arms. "I can carry you if you want. I promise I won't drop you," he joked.

Emerald shook her head and laughed weakly. "It's really okay. If I made it this far, I think I can manage the rest of the way."

Kyle suddenly swooped her up into his arms, and she let out a small surprised yelp. "Don't be stubborn. After all, you are a princess," he managed to say through half-smiling pursed lips still gripping his cigarette.

Emerald rested her head against his chest, feeling the heat permeating from his body. "You are so persuasive," she teased.

"Princess Emerald. I'm gonna have to get used to that."

"Kyle, there is no need for formalities. After all, you met me just as Em."

"Em… Emerald." Kyle smiled. "I like it. Pretty, like you."

Emerald heard a loud click.

"Don't you think about taking another step," said a man's voice. Emerald sensed a body next to them. "Put your hands up," he ordered.

Emerald complied while Kyle lowered her to her feet and did the same. Emerald dared not move, her heart racing, afraid that she was either going to get shot or arrested and sent back to Arcadia. She was too tired and too weak to fight.

"Shit, Ryan, knock it off, will ya?" Kyle cursed, his hands still raised. "It's Kyle!"

"Kyle?" the man's voice repeated. Emerald heard Ryan lower his weapon, then laugh. "Shit! What the hell, man! Never thought I'd see your face again."

The two of them hit knuckles, a strange greeting that Emerald found curious. Ryan gestured for them to follow him, slinging his gun over his shoulder, then turned on a flashlight.

"I was never planning on coming back. But plans change," Kyle said while Emerald trailed behind them. In the distance, Emerald noticed what looked like bonfires, casting their light on a few dwellings and tents.

"Yeah? What plans are those? Big *city* wasn't what you thought?" Ryan laughed.

"Nothing like that." Kyle turned to Emerald, nodding his head toward her. "She's in trouble."

"Really?" The man paused and stared her down, curious. Emerald blushed, but she was sure that no one noticed, as the light from the camp barely illuminated them as they approached. "What kind of trouble?"

"Oh, you know, all of Arcadia, including the King and some crazy ass bionic man is out looking for her," Kyle replied dryly. "Typical day for me."

Ryan took a step forward, eyeing Emerald. "And who might you be?" He shined his flashlight directly on her, then sucked in his breath as he noticed her hair. "*Ho-lee* shit."

He yanked Kyle away from her, pulling him aside and whispering fiercely. Emerald couldn't hear the exchange, but she heard sharp words clashing back and forth, and the phrase "only for one night" from Kyle's mouth.

After several moments, Kyle returned to Emerald, then guided her, following Ryan to the camp.

"What was that all about?" Emerald asked, looking at Ryan.

"Let's just say that they don't like outsiders," Kyle answered casually, not affected by the exchange.

As the two of them reached the outskirts of the camp, Emerald could see a few people standing guard with their guns drawn. Ryan waved to them, and the guns lowered, allowing them to pass.

Inside the camp were beautifully decorated tents in a variety of colors and patterns, easily noticed even with only minimal light from the bonfires. Scattered within the tents were metal trailers and a few stone dwellings.

There were already people hanging out by the bonfire, laughing and drinking. As Ryan, Kyle, and Emerald approached, the wasteland dwellers stopped what they were doing, trying to get a glimpse of the newcomers. There were several whispers, causing heads to appear out of the tent flaps, and faces pressing up against the glass of their trailer windows.

The group began to gather before the main bonfire, and Emerald noticed that the people that came out to see what was happening were mostly women. There were a few sturdy-looking men and some children.

"Kyle!" Emerald heard a man's voice call out from behind. She turned, the wind whipping her deep-green hair in her face. Pushing her ponytailed locks aside, Emerald saw a thin, tall man with dark skin and long black dreadlocks. He was older, his skin weathered along with some gray sprinkled through his locks. He was wearing a long tattered red tunic with an intricate pattern; it billowed in the wind.

"Victor?" Kyle said, pulling Emerald's arm to move closer to him.

Victor shook Kyle's hand, then they shared a big, one-armed hug. Emerald watched the exchange, and his dark eyes noticed her immediately. He stopped, then bowed, falling to his knees.

"Princess," he said, addressing her formally. There were loud whispers within the camp, and suddenly everyone was on their knees.

Emerald whipped around wildly, feeling panicked. "No, no, please."

Everyone eyed her, including Victor. He cracked a light smile, then nodded his head, rising to his feet. The crowd followed suit.

"What brings the princess of Arcadia out to the wastelands?" Victor asked, waving at the crowd to disperse.

"Victor," Kyle said, "there's some troubling shit happening, and she needs to get as far as humanly possible from Arcadia."

Victor nodded at her in acknowledgment, then turned to Kyle. "Indeed, there is."

"What? How do you know? Was Arcadia's broadcast live?"

Victor waved to Ryan, urging him to come closer. He turned to Kyle, then said, "I'll have Ryan show you to your old trailer and have food brought up. Go rest and eat. We'll talk in the morning."

"Thanks. I'm pretty sure I know the way to the trailer."

The cheer on Victor's face faltered, then he composed himself. "Kyle, much has changed since you were last here."

CHAPTER 34

ORANGE

Colors appeared out of the blackness as images slowly morphed from fuzzy blurs to clear outlines. They made shapes, shapes in the image of a public restroom, all colored in shades of blue and orange. His body swayed back and forth. He was unable to get ahold of himself, as he was beyond inebriated.

Drew swung his head back sloppily, relieving himself in the urinal in front of him. After emptying his bladder, he clumsily zipped up his suit pants and fixed his collared shirt. He washed his hands and looked in the shiny mirror before him, gazing at his crooked black glasses through his drunken eyes. He fixed them, then took one last look at his appearance before stumbling out of the bathroom.

Spread out before Drew was a large party, filled with his fellow corporate associate scientists, directors, and other wealthy businesspeople. Air transports flew above the glass ceiling, capturing the night scene of the city. The party guests paid no attention to the aerial landscape. Most were mingling and laughing with the other scientists, drinking and eating food from party platters. It was the first time that Drew had heard some of them laugh. Everyone in the lab worked long hours, and they were all much too serious about their work. Including him.

Drew hadn't even wanted to go to the party. He had always been a loner, and he didn't seem to connect with anyone at work. He preferred his research over a simple party. It was much more exciting than a person. What he was working on would change the face of Arcadia forever. It was groundbreaking, something that would give people hope where there had been none before, and that satisfied Drew more than any party. But she'd convinced him. Between Gwen and work, they never had fun anymore, and she'd insisted that they needed to get out and at socialize like normal people every once in a while.

Who is she? She… she…

Malfunction.

Glitch.

"Looks like I need to call an air taxi. That's a first," she said, laughing. Drew looked at the blurry face in front of him. Everything was in precise detail except her face. It remained fuzzy, nothing more than a blur. "Are you ready to go?"

Drew nodded. "Yes. I think I will be sick soon if we stay any longer," he answered. It was not far from the truth. He hardly ever drank, and now it was catching up to him.

"Okay. Let me say goodbye to a few people, and I'll call the transport service," the woman's voice said. She laughed again. "It is something else seeing you like this. It's funny, really. You are so… sloppy," she remarked, chuckling.

"And so horny." He leaned in to her, grabbing her by the waist, kissing her ear.

"Drew! Not here! Do you want people to find out about us?"

"I don't care what other people think," he whispered in her ear. Her hair had the light scent of flowers, her perfume radiating around her neckline. "Let the world know how I feel!"

"If people find out, they might terminate one of us," she hissed at him. "Do you really want that to happen? Especially after all our hard work?"

He sighed. "No. You're right." He gave her a devious smile, dropping his hands from her waist.

She playfully shoved him away with her purse, then walked away to her other colleagues to say her goodbyes. She returned shortly, dialing the transport service on her communicator.

"Yes, hi, I'd like to request a pick up from Platform 1281…"

The voice of the woman was drowned out as the world spun around Drew.

White noise.

Static.

"Looks like they are ready for us," the woman said as she ended the transmission, fixing her jacket.

Stepping outside, both of them waited for the transport. The lights were vibrant. More so than any other night that he could recall.

The taxi transport pulled up, and the back door opened for them to step inside. They seated themselves in the back end of the vehicle, then the door shut. Drew snatched the woman, reeling her into his arms, kissing her.

"You just couldn't wait, could you?" She giggled, playfully returning his kisses.

There was a loud cough from the front of the transport, breaking the private conversation. "Where to?" the taxi driver asked.

The woman pulled away from him, embarrassed.

"Platform 683-A, please," Drew said, pulling her back toward him, kissing her again.

"Sure thing, let me pull up the coordinates. We'll be off in a sec."

The engines sounded from the transport, and Drew felt them lift off. He paid no attention to the landscape outside the window; his drunkenness really had made him horny.

He felt her shy touch against his leg as they kissed again, and he smiled under their wet kisses. He hoped she was in the mood for some action when they got home.

With a sudden violent force, there was a loud blast from the engine. He felt the weightlessness inside of the transport for a second before his heart dropped into his stomach. The woman was yanked away from him, terrified. The driver was furiously yelling over his communicator, navigating the steering wheel while pushing multiple buttons, but it was no use. They were heading straight toward the ground.

A hard crash rocked his body, and he tried to make sense of the disaster around him. Screams from the woman. Shouts for help from the transport driver. Smoke. Lots of smoke. More screams. Fires. Orange flames engulfing him.

He couldn't move. His right side was lodged in metal, and his body was broken. The heat of the fires incinerated him, melting his flesh as he screamed. Oh God, the heat...

"Drew! Oh my God, oh God... Drew!" she screamed.

Blackness.

His eyes jolted open.

No fires. No screams. Just a constant hum.

He must have been dreaming.

Do machines dream?

He sensed vibrations now.

Malfunction.

Keys typing.

Through the tangle of wires and machines, Drew saw the lab technician Telly glance at him. She was crouched over one of the machines, typing in code while plugging in several devices.

"You okay? What is it?" Telly asked in a soothing voice. She walked over and sat next to him on a stool. There were other members of Telly's team working in the room, several of them working on his circuitry while others sat on their computers, typing away.

No sound came out of his mouth.

Telly rested her hand on his shoulder. "Sorry, Drew. I'm still working on that voice box prototype, but we were held back due to the damage to your circuitry. Fixing that is a priority now." She held up a small flat screen from her lap. The screen had a long, thin cable that connected to the back of his head. "But in the meantime, we have this. Just talk with your mind. My tablet will translate it to text."

Drew nodded, awaiting an order or question.

"What happened to you out there?" Telly asked. Drew saw the team pause for a moment, glancing in their direction curiously.

"I was locked on the target. I had her in my grasp," replied Drew through the tablet.

"How did your circuitry go into overload? The authorities reported that there was purple lightning. Is that true? Did you see purple lightning?"

"Violet, 410 nanometers. Mixed with multiple wavelengths of the spectrum."

Telly sighed. "What are you talking about?"

"The source had multiple frequencies... Able to emit different photon energies."

He remembered seeing the frequencies within the light. It had all the frequencies except one—orange. But the red was not as powerful as the others.

Telly shook her head, confused. "Did this violet lightning cause your system to fail? What happened?"

"I had the target in my possession, but a man interfered with my mission, causing me to release the target, not by choice. I engaged both persons. After that, violet lightning."

"Then?" Telly asked eagerly.

"I continued to pursue the target and the unknown man until the border of Arcadia. I was overcome by a force, which caused me to go off course and crash."

"Force?"

"Affirmative. 410 nanometers."

"Drew, did you see the cause of this lightning? This force?"

"No." His body suddenly shook violently, an electrical current shooting through his body, then stopped. *"I did not see the source."*

"Telly," Robert called out from behind his platform, putting down his tools on a metal tray.

"What?"

"We replaced about thirty-eight percent of his wiring and circuitry. The transfusion is in place, and we restored his main transistors. I think before we replace the remainder of the shorted parts, he needs to rest and let his body recharge with the injected blood."

"Agreed. But all of you must stay on site. I have to report to Director Santiago in twelve hours' time, and I need everyone on standby in case something happens."

"Yes, ma'am," Robert replied. "We have our communicators. Page if you need us. Michael is right outside."

"Thank you."

"What's that? Did I just hear a thank-you from you?" Robert joked.

"Yes, you did. Although I just might take it back if you continue to stand behind me and annoy the hell out of me."

"Good night to you too." Robert chuckled, then walked out of the lab.

Drew watched as Telly waited for Robert and the others to leave the room, then closed the door behind them. Darkness settled in his room, and the familiar bluish light from the observation window appeared. Occasionally, hints of color from the machinery lit up sporadically.

Telly put down the communication tablet on the platform he was plugged into, then walked over to him, staring. Gently touching his hand, she then guiding his hand to the curve of her waist.

Drew continued to look at her, his eyes glowing.

What is she doing?

Her hands traveled across his body, exploring the flesh infused with machinery. She then placed his mechanical hand behind her, then buried her head in his exposed chest.

Drew froze, unaware of what he should do. He needed instruction.

Reaching for his face, Telly touched it softly, keeping her eyes steady on where the fingers were heading.

She continued to move her hands, first to his flesh, then to his mechanical side, watching him as he remained inanimate. After three minutes of contact, she paused in front of him, her eyes firmly studying his.

"Drew… do you remember?" she asked him quietly.

"Remember what?"

Picking up the tablet, she saw the words across the screen, then shot him a look. "Us."

"Negative."

"Do you have any memories at all?"

"Fragments. I cannot distinguish between reality, memories, or my programming."

"Are you able to recall any of them?"

"They disappear two minutes after I awake."

"Then you do dream?"

"Yes."

"Can you tell me about them?"

"I cannot recall any except one."

"Tell me."

"I see a green jewel. I need to replicate the jewel. One hundred times. I cannot replicate the jewel. Because of my failure, I am enslaved to the darkness."

There was a long pause, then her eyes widened.

"What does it mean?"

Cannot compute.

Drew began to shake violently, causing his processor to overclock. Orange light flashed from his cybernetic eye, pushing him to the brink of overload.

Access denied.

Telly laid a hand on him while she adjusted some of the exposed wiring.

Whatever she did, it calmed him. Slowly touching him, her eyes met his.

"Do you feel anything when I touch you?"

Was she trying to confuse him somehow? *Yes. I feel your hand on my face.*

"I meant inside. Did you feel any emotion of any kind?"

Did he? Should he have? It was too much to use his brain processor. *Negative.*

"You must have felt something," she protested.

"Nothing."

Telly began to shed tears, a human response for crying. It seemed familiar, but he couldn't understand why.

"I just want you back," she whispered, rubbing her fingers under her glasses.

"That does not compute."

"Of course it doesn't!" Telly snapped. She threw the tablet across the room, the cord yanking itself out of the back of his neck. As it did so, it caused his neck to whiplash, jerking from the force. "Why should it?" she yelled. "After all, you're mostly machine now!"

Drew looked at her, cocking his head, trying to decipher the situation. He didn't understand why she was reacting the way she was.

Telly slumped to the floor, and Drew could no longer see her. Breathy sobs echoed in the chamber, coming from her direction.

Across the room, the cracked tablet glowed white with his words still on the screen. Why did she throw the device?

***

It needs to be done. She is clearly unstable. I'll be damned if she gets the whole team fired for her outburst. The director needs to know about her behavior.

Michael waited.

Telly came bursting out of Drew's room, then slammed the door button behind her.

"Rough day?" Michael asked from above his computer screen.

She gritted her teeth, then walked furiously out of the lab, the sounds of her feet getting faint.

When he heard no more of her, Michael peeked out of the lab and down the hall.

No one was there. There was no sound coming from the dorm room, and it was closed. All was quiet.

They must still be napping.

Michael quickly bolted to the elevators, then swiped his key card, stepping inside. The glass elevator ascended, giving him a view of the city. The morning sun approached, reminding him of another night of sleep lost.

It was more than apparent now that Telly had an unhealthy attachment to Drew, one that no scientist should ever have to their experiments. Michael had heard her mutter things to Drew over the weeks leading up to the resurrection, things that only girlfriends or wives would say to their significant other. But now, it seemed, her attachment to Drew had escalated even further. It was one thing if she was a bit overprotective about Drew since she worked on him, it was certainly another thing for her to try to advance on him. What was she *thinking*? Was she trying to get romantically involved with company property? With *experiments*? This whole situation proved that he should have been in charge of Lab 34. After all, he had been with the corporation much longer than Telly, and he was long overdue for a promotion. But no, she had to come in and take *his* position. Perhaps after reporting to the director about what he had just witnessed, things would finally change.

The elevator came to its destination, opening its doors to a large outside platform. Immediately, Michael was greeted by one of the corporate guards.

"ID."

Michael flashed his card, and the guard scanned it.

"Clear."

He walked past the guard, then waited in the designated spot for the company transport. He watched as a transport landed for the person in front of him, then waited his turn for the next one to arrive. It only took several minutes.

"Where to?" the driver asked as Michael entered and seated himself on a plush blue seat.

"Corporate level."

"What platform?"

"The director's platform."

"What number is that?" asked the driver.

"I don't know," Michael barked impatiently.

"Okay, hold on. Let me search my database," replied the driver.

"Yes, you do that." Michael rolled his eyes. People who drove transports were complete morons. The driver worked for the company, for Pete's sake; it was his job to know the name of the platforms and where they were located.

"Found it. Platform 2862."

Michael pulled out his communication device, speaking into it. "Dial Director Jonathan."

"*Unable to connect. The director's line is busy,*" replied the computer voice.

"Well, then, dial Director Santiago!" he shouted into the device. He watched as the transport took off, hovering over the grand city, the neon lights competing with the morning sun.

"*Accepted. Now dialing…*"

CHAPTER 35

Familiar sounds from the camp surrounded Kyle, ones that he hadn't heard in years. Children playing and chasing each other while their mothers worked their given chores. Some of the women were huddled in groups as they labored, gossiping about the latest rumors. Others sat alone, singing in the wind. There were men's voices too, but not nearly as many as the women. Surely there had to be more men in the camp. Where the hell were they?

The morning air was brisk, but it was nothing compared to freezing his balls off last night with the authorities chasing his ass. He felt terrible for Emerald, as she had been like a block of ice when they finally arrived in the wastelands.

Kyle finished grabbing some supplies from the commune dwelling. Fresh clothes, dried food, water canteens. All he needed was gas for his bike, and they would be set to cross the wastelands. It wasn't too much farther to Illumina. Once they made it there, Emerald would be safe. Even Kyle knew that the king of Illumina didn't give a shit about the king of Arcadia. He was a bit of a wild card and a nuisance, definitely Kyle's kind of king. He decided if they left the camp at nightfall, it would give them more of a chance of not being spotted on their way.

"Never thought I'd see your sorry ass back here," a familiar voice called out as he was filling the canteens at the water basin.

Kyle turned and saw Garrett. His old best friend hadn't changed much. Same black hair in a faux hawk, same dark eyes, and deep-ebony skin inked with a pattern that mimicked a circuit board on his face.

"Yeah, well, I missed eating dust for breakfast."

"Smart ass." Garrett crouched next to Kyle as he continued to fill the second canteen. "How've you been, man? Besides being on the run from the king himself." Garrett took a drink from his flask, then held it up to salute him. "That, my man, takes some serious balls."

Kyle finished filling the canteen, then snatched the flask from Garrett, taking a swig. The burning liquid felt energizing. "Thanks for asking. I'm doing pretty well, considering all the shit that hit the fan. By the way, thanks for that ID. Came in handy."

"It's no wonder you needed one. Shit. Princess Emerald, huh? Next time you get me involved in one of your schemes, at least tell me who I'm risking my ass for." Garrett laughed, retrieving his flask and taking a drink. "I heard that you had an encounter with a cyborg."

"The crazy ass tried to kill me and kidnap Em."

"Em?" Garrett raised an eyebrow.

"Yeah, Em. You know, Princess Emerald," Kyle said impatiently.

Garrett cracked a smile. "Pet name?"

"Whatever. Forget it." Kyle snatched the flask out of Garrett's hand, guzzling it.

"Well, I have something to show you. It might explain a lot," Garrett said, getting up.

"I have to stop and see Victor first. He said he'd talk to me this morning," Kyle said, lighting a cigarette.

"Don't worry. Victor's already there waiting for us."

Kyle followed Garrett, smoking his cigarette. There had been improvements and changes that happened over the years, but there were still hardly any signs of the men.

"So what's the story with the camp? Where the hell is everyone?" Kyle asked casually.

"Gone."

Kyle exhaled, continuing to study the camp as they zigzagged their way through the colorful tents. "They got smart too, huh?"

"I'll let Victor explain."

"Why you got to be all cryptic and shit?"

"Just hold your ass a little bit longer."

Garrett led Kyle to one of the larger trailers in the camp. Kyle smiled, shaking his head at the contraption.

Good old cyber-drifters. They can't get enough of that techy shit.

Wires were strung out of the tinfoil-covered windows, all connecting to a satellite resting on top of the roof. As Kyle stepped inside, he saw the floor and walls were covered in wires that ran through multiple computers, screens, and keyboards, creating one giant machine. The room itself was in sheer blackness except for the bright colors flashing from the monitors and keyboards. In between all the wires and monitors were stacks of papers, trash, food wrappers, and empty soda cans.

Kyle noticed Victor seated in front of one of the monitors, his chair turned toward Kyle.

"What's with all of this? Why bring me here?" Kyle motioned around with his chin, looking around. Computers bored him to tears. Give him an engine over a computer any day. "Does this have to do with that cyborg?" Kyle turned to face Victor. "I'm sure you heard about it if Garrett already knew."

"That is why I brought you here to talk." Victor motioned for Kyle to have a seat. Kyle obliged, lighting up another cigarette.

"There's no smoking in here," Garrett said.

Annoyed, Kyle exhaled, then rubbed it into the floor, tossed the butt out the door, and seated himself again.

"Victor, what the hell is going on?" Kyle demanded. "Where is everyone? Ryan freaked the hell out last night about Em entering camp, and Garrett just told me that some of the men are gone."

"Kyle, much has changed since you left."

"So everyone keeps telling me," Kyle muttered.

"Most of the men have been arrested."

Kyle shot up. "What? Why? Under whose jurisdiction?"

"Arcadia's," Victor answered calmly. Garrett's eyes darted in his direction, then he turned away to type on the computer.

"On what charge?"

"Violation of Arcadia's Ordinance 1-969."

Rage pumped through Kyle's chest. "And what the hell is that?"

Garrett was still typing on his computer. "A new law that went into effect sometime after you left. It allows the authorities to arrest anyone found in Arcadia's desert territories."

"The fuck is that shit?" Kyle snarled, slamming his hand on the table where the keyboards rested. Garret eyed him, warning him to be careful.

"It happened infrequently during our usual supply runs," Victor said. "Then it started happening more often. At first we thought the men had just decided to abandon the camp. After several runs, we learned the truth."

Kyle's gaze looked at the floor, staring blankly. "If the men went missing, then how did you find out?"

"Because Zayan made it back unseen several years back."

Kyle turned back to face Victor. "Several *years*? You mean to tell me that you've been sitting here for *years*, letting this shit happen and not doing a damn thing about it?"

"Would you calm the fuck down and listen to Victor before running your mouth?" Garrett barked. "What do you think we've been doing this whole time?" Garrett typed at the computer, and two of the screens overhead changed.

"What's this? What am I looking at?" Kyle asked. The monitors streamed unfamiliar code, like a foreign language. "Does this have to do with the missing men?"

"It has everything to do with our missing men. And that cyborg that you encountered," Victor stated, urging Garrett to continue. Garrett began to type again, more screens pulling up different pictures. Some of the faces Kyle recognized. Faces of men he knew growing up. Most of them his age.

"Weeks ago, I finally cracked the code and was able to hack into Arcadia's authorities' mainframe. I was able to look at the case files of our camp's men," Garrett said. "One by one, I discovered that the men were being transferred to a place called Lab 34 immediately after being incarcerated."

"What is Lab 34?" Kyle asked. He hovered over Garrett's shoulder, staring at the computer, as if staring would help him understand what the hell was going on. It was all gibberish to him, and it was pissing him off. "And what the hell is all this?"

"These are the hacked files of Lab 34." Garrett stopped typing, looking over to Victor.

Victor sighed, his weary eyes looking tired. "Our men are being experimented on. The King's corporation is turning them into cyborgs. He's creating an army."

Kyle stared at the screens, dumbfounded. He wanted to punch somebody or something. His people were being experimented on? And to think he saw them first hand down in the lower levels during the riots, gunning people down.

The fuck is wrong with the king of Arcadia? Did Em know of these experiments? Is that why she ran away?

Thinking of Emerald suddenly made his gut twist. He hoped that she knew nothing of this, otherwise he wouldn't know what to think of her.

Kyle stood up and flexed in anger, clenching his jaw. He fumed, fighting a violent urge to punch the computer. Garret noticed his reaction, saying, "Please don't hurt my equipment. I just replaced it recently."

Getting into Victor's face, Kyle snarled, "So what are you planning to do about this, Victor?"

Victor remained calm and collected, ignoring Kyle's demeanor. "I am sure that you have noticed that these things are more powerful than your average robots," he answered.

"Kyle, all of the cyborgs have been infused with special blood," Garrett added. "Some kind of magical blood."

Kyle's gut twisted, spiraling into a bottomless pit. He felt sick. Really sick. If it was the King's corporation experimenting on the wasteland wanderers, then it had to mean that the magical blood had come directly from Emerald. *That* was why she was being chased. She was at the center of the experimentation.

Then Kyle remembered when Emerald had drawn that picture of herself in the band's warehouse. Her, at the center of the wires, connected to machinery.

She knew. She had to.

Garrett pulled up another picture. It was the face of a man in his late forties, shaved head and glasses. It was the cyborg that chased them through Arcadia.

"I recognize him," Kyle said angrily. "Who is he?"

"His name is Andrew Napoli. At least, that was his name before he was resurrected as a cyborg. Goes by Drew now. Apparently he was the only cyborg to develop his own magical properties from the blood sample."

His gut continued to churn while his blood boiled. "Garrett, does it say who the blood donor was?"

Garret shook his head. "No, I can't find anything on it."

"Dammit!" Kyle cursed, running his hands through his hair. His head was spinning, filled with animosity for the king of Arcadia. And now Emerald was involved with this shit too.

Victor raised an eyebrow, cautiously choosing his words before he spoke. Everyone in the camp that knew him understood how much of a hothead he was. "Kyle, you understand that you cannot stay here in the camp longer than another night, right? Everyone is shaken that the princess is in the camp. With the King out searching for his daughter, and our people being experimented on, we can't let you stay here. Not with her, as much as we would love to aid her escape from Damaris. The King is a dangerous man."

Kyle slammed his hand down on the table. "Well, no shit!" He calmed himself somewhat. "Don't worry about it. I was planning to leave at nightfall."

Victor rose, his face serious. "Why was the princess running away from Damaris, exactly? Did she say?"

Kyle suddenly thought of Emerald's magic, but he knew better than to tell Victor. Even though he was pissed to the high heavens that Emerald was the cause of the experimentation, he shut his mouth. Kyle narrowed his eyes, then shrugged. "All she said was that she never left the palace and wanted out."

"I see." Victor remained silent for a few moments, then continued. "Kyle, be careful. There is no way that we can figure out how to stop these things. This technology is greater than many have ever seen, including us. That magical blood gives them what appears to be a significant cell regeneration structure. They are hard to overcome. And if all of Arcadia is looking for the princess, it is only a matter of time before they do find her."

Kyle scowled, irritated at the thought. "I just wish there was a damn thing we could do for our people." Kyle opened the door and left, lighting a cigarette. He had to think.

"Don't blame the princess," Victor called out. "She is an innocent bystander in all of this. I am sure Damaris kept these plans secret to everyone except his Inner Council."

Bullshit. Em knew. She was the damn donor.

"Whatever," Kyle said, walking away, leaving it all behind him. His mind felt messed up all over again. What the fuck was he going to do?

CHAPTER 36

Ayera felt the airship jerk as it made contact with the docking platform. From the deck, she watched the crews secure a plank between her ship to the High Court citadel's platform.

When the plank was set, Ayera quickly crossed the suspended makeshift bridge, trying not to look down at the steel gray clouds below her. A storm was brewing, probably a snow storm, as in this region, this was the time of year that the earth below would be covered in it. But the stormy clouds beneath the bridge did not affect the vivid blue sky and white glowing sun above the atmosphere.

Ayera had only visited the High Court citadel a handful of times, but each time was no less grand. The courtyard held a magnificent white sculpture of the God of Light, holding in his hand a prismatic orb to symbolize the Spectrum of Magic. There were white-marbled stairs lined with massive pillars that led directly into the floating ivory citadel. Clouds floated by in peaceful wisps. This is what Ayera imagined the God of Light's domain would be like. A pure paradise in the heavens.

Worry fluttered through her insides with each passing moment. Of all people, her sister was about to destroy the entire world. Her own *sister*.

It deeply troubled Ayera, knowing that Ikaria had stolen the gifteds' power and murdered three of them. Especially Lord Kohren. Ayera had been attached to him. He was always so attentive to her, and so kind. The only one who ever gave her any attention the last few years besides her sister.

Ayera choked back tears just thinking about Lord Kohren, gone forever in this life. How could Ikaria do such a terrible thing?

If only Ayera hadn't been named heir to the throne, Ikaria wouldn't be consumed with jealousy, craving the crown on her head and the man she loved. She'd be ruling World Sector Six with her cleverness and outsmarting the other sectors. Ayera might have been married off to another lord of the court, one with much more integrity and honor than Cyrus. Ikaria had always been the brighter one between them, completely studious in her younger years, preparing to rule when the time came. Ayera hated studying and never was good at it. She much preferred the art of dance and theatre and had no love to govern. But what she wanted didn't matter, Ayera had to do what her father ordered her to do: be the Empress of World Sector Six and marry Ikaria's fiancé.

The only time Ayera had ever fought her father was when he'd told her to marry Cyrus. Emperor Ojin had been adamant—she must marry him. Ayera knew that the High Court had already approved of the match and pushed her father to not break the pact with World Sector Three. It had been signed by all parties; Cyrus was to marry his daughter. At the time the pact was signed, a vision came to High Priest Auron of Ayera's ascent to the throne, confirmed by High Justice Tyllos of the Yellow. It had put the pact into question, since Cyrus was to marry Ikaria.

But the High Court stepped in, giving judgment in the case. Cyrus was contracted to marry into the family, but no name was specified, and the Emperor Ojin could adhere to the pact by marrying Ayera off instead.

And Ayera had absolutely no say. She had to obey. Otherwise Ikaria would be sent to World Sector Three to be under the close supervision of the high justices. And that was the one thing the Emperor Ojin did not want, as he'd whispered in secret to Ayera. Ikaria was to stay within World Sector Six's court. Ayera's father made her promise that she would do anything and everything to please the High Court and not provoke them. Ikaria would be of great use one day, her father was sure of it, and he didn't want her power handed over to another sector.

Ayera knew that Cyrus and Ikaria had already had each other sexually. It made it even more awful, since Ayera was still a virgin when they wed, knowing that Cyrus had already been active with her sister. Not only that, she was not attracted to Cyrus in the least. Ayera much preferred a man like Lord Kohren, quiet and humble, instead of an angry drunken flirt like Cyrus. He and Ikaria would have made the perfect couple. Ikaria was always angry on the inside, Cyrus was always angry on the outside. Both loved to sample the earthly desires of the flesh.

Not her. Ayera wanted to keep herself pure and do as little of her wifely duties as possible, especially with her lecherous husband. In a way, it would stave off her having an heir, and in return, her sister could have her legitimacy reinstated to the throne, since she was next in line. It was Ayera's silent way of purging the guilt from her body for her assuming the throne and marrying Cyrus, her way of apologizing without words. But now since finding out the truth about her sister's plans, there was no need for silent apologies. Everything had changed.

As Ayera started to ascend the grand steps into the citadel, a court servant dressed in red robes came to meet her. It was High Justice Belinda's servant; Ayera could tell by the color and fashions of the robe.

"Empress Ayera, we have been expecting you," he said, bowing.

"You have?" Ayera asked. She began to walk behind him as he led her the rest of the way up the steps. "How did you know I was coming?"

"I will let the High Court explain," he stated. He led her down the main hall and through the doors into the audience chamber.

This was Ayera's first time in the High Court's audience chamber. The other times she had visited the citadel was when her father was on business for their sector. Never, during her reign, had she ever had to journey to the High Court on official business. The chamber was circular, with white ivory pillars surrounding the room. Half of the room had six white thrones, equally spaced, with nothing but the giant ivory pillars and the open blue sky behind them. Clouds floated gently by in the sky's backdrop.

The High Court justices were already seated upon their thrones. A large colored jewel was set within each of the throne's backing, making it appear that the gem was floating above each justice's head. There was one jewel per color to match the justices' respective colors. However, not every justice perfectly matched their color, as there was no one to represent green and violet magic. In those thrones sat an extra blue and red justice. Two reds, one orange, one yellow, and two blues.

Ayera entered their presence, kneeling to the floor. Her head was bowed so low that it kissed the ground, her hair and kimono flowing behind her.

"High Court Justices," Ayera addressed them.

"Empress Ayera. We know why you seek us," High Justice Belinda called out. Her long scarlet hair flowed down her sides, and her eyes burned with fire, contrasting with her porcelain skin.

"Then you know what I will ask of the High Court," Ayera replied.

"Yes, we do," murmured High Justice Borgen, his voice trembling with the onslaught of age. His long blue hair and beard was more faded than the last time Ayera had seen him. "But we will have to deny your request."

Still kneeling on the floor, Ayera's head shot up to glance at the justices, her dark eyes darting to each of them. For a moment, she thought that they were mistaken about why she had come.

"Forgive me, High Justices, but I don't think you understand. Ikaria has been consuming other gifteds' blood! Auron is sure that she is behind all of the gifted losing their magic! My sector needs reinforcements to put a stop to her!"

"We understand perfectly well, which is why we must deny your request," answered High Justice Tyllos of the Yellow. "I have been granted a vision recently from the God of Light." He gave her a concerned look. "Ikaria is indeed behind the disappearance of magic."

"Then you know the peril our world is in," Ayera declared boldly. "If Ikaria succeeds, she will destroy the future of this earth and all of the magic within it!" Ayera gave a skeptical look to Tyllos, as if he had not heard her properly.

Tyllos gave Ayera a warm smile, his golden eyes lit up like the heavens. "No, child, that will not happen, I can assure you."

"But Auron's vision, it told him so," Ayera countered, turning to face them all in disbelief. She couldn't understand why they didn't feel threatened. "We need to stop her now before any more magic disappears. Don't you see? My sister is seeking the gift of the black!"

"Gift of the black?" High Justice Perserine of the Orange repeated incredulously, then gave a laugh. "There is no such thing."

"Auron has foreseen it. You know that his visions always turn out to be accurate!"

"Perhaps Auron is being influenced by your sister with secular books," Tyllos of the Yellow said. "In *The Spectrum*, there is no mention of the gift of the black, therefore his vision, by all accounts, is false. It is not uncommon for a priest to stray from time to time, to be influenced by worldly things."

"Auron?" Ayera questioned. "He is the most pious man I know out of all the world sectors. I assure you, High Justice, he is not influenced by my sister, nor the darkness."

The justices looked at each other, then Belinda spoke. "Empress, I am sure you did not come here to squabble with us regarding Auron's character."

"Forgive me, High Justice," Ayera said, bowing and lowering her head. "I am desperate to save my gifted from losing their magic."

"I understand your fervor for your people," Belinda said with a nod.

"Then you will send reinforcements?"

"No. Like Tyllos said before, your request is denied. This is not a problem for the High Court. Rather, it is *your* problem."

"What?" Ayera shook her head, shocked at what she was hearing.

"We feel that you must deal with your sister, as she falls under your jurisdiction. And indeed, by Tyllos's account of his vision, she is making the magic disappear in your sector, but she will not destroy our world as Auron has predicted, with some mythical magic that does not exist. No, Tyllos has foreseen that the future will continue despite your sister's meddling behavior.

"As a precaution, we do not wish to aimlessly send our gifted, nor any other gifted from the other sectors, only to have them succumb to your sister's whims. Many of your gifted have already lost their powers due to your sister running amok, and I'm afraid we don't have extra gifted to waste on your sister's menacing behavior."

Ayera stood there stunned, staring at the justices as they sat on their glorious white thrones, as if they were gods themselves on Earth. But what god would not want to stop the darkness?

Her father's words rang in her ears. *Don't ever displease the High Court, my daughter. Stay true to them to keep the peace of the sectors...* But the world was in peril, and Ayera needed help. What else was she supposed to do?

Pushing the thoughts of her father's wishes aside, Ayera looked around at them, questioning her devotion for the first time. "And what if I cannot stop her with the gifted I have? What if she is already too powerful? I don't even know if she has the ability to use her violet magic, but what if she does? Then what happens? Auron thinks that she will travel back in time to collect the gift of the green now that she has acquired the blue gift."

"That is your problem, not the High Court's," Belinda said forcefully. "And if she does succeed in collecting green magic, we will then personally stop her here in the future and find someone more *suitable* to rule in your and your husband's stead." Belinda shot her a cold look. "We gave you strong opinions regarding your sister when you first assumed the throne, did we not?"

"Yes, you did." Ayera nodded in agreement, her eyes lowered. Ayera suddenly felt flustered and angry. The high justices had pressed Ayera early on in her reign about Ikaria being transferred to World Sector Three. But she held her father's words close to her heart, closer than the words of the justices. She had promised her father and wouldn't break that promise unless there was a court order, and then she would have to obey.

"If you had followed our advice regarding your sister at the time, none of this would have happened," Belinda stated coldly.

"Empress Ayera," High Justice Oriel said softly, his ice-blue hair standing out in contrast with his ebony skin, "we know of your unwavering loyalty to the High Court and the world sectors." His pale-blue eyes were like darts into Ayera's soul, but his voice said otherwise. "We would hate to have to remove you from your position as empress."

Ayera looked at him through watery eyes, confused. They didn't want to help her. And now they were threatening to take away her rule. Ayera could not lose the throne; her father would never forgive her in the next life. Her family had held on to the throne for many centuries, and she couldn't be the one that ended their dynasty.

"I wouldn't want to let the High Court down, as that would sadden me greatly," Ayera said smoothly, wiping away her tears, her voice remaining confident. "I will ensure we stop Ikaria with our sector's gifted, however challenging it may be."

Borgen smiled under his long blue-white beard. "We have faith in you, as you have proven yourself in the past," he said in a fatherly fashion.

Ayera nodded. She stood up to leave, but she couldn't help herself. "High Justices, do you know what the gift of the violet does? It would help us prepare more suitably to stop my sister," Ayera asked, hoping there was some good that came out of her meeting.

"Force and control," answered Tyllos. "That includes objects and of the mind."

Ayera's heart stopped, her mind swimming with a thousand thoughts at once. What if Ikaria had the ability to use her magic already and was controlling the court's thoughts. Was that how she got the other gifted to comply? What if what Tyllos said was true? That Auron was being influenced by her sister?

Nonsense. Auron is the strongest person I know!

"Please, Empress, be careful," Tyllos warned.

"I will, High Justice, for all of our sakes," Ayera said, rising from her position to be escorted out of the hall.

All the way back to her airship, Ayera stared blankly ahead in dismay. The more she thought of her audience with the High Court, the more perplexed and disturbed she felt. Ayera was struggling with the fact that the High Court did not want to send reinforcements to her sector, not wanting to lose any more gifteds' magic. And if what they said was true, that Ikaria could *control* people, Ayera would need many more gifted than her sector had to succeed. She needed to overwhelm Ikaria to truly stop her. Surely Ikaria couldn't control more than several people at once, could she? Ayera hoped that was true. But even so, her request had been denied, and no other sector would be coming to their aid.

As Ayera entered her ship to depart, a thought struck her. Something the justices had said.

If Ikaria had the ability of control and force, then how had she made magic disappear from the gifted who lived? Those who had died—their magic had still been intact. Ikaria likely controlled them, forcing them to die, and consumed their magic to gain their power. But to make magic altogether disappear from those who had lived? With Ikaria's powers, it did not seem possible. It didn't fit the description of her magic.

For the first time in her life, Ayera had an ever-so-small inkling that Ikaria was right about the High Court. It was a mere speck, but it was there, festering.

CHAPTER 37

GREEN

The patterned curtains swayed in the breeze, gently flowing back and forth. From where she lay, Emerald watched them tease the wind that flowed through the open window. The hot mattress stuck to her skin, and any time she moved, the plastic peeled away from her body like a sticky bandage. There were no sheets on the mattress, just the plastic encasing and a simple blanket that had been tossed over her.

Kyle was absent from the bed. Though he was gone, the scent of his body mingled with the aura from their lovemaking, lingering, reminding her of the pleasure that had taken place hours ago before they went to sleep.

Emerald stretched out in satisfaction, smiling to herself. *Where did he go?* she wondered.

She thought for a moment, then reasoned that he probably went to fetch supplies and to talk with the head man of the camp. Victor. That's what his name was.

Emerald took in the details of the trailer, intrigued. She and Kyle had entered in the middle of the night, which made it impossible for Emerald to get a good look around. The trailer was tiny, with a few windows decorated with curtains, a small table, a few knickknacks lying about, and a small picture of two people hanging on the wall.

Getting up to inspect it, Emerald realized that the picture was of Kyle when he was a boy, and someone she guessed to be his mother. The woman was quite beautiful, with long light brown hair decorated with heavy golden jewelry. Her clothes were brightly colored, like how Emerald would envision a true gypsy. Even Kyle was dressed in brightly colored garb, something that made Emerald chuckle softly.

Emerald heard the trudging sound of boots climbing the metal steps, then the door swung open.

Kyle appeared at the door, carrying a green canvas backpack, a plastic bin, and a pile of clothes in his arms. He threw the pack to the ground, then tossed the clothes at her.

"Here," he said curtly through his pursed lips, taking a drag of his smoke. "The women gave me some clothes for you."

Emerald dug through the pile of clothes, pulling out a pair of black stretch leggings, a black tank top, socks, and a pair of comfortable-looking black combat boots.

"I know it's nothing *fancy* like what you're used to."

Emerald eyed him for a moment, confused at his sudden coldness. Smiling, she said, "They are more than fine. Please thank the women for me."

He didn't answer, just continued to dig through the supplies, pulling out food rations.

What is going on with him?

"I got us some grub," he said, tossing the rations on the table. "The wasteland folk aren't known for their cooking, just warning you." He began to change into new clothes, facing away from her.

Slowly, Emerald eyed him as she neared the table, then sat down, practically inhaling a bread roll and dried meat. She hadn't realized how hungry she was until the food hit her lips. Her last meal had been back in Arcadia before Kyle's show, more than twenty hours ago.

Cautiously, Emerald asked, "Did something happen this morning? Why are you in a foul mood?"

"I never said that I was," he said defiantly, finishing putting on a clean shirt.

"It is obvious that something is upsetting you," Emerald stated, not accepting his answer.

Kyle stopped all movement, facing her. "Did you know?" he asked bitterly.

Her heart stopped at the sight of his expression. He was angry.

Unsure of his unfounded anger, Emerald shot him a confused look. "Did I know what?"

"About the experiments."

Still not following what Kyle was getting at, Emerald became annoyed. "*What* experiments?"

He leaned into her face, his expression indignant. "The experiments that *your* father is doing on *my* people."

"I have no idea what you are talking about. I do not know of any experiments!"

"Those damn cyborgs are infused with *your* blood. Don't tell me that you don't know anything about that!" he said, raising his voice.

Kyle's words were like a punch to her gut, hitting her, and hitting her hard. It was like he'd opened the floodgates within her mind, and suddenly everything made sense. The weekly blood samples. That was what her father had been doing with her blood—experimenting and creating cyborgs.

Emerald's gaze lowered, knowing that she could no longer meet Kyle's. Her father had used her blood for all the wrong reasons. And now her blood had caused harm to Kyle's people.

Anger ran through her. Anger at her father. Anger at herself for being so naive. Even Derek had questioned it, because he knew too that it wasn't right.

"So you *do* know about it," Kyle snapped.

Alarmed and sick to her stomach, Emerald remained silent. It was all her fault, everything. If she had never been born with magic, none of this would have ever happened. If only she were stronger of character and had questioned her father more often, perhaps this would have never happened.

"Kyle, I didn't know about the experimentation. I had no idea," Emerald whispered in a low voice. "The blood samples, yes, I was aware of it. Of course I was." Her gaze finally met his. "But my father told me it was to monitor my health."

"And you didn't question it? You just gave the blood freely, knowing that you had magic?" Kyle shot back.

"Yes, I did. I never questioned it. Ever," Emerald whispered. "But I should have." Tears welled up inside her eyes. She forced them back, trying to hold them in.

"And what about the drawing?"

"What drawing?"

"On the warehouse wall. You had to have known what was going on! It was clear as day in the picture!"

Before Emerald got a chance to explain about the strange prophetic magic, she was interrupted.

"Knock, knock!"

Emerald and Kyle turned their attention to the door. Garrett stuck his head in, casting a glance at both of them.

"Did I come at a bad time? I didn't hear any fucking," he said jokingly. Emerald shot him a mortified look, while Kyle glared at him.

"What the hell are you doing barging in like this," Kyle snapped.

"I brought you a couple of filled gas cans, asshole," Garrett barked at Kyle, then turned to Emerald. "What the hell is up his ass?"

Emerald remained silent. She felt sick, terrible, saddened, confused… and now abandoned, like she had somehow lost Kyle.

"Is it what we talked about this morning?" Garret asked casually.

"Something like that," Kyle muttered, pushing past him out the door.

After Kyle left, Emerald began to weep quietly. She felt alone, and now she had no one to rely on. It was as though Kyle, who she'd felt united with, had suddenly pulled the connection that held them together.

And her heart ached terribly. She felt lost.

Garrett's footsteps approached her, and he rested a hand on her shoulder. Emerald couldn't even muster up the courage to face him. Had Kyle told the others about her magic?

"Please don't cry, Princess. Kyle's a real asshole sometimes. If you want, I can go pound some sense into him." He paused, then continued, "However, I'll most likely have my ass handed to me, so I'll need you to promise you'll patch me up."

The statement made Emerald laugh in the midst of her sadness. Chuckling while sucking in her tears, she looked at him with bleary eyes. "Thanks, but I really don't want to make things worse than they are. It's just a big misunderstanding. I'll talk to him when he gets back."

"You sure?"

"Yes." Emerald smiled at him, putting her hand on his. "I just want to be left alone for a while."

"Okay. I'll see you later tonight, then," Garrett said in his most cheerful tone. He bowed awkwardly. No doubt it was the first time he ever had to. Emerald chuckled again as he turned away, heading out the door.

Thinking about the cyborgs, her blood, and the experimentation, she thought hard what she could do to stop it. To redeem herself.

What was there for her to do? At this point, all she could do was run.

And now Kyle was angry at her. It was the worst feeling ever.

***

Kyle hadn't returned all day, leaving Emerald in the trailer by herself. She watched the sunset transform a warm sky to a barren void, a void that mirrored how she felt. She was in a foreign place and much too nervous to venture out and make small talk within the camp.

There was a small rap at the door. Emerald sprung up from her seat at the kitchenette table, still sick at heart from Kyle's heated words and bored from the hours that had passed.

Opening the door, Emerald saw Victor, wearing another brightly colored tunic, different from the day before. He had golden bands and cuffs mixed into his dreadlocks, giving him an overall exotic look, as if he were a warrior straight out of a desert tale. Strong and powerful.

"Would you care for a walk, Princess?" he asked, bowing to her.

"Yes, I would very much like that," Emerald agreed. He bowed, then held out his elbow like a formal gentleman at one of the royal balls, and she took it like the princess she was. It felt strange to her, as no one had truly been formal with her for days now. As much as she liked being unknown as a normal citizen of Arcadia, she found she rather missed the formalities of being a princess.

"Have you spoken to Kyle since my conversation with him?" he asked, guiding her out of the trailer.

"Not really. I managed to get a few words in before he went storming off," Emerald said sadly.

"Yes, we all know Kyle can get a bit… heated. Hopefully he will come to his senses."

Hopefully, Emerald thought, her heart aching from Kyle's name even being mentioned.

Victor led her into the center of the camp, escorting her to a large bonfire. He gestured at a bench, and she took the spot.

Kyle was right about the desert. It was very cold at night, a dramatic difference from the heat of the day.

"Does Kyle know?" Victor asked.

Emerald stared at him for a moment, holding her breath. "About what?"

"About you being gifted."

Emerald turned to face him in the firelight, whispering softly, "How did you know?"

A small smile emerged on his face, his eyes locked on to the bonfire, looking deep into the flames. "Because you look exactly like your mother, and she had the gift."

Emerald froze in place at the revelation, dumbfounded. "What?" Emerald whispered slowly. "My mother... was gifted?" She inched closer to him on the bench, eyeing him curiously. "You knew my mother?"

"Yes, very well. Elyathi grew up out here. We were in the same camp."

"This camp?" Emerald asked.

Victor shook his head. "No, Princess. There are hundreds of camps out in the wastelands, and this is just one of them. It was a camp far west from here. It's vacant now, its inhabitants now further west."

"My mother never told me she grew up in the desert."

Victor nodded knowingly. "She did indeed live out here. However, she wasn't born in the wastelands. Several people from her lands brought her to the wastelands in hopes of hiding her. From whom, I do not know. But even so, rumors of her beauty reached Arcadia's royal court and eventually the ear of Prince Damaris. She had just come of age. It was perfect timing. Damaris had been searching for a bride for many years, and no woman delighted him like Elyathi did."

"My mother told me she was raised by the baron of the Twin Kingdoms," Emerald said in disbelief.

Victor laughed. "No one would ever want to hear that Damaris's bride was raised in the wastelands. A person's past can be easily changed whenever a royal is in need of it." He chuckled. "Your mother no doubt was told not to repeat her past, even to her daughter."

Emerald felt relieved. It was the first time that someone could talk freely to her and held no judgment. Besides Kyle.

Kyle... Just thinking his name overwhelmed her with grief all over again.

"I suppose you know why I am being tracked down by that cyborg," Emerald said, looking up from the fire.

"I knew you were the mysterious donor the moment Garrett told me of the magical blood," Victor stated. "Weeks ago."

As his words echoed in the winds, it was like Emerald hadn't heard him. Her thoughts were preoccupied about her mother.

"I can't believe my mother had the gift. All these years, I never knew," Emerald said softly, the thought persisting in her mind.

"She hid it from everyone, including most of the wasteland dwellers. Although she never colored her white hair, she did hide her white eyes with lenses. I assume she hid her secret from your father, and apparently from you too, knowing how dangerous Damaris really is."

Her mother had hidden her gift from Emerald. Her whole life, there had been someone that Emerald could confide in that would truly understand her, but instead her mother had chosen to hide it from everyone, including her. A twang of anger bubbled inside of her. She'd felt so alone her whole life, as if no one understood what being gifted was like, and all the while her mother was right there, hiding her power. Hot tears started to form, but she managed to push them aside, wiping her eyes quickly.

Was she disappointed? By far, yes. But did she blame her mother? No. Knowing what she knew of her father now, Emerald finally understood why her mother chose to keep her secret until her death. But it still upset her.

White magic. There was no passage in *The Spectrum* about a gift of the white that Emerald could recall. What did a white-gifted even have the ability to do? Why hadn't Emerald ever felt her mother's magic within her? She'd felt the other gifteds' power flowing through them…

Emerald stared at the bonfire, kicking the sand underneath the bench absentmindedly. Victor held out his flask, which she accepted gratefully, then guzzled down the hard liquor. She didn't want to think about anything anymore. Kyle's unjustified anger, the missing men and the experiments, and now her mother and her secret. Emerald felt like bursting into tears, but another part of her knew tears were useless.

"Princess, I know how much trouble you are in right now, and I wish I could help you in some way. The only piece of advice I can give you is that you cannot live a life that is not true to yourself. There is a reason why magic was brought back into this world. And you, above all else, have the power to do extraordinary things. You can bring so much *change* to Arcadia and the surrounding kingdoms."

Emerald met his eyes, thinking about what he'd said. She took another drink from the flask. Not saying a word, her watery eyes darted back to the fire, watching the mesmerizing flames, calming her spirit.

After a long pause, Emerald broke the silence. "You're right. I can live a lie no longer. I escaped not wanting to do so, and instead I am doing the same thing out here, hiding the fact that I am a gifted."

Emerald handed back the flask, and suddenly an idea struck her. Perhaps, in an odd way, Kyle was right. She been complacent in the shadow of her father for so many years and hadn't stood up to him. She had never questioned her father's decision regarding the blood. In fact, she never questioned any of his decisions, and instead let him hold her hostage in the confines of the palace.

She had to go back to the palace to confront her father. Maybe with the help of her magic there was a small chance to free the missing wasteland dwellers.

Her heart began beating through her chest hard; she knew what lay ahead of her.

She turned to meet Victor's gaze. "Actually, Victor, there is something you can do to help."

CHAPTER 38

The report was rather tedious, as Telly didn't want to leave out any details for Director Santiago. She sat at her computer station, typing and poring over all the notes she had taken over the last twenty-four hours. She was so engrossed with her report that when someone cleared their throat behind her, she jumped slightly.

"What is it?" Telly asked, annoyed.

She swung her computer chair to find Director Jonathan standing there, and she crossed her legs nervously. She had not expected Jonathan at this time. Not for at least another hour, when her report was actually due.

"Telly, I need to talk to you," he began.

Telly removed her glasses, rubbing the tiredness away from her eyes. She was exhausted and stressed about how much there was to do. She had very little time left to finish her report, and she and her team needed to get Drew back up to full capacity soon, before Councilor Zane put in another call.

"Jonathan, can't this wait? I haven't finished the report yet. It will be done shortly."

"Forget the report for now."

Frowning, Telly gave him her full attention, waiting for him to continue.

"Telly... I don't know how to put this any other way..." Jonathan began, pulling up a chair to sit in front of her.

Telly watched him as he struggled with his words, looking at him curiously. "Director, what is going on?"

He composed himself for a moment, but she saw that he couldn't shake his uncomfortable look. "Director Santiago… heard of an incident that happened a few hours ago."

Confused, Telly shrugged. "I don't know what you are referring to."

"Telly, he found out about your personal attachment to Drew."

Telly eyed him for a moment, cautious about how to proceed with the conversation. "And? How does this relate to some incident from earlier?"

"Let me be blunt. It was discovered that you overreacted with Drew. Asking him about personal questions, memories. And when you didn't like his response, you lost it, breaking company equipment."

Telly's heart stopped in her chest. Someone witnessed her doing that? Who would have reported her?

"You overstepped your bounds, Telly. You see, Director Santiago views your attachment as a liability. And now, with Drew being another means of extraction, and with the King himself personally invested, Drew has become far more valuable than any of the other cyborgs. You understand, don't you?"

The realization finally hit her. He was telling her she would never see Drew again. The shock ran through her body, and paralysis set in.

"So… you're letting me go?" Telly asked slowly. Her hands began to shake with fear.

"No, we are just reassigning you. After all, this is a one-time incident, and you have nothing else on your record. Besides, we would hate to lose a brilliant scientist over something like this. Especially considering your contribution to the advancement of cyborg technology."

Telly paused, tears stinging her eyes. Her nose started to run. "Where am I being transferred to?"

"To the bionic weapons division. You are no longer working with the cyborgs. Director Santiago thinks that would be the best option."

Everything was moving in slow motion. She would never see Drew again. As hard as she had worked to ensure his success, she would no longer work on him. Uncontrollable breathy sobs came quickly, tears following close behind. Jonathan frowned at her sympathetically but said no reassuring words. What was there even to say?

"Please, Director, please don't do this! It is my life's work! Drew and I built this technology together. It is only fair for me to continue to work on him," Telly argued through her tears.

"He will be moved out of the lab anyway, once the target is located and acquired."

Telly paused. "He's going to the palace, isn't he?"

"I am not discussing it."

"It's true, I know it! It's too soon, Director. Even you must know that! Besides, Drew isn't stable in the head. I know he is confused inside, even though he appears to be a complete machine on the outside. He is dreaming, having thoughts, just like us. We need more time with him," Telly pleaded. Her stomach twisted at the thought of Drew at the palace. It left no doubt she would never see him again.

"It doesn't matter what the corporation thinks is best for Drew; it's what His Majesty thinks is best. After all, he owns this corporation. All of the research, the weapons, and the cyborgs; they are all his property. We have *no* say."

Jonathan stood up, gesturing for her to do the same. Telly continued to sob, unable to move her body. After a few moments, he put his hand on her shoulder. "Listen, you get thirty minutes to pack your things, and then I have to escort you out of this level."

Telly looked at him with her swollen eyes, placing her glasses back on her face. She rubbed her throbbing head, tousling her short hair in frustration.

"Can I at least say goodbye?"

The director nodded. "I will give you a moment of privacy." He walked out of the room, leaving her alone.

Telly went into Drew's experimental capsule, walking carefully over the wires, tubes, and cords tangled all around the room. Her eyes were puffy from crying, her poor vision causing her to stumble. As she approached him, she turned on her cracked communication tablet, her hands still shaking. Anguish washed over her, and a deep sadness set in.

She would never see him again. Never. Drew would be transferred to the palace, she to the bionic weapons research level. Tears flooded her eyes again.

Drew's good eye glowed with intense orange power, his cybernetic eye focused on her.

"Drew, I came to say goodbye," she said, choking on her tears. Snot dripped out of her nose, and she wiped it absentmindedly on the sleeve of her lab coat. Her tablet glowed as a message came across the screen.

"Where are you going?" he asked.

"They are transferring me. Apparently there are people who think we shouldn't work together anymore," Telly said, her own words stinging her.

"Goodbye, Tell Me Lots."

Telly's head jerked up as she read his words. Did he remember? She hadn't heard that name in years—not since before the accident. Drew had given her that name before they began to date, when they were working together on research. She was known to blab her mouth about theories and calculations when in the lab. That was why he began to call her Tell Me Lots, to poke fun. It became her personal pet name after they started seeing each other.

She faced the tablet, showing him his words. "Drew, did you really say this?"

He nodded.

"Why did you say this? Are you able to recall memories further back than what you previously told me?" Telly asked, frantically searching his eyes. Her heart raced.

"Yes. They are just longer fragmented memories."

This couldn't be happening to her at a worse time. Drew had called her by their intimate nickname. He was making progress, possibly remembering their past together. And now she was being removed from him, and him from her.

She paused in hesitation, then leaned over him, kissing his cold lips. His lips responded awkwardly, and his body motions were unnatural, but he did return her kiss. He didn't pull away either.

It had been years, and she felt so alone without him. And now he was finally coming back. Only now it was too late.

As their lips parted, Telly searched his piercing orange eyes, noticing new hair growth on his shaved head. It was coming in orange, as bright as his eyes.

Drew's body shook violently. His body jerked, almost knocking into a stainless-steel rolling table, causing the vials of blood and wires to rattle at his violent movements. Telly pushed the table back slightly to get it out of his way, then placed her hand on his.

"Drew, please, don't try to process this situation. You are experiencing feelings that your programming can't handle," she said in a soothing voice. She thought about when she would be transferred. Who would be there for him? No one could calm him down like she could. She couldn't accept this would be the last time she would see him. There had to be another way.

Telly looked back at the table with the glowing blood samples strewn across it. His blood, and several of the donor's. Princess Emerald's blood. The team had been so tired, including her, that they forgotten to store the unused samples back in the sample containment machine. They hadn't even inventoried his yet.

All the cyborg technology. It was Drew's and her technology. They were the founding pillars, with the help of the corporation's blood. She wasn't going to let the corporation get the best of their situation, especially now that she realized that the princess was an unwilling participant in the matter. She felt sorry for her.

Knowing where the surveillance cameras were stationed in the lab, she directed herself with her back facing the camera. Drew eyed her for a moment, then closed his eyes, glowing with a warm orange color. Unsure of what he was doing, Telly continued with a slight movement of one of her hands. She quickly palmed the glowing magical vials, then shoved them up the sleeve of her lab coat. It was then Telly noticed that the security cameras were surrounded with orange magic. Drew had to be altering their image somehow through the equipment.

Drew opened his burning orange-white eyes, then nodded at her, his power fading away.

Where am I going to hide these?

A revolting thought crossed her mind, but it was the only one that would work. Telly quickly ran out of the lab, heading to the bathroom. Jonathan was in the hall, leaning against the opposite wall with his arms crossed, waiting for her.

"Done?"

"Almost. I really have to go the bathroom."

"Can't it wait? You only have fifteen minutes left to get your stuff out of there."

"Jonathan, I am on my period. I need to change my bloody pad before people see it coming through my lab coat."

He scrunched his face up with look of disgust. Her bluntness worked, because he waved frantically for her to go. "Hurry!" he called out impatiently.

Telly ran to the lab bathroom, grabbed one of the feminine pads from the dispenser, then entered a stall. Emptying the four vials from her sleeve, she dropped her pants and placed the delicate glass vials on top of her underwear carefully. She took the sanitary pad, placing the sticky adhesive underside of the pad over the glass vials, securing them. She then pulled up her underwear, situating the vials and pad between her lower lips horizontally, making sure they were in place, then fixed her pants and lab coat.

Walking out of the bathroom, she passed by the director once again.

"Finished?"

"Yes," she stated as she squeezed her thighs together. "I just have to grab my purse from the office."

"I'm coming with you. I have to walk out to the platform to see you off."

"Yes, Director."

CHAPTER 39

❖━━━━━━━━❖

YELLOW

The temple reverberated with the prayers of the yellow-gifted. Each prayer was in a different tempo and pitch, filling the room with heavenly words that flowed like a thousand poetic songs spoken at once.

At the front of his brothers and sisters, Auron stood before them, praying for the Empress's success, and for when they would confront Ikaria. The darkness had to be stopped.

Auron's staff sat on the altar behind the processional pole that held the circular symbol of the Spectrum of Magic. The orb from the staff glowed a muted white, soaking in any daylight that remained. The staff needed to be refreshed; Auron had been indoors for far too long to give it a proper charge.

Only the priests knew the power of Auron's staff, and it remained a secret in World Sector Six. Auron had never used the staff in front of anyone. He didn't want to give away its secret. To all who had encountered Auron, they assumed he had difficulty walking, especially now in his later years. Others thought it was a priestly ornament, showing his status as high priest of World Sector Six.

But what most didn't know was the pure power that the staff held, giving the user an extra surge of power from the light it captured, thus making one's magic spell ten times what their normal power was supposed to be. It had the capacity to hold much daylight, allowing the staff to continuously flow its power to the gifted wielder at a constant pace for a given amount of time.

Auron's ancient ancestors from World Sector Four had devised the staff. The orb itself was made from no material ever recorded or recounted from earth's matter. What Auron had been told by his father was that the staff's crystal was given to the first yellow priest that had ever walked the earth in a vision. As the priest reached out and touched the crystal in his dream, he awoke with it in his hands, declaring immediately that the Light Spirit had blessed him and his people, bestowing the spirit's favor upon them.

The Light Spirit was what his ancestors called the God of Light, recognized as the true god in the ancient times of World Sector Four. It didn't bother Auron that the people of his past called the God of Light something else; many different peoples of the world had different accounts of their experience, describing him in different forms.

But as the world came together after the Apocalypse, the first High Court reestablished a world religion, the only practicing religion that remained on Earth at that time. No one cared for religion before the great catastrophe, as technology ran rampant in the world, leaving only the true religion to stand amassed in the dark world. The High Court at that time saw the Apocalypse for what it was—the God of Light's punishment for the world's societies for abandoning their faith. People who survived began to pray and believe, and *The Spectrum* became widely circulated throughout the early centuries of the Post-Apocalypse Era. And to Auron, it truly was the true religion of mankind, and it proved itself so by surviving all other earthly religions.

Early writings of the Apocalypse described the God of Light hurling massive meteors from the heavens, striking the earth right at the heart of what was currently known as World Sector One. Later, writings pointed to evidence that the use of machines took over mankind and eventually killed off the people of World Sector One, utterly destroying those lands.

After the desolation of World Sector One, the machines went off into the other parts of the world, causing massive destruction before they imploded, leaving behind noxious fumes that sunk into the earth. Either way, technology was the root cause, leaving the whole planet sick to its core.

Auron believed both to be contributing factors to Earth's destruction. He believed that the machines did indeed get out of control, wreaking havoc upon the world. But Auron also believed was that the God of Light wanted to purge the world of what was evil, since mankind created such abominations and abandoned their faith. Thus, the God of Light wiped out the technology with his heavenly meteors, crushing the darkness and destroying all evil. Auron hated what was evil. Technology—it was an abomination from the pits of darkness itself. It was man made, inherently evil, and had no place in the world.

Auron opened his eyes, facing the direction of the altar. He did not see any radiant yellow light reflecting off the walls and pillars of the temple; no priest was enveloped with their magic.

Bowing to the Spectrum symbol on the altar, Auron deemed it safe to turn around. He glanced at the other priests and priestesses, and slowly they began to halt their prayers in the tongue of their heavenly language. They bowed to him, and he nodded in return.

"Keep praying fervently, my brothers and sisters. Do not give up faith, the God of Light will provide for us in our time of need. He *will* stop this plague. Stay strong and vigilant. Good always triumphs over evil."

Auron cast a glance all around him, thinking of Ikaria. He couldn't tell them; he had been ordered not to. Cyrus had selected only a few gifted to be made aware of the sorceress's doings, and none of them were among the yellow-gifted. "Please, be wary of all evil. It could come at any time, and in any form."

It wasn't the best warning, but it was as close as he could get to telling them without breaking his word to the Emperor.

"Yes, High Priest," they murmured back to him.

"You are dismissed."

The priests and priestess, all in their emblazoned robes, golden hair flowing, bowed one last time, then trickled out of the temple.

God help us all, Auron thought as he bowed to the altar one last time and exited the temple.

Auron walked through the citadel, turning this way and that within the intricate maze of halls and doorways, making his way to his chambers. He entered, shutting the door behind him. As soon as the door latched shut, Auron felt an immediate shift in the air, and a knowing feeling came over him.

He turned around to face her. Ikaria sat next to his enchanted fireplace in his oversized velvet chair, dressed in a deep-purple kimono embroidered with black designs. Her hair was completely down, flowing down the swell of her back. Auron noticed that dark violet was growing in the roots of her hair. He hadn't seen it before, most likely from her covering it up with her headdresses and the way she styled her hair. It was the result of her consumption of the other's gifted colors, each color of blood mixing with hers, on the way to complete darkness.

The gift of the black…

Ikaria was casually sprawled back on the sofa, her back against one of the armrests while her legs rested on the other.

"Good evening, Auron," Ikaria said with a smirk upon her face, her narrow eyes glistening with her pale violet color. "I had thought for a moment that you would decide to pray at the temple again for a fourth time rather than retire. It appears that I was mistaken."

Auron hesitated for a second, then turned his bulky body back toward the door. As he grabbed the handle, the door lock snapped shut on its own, glowing violet. He looked back at Ikaria, his heart skipping a beat.

"Come now, Auron. There is no need for that, is there? You just arrived," Ikaria said sarcastically while inspecting her polished nails. Then she rolled her head slightly to see his reaction.

Auron took a deep breath, unsure of what to do. His mind raced through possibilities, but no logical idea came to him. Just then he realized he'd left his staff charging in the temple. It was the only real tool that could stave off Ikaria, at least for the time being. Auron cursed himself for being overly tired. It had caused him to be careless, something he couldn't afford, especially at a time like this. It certainly wasn't the first time he had left his staff at the temple, but it most certainly was the wrong time. There was no other option. He had to confront her.

"Why did you come here?" Auron asked, facing Ikaria directly.

"Now, now, Auron. Don't play the fool with me." Ikaria gave a small, playful laugh, kicking one of her legs up off the armrest, exposing her smooth legs from under her flowing robe. "You know very damn well why I'm here," Ikaria cooed. She smoothed out her hair with one grand stroke, the hair falling perfectly into place.

"I won't go down easily," Auron stated firmly as he summoned a golden, half-dome translucent barrier around him. The yellow magic flowed through him, streaming to the dome, strengthening it.

Ikaria got up slowly, then straightened out her robe with a swift brisk of her hands. "I don't expect you to," she said, glaring at him. "For ten *long* years, I have dreamt of this moment. Over and over again. Don't disappoint me."

Suddenly, the image of Ikaria glowed a bright violet, then faded into thin air. Through the golden barrier, Auron shot his gaze in every direction, trying to see if she had reappeared elsewhere within the room. The air around him shifted again with a warm current.

With a quick jerk of his body, he threw his arms out, summoning the yellow magic, causing the golden barrier surrounding him to liquefy. The magic poured onto his body like water, then encased him entirely, becoming a translucent golden shell.

Ikaria's image appeared a split second later where the barrier had stood a moment before, just as the golden shell assimilated with his body. A glowing, dark-purple ice shard appeared out of the palm of her hand, then broke free. Ikaria grasped the shard, slashing it against his chest. But instead of it piercing his body, the ice shard scraped against the golden barrier, as if the golden magic was smooth as glass but hard as steel, causing the shard to shatter in her hand.

Quickly throwing up her hands, Ikaria's robe fluttered around her, revealing a garter with an enchanted blade. Summoning the dagger to her hands by force of magic, she grasped it, then hurled it at him, letting her violet magic guide its way toward Auron's body. It made contact with his golden shell, shattering it like glass all around him. With another jerk of her hands, his body began to rise in the air, then slammed violently against a wall.

The force of the blow knocked the wind out of his lungs for a moment, leaving him to gasp for air. Still immobile and unable to control his own body, he felt the dark-violet magic surround him, slowly dragging his body to Ikaria's feet. When his body reached hers, he was left suspended in the air right in front of her.

Auron was powerless, but it didn't stop him from drawing more power from his life force to flow over his thoughts.

Ikaria stood, waving her hand for the enchanted blade to return. It followed its master's orders, retreating to her outstretched hand. It gently placed itself in her palm, and the sorceress used it to scrape underneath her fingernails as she flashed him a dark smile.

"I have waited a long time to taste your blood. Did you know that?" Her head angled close to him. Auron was frozen, suspended in the air, unable to move. He had to do something, but what? His power of protection was no match for her control magic, especially since she had multiple abilities.

"The gift of the yellow... I wonder what it tastes like?" she asked herself, not expecting him to answer. She walked casually around him, as if Auron about to die was an ordinary activity for her. "Wrath? No... that was red magic. It made me hate you all the more." She eyed him for a moment, then shot out her hand quickly, burning him with violet flames.

Auron screamed as the flames burned his skin and blistered his flesh. She stopped suddenly, then shot her head in his direction.

"Euphoria?" She laughed while pacing mindlessly around the room in thought. She clutched her enchanted blade, then hurled it.

The blade plunged into Auron's flesh, sending a shocking sensation all over his body.

"No, it can't be that." Ikaria paused, staring off into the distance. "Melancholy? Ah, the taste of blue magic, it made me relive my deepest sadness." She snapped her head, looking at him directly. "The sadness which *you* put in motion."

Auron grimaced in pain, letting out loud grunts. Sweat poured down his brow while he tried to summon the power within his core. He was losing focus because of the pain being inflicted on him.

"Do you know how much I was shamed that day? All because of your vision!"

"You won't win," Auron managed to say out loud.

"Really? By the looks of it, I already have," Ikaria sneered. "But I must say, it is impressive that you constantly stream your magic, surrounding your mind. Very clever."

"It is true. Someone will stop you," Auron managed between gasps.

"I doubt it. You put too much faith in your visions, while I create my own destiny. Besides, what power can take on my magic? Do tell, Auron."

"He is a spirit. A ghost," Auron spat out. "A ghost with the gift of the red."

Ikaria burst out laughing uncontrollably. Throwing back her hands, she created dark-violet electrical currents, then released them, shocking his body. The more she laughed, the greater the lightning, and the more his body jolted from the shocks. He cried out in pain.

"Oh, Auron, really. Stop it now. You are too much," she managed to say between her laughs, pausing the electrical storm. "You put too much faith in the unseen. It's time you start believing in the known."

With that, she threw out both of her arms, and the ground shifted, then formed a giant earth platform, shooting up from the floor. His body hovered over to the makeshift platform, then slammed against it in a prone position. Ikaria lingered over him.

"Don't worry, I will be gentle. Promise."

Her violet magic held his head back, his neck exposed.

Auron felt a sudden, thrashing, violent attack on his consciousness, causing him to jolt wildly. The force rocked his mind, trying to make its way inside into the core of his soul, right where his magic rested. His yellow protection magic responded, concentrating all of its power within his mind.

Ikaria was trying to get inside his thoughts.

He could not let her have his mind. Auron had to reach the Ghost Man. It was the only way that the past could prepare for Ikaria. They had to be warned. Ikaria was too powerful.

Auron closed his eyes, blocking Ikaria's constant waves of mind attacks as his body continued to shake uncontrollably. Drawing upon his yellow power, he felt his body radiate with a vileness so evil that he couldn't believe he was doing it himself.

A burning sensation ran through his body, calling forth the magic as it ran through his life force. The power met resistance within himself, as his magic did not to want to be forced into making visions. It was the dark side of the yellow, from the dark side of the spectrum. The power of creating visions was for the God of Light alone. The magic did not like it, creating a fighting tension of the light and dark power inside of his being. His body tremored, but it was nothing compared to what Ikaria was inflicting on his physical body. The harder he called from within to summon the darkness, the more it burned his soul from within.

Ghost Man, please help us! The future of our world will cease to exist without your help! You must stop Ikaria from getting the gift of the green at all costs!

"Giving up on me so easily?" he heard Ikaria call out. "Auron, I expected much more from you than that."

Ignoring her words, he began to weave a prophetic dream with the yellow magic, sending it into the lifestream—the place where souls, visions, and time flowed to eventually reach the God of Light. Auron hoped that his woven vision would appear to the Ghost Man. If not, hopefully it would go to someone who could at least forewarn him.

The staff… You must use the staff… Especially if she has acquired the gift of the black…

The darkness shook his soul, surging into his physical body, overwhelming him. His mind went dark, causing Auron to abruptly end his prophetic dream-weaving.

Releasing the evilness of the darkness, Auron opened his eyes, seeing Ikaria's violet magic surrounding him.

"Embracing the dark side of your color, I see. Hypocrite." Ikaria wrinkled her nose in disgust. "You are a piece of work, aren't you?"

Auron couldn't do more. He was out of options. What could the power of prophecy and protection have against the power of control? Ikaria didn't just have control over mind and body, but time, the elements, and illusions. There was no way out of it. All he could do was die. He would die a martyr's death. At least he'd warned the past with his woven prophecy through the lifestream.

"Why didn't you take control of me?" Auron managed from his hoarse voice.

"Where's the fun in that? I thought it would be bittersweet for you to play out your little charade with my sister and her pathetic husband, only to realize that all along, I had complete control without even touching my violet magic."

"And all the gifted… What about them? What did they do to you?"

Ikaria stopped for a moment, then gave a small, knowing smile. "I never touched any of them. Well, actually, three of them. The dead ones. The *traitors* to our sector." She leaned over his face, whispering. "You might want to ask the High Court about the others." She stood up, brushing her hair over her shoulder. "But I think you might be a bit busy right now. Perhaps another time."

With a sharp movement of Ikaria's hands, the platform shifted under Auron. He felt the earth reshaping itself into a new form. His body dropped to the ground. An earth spike pierced him in the back, then stabbed through his whole body. Auron fell to the ground.

A flash of white shot across his mind's eye, then went dark. He could feel Ikaria's lips pressing against his stomach, where the flow of his blood was gushing out.

There was no movement from him. No words.

Within the darkness of his mind, Auron saw a beautiful princess with green hair the color of an emerald jewel. She was with the red-gifted man, the Ghost Man from his previous vision, both in a deep embrace.

She was the complement. The complement the man was searching for in the darkness.

CHAPTER 40

❖———————❖

Kyle stumbled through the darkness of the wastelands night, trying to focus on the ground in front of him, which was barely visible in the moonlight. Liquid sloshed around in the cans of beer he clutched, given to him by Garrett earlier from his personal stash. Several were already half empty, consumed by none other than himself. The night was stiller than usual, with no winds and hardly any sounds of the wild animals that normally contributed to the night.

What an asshole he was. A complete fucking dick. Earlier, he'd watched Emerald from afar as she talked with Victor at the camp bonfire. The very image of her made his heart hurt. Really, how could he be mad at someone who was the definition of innocence? There wasn't a rotten bone in Emerald's body, and she always had a positive outlook on her situation, regardless of how much shit was swirling around her. And here he was, stubborn as fuck and hadn't apologized yet. Someone needed to punch him.

After a good amount of time jaunting through the barren land, Kyle caught the outline of a familiar large boulder in the moonlight. Nearing the rock, Kyle yanked a beer from his six pack, pulling it free from the plastic packaging, and set the can on top of the stone. He fumbled around in his jacket until he found his smokes, lit one, then plopped down in front of the boulder.

Kyle took a good long drag of his smoke, then exhaled slowly, feeling the calming sensation run through his lungs. Reaching for another beer, he cracked one open, guzzling all of its contents, then grunted after he finished, tossing the can aside.

"Hey, Mom," Kyle started, lowering his gaze to the ground, almost ashamed. "Long time no talk. It's been a while, huh? Sorry I couldn't get out here earlier, but I had a lot of shit going on. Brought you a cold one. Thought you might like that," Kyle said, pointing to the beer can on top of the rock. "Don't get too excited. It's really not that cold. More like drinking warm piss water, but it gets the job done."

He looked up at the boulder, trying to focus his eyes on his mother's name chiseled in the rock. It was no use. It was too damn dark.

"I finally brought a girl home," Kyle muttered. "After all the years you rode my ass about it, it finally happened. She's a good girl, you'd like her. Bit naive, but sweet. Gorgeous as fuck." He paused, smiling to himself. "And she has magical powers. Can you fucking believe that shit?"

He stared at the boulder as he opened another beer and slammed it. He thought of Emerald and their last moments together. His mood darkened.

"But I fucked up as usual. I can't seem to fucking hold on to anyone..." His voice trailed off. "And this one... she's... *different*. Not like the other dumb broads."

A sinking, shitty feeling came over him, which made him feel worse than moments before. Emerald didn't deserve to be treated the way he treated her. He *hated* himself for being such an asshole. He hadn't even heard Emerald's side of the story; he was too angry and too busy jumping to conclusions to even listen to what she had to say. He cringed just thinking about their exchange, and each time he replayed it in his head, he felt even worse. Emerald had no one else to rely on but him, and he was supposed to protect her. Instead, he'd acted like a jackass in the heat of the moment. If Emerald had really known about the experiments, she would have told him. She'd been completely clueless about his accusations, and he knew deep down she was more than innocent; she'd been manipulated and used. But what was still bothering him was when he'd mentioned the picture. She'd been about to say something regarding it, but like the asshole that he was, he just left angry.

Kyle finished his beer, staring at his mom's grave. His vision began fading in and out from the effects of the alcohol, making his head start to spin.

"I know what you are gonna say, Mom," he mumbled. "You don't need to tell me. I already know. Just let me be for a little while longer, then I'll drag my ass back there and make it right," he said, staring at the rock. "Just let me rest for a moment."

He lay down on the desert ground, staring up at the blurry stars. Each one twinkled with its own brilliance. A gentle wind swept over him, and the rushing sound filled his ears. The sky started to spin, and he closed his eyes, listening to the soft rustles.

***

Kyle rubbed his eyes, confused for a moment about where he was. Realizing he'd passed out at his mother's grave, he shot up, swept the dirt off his face, and headed back to camp.

The moon was still high in the sky, and the camp bonfires were still lit, so it had to be around midnight or so. He and Emerald had to be off to Illumina by morning, and he still had much apologizing to do to Emerald before they took off. Hopefully she'd forgive his asinine behavior.

Nervous about facing her, he slowly climbed the trailer steps, then took a deep breath.

Just suck it up, dipshit. Own it!

Kyle opened the door and stuck his head through it, glancing to his right, then to his left.

Emerald wasn't there.

Flopping on the bed, Kyle lit a cigarette, then kicked off his boots, waiting for her to return.

Maybe she's still with Victor by the bonfire, he thought. *She probably doesn't want to see my ass. I don't blame her. If she doesn't come back soon, I'll go find her.*

As minutes turned into an hour, Kyle started to get anxious. Emerald still hadn't returned, and he was starting to worry he'd truly fucked everything up with her.

Noises erupted outside the trailer, and he heard men talking loudly. Getting up, Kyle put out his cigarette and threw on his boots.

"Kyle!" came a loud, sharp whisper from one of the trailer windows.

Kyle moved toward the whisper, peeking his head between the curtains. He didn't see shit. More noise ensued, and the men's voices outside became more forceful.

Someone had one too many beers.

"Kyle!" the whisper came again.

"What?" Kyle stuck his head out sharply, jerking it around. "Who's there?"

"It's Garrett, asshole!"

"What's going on?" Kyle asked. "Why can't you come knocking on the door like a regular person? You got to be all damn discreet and shit!"

"The authorities are here! They're looking for *her*!" Garrett whispered in a panicked tone. "Get the princess out of here. Victor is buying time!"

Em... Kyle's heart sank, and a feeling of impending doom came over him. "Garrett, she's not with me!"

"Are you serious? Well, she's not out here. You need to find her," Garrett hissed, his face remaining anonymous in the darkness. "They're going to start searching the camp. They were asking about you too."

Fuck me! If Em is captured, I am the world's biggest motherfucking asshole ever.

Kyle climbed out of the small window facing the desert, landing his feet on the dirt quietly. Scaling the backside of the trailer wall, he looked around a corner and spotted the authorities' ground transports flooding their lights throughout the camp as men with guns walked through. Screams and cries echoed throughout as the police ripped through the tents.

Going off his memory of the camp's layout, he dashed toward the first large pile of boulders on the outskirts. It was a damn good thing he'd already put Garrett's gasoline in his bike, otherwise he would be seriously fucked right now. All he had to do was find Emerald. Hopefully she was behind one of the other piles of boulders. Or maybe she had already started to make her way further into the desert.

The last thought unnerved him. She had no supplies to last out there.

Kyle waited as the spotlight from an air transport flashed its rays in front of the boulder he was behind, then sprinted to the next set of boulders after the light drifted away.

His new hiding spot was still at the edge of the camp. The authorities continued to rip through the camp while women screamed and children cried. The few camp men were fighting, but it was hopeless against a large task force such as Arcadia's.

A well-groomed man stepped out of one of the transports, positioning himself front and center.

"Where is she?" the dark-haired man demanded, stepping right in front of Victor. "Where is the princess?"

"She is not here," Victor murmured, bowing. Victor's eyes did not leave the ground, as if he knew who this man was and knew to respect him.

"She was here earlier, a few hours ago! Where did she go?" The man's voice boomed through the camp, echoing off the rocks.

Victor didn't say anything.

"And the man who kidnapped the princess. Tell me where he is!"

"Kidnapped?" Victor repeated incredulously.

The elite got in his face, grabbing Victor by his tunic. "If anything happens to my fiancée, I will ensure that this whole camp is burned to the ground and there is nothing left of it." He threw Victor down and stormed off, his cape flapping in the wind.

That's the asshole Em wanted to marry? Talk about a first-class asswipe.

As Kyle waited for the air transport's spotlight to make its rounds once again, an immense green light exploded in the distance. Kyle's heart sunk into his chest.

Emerald's magic. She must have left the camp hours earlier.

The whole camp erupted into chaos as soon as they saw the burst of green magic. Arcadia's authorities began barking out orders to each other, and the officers retreated into their vehicles. After men ran by Kyle's boulder, he sprinted into the darkness, down the main gravel path to where his bike was parked. Dodging the light from the multitude of transports, Kyle stumbled quickly to his motorcycle.

He started the engine, gunning it down the path. Within seconds, Kyle felt the aerial spotlights on him, though only for a quick moment. They flew away, heading toward the direction of the green magical blast. Other ground transports flew by and ignored him, heading in the direction of the princess.

Kyle made his way to the main road in haste. He knew of another dirt road junction that veered off in Emerald's direction, the only one that wasn't too rocky for his motorcycle. He gripped the handlebars, heading full speed to the junction.

With each minute that ticked by, he was slowly losing pace with the transports. His bike couldn't handle the gravel, unlike the main road. Up ahead, there was another blast, this one closer, and this time it was bright orange.

Shit! It's that damn cyborg!

His bike began to shudder from speeding on the gravel, but he continued to gun it anyway.

"Come on, you piece-of-shit bike!" Kyle cursed loudly. "Don't fucking fail me now!"

The bike continued to move but not as smoothly or as fast as he would have liked.

Closer and closer Kyle came to where the transports were stopped, searchlights beaming on one person—Emerald.

Gunfire erupted from the direction of the transports. A split second later, his tire blew out from underneath him, and he instantly lost control, the bike spinning and flinging him off wildly. Kyle heard his bike crash against a large boulder as his body tumbled violently on the rocky desert ground, landing near Emerald and the authorities.

"Kyle?" he heard Emerald's voice cry out.

His body was racked with pain, but he managed to roll over and weakly look in her direction. Her long green wavy hair swayed in the wild winds, her pale skin cold and iced. Her eyes sparkled bright green. Even now, she was hauntingly beautiful. The cyborg held her tightly in his grasp. She didn't struggle, just stood there being held prisoner, a mortified look on her face as the winds whipped her hair fiercely.

"Em…" he called out hoarsely to her. "What are you doing?"

"I'm going back."

"Don't do this…"

"You were right all along… I never questioned him! I am going to do something about it."

"Look what we have here." Kyle heard a voice say above him. There were more sounds of footsteps shuffling near him, kicking dust in his face.

"It's Kyle Trancer. The one who kidnapped the princess," said another officer.

"Bullshit," Kyle managed as he spit out blood. He made a lousy attempt to get to his knees, but he was badly injured, and he slumped back down on the ground as a circle of policemen hovered over him, snickering. "I ain't no kidnapper…" Kyle coughed.

The authorities continued to laugh as he heard Emerald's faint cries.

"He didn't do anything! I was the one who ran away. Please, just let him be…" Kyle heard Emerald say.

Kyle grunted. "You hear that? I didn't do nothing."

One of the men pulled out a sedative in a syringe, startling Emerald. They injected her without warning, and she cried out in shock.

"We heard it," one of the officers said. "We heard it loud and clear."

"You fucking assholes!" Kyle managed before the hard force of a police baton bashed him over the head, rendering him incapacitated. The world went black and was replaced with twinkling white specks. The taste of iron filled his mouth as he coughed up more blood.

"Kyle!" he heard Emerald cry out.

"Em…"

The last thing he remembered in his blackened vision was a green glow and the words "Leave him."

CHAPTER 41

Derek ran down the transport ramp out into the cold open desert. White floodlights were shining in the area, while armed men encircled a perimeter. There were loud hovering beats sounding above him from the transports that hadn't landed yet.

A group of men had swarmed a location near a pile of rocks. Derek ran over, pushing the men aside.

A man with white hair lay there, bloodied. It was the man that Emerald had escaped with on the motorcycle.

Rage twisted within Derek at the sight of him. With a sharp swing of his boot, Derek kicked him hard. The man's unresponsive body twitched, then remained still once again.

"He's still alive," one of the authorities stated. "What should we do with him?"

"Leave him. Let him suffer out here. Better he dies in the wastelands than in Arcadia's cells." Derek looked around. "Where is she?"

At that moment, his own question was answered. Out of the darkness, an orange glow appeared before him, causing Derek to stumble backward in surprise. The orange began to fade, and eventually Derek could make out the shape of a man, and he was holding an unconscious Emerald in his arms. The cyborg had very mechanical movements, making him seem decidedly inhuman. His eyes glowed at Derek in acknowledgment.

Derek had seen the cyborg for a brief moment at the crash site when the scientists retrieved him, but it was nothing compared to seeing it move when it was alive and walking around.

Frightened, Derek stared at the man, then hesitantly held out his arms, waiting for the princess to be handed over.

The cyborg's burning orange eyes pierced through the flashing floodlights, causing the hair on the back of Derek's neck to stand on end. He approached Derek with his mechanical movements, twitching strangely every so often while the circuitry shimmered orange.

Realization shot through Derek. This was what Ikaria wanted to bring to the future. He tensed. She could have them for all Derek cared. Such things shouldn't even exist as far as he was concerned. They were what Damaris had intended to send and conquer York. Once again, Derek had no one to thank but the wicked witch from the future herself. If she hadn't interfered when she did, York would have been overrun by a cyborg army.

The cyborg continued to look at Derek with empty, emotionless eyes. He lifted Emerald, extending her out toward Derek. He waited patiently, his arms outstretched with the limp princess.

Approaching with caution, Derek slowly took Emerald into his arms. She was unconscious, her body lifeless. The cyborg watched him, causing Derek another wave of uneasiness.

Emerald's breathing was slow but steady. She was in a deep sleep.

"What happened to her?" Derek demanded.

The mechanical man cocked his head, then his eyes flashed orange brightly.

"Can you not speak?"

The man nodded, then melted away into the night.

"Can someone tell me what happened to the princess?" Derek yelled, jerking his head around at the authorities around him.

"We had to sedate her, Your Highness," said an officer who approached. "It was best to be safe in case she tried to run again."

"So you thought it best to drug her?" Derek snarled. "She is a princess, not some wild savage to be tranquilized!" Angrily, he turned away from the officer, not letting him further explain himself. Derek fumed all the way back to the transport with Emerald in his arms. He sat down inside, laying her down on the backseat, positioning her head in his lap. He watched her delicate, dirty face as she breathed in and out while her windswept hair fell across her bare shoulders. Derek couldn't believe Emerald was wearing such poor, tattered garments. They were cheap and unfit for someone of her status.

With a gentle stroke, Derek whisked away the long strands of loose hair covering her face and tucked them behind her ear. As he did so, he noticed three piercings, lining the upper ridge of her ear, curved black spikes peeking out. With a sudden burst of jealousy, Derek's heart raged, seeing the rebellious man's influence on Emerald.

No matter, the man was now dead. Or would be soon.

CHAPTER 42

Kyle…

Emerald was alone.

Kyle, I'm sorry. So sorry…

Remnants of the last moment when Emerald saw Kyle's bloodied head and lifeless body in the wastelands stood still in her mind. Through her drugged state, she managed to reach out past the authorities and heal him, or at least she hoped she did, because she didn't remember anything beyond that point.

Please be okay…

Emerald found herself in a strange prismatic room that was not familiar to her. The walls themselves looked like they had been cut from one large stone, with intricate details delicately carved throughout and no cracks in the corners to be found. On one side of the room was a glass door that led outside to a private deck. Next to that door was a window overlooking an endless sky, with no sign of the ground below. In the middle of the room was a fire pit. Emerald felt a magical connection to it; it was not a normal fire fueled by wood. No, it was fueled by magic.

Emerald turned away from the fire and saw a tall, slender woman sitting at a vanity, and two servants were fixing her long, floor-length violet hair. Startled, she got up and hid behind a couch in the far corner of the room where the door was.

What is going on? How did I get here?

Curious, Emerald peered at the woman from behind the couch. The woman was gorgeous. She had narrow violet eyes and a long neck that she held high. Her proud face remained perfectly still as one of the servants painted her lips a bright fuchsia.

She has the gift!

The servant women fixed the violet maiden's hair into a large ponytail, split in two sections, then secured it with large fuchsia and silver hair combs. The regal woman stood up, her silky white under-robe flowing around her slender legs. She held her hands out as the two servants retrieved a lavender kimono embroidered with silver and pink designs. The woman gazed in her vanity mirror, appearing satisfied at her appearance, then fixed her bust line, opening the robe slightly to reveal her cleavage.

As the servants finished dressing the woman, another servant dressed in similar robes came into the room, then bowed to the violet woman.

"Princess Ikaria, Emperor Ojin has summoned you to the private hall," the servant said.

"It must be something to do with the ceremony," Ikaria stated, still looking at her reflection. "What does Father want this time?"

"I don't know, Princess, but he wanted you to come right away," the servant urged.

"Fine." Ikaria waved at her servants to open her door, turning and heading in Emerald's direction.

Emerald quickly ducked her head behind the couch again, but it was too late. The violet woman looked directly at her. Emerald's heart stopped, scared of what the princess might do or say. But to her relief, neither the princess nor her entourage of servants seemed to notice her as they exited the room.

Emerald exhaled in relief.

What is going on?

It was like Emerald didn't even exist, or better yet, was invisible to everyone.

Maybe this is a dream?

Emerald peeked out from behind the door, then decided to follow the princess, walking down the hall behind Ikaria's servants. The group of women stopped suddenly, causing Emerald to walk right through one the body of one of the servants, as if she were a ghost.

The princess turned her delicate neck, flashing her light violet eyes. "Do not let the kimono drag on the ground. I cannot get it dirty before the ceremony!" She turned away, waiting for her garment to be held up. The servants quickly picked up the back of the robe, ensuring that it did not drag on the marbled floors.

The group of women approached what looked like an audience hall. It was so expansive that Emerald knew she was in either a palace or castle. There was another set of women servants standing outside the entrance wearing robes similar to what the violet princess was wearing, but in a different color, a light gold.

The servants dressed in gold bowed low to Ikaria. Ikaria continued to hold her pose, not greeting them in return. Just then, the door in front of her swung open.

Through the doorway, a younger woman emerged who looked just like the violet woman, albeit with dark features. She was shorter, smaller, and had long flowing black hair, dark eyes, and small lips. The woman's eyes looked similar to Ikaria's—narrow, elongated, but not nearly as thin.

The smaller woman lowered her eyes to Princess Ikaria. "Princess," she said quietly, bowing her head.

Ikaria acknowledged her with a bow. "Sister," she said in response. The black-haired woman and her servants walked away, disappearing down the hall as Ikaria entered the private hall alone, her servants waiting outside. Emerald slipped into the hall after Princess Ikaria.

The black marbled floors in the hall were highly polished, and the blackened glass walls and ceiling echoed eternal images of the people within the room. Emerald walked up to one of the walls, seeing if her reflection was there. To her dismay, her image was unseen, and all she saw was a set of tall stairs leading to a marbled circular platform in the middle of the room. Several white lights illuminated the top of the platform, highlighting two thrones.

On one of the thrones sat a man with the same features as the two sisters. He was dressed in the most ornate robe Emerald had ever seen, with a golden scepter in his hand and a large golden crown. Next to him was his wife, no doubt, dressed in a similar fashion.

Six people stood on the far side of the thrones, all perfectly composed. She assumed that they were some people of importance by the way they held themselves high and how elaborately dressed they were, more so than the man who sat on the throne. What was even more fascinating was that all six people had the gift. There were two red-gifted, one orange, one yellow, and two blues.

It was so beautiful to Emerald, seeing people like her having magic. She felt power radiating from the gifted. It was as if gifted were meant to be with other gifted, that this was magic in its natural form, all of the colors coming together to form the God of Light's power, forming perfect harmony. It was only natural to feel drawn to the others.

To the right of the thrones was another gifted man with dark skin the color of ebony, with stubby yellow hair. He had the most intense golden eyes Emerald had ever seen. The man was dressed in elaborate golden pants and a gold shirt a collar and large sleeves. In his hand he held a long staff with a translucent prismatic crystal orb mounted on the top.

Ikaria approached her father, giving him a deep bow, then turned to the six gifted off to the side, doing the same for them.

"It is an honor to be in the presence of the High Court," Ikaria murmured.

The High Court nodded slightly, holding their posture. It was apparent to Emerald that these people were in charge and not the Emperor himself.

"You summoned me, Father?" Ikaria's voice echoed through the chamber.

"Ikaria… there has been a vision," her father said.

Emerald could see the anguish in the Emperor's eyes for what he was about to say. He closed his heavy eyes while the Empress put her hand gently on her husband's hand. The whole room was silent, waiting for the Emperor to continue.

Ikaria looked at her father, then looked around at the other gifted, her face now wearing a mask of worry.

"What is it, Father?"

The Emperor sighed loudly, then opened his narrow eyes. "I am sorry to say this, my daughter, but you are not in the future to rule this sector. Your sister has been seen in your place."

Emerald saw the shock on Ikaria's face. She was stunned speechless by the news. Ikaria turned to her mother, shaking her head in panic and disbelief.

"I don't… understand," she said, her voice trembling.

One of the members of the High Court stepped forward. He was an older man with startling blue eyes, dressed in a silver robe with a circular back piece showing his authority. His hair and beard were mostly white, but Emerald could still see the blue that had faded away from it.

"My dear, as much as we know this unfortunate news is hard for you to take, we must always follow the visions from the yellow-gifted." He paused. "Always."

Ikaria shot him a look, her violet eyes intensifying.

The old man noticed Ikaria's glare, continuing. "We must all do our duty to our sector." He returned her look with serious eyes, almost giving her an indirect warning. "And follow what the magic has directed us to do."

Emerald felt the air thicken as emotions flooded in the room. The only ones in the room that didn't appear to have any sort of emotion were the members of the High Court. They appeared to be gloating. Nothing on their faces showed it, but Emerald could sense it.

"You. I suppose this was all *your* doing!" Ikaria raised her voice, pointing a finger at the man with the staff. He raised an eyebrow but didn't move or speak otherwise. "Typical," Ikaria spat under her breath viciously. "Just because I don't fit the ordinary school of thinking that the court has adopted, doesn't mean I am not fit to rule!"

The golden man eyed Ikaria, remaining silent. Just by his look, Emerald could see that it was his vision that had brought about this change in plans.

Another member of the High Court spoke up. "Do not blame Auron. This is exactly why you are not fit to rule," said a middle-aged woman with long red hair and flaming eyes. "We have heard several reports about your... fascination with technology. One would think you would like to introduce it back into society."

"So I am being denied my right to rule because of some rumored reports?" Ikaria asked the woman, scoffing.

"No, Princess. You simply were not seen in the yellow's vision as the future Empress, unlike your sister, who was. You are making this more difficult for yourself than it needs to be."

At the woman's cruel words, Ikaria fell silent, her entire body trembling now. Then she whirled in the direction of her father, collapsing on the floor, sobbing. "Why have you done this, Father?"

No one said anything. They merely continued to watch as Ikaria sobbed. Her tears sprinkled the floor, creating small little reflections, her heated breaths making cloudy impressions in the shiny floor.

Emerald felt sorry for this Princess Ikaria. Even though the woman appeared to be self-centered, she felt the pain radiating from the woman's soul. It was genuine. Raw. Emerald would never wish ill toward the proud, even if they deserved it. It seemed like everyone was against her.

I wonder what they meant about introducing technology into society? Am I somewhere in the past that doesn't have technology? Or possibly the future? Or is this all a dream? Do I need to wake up?

The sobs continued to echo through the hall, and finally, the Emperor spoke.

"We will ensure that you have a position at court when your sister assumes the throne," the Emperor said, not unkindly. "Until then, you will continue your studies on magic. Hopefully you will discover how to wield your violet magic to better the court and our sector."

Silence settled upon the room. Ikaria lifted her head, glancing at her father with a tear-stained face. Her narrow eyes were bloodshot, but the beautiful halo of pale purple irises within her pupils still burned bright.

"Yes, Father," Ikaria answered in a whisper, then bowed her head.

Walking over to the sobbing princess, Emerald placed a hand on her shoulder. Ikaria suddenly stopped sniffling, and Emerald could sense a calm, bitter resentment within.

At that moment, both blue-gifted members of the High Court turned sharply at Emerald.

"Who are you?" the man with the beard called out.

"How did you get here?" the other one asked.

Emerald looked behind her in case he was talking to someone else. There was no one behind her. They were talking to her.

Emerald stumbled backward, mortified. "Please, I didn't mean to intrude. I don't know how I got here!" Emerald answered, her heart racing. Her head whipped wildly as she glanced in every direction. No one saw her but the blue-gifted men, and Emerald could tell they were confused and had no idea who they were talking to.

"What is the meaning of this?" the Emperor asked, puzzled.

Both blue-gifted men of the High Court gave Emerald a dark look and jerked their hands outward, calling upon their blue magic.

The world quickly started shifting in all-blue tones, and the movements of the people slowed in motion.

Time was freezing.

I just want to go back to my time! All I want to do is see Kyle one more time…

Emerald cried in her mind.

Emerald closed her eyes, calling forth her power. A deep sadness washed over her as she remembered once again that Kyle was gone, angry with her. But he'd come for her. He didn't want her to go. That thought in itself gave her comfort, even though she was alone again.

Emerald felt a surge of power flowing through her core. It was not her life-giving magic. It was one she had accidentally stumbled across before, one that was close to her green magic. The magic continued to feed off her thoughts of Kyle, growing in size, welling up in her soul.

With a sudden flash, her eyes opened, and Emerald extended her hands, causing a massive green-yellow transparent barrier to engulf her just as the men's blue power struck her. Their blue magic was immediately absorbed into her green shield, saving her from being frozen in time. With another movement of her arms, Emerald shot another blast of magic around her. This time, the magic was green-blue.

Like a giant tidal wave, the magic washed over her.

Wake up, Emerald! Wake up! Emerald ordered herself.

Emerald saw space, stars, and galaxies swirl around her, fading from greenish-blue to the blackest night.

Wake up!

***

She heard sounds at first. Familiar sounds. Glacia's low humming mixed with muffled sounds of the city.

Her eyes felt heavy, but Emerald managed to open them. She was back at the palace in her quarters.

What happened? Had she been dreaming? Why did she feel so tired? The recent events were such a blur, and Emerald had a hard time gathering her thoughts. It was like someone was tickling her mind, leaving her unable to complete a coherent thought. She couldn't muster up the energy to use her voice, just a small moan.

Just as Emerald made a sound, she heard soft footsteps nearby. They were Glacia's, as she had a particular walk about her.

"Princess," Glacia whispered under her breath, blotting a damp rag on her forehead. "I was so worried about you."

Emerald tried to move her lips, but her voice cracked, and the muscles in her mouth felt stiff.

Glacia noticed and fetched a glass of water, then sat Emerald up to drink it.

The iced water shocked her system, giving her the jolt she needed to awaken her slow-moving body. Emerald closed her eyes, continuing to drink the water, shutting out the sounds and sights around her.

Kyle's image filled her mind. He had come for her, out in the wastelands. He didn't want her to leave. Neither did she, but she had no choice. She couldn't keep running from her father, and she had to help the desert peoples. A pang of sadness filled her and she recalled leaving Kyle the way she did. But in the end, he was right. She had to do something. Emerald had let her father have his way over everyone long enough. It had to stop.

"Glacia, how long was I out?"

"About sixteen hours or so," Glacia replied, blotting her forehead again, wiping the wet hair away from her face. "We have been so worried about you. Prince Derek has not left your sitting room, waiting for you to wake."

"Derek?" Emerald's mind was still clouded with fog, and Derek was lost within it. "He is still here in Arcadia?"

"Well, yes. Your father has accepted Derek's proposal."

Emerald's gaze suddenly jerked toward Glacia, and the fog of her mind lifted. "*What*? He has?" Emerald asked in disbelief.

Glacia stilled for a moment, then continued. "Princess, your father has fallen very ill."

Emerald's gaze met Glacia's. "Tell me what has happened."

"The night after you have left, it was rumored that your father was out of sorts, and he signed Arcadia away to Derek, naming him heir. Since then, the King has been in his chambers and sees no one but Derek or the Inner Council. It has been whispered that your father sees them once a day to give direction and refuses to do anything else."

Shocked ran through Emerald. "Truly?"

"Yes, Princess. I am sure you have much to talk about when you see Prince Derek. Shall I let him know you are awake?"

Emerald shook her head. "No, not yet. Let me gather my senses."

Glacia bowed, then disappeared into Emerald's bathroom, starting the bath water.

Prince Derek... heir to Arcadia now? My father fallen ill?

If what Glacia said was correct, Emerald couldn't confront her father about using magic. He was too ill. Besides, if she married Derek, she wouldn't have to worry about her father anymore. Derek would listen to her about the desert peoples and the experiments conducted on them. He would put a stop it, surely. And she could convince Derek to stop the taxes on the lower levels. The two of them could unite the kingdoms, ensuring that her father's harsh rule would end.

Emerald's head was spinning at the thought of all the good she could do marrying Derek.

A sudden, conflicted feeling overcame her. Kyle. She would have to put Kyle behind her. Out of her thoughts. And that depressed Emerald. Would he ever forgive her? He had to understand that it was the best for everyone. For his people and for Arcadia. She was going to right her father's wrongs. But why did she feel so terrible about it? The mere thought made her feel sick deep within her soul and her heart heavy with grief. Part of her wanted to hop on the back of Kyle's motorcycle and just forget the world around her. But she couldn't do that. She had done that for the last week, and it did nothing to help Arcadia. The city was left in ruin, taxes were still high, and cyborgs were roaming the city.

She felt so confused.

Emerald could hear the bath water filling the tub from where she was sitting, and every so often Glacia swished the water with her hand, mixing oils into the water. Out of the corner of her eye, Emerald saw the air by her window fluctuate, like a drop of water falling into a pool, causing the image of the city to flutter. It came to a stop as a shadowy image of a man began to form in its place.

Emerald immediately recognized the image. The orange-gifted cyborg.

Emerald shot up weakly, and through her muddled and groggy mind, attempted to call forth her power. A faint stream of dark-green magic flew at the cyborg.

Just as the green power was about to strike him, the bionic man cast a transparent orange-yellow shield as big as his body, blocking Emerald's magic. He did not even flinch when the power hit, and he remained standing there with glowing orange eyes void of emotion.

Weakened by the sedatives and from using her power, Emerald collapsed on the bed. She struggled to roll over, facing the cyborg.

"Get out of here!"

Glacia came running out of the bathroom, towel in hand. "Princess, what is going on?"

Emerald shot her hand up, pointing to the cyborg.

Glacia looked at the cyborg, then sighed. Walking over to her, Glacia helped Emerald up out of bed. "Princess," she whispered, "you are now being monitored at all times. King Damaris's orders. That *thing* has been ordered to shadow you."

Emerald sighed in disgust. Just another way for her father to keep her prisoner. But if what Glacia said was true, Derek would be Arcadia's new king, and she would only have to put up with it for a short while.

The cyborg continued to stare at her with his alarming expression. Emerald never really had a good look at him when she and Kyle were being chased by him. This cyborg was once a person too, Emerald reminded herself. He was programmed to follow orders. Just like all the other desert wanderers who had been experimented on. They were all following orders.

Kyle, I will free your people. I promise. Emerald hoped that when she did free them, they would be capable of living a somewhat normal life. Perhaps they were too far gone as cyborgs, but she had to hope that they weren't.

"Do you have a name?"

The cyborg remained motionless, only flashing his eyes a bright intense orange.

"Princess," Glacia whispered, "he doesn't talk. At least, I don't think he can. I heard someone refer to him as Drew."

Drew cocked his head, clearly understanding their conversation was about him.

"Has he been here this whole time?" Emerald whispered back.

"Yes, ever since you were brought back to the palace, he's lurked in the shadows of your chambers. Sometimes you see him, other times you don't." Glacia shuddered. "It's like I can sense him in the room, but I never know where he is."

Emerald glanced at Drew. He stood still, eyes locked onto hers.

"At least you can give me the decency of feeling like I have privacy," Emerald said, waving her hand at him.

Unexpectedly, the cyborg listened to her request, fading back into the imagery of her chambers.

Emerald remained still while Glacia retreated into her wardrobe. The silence made Emerald think of Kyle again. She hadn't been away from him for more than a day, but she missed him terribly. His wild spirit, crude language, his singing… The pain of being separated from him flooded her mind all over again.

Emerald walked over to where her paints were stored. The picture of the wild woman still stood on her easel.

Grabbing her old painting, Emerald threw it aside, grabbing a fresh canvas.

"Princess, let's get you cleaned up. You will feel much better after you have a hot soak," Glacia called out.

"No. I need to do this," Emerald answered.

Then she began to paint. And paint. She painted until her red paint was gone.

CHAPTER 43

Derek waited anxiously in Emerald's sitting room for hours, hearing muffled voices behind her chamber doors. As each minute passed, he became increasingly impatient.

He just needed to see her again.

Derek paced around in front of the fireplace, watching his shadow as he moved about. Firelight danced on walls while the light of the flames refracted off the silver ornaments throughout. The warm orange tone of the light didn't comfort him. His insides were all knotted up.

What was taking Emerald so long? It sounded like she had finally awoken. Had her handmaiden forgotten about him? Was it that Emerald did not want to see him?

Doubt shadowed his thoughts as he thought about the man who had been seen with Emerald. A twinge of jealousy sprung anew, and he began to feel sick all over again.

The muffled voices became louder. Emerald and Glacia were coming toward the door. Derek quickly composed himself, straightening the black-and-white puff sleeves on his jacket and tossing his hand through his curls, quickly fixing his hair.

The door opened, and a soft white light emerged, gracing the sitting room. He saw Glacia first, then Emerald.

Derek held his breath while he took in Emerald's beauty. Her long green waves were loose down her back and sides, with a simple silver circlet that framed her porcelain face. Her green eyes sparkled while her soft pink lips glimmered. She was dressed in a pale green gown that accentuated every curve of her body. His cheeks began to burn as he took in her figure.

"Princess," Derek said, bowing to her in reverence. "You have no idea the state of torture I was in during your absence, knowing that you were gone."

"Derek," Emerald said, nodding her head in acknowledgment. She seated herself on one of the sofas, then Derek followed suit and sat directly across from her. "I appreciate your concern for me," she whispered solemnly.

She didn't say anything else, which made Derek's nerves stand on edge. Even her greeting didn't seem as joyous as he thought it would have been.

Derek leaned in, offering his hand. "Princess, I am so relieved that you are all right." He noticed she did not accept his hand, which made him lean in further to her. "I was worried about you."

"Thank you, Derek. I really am all right, minus the fact that the authorities drugged me. I still feel drowsy." Emerald glanced at him, then took his hand hesitantly. "But I must say, I was a bit surprised that you hadn't left Arcadia yet, given the circumstances."

"I couldn't leave you knowing that you were all alone in Arcadia. Besides, I was unwilling to take no for an answer from your father." Derek held her hand in front of him, then kissed it. "I was willing to do whatever I had to in order to win your father over."

"How did you convince my father? He was adamantly against the match," Emerald asked curiously. "Especially of you."

Derek thought of Ikaria for a moment, then pushed it aside. "Never mind all the details," he said smoothly. "The important thing is that you are here now, and that we will be married."

"And what of my father? What will happen to him?"

"He will rule up until our wedding, then he will step aside. We will grant him the title of Lord Father of Arcadia, and he will settle in the western sector."

"And when are we to wed?"

"However long it takes for the servants to plan the wedding. Everyone in the palace has been working quickly to ensure that it could take place once they found you."

Emerald paused in thought. "I see."

"Soon after the wedding, there will be an official coronation for both of us, and a transfer of my new Inner Council. After that, your father will retire."

"I can't get over the fact my father agreed to all of this…" Emerald said in disbelief.

"Does it not make you happy?"

Emerald bit her lip, then nodded. "It does. It's just, all of it is happening so fast. I just got back here and learned of all of this…" Her voice trailed off, her face distant.

Derek was taken aback. He would have thought Emerald would be ecstatic considering all the years she had been locked away in the palace by her father, but by the words that she spoke, it was almost as if she had no opinion on the matter. Derek felt a sharp pain twisting in his insides, and he felt sick all over again.

His thumb lightly caressed her hand as he asked, "Princess, you still want to marry, do you not?"

Emerald's eyes immediately met his, frozen. Then with a simple smile, she gazed at his hand, shying away from him slightly. "Yes, of course."

It has to be that man she was with. This is his doing! He's poisoned her mind.

The mere thought of the man with Emerald burned deep within Derek. Rage brewed while hatred fill his heart. To think that Emerald even *touched* another man as they escaped Arcadia made him sick. Really sick.

"It's that man, isn't it?" Derek asked abruptly before he could stop himself. "That one you were on the motorcycle with. You are thinking of him." He couldn't believe he'd just spoken his thoughts. But it was too late. Besides, it had to be said at some point, just so he could move on.

Emerald held her breath, shaking her head profusely. "No. No, you are mistaken."

"Good." Derek leaned in, brushing her green hair aside, kissing her forehead. "I cannot bear to think of you with anyone else."

His heart raced as he moved his hand across her soft skin, his senses filling with desire. Derek closed his eyes, taking in Emerald's scent, kissing her lips.

She hesitantly kissed him back.

"I have waited so long for you," Derek whispered. "I will do anything to please you, Emerald."

"Thank you," she whispered back.

His desire for Emerald overwhelmed him, urging him to continue.

Leaning in to kiss her again, he felt her hand on his chest, slightly holding him back.

"Not now, Derek," Emerald said, her voice faltering. "I need some time to adjust."

Anger erupted within as Derek backed away from her. He felt completely rejected, like there was an unknown wall that kept him separated from her.

Emerald gave him a weak smile, then placed her hand on his.

"I just need some time."

As he watched her walk back into her bedchambers, a violent rage filled him.

It *was* the other man. Kyle Trancer.

How he *hated* that man.

CHAPTER 44

◇━━━━━━━━◇

Dawn kissed the sky as Kyle continued to wander endlessly through the wastelands. He was so damn cold, holding his hands under his armpits to keep warm. He would give anything to have a drink of water. His thirst was a problem that would end his life if he didn't find something soon, and he was sorely regretting the earlier beers. If it came to it, he would be willing to drink his own piss to survive. Not his first choice, but it was better than being a scrap of meat for the vultures.

Kyle found himself on the main road, finally getting a sense what direction the camp was in. He hoped to God that Arcadia's authorities hadn't destroyed the camp. Everyone had hated the idea of having the princess in the compound, and if it was ruined, they would hate him too. Not that he cared; Emerald was worth all the hate.

Replaying last night in his head, the only answer he came up with for why he was still alive was that Emerald must have healed him. His body had been pretty fucked from the crash, and his head beaten badly by the police. He remembered bright-green light filling his vision. That had to have been her magic. There was no other real explanation why he'd survived. He recalled her standing out in the cold winds, waiting to be taken back into the city. All because of him. His assholeness prompted her to go back. God, he hated himself.

Kyle stumbled along the road with the morning sun on his back. Every minute, he hoped that a transport would pass by for him to hitch a ride. It was the main road after all, and he was sure someone would drive by and spot him. Hopefully.

Hours passed, and the sun hit high noon. The morning chill was replaced with scorching heat. With every step he took, the sun's sweltering heat sapped his energy, and he began to wear down, drained and tired to the bones.

Kyle saw two motorcycles driving toward him in the distance. As they came into view, Kyle recognized them as members from his home camp.

Thank fucking God.

"Kyle!" Jared yelled as he pulled up. "They didn't take you!"

"Shit, we were looking for you," Reila said.

Jared got off his motorcycle, grabbing Kyle as he stumbled. Reila pulled out a canteen and shoved it in Kyle's face. He accepted, drinking until it was almost empty.

"Thanks," Kyle said, out of breath, feeling light-headed. He guzzled the last of the water, then wiped the excess running down his chin with the back of his hand.

"We passed by this spot earlier looking for you."

"Yeah, I was off the main road. Out in the middle of butt fuck nowhere," Kyle replied, pointing weakly. "It's hotter than hell out here."

Reila lit a cigarette, then took a long drag. "Glad we found you. Looks like they took your girlfriend, though. Kinda seemed like she wanted to get caught to me," Reila said under her breath.

Kyle shot her a look, and Reila shrugged.

"I'm going after her," Kyle said, then suddenly collapsed.

Jared caught him, pushing his body toward one of the bikes. "Not like that, you aren't. You need to at least get some supplies before you head back to Arcadia."

Kyle seated himself on Jared's bike. "I hate when you're fucking right."

"I know. That's why I am the most hated man in our camp," Jared said, then paused. "Correction. I *was* the most hated man."

"I can only guess who's the most hated man now," Kyle remarked sarcastically.

"You got it," he said, smiling.

Jared hopped onto his motorcycle, and Kyle held on behind him. Reila tossed her cigarette butt, then both she and Jared started their engines and pulled away, heading toward the camp.

***

Reila, Jared, and Kyle arrived at the camp within the hour. As they entered, Kyle saw the camp was in disarray. Some of the men and women were repairing tents while others cleaned up shattered glass and broken metal from the trailer windows and doors. Victor was at the center, giving out orders for those who needed further instruction. Kyle watched him pause as he noticed the motorcycles pull up.

"Thank goodness you are alive," Victor said, meeting them.

"Thanks to these two," Kyle said, getting off Jared's bike. His body was sore and ached when he moved.

"Don't ask me to save this asshole again," Reila said under her breath, parking her bike. "Because of him, my tent is destroyed."

Jared and Reila jumped off their bikes, then patted Victor's shoulders. Victor returned the greeting, then Kyle nodded in thanks to Reila and Jared, and the two of them went wandering into the camp to help the others.

"She's gone," Victor said to Kyle.

It was an obvious statement, but there didn't seem to be much else to say.

"Fucking assholes," Kyle said, thinking of the authorities, the King, and the prince. "And now, somehow, I have to go find her." Kyle turned to face Victor head on. "Victor, I *have* to get her back. Our people are going to continue to get fucked if we don't."

"I know."

"What do you mean you know?" Kyle narrowed his eyes. "How much do you know?"

"Everything," Victor said firmly. "Her blood is the one being infused into the cyborgs." Kyle was about to open his mouth in protest, but Victor interrupted him. "You were *supposed* to be protecting her. But like a damn fool, you took out your anger on the wrong person."

He was right. Kyle only had himself to blame. It pissed him off even more that yet another person was reminding him of his faults.

"Okay, all right! I'm an asshole! Can we please stop reminding me of that fact?"

"No," Victor said sharply. "Because if you weren't such a damn fool and didn't leave her alone all day, she might have not felt like she should go back to her father. She probably would be on the way to Illumina with you."

Victor paused, closing his eyes, sighing. "But I understand why she did it."

"Why? Why the hell did she leave?" Kyle ran his hands through his sweaty hair.

Victor opened his eyes, staring at Kyle sternly. "Probably because she thought that by going back, she would be able to stop her father from continuing to experiment on our people."

"Well, fuck." Deflated, Kyle plopped down and lit a cigarette. Tossing his head back, he puffed while he watched the barren blue sky, trying to think what he needed to do.

"Come," he heard Victor's say.

"Victor, I really don't have time for this shit. I just need a moment, then I have to be on my way. You understand why."

Kyle saw a single black bird fly by in the blue void. That was how he felt without Emerald. Alone.

"Precisely," he said. "That is why you must come with me before you go after the princess."

Kyle eyed Victor suspiciously, but Victor didn't budge from his spot, waiting for Kyle to follow.

"Fine. But keep it short."

As Victor led Kyle through the camp, he motioned for Garrett to follow them. Garrett ran up alongside them, along with another woman Kyle wasn't familiar with.

Kyle nodded at Garrett, silently greeting him.

"Hey, man," Garrett said, following behind Victor.

"What's going on?"

Garrett eyed the back of Victor's head, then looked at Kyle. "You'll see…"

The three of them followed Victor to his dwelling. Victor brushed aside a woven blanket that hung in the doorway, and the four of them made their way inside. Garrett seated himself on a rugged chair. The woman remained standing.

Victor shoved aside a stack of papers and books, revealing an old computer in the shape of a box from behind them. After sliding open the computer monitor screen itself, Victor pulled out a small carved wooden box. Garrett rose to his feet while the woman watched.

The hell is he doing?

Victor opened the box carefully, pulling out a vial of glowing red fluid. Victor held the vial in front of Kyle, motioning for him to take it.

"Is this... blood?" Kyle asked.

"Emerald's blood," Victor said. "She asked me to give you when the time came. Now I understand why."

"When did she give this to you?"

"We drew her blood after I talked with her last night."

Kyle looked at the vial, mesmerized by the glow. Emerald wanted him to have it. She wanted him to be gifted like her. God, he only hoped that she still felt for him what he did for her. If only he could relive yesterday all over again. Like Victor said, he was a damn fool.

Pushing his thoughts aside, Kyle snatched the vial from Victor's hand, looking into its red depths in the light.

"You realize what this means?" Victor asked him softly.

"Hell yes, I realize what this means. Inject this shit into me so I can go get her!" Kyle said, jumping to his feet.

"Kyle, injecting yourself with magical blood doesn't guarantee that it will give you her power," Garrett interjected. "When I hacked into the files of Lab 34, only one out of *nine hundred* men took to the magic. Think about that. Only *one*. That one being Drew, the orange guy who chased you guys."

"But it's worth a damn try." Kyle continued staring into the blood's light.

"Yes, it is," Victor stated. "If it works, it means you can aid Emerald and redeem our people. Hopefully she can change the King's mind. Or remove him by force, if necessary."

"I'll do whatever I can, you can bet your ass on that," Kyle said. "First priority is Em's safety."

Emerald. Just saying her name made him feel incomplete, like his other half was missing. She was the only pure light within the fucked-up world. He had to get her out.

Garrett turned to the woman. "Do you have what we need?"

She nodded in response, pulling supplies out of her pack.

"Yes, let's get this shit done," Kyle agreed.

"Get in the chair," Garrett directed him, and Kyle did so. He turned to Victor. "Do you have any belts?"

Victor nodded, then walked into the next room.

"Belts?" Kyle asked, snapping his full attention at Garrett. "What the fuck?"

"Dude, if you'd seen the reports I've seen, you'd know why," Garrett answered. "Trust me. It's good for both of us."

Kyle's heart began to race. What if his body didn't accept the blood? Or better yet, what if the magic decided that he was nothing but a piece of shit for abandoning one of their own?

God, if you really exist, now is the time to lend me a hand.

The woman returned with a needle. Victor appeared, securing Kyle's limbs tight against the chair with the belts he'd brought back. Kyle couldn't move except his neck.

Damn, they're serious.

The woman took out a syringe, sucking Emerald's blood in via the needle.

"I would say this isn't going to hurt, but I have no idea," she said matter-of-factly.

"I'm ready," Kyle said. He clenched his fists and closed his eyes, waiting in anticipation.

Hold on, Em. I'm coming, he thought desperately. *I promise you, I will never, ever pull that shit again.*

Kyle felt the prick of the needle in his arm burn as the blood began to seep into his bloodstream. Sweat rolled down his brow as his body became hot, burning within.

His heart began to beat quickly, pumping hard. With each heartbeat, its pace increased; first it was slow, but as it continued, it became rapid, so rapid that Kyle was sure it wasn't humanly possible for a heart to beat as fast as his was. The sound of his heartbeats pounded through his ears until he heard no more whispers from the others in the room. The pain, the suffering, what he'd said to Emerald, he was reminded of it each time his heart hammered through his chest, spreading so quickly and so violently that it burned. Burned his very inward soul.

Kyle screamed, and his eyes shot open.

Red. There was nothing but red as far as his eyes could see. He was no longer strapped in the chair, but he was standing in the crimson void.

Through the red, Emerald appeared, her oh-so-gorgeous image dancing with fierceness within the red vast space.

I never meant to push you away...

The fires inside of his soul ignited, flaring.

Startled, Kyle tried to pat it out.

Instead it fought back, expanding in size.

Kyle rolled to the ground, hoping to extinguish it.

Like wildfire, his inner self was set ablaze instantly, melting away his insides into a pool of nothingness.

You left me, Kyle… You left me all alone. Why did you leave me?

"I'm sorry, Em! I fucked up! I should have never left you alone!" Kyle yelled in agony. "I'm sorry…"

No one heard him; it was no use. He was talking inside the expanse of his mind. His body was being consumed by the red flames. They were eating away at his existence, and there was no one there to help. Just him in the crazy ass red space, waiting to die.

Screaming from the excruciating pain, Kyle saw Emerald was suddenly gone from the fires. All that remained were the flames from within his soul, colored in red.

He looked down at his hands, watched as his flesh melted in the hellfires emitting from his palms.

"Fuck you, flames!" he cursed at them.

The flames grew larger, spreading throughout his being harder and faster, his soul disappearing at a much more rapid pace than before. All of him was being taken away by the magic.

We are in charge! The flames hissed and crackled, igniting pain through his spirit.

"The hell you are!"

Kyle doubled over in pain, writhing in the red flames. Struggling, he ordered himself to get up, but his body refused. Instead, the fire spread, creating a wall of flames around him in his crimson world. A strong gust of ruby-tinted winds blew through the fires, feeding their frenzy, enlarging them tenfold.

What the hell am I going to do?

Smoke filled his lungs. He coughed constantly as he struggled through the fiery damnation.

If I only had water. Just a little bit of water…

Through the smoke, raging red waters came in full force toward him. They ripped through the wall of flames, dowsing them. The waters formed a new path through the fires, then violently rushed over him.

Kyle couldn't move, as his body was badly burnt from the inside out.

The rushing red water grew, submersing his soul. Before he knew it, Kyle was drowning in its red depths. The crimson waters were too deep and continued to pull him under. Fighting the current, Kyle frantically paddled to the surface, but the water kept coming.

Through the red murkiness, he saw a dark object obstructing the ruby waters above. It grew in size slowly, but he knew it could be his saving grace from the deadly waters. It was dry land.

The moment Kyle thought of the island above him, he was no longer in the water. Instead he was in a red rocky desert wasteland. Its appearance mimicked his homeland, the same rock formations and the same outcroppings. He even saw the camp far off in the distance in shades of red.

A revitalizing wind embraced him in their folds. The red magical air was illuminated within the winds as it brushed against his skin and eventually rested in place, making him whole. The gentle winds continued to flow, filling him with the power of the red magic.

They were giving him a second life. A new life.

You must go to your princess, the red magic softly whispered in his ears.

CHAPTER 45

The soft leather of her sofa did not bring comfort to Telly. She sat in the black folds of the couch, staring out of her apartment window. Arcadia's mid-levels were lit up in all colors, dazzling its citizens. Ground transports sped across highways woven through the city while their air counterparts flashed in the sky like magnificent twinkling stars.

Depression settled in her bones. Drew was gone. She would see him no more. It was like losing him all over again, but this time there was no hope.

Reaching over to the coffee table, she picked up a thin brown package, then unwrapped the contents, revealing a small book. The stolen vials of blood already sat on the table with her work bag.

The Spectrum. The bible for the so-called gifted, or believers of the gifted.

There was no print or embellishments on the cover; it was just tattered and weathered from years of the previous owner's use. Telly had had to bend over backward to get a copy of the book, scouring online to purchase it. No one had digitized a copy of it for online use, not even any of the world cathedrals or churches that remained open. People had little use for myths in this modern age, Telly told herself, or the fact that no one cared. No one except her, apparently.

"Mom, what are you doing?"

Startled, Telly turned to see her daughter's head poking out from the hallway. She dropped *The Spectrum* on the couch.

"Gwen, it's way past your bedtime."

"But you're up too!" the teen protested.

"Just go back to bed."

"Whoa, did you really get a *physical* book?" Gwen asked, approaching curiously, trying to get a peek of the book's cover. "How come it's not digital? What book is it?"

Telly pushed the book behind her. "Just go to sleep."

"Can you at least tell me what book you got?" Gwen quickly ran up to her side, snatching the book.

Telly leapt up from the couch, running after Gwen. "Hand it over to me right this instant!"

"Since when did you get religious, Mom?" Gwen said, flipping through the book.

"I didn't," Telly snapped, yanking the book out of Gwen's hands. "Now go to your room before I decide to ground your butt."

"Fine," Gwen huffed as she walked toward her room. "Why does everything have to be a secret with you?" she muttered as she slammed the door behind her. A few seconds later, muffled music could be heard coming from the teen's room.

Telly was about to go into her room to make a point but decided to let it go. She didn't feel like getting into an argument tonight. She didn't have the energy.

Telly waited, listening to the music coming from Gwen's room, then opened the book. The smell of the pages was stale, and the paper crumbled as she flipped to the beginning.

In the beginning, the God of Light shone his light upon the earth. Ruling with his right hand, the God of Light held the light of the world, power that no man or being under him could ever possess, for the power was too great for any other being on the earth.

The Lord of Darkness desired power and longed to hold the earth as his dominion. Above all, he coveted the God of Light's pure light, the power to overcome heaven and earth.

The Lord of Darkness gathered his demons, and a war in heaven broke out. The angels of light battled the demons of darkness. The God of Light burned his light, eradicating any darkness that entered the heavens, then hurled the Lord of Darkness to the earth's dark corners, never to allow him to step foot in the heavens again.

After the Lord of Darkness was abolished from the skies, the God of

Light hurled the brilliant light of his right hand to the earth, shattering it amongst the peoples. For no person, nor any being besides the God of Light himself, should possess the Spectrum of Magic.

And thus, it was so. The fragmented light split into the colors of the world. Each color chose an inhabitant of the earth, transforming them into the Gifted.

Telly turned her focus to the stolen vials of blood, each one of them laid out in a straight fashion on the glass top of her coffee table. It wouldn't change her decision.

Getting up from the couch, Telly went into the kitchen and found a wooden spoon in the utensil drawer. It was still brand new, never been used. That showed how much cooking she actually did. In fact, almost all of her cooking utensils hadn't been soiled, save for a couple of them. She grabbed the spoon from the drawer, then walked back over to the couch, seating herself quietly once again while setting the wooden spoon on the coffee table.

She reached for her work bag, pulling out a sterile syringe.

Her heart pounded in her chest, adding to the feeling of nervousness at what she was about to do. She took a deep breath, then exhaled, trying to calm her nerves. A loose piece of blonde hair flopped in front of her face, and Telly yanked it back, securing it with her hair clip.

Telly reached for the blood sample that was Drew's, then held it gently in her hands. She studied it in the lamp light as if it was the first time she was truly seeing the magical blood.

Drew. How I miss you already, she thought sadly, watching the blood pulsate a deep glow.

Turning her attention to the wooden spoon, Telly grabbed it, then bit the middle of the handle, her teeth clamping down on the awful taste of the wood.

Grasping the syringe, Telly filled it with the blood slowly.

Pulling back the sleeve of her sweater, she made a fist. Her veins popped out, giving her a clear sign where they were. She took a deep breath, held it, then plunged the needle into her vein.

A burning sensation tingled her insides for a second, then like wildfire, the tingling was replaced with wild hellish flames that ran rampant through her body instantly, setting her soul ablaze.

Grunting through the wooden spoon, Telly fell into the sofa, flailing. She tried to grab on to something, anything, to ground herself, but it was no use; her body rolled and thrashed within the folds of the couch as she gasped for breath. Her head jerked back violently as the spoon flew from her mouth, and suddenly she found herself suffocating in an orange world as Gwen's music continued to play in the background.

You don't believe! hissed the magic.

"I don't know what to believe!" Telly cried.

So be it! the magic answered.

Agony consumed her body, paralyzing her with an immense fear so strong she'd never felt anything like it. Through the orange world, she saw Drew as he was before the accident. He was the only thing that made her truly happy in life. Him and Gwen.

"Drew!" Telly called out hoarsely, still writhing in pain. She stretched out her hand in the hope that he would take it.

Instead, the image of him faded before her eyes into the vast orange space, leaving her soul tormented in an orange hell as she screamed his name.

CHAPTER 46

He was going to be the world's hero, and everyone would worship him for his heroic deeds. After all, according to Auron, the Ghost Man would indeed stop Ikaria. The prophecy was meant for him, there was no doubt about it. And no one longed for him more than Ikaria herself. Cyrus would use that to his advantage.

Cyrus pictured in his mind the praise he would receive from the High Court if he personally stopped Ikaria. Perhaps they would even bestow their special blessings upon him, the ones that were meant for only the elite. He already had been graciously given their courtly favors. But he wanted more. To receive any blessing from the High Court was a gift from the God of Light himself. And that gift of power was what he desired most.

Ikaria. Still wallowing in her misery over the loss of her right to the throne, and still pining over him like a jilted lover. Cyrus had caught Ikaria's stares from time to time while he engaged with private flirtations with the younger women of the court. At one time, she was renowned for her unique beauty and elegance, and rightfully so. She was tall like him, with wondrous curves that made any man firm. Her pale violet eyes were fierce, and her long neck demanded to be kissed. He wouldn't necessarily say that he once loved her, but she did make him feel delightfully good. They would have made a great match, as they were both beautiful people, and would have produced beautiful offspring. But since she was not named heir to the throne for World Sector Six, he had to pursue his orders, and his ambitions, to marry the named heir.

And it turned out to be her sister, Ayera.

Empress Ayera was indeed very lovely to look at. She was a smaller, softer version of Ikaria. However, she was a completely uninteresting lover. Ayera hardly ever seemed interested in him sexually, which led him to seek satisfaction elsewhere. She probably had some hang-up from her sister's jealousy, which caused her to be sexually cold toward him. Once or twice the thought of Ayera preferring women to men had crossed his mind. No matter, Cyrus found plenty of women willing to fulfill his manly needs.

Cyrus walked alone in the crystal halls with the light of the moon reflecting upon him. As he approached Ikaria's chambers, he paused for a moment before knocking. They hadn't spoken privately since they were engaged. That was years ago. He had heard reports of Ikaria's enraged fits and uncontrollable sobs when word was spread throughout the sector that he was betrothed to Ayera. Even her desperate letters, begging him to come and comfort her, had gone ignored. Ikaria had taken it all so personally. Cyrus was just doing his duty and honoring his pact while fulfilling the one wish that he most desired: becoming the emperor.

Cyrus gave a demanding knock. Suri, Ikaria's servant girl, opened the door, wearing a violet yukata that clung to her elongated thin frame. When Suri noticed him, her eyes widened, then she quickly bowed, keeping her head lowered.

"Emperor Cyrus, how—" Suri said quietly.

"I need to see Ikaria. Now."

Bowing again quickly, she gestured for him to come in. "Enchantress Ikaria is out on her private viewing platform. I will fetch her for you."

"That is not necessary, I will go and see her myself," Cyrus stated. Even her servants talked like Ikaria, very masked, very polite, yet with a hint of spite behind them. It annoyed Cyrus greatly and made his skin crawl.

Cyrus marched through Ikaria's chambers with Suri trailing behind him. She ran up in front of him when he arrived at the balcony exit, unsealing the airtight door and holding it open. A strong airflow entered Ikaria's chamber as he stepped outside onto the balcony. Behind him, Suri closed the door.

The high-altitude air was especially chilly tonight, causing Cyrus to cover his shoulders with the warmth of his cape.

"Emperor Cyrus," Ikaria's voice pierced the air.

Glancing in her direction, Cyrus saw Ikaria in the nude, soaking in a brightly lit spa. Immersed in the whirling hot water, Ikaria took a long drink from her goblet, her wet hair wrapped around her exposed breasts. As Cyrus approached, Ikaria emerged from the water, standing up seductively. The frigid air tightened her nipples as steam emitted from her body.

She saw his wandering eyes gaze at her chest, then flashed a wicked smile, giving him a slight bow. "I was just having my evening soak. Please, won't you join me?" Ikaria said in a smooth voice. She sat back down on the underwater bench, taking a drink of her dark wine.

"You know that I cannot. Besides, I came here to talk to you."

Ikaria laughed. "What's this? The Emperor suddenly has morals?" Ikaria fake gasped, then placed her hands to her upper chest in mockery. "I was under the impression that you liked to have fun at night. Or is it that I am too old for you now. I see your tastes have changed to a younger type."

Cyrus fumed. "I did not come here to discuss what I do outside of daily court activities."

"No. I suppose not. But when they are tied together with your nightly activities, it is so hard to distinguish what is what." Ikaria shot him a look. "Oh, stop. Do you think I care what you do with your male part? If I truly did, my sister would have heard about it by now."

The more he looked at the hot tub, the more inviting it became. Steam rose from the glowing cyan pool, reflecting all of Ikaria's upper body while her lowers were submerged in the misting whirlpools. Her violet hair flowed in every direction, entrancing him.

He knew privately that Ikaria still wanted him; her wounded eyes told him so. Besides, the air was much too cold, and the hot water, wine, and her luscious breasts looked much more inviting. He could have a bit of pleasure before rescuing the fate of the world. Ikaria had always had the best body out of any woman at court.

"You have a way with words, I will give you that," Cyrus stated.

"More like a way with my body," Ikaria answered, revealing a seductive smile.

Cyrus laughed, then stripped off his clothes and entered the tub. Ikaria finished the last of her wine, then poured another glass from a silver pitcher that sat on a nearby table. She handed it to him, as she only had one chalice out on the deck. Cyrus accepted, tasting the coolness of the wine as it flowed down his tongue while watching Ikaria's hair swirl around her. She floated closer to him in the water, then took the half-empty glass from his hand.

"So why are you really here?" She eyed him, taking a drink, then handed him back the glass.

"I have heard rumors that Ayera assigned you to study with Kohren. That is, before he passed."

"Truly unfortunate. Another death by the plague. The pain must have been unbearable for him to commit suicide." Ikaria threw back her head, resting it on the edge of the hot tub.

Cyrus sighed, eyeing her every movement. Of course she was playing it off that the plague took Kohren. It was too easy for her. "Did Kohren find anything in regard to the plague before he died?" Cyrus wasn't expecting a truthful answer, but it didn't hurt to ask.

Ikaria laughed, moving herself closer to him. "Come now, Cyrus. Did you really come here to talk about the plague?" Her hand was suddenly on his chest, her violet eyes smiling. Her fingers trailed along his muscles, slowly moving their way downward. "Or did you have something else in mind?"

His mind fluttered with distraction. She always knew how to tease him, to make him forget his words. "No, I didn't," Cyrus managed.

"Good, because this conversation is starting to bore me."

Her hand continued to wander over his body as her eyes burned with desire. Ikaria paused for a moment, making Cyrus question if she was going to either use her power against him or try to seduce him. Then Ikaria floated away in the water to the other side of the tub, taking another drink of wine. An alluring smile tinged her lips as Ikaria arose from the hot waters, toweling her body for a moment, then slipped on her lavender kimono. "Come. I am need of warmth by the fire."

Cyrus arose, then took the towel, drying himself in the frigid air. He went to reach for his clothes, but Ikaria shook her head, waiting at the sealed door. Taking the hint, he wrapped his lowers in the towel, and the two went inside to her quarters.

Suri opened the sealed door, and Ikaria seated herself on a chair in the middle of the room, next to her enchanted fire pit. Cyrus sat down on the other matching chair, then realized they were the thrones that he'd given to her as an engagement present.

"You still have these?" Cyrus asked, feeling slightly warm from the wine and the fire. He leaned back in the plush purple velvet of the padding, running his hands over the silver swirls on the armrest.

"I do. They are my most favorite chairs. They help give me the clarity I need for each day." Ikaria smiled at him. She held up her glass, waiting for Suri to fill it.

The servant girl came, then bowed. "I am sorry, mistress, but there is no more wine in your chambers. I need to make a run to the citadel's cellars."

Ikaria shrugged. "Well, then you better be off. We mustn't keep His Majesty waiting."

The girl bowed, then scuttled out the door.

"Can she be trusted?" Cyrus said. The last thing he needed was word around the court that he'd slept with Ikaria before vanquishing her.

"She has served me for many years. There is no need to worry."

"Good." Cyrus smiled, leaning his torso over near the fire, feeling the remains of the cold air from the patio melting from his body. Ikaria smiled back at him, her violet eyes flashing with a twinkle. She leaned back in her chair, then glanced at him. The folds of her kimono began to loosen, exposing a good portion of her chest.

Cyrus became instantly aroused. He gave her a wanting smile as the towel around him shifted to expose his body. He couldn't help himself. Her curves were too tempting.

Ikaria gave a dirty laugh. "You want me, don't you?"

"I would be lying if I said I didn't."

Ikaria slowly stalked her way toward him, her face and body an inch apart from his.

Her inviting, lustful eyes instantly transformed into animosity, the hatred piercing him. With a hard slap, Ikaria struck him hard across his cheek, causing his flesh to sting where she hit him. She jerked her body upright while straightening her kimono, making sure she was covered.

"Shame on you," she spat out venomously, striking him again harder against his face. "You already have a wife. My *sister*. You have made a fool out of her, just like how you did me. Did you honestly believe that I would go running into bed with you after all this time, especially after you so *politely* broke off our engagement?"

Enraged, Cyrus shot up from his chair, hurling it aside. He called upon his strength, the hidden magic that was ghosted from all World Sector Six, and power coursed through his veins, gathering within his hands.

Releasing his power, pink ice enveloped Ikaria, causing her lower body to freeze into place. Cyrus felt the orange illusion spells that had been cast on him lifting, and his true color became apparent in his hair and eyes.

With another quick jerk of his hands, he beckoned his power, releasing a sweeping pink hailstorm within the chamber, icy stones pelting in Ikaria's direction.

Ikaria remained still, laughing. Her hand lazily flipped palm up, casting a protective spell to surround her as the pink hailstorm went around the barrier. "Pathetic," she called out from within.

With a swift movement of her hands, a violet magic instantly impaled his mind, causing him to cry out. The pink hailstorm stopped suddenly, and Cyrus tumbled to the floor. Explosive pains erupted in his mind, making him grunt. His mouth felt wired shut, as if an outside force were holding his jaw in place.

"Not even a true color. A reject, a mere tint." Ikaria laughed, then swept her hair behind her shoulders. "Only to have water and ice aid you? So deplorable that you caused the gift of the red to rebuke you. Clearly, the God of Light doesn't favor you, does he, Your Majesty?"

Before he could respond, a violet rushing glow ran past him, turning the throne that he had been sitting on upright. The glow then surrounded him, swirling around quickly, causing his whole body to hover toward the throne, then forced him to sit on it. Cyrus tried to break free from the stronghold that held him hostage, but the force was too strong. The mere thought of him doing so sent stabbing pains through his mind.

Ikaria's laughs filled the chamber while her magic forced his body to sit up perfectly straight on the throne. Cyrus felt the towel around his lowers fall, exposing him. "It was so poetic that you thought you were Auron's Ghost Man," Ikaria said mockingly. "Your red tinted color 'masked.' A ghost."

Cyrus sneered. "You know of Auron's prophecy?"

"The fool told me before I consumed his blood just a few hours ago."

Full of fervor, Cyrus focused his energy on summoning his magic. In response, Ikaria slammed another spasm of agony into his mind. His body began to compress with a great force, making it difficult to breathe. The violet glow that surrounded him lit up brighter as the force became more intense. His mouth still moved slightly as he gasped for air. The force became greater and much stronger. His chest was collapsing.

"Oh, Cyrus, as much as I admire your zeal, this is just sad," Ikaria said, standing before him. She leaned over him, whispering in his ear. "You thought you had me fooled. I knew of your power *years* ago. I felt it within your mind, after you 'broke' me. I have you to thank. If you hadn't been such an ass, I would have remained powerless, unable to wield my magic."

Cyrus's eyes went wide, shooting her a look. "You knew this whole time?"

"I saw your little pretty pink hair and eyes within my mind's eye. And when I had consumed the Lady Yasmin's blood, the orange magic allowed me to see it barely peeking through the spells that the orange-gifted cast on you. Tell me, were you born *deformed*, or are you some failed High Court experiment? Oh, let me guess, they *blessed* you." Ikaria laughed, flashing him a wicked smile. "Some blessing."

"You have no idea what you are doing!"

"I know exactly what I am doing."

"You think you can take on the High Court? Well, I would like to see you try," Cyrus scoffed. "You are no match for them! They are most powerful and will slaughter you before you can even wave your finger!"

"Always the dramatic one, you were." Ikaria waved him away. "I hope you are comfortable. It's going to be a long night."

Cords from her canopy bed, basked in violet magic, whipped around him, tying him in place. They were as forceful as her magic squeezing him and secured him firmly to the throne.

"What are you afraid of? Kill me! Or do you not have the stomach for it?"

"No. I'm not going to kill you. Not yet, anyway. I will let you rot in that throne for ten long years, then kill you. After all, it's only fair. That is essentially what you did to me. Besides, it will give you time to contemplate how you behaved toward me, in the very gift that was to speak of our engagement. I think it's a rather fitting punishment, don't you agree?"

"I will have you arrested!" Cyrus forced out of his mouth.

"I doubt it. And good luck if you are counting on the High Court to rescue you. They do not care for their underlings. Just look at the case of Kohren. I know he gave word to them about me, and they didn't even lift a finger to help him. I can safely say that they will not grant my sister's request. And besides, how will you arrest me if no one discovers that you are here?"

Cyrus's anger melted into fear. He shook his head, shoving the thought away. The High Court would help him. He was sure of it. After all, his sector did everything they had ever asked, gathering information on Ikaria's magic, divulging any secrets of the court to them, granting their spies court positions, and even handing them over secret scrolls and artifacts. They would aid him, he was sure of it.

Furious, Cyrus tried to yell, but his mouth was stuck shut. He struggled with the invisible force crushing him along with the enchanted cord, fighting against the violet magic. Where was that servant girl? Perhaps she would discover them.

"Now, if you will excuse me, I have other evening engagements. And Cyrus," Ikaria added, "don't count on Suri."

Cyrus shot her a look. She had read his mind.

"Like I said before, she is quite loyal to me. I dare say that she is one of the only people who has truly loved me."

Ikaria snapped her fingers, then the firelight died out, leaving him alone in the cold darkness of her chambers.

CHAPTER 47

GREEN

Emerald set down her charcoal, studying the completed drawing. Kyle's face peered back at her, giving one of his angry snarls within the dark thick lines. If circumstances were different, she would have chuckled at his expression; she had always thought his scowls were somewhat amusing. But circumstances were not different. An emptiness continued to grow in the pit of her stomach, an endless void that she couldn't fill. The more she tried to fill it, the more barren it became.

She missed Kyle.

What was he doing now? Had Victor given him her blood? She'd wanted Kyle to have it in case she didn't succeed with her father, so that he could in turn help his people. But since she didn't need to confront her father anymore, Emerald could consider it more like a parting gift. She wasn't even sure that his body would accept the magic and take on the powerful effects that it gave. Hopefully it did and gave him something to remember her by.

Emerald grabbed a piece of tape, then hung the sketch next to her last painting of Kyle on the wall that was in several shades of red. Red. If the magic indeed chose Kyle, he would have the gift of the red. Elements, Emerald recalled reading in *The Spectrum* years ago; that was the power of red magic. It would definitely suit Kyle, as wild as he was. No man could tame fire or the strength of the winds and water, nor any building withstand the destructive force of the earth. And with Kyle, he fit right in with it all.

An unsettling thought struck her. Once she was married, there would be no relationship with Kyle whatsoever. It would be the ultimate end to whatever they had. That thought made her even more depressed.

"Who is this mystery man?"

Startled, Emerald whirled around and saw Glacia staring at her picture.

"You have been back at the palace now for a few days, and you have not told me about him," Glacia said. "In fact, you haven't told me much about anything. I have been waiting, but I can no longer contain myself."

"Just someone I met. He plays in a band."

"So vague." Glacia sighed loudly. "Could you at least give me something more than that? It's me, Princess." Glacia turned her attention to the copy of Remy's old band flyer, the one before Emerald made them a new one. "Disorderly Conduct, huh? Never heard of them."

Emerald stared at the picture, taking in Kyle's image. She was afraid that she would forget his image. His features. His eyes, his face, his hair… She couldn't let them fade from her memory.

Not alluding to any details, Emerald muttered, "It does not really matter anymore. Besides, I am going to marry Derek, am I not?"

"If it didn't really matter, you wouldn't be drawing him," Glacia pointed out. "Speaking of Derek, you need to hurry up and get ready for dinner. You haven't been seeing the prince very much, and he will start to wonder why you continue to hide from him."

She groaned, turning away. "I'm not hiding," Emerald said defensively. She just didn't feel like seeing anyone, including Derek.

"Really? Then what are you doing?"

"I just need time to myself."

"Right." Glacia rolled her eyes. "Princess, you had twenty-four *years* of time to yourself."

"Glacia, would it be terrible to say that I no longer wish to get married? Is that selfish of me to even think that, considering it would benefit Arcadia if I did so?"

Emerald watched as Glacia tossed a gown on her bed, then began rummaging in her wardrobe to find shoes. "Everyone has doubts. It's just how you act upon them," Glacia called out. "And if you are thinking about that mystery man that you refuse to tell me about, you should at least try to put him aside."

Emerald began to undress, then slipped on the dark emerald-green gown. "I know. It's not like anything could ever become of us…"

Glacia came back, then zipped her up, turning Emerald's body to face her. "Princess, I won't lie. I can't say love is easy, because it's not. Your heart is somewhere else, and that is okay. It happens to us all." Glacia turned her around, giving Emerald the space to seat herself at the vanity, then began to run a comb through her hair. "Please, try and take comfort in Prince Derek. He was truly worried for you. Every waking hour he was on pins and needles, praying for your safety. He cares for you, and that is hard to find in a man. I mean, he has waited *years* to be with you. Most any other man would have given up and moved on."

Glacia continued to style her hair for the evening's dinner while Emerald sat in silence.

I am going to marry Derek, she told herself. But her insides churned in confusion.

In the corner of her eye, Emerald saw a fading flash of orange by the new picture of Kyle. The cyborg. Always watching what she was doing, always studying her drawings as if there was a message for him written within. Emerald couldn't get away from him. And he couldn't get away from her. Her father had ordered him to watch her, and there was nothing the cyborg could do to override his instructions. Even while incapacitated, he could still chain her down.

She thought sadly of who the cyborg was before, and how he had no say in his own life. In a way, they were the same.

CHAPTER 48

Derek sat in the King's private dining room, glancing at the empty chair that sat diagonally from him. Emerald was late.

A servant came by, offering Derek his third glass of wine. The dark liquor made his blood boil instead of calming him down. He glanced over at his polished reflection in the sleek blackness of the marbled walls. He looked the best he had ever looked, dressed in his most expensive royal garb and glittering gems.

Why hadn't Emerald arrived yet?

She had shut herself away from Derek the last few days, only making brief appearances to meet with him. No matter how much he tried to lighten her mood, Emerald seemed distant. Her eyes stared at nothing, not truly focusing on the world around her. Not even the wedding planning seemed to make her happy, which made Derek stir with anguish.

If Emerald hadn't left the palace, none of this would have happened. She had been perfectly in love with him, and he her, before she had escaped. But since the princess's return, Derek could tell her heart was not convinced. And that thought made Derek worry. Immensely.

Was it that man, Kyle, or was it the freedom she had tasted? Derek had a feeling that it was the man, in which case, only time could make her forget about him. And she would forget him eventually. After all, when Derek's transport arrived in the wastelands, Kyle Trancer was half dead. The only thing that likely remained of the man was his bones, as the vultures had probably picked away his flesh.

And if he'd somehow survived his injuries, he probably died of dehydration, starvation, or crawled his way back into the lower levels of Arcadia where he belonged. He didn't deserve to even be in the *presence* of the princess. The man was a nobody. Derek had waited his whole life to be with Emerald, and he wasn't going to let some piece of filth get in the way of his happiness. And when Damaris finally stepped down, Derek would officially be declared king. And Derek would allow Emerald to have her freedom—on the upper levels, of course, like any other royal.

Just when Derek was about to start his fourth glass of wine, a shocking pain ran through him. His wine glass fell on the floor, shattering into pieces, as his body went numb.

Why haven't you gotten the blood for me? We had a deal!

Another lance of pain twisted Derek on the inside, causing him to slump over in his chair. One of the dinner attendants noticed and came running to him.

"Your Highness, are you unwell?"

Derek grimaced, waving him away. "Yes, but it's just a small headache. I'll be okay. Leave me be."

The dinner attendant stared at him with concern, hesitantly backing away.

"I said let me *be*!" Derek yelled as he slammed his hand on the table.

The dinner attendant blinked at his sharp words. He bowed, then hurriedly scuttled away while Derek's chest pains continued to rock through him.

I want my blood. Now! I grow impatient waiting for you.

I cannot... I just cannot hurt her! She will hardly even see me! Derek snapped at Ikaria's voice in his head.

That's not my problem. Get me her blood before I change my mind and have Damaris take everything back from you.

Just give me more time! Derek answered. *I'll find a way.*

You had better.

Right at that moment, Emerald appeared across the dining hall. His heart skipped a beat just seeing her walk gracefully across the hall, her bright image sweeping through the darkness of the marbled floors. She was his, soon to be his queen.

Emerald approached, bowing slightly. Her green eyes met his, devoid of her once vibrant enthusiasm, replaced with a pitted despair. Her attention turned to the shattered glass on the floor, but she made no remark or expression regarding it.

"Derek, please forgive me for being late. I was caught up in something and didn't realize the time." She took her chair, then accepted a servant's glass of wine. The servants began bringing out the dinner for the two of them.

"What kept you?" Derek asked, realizing that the edge in his voice made the question sound harsher than he'd intended.

"I was painting."

"Painting what?"

Emerald hesitated. Her silence told him more than anything else could have. Sweat began to bead on his forehead, and his body became flush.

"Emerald, is everything all right?"

Emerald bit her lip and lowered her eyes. "Yes, Derek, everything is fine. Why do you ask?"

"It is just... since you have been back at the palace, you seem melancholy," Derek began, reaching for her hand across the table, gently touching her fingers. "What happened to you out there? Who was that nobody that you were on the run with? You have hardly told me anything, and it has been days since you have been back—"

"He is not a nobody," Emerald interrupted.

Derek's chest flared up in a rage, but he managed to keep it down. He put down his fork and slid the plate away, annoyed. "Fine. He is not a nobody. That *man*... Who is he? How did you end up with him?"

"He saved me in the lower levels from another man that was harassing me."

"*Saved* you?" Derek repeated the word out loud. "And you willingly went riding with a stranger from the lower levels? Just like that?"

Derek could have sworn he heard Ikaria's laugh in the back of his mind at that moment, but with all the pent-up frustration flooding through his mind, he wasn't quite sure.

"Derek, can we please talk about something else?"

Leaning in, Derek whispered sharply, "Emerald, if we are to wed, you must be willing to trust me. That means no secrets between us. Including what all happened to you outside of the palace."

"There are no secrets between us."

"Really? What about your power? You have not confided in me about that."

Emerald gasped, her eyes wide. The servants paused for a second as they filled their wine glasses in disbelief, then immediately filed out of the room in haste.

"Your expression tells me everything. You did not trust me, did you?" Derek muttered flatly. "Just like how you will not talk to me about what happened outside of these palace walls."

"Derek... I... hardly anyone knows about that."

"But I bet Kyle knows about it, *doesn't he*? You were spotted with him when you used your magic to escape Arcadia." The last statement slipped out his mouth unintentionally, but he had thought about it constantly.

Emerald's eyes began to tear, which then made Derek feel awful. Why was it that everything that came out of his mouth sounded worse than it was? It was that damn witch in the back of his mind. He never was short with anyone, and now she was making all sorts of trouble.

"What is wrong with you? Why are you being like this?" Emerald whispered, her eyes filled with tears.

Ikaria's laugh echoed in Derek mind for certain, causing him to flinch. Leaning over the table, Derek stroked Emerald's face gently as a tear ran down her cheek. "Emerald, I... I didn't mean what I said. I just can't... I can't bear the thought of someone else invading your thoughts. Please, let us pick up where we left off before you ran away," Derek whispered in her ear, stroking her hair.

Another tear ran down her cheek as she rose from her seat. "I need time to think."

"About what?"

"About us."

Derek shot up, grabbing her hand and pulling her back to him. Lowering his voice, he stated, "You want to go back to the life you had with your father? *Truly*? With me, I would give you the world. Your freedom!"

Emerald flashed her green eyes, piercing him. "At what cost?" Looking at the hand that held her arm, she shoved it away, then took off.

"Where are you going?" Derek roared.

Emerald quickly spun around to face him. "Anywhere but here! You are worse than my father!" Her bright-green eyes flashed of bitterness, then she quickly ran out the door. As she did so, several servants came into the room with more wine and food.

Derek became acutely aware of the servants' reactions as the princess ran past them. Embarrassment came over him, which fueled his temper even further.

Shooting up from his seat, Derek threw it aside violently, sending it smashing to the floor. He ran after Emerald. Anyone who stood in his way—servants, guards—Derek pushed them aside. And each time he did so, it made him even more angry. It felt good releasing his pent-up rage on those around him.

As Derek was about to exit the room, a man who was as nearly tall and muscular as him stood in the entrance, blocking his way.

"Move!" Derek snapped at the man, attempting to push him aside.

The man didn't budge from Derek's force, but instead remained in his position, staring at Derek, flashing his orange eyes.

Suddenly, Derek became acutely aware that it was the cyborg that was in front of him, masking himself as a noble. His cybernetic eye and the circuitry were gone, and instead the cyborg wore a rich black robe and thick black-framed glasses. The cyborg was far from acting like a lord, as his movements were still completely mechanical.

The intense orange glow of his eyes flashed one last time, almost as if the machine was threatening him to stay away from Emerald. But Derek would be damned if he was going to let this cyborg stand in the way of him and Emerald. He would not be intimidated.

"Let's get this straight, *robot*," Derek said, getting into the cyborg's face. "If you ever come between me and her, I will have you dismantled for parts!" He dodged to the side of the cyborg, then briskly ran down the corridor. Derek looked every which way for Emerald, but she was nowhere to be seen.

There were no signs of the princess, so Derek could only guess that she had retreated to her quarters. Quickly picking up the pace, Derek made his way through the palace halls, then to Emerald's private elevator lift.

As the lift ascended to her tower, Derek watched the city, fireworks twinkling all its colors within the nighttime sky. Everyone was celebrating the news of their engagement, but he was far from celebrating. He was chasing after his fiancée like a blasted fool.

I just need to apologize... Hopefully she will understand. He clenched his jaw, angry that Emerald had said he was worse than Damaris. Did she not understand what he had been going through just to free her?

Derek came to the double doors of her quarters, knocking loudly.

"Princess, it's Derek!"

There was no answer.

He knocked again, resting his head on the double doors, sighing. "I'm so sorry, Emerald. Please… let me in."

There was a click of the lock, and one of the doors opened. Derek was about to get down on his knees to beg Emerald to forgive his behavior from earlier, but instead Glacia met his glance.

"Prince Derek? Why aren't you at dinner?"

"Please, let me see Emerald."

"She's not here, Your Highness."

"I don't believe it. She has to be here!" Derek snapped. "Let me see her!"

He pushed Glacia aside, then stormed through Emerald's chambers. Glacia ran behind him, confused at what was happening.

"My Prince? I told you, she is not here!"

Derek ignored her, hastily opening the door leading to Emerald's bedchambers.

What met his gaze was not the princess. It was *him*. Not him physically, but drawings and paintings, plastered all over the wall. There were many pictures, so many that Derek couldn't even begin to count. His face, everywhere, and they were all staring at him, almost mocking Derek for daring to try to make Emerald happy.

Glacia slowly approached behind him, a mask of fear on her face at her failure to keep Emerald's secret. One that was worse than her hiding her magic.

Emerald was in love. And it wasn't with him.

Never had Derek felt so furious in all his life.

Anger mixed with envy poured through his veins, burning deep within his soul. His hands shook with pure animosity for the man who had captured Emerald's heart, keeping it out of Derek's reach. Her love was meant for him, not some trash from the lower levels.

Furiously, Derek lunged at the wall, tearing and shredding each and every picture. Hatred consumed him, flamed his entire being as he worked fervently to purge the man from Emerald's life. With each rip, each shred of paper, Derek felt that he was removing a piece of that man from her life permanently. He needed to be gone and out of Emerald's life once and for all.

Once the last picture was in a thousand pieces on the floor, Derek turned to Glacia. "No more! You understand? I will not tolerate having my fiancée in love with another man! She is forbidden from drawing him!" He lowered his head to meet her face to face, snarling his words out, "That is an order. I may not be king yet, but I will be soon."

Glacia silently nodded, then shied away while Derek stormed past her, slamming the door shut.

***

Rage filled him.

The images of Kyle flashed in his mind, haunting him, all of them burning with Emerald's red paint. The thought of all those pictures fanned the flames of his wrath, growing by the minute. A feeling of unrequited desire for Emerald clenched him while a feeling of hatred swelled for the man that held her heart hostage.

Damn that man!

As soon as Derek entered his bedroom, he tore off his jacket, ripping the top silver clasps from the black silk shirt that was snug against his neck.

"I need a damn drink!" he barked at his servants, who were in the sitting quarters. Silas appeared almost immediately with a chalice in his hands and offered it to the prince. Derek snatched it, drinking the dark red wine while waving Silas away. He slurped his drink, not minding his manners in the least, then quickly wiped his mouth with the sleeve of his shirt. All he wanted was his pain to go away.

Derek turned to his vanity, staring at the holographic image of the violet circlet. It teased him, as if Ikaria knew exactly what had happened and was daring him to take it.

"Are you happy now?" Derek roared at the circlet, kicking the vanity as hard as he could. The circlet responded by glowing a brighter purple, and a faint laugh echoed in his mind. "I will get your damn blood!" Derek kicked it aggressively once more.

Good. It's about time.

"Damn you, witch! This is all your fault," Derek cursed. "You just had to interfere with everything, didn't you? And now, she does not want me! I am nothing without her! I have lived every moment for her, and now... I am nothing!" Derek shouted, giving the vanity one last hard kick.

You will soon have her back. Just give me the blood, and the circlet is yours. She will be back in your good graces again, you'll see.

The pain in his chest flared up, nearly suffocating him. Derek weakly grabbed the nearest sofa, flopping himself on it, facedown. The soft velvet material was the most affection that he had gotten in the last few days, as Emerald was seemingly cold and distant with him.

Derek rolled over on the sofa, trying to catch his breath. The circlet was straight in his line of view, glowing brightly before his eyes. It was like he couldn't see anything else in the room except the vivid deep-violet crown, its power drowning out all other surroundings.

The circlet. The idea of its power came into his mind, toying with him. If he chose to use the circlet, Emerald would become his...

His stomach suddenly felt sick at the mere thought.

No. That's not right, Derek told himself.

He quickly glanced away. Slowly, as if the jewelry was demanding his attention like a powerful magnet, Derek turned his eyes back to the beauty of its magic.

What about the kingdom of Arcadia? Without the witch's help, Damaris would have been still ruling, letting his kingdom collapse due to finances, or worse, going to war with York. I have been named heir to Arcadia and can make it right.

And what of Emerald? He was expected to marry the princess, and the whole kingdom was looking forward to their union. If he didn't follow through and marry her, Damaris would still rule by law.

Emerald is too innocent! She just happened to be fascinated by the first man she met outside of the palace, no doubt. She is just not thinking clearly. She cannot stay here under Damaris's rule. That is something she never wanted.

With each breath he took, Derek began to rationalize the use of the circlet's power. The more he thought of it, the steadier his breathing became until his pain was fully subsided. After, he stood up and took another drink of his wine, then glanced at the transparent crown once more.

"Silas!" His servant peeked through the bedroom door, waiting for

Derek's order. "Get me a change of clothes. I am drenched in this wretched outfit. And ready my transport."

Silas eyed him, bowing. "Where are you off to this evening?"

"To one of the clubs in the upper levels. Since my evening is completely shot, I might as well talk politics and drink with the other lords of Arcadia. God knows that I am completely cursed when it comes to courting the princess."

"She'll come around, Your Highness."

"I hope so. I don't know how much more I can take of this, Silas."

"Also, Your Highness, might I inform you that the same woman who has been requesting an audience since yesterday has come to see if you are now free."

"Again? Who is this person?" Derek asked, quickly ripping off his sweaty shirt and snatching up his earrings and rings. Silas handed him a clean blue satin shirt with black trim and black clasps.

"The woman says her name is Telly Hearly. She claims that she is from some Lab 34, I think it was. How shall I respond?"

"Silas, I don't have time for visitors. I have a lot going on right now, as you can see. I need some time to cool off."

"She is insistent."

"No. No visitors. Period. Not until after the wedding."

"Yes, Your Highness."

Silas helped Derek get cleaned up from the evening, then escorted him to the royal transport platform. Derek entered the transport, seating himself in his favorite spot, in the very back. Two other guards entered the transport, seating themselves in the front, then closed the inside divider, allowing the prince privacy.

Derek stared out the windows as the transport took off, the tops of the skyscrapers becoming distant among the city lights. Higher and higher the transport flew until all Derek saw was a blur of lights in all colors of the spectrum and the blackness of the ocean off in the distance.

Turning away from the window, Derek noticed the air in front of him ripple. In a matter of seconds, an image of a woman assimilated before his eyes—short blonde hair and thick-rimmed glasses. She sat silently, seated directly across from him, gun in hand.

Shock ran through Derek. He couldn't tell what was the more shocking of the two—the woman appearing before him or the gun in her hand, aiming right at him.

"Don't even think about calling out to your guards," she said, her eyes narrowing. They were pale orange, glowing. She had magic.

Derek suddenly realized he had seen this woman before; she'd been at the cyborg's crash site days ago.

Taking in a breath, he knew better than to try to resist a gifted person. Between Ikaria's mental mind games and Emerald's wild police chase, Derek decided it was best not to aggravate someone with magic. It was bad enough with Ikaria constantly invading his thoughts.

"How did you get in here?" Derek whispered fiercely.

"I snuck in. The door was wide open."

"Are you the one who keeps pestering Silas to see me?"

"Yes. Telly Hearly, Your Highness. Why have you denied my request?" The woman continued to hold the gun steady, but by all accounts, she was doing a terrible job. If Derek had to guess, she had never held a gun in her life before this moment.

"Honestly?" Derek scoffed at the question. "I do not have the time to grant an audience to anyone who asks of it. As you can see, I am engaged and about to inherit a kingdom," Derek said dryly. His eyes shifted to hers. "You have magic? Like that cyborg you work on?"

"The magic decided I was only partially worthy of its power."

"What is that supposed to mean?"

"I didn't fully believe, so it didn't grant me the full potential of the color's magic."

One of the guards faces appeared through the plexi divider of the transport, looking concerned.

"Your Highness, who are you talking to?"

Derek's eyes swept from the guard, then to Telly, who continued to point the gun at him. Realizing that the guards couldn't see her due to her spell, Derek shook his head. "No one. I am just talking out loud to myself."

At this point, everyone in the palace probably thought Derek was crazy. He was randomly breaking out in chills and fevers, talking to himself out loud, and he was short with everyone. Soon everyone would think the worst of him. He just needed to hurry up and get rid of that witch and things could go back to normal.

Derek paused and smiled to the guard, who then disappeared behind the divider. After he deemed it safe, Derek continued. "Are you working with *her*?" he whispered, referring to Ikaria.

Telly looked confused for a moment. "Her? I don't know who you are referring to." Telly inched closer to him. "Your Highness, I have come to beg a favor of you regarding the cyborg."

"With a gun?"

"I would do anything for love," she said, speaking her words firmly as her glassy eyes began to tear. "Wouldn't you?"

Derek was about to argue, but then he stopped himself. They were both in the same position, though certainly under different circumstances. He would indeed do anything for Emerald; he had already conspired with a witch from the future, something he would never normally think of doing. But if it helped him get Emerald, he would do it, even if the price he had to pay was using the enchanted circlet. And by the looks of it, this woman Telly was just as desperate as he was, pointing a gun on a royal prince.

"The corporation recently transferred me out of the cyborg division. A division that Drew and I had *years* of research poured into," Telly continued.

"Who's Drew?"

"The cyborg that is now with the princess."

"He has a name?"

"Well, of course he does. That was his name before he was resurrected."

"Are you asking that I request the head director of the corporation put you back on the team? Because if you are, I have no say over such matters."

"You are engaged to the princess, are you not?" A few silent tears fell from her cheeks, then she flashed her helpless pale-orange eyes at him. "Your Highness, please, hear me out. Drew is not ready to be alone, not without me. His memories are returning, and it could be quite confusing, especially with the power that has been given to him. Damaris now wants him for weekly extractions, and a week is not nearly enough time in between each extraction period for recovery. He needs to be back in the lab, under supervision of those who can *help* him."

That robot indeed needed to be back in a lab, far away from him and Emerald. That damn thing was becoming a nuisance.

"Please, is there nothing that you can do? I will do anything that you ask."

Derek thought for one moment. At one point or another, this woman had had access to Emerald's blood. Perhaps she still had access to it. If she did, Derek could forgo causing any sort of direct harm to Emerald.

"Are you able to retrieve a certain person's blood for me?" he asked quietly.

Under a wet sniffle, Telly revealed a hopeful smile, knowing what he was referring to. "Whose blood? The princess's or Drew's?"

"The princess."

"How much blood do you need?"

"One vial."

Telly wiped away her tears from behind her glasses, then flashed her tangerine eyes. "How soon do you need it?"

"The sooner, the better, for all of us."

"Give me two hours," she replied, smiling under her tears. "Where should I deliver it to?"

"To my palace chambers. Sapphire Quarters."

"It will be done in no time."

Derek turned his attention to the guards up at the front, knocking at the divider. "Turn this transport around," Derek ordered, calling out to them.

"Your Highness? But we are almost at your destination."

"I don't care. I'm feeling lucky right now," he said, smirking to himself.

CHAPTER 49

GREEN

Emerald stood against the garden's balcony, watching the mesmerizing fireworks display that the city put on. Arcadia was celebrating the engagement of their princess to Prince Derek, and every night there was a grand fireworks display off the oceanfront. It would continue until they were wed, and that night would be the biggest fireworks display of them all.

Knots tightened in Emerald's stomach just thinking of the wedding.

Derek… Why was he acting so possessive? For all the years that Emerald had known him, Derek had never acted the way he had at dinner. Quick tempered, irritable, and jealous… Those were not qualities that Derek was ever known for. But since she had been back at the palace, Derek wanted to know what she was doing at all times, and he'd become aggressive, insisting on seeing her every moment, which made Emerald want to see him as little as possible.

Her emerald engagement ring captured the light of the fireworks, each color splashing its light across the shiny cut of the jewel. Red fireworks flared up, complementing the green color of the gem.

Kyle…

She missed him terribly. What would she give to see him that very moment. If only she could kiss him one more time or hear him say her name again. But she knew that that was not going to happen, and that for the good of Arcadia, she needed to wed Derek before the city fell apart financially. She had to take responsibility for her people, even though it was not her heart's desire.

When the last firework flashed across the sky, Emerald exited the gardens and headed into the palace, carefully avoiding any route that Derek might take to his room or hers to find her.

As she came upon her main chamber's door, Emerald heard Glacia's muffled cries behind the thick wood. Concerned, Emerald quickly swung open her door, running across her sitting room and into her bedroom, where the sounds were coming from.

Glacia sat in the middle of the floor, thousands of torn up pieces of paper scattered around her. Emerald suddenly realized that they were pieces of her pictures of Kyle, as her wall was completely barren.

Emerald gasped, falling to her knees. "Glacia, what has happened?"

"The prince…" Glacia forced out of her mouth between the sobs.

"He came here? Into my bedroom?"

Glacia nodded, words not coming out of her mouth as she continued to cry.

Emerald clutched the shredded pieces, then burst out crying. Those drawings had been one of the two things she had of Kyle, the other being her memories. But the drawings made him real to her, whereas the memories were fading fantasies.

"Why… Why would he do such a thing?"

Glacia rubbed the tears from her eyes, leaning Emerald into her arms. "He was so angry, Princess. So angry. Your intuition about him was right. No wonder you were having doubts."

Emerald held Glacia as she stared at the distorted pieces of Kyle that lay all across the room, tears streaming down her face. Never had she thought it would come to this. Never in her life had she felt so violated, so intruded upon. She couldn't marry Derek. Between dinner and his fitful rage against her drawings, what else was he capable of? The thought of it sent a shiver down her spine. He was no longer safe, and she felt no love for him whatsoever. Especially not after this. All that was left for Derek was resentment.

"I can't marry him," Emerald angrily whispered to Glacia. "I won't."

Glacia looked at her with her glassy eyes. "What about the kingdom? You won't be queen unless you marry the prince under your father's terms."

"I'll find another way. I must go to my father."

"But he refuses to see anyone. Even you."

Something isn't right about Father. Why has he not seen me? Is he truly sick as he claims he is? Why hasn't he asked for healing from me? Why does he refuse to see just about everyone except Derek? How did Derek persuade him anyway? Questions flooded Emerald's mind, as she suddenly realized that everything was off.

Emerald turned her attention back to the scraps of paper, disheartened. Glacia noticed the expression on her face, shaking her head in shame.

"I'm sorry, Princess. I tried to stop Derek from entering the room, but he was determined to see you."

"It's not your fault, Glacia. I just can't believe the audacity he had to try and follow me to my chambers." Emerald smiled weakly at Glacia through her tears. "Perhaps if I'd come here instead, I could have saved my pictures."

Glacia started picking up all the pieces off the floor, gathering them into a pile. "What are you going to do?" she asked.

What *was* she going to do about Derek if she wasn't going to marry him?

"Tomorrow, I will break it off. I cannot bear the thought of seeing him another minute. I have already had enough of him today," Emerald answered, helping Glacia gather the scraps.

"I am ashamed that I tried to persuade you to be with him," Glacia said, sucking in her breath.

"You didn't know. I didn't know…" Emerald answered, stopping in midsentence.

The cyborg faded into view, glowing an intense orange. He cocked his head, his gaze fixated on the scraps of paper. His eyes glowed with the cybernetic eye, brighter than his original.

"What do you want?" Emerald said to him stiffly as a fresh tear streamed down her face.

The cyborg approached her in a mechanical fashion, holding out his hands.

"No. You can't have them!" Emerald clutched the paper shreds to her body as if her life depended on it.

His eyes flashed at Emerald, then he swiped his hand, grabbing all the scraps from her. His movement startled her, causing her to let go of the pile.

"Don't take them!" Emerald cried, trying to push him back.

His eyes flared in response, not releasing his grip on them. Instead, something in him glitched, then he mechanically moved to her art desk, flopping the stack down onto the table.

Placing his hands on the pile, the cyborg closed his eyes.

Curiously, Emerald watched as his body began to shimmer a bright orange. The orange light swirled all around the cyborg, and he burned as bright as day. Magic began to gather in his hands, pulsating as it grew. With a sudden jolt, he released the power and the orange light surrounded the scraps of paper, as if the magic were a light dust resting upon them. After several moments, the orange glow faded away, and the magic was gone.

The cyborg opened his eyes, then collected the pile in his hands. Extending it outward for Emerald to take, Emerald saw that the pictures were whole again, as if they had never been damaged in the first place.

Thumbing through the whole pile, Emerald was in awe as she saw that each picture was fully intact. All of Kyle's faces were restored.

Quickly looking up at the cyborg, she began to tear up all over again. "Thank you," she whispered.

The cyborg cocked his head in response, then faded away into the nothingness of her room.

Holding the pictures close, Emerald realized that there was hope for the machines. They still had a soul in them. With much help and rehabilitation, maybe they could live a somewhat normal life. Maybe.

"That's impossible," Glacia said in disbelief, taking the pictures from Emerald's hand. She began to tape them up on the wall, back in their original spots. "Princess, I think that thing is looking out for you."

"Isn't he supposed to be watching me at all times?"

"I didn't mean it like that. I think he wants to *help* you."

It did seem like the cyborg was protecting her more than keeping her prisoner. And her father… What was he doing?

It was time to pay a visit to him.

CHAPTER 50

❖————————❖

YELLOW

A cool feeling flowed throughout his body, restoring his soul. Breath entered his lungs once more, causing his body to gasp for life-giving air. Was he dead?

Panic set in, and Auron began to breathe in an abnormal pattern. His mind and body felt heavy, and his heart raced.

"Just breathe," called out a gentle feminine voice.

Auron obeyed the voice and concentrated on each breath. Another cool healing wave washed over him, calming his mind and steadying his breathing.

Auron was sure that he was on the brink of death and just about to pass into the God of Light's paradise. Or maybe he had died, and his soul was awaiting the God of Light's judgment in purgatory, then was miraculously brought back to the land of the living. Either way, it had not been his time to die yet, for the God of Light willed him to live.

"You were almost dead," the voice told him.

"I… didn't die?"

"No. Your protection magic kept you from dying. It seems that the gods willed you to live."

"You mean the God of Light," Auron corrected the voice.

Still lying on the ground, Auron slowly opened his eyes. His vision was nothing more than blurry colors in large blotchy shapes with all the fine details distorted. His body was completely immobile. Cramps sporadically shot through his lungs, causing Auron to continue to cling to life with every breath he consumed. Gradually, the fuzzy outlines began to take shape.

A dark-purple figure entered his line of sight, causing alarm. Auron gasped, then quickly struggled to summon his power.

The dark shadow laid one of her small hands on his chest. "I am not going to hurt you," she whispered. The woman's voice was rather soothing, just like the magic that restored life to his broken body. Her gentle hands assisted Auron's hefty body to a sitting position, causing much strain. In response, he coughed up a bit of blood that was hanging in his throat, his husky shoulders jerking as he did so.

Suddenly a bright violet glow filled his eyes, and another healing wave flowed through his body. This time, it restored his insides. Auron could feel the organs in his body mending, the impaled flesh knitting together, tingling throughout his whole body.

When the glow subsided, Auron's aches had vanished, and his vision was crystal clear. His chambers looked as they always had been, as if the battle between him and Ikaria had never happened. There was no shifted earth, no spikes in the ground, no damage. He didn't even see the blood from his body. It was like he had dreamt the whole incident, and everything regarding it remained fuzzy in his mind.

Auron turned his attention to the woman, seeing her for the first time. An outlandish, wild woman sat beside him. She looked younger than him, roughly in her midthirties. Her head was shaved on both sides of her scalp, while the top portion of her hair remained long, styled to stick straight up like a razor blade, colored purple. One of her ears was completely pierced from bottom to top with dangling silver earrings and hoops. The other ear had just one simple stud, and there was a nose ring in her left nostril. A small purple jewel sparkled in the middle of her forehead. Her feminine voice did not match her harsh appearance, as her rigid, straight figure was dressed in tight black clothes and thigh-high black boots.

"Your magic is missing," said the woman. "No wonder you couldn't heal yourself."

"Missing?" Auron sat there, rubbing his face, trying to grasp the situation.

"You are missing your adjacent colors. If you had them, you could have healed yourself to a somewhat better state than how I found you."

"Adjacent colors?" Auron questioned, giving her a confused look. He was missing magic? "Who are you?"

"I received your message. More like your warning."

"I believe you are too late," Auron said, coughing out the remaining blood in his lungs. He eyed her, noticing that her hair was too dark of a violet to be her true gifted color. "And it seems that the message went to the wrong person. I was trying to reach a man with the gift of the red. The Ghost Man."

The woman nodded, offering her hand. "I know. That's why I am here. I am trying to find your Ghost Man. Your message went farther back in time than you intended, reaching me."

"How far back?"

The woman paused for a moment. "Almost to the beginning of time."

Auron groaned. Ikaria had his power and was probably well on her way to leaving their time, and all the while, his message had failed. He needed to find the Emperor before Ikaria did anything. The Empress was to arrive back at the citadel tonight. Hopefully she brought with her reinforcements from the High Court. That is, if they weren't already too late.

"Then why are you here? What of the Ghost Man?" He took her hand, and she helped him to his feet. His body still felt clumsy from the battle that had taken place hours prior.

"I have spent many years traveling all of time in search of this Ghost Man. To my dismay, I have found no trace of him. It's like he doesn't exist."

"Surely the vision gave you the sense that the Ghost Man wasn't in this era," Auron asked.

"I thought I was close to finding him in another time, but it was just a non-gifted, leading me to another dead end. After exhausting all of my options, I decided to find the source of the vision to get more clues on where to search for this red-gifted man."

Auron thought immediately of the vision when he was dying. That had not been included in his cry for help, as his message had already been sent out after he transmitted it within the lifestream. There was a princess. His complement.

"If you find a princess, one who has the gift of the green, you should find him."

The woman's face dropped at his statement. Auron could tell she knew exactly who he was talking about. "Truly? Are you sure?"

"Yes, without a doubt. She is his complement."

"If that is true, then I must get back to the past."

This woman had the violet gift, just like Ikaria. But there was no way she would have been able to travel time with her given color and how dark purple her hair was.

She has consumed other colors.

"How many colors have you absorbed?" Auron said, his voice coming out a bit harsher than he intended. "You can heal. And time travel."

"I have absorbed all but two colors." Her purple eyes glanced at him as if she knew his thoughts. Auron saw the shame within their amethyst depths.

"I know what you are thinking. I have felt the same way for the last how many years that I have traveled. I have defied the laws of the gods, an action that has haunted me every day of my life," she said sadly. "But remorse and shame are the prices I pay to save the future."

"I see."

Auron had no other words for her. Her sins obviously affected her, just by listening to the weight of her heart while she spoke.

"Before I go," she said, "I need to know what this staff that was whispered of in the vision looks like. There was no imagery, as if the dream had been cut off."

"I wasn't able to weave the full message. For that, I am sorry. I was overcome by the sorceress's magic," Auron said.

"Where can I find it?"

"I was hoping the Ghost Man would find it back in time with my ancestors, but since you are here and have healed me, we can simply go retrieve it now," Auron said quickly. "I forgot it in the temple while I was meditating on my nightly prayers. Let us hope that it's still there, given the circumstances. The one who seeks to destroy us all might have it in her possession, knowing how cunning she is. If she does, there will be no chance in stopping her."

"Who is this sorceress you speak of?" the woman asked.

"I will tell you on the way," Auron answered. He held out his hands, summoning his yellow protection magic around them. The magical barrier encased them in a shimmering golden color.

"No need," she said, summoning her own barrier in a transparent violet. "I have my own." She nodded her head at him, motioning that she was ready to go. "Geeta."

"What?"

"That's my name. Geeta."

"Auron."

They made their way out of his chambers and through the citadel halls. As they turned around another corner, the walls began to shake violently, and the ground shifted. There were forceful booms, sounds that only magic could make, while screams and shouts echoed through the halls.

Auron and Geeta gave each other a knowing look. Auron had to choose between getting the staff first or what sounded like a confrontation with Ikaria. If they went to get the staff, it might be too late. The temple was on the other side of the citadel. They didn't have the time to do both. The Empress most likely had her reinforcements, and they were confronting her now. He made his decision.

"We need to try and stop Ikaria in this time at all costs. She can't travel back," Auron called out, leading the way through the corridors, running as fast as he could. "With your power, perhaps we might have a chance!"

"I will do what I can," Geeta said, sprinting right behind him.

CHAPTER 51

VIOLET

Y ou sent for me, sister?"

Ikaria strutted through the main audience hall, swaying her hips while the high heels of her shoes clacked firmly across the polished black marbled floors. Her hair, along with the fabrics of her headdress, flowed behind her, gracefully following her provocative moves. She heard the doors close as the guards blocked the entrance. Within the shadows of the hall, Ikaria saw the air ripple and move from her acquired orange magic. The illusionists. Now that they didn't have to mask the Emperor's appearance, they were solely concentrated on fooling her, hiding in the shadows.

This ought to be fun. Ikaria glanced out of the corner of her eye, trying to get a count and location on where all the orange-gifted were hiding. *Derek had better pull through and get that blood.*

Ikaria could take down the gifted, but it would still be challenging. She didn't have all of the colors of magic, which meant she could still be overwhelmed.

Ayera was seated on her throne, casting a glance down on Ikaria, who stood at the bottom of the stairs that led to the royal platform. The Emperor's seat was empty. Cyrus was probably still struggling back in her chambers, cursing her existence. The mere thought satisfied Ikaria immensely. Cyrus thought he was this so-called Ghost Man, with his tinted gift being masked or ghosted from the court. Clever, but wrong he was.

Ikaria gave Ayera a swift bow, then rose steadily, eyeing her sister. "What is with all of the formalities? Summoning me to the audience hall, with guards... and gifted?" Ikaria gestured around her at the invisible orange-gifted.

Ignoring the question, Ayera pressed on. "Ikaria, have you seen the Emperor as of late? Ever since I returned, no one has seen him."

Ikaria sneered. "How am I to know, sister? I am not your husband's *keeper.*"

"And Auron?" Ayera stated with grave concern. "I summoned him here earlier, but he has not yet come. I am told his chambers are empty."

Clever little Suri, masking Auron's body. Shrugging, Ikaria dismissed Ayera. "How am I to know where that priest is at? Probably off at the temple doing what priests do... praying. At least, that is what I am told they do."

"I am being serious, sister."

"So am I," Ikaria said darkly.

Ayera shot up from her throne, and Ikaria saw the airflow glide around her sister swiftly. The currents of the gifted moving around caught Ayera's hair in their wind, the long strands floating behind the Empress. They were getting into position to protect her. Through the illusion spells, Ikaria could see many of the gifted from World Sector Six—reds, oranges, and yellows.

"You know, Auron had a vision," Ayera said.

"He's always sticking his nose where it doesn't belong," Ikaria said, casually walking to the side of the royal platform, seemingly uninterested. "Let me guess. He told you that I am the *cause* of this magical plague, and that I am consuming everyone's power and absorbing the colors to complete the Spectrum of Magic. Did I sum that up correctly?"

Ayera's eyes suddenly watered, tears holding fast within the corners. Ayera looked terrified at the confrontation at hand. Loathing twisted inside Ikaria.

My sister doesn't have the stomach to be Empress...

"Is it true?" Ayera whispered. "Have you been absorbing others' power? Are you the cause of this plague?"

Ikaria narrowed her violet eyes. "That is what the High Court would have you believe. But they are the cause of the disappearance of magic, not me."

"Nonsense."

"It's true. Did you know that I found a book in our library, detailing any and all laws of magic?"

"You never told me of such a book."

Ikaria ignored her. "It said that all gifted have the ability to tap into colors that are next to theirs in the Spectrum of Magic. We gifted should have felt these other colors throughout our lives, and yet no one in the future has this ability. Don't you find that odd?"

"Why didn't you show this to me?"

"Because Lord Kohren was acting as a spy for the High Court! I was protecting you and this sector by not speaking of it! I knew that if I did, he would have found out about it and delivered that book to them. But he found it anyway, it seems. And now the High Court has likely destroyed that knowledge."

"They don't have spies, sister," Ayera said, sounding exhausted. "Why would they? We are under their law, and we faithfully abide by it!"

"Because they need my magic!" Ikaria cried. "Just ask your husband. Or maybe ask some of your orange-gifted. They have been masking his magic. In fact," she said, looking around the room with disdain, "they are all working together, since they have the ability to see right through their spells. They all *know*."

Ayera's face looked like it had been hit.

"They have been lying to you, sister. All of them. How convenient is it that the High Court has total control over the laws and magic? And how they want us to not be aware of our adjacent colors! Let's not forget their technological ban, enforced by them and the previous High Courts. And yet they themselves are using the old technology artifacts found on Earth to develop their own technology, making them even more powerful. Sister, they have the ability to *take away magic*, as well as give it to their spies, their supporters. What do you think their 'blessings' consist of?"

"Heresy!" Ayera said vehemently. "That is against the law of magic!"

"Precisely, sister. And who gets to decide the law of magic? Who keeps them in check? I think you know the answer to that one. Don't you see, sister? The High Court wants complete control over everything. Magic, technology, the world sectors. Complete control. They are trying to complete the Spectrum of Magic for themselves." Ikaria narrowed her eyes, whirling around at the invisible shapes hovering around her. "You know deep down that they killed Father and Mother. Why else would they press for you to be named heir the moment before I was to be named?"

"My coronation had nothing to do with that! Auron had a—"

"Yes, yes. Auron had a vision," Ikaria said mockingly. "A vision that was false. Any yellow can alter a prophecy. They planted that vision in his head so I wouldn't become Empress, because Father trusted Auron more than anyone else. In their eyes, Father needed to be gone for our stance on technology. We were a *threat* to their so-called peace. They murdered our parents to ensure they had a complacent person on the throne, with a sworn supporter as your husband. I guarantee Cyrus knew of the plot to kill our parents. Why else would he be so anxious to marry either one of us? He got what he wanted— to rule."

Ayera's tears began to flow from her cheeks, but her face remained still, her hair whipping around her. "That is what you really believe?"

"Yes. It is," Ikaria said sharply. "The High Court must be stopped. We can no longer idly sit by and let them have supreme rule and authority over all the sectors. Certainly not this sector." Ikaria boldly stood at the bottom of the throne's steps, facing her sister straight on. "Tell me, sister, with you as Empress of World Sector Six, are you just going to sit there and twiddle your thumbs while they take our technological artifacts away, all while letting them enforce more ridiculous laws on magic, continuing to suck everyone's power away?" Ikaria's voice echoed through the halls.

Ikaria watched Ayera's face twist with worry and confusion, standing in silence. Ikaria felt it, the many doubts swimming about in her mind. And there was a promise… one between her sister and their father… hidden away within the depths of Ayera's thoughts.

Ikaria swung around wildly, watching the invisible gifted. "Well, I for one, will not," Ikaria said, more as a threat to the invisible gifted. "I will do everything in my power to ensure they go down screaming. They fear me most, because I have what they don't: violet magic. And it aggravates them that they cannot control *me*. I am their worst nightmare, and they don't know how to stop me. That is why they wanted Father to send me to World Sector Three. But Father was smart enough to know that they wanted to contain my power and take it away!"

Ayera gasped, and her face went white. "How did you know about them asking Father to transfer you to World Sector Three?" Unsure of herself, Ayera shook her head, blinking away her tears. "I… I just don't believe you, sister. Just listen to yourself. Is it true that you have consumed other gifteds' blood? Or is that a lie too?"

"Four gifted in total, sister. All for a good cause," Ikaria said, no longer feeling the need to hide.

"And all this time… you have been hiding your power from the court… and from me." A deep sadness resonated in Ayera's accusation. "You didn't trust me. And yet I trusted you to find the out about the plague. Instead you killed four of our gifted and hid your powers from your own sister." Ayera's face hardened, shooting her a look of disgust.

"Spies, sister. *Spies*," Ikaria corrected her.

"*Witch!*" Ayera screamed. "Arrest her!" She shot out her finger at Ikaria, her eyes filled with rage and mixed with tears.

"So this is how it is, sister," Ikaria said in a condescending tone, narrowing her eyes. "Going to take me down with a pack of gifted like some wild beast out of control? I expected better of you," Ikaria sneered. "Have it your way."

With bright flashes of orange from every direction, the air materialized into the gifted. They instantly cast golden barriers surrounding themselves and Ayera, glowing with intense golden light. The room began to morph and twist, then suddenly the walls began to shift toward Ikaria. A large ring of glowing red ice and stone formed around her, trying to barricade her from all sides.

"Weak," Ikaria said contemptuously, amused at their attempt. She stretched her arms to the sky, burning with her dark-violet power. The walls, ice, and all of the gifted slammed back into various parts of the audience hall. The impact boomed, and crumbling sounds echoed from citadel's walls.

"You want to play games? Let's play, shall we?" Ikaria twirled to face the gifted, smiling at them mockingly as they recovered from the impact.

With all her powers combined, Ikaria melted away everyone's barriers while the world turned a deep purple, freezing them in time. A violent storm formed in the chamber, growing in size, swelling until the chamber could no longer contain it. The storm flashed violet lightning and whipped snow, hail, and glowing purple ice shards in all directions, smashing into the gifted, who remained frozen and helpless.

Except her sister. Ikaria protected her sister with her magic, casting a barrier around her. She couldn't harm her sister.

Ikaria began to laugh, as no one had time magic to stop her.

Through the heavy whirling snow and ice, Ayera watched her with sadness and awe as the gifted were pelted by the storm. Ikaria willed time to not allow them to move.

The violet ice whipped every which way at them within the cold, circling violet storm.

"We both know that I would have been the better ruler, sister," Ikaria snarled. "The throne is *mine*. It always was and always will be. I will take back what's rightfully mine, and then I will use all of my powers to shred the High Court into oblivion!" Ikaria flashed her younger sister a look of disapproval, her violet eyes glowing. The winds and ice continued to whip around her, her hair flying wildly. "And when I am Empress, I will restore the ancient ways with technology and heal our lands using the blood of the green! Without your support!"

"Not if I have anything to say about it!" called out a familiar voice.

A purplish-red burst of hot wind filled the chamber, counteracting Ikaria's ice storm. The snow and ice dissipated, creating slush waters at her feet. Ikaria was instantly surrounded by a purple magical force crushing her body.

Someone else had *her* color.

It had to be that gifted that Derek warned her about.

Snarling, Ikaria closed her eyes, sensing the minds who filled the chamber. Locating the mysterious caster, Ikaria then sent a forceful blow toward the violet caster's mind and felt the purple magic that surrounded the unknown violet caster flee.

Ikaria had stunned the woman temporarily.

Whipping her hair aside, Ikaria summoned her own violet protection barrier once again, reinforcing it through her mind. From the translucent violet barrier, Ikaria caught Auron's image next to the unfamiliar violet-gifted. He had been completely healed.

Always a thorn in my side, that damn priest!

Extending her arms, Ikaria sent a mind-shocking wave to the mysterious gifted woman, but she had her mind shielded with magic, mixing violet magic with the gift of the yellow.

This woman has consumed other colors too.

The violet woman charged at Ikaria while casting a large forceful blow toward her. Ikaria flashed out of her spot using dimensional magic, reappearing right behind the woman. Quickly summoning the gift of the orange, Ikaria caused the room to shift in different positions, making the woman confused about where Ikaria had appeared. With a flash of ice, Ikaria struck the woman in the middle of her chest, but her body was doused with Auron's magic, and the blow was not fatal.

"I see you have a friend with unique talents, Auron. Such a fraudulent priest you are, hanging around with sinners."

"She's here to stop you!" he said.

"Ah, I see. Your vision proved to be false, after all. She is no man, and she does not have the gift of the red."

Combining her magics, Ikaria constructed a complete circular force barrier around herself, crackling with violet lightning. The barrier began to grow in size as Ikaria funneled magic to it, intensifying the barrier. The purple-gifted woman began to unfreeze the other gifted, and the world faded back to its true color. One by one, the yellow-gifted began to counteract Ikaria's spell by siphoning the protection magic away from her barrier.

Any time now, Derek!

The purple-gifted woman joined in with the yellow-gifted, and they all worked on melting away her barrier. Ikaria grimaced, continuing to flow her magic to the barrier, but they were faster and stronger together.

Ikaria couldn't keep this up forever.

Then she heard Derek's call through time. He had the blood. Through the barrier, Ikaria glanced at her sister, giving her a smug look.

"Goodbye, sister. The next time you see me, I will have completed the Spectrum of Magic. There will be no stopping me." Ikaria's eyes burned violet-white as she laughed, and her body started to disappear slowly inside the barrier.

Auron, the purple-gifted woman, and the yellow-gifted intensified their magic, hoping to break the barrier before she disappeared, but it was too late. They couldn't penetrate the magical blockade fast enough.

With a sudden motion of her hands, Ikaria called forth time, letting its waters rush through her soul, and at the same time, released her barrier magic. The dark-violet magic exploded, shattering everything in it.

Then there were stars. A multitude of stars.

She was in the space-time continuum.

CHAPTER 52

The vial of blood had an odd glow to it, pulsating a brilliant red. Derek could feel the warmness of the blood through the glass vial. Emerald's blood. The secret she had been hiding from him, her being one of the gifted.

Even if she had confided in him years ago, Derek doubted that he would have believed it at the time. Now, with a sorceress invading his mind, a magical cyborg, and a disappearing scientist, it was hard not to believe in magic. Yes, it was very real. And her blood was the cause of all the events spiraling out of control.

It's for her own good, he told himself. *She needs to be queen of Arcadia. The people need her. I need her.*

He had wanted her for so long, and finally, he was about to have her. If she was going to be stubborn about marrying him, then he was just going to have to make the decision for her.

"Leave me," Derek ordered the servant who had delivered the blood. The servant bowed, then left the room, and Derek locked the door behind him.

Derek stared at the blood, sucking in his breath, watching the liquid illuminate its eerie essence.

I hope I don't regret this.

Derek glanced at the vial one last time, then closed his eyes. He clenched his teeth, not wanting to follow through with what he was about to do. If he did it, it meant he was indefinitely helping that witch. But was she all that bad?

Yes, she is! he told himself. But she had helped him as promised… And

Emerald. He had to help Emerald. She couldn't live under her father's tyranny.

Determined, Derek took one last deep breath. "Ikaria!" he called out.

There was a long pause. The air remained still, unmoving.

Perhaps Ikaria hadn't heard him. Derek looked around, wondering if he was crazy and it was all a dream, but the glow of the circlet on his vanity remained.

A moment later, the air rippled, and a transparent figure began to emerge. Slowly, the body became more opaque, and Ikaria's hourglass figure appeared in front of him.

She gave a long stretch, extending her body and sticking her chest out, her corset doing a poor job containing her ample breasts. She snapped back into place, then held out her hand, waiting for him to hand over the blood.

Derek clenched the vial involuntarily, then hesitantly placed it in her extended hand. Ikaria lifted the vial in front of her eyes, examining the blood to ensure it was magical. Then she smiled, letting out a joyous laugh.

"What took you so long?" she asked coyly. "I was in the middle of something when you called."

Derek narrowed his eyes. "Really? After all this time hounding me, you are suddenly in the middle of something?"

Ikaria held up a hand. "You really are too serious, my prince. You need to lighten up a little."

Her violet eyes looked to him as she raised the vial in front of her face, giving him a wicked smile. Ikaria popped off the cork, then raised the vial as if proposing a toast at a feast. Only this feast was far from ordinary.

"If this is anything like orange blood, I'll be in for a real treat," she said, eyeing him. She began to lick the contents of the blood, slowly and sensually, never taking her eyes off Derek, making him feel uncomfortable. Then she drank half of the vial with a swift flick of her wrist.

Derek blushed, looking down at the ground.

"Do not be embarrassed, my prince," she said as she swallowed the blood. Ikaria handed him the half-empty vial.

"Why are you giving me this?" Derek asked.

Ikaria flopped onto his bed, making herself comfortable as she sprawled her legs. "Because, it is your turn," Ikaria she said casually.

"My turn?"

Ikaria laughed, her violet eyes flashing at him brightly, her hair flinging back. "I've seen you in awe of the gift. Power is so... desirable. How much more fitting of a king you would be if the gift chose you? A king to match a gifted queen."

Derek looked down at the vial, watching the blood pulsate. Deep down, he wanted that power. Thinking of all he could do with that power, it was tempting. He could use it for good, for his people, and for Emerald.

Ikaria's last words rang in his head. *If the gift chose you.*

He looked over at Ikaria as she threw back her head in ecstasy. A darkness had formed around her, misting and swirling around her body as the magic worked through her system. Through the darkness, an intense black power radiated from Ikaria's heart as she began to thrash on his bed, appearing to be in intense pain and intense pleasure.

Derek closed his eyes as Ikaria's climaxing cries filled the room. Trying to block out the noise, Derek thought of Emerald. How much he wanted her, how much he desired a simple smile from her. How much he burned for her. With power, Emerald could confide in him, feel close to him...

He slowly raised the vial to his lips, hesitating. Then, pushing back all arguments that arose in his head, Derek quickly drank the glowing liquid.

A horrible death grip immediately filled Derek's lungs. It was as if time had stopped his body, freezing him into an eternal state. He couldn't breathe. The more he tried to, the more fear and paranoia poured over his soul, sinking him to the depths of his heart.

A sharp pain shocked him throughout his being, stabbing deeper and deeper into his core. Derek crumpled to the couch in a fetal position, sweating more than he did with his mysterious sickness.

His heart began to beat rapidly. It pounded through his chest, beating with such ferocity that it pushed him to the verge of a panic attack. He ripped off most of his clothes, then melted to the floor, the pain becoming more intense by the minute.

Images from different times, the past, present, and future, flashed before him. They were constantly changing, moving, flowing through the river of time. Each one flashed as his heart beat quicker, like the beat of a song gone mad.

Emerald stood before his eyes with that man from the lower levels. She was cradled in his arms, a bright smile on her face. But instead of enraging him, the image saddened him, drove his soul into a deep depression.

Derek cried out for Emerald, holding out his hand for her to take it, but she turned away.

The image of her disappeared, leaving him alone in the blue void. Grief bled through his heart, and his existence became desolate. He had no reason to live without her.

He sunk to the bottom of his sadness, letting it envelop his soul. His vision became a blur within a sapphire world, drowning in a pit of nothingness while the sounds of Ikaria's climatic, erotic laughs echoed in his ears.

CHAPTER 53

Vulnerable. That was how Ayera felt. Completely vulnerable.

Ayera shifted her eyes around the room, watching a few of the orange-gifted dissolve away, becoming unseen once again. Shivering, Ayera felt their eyes still on her, watching her every movement and expression.

Was what Ikaria said about Cyrus true? Were all the orange-gifted keeping his secret from her? Were the other red- and yellow-gifted aware of his power as well?

She felt like a fool.

Angrily, Ayera wiped away a tear.

Whether it was true or false, the High Court would no doubt find out what had taken place today. She had failed, and Ikaria had succeeded in her plan to travel back in time. World Sector Six hadn't been able to stop her.

Auron slowly approached the platform with the mysterious violet-gifted woman, both waiting for her to speak. The other gifted that remained were just as shocked as Ayera. The revelation of spies within World Sector Six's court, the unknown ability of adjacent magic, or Ikaria having the ability to wield her own magic with other colors… it was a lot to take in.

Ayera whipped around. "No one is to leave this chamber! I want everyone to be seen!" she ordered, her voice booming through the hall.

The orange-gifted that remained turned to face their invisible counterparts, while the other gifted eyed the room curiously, waiting for them to follow orders.

The few gifted didn't appear, which made Ayera furious. They had no respect for her or her command.

"Arrest those who choose not to obey!" Ayera said.

The violet-gifted woman headed for the doors, outstretching her palms. The doors clicked into a locked position. With another swift gesture from the woman, violet magic flowed through the air, ribboning around invisible bodies. The violet woman swept her hand, and the violet-magic-infused bodies were hurled to the foot of Ayera's platform.

The violet woman returned, then bowed. "I believe they were attempting to leave, Your Majesty."

"I suspected as much." Ayera narrowed her tear-stained eyes. "Show yourselves!"

The orange-gifted appeared gradually, struggling within the confines of the violet magic that bound them.

"Were you the ones masking the Emperor? Tell me! Were you and all your orange-gifted friends in on the Emperor's secret?"

One of the orange-gifted, Mikko, spoke. "No, Your Majesty. There were only three of us."

"I want the truth!" Ayera shouted.

"It is the truth, Empress."

Ayera turned to the other orange-gifted, shaking with anger, pointing. "And you all, if what he says is true, why did you not see what they were doing? Did you not see the Emperor cloaked within their spells?"

Another orange-gifted, Jonas, answered. "Empress, we have never seen the Emperor masked with magic. We saw him as you did, with brown hair and eyes. I can say for certain, at least for me, we have not seen anything that was out of the ordinary."

"I do not stand for liars, Sir Jonas!"

"I swear it!"

"Your Majesty, what he says is true," the violet woman said.

Ayera eyed the woman. "How do you know?"

"Because I can feel their minds. He isn't lying." The woman walked over to the group of magically bound men and gave them a kick with her boot. "But these guys, they are at fault."

"I see." Ayera watched the men as they lowered their gaze. "How is it that you are able to fool the other orange-gifted?"

The men remained silent.

"That was an order, *sirs*."

They continued their silence, glaring at her.

"Their magic has been intensified by infusion," the violet woman said, staring at them curiously. "By… a blessing?" The woman glanced over at Mikko, raising an eyebrow.

"Did you sense that too, stranger?" Ayera asked hesitantly.

"No, I just heard their thoughts."

The men glared at the woman and grunted, trying to break free from her magic.

"Take them away. I want them on lockdown in the dungeons, and I want five gifted stationed at all times. Lord Nathan!"

"Yes, Your Majesty." The man stepped forward, his red hair glistening.

"I put you in charge of this task. You are to assemble teams and ensure that each group is balanced with different colors of gifted."

The man bowed low, then glanced hesitantly at the entrapped men.

"Remove them from my sight before I do something that I regret!" Ayera snapped. "And as for everyone else, I want everyone out. Now!"

Auron and the violet woman were about to leave, but Ayera called out, "Not you, Auron. And your acquaintance. You two may stay."

Auron and the violet woman stood before her as the others gave them curious looks. Some of the gifted melted out of sight while others exited the hall's doors, following the string of guards and gifted escorting the magically bound men. As the last of the gifted exited the hall, the doors closed behind them.

"Empress…" Auron began.

Ayera held out her hand to silence him, then let out a loud sob, staggering backward into her throne. "I don't even know if I can speak my thoughts, Auron. I… I don't know what to think."

Auron frowned. Ayera was sure he didn't know what to make of the situation either.

"What happened with the High Court, Empress?" he asked earnestly. "Why did they not send you reinforcements?"

Ayera scoffed at the mention of them. No wonder why Ikaria hated them so. The more that was revealed, the more ammunition Ikaria had against them, and it forced her to consider that her sister's concerns about them held some truth. She seldom agreed with Ikaria, and now was not the best time to start. Or was it?

"Auron, the High Court did not want to send any gifted to help. Instead, they pushed the problem back on us." Ayera's eyes met his. "They also said that your vision was not true, the part about Ikaria destroying the world; Tyllos said it wouldn't happen. Furthermore, they made it very clear if we do not put a stop to my sister, I would be dethroned." Ayera sighed, waving her hand aimlessly at her throne. "I think I shall not be seated up here much longer unless we do something about it. Perhaps I have already lost it."

Auron looked like he had been slapped by the God of Light himself. "Truly, Empress? How could they say that? I have been proven correct every time!"

"Something is going on here," Ayera said quietly. "And with Cyrus... Why were we not made aware? And these 'blessings'? What are they?" Ayera turned to the violet woman, hoping for answers.

"I didn't hear much, Empress," the woman answered immediately, sensing her question. "They were trying hard not to think, as if they understood my power. I only heard the word 'blessings' and a thought of some kind of super power to enhance their magic."

Ayera studied the woman for a moment. She was bizarre, like no one Ayera had ever seen. Her hair was wild, her fashions strange. She was a unique gifted, without a doubt. "Who are you, stranger?" Ayera asked.

"Geeta, Your Majesty."

"Where did you come from, Geeta?"

"The past."

Auron stepped forward, bowing. "Empress, allow me to explain. Your sister was secretly waiting for me in my chambers earlier this evening. Upon entering, a battle ensued between us." Auron paused, then lowered his gaze. "She easily overwhelmed me, causing me to lose consciousness. I was on the brink of death, or perhaps I really did pass away. It was hard to tell. But before I thought I had passed into the God of Light's realm, I sent a message, using all my power, to reach the Ghost Man."

Ayera's eyes flickered to the strange violet woman. "Is she the Ghost Man?"

The woman bowed as if it came naturally to her, unlike her unnatural appearance. "No, I am not. Auron's message reached further back in time than he intended. I came to help find the man in Auron's vision and to help stop the destruction of the earth."

It seemed that Geeta was the only one Ayera could trust besides Auron.

The God of Darkness take the orange-gifted for their deception! And Cyrus, he had deceived her too, just like he had with her sister. No wonder Ikaria wanted vengeance. And where was he? Was he even alive? Had Ikaria killed him too?

"What now, Empress? What do we do about Ikaria?" Auron asked quietly.

Ayera shifted in her seat. "She must not return to this time era." The coldness of the throne sent a chill up her spine. The words of the High Court echoed in her head. She couldn't lose her father's throne. She would be the biggest disappointment of World Sector Six.

"I concur, Empress," Auron agreed. "If she returns with the gift of the black, it will be too late. She must be stopped back in time. Empress, whatever High Justice Tyllos thinks, I am sure that my vision is correct." Auron's voice shook, as if he was hesitant about the whole situation. She didn't blame him; she was feeling the same as he did.

"I agree with you, Auron."

He paused in thought. "What if we sent our sector's gifted back in time to stop Ikaria?"

"But how would that be any different than what just took place? We couldn't take her on in *this* era!"

"But the Ghost Man is back in the other time, along with this green-gifted princess. With those two, and with Geeta and our gifted, it would boost our chances in stopping Ikaria. And perhaps I can persuade the gifted in the other sectors..."

Ayera paused at his proposed plan. It sure sounded a lot better than doing nothing. For some reason, the High Court said they would stop Ikaria if she came back to this time. That didn't sit well with her. Minute by minute, her faith in the High Court was dissolving.

"You think you can persuade other sectors?"

"My old sector, Sector Four, would aid us, I am sure of it. My niece Vala has much influence in that court." Auron paused, then lowered his eyes. "But as far as the other sectors, I do not know."

"And how do we get to the past?" Ayera asked. "We would need your niece to come with us. We have no blue-gifted here, and she is the only blue-gifted that we have connections with in any of the world sectors. We must pray with all our hearts that she will be willing to help us."

"Do not worry about that, Empress. I will ensure that she will help us."

Geeta cleared her throat gently, getting Ayera's and Auron's attention. "There is one problem, Empress. If the gifted travel back in time without the blood of the green, they would not be able to stay in that time era for long. Their bodies would disintegrate within minutes without that blood. You might have fifteen minutes at most. It's the God of the Blue's design, limiting how much power a blue-gifted has over the flow of time."

God of the Blue? Never had Ayera heard of that god before. Doesn't she mean the God of Light, or his angels? This violet woman had some rather strange notions.

"Maybe… this green-gifted princess could help us by offering her blood?" Ayera suggested quietly.

Auron and Geeta stood in silence, slowly meeting her gaze.

"Empress? You cannot be serious…" Auron said, aghast. "That is against the God of Light's laws. The gifted cannot consume another gifted's blood! You know that! You yourself have preached against it!"

Ayera rubbed her eyes, feeling very tired. She had. She was completely against breaking any laws that the High Court and the God of Light had established. But everything had changed. No help from the High Court was coming, and her sister had consumed almost all of the magics, traveling back in time to disrupt everything, all to destroy the High Court and claim the throne, only to destroy the future of the planet in the process. This was no time to follow the rules. And something in her gut was telling her that the High Court could not stop her sister in this time if Ikaria succeeded.

"Perhaps, Auron, it is time we reevaluate the rules. And time to break them. To do what is right." Auron opened his mouth in protest, but Ayera continued. "I know exactly how you feel, and I don't like it, just as much as you. But if my sister does make it back to our time, then we are all doomed, just as your vision states. We must do what is necessary to stop her in the past. Even if it is by defying the God of Light's laws."

"What of this princess? She cannot possibly give her blood to an army of gifted," Geeta said. "She would die as a result."

Ayera sighed heavily. Geeta was right. "Then we must fight until we disintegrate," Ayera answered. "Perhaps if Vala can get us to the right time and exact place, fifteen minutes will be enough to stop Ikaria."

Auron's troubled face met hers, while Geeta nodded in approval.

"We will prepare our gifted," Ayera said. "Geeta, we need you to find the

Ghost Man. We will decide upon a time and place to meet you in the past. Meanwhile, Auron, you must travel quickly to World Sector Four."

"I can take you there. No need to travel," Geeta offered.

Auron turned to Ayera. "Should we tell the other gifted about what will happen to them back in time?"

"It's your choice. I will leave that up to you. Perhaps if you do, it will make them fight even harder."

"And what of the Emperor?"

Ayera sighed. What was she to do with him? Ayera turned to Geeta. "Might I ask a favor before you and Auron leave?"

"I would be glad to assist you," Geeta answered.

"It will not take long." Ayera stood up, looking down on the two of them. "Auron, please fetch an orange-gifted whom you trust. Take whomever you select, along with Geeta, and find the Emperor. He has to be here somewhere, either dead or alive, masked by Ikaria's magic. Once you have located him, lock him up if he is still alive."

"Empress… are you sure about this? He is our *Emperor*." Auron shook his head in disbelief.

"Yes, and he also has deceived us all. The God of Light take me now, but I believe my sister about Cyrus. Have Geeta and the orange-gifted spellbind and enchant one of our dungeons to hold my sister. We need a place that Ikaria's magic can be contained."

"Empress, even with that combination, she might still be able to overcome an enchanted room," Geeta said.

"Do whatever you can. We need her somewhere where she can meddle with our sector's affairs no longer. That is, if we succeed in the past."

"Right away, Empress," Auron said.

"Send word when you find Cyrus, Auron. I have many questions for him if he is truly alive," Ayera said, nodding politely to the priest and Geeta, then dismissed them before they bowed and walked out.

Yes, she had many questions for her husband indeed.

***

"Your Majesty, we found the Emperor. He is alive. Auron and the violet-gifted woman are with him now."

Ayera shot up from her chair in her council room, throwing down a missive that she had been attempting to write. "Where is he, Lord Jian?"

"He is in Sorceress Ikaria's chambers, Empress." The orange-gifted bowed, his sparkling mandarin-orange eyes meeting hers. "It appeared that he was being held hostage. He was bound with your sister's magic, and well…" The lord cleared his throat, clearly uncomfortable.

"And?"

"He was completely nude, Your Majesty," Lord Jian answered, turning red in the cheeks. "And masked with an illusion spell, I might add. The violet woman is holding him with her magic now."

Ayera frowned. So her husband just couldn't help himself. Had Ikaria had her way with Cyrus just to stick it to her? Or was it all a trap to get Cyrus to step aside?

Not wanting to think about it any further, Ayera turned to Jian. "Thank you for your assistance, Lord Jian. Take me to him now."

Jian bowed, then moved toward the council room exit, waiting for Ayera to follow suit. They walked swiftly through the corridors until they came upon Ikaria's chambers. As Lord Jian opened the door, Ayera immediately saw Cyrus's face, and he had light pink hair and magenta eyes.

He was angry.

And just like Lord Jian had said, Cyrus was naked, bound by a magical violet cord. Auron was in the room, averting his eyes while Geeta stood beside the chair holding Cyrus with her magic, funneling her violet power into the cord.

Cyrus turned to her immediately, his body struggling within the confines of the magic.

"Ayera! What is the meaning of this? Why have you not set me free? I demand you do so at once!" Cyrus barked. "Or are you working with your sister, too?" His spiteful eyes narrowed.

Ayera raised an eyebrow, then glanced at his naked flesh. He looked so pitiful. She could only imagine Ikaria gloating over Cyrus's woe and humiliation.

"Why are you naked?" Ayera asked innocently. She knew why, and she had always pretended not to notice Cyrus's lust for other women. But it couldn't be helped. He was such a fool, and she wanted him to understand how foolish he had been for deceiving her.

"Your sister tried to seduce me, that *witch*!" Cyrus snapped. "I *knew* she was nothing but trouble! If only you had listened to me about heeding the High Court's counsel, we wouldn't be in this predicament!"

"You mean *you* wouldn't be in this predicament," Ayera corrected him.

"Now's not the time to get smart with me, Ayera. Have them unbind me right this instant!"

"No," Ayera stated firmly. "You are under arrest for treason."

Cyrus scoffed, his face a mask of incredulity. "On what grounds?" He laughed as if she'd just told a joke.

"For conspiring with the other orange-gifted to conceal your identity. That is a big offense in our world sector. You know that."

Ayera knew he was secretly involved with the High Court, but she had to tread carefully.

"The High Court gave me their approval to do so!" Cyrus argued.

"Well, in order to corroborate your story, I must send an envoy to the High Court and see if what you say is true. In the meantime, you will be locked up."

"This is ridiculous! You think you will lock me up?" Cyrus spat. "Go ahead, make enemies with the other world sectors! The High Court will excommunicate you, you shall see! Maybe then I will be rid of a stiff little bitch such as yourself and get myself a wife of my choosing!"

"Your Majesty?" Auron said quietly from behind as his mouth dropped in shock.

Ayera frowned. His words didn't hurt, but they did ring true. She really was a stiff woman. Did everyone see her like that?

Geeta noticed her expression, then gave Cyrus a hard kick in the shin. "I know many men like you. All have seen unfortunate ends," she said through gritted teeth.

"Don't trouble yourself, Geeta," Ayera said. She turned to Cyrus. "Before we put you away, I must know why you chose to hide your power. Why do so? It is such a waste of time. Your whole life a facade! We are free peoples of magic; it serves no purpose for you to hide."

"To hell with you if you think I'm going to answer!" Cyrus spit out.

"Does it have anything to do with the 'blessings'?" Ayera asked slowly, suspicion growing in her mind at his reaction.

Cyrus paused, just for a split second, but that second was enough to confirm it.

"I answer to no one but the High Court!" Cyrus said.

"You are correct, Your Majesty," said Geeta. "It does have to do with the blessings. I can feel his power; it is foreign, something he wasn't born with."

"You don't know anything, *witch*! That's what all the violet-gifted are! Witches!"

"Take him away!" Ayera ordered.

Geeta funneled her violet magic to the Emperor, forcing his body to stand. As they walked out of the chambers, violet magic floated through the air, picking up one of Ikaria's bedsheets, then made its way back to the Emperor, covering his lowers.

"Auron, before you leave," Ayera said.

"Yes, Your Majesty?"

"Make sure Lord Nathan rotates his team of guards on the Emperor."

Auron bowed. "Yes, Empress."

"Please hurry yourself to World Sector Four. Time is running out, and we need far more gifted than what we have. I will pray for your success. Heavens know, we need it."

CHAPTER 54

❖————————————❖

ORANGE

Why did she create images of the same man, over and over again? Always the same pigmented colors of the spectrum's wavelength. 620–750 nanometers.

Malfunction.

There were sixty-two pictures in total. Sixty-three after she finished this one.

Drew watched silently as the princess confidently painted with each brush stroke in shades of red on her canvas. How she worked was like how his memories were returning to him. Patches of paint slowly formed an image, like a camera lens that was blurry, now coming into focus. It was like his dream, the same one he had been having since his awakening. Slowly, the dream was starting to make sense to him, but he hadn't quite figured out all the details. The green jewel he needed to replicate one hundred times.

He figured out it was the princess that he needed to replicate, but why?

Malfunction.

What purpose would it serve?

Drew glitched at the thought.

He's trying to think like a human… said a voice, laughing within the network. *Don't we all wish we were human again?*

Ignoring the voice, Drew continued to watch the princess Emerald. This man that the princess painted, he was the same man who Drew had fought when he had been ordered to capture her. To Drew, it seemed that she didn't want to be taken away and escorted back to her home. But who was he to stand against his orders? It was hopeless even if he tried—his programming wouldn't allow it. Like the other voices in the network said before, he was no longer human. Only a fraction.

But something was bothering him on the inside. He had felt compelled to help fix the princess's drawings. It wasn't an order, but it wasn't necessarily going against his programming either. He had a strange feeling... He'd *wanted* to help her. It felt good to his circuits, and right on the inside.

Telly. He had just started to remember their past before she left the lab. Just mere fragments, but it was enough for him to piece the memories together to give him enough information. The corporation. They took her away from him. Inside, he felt no joy, only anger toward the company. And what about Gwen? What had happened to their daughter? He had so many questions to ask Telly, but she was gone now, and he was at the palace, ordered to guard the princess.

Drew convulsed at his thoughts, which caused him to flash orange in and out of view like a broken screen.

The princess looked up from her painting, eyes concerned.

There he goes again, said another voice in the computerized stream. *Trying to process his past...*

It's useless, an electronic voice called out in the network.

"Are you... okay?" Emerald asked, pausing.

Drew blinked with his good left eye, suddenly aware she was talking to him. He nodded, using the only form of communication he had. Telly had the tablet.

"You scared me for a moment. I keep forgetting that you are there."

He did too. Half of the time he lived in his dreams, where he felt more real than reality itself.

The princess faintly smiled, then turned her attention back to her picture, working swiftly.

The princess. The dreams are always of the princess. And the darkness. Every dream, it showed Drew what he needed to accomplish: to replicate the princess. The last dream he had, she was traveling to another time. But he couldn't let her. There was darkness beyond the portal of time. He had to protect her from the darkness. He copied her one hundred times, filling the skies of Arcadia.

We need her one hundred times... echoed the voice in the dream.

One hundred times... I need to replicate the Princess one hundred times, Drew thought.

Malfunction.

Are you trying to override your programming? called out a voice within the network. *Because if you are trying to have thoughts outside your capabilities, it will result in overload.*

Do you know about my dreams? Drew asked the network.

Dreams? Machines don't dream, laughed another voice. *We just sleep.*

I don't! Drew argued with the voices. *My dreams tell me that I have to replicate the princess one hundred times!*

Good luck with that, another voice said.

I can do it, Drew insisted. *I have been given the gift, as records state. 590-620 nanometers in color. I just need to figure out why, and I can do it!*

There is no why. We don't question. We follow orders, replied the voice.

There is no free will with the master, said another voice within the stream.

Who is the master? Drew asked the voice.

He doesn't know the master? an incredulous voice asked.

The one who gives the orders.

But anyone can give us orders! Drew argued inside the network.

Not just anyone. The one who has the master gauntlet. It controls us all, overriding anyone's orders...

Master gauntlet?

The master lies dormant right now. But he will awake soon. We are on standby.

Drew shuddered, trying to process what it all meant. Who was the master? The more he tried to process who the master was, the more he flickered nonstop like a fading star. The orange magic that pumped through his veins became so intense that Drew was on the brink of going into shock. Shaking violently, sparks began to shoot out of his circuitry as he swung wildly at the wall with his metal hand, trying to stabilize himself. Instead, the metal hand screeched against the wall, missing his grip entirely and falling to the floor.

The princess stopped painting while her handmaiden backed away into a corner, holding her hands up for protection. Her hands would not stop his magic. Humans didn't use logic in dire situations, Drew had come to realize. Their actions were the results of their emotions. This handmaiden was acting on fear.

In a split second, the princess extended her hand, summoning a translucent green-yellow half-dome barrier in front of her. Funneling her power through her hand, bright-green magic pulsated into the protective dome, strengthening it.

Slowly, she walked toward him as the sparks from his orange magic bounced off her transparent shield. Drew continued to shake, watching her approach with caution. She lowered her body to meet his, then reached out her other arm, the one that funneled no magic.

Through the sparks emitting from his body, Emerald laid a hand on his arm, a friendly gesture to calm him. Her touch… the feeling of her hand gave him a sense of peace, a tranquil sensation that someone cared.

Drew's heavy breathing subsided while the sparking from his circuitry slowly came to a halt.

An awareness came over Drew. The princess cared about him, and she wanted to help him. How could he possibly know that? His program scan didn't tell him, and she didn't say. It was a feeling… a knowing.

He jolted again.

"What have they done to you?" the princess whispered, staring deep into his good eye, wisping away her barrier.

Malfunction.

"Why did they make it so that you can't talk?"

Drew cocked his head at her, unsure of how to answer. All he could do was continue to breathe from his episode.

"Well, I'm going to fix that. Or at least try," she said firmly. She hesitated, then continued, "That is, if you will allow me to."

Fix me?

Drew nodded in response, waiting curiously for what was going to happen.

Princess Emerald closed her eyes, laying a hand on his throat. Drew could feel the coolness of her skin against his hot flesh, alleviating the heat from within. With a sudden burst, a green glow began to beat brightly in her hand. The magic burned into a bright whitish-green color, basking the whole room in its light.

A pulsating sensation came over Drew, beating to the same time as his heart. Faster and faster the beating magic continued, pumping through his body, then settling in his neck. The wires within began to shift uncomfortably as the power continued to pour in.

The uncomfortable feeling turned into sharp, stabbing pains, and his body felt like it wanted to reject his circuitry, to purge its unnaturalness. He jolted violently in response.

The green magic halted swiftly while his insides stopped shifting, and then the room was no longer colored in hues of green.

"It's all wrong," Emerald said quietly, her face downcast. "Your body is too... artificial. I'm so sorry that I couldn't heal you." She smiled sadly at him, laying her hand on his. "I don't know what they put you all through, but I swear I am going to see that you and the others are freed, regardless of who is sitting on the throne. I will find a way."

Her words resonated with him, deepening his resolve for the need to protect her. She wanted to help him... She wanted to help all of the cyborgs. And for that, if it was in his power, he was going to help her in any way he could.

Drew nodded in response, fading back into the air once again as the orange magic enveloped his being.

CHAPTER 55

YELLOW

Auron gripped Geeta's hand tightly as they flew across the world of blues and violets. The skies were dotted with small floating sky citadels and airships, all void of motion within Geeta's time-dimension spell. Her free hand held his staff, its crystal orb glowing a bright violet-blue.

Auron's directions were a bit rough, as he hadn't frequented World Sector Four by use of airships in a while. Hopefully he was guiding her in the right direction. It was hard to follow the sun since it was a little after midday, and its placement was directly above them. He should be in prayer at this time, but it was no time for prayer.

"Don't let go of my hand, otherwise you will end up in whatever part of the world we are in. Not to mention, you will fall aimlessly to the earth…"

Auron gave Geeta a weak smile, trying not to look directly below. Air travel always made him woozy, and especially now that he had nothing underneath his feet. It was just him and the air that floated around him. At any time, he could heave up his morning meal.

"I don't plan on letting go," Auron stated. "As much as I would love to see Earth's ground, I do not want to visit it the unconventional way. And even if I were to survive the fall, my lungs couldn't endure for that long on the surface."

"Is that why the future took to the skies? Is there no place that is inhabitable on the surface below?"

"There are a few patches of land deemed safe, but even then, the toxic winds blow in, and the dwellers have to take shelter for months at a time.

They've built specific buildings designed to filter out the poison."

"I see. And your sky citadels... all have been enchanted by the red, orange, and blue-gifted, I take it? Red for the earthen materials, the ground that it sits on and the winds that uphold it. Blue for the placement within the earth's dimensional space and orange to bind them together?"

"Correct. It takes months of funneling their magic at a constant stream to build one of the citadels. Many gifted are rotated in and out for food and sleep, but that's about it."

Geeta glanced at one of the small citadels as they passed by, smiling. "It's remarkable...I never thought the future would come to this. The beauty of the sky citadels are just as captivating as the skyscrapers of the past."

Auron frowned. "The city-kingdoms of old deserved their destruction."

"Oh? How's that?" Geeta's nostrils flared at his statement.

"Because people forgot about their creator and instead put faith in their machines and technology."

"You are right about the people forgoing religion for technology, but I disagree that they deserved their demise."

Auron was a bit amused at her statement. "And why is that?"

She eyed him with her glowing purple eyes. "I've been to the past; I have seen the great city-kingdoms. And what the humans have created is *beautiful*. The gods have blessed us with vision, creativity, and intelligence. And what the people did with their God-given talents, it is breathtaking."

"Don't tell me that you are swayed by the darkness too, friend," Auron said. "Technology was the cause of Earth's demise. Surely even you can see past the beauty of the machines and see them for what they are—instruments of darkness."

"I *do* see them for what they are—tools. It's what the person does with those tools that makes it bad or good." Geeta sighed, then turned her gaze away, looking into the distance. "I have seen many people in the past that were clothed as priests of light, only to have darkness consume their hearts. I have also seen machines with souls that were sent out to do bad, but underneath had hearts that were pure."

Machines with souls? Now that was beyond ridiculous. Geeta was definitely misguided in her beliefs, especially regarding the machines.

They continued to move quickly through the dimensional airspace, Geeta effortlessly guiding them with the power of flight. Auron now fully understood the power of the blue-gifted. He had known that the blue-gifted could move as they pleased within the time-and-space dimensional world. They could have walked, crawled, or jumped in the air without weight and so forth, but floating quickly seemed much more effortless than walking. When the blue-gifted disappeared and reappeared in a second, it took the gifted moments, even hours, in their dimensional time world to get to one spot to another. To the regular person, it was instantaneous. But for the blue-gifted, it was long and drawn out. It gave Auron a new appreciation for their power.

"It's too bad it takes so long within this spell to travel. I can't believe this is what the blue-gifted do. What's the point of traveling within a spell if you can just walk?" Auron said, not expecting Geeta to answer. Kohren seemed to always want to flash into different places rather than walk, Auron thought. Maybe he just wanted to exercise his power occasionally.

"I know for a fact they can flash from one place to another within the dimensional world," Geeta said, giving Auron a crooked smile. "I just haven't figured out how. I was never good at casting blue-violet magic. Couldn't harness its power unlike my other color, red-violet. In fact, I would say I have close to the full casting potential of red, whereas blue just fizzles for me. I have even consumed blue-gifted blood, and yet I still cannot seem to grasp the potential of this color." Geeta eyed him for a moment as her earrings dangled from the force of their bodies being pushed through the skies. "You never told me why you are missing magic, by the way."

"I don't know. I never knew us gifted had that kind of potential," Auron said truthfully. "It's not mentioned in *The Spectrum*, nor has any gifted ever had that kind of power in my lifetime."

"Hmm," Geeta said, flaring her nose again. "It's something for you future gifted to dig into. The gods blessed us with our analogous magics, and some are so fortunate to be able to use the full power of the adjacent magics, or almost all of it. Like me and my red magic. Especially if the future is in need of healing. You should have that magic and be able to cast some healing and illusion spells. It's strange you do not."

To think he could heal with the power of what is called analogous magic. Auron recalled Ikaria mentioning that while he and Geeta tried to stop her from traveling back in time. She was certainly aware of that power. That thought scared him.

Auron and Geeta saw two other floating citadels in the distance, and he recognized their structures at once. The two citadels were linked by a long bridge, unifying them as one. It was one of the more unique citadels in the world, housing many of World Sector Four's people.

"World Sector Four's court citadel is close," Auron said. "Just keep heading in this direction."

As time passed, World Sector Four's court citadel appeared off in the clouds. The sunlight caught its reflective metal shell, gleaming in the sky. The floating earth chunk that the citadel was situated on was heavily eroded, the rock below jagged to a sharp point, with vines intertwining and wrapping the bottom. How Auron missed his old home.

"Over on that platform. That's where they receive visitors," Auron said to Geeta, pointing to the eastern platform.

She nodded, quickly floating over to the dock, and they landed their weightless feet on the platform. Auron saw the guards posted out front, frozen in time, unable to see the two of them within the blue-violet world.

Geeta let go of Auron's hand, and their bodies emitted a violet flash, startling the guards.

They blinked for a moment, catching their breath, then saw Auron's face.

"High Priest Auron?" one of the guards said. They looked to Geeta, and their eyes went wide. It was likely the first time they had ever seen a violet-gifted. Especially one who had the powers of blue magic.

"Yes. I am here to see the Lady Vala," Auron said. He turned to Geeta, then nodded in appreciation. "Thank you. Without your help, I would have wasted time on the airship."

"Anytime," Geeta said, nodding. "I wish you many blessings of the gods for your success."

"I will ensure we get more gifted to help our cause," Auron assured her.

"Good. I will be waiting for you in the past. Don't be late," she said firmly. "I will see that the Ghost Man gets this." She held up the staff, her hand clenched firmly around it.

Geeta flashed Auron a small half smile as her body radiated a bright purple. A violet-blue time portal appeared under her feet, then shot upward, erasing her body as it moved over her. With a twinkling flash, Geeta was gone.

Auron had to admit, the woman was rather odd and very perplexing. Geeta appeared delicate at times, and other times she was hard. She loved her gods but embraced the technology of old. She was a saint to help but a sinner by her blood consumption. She was certainly the most unique gifted that Auron had never met in his lifetime.

The guards led Auron into the depths of the citadel, passing its golden halls etched with geometric designs. Enchanted orange-glowing glass orbs were spread out above the hallways, hovering, giving the golden halls an even more golden appearance, if that was possible.

They came to an elaborate set of doors and knocked.

A woman with deep eyes and chestnut hair opened the door. She saw Auron's face, then let out an audible gasp, bowing immediately.

"High Priest Auron. I assume that you have come to see the Lady Vala."

"I have. Is she here?"

"No, she is at court right now. But come inside and make yourself comfortable while I go fetch her."

"Thank you, Katrina."

The servant ran off with the guards as Auron entered Vala's chambers. He walked a few steps in, admiring how richly decorated her quarters were. The entry room was large, with windows that stretched from floor to ceiling and covered the entire wall. Sunlight poured into her chambers, basking her richly decorated and embroidered furniture, seating cushions, and thick tapestries in a warm light. Her chambers were much more colorful than World Sector Six's designs and interiors, dabbed with reds, oranges, and violets, with a few hints of blue.

Auron smiled. Vala always had said that the God of Light accidentally made her blue-gifted while she was secretly meant to be red. If one were to judge her by her room's appearance, red was her main color, with the accents of the colors that fell next to it in the spectrum close seconds. Blue was only slightly scattered in, as if his niece was still in denial about being born with blue magic.

The doors opened, and Vala and Katrina appeared. Vala had on a traditional blue dress in the fashion of World Sector Four's design. Auron noticed that she had cut her tight cobalt curls since the last time he had seen her, giving much definition to her face, framing it beautifully. Vala wore a thick golden circlet with a sapphire set in the middle, distinguishing herself as a gifted lady of the court, and had decorated herself with large golden earrings and a golden necklace that covered most of her neck and chest. Her makeup was based on gold, bring contrast to her ebony skin and water-blue eyes.

"Uncle?" Vala smiled, running over to greet him with a quick hug. "What brings you here?"

Auron returned her embrace, meeting her gaze. "Vala, I have come here on urgent business."

"What is it, Uncle?" Vala waved her hand to her servant, then took a seat on one of the plush sitting cushions. The maid returned with hot tea.

"I need your help, and so does World Sector Six." Auron paused, shaking his head. "No, that is inaccurate. The whole *future* needs your help."

Vala put down her teacup gently on the sitting table before her, not making a sound when the cup touched the surface. "Have you had a vision, Uncle? Tell me," she whispered in a serious tone. One thing Auron could count on: Vala always took his visions seriously.

"Yes, I have. Surely you have heard of the plague upon our sector?"

"It is known throughout all the sectors. This isn't old news. It started years ago."

"And have you ever wondered why it hasn't spread into the other sectors?"

Vala took a sip of her tea again, studying Auron's expression. "Everyone is prepared in case it does spread, but no one has ever questioned why it hasn't. It's only a matter of time before the other sectors become like yours."

"No. It's attributed to one person. Our very own court sorceress. *She* is taking away the power," Auron said.

Vala gasped. "Ikaria? This is what your vision has told you?"

"Yes. And even worse, she has now traveled back in time to complete the Spectrum of Magic."

Vala's face dropped, shocked at what he had said. "But... that's heresy, Uncle. How...?"

"If she does indeed complete the Spectrum of Magic, she will be bestowed with the gift of the black."

Vala almost dropped her teacup as her hands began to shake uncontrollably. "Gift of the black? Uncle... is that even a real thing?"

"Yes. A power so great, it could bring an end to the Earth's existence."

She sat in silence. Auron could tell she was afraid. "And I suppose you want me to travel back with you to help stop her?" she said finally.

"All of our sector's gifted are preparing to travel back in time," Auron replied. "But we need more gifted, and we need someone to port us to the past. We don't have any blue-gifted in our sector. Not after Kohren's death."

Vala's face jerked to his, her expression steady. "Lord Kohren?"

"Had you not heard? He was murdered by Ikaria herself."

She took a deep breath, then tapped the ring of her teacup gently in thought. "How many gifted do you need, Uncle?"

"I was hoping to get about forty."

"*Forty?*" Vala said incredulously, her eyes bulging. She nearly spat out some tea. "That many? I don't even know if I can get five, let alone forty."

"We need that many if we are to overpower Ikaria," Auron insisted, his face grim. "We couldn't stop her with our own gifted. You still have hundreds in this sector. There has to be at least some who are willing to help."

"I don't know, Uncle," Vala said hesitantly. "It's interesting that the same day you arrived, a High Court courier brought a message to our sector."

It was Auron's turn to raise an eyebrow. "What did it say?"

Vala's ocean-blue eyes locked onto his. "It said that none of the world sectors are to help out the other sectors. Pretty vague. Everyone at court was baffled by it. But now I understand the message."

Auron sat back in his pillow, stunned. It was as if the High Court was trying to counter everything Ayera and their sector did. They truly wanted Ayera to fail.

"I guess that means that you will not help us..." Auron's voice trailed off.

"I never said that, Uncle," Vala said, and she gave him a big, bright smile. "It just means that it will be hard to convince anyone to help. Especially since the High Court ordered it; we could be arrested. But I do know of a few gifted in our sector who have become quite disenchanted with the High Court. I will talk to them."

"Thank you. Travel to our sector when you are ready. Our gifted will be ready to leave at a moment's notice."

"Yes, Uncle. Give me three days; I will be in your sector by then."

Auron paused for a moment, thinking about what Geeta had said about the gifted traveling back in time. It would mean their deaths. He couldn't hold that information inside and expect the God of Light to welcome him into paradise. Saying nothing was still deceit, even through omission. He had to tell her.

"There is one thing I should mention. And it may change everyone's minds, including yours," Auron said.

Vala sipped her tea one last time, then got up from her pillow to escort him out. "What is it?"

Auron paused, then took in a deep breath. "There is a likely chance that every one of us in the future will perish in the past. I was informed that our bodies cannot withstand being in another era, and thus our bodies will disintegrate after a certain amount of time. Depending how quickly we defeat Ikaria, there is a good chance we will die soon after."

Vala's warm face went still.

"But it won't really matter, because if Ikaria succeeds in traveling back to our time era, the whole world will be destroyed, and we will perish anyway. We will die in the past or die in the present. I have foreseen it, and it *will* happen unless we stop her." Auron turned to his niece, put his hand on her shoulder. "I will understand if you do not want to help."

Vala was slow to answer but finally broke the silence. "As much as I don't want to die, I will still help. I do not want to be one of those gifted who do not use their God-given gift. Perhaps this is my calling, and this is the very reason why the God of Light bestowed the gift of the blue upon me."

Auron smiled, and Vala gave him a quick hug. "I will see you in three days' time. Hopefully with more gifted other than yourself."

"Your name has much sway in this court, Uncle. Your visions have always been deemed exact and accurate," she said with a small smile. "And it always helps that your heritage dates back to the first priest. That says something in itself. I merely have to vouch for you, and it could influence people. Wish me luck."

Auron bowed one last time, heading for the door. "I pray they will understand the extremity of the situation."

Auron was about to walk out of her chambers, then stopped, realizing he hadn't taken an airship there. Geeta had brought him, and now he was stranded.

Turning to Vala, he asked, "Actually, I will need help getting back to my sector…"

Vala grinned.

CHAPTER 56

◇—◇

BLUE

The God of Light fragmented the light in his right hand, each strand becoming a new color into the world. Blue arose from the colored depths, and with it, sadness came upon the earth, bearing terrible darkness. Then the God of Light took dimensions within the sadness, bending it, then bestowing it to his chosen, allowing the gifted to travel across the chasms of time and space.

—account of Ardashir Rahbar's vision, 2594 B.E.

The cold hard floor was uncomfortable, causing Derek to wake from his sleep. His body was stiff from the discomfort of lying on the ground.

Through a window, Derek saw gray, thundering clouds that filled the sky, hiding the tops of the other skyscrapers. His head ached, and he gave it a good rub to alleviate the pain. It didn't help. He felt like he had the worst hangover ever, like he'd drunk too much wine at a party. But there had been no party, and no wine.

Derek's thoughts turned to the sorceress. He recalled a darkness forming around her, and her orgasmic screams echoing in his ears. Then there was blue. Blue... from Emerald's blood.

He had drunk Emerald's blood.

Derek shuddered at the thought. His heart felt heavy, causing his body to twitch in disgust. Bile shot up his throat.

Derek ran to the bathroom, vomiting everything he had inside. His mind was the clearest it had been since Ikaria had first appeared to him. How could he live with himself? He'd wanted Emerald so bad that he let Ikaria warp the mind of Damaris and had let her convince him to drink Emerald's enchanted blood. He was so caught up with his emotions that it controlled his reckless actions.

After he finished showering and brushing his teeth, he walked back into his bedroom with a towel wrapped around his lowers, and there was Ikaria. She lazily opened her eyes, giving him a wicked smile.

"Good morning, my prince," she said, smiling and flashing her dark eyes. "Did you sleep well?"

Her eyes were no longer violet. Instead, they were the color of polished onyx.

Derek quickly averted his gaze, as her breasts were practically falling out of her armored corset.

"You need to leave," he said. "If someone walks in, they might think… that I was unfaithful to the princess."

"Oh, quiet, you. No one has morals in this time. Except you, perhaps." She gave him a wicked look, then sat in a chair next to his bed. "Hello? Can I get some wine, please?" Ikaria called out to one of his servants in the sitting room.

Silas appeared, giving Derek and Ikaria a questionable look.

"The prince and I would like a glass of wine," Ikaria said, smiling.

"This isn't what you think," Derek told Silas, then immediately turned to Ikaria. "I just woke up. I don't need wine. What I need is for you to get out of here while I change."

Ikaria didn't budge. Instead she looked at Silas. "Well, are you going to get me a drink or do I have to serve myself?"

Silas bowed to Ikaria. "Forgive me, madam, but the master said—"

"I don't have time for this," Ikaria said, sighing. Her eyes began to burn a radiant black. Derek quickly jerked his head in Silas's direction, morbidly curious to see Ikaria's spell on his servant.

Silas bowed to Ikaria mindlessly, then left the room, most likely to fetch her a drink.

Derek opened his mouth in protest, then closed it as he watched her magic control Silas's body. The use of her magic and the power it radiated amazed him, though he felt sorry for Silas.

"Is that what a woman needs to do to get service around here?" Ikaria sprawled herself on one of Derek's plush blue chairs, making herself comfortable.

Silas returned immediately, offering him and the sorceress a glass, then vacated the room. She glanced casually in Derek's direction, studying him. "You don't look any different."

"Different? You mean from the magic?"

Ikaria nodded. "Usually the magic changes your eyes, but I suppose since your eyes were already a pale blue, the gift didn't find it necessary. But your hair will grow in blue." She leaned in, and a wicked smile appeared. "I wonder if your hair will be deep blue? That would suit you, wouldn't it?"

Had he truly received the magic? He had dreamt in shades of blue, but had he actually received that power? He didn't feel anything.

"Are you sure that I have magic?"

"I can feel it flowing through you. With this green magic mixed in my blood... I can feel other magics in my presence." She turned to face him, indifferently drinking her wine. "You have been given a deep, strong magic, my prince."

Derek quickly sat down next to her, at full attention. He remembered seeing images from the past, present, and future. He saw different peoples, extraordinary cities, and fantastical lands.

"Does the... I mean, does my magic allow me to see things from other times?"

"Yes, my prince. The gift of the blue is the magic of time and space dimensions. You have the ability to glance into time—forward and backward, as well as stop it. You can also travel through time and dimensions. However, you will need some help from the gift of the green to stay in another time, as your body would dissolve into nothingness."

It finally struck him. That was why Ikaria never traveled back in time with her body. That was why she needed the green blood.

"Why is that? It seems that puts this blue color at a disadvantage."

"Apparently the God of Light wanted to be cruel. Who knows." Ikaria shrugged. "It is said that one is not meant to interrupt the flow of time. That it's time's way of paying back in retribution if a gifted dared to do so, causing them to wither away. It is a violation of magic to inherit another gifted's power, so no blue-gifted would ever dream of consuming green-gifted blood."

Derek's eyes sharply locked onto hers. "Violation of magic? You mean… you just… we…"

Ikaria laughed. "How does it feel in that moral soul of yours, that you, a common man, inherited great power and impossible abilities?"

He lowered his eyes, then took the cup of wine that he'd refused to drink, finally taking a sip. "I… don't feel like I have done anything wrong," he said quietly. It was true, he actually felt empowered, like he had the ability to control his terrible luck for the first time since coming to Arcadia.

Ikaria leaned in. "Neither do I." She snapped her head back, drinking the wine casually. "And that is where I differ with all the other gifted."

The power… he could feel it now. It ran wildly through his veins, gathering more energy with every heartbeat. It felt invigorating. He felt the urge, the *desire*, to tap into it.

"How do I… use my power?" Derek asked curiously.

"You want me to throw in a teaching lesson too? That will cost you more cyborgs."

"I don't care about the cyborgs."

"Fine." Ikaria smiled, leaning back in the sofa, kicking up her legs and caressing them. "You must be able to tap into your emotions, which are attached to your core being. Each magic is associated with a feeling. In your case, it would be sadness and depression. It should be rather easy for you, considering everything that's happened to you."

"Thanks for making me feel worse," he said flatly.

"That is what I am here for," Ikaria said, lazily eyeing her goblet. "Just close your eyes. Think about your *pain*, your *sadness*. Remember the princess is in love with another man. If that doesn't give you a shove, I don't know what will."

He shot her a look at the mention of Emerald. Ikaria gave him a crooked half smile, narrowing her black eyes, daring him.

"Will I be able to use it right away?"

"It depends. Some people have a natural talent like myself. Others need lots of practice."

"Natural talent?"

"Yes. It's just like anything else," Ikaria said. "Some people can pick up an instrument, practice very little, and be the most talented musician. Others can practice their whole life and just be mediocre. But one thing is common with everyone: You won't be able to use your magic unless you use the specific emotion that is tied to that particular color." She fluttered her hand, gesturing to him. "Go on, try it."

Derek took a deep breath, then shut out the world around him, thinking only of Emerald. Her words. Her last words.

I need time to think.

About what?

About us.

The conversation played over and over in his mind, digging into his soul.

Pictures flooded his mind. Pictures that hung all over Emerald's room. Pictures of that man…

Out of the blue darkness of his heart, Derek saw Emerald.

Emerald? Derek called out to her.

Emerald spun around in every direction, her gaze searching. When she made another swift turn of her body, a look of recognition came over her face.

Emerald! I'm here! Derek called out to her.

The princess ran in the same direction that her eyes were locked upon. Moments later, she landed into a man's arms, embracing him.

It was that man. *Kyle.*

Time slowed.

Emerald smiled at Kyle, the one who stole her affections. Her hands ran up his chest and around his neck, pulling him close. Their motions were slow, and every second seemed like an eternity.

Kyle's lips closed in onto Emerald's, gently kissing her.

Time halted.

No, Derek screamed in his heart! *I cannot let you go! I won't let you go! You are* mine!

The image of Emerald looked so happy, so enraptured by the other man. She answered Kyle's kisses back with passion. Her hands savagely combed the back of his neck and up through his white hair. Each moment her kisses became more climactic. And they didn't stop.

NO!

Derek jerked his eyes open. The world had a blue tint to it, and the air felt incredibly still around him. He glanced at the window outside—the city was paused. The air transports were frozen in midair. The people within the platforms, the skyways, all were like still ants, unmoving. There was even a lightning bolt frozen in time, a rod joining heaven and earth. Derek looked over at Ikaria, who seemed to be the only one with the ability to move, all in full color.

"Very good, my prince," she said, smiling. "I had to give you a little push, though. Sorry about that," she said nonchalantly.

Derek looked at her within the frozen world. "You placed that image in my mind?"

"Well, yes. You are so simple, driven by only one passion. Didn't it make it easy for you?"

"I guess. But why is it that you are moving?" he wondered, looking at his hands where he felt the magic release.

"No one can stop me from moving, my dear prince. Unless there is someone who is as talented or as powerful as me."

"You mean it's hard to get rid of you?" Derek muttered.

Ikaria laughed at his poor joke. "I am afraid that you will never be able to get rid of me. Especially now that I have the gift of the black."

"Is that why your eyes have changed? You have black magic?"

"Precisely. There is no stopping my magic, and I have you to thank for that." Ikaria smiled wickedly at him.

"Is that supposed to make me feel better?"

"I would think it would be at least a highlight of your time here in Arcadia."

Derek sighed. Ikaria irritated him to no end. But he apparently wouldn't be ridding himself of her. Not yet anyway.

Ikaria noticed his disgruntled look. "I have a little secret that can cheer you up."

"I don't like your secrets. The last one was about my father having an affair, and I am still processing that one."

"Oh, hush. It's nothing like that." Ikaria laughed. "It's about your magic. All gifted have the power to tap into colors that are next to yours in the spectrum. You can possess certain abilities of the power of violet and green, but only to a small degree."

Derek looked at Ikaria in full color within the blue world, trying to search his power deep within his soul. His power was like a soft breeze, gently running through his body. He did feel the other strange powers within, tingling within his blood. They were there, but not as prominent as the blue that spoke to him.

The blue magic grew within him, making him aware of being devoid of Emerald, painfully crushing his insides. Pushing back his thoughts and his feelings, the azure world melted away into color, and the world instantly came back to life.

His heart raced at the feeling of the power that rocked his body. It made him feel so alive, like his soul had awakened for the first time in his life. The thought of being in the presence of Emerald was the only other comparison he could ever make, although he didn't have her. Not yet.

He had a lot to think about as well.

First things first. I must go see Emerald.

Derek turned to Ikaria, casting her a glance. "I need to get dressed," he said, waving her away.

"By all means, get dressed. I need some good morning entertainment."

Derek gave her a look of annoyance. "I need my privacy. I am going to dress now," he repeated firmly.

"Don't worry, my prince. You aren't my type anyway. If you were blond, on the other hand, I would have had my way with you several times already."

"You are sickening," Derek said in disgust. He gave her a cold hard stare, then went to his wardrobe to look for some garments to wear for the day.

Silas came back with another glass of wine, offering it to Ikaria. She took the glass, then took a long, deep drink. "I beg to differ, my prince. Don't play innocent with me. I have seen your dirty mind playing with Emerald the last week or so."

Derek jerked his head in her direction.

Ikaria didn't even flinch, staying focused on her glass of wine, admiring the shape of it.

"Wonderful," he said sarcastically.

"I must say, with how much you think of her, you almost had me convinced that I needed to fornicate with her too."

Derek's mouth dropped, dumbstruck. "Those are my most private thoughts! Those are meant for *me*, and me alone!"

"Nothing is private with me, my prince. What is it about the princess, anyway?"

"Get out of here!" Derek roared, running his fingers through his sweaty curls.

"Fine." Ikaria got up, downing her glass of wine, then strutted past him. "I was getting bored with you, anyway. So dull, you are."

She turned her head slightly, then held out her hand in the direction of the vanity. Slowly, the floating holographic circlet became opaque, then dropped onto the vanity with a clink. "As promised," she said, referring to the circlet. "Come talk to me when you have finally had a good romp with your princess, as I can see you have much frustration that you need to get out. I, on the other hand, have business to take care of."

Derek watched her about to leave, then called out. "What are you going to do? Aren't you not supposed to disrupt time?"

"Has that stopped either one of us?" she asked, fading away into the air.

Derek walked to the vanity and picked up the crown. It still had a violet glow, but it was solid in his hands.

He felt violet power surging from the metal, vibrating through his body, mixing with his blue magic.

It made him feel alive. So very alive. And in control.

In the back of his mind, he felt a small hint of guilt poke at him. Clenching the circlet, Derek turned away, thinking of the odd scientist.

"Silas!"

Silas entered almost immediately, glancing cautiously around the room. "Yes, Your Highness?"

"Find the number for the head director of the King's corporation. I would like to talk to them within the hour."

"Yes, Your Highness."

It was time for him to honor his end of the bargain.

CHAPTER 57

BLACK

The Lord of Darkness called upon me into his service, in exchange for his eternal power. The darkness, the ultimate combination of all colors of the spectrum, empowered my spirit, and emboldened my heart. He commanded my life-force and consumed by whole being. I was no longer on my own, for he was there with me in everything I did.

—from the banned works of Dreyfus the Elder, 1379 B.E.

Ikaria stopped and lingered occasionally as she walked through the palace, touching each and every one of the technological devices that were scattered throughout the halls. Lords and ladies passing by gave her curious looks as she caressed the machinery. Some were heard making comments on who the new woman in the palace was, but most continued down the halls to their intended destinations in silence. Ikaria didn't care what anyone thought. Had she ever? She was stopped and questioned by guards a few times, but Ikaria just told them that she was Derek's royal advisor from the Kingdom of York, and they let her be. After all, he was soon to be king of Arcadia.

When Ikaria had completed the Spectrum of Magic, the gift of the black spoke inside of her, granting Ikaria a power of her choosing. Not only did the black gift amplify her magic, it blessed her with her greatest desire—to understand how the machines worked, from their conception to when they were built to their engineering and design and how they ran. The knowledge was far greater than any book that Ikaria had read, and she hungered to know more. With each new heightened awareness, Ikaria thought of the countless possibilities that could change the face of the future, starting with World Sector Six. And she had information that *no one*, not even the High Court, could steal from her because it was stored within her consciousness.

After absorbing much information from the countless technological mechanisms, Ikaria finally made her way to the outside of King Damaris's chambers, stopping in front of the guards. The thought of King Damaris gave Ikaria a stir within. She had always wanted to see King Damaris for herself in the flesh instead of inside his mind. Ikaria never had cared for older men, but Damaris was an exception, as handsome as he was for his age.

"I am sorry, miss, but you are not supposed to be here," one of the two guards told her firmly. The other guard lowered his eyes to her cleavage.

Responding, Ikaria gave a small, pleasant smile. "I would like to request an audience with His Majesty."

"His Majesty doesn't want to see anybody."

"Oh, His Majesty will want to see me." Ikaria grinned, sweeping back her violet hair.

"And you are?" inquired the guard.

"I am from York. Tell the King that Derek's royal advisor is here to see him," Ikaria said, looking a bit annoyed, pretending that they should know who she was.

They both opened their eyes at the mention of her title, then exchanged looks. The guard who'd spoken disappeared inside Damaris's chambers, while the other guard studied her. Ikaria decided to toy with him by sticking out her chest and taking a deep breath. The guard saw the exposed tops of her breasts rise out of her corset as she breathed, then quickly looked away, his brow moistening with sweat.

The other guard returned, then motioned for Ikaria to enter.

Playfully, Ikaria smiled at the flustered guard, then ran her finger across his chest as she walked past him. His cheeks turned red as he lowered his gaze.

Men were so easy to manipulate. Give them a bit of skin and you had them wrapped around your finger. Ikaria didn't even have to use her black magic, nor her old violet magic, that was just how easy it was to control their lustful minds. Especially Derek. All he wanted was Princess Emerald, and all Ikaria would have to do was give him the princess in exchange for the whole kingdom of Arcadia if she so desired. But this was about revenge on the High Court, not about ruling Arcadia.

I can't wait to wipe those smug looks off their faces, especially that High Justice bitch, Belinda. Ikaria let out a small laugh just thinking about the High Court trying to stop her and the cyborgs. They would soon face their doom.

Ikaria entered Damaris's sitting room, gracefully scanning the chamber to get a glimpse of the King himself. The light of the day flowed through the paneled glass, capturing the white-marbled room flecked with gold. She spotted Damaris, seated in one of his chairs, alone. He was just as handsome as she'd seen him in Derek's mind, but he was much more attractive in person.

His chiseled face complemented his light-green eyes and thick blond eyebrows. His hair was long blond silk, flowing down his back, with a simple golden circlet adorning his forehead. He looked so regal in his red velvet and silks. And underneath his robes, Ikaria could see that Damaris was extremely fit for someone in his fifties. Her lowers stirred with a burning sensation just taking in the King's form. He was a bit older than she would have preferred, but she didn't mind. It just made the game new to her.

I suppose I should let him have his mind for a little while, she said, smiling to herself.

Slowly, Ikaria began to pull away her magic. She loved to let the host have a bit of control for the fun they were about to have.

"The guard outside told me you were an advisor from York," Damaris called out as Ikaria approached him. "This is the first I have heard he had such a position. Why didn't you escort the fool here when he first arrived?"

Trying to call my bluff, I see.

"I had other business to attend to," Ikaria hinted with a small smile. "You know how that is."

A sudden look of recognition came over Damaris's face, then quickly morphed into a scowl. "It is *you.* The one in my thoughts, paralyzing my mind! Forcing me to give up my throne to that worthless prince! Now I understand!"

"Oh, come now, my king. It's all for the best." Ikaria walked toward his seat, swaying her hips and bowing before him.

"Best for whom? York? I think not!"

"I think you are mistaken."

"Then whom?"

"For Arcadia." Ikaria walked over to a nearby chalice, pouring a cup of wine. She returned, hovering over his chair, taking a long drink, then offered him the cup. Damaris snatched the goblet, downing the glass. "You see, your daughter needs to produce offspring to ensure the future gifteds' survival. She certainly cannot do that under your strict supervision, can she now?"

"The future? Bah, I do not care for the future. I care only about the here and now." Damaris glanced at her. "My daughter doesn't need to procreate. She needs to stay right here with me."

"I'm afraid I disagree."

"Is that what your magic tells you? To halt my plans of conquering? Because if that is so, you can forget about it and go crawling back to York empty-handed."

"My king, I came here to ensure that you follow through with your end of the bargain."

"Bargain? There is no bargain." Damaris laughed. "I see that the King of York is using a gifted to one-up me. Forcing me with crafty spells to give up my kingdom. Well, I am not afraid of any gifted. Especially you."

"We are the same, you and I. Not afraid of anyone or anything."

Damaris swished his chalice around, taking another drink. "Why is it that you conspire with Samir? If you truly are able to see the future, you would see that I was granted a vision that my kingdom would reign over all others, a vision that came from the God of Light himself. But it appears that York has more sway over you than the God of Light. That makes you just another pathetic hound dog, eating out of Samir's lap."

"You are sorely mistaken, my king," said Ikaria. "It wasn't the King of York that sent me. I sent myself. You see, I do as I please. No one has authority over me, including this Samir, King of York, or even the God of Light himself." Ikaria moved closer to Damaris, sliding a hand across his back alluringly. "But I can be convinced to change my mind and work toward Arcadia's favor." Ikaria smiled wickedly at him.

For the first time, Damaris's face returned her smile, then he bellowed out a loud laugh, amused. "Convinced? Really?"

"Why yes, my king. I am just a mere person, just like anyone else." Ikaria came closer to him, brushing her finger across his body. "Minds can easily be persuaded."

Damaris gave a small smile, taking a drink of his wine. Ikaria lowered into his view and took the cup from his hands, then licked it seductively before placing it on an end table.

"Let me have a look at you," he said, motioning for her.

Ikaria gave him a sly grin, then stood in front of him, striking an erotic pose.

"Tell me, what motivates one such as yourself? Rule? Power?" Damaris's eyes were fixated on her, taking in the curves of her body.

"Let's not talk about business right now," Ikaria said, crawling into his lap.

"Agreed."

Ikaria ran her fingers through his blond hair, then patted it gently. "I have a thing for blonds, and I know you have a thing for my kind." She moved her position, then straddled him, both her legs locked onto his body.

"You saw that in my mind, did you?"

"Indeed," she whispered in his ear, massaging his earlobe slowly between her lips. She could feel the hot breath of his mouth on her neck, which caused her senses to run wild. A shudder ran through her body as she sensually kissed his ears.

His mind was wide open, ready for her to invade once again. But it was different controlling him from the same time era, instead of across time. The inside of his dark mind was so vibrant, so beautiful, and so erotic.

Damaris continued to kiss her neck fiercely. Ikaria moaned softly, pleased at his touch. They would have made a great pair if circumstances had been different.

"We are going to continue to play by my rules," she whispered in his ear.

Damaris immediately snapped away, glaring at her. "I thought you said that I could change your mind about Arcadia."

"Sorry to disappoint you, my king, but I lied. I don't ever change my mind once it's made up."

At once, she summoned her black magic, taking hold of his mind. His eyes instantly went vacant, awaiting her direction.

"I didn't tell you to stop…" she stated as she kissed his ear.

Damaris resumed kissing her but no longer made conversation.

"I have a perfect wedding gift for you to give the happy couple," Ikaria whispered, moving her hands further down his body. "But before we get started, I will be needing this…"

Ikaria traveled her free hand down to Damaris's hand, meeting it, his hand encased in cold, hard metal. She pushed the edge of his robed sleeve back, revealing a metal gauntlet with a large colorless orb in the middle. Through the glasslike sphere, Ikaria saw intricate wires running to and from it. Ever so delicately, she slipped the mechanical gauntlet off his hand and fastened it onto hers. Immediately, Ikaria felt the black gift working through her, giving her understanding of the delicate device.

"Thank you, my king. You have given me my wildest fantasy," she said breathlessly, looking at her new toy.

Then she began to ravage him with her kisses.

CHAPTER 58

GREEN

"I have come to see my father," Emerald stated, standing boldly in front the King's guards posted outside his chambers.

"I am sorry, Princess, but His Majesty already has a visitor."

"Is Derek with him? Let me talk to them!" Emerald demanded.

"No, it is the Prince of York's advisor."

"Advisor?" Emerald said, bewildered. Derek had never told her that he had an advisor.

"Yes. She just went inside about ten minutes ago. We were given very strict orders not to let anyone in."

"She?"

The guard blinked at her. "Hasn't the prince told you about Advisor Ikaria?"

"It seems that no one tells me anything, quite honestly," Emerald replied, frustrated. "Please, sirs, just let me see my father. I was told that he has been very ill." She leaned in, lowering her voice to a whisper. "I think you both know that I have the ability to help him. Please reconsider."

"We know you can help, Princess," the guard said quietly. "But we still can't let you through. I am truly sorry. I think the best option you have is to talk with the prince. Perhaps he can put in a word to change your father's mind, or you could come back later and see if His Majesty is accepting any other visitors." He nodded his head in respect but otherwise made no other movement from the door.

Derek putting in a word for me? Emerald thought. It was as if she had stepped into a backward reality or some kind of strange dream.

Derek. He never did tell her how he'd convinced her father to let him marry her. And why had her father fallen ill so suddenly? Why hadn't he called on her? And why was Derek the only person allowed to see her father besides his royal advisor? And who was this advisor anyway?

Something was going on. Emerald felt it deep down, and a deep concern consumed her. Emerald turned to the guards, giving them a weak smile. "I shall come back later. Please, if you see my father, tell him that I called on him."

"Yes, Princess," they said in unison, nodding.

As Emerald walked back to her chambers, her thoughts wavered between her situation and Kyle. How she wished she could be with him, in the safety of his quaint apartment, hidden from the upper levels. Her world was drowning her, and now she felt trapped. Trapped by the very man she had hoped to marry all these years.

What would Kyle do in my situation? Emerald could already hear Kyle's voice. *Tell the asshole to go packing back to where he came from.* She smiled to herself. That was definitely what he would say.

If her father wouldn't see her, then she would have to take it upon herself to end the engagement. Emerald didn't care what kind of agreement her father and Derek had. She was not a prize to be won or an agreement to be bartered with. She was a princess. And she was not going to live a life of unhappiness anymore.

First, she had to talk to Derek. Then she would go find Kyle.

CHAPTER 59

BLUE

It was nearly evening. Derek anxiously waited for Emerald, sitting completely upright on the audience chamber's metal throne. He watched as raindrops splattered against the paneled glass, creating an electric-green pattern that captured the glow of the palace from outside. Loud rumblings of thunder sounded.

Emerald had finally sent word that she would see him.

Derek had not seen her since the incident with her drawings. He had called upon her countless times, and every time she never showed, nor gave word. It was torture not seeing Emerald's angelic face. The face that kept him going all these years, the face that gave Derek hope for his future. Well, *their* future, he should say. He desperately wanted nothing standing between them, but the more he tried to fix the situation and apologize, the more she refused to see him. It pained him to be withheld from her. She was his *life*. They were about to be married, and it was about time they put this whole thing past them.

Derek got up, pacing evenly around the throne a few times, then sat back down, unsure how to handle his excessive nervousness. There was not a soul in the hall, as most of the councilors and lords had retired for the evening. The servants were too busy preparing for the royal event, working nonstop to ensure that the wedding was the grandest one the world had ever seen. It was set for tomorrow, and soon Emerald would be his by right.

Ikaria had been gone most of the day and hadn't returned from wherever she had gone, but Derek did not mind. He wasn't in the mood to handle her vile comments and crude sexual humor. He was tired of her and just wanted her gone.

Derek reached inside his tunic and felt the cold metal circlet within his hands. Dark magic radiated from it. A feeling of guilt ran through him again, but his logic, along with his newfound power, pushed away the guilt, leaving him with a sense of resolve. It was all for the best.

A shadowy figure walked toward him, a most beautiful shadow, belonging to the one who had captured his heart. Lightning crashed within the skies outside, illuminating the deep-blue room with a bright white, giving Derek a glimpse of Emerald walking toward him, her maidens behind her.

"Princess," Derek said, rising from his seat and bowing deeply before her. He took Emerald's hand, then softly kissed it. Something caught his attention—Emerald wasn't wearing her engagement ring.

Emerald raised an eyebrow at his expression, then immediately snapped her hand away. "Derek," she said, rather coldly, "why is it that my father refuses to see everyone except you and now your advisor?"

"Your father decided it was best that I alone see him, as well as my advisor, since he is transferring matters of state over to me," Derek said quickly.

"But why won't he see me? Did he say?" Emerald pressed.

Derek shrugged, pretending he didn't know. "I couldn't tell you, Princess. I have asked him the same thing. In fact, I urged him to see you, but he wouldn't listen," Derek said, the lie heavy on his lips. "Please, let's not talk about your father." His face turned serious, glancing at the handmaidens. "Might I have a word alone with you? I have been anxious to see you all day."

Emerald continued to stare at him with hesitation but finally nodded. Waving her hand toward her handmaidens, she said, "You are dismissed. Please wait outside the hall for me."

Derek watched the women leave the hall single file. One head turned back before she exited the hall, peering at him harshly. It was Emerald's first handmaiden, Glacia. Her hazel eyes pierced right through his heart, as if she could see his intentions. She glanced at him for a second, then disappeared behind the door with the other maidens.

Derek swallowed his nerves, then began in an even voice, "Emerald, I have been wanting to apologize to you for the way I behaved. I... I don't know what came over me, but I am sorry and ashamed for what I did. I was completely out of line. How I acted was the last thing I ever wanted to do to you." He leaned in closer, then held her hand, kissing it gently once again.

Emerald withdrew her hand after he kissed it, taking a step back from his space. "You are right. You were completely out of line," she said coldly. "You violated my personal space and destroyed my drawings, after I specifically told you I needed time to think. What good did you think would come of it? Please, tell me."

Yes, Derek, do tell! Ikaria mocked inside of his mind.

Shut up! Derek answered the sorceress.

"You are my fiancée," Derek said, scowling at Emerald, frustrated. "You are *supposed* to be devoted to one person: me. Instead you have refused to see me since you came back to the palace. And what's worse is you spend all your time drawing pictures of another man! Don't tell me you wouldn't be the least bit angry if you were me!" Derek stepped toward her, getting close. "Please, Emerald, the thought of another man with you… I cannot bear it! I want you to be mine. Fully mine!"

Emerald began to back away from him, her bright-green eyes wide.

Derek saw it. Fear. Emerald feared him.

Thunder pummeled the halls again, causing the room to shake slightly.

"Derek… I am not marrying you," Emerald said in a whisper.

I told you that you would be needing the circlet, Ikaria said within his thoughts. *If you would have believed me in the first place, you wouldn't be in this situation now.*

Ignoring Ikaria, Derek inched closer to Emerald, furious. "I don't accept that. I won't! I cannot live without you. You are the air I breathe. I *need* you! Don't you see? I have done everything possible, all for you! And I will continue to do anything to keep you." Derek paused, taking a deep breath as he leaned into her, smelling the sweet fragrance of her hair, then caressed her delicate locks. He put his hand under her chin, lifting her face to meet his gaze. She was so beautiful.

Forcing her head away from his touch, Emerald continued to back away until she could no more, her backside meeting a wall. "Derek…" she said hesitantly, "I think it's best… that we say goodbye."

"Say goodbye? Why would I say goodbye?" Derek planted his hands on each side of Emerald's shoulders, trapping her against the wall and pinning her in place. "Did you not hear what I said? You are *everything* to me, and I cannot live without you!"

The blue magic began to gather within his veins, slowly building up with each heartbeat. Ikaria's laugh echoed in his mind as the power inside of him increased.

Emerald shook her head in alarm and struggled, trying to get away from him without success. "Derek, please, you are scaring me!" Emerald finally wrenched herself from underneath his hands, inching away from him.

"I will not say goodbye to you!" Derek roared.

With a flash of his hand, Derek released the sadness of his soul. The blue magic burned brightly, flowing violently like a twisting, glowing stream of blue energy toward Emerald.

Her eyes went wide in disbelief, then she quickly brought up her hand in response to his power. A greenish-yellow barrier formed instantly, encasing her in a mass of energy.

But it was too late.

Derek slowed time, allowing his blue stream of power to seep into the barrier where it hadn't completely finished forming yet. The blue magic bound Emerald, then Derek allowed time to flow once again.

"I can't move!" Emerald exclaimed, panicking. Her lower body was frozen in time, his blue magic shackling her. Her neck and face jerked every which way as she struggled. "Please, Derek, release me!" she begged, shedding a tear.

A sudden force pushed Derek's body violently, crashing him against one of the walls, knocking the air out of his lungs.

Gasping for air, Derek tried to see what had hit him. A glowing orange light filled the hall, revealing the cyborg.

"Help me!" Emerald cried out.

Attempting to catch his breath, Derek snarled. "Damn robot, you obey *me!*"

Its cybernetic eye made a mechanical sound as it focused on Derek. In less than a heartbeat, the cyborg shot out a giant wave of orange ice, freezing Derek's feet into place.

Derek swung his hands back, then outstretched them, pouring a blue stream of time magic, hurling it in the cyborg's direction. He was a second too late, as the cyborg flashed orange, disappearing. Derek broke free from the ice and whirled around wildly, knowing that the cyborg would appear at any moment. Emerald's sobs could be heard echoing through the hall.

Then the room began to fade into hues of orange, slowly morphing into a deep rocky pit filled with lava.

Derek found himself situated on a boulder, hot bubbling lava all around him. Confused, Derek looked around at the high jagged walls that held him prisoner.

This isn't real... The robot is playing games with me!

"Show yourself, you coward!" Derek yelled, his voice reverberating against the rocky walls.

It's all an illusion. The lava can't be hot. It's not real!

To test his theory, quickly Derek hovered his hands over the lava and hissed, pulling them back. It *felt* hot, but was it because Derek's eyes were deceiving him, or could his mind and body actually make him feel the heat?

There was a sudden gust of air behind him, and he was knocked to the ground, his face landing a few inches from the boiling lava.

It was really hot, Derek decided.

Derek shot up angrily, only to be pummeled back to the ground by an invisible force. Kicking his feet upward, he felt his feet make contact with the unseen momentum. But somehow Derek knew that he hadn't even stunned the robot.

Crawling away from the blazing lava, Derek eyed his surroundings. There were no protruding rocks coming out of the walls that he could use to climb out. He was stuck inside the illusion.

The lava began to rise, causing the boulder that Derek stood on to slowly shrink. He had to do something fast. Could he freeze time in an illusion? He doubted it.

"You are nothing more than worthless piece of scrap metal!" Derek taunted, turning every which way.

The air quickly shifted once again.

Grasping at the makeshift air, Derek felt the mechanical arm of the cyborg, then latched on to him. Filling his veins with the deep magic that ran through his soul, Derek unleashed the blue energy. The massive tidal wave of magic enveloped the invisible cyborg. Derek felt the magic freeze him into place, stopping the machine's body in time.

Stunned, the cyborg materialized before his eyes. As he did so, the rocky terrain melted back into the palace hall, wiping away the magical illusion. Near the hall's entrance, Derek spotted Emerald fleeing the room, free from his magic. He must have let it slip while he was fighting the cyborg.

"Where are you going? Back to *Kyle?*" Derek roared jealously.

"Leave me alone!" Emerald yelled, running away and not looking back.

Breathing heavily, Derek mustered up his strength and power. A deep envy that he had never felt before consumed him. Envy of the man who stole Emerald's heart. The jealousy mixed with his sadness, forming inside him, and he realized it was a new magic.

Unleashing the new power, a roaring blue-violet force of energy raged out of him, encompassing Emerald. It took hold of the princess, forcing her to slide back toward Derek, and the doors barred themselves on the inside. With another surge of his power, Emerald was locked into place, next to him once more.

Derek noticed that the cyborg was moving his mouth awkwardly. Derek's magic had him stopped, and all but his head was immobile. More air was coming from the cyborg's mouth as he continued to mechanically open his jaw, his lips moving in unfamiliar actions.

The robot is trying to talk.

Derek laughed, amused that the cyborg was struggling to use his voice. Derek turned to Emerald, seeing her eyes full of tears. It pained him to see her in such a state.

Loud air came out of the cyborg's voice box a few times. Derek turned his attention back to it, annoyed.

Then it spoke.

"N-NO!" it roared.

Sneering, Derek stretched out his hand carelessly, stopping time on the cyborg's entire body. The cyborg's head froze, his mouth open in his attempt to talk.

Running his fingers back through his thick curls, Derek charismatically walked toward Emerald, his eyes fixated on every detail of her body. He couldn't help it, she was too beautiful not to stare.

Tears were rolling down her face, and she cringed away from him as he approached. The more she cried, the more aggravated he became. She was so blinded by the other man that she couldn't see how much Derek loved her. He was doing this for *her*.

Derek came within an inch of her, smelling her fragrant hair, touching her bare shoulders. Her skin felt like a smooth cream, and her eyes sparkled behind those tears, just like how he'd thought of her every day in his fantasies. He grabbed a lock of her hair, closing it in his hands as he gently kissed it. His passion for her made his blood burn. He wanted her. Badly.

"There is no need to be afraid anymore, my sweet princess. I can protect you," he said softly, continuing to kiss her hair. "I have magic now, just like you."

"Please, Derek, don't do this," Emerald cried, unable to move her body. "Please…"

"Why? After all, you told me that your feelings were true for me," he said, hovering over her. "I believe the words in your note were, 'My heart was sincere when I said that I wanted nothing more than for us to be together.'"

"I'm not in love with you!" Emerald countered fiercely through her tears. "I will never be in love with you!"

"Do you know what I have done for you?" Derek said, his eyes flaring. "If only you knew the torture I have endured every day since I have known you. You robbed me of my every thought, haunted my dreams at night. My heart is held hostage, and the only person who can free it is you."

Derek dove in to kiss her. Emerald turned her head to the side, trying to evade his lips.

"Glacia! Celeste! Help me!" Emerald screamed.

Instantly, Derek summoned up the sorrows of his heart. The sadness ate away at the insides of his flesh, burning with the deep blue of the night.

Time! Bend to my will!

A deep-blue glow emitted from his hand, then a giant flash of blue surrounded the world.

The room became still and silent, painted in hues of blue. Time had stopped, all but him.

Derek approached Emerald, pulling the circlet out of his tunic. His hands were sweaty, afraid to drop such an extravagant piece of jewelry. The position that the princess was locked in looked like she was waiting to be danced with. So elegant, so captivating.

Derek took in her lovely porcelain complexion, then moved his gaze to her breasts. The dress was low cut, making it easy to feast his eyes on her flesh. His cheeks became flushed as an insatiable lust for her filled him.

Derek moved in and kissed her still, soft lips. "You leave me no choice, my princess. I didn't want to have to do this, but I have given you every opportunity without the use of magic," he said in a whisper, staring into her eyes.

He leaned in and gave her another kiss. Even though her lips didn't kiss back, he felt the pressure within his body and mind melt away. He would finally be able to be live freely with her, satisfying any and all urges that he had for so long. She was his.

Derek gave Emerald one final glance, then slipped the circlet on her head. He felt a magnetic pull from the crown as it tightly secured itself on her forehead. Derek took a step back, wanting to see if the magic of the circlet had taken effect.

He pulled his hand out once more, concentrating the magic within his palms.

Time, continue!

The blueness of the still world dispersed, vanishing back into color as he lowered his hands. Flashes from the storm illuminated the hall, reflecting blue and white colors against the marble pillars. Hard rain could be heard pattering on the windows, and the thunder boomed.

"Derek?" Emerald said with a dazed look on her face.

Derek remained still, watching her. Thoughts of their kiss flooded his mind. Her delicate, soft lips brushing against his.

The circlet on Emerald's head began to glow a deep purple. Emerald glanced at him, then smiled. An eager look came over her face.

Emerald moved closer to him seductively. When she couldn't get any closer, Emerald placed her arms on Derek's shoulders, then yanked him to her, kissing him wildly.

Her intensity made Derek want her even more. So much more.

Almost like she could sense his desire, she continued to kiss him fiercely, burying her hands under his shirt. Her touch made him gasp softly.

He returned her kisses, over and over again. His body needed her.

"Come," Emerald said, pulling away from him, holding his hand. Her eyes were empty, void of pupils, but her body was completely alive.

"Where are we going?" Derek asked, eyeing her curiously.

"You need me," she said. "And this place is not suitable."

Derek broke out in laughter, pleased. Emerald's hand continued to tease the inside of his shirt. As much as he wanted to take her to bed here and now, Derek still felt a sense of moral obligation to wait until after the ceremony.

"As tempting as that offer is, let us wait until tomorrow night, Princess. I want to start our marriage off right."

Emerald smiled at him with vacant eyes, then nodded. "Yes, my prince."

Derek paused for a moment, considering going back on his word. His lust was quenched for the moment, but it left him feeling high and dry, wanting, no, needing more of her.

It was like Emerald had heard his thoughts, because a moment later, she pushed him onto the throne, covering him with soft kisses, sending him into a state of bliss.

Her body was pure ecstasy.

Derek met her with kisses of his own, pulling her body close to his.

I don't know why you didn't do this sooner. It feels good, doesn't it? Ikaria murmured in his mind.

Can I have some privacy at least?

As you wish, my prince.

Emerald continued to run her hands all over his body, loosening his shirt, her fiery kisses moving up and down his neck.

The witch was right. It felt more than good.

CHAPTER 60

ORANGE

The sparkling green jewel looked so vibrant in the dark world. It pulsated life, its rays piercing the black skies.

Drew watched the giant gem continue to radiate its green light as he anxiously walked toward it. In this world, he had his body, the body before the accident. He wasn't a machine, nor was he controlled by a program.

He was free.

Drew stopped a foot away from the jewel, contemplating if he should touch it. Curiosity got the best of him, and he leaned over, laying his hand on the cool, hard surface of the emerald.

Underneath his hand, blood began to seep out of the gem. Surprised, Drew removed his hand, taking a step back. With each pulse of light, blood continued to flow from the gem's core, as if its heart were bleeding. The blood streamed down faster as the jewel's heart quickened. Frantically, Drew placed both hands on the emerald, trying to suppress the bleeding.

But the blood continued to pour out. It kept oozing blood until the world was drowning in it.

Thunder rumbled, and a green flash of lightning crackled across the sky. Bloodied rains began showering down from the dark heavens, contributing to the flooding bloody waters.

Drew flailed in the ocean of blood in a panic. The only thing that remained constant was the glowing green emerald, still beating on a rock, high above the crimson waters. He never knew how to swim in his past life, and he was having a hard time keeping his head above the blood.

Torrents of blood hit his face, splashing his bifocals with ruby streams of liquid. Quickly, he tried to wipe it off with his hands, but instead he just smeared it around the lenses.

"I give up!" Drew yelled at the sky through the bloodied crimson rains. "I don't know what this all means! It has to do with the princess, but what? What should I do?"

We need her blood. One hundred times... the voice in the skies rumbled with thunder. *You are gifted, are you not?*

"Yes!"

Then use your power.

Drew jolted his eyes open.

His cybernetic eye scanned the room, telling him he was still in the audience hall of the palace. The dangerous man with the gift of the spectrum, in the wavelength of 450-495 nanometers, was gone, along with the princess.

Malfunction.

Drew glitched, shuddering from his circuitry. He could move. He was free from the prince's magic, no longer paused in time.

Where had the princess gone? Was she okay? What had happened after he was paused in time?

Malfunction.

Drew noticed an odd, impossible light, its color absent from the spectrum. Black.

A woman appeared within a black glowing mist, giving him a faint smile. Long violet hair and strange black eyes that made his circuits go haywire. She arched her back and held her head high as she moved, walking toward him in a predatory sort of way.

"So, I heard that you had a little misunderstanding with the prince?" she said, winking and laying her hands on his chest. "But don't mind Derek, he can get a little carried away. He means well."

Drew watched her hands move across his body while her eyes sparkled. Was her look that of excitement? He felt like he should flee from this woman, but his circuitry couldn't comply.

Malfunction.

"I wonder what it's like with a machine?" she wondered aloud, laughing.

Why was she laughing?

Her black eyes glistened, peering right at him as she leaned in. "You know, you now have to do what I say."

Confused, Drew gave her a blank stare, cocking his head.

In response, she held up her hand, revealing a silver gauntlet with a glowing orb on the backside of the hand.

The master gauntlet. It was what the others in the network had warned him about. She was the new master.

Drew felt an instant attachment to the device, drawn to its energy. His mind started to feel fuzzy, as if he wasn't there inside his mind. His face and body tingled, then turned numb. He no longer had control of his limbs.

The woman moved her fingers slightly, running her gauntlet hand down his body, stopping before his lowers, resting her hand.

He didn't move. He *couldn't* move. How he wanted to.

Access denied.

"Not today, my lovely piece of machine. We must play a different day," she said, flashing a smile at him. "However, I came here to tell you to play nice with the prince. Your job is to protect both him and the princess and ensure that they have their wedding. After all, we must not give the High Court the history that it wants." The woman's eyes lowered to his male anatomy. "We just have a little while longer before you travel back with me to my time. Then"—she paused for a moment—"we can play, you and I."

Negative, Drew answered in his head. *I cannot leave Telly.*

A voice in the network laughed, echoing in his head. *You cannot disobey the master! Can't you feel the suppression of your body? Your mind? It's futile.*

Only the master can guide us, called out another computerized voice.

I can't go with her! There is something I must do, answered Drew.

Do? There is nothing for us to do but follow orders! You cannot act outside your programming, however human you think you are, the computerized voice replied.

We are cyborgs. Built with a purpose, another voice called out within the network.

A purpose to destroy and conquer, whispered another. *There is no hope. We will never be free.*

No, I don't believe that! Drew argued back within the network.

The woman studied him for a moment, curious. "It's so fascinating," she said, gently stroking his shaved head. "You are the only one whose thoughts I cannot see with my power, even with my new black gift." Her finger ran down his face to where circuits were exposed, then touched his lips. "I wonder what you are hiding in there?" She paused, about to lean in, then stopped. "So much power, so much information. You and I, we are going to do so much together, along with the princess."

The princess. Was the princess going to help this woman too?

Malfunction.

Confusion ran through his circuits. His programming told him to trust this woman, but his mind screamed constant warnings. Drew stood there silently, unable to override her or her orders.

He had no choice. The master was in control.

CHAPTER 61

RED

I turned my head toward the fiery heavens and saw the Angel of the Red, the Keeper of the Elements. In spirit form, he took me to the four corners of the earth. "Come," he said, "I will show you what the God of Light has shown me." I looked and saw the gift of the red flowing forth from all four corners, and in each corner, a different power arose. Winds blew from the north, waters flowed from the east, fires burned from the west, and the earth shook from the south. They came and filled my soul, instilling me with their ancient wisdom.

—excerpt from *The Spectrum*, Chapter of the Red,
recorded by Varian Hardenburg, 521 M.E.

Half of the camp was charred when Kyle gained consciousness. He was face down on the hot, dry, rocky dirt, centered within a scorched radius of the desert. His clothes had been incinerated, leaving the backside of his naked body exposed to the wasteland's hot elements.

Slightly lifting his head off the gravel, Kyle saw that many of the camp dwellers were gathering around, noticing that he was moving. As his body stirred, the women who had children covered their offspring's eyes, immediately shooing them away from the incident. From behind him, Kyle heard loud trudging footsteps grating along the pebbles with each step.

"I wasn't sure if you were going to make it," he heard Victor say.

Kyle stumbled to his feet, exposing his naked flesh to the remaining onlookers of the camp. Glaring at them he grumbled, "Do you mind? Why don't you all take a picture while you're at it?" Instantly, the camp dwellers dispersed, except Victor, who tossed a blanket at him. "You know, you could have given me this when I was passed out," Kyle muttered.

Victor put his arm around him and chuckled, helping Kyle remain steady. "We did. Several times. Each time the blanket would catch fire and burn up."

"Damn. Seriously?" Kyle looked around at the damage throughout the charred area, awestruck. "Did I do that?"

"Yes. Luckily, when we realized that the magic you were succumbing to was getting out of control, we evacuated the camp, leaving you here."

"Thanks," Kyle muttered. "Glad to know that I have friends that'll be there for me. How long was I out?"

"Almost a week now."

Kyle turned sharply to Victor. "A *week*? Why the hell didn't you wake me up?"

"We tried, but you were in some type of magical coma. The only thing we could do was pour water on your body. Your skin absorbed it somehow, allowing you to stay hydrated."

The image of Emerald came to his mind, her dancing in the flames of his vision. Kyle had to get to her, but he didn't have any means to get back to Arcadia. His bike was somewhere out in the wastelands, wrecked.

Kyle snarled, pissed at himself. Pissed that he'd fucked up so hard this time. His anger burned inside of him, and he was going to explode if he didn't get a move on to find Emerald. He had already wasted days. Fucking days.

He turned to Victor. "I need to go. Now."

"Yes, I think it's best if you hurry." Victor led him to Garrett's trailer, and both entered. Garrett had already laid clothes out for Kyle on his chair. Black leather, his favorite.

Kyle snatched up the pants, yanking them on.

"The princess is to marry soon," Victor called out.

Kyle spun around in Victor's direction, latching on to his tunic. "What the hell did you just say?"

"She's getting married to the Prince of York. The one that threatened our camp."

Kyle's heart sank in his chest. "Well, shit. I can't go and stop her, then. Maybe she wants to get married to that asshole. Maybe... maybe it's her way of helping us."

The news hurt. He never liked admitting that kind of emotional crap, but it hurt. Bad.

"I don't like him. There is a darkness to him." Victor paused. "Before she left the camp, the princess told me that she had to go back to Arcadia to face her father. Somehow, I don't think it's going as planned. I can sense it."

Did Emerald really want to get married to the prince? She'd told Kyle that she did at one point, but did she really want to now? Somehow, Kyle doubted it. Victor was right. The prince did seem like a control freak and was obsessed as hell with finding her. Kyle had a bad feeling about the whole thing, and it didn't sit right with him. Deep down, he knew the way Emerald felt about him, and what they had. Kyle wasn't willing to let it go without hearing her say it. If Emerald really wanted to marry that fucking asshole, Kyle would accept it and walk away.

Kyle sighed loudly, running his fingers through his hair, frustrated. "Fuck! What am I supposed to do? Waltz into Arcadia, break up a royal wedding, and say, 'Princess, I think you're making a big mistake?'"

"Sounds about right," Garrett said, inserting himself into the conversation. "Kyle, how does it feel, man? Do you feel any different?"

"I'm mad as hell, that's how I feel," Kyle said, throwing the shirt over his head.

Garrett jolted back when Kyle glanced at him, a look of shock on his face. "Damn," he cursed under his breath.

"What?" Kyle demanded.

"Your eyes… They've changed."

Kyle quickly rummaged around Garrett's trailer, looking for anything to cast his reflection. Garrett helped, hurrying over to a messy counter and shoving the clutter aside, revealing a small mirror. He handed it to Kyle.

Peering into the glass, Kyle saw his new eyes. Eyes the color of sparkling rubies. He hovered close to the glass, almost pressing against it to stare at his appearance, amazed at the change.

"Well, I'll be damned. Literally." He casually tossed the mirror to Garrett, who caught it.

Garrett chuckled. "Well, I don't think you should consider your power being damned."

"Whatever. At least I'll scare the hell out of Arcadia when I arrive. Do you have any smokes? My head is killing me."

Garrett handed him a pack of cigarettes, and Kyle shoved them inside the borrowed studded black leather jacket.

Kyle held out his hand. "And your keys."

"Keys?" Garrett asked, staring at him blankly.

"Yes, the damn keys to your bike," Kyle said, still holding out his hands, waiting for Garrett to respond. "If I'm gonna stop Emerald from marrying that guy, I can't just fucking walk my ass back there." Kyle paused for a moment, rubbing his head. "I can't believe this is happening."

Garrett looked to Victor, who gave him a nod. Sighing loudly, Garrett fetched the keys to his motorcycle, then hesitantly slammed them into Kyle's extended hand. "Don't fuck up my bike. I just built the damn thing."

"I can't promise you shit, but I'll try and be good to it," Kyle said, pulling out a cigarette and shoving it between his lips.

The moment Kyle thought about needing to light the cigarette, flames flared up from his hand, charring the cigarette.

Garrett and Victor jumped back, shocked. The flames continued to burn in Kyle's hand.

I know you're just as pissed as I am, Kyle told the flames, *but together we will get Em back.*

With one solid wave of his flaming hand, they disappeared, and his skin was unharmed.

Spitting out the charred cigarette, Kyle reached for another one, placing it between his lips. Victor and Garrett watch him curiously as he raised two fingers. A small flame ignited from the tips, lighting his cigarette. Victor and Garrett both stood in astonishment, then smiled at each other at the awesomeness of the power.

Kyle inhaled his cigarette the longest he could, feeling the buzz of the nicotine. Exhaling, he held the cigarette in his mouth and studied his fingers. "Damn, that's useful." He turned to Victor and Garrett, nodding. "Time to haul ass back to Arcadia."

"Be safe," Victor said. "Watch out for those cyborgs. And Damaris."

"Yeah. I have no clue what I'm gonna do about that, but I am going to try my damnedest," Kyle said, stepping out of the trailer.

"At least come back to return my damn bike," Garrett called out.

Ignoring Garrett's statement, Kyle exited into the hot sun, walking down the trailer's metal steps while taking another drag. Circling the camper, he came to where Garrett's bike was parked.

Taking one last puff of his cigarette, he held it between his fingers and pinched it. Power surged through him, calling forth the water element that he'd conquered in his vision. The power obeyed from within, racing through his blood and into his fingertips.

Suddenly the cigarette cherry sizzled as if it had been doused in water. Kyle froze the moisture in retribution for trying to drown him earlier within the confines of his mind.

Let's see you fuck with me now, damn cyborg!

Kyle hopped on the bike, started the engine, and took off.

CHAPTER 62

All night and into the morning, Glacia had been worried for Emerald. When the princess returned to her quarters in the wee hours of the morning, it was apparent that Emerald was not herself. Her face had been expressionless, her eyes vacant, and she only spoke when spoken to. Her bodice had been slightly undone and her hair disheveled, which was a cause for concern. Emerald didn't say a word about Derek, but instead went right to bed in her evening attire. Glacia wondered if Derek and Emerald had made up. By the looks of it, Emerald did more than make up with the prince, causing Glacia's stomach to churn.

Glacia placed her hand over the doorknob to Emerald's bedroom, pausing.

"What's wrong?" Celeste called out from the sitting area. The other handmaidens paid no attention, going about their morning activities.

"Nothing," Glacia lied, sighing. How she wished it was nothing.

Turning the knob, Glacia stepped into Emerald's bedroom. Emerald sat up from her bed in an unusual manner.

"Good morning, Princess. Did you sleep well?" Glacia asked, giving her usual bow.

"Yes," Emerald replied, her eyes void of life.

A shiver ran down Glacia's spine at the unusualness of Emerald's movement, or lack thereof. Trying to ignore Emerald's odd behavior, Glacia continued, "Princess, shall we get you dressed? I am sure that you will want to get out of that gown. I don't know how you could have even slept in that thing. It must have been terribly uncomfortable."

Emerald didn't answer. She rose from her bed and pulled up her hair, waiting for Glacia to undo her gown.

Glacia hesitantly walked toward Emerald, then began to unlace her bodice. Emerald touched her circlet, cradling it against her head. It was a new headpiece, one that Glacia had not seen before.

"New circlet, Princess?"

"Yes. A gift from Derek," Emerald said without emotion.

Glacia pulled Emerald toward her, whispering, "Is everything okay?"

Emerald glanced at her with void eyes. "Yes, why wouldn't it be? Today is my wedding day."

"Wedding?" Glacia echoed, stunned. "Princess, what happened? I thought you were going to break it off with Derek."

"Why would I do such a thing? I want to be with him."

"You do?" Glacia asked incredulously.

Emerald paused, looking confused. "Why, yes, of course."

At that moment, Drew appeared in one of the corners of the bedroom. He gave Glacia a look of warning, then shook his head. Although he never talked, Glacia knew what he was trying to say. Emerald was not herself.

The cyborg frowned, then sighed silently.

Turning quickly to Emerald, Glacia asked, "Princess, if Prince Derek has done something to you, please tell me."

"He has done nothing to me."

Glacia lowered her voice. "Did he have you?" she asked in a whisper.

"No."

Glacia sighed with relief, but it didn't help much. The gut-wrenching feeling returned. Everything wasn't all right. But what could she do if Emerald wouldn't confide in her?

"I need to get ready for my wedding," Emerald said.

Hesitantly, Glacia bowed while Drew disappeared back into the void. "I will draw a bath for you. There is much to do before this evening," Glacia said.

"Yes, thank you."

Emerald walked into her private bathroom completely naked as Glacia followed anxiously. The handmaiden began to fill the tub with hot water, scenting the water with lavender oils. Emerald had removed all of her jewelry but the circlet.

There was noise coming from the bedroom, and Celeste appeared at the bathroom door. "Princess, the prince's advisor, Ikaria, is here to see you."

"Bring her here."

Glacia's jaw dropped, then shot a look to Emerald to see if she was serious. "Princess, do you really want a stranger to see you unclothed? I can have Celeste serve her some wine and have her wait in the sitting room until we are finished."

"Bring her here," Emerald repeated herself.

Had she stepped into an alternate universe? Glacia couldn't believe Emerald was insisting on seeing the advisor while having her bath. She was completely out of her mind.

"Yes, Princess," Glacia said slowly. She opened the door to fetch Ikaria, but the woman was already standing in the doorway with a deep smile. Her narrow eyes flashed as she strutted in, then she bowed to Emerald.

"Princess, I am here to bathe you," Ikaria said smoothly, walking over to the tub, getting on her knees. "The prince told me to take good care of you today, and I intend to do so."

Glacia had never seen Ikaria before, but she had heard the wild gossip throughout the palace. She was as beautiful as the rumors claimed. The woman had beautiful violet hair and mysterious black eyes. She wore half of her hair down and half of her hair in a top-knot split ponytail, fastened with several large ornate hair sticks. She was dressed quite provocatively in a fashion that Glacia had never seen before. A revealing armorlike silver top and jewelry and flowing black skirts with high slits.

"Advisor Ikaria," Glacia said, bowing, "I can assure you, there is no need. I have been assigned to the princess for years, and have always given her a bath."

"I will have Ikaria give me my bath and dress me as well," Emerald stated. "You may wait out in the sitting room."

"What?" Glacia asked, stunned. On Emerald's wedding day, Glacia wasn't to dress her best friend?

"You heard me. Now, please wait for me in the sitting room."

Ikaria and Emerald looked at Glacia, waiting for her to leave. Hurt and confused, Glacia promptly bowed, finally accepting her orders. Ikaria flashed a smile at her as Glacia left the bathroom.

As she walked back into the sitting room, Glacia's mind raced. She couldn't accept the fact that Emerald wanted Ikaria to bathe her. It had always been their private time to tell jokes, gossip about the kingdoms, and utter a few laughs before they had to act serious again in front of the royals. Something was very wrong, and Glacia suspected that Emerald was under the influence of some kind of spell. Maybe Emerald's magic was going haywire? It had to be. What else could possibly be affecting her? She was clearly not herself.

Determined to figure out what was going on, Glacia quietly made her way back to the bathroom door, peeking through the crack while listening in on the conversation.

"I have seen you before," she heard Emerald say as Ikaria began to wash her hair. Glacia noted that the advisor took care not to remove the circlet from Emerald's head, simply washing the hair around it.

"Nonsense, my princess. We have never met."

"There were strange people with you. Gifted people. Your sister… she was to be named Empress."

Ikaria stopped lathering Emerald's hair, quickly jerking her by the arm. "And where did you hear that?" she demanded sharply.

"I saw it in my dreams."

The advisor quieted, then finally resumed shampooing Emerald's hair. "What else did you see in your dreams?"

"Two blue-gifted men. They wanted my power. They tried to stop me."

A sneer flashed on Ikaria's face as she washed the suds out of Emerald's hair. "All this time I wondered what the interruption was on that day. And now I finally understand. That is how they discovered you. They just needed to find out when you were from. Interesting." Ikaria massaged conditioner through Emerald's long locks, deep in thought. "I think it's in everyone's best interest that I make your circlet stronger. I can't have you talking about such things."

Ikaria laid a hand directly on Emerald's forehead, where the jewel was in the circlet. Slowly, an eerie black glow began to form around her. The mass of energy began to glow brighter with each passing moment, then gathered to Ikaria's hand. Then with a sudden whoosh, the power swirled away from Ikaria, sucked into the circlet's jewel.

Glacia gasped at the sight, slowly backing away while her heart hammered in her chest.

"Do not toy with the circlet, you understand?" Glacia heard Ikaria say to the princess. "It would be near impossible to remove it anyway, but we don't want your mind to go unhinged if someone tried."

"Yes, Princess Ikaria."

Princess? Princess of where?

"Do not say anything further about me, not ever. You will address me as Advisor for the time being."

"Yes, Advisor."

Fear gripped Glacia. What should she do? Emerald was being controlled somehow by magic through that crown. And if the gift was really from Derek, as Emerald had said earlier, then Derek was behind it. He had used magic to manipulate Emerald's mind.

That is why she changed her mind suddenly about marrying him!

Glacia felt sickened at the thought of Derek's deceit. He was not what anyone thought he was. He was not the perfect prince; he was a monster. Using magic to subdue Emerald, fits of jealous rage… Glacia had to get Emerald away from both that witch and the prince.

Glacia's heart continued to race at the thought that a woman with powerful magic was in the same quarters as her.

Act normal, Glacia! she ordered herself. Her mind raced as she tried to calm herself. Then something came to her. She needed to find the man in Emerald's pictures.

What did Glacia know about the guy? Not much. She knew what he looked like through Emerald's drawings. And that he played in a band.

Glacia ran over to the drawings that were hung back up on the wall, searching until she saw a flyer taped next to one of the pictures. "Disorderly Conduct," read the band's name.

"Servant girl," Ikaria said as she and Emerald emerged from the bathroom. "I would like some wine. Don't tarry too long. We have much to do today to ensure that the princess has the perfect wedding."

"Yes, my lady," Glacia said, bowing low.

"That's Advisor Ikaria to you," the woman corrected her.

Glacia nodded, then went to the next room to fetch the liquor. As she returned, she saw Celeste making Ikaria comfortable on a sofa near the princess, propping a few pillows behind her.

Glacia set down the delicate glass of wine on the table next to the advisor, then bowed.

Ikaria flashed her black eyes, giving Glacia a crooked grin. "About time," she said, then smirked, taking a drink.

Take a deep breath, Glacia. Stay calm.

***

"Glacia, I found it," Cyndi said quietly. Emerald's third handmaiden handed her the communication device with the phone number on the screen. "His name is Kyle. The venue said that is the only contact number they have on file."

"Thank you," Glacia said, clutching the device nervously, then slipping it inside her dress pocket. "I am going to go out for a minute. If anyone asks where I'm at, tell them I went to fetch the princess more coffee."

"But we were ordered to stay with the princess all day. We aren't supposed to leave!" Tamara, the fourth handmaiden, whispered.

"Well, I don't care what happens!" Glacia whispered back fiercely. "We have to do something!"

Tamara went silent while the other two handmaidens nodded in response. As the day went on, all of the handmaidens could plainly see what Glacia had first noticed—Emerald was not herself. Cyndi bit her nails nervously, while Tamara and Ophelia paced around the room anxiously. Celeste was absent, as she had been ordered to style Emerald's hair, since she was the best of the handmaidens with hair, but Glacia could guarantee that she was feeling the same as the others, especially in the presence of the advisor.

Right when Glacia was about to leave, Drew came into view off to the side. He glanced at Glacia, not making any movement.

Glacia froze for a second, unsure of what he was about to do.

The cyborg continued to stare at her, then closed his eyes. He stretched out his arm, the arm that wasn't part machinery, and orange dust appeared, whirling in Glacia's direction. The glowing dust settled on her skin, then Glacia saw her body start to morph, while the other handmaidens silently gaped.

Gazing at her new hands, Glacia ran in front of the mirror, seeing the advisor's reflection staring back at her. Turning quickly to the cyborg, he gave her a small nod, then disappeared.

By the God of Light! He just made me look like the advisor! Her head raced with the thought. The handmaidens remained silent, in awe of the cyborg's power.

"Hurry," Cyndi said, breaking the silence.

Without another word, Glacia slipped out of the sitting room and exited Emerald's chambers. There were guards posted outside, and they gave Glacia, or rather, Advisor Ikaria, a nod. Glacia was about to bow back in response but caught herself, straightening her posture and holding her chin up high. She then harrumphed, hurrying down the stairs.

She'd only been around her in a limited capacity, but it was what she thought the advisor would do.

Three levels below Emerald's chambers, Glacia exited the staircase, then slipped down a hall. This floor was mostly unused, except for small matters of state. There was complete silence but for the echoes of Glacia's footsteps. Most of the meeting rooms were empty, and one of them in particular hadn't been used in years.

Cautiously looking around at her surroundings, Glacia went inside the abandoned room, then locked the door. She sat down at a small desk, which was equipped with a blank notepad, pen, and a palace tablet.

Glacia looked down to where her dress was but saw Ikaria's outfit instead. But she *felt* her own dress flowing around her body, with the weight of the communication device. It had to be the magic making her dress appear like the advisor's, but underneath the magic, she still had her original garments.

Glacia felt around for the device, then delved into her invisible pocket, and the device was in her hand as it emerged.

Such a handy trick!

The communication device still had the number entered on the screen. All she had to do was press the call button. Why was she so scared?

Scared at getting caught... I will be toast if the advisor finds out...

Taking a deep gulp, Glacia pushed the button, hearing the device dial the number.

One ring. Two rings. Three rings... Four...

"Yeah?" said a male voice on the line.

Glacia took a breath, then faltered for a moment. "Um, hi. I am trying to reach Kyle? Is he available?"

"Who is this? Is this Em?" the voice asked.

Em? Is he talking about the princess?

"Do you mean Em as in Princess Emerald?"

"Wait, *what*? Em, is that you?"

"No, but this is her handmaiden, Glacia. I really need to talk to Kyle. Emerald is in trouble!" Glacia pleaded into the device.

"Handmaiden? Emerald?" the voice echoed. "Oh, shit. No wonder the police were drilling us!"

Glacia heard the other person rummaging around, with more male voices in the background. There was some fighting over the device, then more noise.

"Listen, you tell that asshole that I was arrested because of him!" a new male voice shouted.

"I'm… sorry?" Glacia said, confused. "So you don't know where Kyle is? The princess is in trouble, and I need to tell him. She needs help!"

"Princess? Are you talking about Em?"

"Yes! She is Princess Emerald!"

"Holy shit!" the voice exclaimed. More muffled noises could be heard. "Hey, Remy, Em is Princess Emerald! Can you believe that shit? How the fuck did homeboy end up so lucky?" the voice called out to the background.

"May I talk to Kyle, please?" Glacia said hurriedly. She did not want to be caught, and the conversation was going nowhere. Was Kyle like these men on the phone?

"We don't know where the hell he is. The middle of our gig, he goes chasing after Em and some weirdo. After hours of arguing with the police and telling them we had no idea what kind of trouble homeboy got himself into, they finally let us go. So if you see that asshole, tell him thanks a fucking bunch."

Glacia's heart dropped. Not even Kyle's band knew where he was. No one could help.

"Please, if you see him, tell him what I have told you. If you could, can you take down this number? I might not be able to answer this device, but I will get your message if you leave one."

"I guess. Damn, I still can't believe that bastard and the princess… together. Wow. I didn't see this one coming."

"What is your name, in case I need to call back?" Glacia asked.

"Diego."

"I'm Glacia. Please, make sure he gets my message if you see him."

Glacia gave the number to him, then politely hung up, staring at the screen, lost in thought. Her head was swimming. Kyle couldn't be reached, and it felt like she had no other options.

Then a thought struck her. Haze. Maybe he could help.

Quickly putting the device back into her pocket, Glacia slipped out of the room, making her way in haste back to Emerald's quarters.

CHAPTER 63

RED

A violent, raging red thunderstorm trailed Kyle, leaving a path of devastation behind as he drove furiously toward Arcadia. The wild red winds whipped through his hair while the hard rains drenched him. With each second, his fury channeled the magic, calling forth the elements, destroying everything along the way. The more anger he felt, the greater the crimson storms and ruby vortexes ripped through the wastelands and into the city.

No one was going to mess with him now. Not Arcadia's force. Not the prince. Not even the fucking King himself. He just had to see Emerald. One word from her. Just one. That was all he needed to know if she really wanted to get married.

Arcadia shone in all its glorious lights as Kyle approached. Night had fallen, and the traffic was backed up due to the rains, but it didn't slow him down. The power of the elements enveloped him, making his motorcycle lighter, fast as hell, and more maneuverable, with the power of the winds on his side. The water on the roads obeyed his thoughts and allowed his bike to glide through the streets effortlessly.

Kyle dodged the ground vehicles, the furious winds causing massive damage from behind. Air transports that caught up in Kyle's red current were flung in all different directions, slamming across the city. The earth rumbled and quaked as he drove, shaking some of the ground vehicles aside, creating a clear path for Kyle to maintain his speed.

It didn't take long for the authorities to appear. It was hard for Kyle to go unnoticed with the havoc he was inflicting upon Arcadia.

Kyle's vision was suddenly flooded with a bright white light. More lights followed suit, and he heard the hovering sounds of the transports above, following his path.

Come get me, assholes, he taunted them within his mind. *I'd like to see you try.*

He could hear them over the megaphone from above, yelling at him to stop. Other ground vehicles pulled in from behind in pursuit, yelling through their intercoms, telling him to surrender. Either way, he wasn't going to give in to their bullshit. Any other time he probably would have.

This time it was different.

Funneling rage into his power, Kyle spoke to the winds through his mind, letting them guide his motorcycle. They steadied the bike for him, his motorcycle being enveloped by glowing red current. He let go of the handlebars, trusting the magic. His bike was wobbling unsteadily.

Stay still, he ordered the bike.

A feeling of another power, one that he hadn't felt before, surged through his blood. It was a forceful power, ripping through his body. Suddenly that power began to control the motorcycle through the streets, driving it for him, glowing with a red-violet intensity. Kyle didn't have to tell the power where he was going. It knew his mind, automatically sending him toward his destination.

The Holy Cathedral of Light. Garrett had better be right with his information, because Kyle had no time to fuck this one up.

Kyle looked behind him, seeing that only the larger ground vehicles could weather his storm; the small units couldn't manage. However, the transports that remained were gaining on him.

Swiftly, Kyle raised his hands, summoning bright ruby-red flames. With a large downward swoop of his arms, he ignited a tremendous fireball within his palms, then hurled it at the ground behind the motorcycle. As soon as the fireball met the ground, it transformed into two giant walls of fire behind him.

Sounds of the megaphone repeated above as spotlights shone on him, illuminating him for all of Arcadia to see. Eventually, someone was going to get tired of the chase, and it sure as hell wasn't going to be him.

After several more minutes, Kyle finally made it into Arcadia's western sector. Passing another intersection, he knew he was close.

Racing toward the building that the crystal cathedral was on top on, Kyle saw a multitude of authorities surrounding the ground level of the building. There was a swarm of police vehicles and transports, and many of the palace guards were situated among them. No doubt it would be the same on every platform while the princess and prince were attending their ceremony.

Gathering up his courage, Kyle jumped off the moving motorcycle, summoning his magic. The red winds encircled him, catching him in midair, and he hovered for a second. Kyle saw Garrett's motorcycle continue to plow forward into the crowd of authorities, slamming into one of the police transports.

Sorry, man, Kyle thought to Garrett. *That's why I make no promises.* He could hear Garrett now. He'd probably get an earful of choice words the next time he saw him.

The red winds guided Kyle down gently, releasing him from their grasp. The authorities began to charge while transports drove toward him.

Kyle had to make a decision, and quick. He looked toward the building, then an idea struck him.

With all of his strength from within, he called forth the waters from his soul. The red floods and magical waters coursed through his veins, surging through his hands. Kyle shot his hands downward, letting the water spray like a high-pressure hose. The more raging power he fed it, the more forcefully it sprayed the water. Higher and higher he rose, freezing the water as it left his hands, shooting him upward to the mid-levels.

Kyle had created two extremely tall blocks of red glowing ice under his hands. Loud cracks could be heard from below; the authorities were shooting at the ice. Kyle could sense the power within the ice, and it sure as hell wasn't going to hold much longer.

Trusting the elements, he threw his head backward, allowing the winds to surround him completely. Kyle removed his hands from the ice blocks, floating in the air for a moment. He looked down below and saw nothing but small black figures running around in the golden lights of the building and through the skyways. Damn, he was far up.

Hovering within the wet storms, Kyle began shooting large sheets of ice through the air from his hands. He let the winds take over, and they surrounded the glowing red ice, creating floating steps to the cathedral.

Kyle hopped onto the first step, still slick from the rains, and glided quickly across. He stopped near the edge, breathing a sigh of relief. Then a crack appeared. It couldn't handle the pressure of his weight.

He jumped to the next one, and the next, creating new sheets of ice upward, sliding across the sheets, looking at his goal through the raindrops slapping his face. As he left each step, the ice sheets fell on the city below, causing panic within the crowds and the authorities.

More gunshots. A strong force of wind raced by him.

Guns were firing at him from the air transports.

Damn! Winds, a little help right now would be useful.

A gush of red wind flew from his body, almost like a transparent barrier had surrounded him. The bullets made contact with it but then spun out in all different directions, missing Kyle completely.

Air transports hovered nearby, and more gunshots ricocheted away. Kyle summoned a barrier of ice in front of him, shielding him from the bullets. With a quick whip of his hands, red lightning bolted down on transports, causing them to spin out of control.

Soaked, Kyle jumped off the last ice step, making it onto the main entrance platform of the cathedral, where all the transports were to dock. The remaining red ice cracked, then fell to the city depths below. More air transports followed, initiating landings on the platform. Men poured out, guns drawn.

Emerald appeared in his mind. Kyle couldn't let her marry the prince without him really knowing how she felt about him. He couldn't fail her this time.

He heard guards circling him, all heavily armed. A swarm of authorities appeared in front of Kyle, all ready to fire.

Well, shit, this isn't looking so good.

He pulled out a cigarette, placing it in his mouth, then lit it with a magical flame that appeared from one of his fingertips. He then began to puff it casually as he held his hands up in surrender.

The authorities exchanged looks as if he was crazy.

"You are surrounded," one of the captains called out.

"Yeah, I'm pretty fucked, aren't I?" Kyle said calmly.

"Stand down," the captain said.

Kyle took one last drag. The taste of the tobacco felt soothing, but didn't take the edge off his anger. It made him pause for a moment to reflect how determined he was.

He released the cigarette from his mouth, and it fell gently to the ground. When the burning cherry touched the platform, Kyle swooped his hands in a downward motion, creating a massive flaming explosion.

There was an instant fire and smoke barricade between Kyle and the authorities. Through the roaring fires, Kyle heard the platform begin to crumble. The other men yelled in confusion, running in the chaos to evacuate. Kyle passed several of them as he continued to near the entrance. One of the men saw Kyle through the flames and was about to take action, but it was too late. The wall of flames flared up between them as Kyle entered the cathedral.

Once inside, Kyle found himself in a grand foyer made of gold and crystal, decorated with canvas paintings of the God of Light. He shuddered, feeling unwanted in such a holy place.

What Kyle had told Emerald was true—he never gave the God of Light much thought. He did believe there was a god, but he'd never felt the need to pursue religion much further than that. Even with his newfound gift, he felt like it was a gift given directly from Emerald, not from God. What god in their right mind would give an asshole such as himself such a divine gift, anyway?

Kyle had no idea what direction or hallway to take, as there were no signs and no great entrance into the main sanctuary. He decided to take the middle hallway, as logic said that the sanctuary would be at the heart of the building. Hopefully.

Running down the shimmering golden halls, Kyle saw more guards running toward him, guns readied. Kyle gathered that they'd heard the platform squabble outside. As both parties approached, the guards began shooting.

Swinging his hand in an upward motion, Kyle created a red ice wall, letting the bullets bury themselves uselessly.

"Where is Princess Emerald?" Kyle yelled through the ice. The guards looked awestruck, staring wide eyed at the magical red ice. "I don't want to hurt you!"

The raised their guns, about to shoot again.

"Please don't," Kyle said flatly. "I'm already having a shitty day. I woke my ass up out in the desert completely butt-ass naked, barreled through most of Arcadia, and just blew up half the platform out there." The guards' eyes looked worried, and they glanced at each other. "I really don't want to hurt anyone. I just need to find the princess."

"She's down the next hall," called out a voice from behind.

Kyle looked over his shoulder and saw five women in long white dresses. One woman with long brown hair stepped forward.

"You're him! The one in her drawings," the woman said.

Emerald. She had been thinking of him. The thought renewed his hope.

The guards began to shoot the barricade.

"I have been looking for you," the woman shouted over the noise. "They have her now, under their control. A spell of some sort!" The other women went pale, afraid to even speak. All of them looked terrified, grasping on to each other as the bullets continued to ring out.

The ice barricade began to crack. Summoning power from within, Kyle shot another glowing red wall of ice, this time thicker than the last. The guards stopped firing.

Turning back to the woman, he asked, "Whose spell?"

The woman's hazel eyes met his, inwardly pleading with him. "The prince's new advisor, Ikaria. She is controlling the princess. I think it's the circlet she is wearing. It glows a strange purplish-black color, controlling her mind." The maiden lowered her voice to a whisper. "Emerald didn't want to marry the prince. She went to break off the engagement with Derek but returned soon after under the influence of that advisor's magic. I know that the prince is behind it too."

Kyle's blood burned, and the fire within him couldn't be held back any longer. "God damn it!" he yelled, flames burning from his hands. He wanted to explode in the flames and let his soul burn with them, but the thought of Emerald imprisoned made him pull back.

The maiden stepped backward at the sight of his magic but otherwise wasn't surprised by it. It appeared it wasn't the first time she had seen magic.

Extinguishing the flames, he ran past the handmaidens to the next hallway, where the woman was pointing.

"Please, you have to help her!" the maiden called out.

Believe me, she's not marrying anyone tonight. Not if I have a damn say in all of this! Kyle turned down the next corridor to the sanctuary.

***

In the distance, Kyle heard the sound of an organ. The solemn tune echoed through the halls, nauseating him.

The wedding had started.

"Hold on, Em!" he yelled. "Don't marry that shithead!"

Kyle ran down the hall, turning to the next corridor over where the handmaiden had pointed. At the end of the hall stood the entrance of the main sanctuary.

Guards were stationed outside the doors, and they immediately saw Kyle approaching. They drew their guns.

Anger burned within Kyle's soul, and a fiery red glow enveloped him, daring the guards to stop him. They shot their weapons, but it was too late.

Kyle was one step ahead.

A red-violet magic flared up from Kyle's hands, causing all of the bullets to jam up in their weapons. Kyle flashed them a look of annoyance, then raised a hand, transferring his energy.

The guards' weapons burned a bright red, then quickly turned a hot white. They screamed, dropping their scalding weapons, and their guns continued to smoke on the ground. Flashing his hands one more time, Kyle beckoned forth the power of the earth.

The earth responded. Giant rocks formed around the guards' legs, cementing them into place.

That should keep them busy for a while, Kyle thought.

The music had stopped playing, and Kyle heard echoes of the ceremony starting. He felt sick all over again, his guts churning.

Just as Kyle was about to burst through the main sanctuary doors, he felt a sharp, violent jab in his side, punching him with an immense velocity, pinning his body against the wall.

The cyborg flashed into view, his eyes a bright vivid orange. Kyle struggled, unable to budge from the machine's grasp. He placed his boot on the back of the wall, then pushed, forcing the cyborg to tumble with Kyle away from the wall. Calling forth the elements, red lightning forked from Kyle's body to the cyborg's, causing the cyborg to lose his grip.

The machine narrowed his glowing natural eye while the cybernetic lens made a sound, focusing on Kyle. He looked furious as hell.

The cyborg stretched out his mechanical hand, the tubes and wiring wriggling free from the damage that Kyle had caused. With a sudden jolt, five long, sharp blades appeared from his fingers and a ball of orange-red flames at the center of his palm. The cyborg's image faded and shimmered orange as he began to multiply himself, surrounding Kyle.

The copies charged toward him, shooting their flames, blades ready to piece him.

"Oh, no you don't," Kyle yelled at him. "Fire likes me better!"

Reaching toward the flames, Kyle waved his arms, snuffing out all the fires within the copies of the cyborg's hands. Pushing back his hand with much strength, a great wall of earth shot up around Kyle, then tidal waved toward all the copies of the cyborg. It knocked down the real one, causing all the other illusions to disappear like bubbles being popped.

Kyle threw back his hands, summoning frozen waters. Red ice encased the cyborg, freezing him in a solid block. Kyle saw the cyborg's body illuminate to a bright orange, then he began to melt the ice from inside.

He didn't have much time until the damn thing freed itself.

With no time to spare, Kyle ran, moving quickly up the stairs, then burst through the sanctuary doors.

Emerald was the first thing he saw. Her long beautiful emerald-green hair flowed down her shoulders. She was dressed in a white and silver gown, and her veil had been pulled back.

Kyle's heart burst. Emerald was locked in a kiss with the prince.

He was too late. Just one fucking moment too late.

"NO!" Kyle screamed from the entrance.

With sudden alarm, Emerald and Prince Derek pulled apart, glancing in his direction. Emerald looked over her shoulder, gazing directly at Kyle, past his eyes and right into his heart. Her vacant expression told him all he needed to know.

Derek's eyes flashed in anger at being interrupted.

"EM!" Kyle ran straight toward Emerald down the aisle and past the wedding guests.

Emerald gave him a confused look, remaining silent.

A deep-blue magic blazed from the prince's body, enveloping him entirely. A blue hue poured over the sanctuary, casting the whole hall in its color.

Everything became eerily still. The priest, the wedding guests, the flickering of the candles. Even the dust particles had been frozen in time. Everything except Kyle, Prince Derek, and Emerald.

"I am sorry, but you were not on the guest list," Derek said to Kyle smugly. Emerald shied away behind Derek, then put her arms around the prince, peeking at Kyle from behind.

"What the fuck did you do to her?" Kyle snarled. He whipped out his hands, calling upon red lightning from within. The elements responded to his need, flashing in Derek's direction. Emerald returned to her position behind Derek's back for safety.

Before the lightning hit the prince, it froze midair, inches away, and turned blue.

"Two can play at this game," Derek called out, laughing. A blue glow began to swirl around the prince, pulsating blue energy.

"Come and try, asshole!" Kyle shouted. He funneled his fury, channeling the earth to aid him.

Roaring at the top of his lungs, Kyle began to charge toward Derek, shifting the floor of the cathedral below him. The ground rippled forward with Kyle as he moved, responding to his command. As he neared the prince, Kyle quickly assessed where Emerald was standing, ensuring that she would not be caught in the line of debris. Luckily, she had retreated away from the prince as she saw Kyle's magic coming at Derek with full force.

As Kyle was ready to unleash the tidal wave of a crumbled mass of stones and bury Derek within, the prince suddenly released the blue magic that enveloped him, causing the room to flash with a burning blue intensity.

Kyle was basked in glowing sapphire magic, and the only movement he could feel was in his face and the beating of his heart.

Derek flashed him a wicked smile, laughing.

"Just what the hell is so funny?" Kyle forced out of his mouth. He tried to wriggle his body from the blue power, but it remained still. The blue magic had frozen his body while the time magic funneled around him.

"You. I can't believe she was persuaded by someone like *you*," Derek said, then turned to Emerald. "Come, my love, let's not have this man ruin our wedding."

Emerald nodded in agreement, flashing a look of displeasure at Kyle.

"Em! Whatever the hell is going on, snap out of it!" Kyle managed to yell.

The blue magic began to intensify, vibrantly swirling around Kyle. A strange feeling took hold of him, as if his body was slowly fading away to another time or place. Grunting, Kyle beckoned his elemental power to surge through his body, hoping it could break the time magic's grasp. Instead of answering him, the azure power swelled in size around Kyle as his body became transparent within the magic.

Kyle could see Emerald through the sapphire magic, her eyes burning a dark green. She gave him a look of disdain, her ruby-red lips sneering. "You... you ruined the day I have been waiting for," she said in an empty voice.

"The hell I did! Em, snap out of it!"

With a jolt of her arms outstretched, Emerald emitted a dark-green halo around her body, enveloped in a dark energy.

The dark-green wave bolted from her body to his. Pain instantly cut through Kyle. The immediate overwhelming feeling of his flesh being pulled apart came over him, gripping his soul. The eerie green magic clung to his life-force, then both flew from his body, draining back into Emerald's outstretched hand.

Second by second, Kyle's power left him until there was almost nothing left.

Kyle heard Derek's laugh echo throughout the sanctuary as his vision went dark. Twinkling white stars appeared in his eyes. Kyle would have doubled over, but the prince's magic kept his body frozen, denying him any motion. Kyle felt his body shift from the cathedral to another plane of existence intermittently. An unfamiliar time or place. It was pitch black, cold. So very cold.

"Em... for God's sake, please..." Kyle managed.

Every word was too much effort, the pain increasing every second. Kyle had very little magic and soul left in him, but somehow the red magic that remained continued to cling to him. It didn't want to leave, causing friction between Emerald's dark magic, Prince Derek's, and his own.

Dammit! I can't die yet! Kyle told his magic. *I can't leave Emerald in this mess!*

Mustering the little energy he had left from within, Kyle felt the strange, terrible magic that he felt earlier, a magic that wasn't the elements. A terrible force from within answered him.

Burning with red-violet magic, Kyle screamed, "EMERALD!"

Instantly, Emerald's dark life-draining magic stopped. Kyle felt his vision returning as Emerald's soul-ripping magic dispersed.

"Kyle?" her voice echoed in the blue world. Her eyes went wide, then she wildly turned around in confusion, suddenly conscious.

Kyle managed a faint smile. He felt weak at the expenditure of Emerald's draining power, and his life-force was nearly gone, all the while still in the throes of the prince's magic. But seeing her face made it all worthwhile and renewed his determination to save her.

"You need to leave, now!" yelled Derek. His eyes glowed a fierce blue, burning with magical power.

Kyle's body began rapidly fading away to the foreign, dark world with Derek's magic. He heard the prince yell something at Emerald, causing her to return to her vacant state.

Kyle tried to muster up his power to call upon the wind, but nothing answered him. Derek's magic was too great, and Kyle had nothing left in his soul to give. He shook violently from the cold. His body was nearly in the alternate universe.

Grunting, Kyle screamed in frustration, hoping that the God of Light would somehow intervene.

But instead of the God of Light responding, a flashing purple magic answered. Vivid, glowing violet magic encased him, creating a shield of protection. Kyle was still unable to move, but at least he was no longer fading into oblivion or another dimension.

Through the glowing purple barrier, Kyle saw Derek, aghast, spinning around to find the new source of magic. Another blast of purple magic shot Kyle's way, penetrating the barrier and into his soul. Kyle felt a healing wave of magic, returning his power and strength and renewing his spirit.

"Who are you?" Derek called out in bewilderment.

"Someone who has come to put a stop to this," a woman's voice answered.

Another surge of violet magic penetrated Kyle's protective barrier, causing the blue magic to disperse, allowing Kyle movement once again.

Kyle drew renewed strength from his magic, feeling a new powerful force from within. Shooting his hands up over his head, red lightning grew within his grasp, swelling in size and power. He felt the forceful magic flowing over him, enhancing his lightning, growing with rage. He shot out his hands, casting the massive red sparks at Derek.

Derek sneered, yanking Emerald toward him, holding her. Suddenly, blue magic washed over them, and they disappeared where the red lightning landed. As quickly as Derek and Emerald disappeared, a mysterious dark woman reappeared in their place. The red lightning struck the woman, but she flashed one of her fingers, and a transparent black half-dome barrier appeared in front of her, blocking Kyle's magic. Derek and Emerald reappeared off to the side of her, the prince's eyes narrowed at Kyle.

This dark woman had to be the prince's advisor, Ikaria, the woman that the handmaiden warned Kyle about. She was the one behind Emerald losing control of herself.

Kyle glared at Ikaria with hatred, funneling his fury through his veins. The fires of Kyle's soul raged, burning within the palms of his hands. Charging toward the advisor, another power flowed over him, in the color of purple, multiplying his power tenfold. He released the fire from his hands, hurling the fireball at the woman.

Ikaria raised her eyebrow, uninterested. The fireball made contact with a black transparent barrier, flashing into view as soon as the fire struck. The magical barrier absorbed the fire, quenching it.

Fuck this shit. I need to get Emerald out of here!

The advisor laughed at him as if she'd heard his thoughts. "Yes, you do," Ikaria agreed, giving him a wicked smile. "However, that's not going to happen. The princess isn't going anywhere. Not today, at least."

She stretched out her hand, and Kyle's body instantly flew across the sanctuary in her direction. Her black magic pulled him, not allowing him any control over his body.

But when Kyle was halfway to Ikaria, another woman appeared. A woman that Kyle had seen before out at the edge of Arcadia's borders. Dressed in tight black leather and thigh-high boots, the olive-skinned woman still rocked the purple mohawk, earrings, and the small jewel on her forehead. In her hand she held a large staff, its orb glowing a vibrant purple color.

The mohawked woman released a colossal purple shock wave of epic proportions, slamming everyone back into various parts of the sanctuary, all except Ikaria. The woman's violet eyes glowed a hot-white purple, matching the color of the orb of the staff, and she extended her hand in the advisor's direction.

"Well, well, well. If it isn't *you*," Ikaria said, eyeing the staff in the woman's hands. "The strange gifted working for the High Court. They always seem to find someone foolish enough to try and take me out. Sadly for you, I always survive."

"I won't let you destroy this earth!" the woman called out, enraptured in an intense purple magic. The violet power swirled around the woman, then drained into the staff. With a sudden jolt, the woman flashed the staff forward, releasing the magic.

Ikaria suddenly bent over, shrieking, her face strained with pain. She continued to yell in frustration as she fought off the woman's invisible magic. "You can't get inside my head," Ikaria screeched, shooting black lightning aimlessly in the other woman's direction.

The mohawked woman disappeared, then reappeared from the side.

"You are right. It would be difficult to unlock your mind, as we are the same," the woman agreed, flashing her staff again. "But I can get inside hers." Turning her staff, she aimed at Emerald, shooting violet magic toward her. Emerald doubled over, falling to her knees.

Ikaria screamed, stretching her arms out to her sides, summoning a vortex of black magic. The magical black void swirled through the sanctuary, blowing everyone aside as if they were leaves in the wind. All those not locked in time were flung to the ground as they tried to move through the magic that whipped violently against their bodies. Ikaria's eyes narrowed as the magic intensified, the vortex glowing onyx.

Kyle felt the sorceress's magical grip release him, allowing him to control his body once more. He crawled toward Emerald, but met Derek blocking his path. He felt powerless. The force of the vortex was too great. But he knew that Derek felt the same, as the prince was struggling through the violent force.

As Kyle neared Derek, he yanked the prince's leg, pulling him forward then pinning him to the ground. Derek fought back, struggling against Kyle and the force of the winds. Derek had more bulk, and both knew the prince would soon overcome Kyle's inferior strength. But that didn't stop him from giving the prince a solid punch.

"Kyle!" Emerald's voice echoed in the wind from behind Derek.

Kyle turned and saw her beautiful face, her eyes full of life. "Em!" he called back to her.

Caught off guard, Derek landed a sharp punch in Kyle's side, then another blow to his face. He fought back, both men wrestling and throwing punches. Between the blows, Kyle caught a glimpse of the mohawked woman struggling within the violent black force, funneling her violet magic to the staff, attempting to counter Ikaria's magic and defuse the situation.

Emerald turned sharply, facing Ikaria, closing her eyes. A sweeping magical force filled the room. Swirling dark-green magic followed the path of the vortex, then shot into the sorceress. Emerald's magic began pulling the life-force from the advisor, and the woman shrieked in agony.

The black vortex stopped, and everyone had free movement again. It was just enough time for Kyle to land a final blow to the prince. Derek slumped to the floor, momentarily stunned.

Kyle grabbed Emerald's hand, and they split toward the entrance of the sanctuary. He saw the mohawked woman shoot her violet magic, casting a protection spell over the three of them as they bolted toward the exit.

Ikaria's eerie laugh echoed throughout the church.

Emerald stopped running, yanking away from Kyle. Kyle looked at her for a moment, thinking that she'd lost hold of him. Grabbing her hand, Kyle began to run again. Emerald didn't move. Instead she released Kyle's grasp once again, backing away from him.

"What are you doing?"

She responded with vacant eyes once more, the crown on her head glowing a blackish-purple.

"No... No! This can't be happening!" Kyle yelled. "Em, you have to come with me!" He took her hand, pleading with her.

She eyed it coldly, stepping back toward Derek.

The mohawked woman grabbed Kyle's hand, pulling him away from the sanctuary. Burning with anger, Kyle flung the woman aside and ran toward Emerald.

More laughs came from Ikaria as she summoned her black magic, knocking him to his feet.

"You can't have her against her will!" Kyle shouted. "She doesn't want to be with any of you assholes!" He tried to get up but fell right back down again. The black magic was controlling his limbs entirely.

Ikaria summoned a massive black ice shield between Kyle and Emerald. Through the distorted dark ice, Kyle saw the woman's image laugh again in amusement as she watched him struggle.

A sudden blast of black magic exploded, burning Kyle's retinas. The only thing he felt was a hand grabbing his.

Then the black magic within the holy sanctuary melted away, replaced with violet light.

CHAPTER 64

RED

An outline of an apartment morphed into view while walls began to take form around Kyle. He was in a small room decorated in heavy beads and fabrics. Familiar skyscrapers and skyways were outlined behind a cloth that hung over the single window.

Kyle had no idea where in Arcadia he was, but one thing was for sure—Emerald wasn't with him.

The mohawked woman reappeared next to him, holding the staff in her hands. The orb's violet magic began to fade away, returning to its original prismatic color.

"What the fuck?" Kyle cursed loudly. "Why did you make us come here? Em is still back at the cathedral!"

"You're welcome," the woman remarked, annoyed.

"Seriously, if I needed your help, I would have asked!"

The woman lifted one of her eyebrows, and her large earrings dangled. "Really? I just saved your butt. You had almost no life, and no magic within you, and I restored it." She cocked her head. "You would have been a heaping pile of flesh if I hadn't come."

Kyle marched right in front of the woman, getting in her face. "I went there to get Em away from those assholes! And instead she's still with them, and I am in God knows where with who knows who!"

"Geeta. Now you know."

"Fine. Geeta. But what the hell?"

"There was no way you would have left that place alive. That sorceress has completed the Spectrum of Magic and has immense power. Power you can't even begin to fathom. Even I could only hold her off for just a fraction of time," the woman said, seating herself on a large embroidered pillow on the floor. She placed the staff next to her gently, propping it against the side of the wall.

"I don't believe that for one second. I just needed more time, and I would have kicked that sorceress's ass!"

Geeta didn't even glance at him. Instead she closed her weary eyes, sighing.

Kyle began to pace within the apartment's confined space, frustrated. "We need to go back and get Em!"

"No."

"What do you mean, *no?*"

"I mean precisely what I said. No," Geeta said smoothly, her eyes remaining closed in meditation.

"Well, I don't need you to tell me what to do. I'm going back," Kyle snarled, heading for the door.

"You don't have the strength to beat the sorceress. Not yet, anyway." Geeta opened her eyes, staring right at him. "We will get the princess, believe me. Reinforcements from the future are coming in two days."

"Then why did you come to help me if you were waiting for so-called reinforcements?" Kyle asked, irritated. He removed a cigarette from his pack, then lit it, inhaling the smoke deep into his lungs. The nicotine calmed him down slightly, but not by much. His hands were still shaking from the amount of power he had exhausted at the cathedral, and he was so angry that Emerald had been left behind. He resumed pacing furiously around the room, unsure of what to do.

"Because you needed *that* to defeat the sorceress," Geeta said as her eyes moved to where the staff was resting in the corner. "It's for you."

"For me?"

Geeta nodded, gesturing for him to take it.

Kyle hesitantly moved toward the staff, studying it. As soon as he picked it up, he felt a deep connection with the staff. The orb turned an intense crimson red as his magic began channeling into it, amplifying his power.

This staff doesn't mess around.

Geeta watched him take in the beauty of the magical device. "I have been searching all of time for you," she said. "I thought I had almost found you before, however, you did not have the gift at the time. It deterred me, causing me to keep searching."

"Why?" he asked, looking at her with curious awe. "Why were you looking for me? And why are you giving this staff to me?"

Nothing makes sense anymore, dammit. Kyle pulled out his pocket flask, then took a long swig, grimacing.

Geeta flashed him a dirty look as he drank his liquor but otherwise didn't protest. "You, by some miracle, will be the one to defeat the sorceress. According to prophecy."

"Great," Kyle said eagerly. "If I'm the one to beat the sorceress, let's get this shit done and go back there!"

Geeta yanked the staff away protectively. "Don't be stupid! Would you calm down for at least one moment?"

Kyle shot her a look but remained quiet.

"I received a message that was for you, back in my time. It came from a priest from the future, prophesizing that the Ghost Man, you, will be the one to defeat Ikaria, the sorceress you encountered at the cathedral. He also predicted that the staff was the key to you defeating her. And now, here I am, giving it to you. I will aid you in defeating her, although now I am not so sure handing the staff over is the wisest thing to do." Geeta glanced at him, then glared at his flask.

"Thanks. I appreciate the compliment," Kyle muttered, taking another drink and another drag. "So why did this priest think I was this Ghost Man? Someone who can stop the sorceress... Ikar... Whatever the hell her name is. What the hell kind of name is Ghost Man, anyway? I ain't dead."

"Ikaria. And I agree, I don't know how you are going to stop this woman, considering you use your gift recklessly. I am beginning to think the gods made a mistake naming you the one in the prophecy." She frowned at him disapprovingly. "What were you thinking, running through Arcadia burning through your power without any focus, taking down half the city with you?"

"What can I say? I have a natural talent for fucking shit up," Kyle remarked sarcastically. Damn, that woman annoyed him. Out of protest, Kyle exhaled his smoke straight into Geeta's face, then took another drink.

She narrowed her eyes at him. "This is serious. I don't think you understand that the fate of the world is in your hands. And here you are, barely able to control your power, hardly able to tap into your analogous colors. And drinking and smoking at a time like this!" Geeta huffed. She got up from her pillow, snatched the cigarette from his lips, then dropped it to the floor and smashed it underneath her boot.

Kyle shot up, getting in her face. "I take this damned seriously. The fucking dream team has my woman, and I'm stuck here getting insulted by some chick that criticizes my habits." He drank the last of his liquor, slamming down the flask on a nearby table. "I never fucking asked to be the one to stop this damned sorceress! Oh, and by the way, it's not my fault that I don't know my abilities. What am I? A mind reader? Am I supposed to instantly know what the fuck to do? Just to fill you in, I just received my new power *days* ago!"

Geeta remained silent, lowering her eyes. There was an awkward pause, making Kyle feel shitty about going off on her.

After a minute, Geeta broke the silence. "You are right," she said softly, raising her violet eyes, meeting his. "All this time, I was expecting someone who had mastered their magic. But it isn't your fault. I am sorry."

Kyle uncomfortably scratched the back of his head. "I didn't mean to be an asshole. Every moment Em is away from me, I just... can't..."

Geeta watched him struggle with what he was trying to say. Kyle couldn't find the words he was looking for. Not out loud, at least. He flashed his ruby eyes at her. "Do you understand? I *need* to rescue Em. She needs me, and I..." His voice trailed as Geeta raised an eyebrow. "Well, forget it. You get the point."

Geeta gave him a solemn look, then turned her back to him, glancing at a display of gods on a nearby pedestal. "I do not understand," she said quietly, "as I have never loved as you do. But I will do my best to help you get her back." Geeta turned her head slightly, looking over her shoulder. "Please, let me atone for my sins these last few hours of the night. I will teach you what I know tomorrow. Get some rest."

"And I'm supposed to sleep at a time like this? Just like that, huh?"

"Just like that, tough guy," Geeta remarked as she began her meditation.

Frustrated, Kyle kicked one of the sitting pillows furiously, then plopped down. He fumed. How in the hell could he sit around in this unknown apartment, knowing that Emerald was in peril? But Geeta was right, his energy was spent. His red fire magic raged in his life-force, angry at him for not going back to Emerald, but the red water magic remained calm inside, reminding him that Geeta was correct, telling him he had to be patient in order to get Emerald back.

Kyle continued to watch Geeta's strange meditation, his head a bit buzzed. It was a welcome feeling. Being drunk made it easier to dull his anguish over Emerald. God, he missed her. He was so furious that the asshole prince still had her.

The flames from Geeta's candles were nothing more than a blur in his eyes, while the spicy scent of her incense continued to mingle with the smoke of his cigarette. As Kyle's heavy eyes closed, the image of Geeta praying echoed in his mind, and he continued to hear her soft whispers, begging for forgiveness to her gods.

CHAPTER 65

BLUE

The wedding feast was extravagant, just as Derek expected. The main hall was adorned with elaborate white decorations, fabrics, flowers, and festive beading strung all throughout the room. The contrast of the white ornamentation against the black marble made the elegant displays stand out all the more. The servants had done a fine job planning the details of the reception.

Every wealthy lord, duke, and baron from Arcadia and York were in attendance, along with the royals that reigned in Olympia, the Twin Kingdoms, and the Second Kingdom. Of course, Derek's parents were there, as they wouldn't miss his wedding for the world. King Samir had a permanent worried expression on his face throughout the entire wedding, likely expecting that Damaris would somehow trick the York royals with one of his undermining plans. Perhaps he fretted about Damaris announcing the secret between them, the one dealing with Queen Elyathi. But Derek knew better and did not dare utter a word to his father about the power that Ikaria held over Damaris. He let his father remain disturbed.

Emerald was seated next to Derek, frozen in her throne without any expression, staring at the guests in silence. He had to admit it bothered him that Emerald wasn't herself and just an empty shell waiting to be ordered around or given some bit of instruction. In fact, Derek hated it, and as the night wore on, he realized he also hated himself for tricking her into wearing the enchanted circlet. But he did find solace in her touch and the comfort of her kisses. He couldn't help but succumb to his fantasies and desires, which trumped her empty shell.

Derek scowled as his thoughts turned to that man interfering with the wedding. Hearing Emerald call out to him in desperation in her moment of being conscious filled him with wild jealousy. Yes, it was all the more the reason to keep her subdued. Emerald would ruin the kingdom of Arcadia over that punk, who was nothing more than trash from the lower levels. Derek couldn't have that.

Food was being served to the wedding party, but Derek wasn't hungry. Sautéed fish in butter and herbs, spiced dishes. All dishes that Derek would normally love to indulge in. But the thought of Emerald compromised continued to eat at his soul while his jealousy and hatred for Kyle consumed him. In the corner of his eye, he noticed that Emerald hadn't touched her food, either.

"My love, please eat. You hardly ate anything all day," Derek urged her.

Emerald glanced at him with vacant eyes, then nodded.

Derek rubbed his chin with his jeweled fingers as he watched Emerald pick up her fork to start in on her dinner. She gracefully ate her food slowly, ensuring that nothing fell on her pearly white satin dress. Derek gave her a smile, admiring her beauty and grace. She then returned his admiration with vacant eyes and a void expression.

Guilt stabbed his gut. Turning his attention to take his mind off his shame, Derek took a drink of wine while his gaze wandered to the wedding guests. His thoughts kept returning to that crazy mohawked woman with violet magic. Perhaps Ikaria knew more about her. The violet woman was clearly aiding that rocker, especially after what happened at the wedding.

As Derek continued to peer into the crowd, he felt a set of eyes on him. Turning his gaze, he met Glacia's stare from far off. As soon as he made eye contact, she turned away, slipping into the crowd. Her accusatory stare said it all. Somehow Glacia knew what he had done; he could feel it by the intensity of her stares. Derek had to ensure she no longer worked at the palace after the wedding. He couldn't let anyone near the princess who was suspicious of him in any way.

"Princess, shall we take a few snaps of you and the prince together to commemorate this splendid event?" Derek heard a voice ask.

He turned his attention to see Haze, Emerald's photographer friend, standing right in front of the table.

Not this guy. Derek gritted his teeth. "That is not necessary," Derek said, putting his arm around Emerald, pulling her close. "I think we've had enough pictures for one evening." Derek flashed Haze a fake smile, eyeing him.

"Very true, Your Highness, but perhaps the princess would like some shots by herself to show off her glorious gown. I haven't gotten a good shot of the details, and you know that the media is chomping at the bit to see all this beading work," Haze said, giving him a half smile, then turning to Emerald. "What do you think, Princess? Would you like to get some close-ups?"

Damn this man.

"I…" Emerald began, unsure of how to answer.

"She doesn't want any," Derek answered quickly, narrowing his eyes.

Haze looked at Emerald, then frowned ever so slightly, enough for Derek to even question that it happened. "If that is what the princess wishes," Haze said.

"It is," Derek said curtly.

"Yes. Derek is right," Emerald murmured. "No shots are necessary right now."

"You see? She is much too tired and overwhelmed with all this commotion. She is not used to this sort of thing and just wants to eat her meal in peace." Derek held Emerald closely, giving Haze a look of warning.

"Yes, Your Highness." Haze glanced at Emerald, then back to Derek. "So sorry to interrupt your dinner." Haze bowed curtly, then wandered away to one of the visiting royals in the crowd, taking pictures.

He needs to go, too. They all need to go!

"You didn't tell me that this time era was so much fun," Ikaria said, traipsing before Derek and slamming a glass of wine as she took her seat beside him. A few of the lords glanced in her direction, some giving questioning looks, others admiring her half-exposed figure.

"Would you keep your voice down?" Derek snapped in a hushed voice, glaring at her.

"What's the matter with you?" Ikaria asked, holding out her empty glass, waiting for a servant to fill it. It didn't take long for someone to arrive, as it seemed the servants were nervous around her.

"I don't like that photographer. And the princess's first handmaiden."

"I don't, either. Shall I get rid of them?" Ikaria laughed, slinking in her seat.

"By getting rid of them... What do you mean by that?" Derek eyed her.

"I think you know the answer to that."

"If that's the case," Derek said, "then no. I will deal with them. I do not want anyone dying on my account!" he whispered harshly.

"Good. I'm not in the mood anyway. This party is much too entertaining."

"Don't they have parties in the future?"

"My father never hosted parties such as these, and my sister, ugh." Ikaria rolled her eyes. "Well, she is just as dull as him." She arched her back, finishing the glass within seconds. "I was overdue for some drinking, dancing, and much-needed flirting. I daresay that I will freely be able to have my way with that blond lord over there. Would you introduce me to him?"

Derek answered with a nasty look, making Ikaria laugh. "No matter, I can work my way over to him later this evening."

A silver glimmer caught Derek's eye, coming from Ikaria's hand. She was wearing a gauntlet. No, not just any gauntlet, the same gauntlet that King Damaris wore.

"Where did you get that?" Derek asked.

"Oh, this is just a little souvenir that Damaris gave me. He wanted to give me something to remember him by."

Derek raised an eyebrow. "I doubt that." He took a drink of his wine. The bitter liquid made his heart burn with rage thinking about everyone. That damn photographer. And that knowing handmaiden. And to top it all off... that degenerate. He had red magic. Maybe that was why Emerald was so infatuated with him. And the fool had come so close to stopping the whole ceremony. It seemed his patch of good luck was wearing thin once again.

"Aren't you concerned what happened tonight?" Derek asked, troubled.

"Not in the least," Ikaria said casually, trying to make eye contact with the elegant blond lord.

"Why not?" he asked. "Those two people with magic tried to take my bride away, nearly ruining the wedding while doing so, and they seemed intent on wanting to stop you."

"The wedding wasn't ruined, my prince. Time was frozen, and I cleaned up the mess before you continued it," Ikaria said matter-of-factly. "No one knows anything but you and I."

"And what of the other woman with purple magic?" Derek asked, sneering. "Do you know anything else about her? She obviously was helping that man with the red magic."

Ikaria shrugged as if unaffected by their encounter. "I don't really care."

"You seemed worried about that woman before."

"It's different now. I have completed the Spectrum of Magic."

"And just because you did so, all your concerns have diminished?"

Ikaria gave him a sweet but menacing smile. "My dear prince, like I said before, whoever that woman is with the violet magic, she is most likely working for my sister, or worse, the High Court in my time. They are a bunch of hacks and has-beens, trying to keep my world subdued with their ultimate hold over all the world sectors. That woman was probably sent by them to steal your princess away from you.

"She won't be the first, nor the last. I expect others to follow suit. You see, they think they are the God of Light's gift to mankind, keeping the laws of magic in check. They are afraid of technology and other gifteds' magic that they do not control. Like your princess's and mine." Ikaria laughed and glanced out of the corner of her elongated eyes, watching his expression before continuing. "They *should* be scared. Especially now that I have the power to stop them. They need to be disbanded, or better yet, terminated from society. Think of Damaris. He was a threat to the peace of Arcadia, was he not?"

"Yes, of course," said Derek. "He was willing to sacrifice many for his obsession over magic and technology through financial loss. Countless lives would have been lost going to war with York for no reason. And he lost all respect from his daughter." A sinking feeling fluttered in his stomach when he mentioned Emerald.

"And so is the High Court. They are willing to sacrifice anything to get what they want. That is why I need your cyborgs. Although I have the power to stop them with just my magic, the cyborgs will help solidify my plan to remove High Court from their position."

"You will have the army I promised you."

"I know, I can still read your thoughts."

Derek shot her a look.

"Don't worry, I haven't been reading them too much." Ikaria looked at him playfully. "Only the entertaining ones." She leaned back in the chair, flashing him a wicked, dry grin.

"So you really aren't the least bit concerned with the others trying to stop you?" Derek asked as he picked at his food.

"My dear Derek, I have the ultimate power flowing through my body, as if the hand of God himself has touched me. Won't the High Court be surprised to learn that the God of Light is on my side?" She laughed.

"No offense, but I highly doubt any god would be on your side after murdering this High Court of yours."

"All justified for a greater cause."

Derek smirked. "I have never pegged you for a devoted follower of any faith."

Ikaria eyed the blond lord across the room, finally getting his attention. She sat up straight, sticking out her bust seductively. "Let's just say I have different ideas of the God of Light, unlike everyone else." The man held out his glass from afar, then toasted silently to her. Ikaria did the same, then the two of them drank in unison. "Now, if you will excuse me, I need some fresh nightly entertainment."

Ikaria rose from her seat, taking the first step down from the platform, then turned her head toward him slightly.

"By the way, I have a wedding gift for you. It should arrive shortly." Ikaria's black eyes flashed at him as she turned away. "You can thank me in the morning."

"Do I really want it?"

"Oh, you will want this gift, that I can assure you."

Ikaria walked down the platform. With each step, the high slits of her dress exposed more of her thighs, catching stares from the men of the court and a few women. She advanced to the blond lord in the crowd, then the two slipped away out of the hall.

What could Ikaria possibly give him for a wedding gift? The thought of her even doing so worried Derek. She was not the generous type unless there was a motive behind it.

Turning to Emerald, Derek drank his wine, taking in her beauty. The redness of her lips, the soft, flowing green tresses. Several long locks graced the sides of her breasts. When was dinner going to end so he could have her?

During the meal's fifth course, a thousand chinking sounds were heard through the hall. Damaris appeared in front of the royal party table, waiting to address the crowd. The goblet sounds slowly died off, leaving the room in silence except for a few joyful whispers. Derek eyed the vacant King, then glanced out to the people gathered, who were waiting in anticipation of the King's speech.

"My dear lords and ladies, thank you for joining us in this wondrous event for the marriage between the Kingdom of Arcadia and the Kingdom of York," Damaris said animatedly, obviously being puppeted by Ikaria.

Was this going to be his wedding gift?

Derek slunk into his throne slightly, anxiously watching while the crowd cheered and raised their goblets. The sinking feeling returned, twisting in Derek's stomach.

"You all know by now the news of my latest declaration, that this fine young man"—Damaris gestured to Derek—"is now the heir to Arcadia. I couldn't be any happier." Claps from the crowd ensued, and Derek's nerves began to race through his body. "No one could ask for a more perfect heir, nor a more perfect match than Prince Derek to my beautiful daughter, Princess Emerald."

Damaris paused for a moment, eyeing the crowd before he continued. "I was never known to be a reasonable ruler, nor a kind one. King Samir can vouch for that."

Derek's father turned beet red under his dark curls while the crowd momentarily glanced in his direction. His mother lowered her gaze, completely embarrassed.

What is Ikaria doing? Derek thought furiously. *She had better not mention anything about my father and Elyathi!*

"I have done many horrible things to this kingdom and have never been the ruler that I should have become." The crowd began to eye each other, raising their eyebrows in surprise. "Instead, I have been unfair, unjust, manipulated, and controlled by a kingdom far greater than this one, all working toward *their* purpose, *their* goal. And in the process, I have destroyed relations with York, something I regret deeply."

The partygoers began to whisper wildly amongst each other, giving puzzled faces. Even Derek's father and mother were flabbergasted.

Damaris cleared his throat loudly, and the noises died down, waiting for him to continue. "And for all the sins that I have committed, I cannot continue to rule Arcadia. I have been controlled by delusions of grandeur for far too long, and it is time someone took control of Arcadia before it is too late. And that is why I am now stepping aside and letting a new ruler ascend to Arcadia's throne. Citizens of Arcadia, look now to your future king. King Derek!"

Just as the crowd began to clap, Damaris flashed a knife in his hand. With a quick gesture, Damaris slit his own throat, the skin peeling apart effortlessly. Blood spurted out of Damaris's body as it slumped to the floor, lifeless. He remained inanimate, his garments soaking up the blood.

Derek shot up from his seat, mortified. There were screams, gasps, and cries from the crowd. Panic set in, causing confusion with the guests. Some ran amok, fleeing the horrifying scene, while others remained frozen in shock. Councilor Emerys, along with the guards, ran over to the King's limp body, propping him up to see if he had any life left in him, while the remaining Inner Council stood aghast. As Emerys held Damaris's body, he was met with more gushing of blood from the neck. The King remained unresponsive. Even Derek's parents had no idea what to do, his father nearly stumbling to a nearby chair while his mother fainted, collapsing onto the floor.

Seeing Damaris dead made Derek recall just how cruel Damaris had been, and the thought crossed his mind that his demise was well deserved. Derek felt terrible for even thinking it, but he was reminded of how hateful the King was to everyone, including his daughter and his wife, Queen Elyathi. No wonder the Queen had planned to run off with his father. She had every cause to do so, considering she was also treated like a prisoner, the same as Emerald.

Damaris deserved this, Derek thought. *For all the hell he gave everyone over the years. Emerald, his citizens, Arcadia's stock markets... He ruined so many lives.*

Derek heard the other members of the council yelling at Emerald, silently pleading with desperate faces. They wanted her to use her healing powers but couldn't say it plainly in front of the guests.

Turning to Emerald, Derek gave her a look, reminding her how cruel Damaris really was to her, how she'd been a prisoner her whole life. The King didn't deserve to be healed. Then he remembered that he didn't need to convince her.

Emerald remained seated, her eyes coldly calculating the situation, then bowed her head. Her gaze fell on Emerys, and Emerald shook her head, silently refusing to help. Derek knew she wouldn't do anything unless he commanded it out loud or in his mind, and he wasn't changing his mind. He couldn't risk her using her power anyway; there were too many people that were still in the hall. If everyone found out about her, they would face a slew of problems, especially with the media blasting the news everywhere. Other kingdoms would possibly try to kidnap her. Any he didn't need any more problems. He had enough as it was.

The guards and councilors flashed their faces toward Derek, awaiting to be instructed.

"Your Highness…" Emerys began, suddenly realizing that the title no longer suited Derek. "Your Majesty, what shall we do?"

"Get everyone out of here now and shut down the palace when the final guest has gone. Get the coroner immediately and prepare for a state funeral. We cannot further celebrate my happy event with this unfortunate outcome. Damaris deserves to have his moment of silence met with our bereavement."

"Yes, Your Majesty," murmured the councilors. They immediately turned away and started barking orders to the guards.

Derek held out his hand, waiting for Emerald to take it. The new queen arose from her seat, then gently took his hand, and Derek escorted her down the platform.

Another guilty pang ran through his body as Derek led Emerald out of the hall.

Some present! Damn that Ikaria. What a mess. I never asked for the death of the King…

But as much as Derek told himself that he didn't want Damaris gone, he had much satisfaction that now no one stood in his way between him and Emerald.

And now they could freely rule Arcadia.

CHAPTER 66

RED

*K*yle... her soft voice whispered.
It was cold. So very cold.

Em? Is that you?

Wake up, Kyle!

Kyle felt his head resting in Emerald's lap, her hands gently playing with his hair. Tiredly, he opened his eyes, revealing her face peering down at him. She was just as beautiful and delicate as the first night he had seen her at the venue. A warm wave flowed through his body, eradicating the icy feeling and lifting his spirits. There, in the darkness, she held him close.

Can't I just stay here with you? Don't make me go back. I don't want to be anywhere that you aren't.

He felt a slight touch of her hand on his chest, playing with his necklaces, wrapping it around one of her fingers. Her life-giving eyes smiled as her face leaned over to kiss him.

As their lips met, violet light burst from Emerald's body, instantly becoming entwined with a stream of black magic. The dark magic began to force Emerald's body away, pushing with a translucent black wind. Emerald jutted her hand out to grasp onto Kyle, but it was too late. The force was too fast and too powerful. Sheer terror and panic radiated from her face. Wicked laughs of a woman echoed in the arid space, reverberating over and over again.

Emerald! Kyle screamed.

Kyle! Don't leave me here alone!

I won't! I promise!

Kyle felt a sudden, hard kick to his side. He shot up from the floor, confused. Through his tired bleary eyes, a violet blob approached. Seeing the purple pissed him off, thinking of the power that held Emerald's mind and soul hostage.

Damn that violet magic all to hell!

Crimson fire ignited from his hands, which he instantly shot in the direction of the purple blur.

Geeta held out one of her hands, freezing the fireball in front of her. The ball of flames immediately crystallized into amethyst ice particles. Geeta wafted her hand, wisping them away.

"Come. Let's begin," she said, turning away toward the door, unaffected by what just happened.

"I didn't mean to do that…" Kyle said, feeling it necessary to explain. The dream had felt so real, like he was there with Emerald.

Geeta remained silent. Either she hadn't heard him or was flat-out ignoring him. Kyle guessed it was the latter.

"Where are we going?" Kyle noticed a black T-shirt next to where he was. "What's that?" he asked, pointing to the shirt.

"For you. I thought you might like some clean clothes. I don't own any men's pants, but I do have a few shirts. You're thin enough."

"Thanks. An old boyfriend?" Kyle asked as he changed into the shirt. The shirt was tight on him, but at least it was clean.

Geeta shot him a look of annoyance. "No boyfriends. I'm not like that," she huffed. "They are *my* clothes."

"Okay, all right, whatever you say…" Kyle shrugged, lighting a cigarette. Apparently the woman was pretty touchy, but what did he expect?

Geeta led Kyle outside the hallway and to the building's elevator, both stepping inside.

"So, that's your place back there, I take it?" Kyle watched as the elevator doors closed.

"Yes."

"Out of curiosity, if you travel through time, why do you have an apartment here in Arcadia?"

"I need some place to rest and pray."

"Well, that's great and all, but why pick this time, and Arcadia of all places? Couldn't you have picked a better time or a more luxurious city?"

Kyle asked, watching the glowing buttons of the elevators as they continued to ascend.

"I had a feeling about this time. Whenever I traveled through each time era, this particular era always gave me a strange feeling that I needed to be here." Her purple eyes flashed, meeting his. "My instincts seemed to be right, as my prayers were answered finding you." Her face turned away, patiently waiting for the elevator to make it to the top. "And the fact is, this time resonates with me. The culture, the openness of the people and views... It was the first and only time I felt like I was where I belonged."

"Makes sense, I guess," Kyle said, shrugging. "I suppose that's why you dress like an Arcadian too, right?"

"Yep."

The elevator stopped at another level, and more people poured into it. A few stared at Geeta's wild hair, still sticking up straight as a razor. Geeta's fashions were more from the lower levels than the mid-levels, where their elevator was stopped. "So where are we going, anyway? You didn't say."

Geeta raised an eyebrow, glancing at the others in the elevator. "All the way up," she stated, then looked away.

The elevator climbed as high as their keycards would allow, then dinged at the highest point of the mid-levels. Kyle and Geeta stepped out along with a few other people that were in the elevator and were met with a widespread marbled floor and high ceilings.

Kyle sucked in his breath, taking in the building's decor. The walls were made of glass panels with gold designs, and several resting areas had expensive lounge chairs, tables, lamps, and businesses scattered throughout. Never had Kyle been somewhere so extravagant. Other than the cathedral, that is. He felt so dirty and out of place compared to the clean, attractive architecture.

I wonder if Em felt the same way being in the lower levels.

Geeta led him through the floor's connecting hub, exiting through large glass doors out onto an open platform, then stopped by the platform railing outside, where the corner of the platform and the building met.

Kyle leaned against the railing, wishing they were in the upper levels, wanting to see the palace where Emerald was at. Instead, he saw nothing but giant buildings towering before him, overshadowing the bright, sunny sky.

"Ready?" Geeta asked, waiting for him.

"Sure as hell am," Kyle stated, looking down at the city beneath their platform. "You wanna jump?"

"No, I don't. It makes me sick." Geeta gave him a look of disgust. "Fly up to the top with your elements," she said. "I'll meet you up there." She paused for a moment, glancing at him. "You can fly, can't you?"

Kyle nodded. "I did it yesterday."

"Good. Then I will see you up there. And don't come flying up until you have made yourself invisible with the gift of the orange. We don't want you to cause any more of a ruckus than you already have."

"Well, how in the hell am I supposed to do that? I have red magic, remember?"

"You have the ability. Just think happy thoughts," Geeta said. With that, a purple glow emitted from her, and she was gone.

Her magic was very similar to Prince Derek's, in how she flashed before Kyle's eyes. He somehow felt in his life-force that she didn't go invisible with her magic, but instead used her power to appear in another place.

Just think happy thoughts. Geeta's words echoed in his head. "Really helpful," Kyle said sarcastically under his breath.

Kyle glanced around at the people that filled the platform, wondering if anyone was paying any attention to him. There were too many people to single him out, as there was too much traffic between the air transports, people riding the escalators, and crowds walking the skyways for anyone to notice. He could just fly up there anyway and meet Geeta. But a feeling stopped him, reminding him that he had to learn the full power of his abilities.

What made him happy? Well, shit, Emerald, by far. His music and his motorcycle did too, but those things couldn't fill the void compared to how Emerald made him feel. More alive than his music, that was for sure.

Closing his eyes, he thought of Emerald. Her smile. The innocence that radiated from her. Her touch.

A warmness flowed within him, stirring his soul. Drawing upon the feeling with the power behind it, he focused it within, letting it flow through him.

Kyle felt his body fading away. Upon opening his eyes, he saw that he was melting into the background with a transparent red-orange color surrounding him, like rippling water. Satisfied, Kyle beckoned the elements to him so he could be airborne.

Immediately, Kyle rippled back into view, the red-orange magic dissipating.

Shit! I just had it!

Again, Kyle turned his focus to Emerald, thinking of the times they were together. The red-orange magic came over him again, wavering in and out of existence. The more Kyle tried, the harder it became, with the magic distracting his focus.

Grunting, Kyle ignored the magic and returned his thoughts to Emerald, continuing to find the times when they were happy. The red-orange magic flowed through him steadily, dissolving him once again. Pictures of Emerald flooded his mind—the time they met, taking Emerald to the beach at night, having sex after the paint fight. Damn, that was a hot memory. The time where they were in the open desert, Emerald being taken away by the authorities... Emerald dressed in white satin, being married off against her will to a motherfucking asshole...

With that thought, Kyle's body returned to the visible world as the magic wafted away.

"Fuck!" he yelled. Frustrated, he kicked a nearby trashcan, catching a few glances from nearby people making their way to the air transports. "Goddammit!" Kyle furiously kicked a trash can again, then lit a cigarette and slumped to the ground, resting his back on the trash can. The thought of Emerald being unknowingly being forced to kiss the world's biggest dick infuriated him, causing him to make a fist, swinging his hand back and punching the metallic bin a few more times. God, he hated that guy. Kyle pulled out his pocket flask and, realizing it was empty, chucked it across the platform, still aggravated.

At this point, I'll be spending all damn day down here, and I only have two days to learn as much as I can!

Kyle smoked his cigarette until the cherry met the filter, then he got up, trying his luck again. What he met instead was failure. Complete fucking failure. He continued to fail for hours. Every so often, he had to wait for people to come and go until it was safe to attempt summoning the orange magic. Luckily, the corner where he practiced was tucked away and out of sight for the majority of the passersby.

The bright sun's rays that shone between the small cracks of the buildings began to deepen to a warm orange. The sun was setting, and soon the day would give way to night. Kyle wasn't even close to mastering orange magic, and Geeta hadn't even bothered to check on him. What a master she was, leaving him to figure it out for himself. Wasn't she supposed to be training him? He was burning daylight trying to figure out how to turn invisible, with no help from her whatsoever.

All Kyle wanted to do was forgo all this bullshit and rescue Emerald. None of this magic stuff. No random punk chick from some random time telling him that he was the one in some damn prophecy. No palace, no royals, no king, no sorceress, no prince… none of that. He just wanted Emerald with him, cheering him on at his show on some of the nights, the two of them alone on vacant platforms, drinking and watching the city from afar on other nights. Motorcycle rides, stealing kisses from her in the darkness of the night. Was that all too damn much to ask?

Those thoughts continued to flow through Kyle's mind, giving him a sense of ease within his soul. The more he dwelled on the thoughts, the more he aware he became of the magic flowing through him. Both magics were present, growing stronger and more powerful with each second. The red and the orange began to fuse together, working in harmony as one.

The new magic awaited his command.

What are you waiting for? he told the power within his mind. *Let's do this!*

The magic was suddenly unleashed, and the bright red-orange magic quickly faded him away, the winds swirling around his invisible body. The strong current held him within its power, giving Kyle the authority over it.

He flew up in the air, rapidly approaching the top of the building.

Geeta waited patiently, arms crossed. Kyle released the red-orange power of illusion, appearing before her.

"About time," she said, walking toward the edge of the building.

"That's it? That's all you have to say? No 'hey, good job, Kyle'?"

Ignoring him, Geeta continued. "We need to keep going higher, to the northwestern part of the city. We can practice on the Unimark Corporation building, since it's one of the tallest ones. It has no guards at the top and is also so high up that no one will see us up there. I will fly with you for just a few minutes, then meet up with you."

"Just out of curiosity, how many damn powers do you have?" Kyle asked, gathering the wind with him once again.

"Enough to make me unclean," she said, gathering her own violet wind around her.

What the hell does she mean by that? Kyle wondered.

They both took off, soaring through the skies. Kyle had his red wind, Geeta had her violet cyclone.

"It would probably be best if you disappear again. We don't want to startle the air transports," she yelled as they flew. He nodded in agreement, fading away into nothingness. He still saw her violet wind disappear entirely, and her presence was gone. As for Kyle, his red gusts were still visible, but at least the pilots wouldn't see his body within the storm.

Reaching the Unimark building, Kyle released his magic, settling on the rooftop. He looked around to see where Geeta had landed. Within a split second, Geeta flashed a violet-blue magic, appearing instantly before him, the staff in her hand.

"There," Geeta said, stooping to retie a boot lace. "This will keep us out of sight from all of the air traffic below."

"When did you grab the staff?"

"Just now. I didn't want people to give questioning looks when I rode the elevator with you. I decided it was best to grab it while we were on our way over here." She pointed to a large duct. "Stand over there."

Kyle complied, having no idea what Geeta was about to do. If it was going to help him rescue Emerald somehow, he was willing to learn whatever Geeta had planned.

Geeta leaned the staff against an outcropping of the building gently, letting it rest for the time being. "You are already aware of your main color, red, which gifts you the power of the elements. However, you are extremely sloppy with it."

Kyle flashed her a look. "What do you mean sloppy?"

"You need to learn to control your anger," she stated coolly. "Otherwise it will get you killed."

"Doesn't the red power fuel off my anger?"

"Yes. But without controlling it, it could turn into wrath, which leads to a darker magic. The magic you saw the sorceress use at the cathedral, most of it radiated with a dark force," Geeta said, flashing her deep-purple eyes.

"Well, she was using black magic."

"That is not what I meant."

"What's wrong with it, anyway?" Kyle asked, confused.

"Everything! When you call upon the darkness of the colors, it can *change* you. The darkness twists you to do terrible things," Geeta said as her face hardened, her eyes full of pain. She flinched. "The perfect example is Prince Derek."

"You think he's influenced by dark magic?" Kyle asked. Not like he cared in any way for that piece of shit.

"Yes. I heard his thoughts and his struggles," Geeta said. "He is so wrapped up in his desire for the princess that it caused him to be influenced by dark thoughts, and now, dark magic. He has openly given his mind over to the sorceress, without even knowing it. She can possess him at any moment, and in a single heartbeat." Geeta shivered, then turned away. "When you draw your strength from within, remember to keep it to the lighter side of the emotion, not the darker. Now come, let's duel."

What Geeta said sounded more like a philosophy than practice. Geeta motioned to him from across the building, silently telling him to go.

Kyle ignited the fires within him, gathering them in his hands, then instantly stretched out his arms. His muscles flexed with the iron strength of the ruby flames, and he cast them toward Geeta.

She swung her hands in a side-sweeping motion. Violet waters shot directly to the flames, counteracting the heat and dousing them into nothingness.

Determined, Kyle decided to summon the storms, casting red lightning toward her. The sparks shot across the building, with Geeta suddenly dodging it with magic, sliding her body ten feet to the side. Kyle gathered the winds, sending them dancing through his fingertips, then shot them toward her. Geeta instantly cast a reflective purple shield. The sparks completely absorbed into it as the winds bounced off.

"I see what you mean. You get to use pretty much any damned power, while I have just the red," he said, frustrated.

"So does Ikaria," Geeta shot back. "You must figure out ways around her power, as she has even more colors than I do in the spectrum."

"How many do you have, exactly? You never answered me earlier."

"Four. But you can almost say five. I have nearly the full potential of one of my adjacent colors."

"Adjacent colors? What the hell is that?"

"Adjacent colors are the colors next to your main color. In your case, it would be violet and orange. You are able to tap into those as well, as I had you do in your exercise earlier with the orange magic, but you will never have the full potential of that magic as a person born with them, unless you are extremely powerful. You will need to explore those powers and learn to hone your red magic as well. For now, you're able to utilize your analogous colors, which is basically calling upon a small portion of the violet and orange magic, it being characterized as red-violet and red-orange."

"Adjacent colors... analogous colors... great," Kyle muttered. "This is beginning to sound like a damn art lesson."

Geeta ignored him, then cocked her head. "Come at me again."

Summoning red ice shards, Kyle quickly shot them at Geeta. In response, Geeta held out one hand, stopping them in midair. Within seconds, they melted, falling from the air into a puddle on the ground. Kyle again hurled larger ones, then she quickly dodged them, her body completely evading the ice.

Kyle grasped the invisible air, pulling it up with his muscles as if lifting something incredibly heavy. A huge red wall of ice shot up in front of him. Kyle swung his hands, and the wall of ice began to be pushed by a powerful force. Kyle's force. Geeta countered with her force, her native color of violet, controlling the wall of ice. They both fought, pushing the oversized giant ice wall, but she was too strong. Finally, he lost control, and the ice wall was hurled off the rooftop. Immediately, Geeta summoned violet fire, shooting it at the falling ice. The fire made contact, and the ice dissipated in the atmosphere and drizzled down on Arcadia's recipients.

Damn. She was more powerful than he'd thought. He was amazed at her abilities when he first came across her, but he'd no idea the extent of it. Geeta was beyond powerful. And she was only able to hold off the sorceress for just a moment? Perhaps Geeta was right, and maybe this future priest had made a mistake on him. More and more, Kyle was feeling fucked. But at least he would be fucked trying to get Emerald back. He would go to hell and back for her.

Breathing heavily, Kyle collapsed to the ground, sweating. His energy was spent. Geeta was too powerful. He heard her footsteps approaching him as he rolled over.

"You have talent, I will give you that. But it's not enough to go defeat Ikaria," her voice said evenly.

Scowling, Kyle spat. "Well, what do you suggest? I am open to ideas."

"Practice. Every day. Until you have mastered your abilities," she said as her one long metal earring jingled.

Kyle laughed. "Every day, huh? Well, according to you, we only have two days until whoever the hell shows up to help us."

Geeta shook her head. "Not unless I freeze time."

"Freeze time?"

"You need all the help you can get at this point," Geeta said. She walked over to the staff, then clutched it within her hands. Closing her eyes, her body began to glow a vibrant purple color while the prismatic orb mimicked her. Each second, the power intensified within her body, and within the orb, the white-hot violet magic funneled between each other. Suddenly, Geeta let out a loud roar, releasing the magic between her and the staff. Not even within a blink of an eye, the whole world froze, and everything was painted in violet-blue hues.

All was still, besides Kyle and Geeta, who were in full color.

CHAPTER 67

GREEN

Suresh's magic wafted away, leaving him in complete darkness. There was no light from his surroundings. Not from the sun, nor from any object, magical or not. Only screams. Screams of millions of people crying out in agony.

What is happening?

Suresh spun around, trying to get a grasp of his whereabouts. Finally, moonlight peeked out from dark clouds that blanketed the sky. But the moonlight was not normal; it was deep red, as if the moon itself was weeping blood.

A massive dark object came into view, blocking the moon's eerie red light. No, it was not one, but many objects. Too many to even count.

A sizzling sound ensued, and moment by moment, the sound became louder. An aura enveloped the objects, and Suresh finally understood what they were—meteors. The meteors grew larger, streaking across the sky, and several were heading right toward him.

With no time to think, Suresh launched himself into a full sprint, looking for any sort of shelter. Through the darkness, he barely made out the red outlines of thousands of destroyed buildings toppled over. He tripped over tangles of metal debris from the destruction of the buildings.

"Hurry!" cried a woman from a nearby mass of large debris. "In here!"

Running in the direction of the voice, Suresh saw a bright flash of the woman's sparkling fabrics glittering against the darkness, capturing the light emitted from the magical crimson meteors.

Dodging underneath a large beam of what looked like an old building, Suresh slid inside, making it just in time. At that moment, one of the meteorites stuck the earth nearby, quaking the ground. A loud boom shattered his ears, rattling the beams of the destroyed building.

Suresh turned back to the woman, noticing she had two young children hiding behind her.

"What is happening?" Suresh asked the woman, shaking his hair free of dirt.

The woman gave a confused look. "Surely you can see for yourself," she replied, eyeing Suresh as if he was crazy. The ground shook again.

Trying to better word it without sounding completely mad, he tried to come up with a better question. "How long has this been going on? I... I just awoke from a deep sleep..."

"And you have been sleeping through the showers this whole time?"

"Yes..."

The woman studied him, then one of her children nudged her arm, forcing her to stop staring. She wrapped her arms around her son, hugging him closely. "It's been happening for at least two days. It first was reported that the meteorites hit on the other side of the world, until all transmissions and devices blacked out. Now no one knows what happened after that besides what we see here. But they said before everything went dark that most of the meteorites landed on the other side, and we are getting the straggler shards of the comet."

There was another sudden boom, and the building debris shifted. Small flecks of dust and metal showered on Suresh, the woman, and her children. Another rocking of the earth, and the building started moving.

"Oh God, oh my God!" the woman exclaimed, grabbing her children. With a burst of panic, she yanked them out of the building, Suresh trailing right behind her. He caught the hem of her sleeve, holding on to it.

"Grab on to me!" Suresh told them.

"We have no time! The building is... Oh God!" the woman screamed, pulling her children away, running.

Suresh heard the building start to topple, its metal creaking while the last of the unbroken windows shattered. He ran after the woman, lunging toward her and her children. Within a second, he caught up, putting his arms around all of them, making sure his skin touched each one.

Suddenly, a bright burst of deep greenish-blue magic burst from his body, enveloping them entirely. Not even a split second later, they appeared miles away from the decimated city, on the outskirts of a mountain range.

The children stood wide eyed, while the woman took a step back as Suresh's power faded. "You… you have the power of the gods…" she started. "They are real."

Suresh only could nod, not wanting to elaborate. He pointed over to a nearby cave, one he'd seen as they traveled through the magical dimension to bring them there safely.

"Get inside there," he instructed. "You will be safe."

"Can you… will you stop this destruction?" the woman asked, as the earth shook again. One of the children lost their foothold, stumbling to the ground.

"I can't. It is far beyond my capability," Suresh answered. "I'm not even supposed to be here. Now please, get inside the cave before the next wave of meteors comes."

The woman nodded, grabbing her children. "Thank you."

Suresh heard more sizzling sounds, and a deep-red glow burned in the sky.

Summoning time magic once again, Suresh's magic whirled around him, then washed over his body, shooting him back into the space-time continuum. His body hurled across the glowing paths until he hit an invisible one, its solidifying mass bumping his back. He rolled a few more feet, then halted, remaining on the starry path, lying still, catching his breath.

The destruction of the Earth… was that because Geeta didn't succeed? He hoped not, otherwise he and the future would soon fade away. Did he still have time to find Ghost Man?

I have to hurry. The Earth is in danger!

Suresh looked over, still lying on the ground, studying all the portals. As he scanned the sky, one stuck out to him.

The portal was not rippling or swirling like the others. It was violet, frozen of any motion.

Geeta. He had finally found her.

Suresh smiled in relief, sure that he finally knew where Geeta was. He leapt to his feet, then ran toward the strange portal.

Cautiously, Suresh touched the portal to see if he could enter it. His finger disappeared behind the violet light of the portal, but the light of it remained still.

Geeta, I'm coming!

CHAPTER 68

RED

Hours melted into days, days into weeks. Weeks then turned into months. No matter how long it had been, Kyle had been living the same damn day, frozen in time. How many days had it been since he met Geeta? It had been so long that Kyle had lost track.

After the first month, after they'd continued to train in the eerie evening sunset of Geeta's violet world, Kyle had had enough. He was tired of seeing the purple light. He would rather have the violet darkness around him so he could at least get some sleep. He constantly grumbled to Geeta about it, and eventually she gave in. They lived an hour in real time that same day they first began training, then she froze time again.

Every day Geeta grilled Kyle on his power, and the two of them dueled until he physically couldn't take it anymore. Kyle never won the duels. As much as he took her instruction, with the combination of his elements and analogous colors, it was never enough to overwhelm Geeta. He had come close once, but Kyle had a feeling it wasn't because of him, rather it was that Geeta had been overly tired that day.

Time had been taking a toll on them. Kyle could see the slight changes in his body and face from the daily practice. Even though he was thin, he now had more upper body strength, the training having transformed his body into something greater. His body was leaner, more cut, and his biceps were larger, causing his tattoos to bulge out from the curve of his upper arm. His jaw was more defined, with slight stubble, and his hair had started growing in red, matching his ruby-red eyes. His red hair had bothered him at first, and he bleached it constantly because of it. But after a while, Kyle got tired of doing it, as it was a pain in the ass, and the red was starting to grow on him. He now had an inch of crimson red with the tips of his spiked hair frosted white from his old growth.

Since time was frozen, Kyle had taken stuff from stores, as both he and Geeta needed to eat. Kyle could see that it bothered Geeta greatly, but he didn't give a damn. He and Geeta couldn't go hungry, and in a way, it was payback for the stores that had taxed the hell out of him. And he was saving the world. It was the small price for the stores to pay for saving Arcadia.

Kyle threw on a clean shirt and pants for the day, waiting for Geeta to finish her prayers so they could start their daily duel. He had never watched her pray since that first night, as it made him feel uncomfortable and completely out of place. Maybe even a little guilty that he had never prayed himself. The closest he had ever gotten to a prayer was when he called out to the God of Light for help when he was about to get injected with Emerald's blood. If you could even consider that communing with the divine.

Geeta was the complete opposite of him with her being so religious with her gods. Kyle had wondered for months if her gods were similar to the God of Light. He finally asked her one night about her old gods. Geeta had told him that her beliefs were different than that of the God of Light, but it was a similar concept with more gods—that each of her color gods combined equaled complete holiness. It all was good versus evil, no matter the details of the religions, she stressed.

As Kyle waited impatiently for Geeta to finish, he grabbed his guitar and stepped outside onto the apartment's patio, which was no bigger than the bathroom inside. Strumming his guitar, Kyle played the same tune he had played every night whenever Geeta was praying.

One of the first nights when the world was frozen, Kyle had retrieved his guitar from his apartment. At that time, a new melody came to his mind, and he couldn't get it out of his head. Kyle knew he had to get it out, as it was burning inside him, and the only way for him to do so was to play it.

The song was about Emerald. A way for Kyle to channel his energy, his drive, and his determination to get her back. Through his singing and playing the melody within his fingertips, he felt deep within that he was creating a spell, strengthening his heart with the entrancing music.

Kyle could have stayed at his apartment and met Geeta routinely to train instead of staying at her place, but within the empty, stale world, it was lonely. He felt he was better off with someone who actually moved instead of seeing Rosie frozen outside her door, eternally locked in a pose, grabbing one of her magazines with Zaphod on her shoulder.

During the second chorus of his song, Kyle heard the sliding glass door open and then silence. Geeta was listening patiently to his words. Kyle stopped mid-song, slightly embarrassed, as he'd never been one to sing love songs, especially in front of others. Besides, it was private. Between him and Emerald.

"She's lucky to have someone like you who loves her," Geeta stated, waiting by the door. "You are her true complement."

"Complement?" Kyle asked, setting down the guitar and lighting up a cigarette. "You mean like a partner?"

Geeta raised an eyebrow, her mouth revealing a half smile, amused at his statement. It was one of the first times he had seen her smile. It was very strange.

"You could say that. Each color has an opposite in the spectrum. It is more apparent when you bend the spectrum line in a circle. For you, being red-gifted, your opposite would be green. And as little as I know of Princess Emerald, you both seem very polarized as far as your personalities go, and your magics. However, being so opposite, you end up complementing each other."

"So complements are couples, basically?"

"Not exactly. Complements *could* be two gifted in love who are opposite colors, as many have thought in my time. But really it's the soul of the person, and the magic that lies underneath in their life-force that works together as one. There is a saying from the Rainbow Mantras, written by my people. It states: The creation of light is through complements, for each color yearns for its other half. The two colors opposite can eradicate all shades of darkness."

That statement couldn't have been more perfect for describing how much he longed for Emerald. He needed her. He *yearned* for her.

"Then you can understand why I need to get Em back," Kyle stated, exhaling the smoke from his lips, his eyes meeting hers. "I just want to be with her."

"I know." Geeta nodded. "It must be painful knowing that your other half, their magic and their soul, is kept apart from you. Especially in her circumstance."

"It's like someone ripping my heart out of my fucking body every day and burning it."

Geeta remained silent, then continued softly, "I can't imagine."

"Yeah, well, you don't want to. It's shitty." Kyle finished his cigarette, flinging it over the edge of the patio. "Let's go. Talking about it is depressing me, and I can't break my focus now."

"Agreed."

***

The Unimark Corporation's neon sign and brightly lit windows were all colored a violet tint, just as the other lights in Arcadia. Shades of violet-blue. Kyle was so sick of seeing violet that he was always excited to duel, since he got to see his red magic. The only other time he got to see color was when he touched an object. And, of course, he and Geeta remained in color as well. He would probably would have gone insane were that not the case.

Geeta was already waiting for him on the rooftop, as usual. Why couldn't he just disappear and reappear instantly with Geeta? It would save so much time instead of flying there. She almost always insisted on him practicing his power, even though flying came naturally to him. On some days, Geeta would extend her hand and use her power so that they could travel together, but that was when she was in a good mood. Geeta hardly ever seemed to be in a good mood, and today was no exception.

As Kyle released the red winds that swirled around him, he fell lightly onto the rooftop, feet first. Geeta nodded in approval, noticing how much more restraint he showed now. What she had taught him about restraint had helped Kyle hone his abilities more, resulting in the spell being more powerful. But Kyle didn't always think Geeta was right about not using his raw emotions to unleash the wilder part of his magic. There was always a storm brewing inside his being, making him feel like his chest was going to explode at any moment if he didn't expend his energy quickly. The force inside of him demanded it constantly, and it nagged at him every time he chose to restrain himself in his casting.

Geeta had the staff in her hands and was gesturing for him to take it.

"Wow, this is a first. You are actually letting me use the staff today?"

She handed it over to him. "Today there will be no duel. Instead, I want you to try and enter my mind using the full power of your adjacent color, violet," Geeta said, not moving from her spot. "You have shown me that you can use your analogous colors, but you have yet to use the full force of your adjacent colors. That is something you must be able to master, especially violet magic." Geeta's long dangling earrings swung as she motioned to the staff. "You should use the staff to amplify your magic, as this task will be extremely difficult for you."

"You know, I've used my violet magic before in our duels, and even a bit when I was at the cathedral," Kyle said.

"That's very true, but it was all by accident when you did it. And every time it was the physical force side of the gift of the violet. You've never cast mental force using violet magic, have you?"

As soon as she said that, he realized that he had. The moment he yelled Emerald's name in the cathedral, he'd broken her mind from Ikaria's magic for just a second. He had thought it was his voice that woke her from her spell, but when he looked back upon the situation with what he knew now, it was his magic.

"Are you sure you want me to use the staff for this? Won't it be too easy for me?"

"Positive. It is nearly impossible to get into the mind of a violet-gifted. You will need all the help you can get."

Kyle paused, glancing at her suspiciously. "Wait, is this some kind of trick? You've always said we shouldn't tap into the darker side of our magic. And now it's okay? What gives?"

Geeta let out a sigh, then sat down on the ground. "You entering my mind is not using the darker side of the violet power." Geeta nodded her head, waiting for Kyle to sit down.

"But I thought you had said before that entering another's mind *is* the darker side," Kyle countered.

"Entering someone's mind, no. Possession of one's mind and body, that is a whole other story. Now enough talk, and sit your butt down."

Kyle complied, resting the staff in his lap, both hands grasping the metal. Closing his eyes, Kyle focused on seeing the violet within his life-force. Through the red magic that pumped in his veins, Kyle saw the violet color seep forward, slowly running its course through his body.

He had never had an opinion on the color violet before. But with months of training in a frozen purple world and discovering what emotion violet magic fed off of, Kyle didn't like using it. It made him feel funny, and not like how he was supposed to. Violet magic fed off jealousy. He could see why red and violet were next to each other in the spectrum, as the darker side of red was wrath, and the darker side of violet was hatred. Similar in aspects, but Kyle viewed wrath as a bit lighter of an emotion than hatred, if one could even make sense of that statement.

Kyle was never one to be a jealous person, as there was nothing to be jealous of in the world. But now, Kyle could understand the emotion, now that Prince Derek had married Emerald and had her as his own. That was something for Kyle to be jealous of. And that made him angry, very incredibly angry. The prince had forced the princess to marry him against her will.

Bastard!

Violet jealousy filled Kyle's life-force, completely encasing him within the purple feeling. Kyle continued to picture Prince Derek the moment he saw him embrace and kiss Emerald at the wedding. Kyle's veins began to vibrate, buzzing with intense jealousy. Darkness began to emerge with the hatred, but Kyle pushed it back.

Don't even fucking think about it! You won't control me, darkness!

Feeling the magic flowing through his body, he released the power into the staff, sensing the orb glowing with a red-violet intensity. Red would always be present in his casting of magic.

Violet magic began funneling from his body as it poured over Geeta. In his mind's eye, Kyle saw the inner workings of Geeta's mind, barricaded and shielded. The complex maze of doors and windows remained shut, all shielded with an intense magic. Sensing the power, Kyle knew that Geeta was using a different color magic to guard her mind—yellow magic, though it appeared violet from her life-force. Protection magic.

Kyle's spirit shifted in Geeta's mind maze, hoping to open each door and window one by one. The protection magic was so intense that it burned him as he neared each entry.

Well, shit, how in the hell am I supposed to get inside her mind?

A swift wind blew over his spirit, and Kyle suddenly felt his mind under attack. With a sharp, forceful blow, he was back in his own mind.

Opening his eyes, he saw Geeta remained seated across from him, narrowing her eyes at him.

"What did you think you were doing? I said for you to enter my mind, not *break* into it!" she scolded him, getting up from her spot.

"I thought that was what I was doing!" Kyle snarled back.

Geeta whirled her hand forward, her violet magic bursting from the palms of her hand. The power picked up Kyle's body, flinging him hard against the cement escape door of the building. "Nobody is allowed to see my thoughts. *Nobody!*" Geeta yelled.

"What the fuck is wrong with you? It was a misunderstanding. You need to chill out! I didn't see anything, and even if I had, I wouldn't have cared. I've seen a lot of shit in my time, and nothing would surprise me. Not now, anyway!"

Geeta's bitter face remained motionless. After a few moments, her eyes lowered, and she turned her head. "I am ashamed," she spoke softly.

"Ashamed of what?"

Her hard face softened, and her eyes started to water. No tears fell, but just the flooding of her eyes made him feel like shit. "I'm done for today," she whispered with a jittery voice.

Geeta suddenly flashed violet, disappearing, leaving Kyle behind. Kyle walked over to the staff, picked it up, then closed his eyes. He breathed in deeply, focusing on the power of the staff, bonding with his magic.

Well, she might be done, but I sure as hell am not!

Then Kyle began to practice on his own. Not with restraint but with his raw emotions.

Boy, did it ever feel good.

CHAPTER 69

❖━━━━━━❖

YELLOW

"Iigh Priest Auron? Are you okay?" a younger priest called out within the temple.

Auron shook his head, realizing that it was way past time for his ritual meditations. The moon was full in view between the columns of the temple.

He'd had the same vision again. The gifteds' bodies melting all around him, their bloodcurdling screams of agony cursing him for taking them to the past. They all blamed him for their demise.

"You have been staring at the same spot for more than twenty minutes," the boy continued.

"Yes, my son, all is well," Auron answered. "I was just heavily in thought." How he wished that were true.

The young yellow-gifted priest walked up to him anxiously. His hands jittered while his body moved awkwardly. He glanced down at the floor for a moment, then shyly looked up to Auron. "Might I confess something to you?" he asked while his foot shuffled the floor.

"You may." Auron nodded, gesturing for the boy to continue.

"I have been praying that the God of Light gives me strength for what is about to take place. I fear that I will not have the courage to do so. I know that we are to die, almost without a doubt, but at the same time, I am scared to die. I should feel delighted that we are to do the God of Light's work by eradicating the darkness, but I can't help but feel that I wish we didn't have to be the ones to do so. I feel so guilty by just thinking it."

Surprised by the boy's honesty, Auron gave him a warm smile, then stated, "I must tell you, child, that I, too, am afraid."

The boy's face was awestruck. "You are? But you are the high priest!"

"Yes, but I also have feelings just like you. I, too, would prefer someone else do what we are called to do. But it is not so. We must follow through on our calling, otherwise our faith is false."

Somehow, Auron didn't believe his own words. All he could hear were the screams in his vision.

"But what god would ask so many gifted to die for the sins of one person? Surely that is not fair," the boy stated.

It wasn't fair. Auron was still wrapping his head around that fact. Maybe he didn't have the faith he should have; maybe it had never been strong to begin with. The images of the disintegrating gifted and their cries filled Auron once again, causing him to shudder.

Why was he suddenly feeling like this?

***

The food grew cold as Ayera picked at her plate. She had no hunger, and her nerves were overwhelming her. She hardly ever drank wine but decided to have a glass for tonight's meal. It was left untouched.

If her gifted traveled to the past and perished, she would lose her throne, the throne that her family had occupied for centuries. All because she was an unfit ruler in the first place.

There was a quiet knock on the dining chamber's door.

"Come in," Ayera called out, pushing the plate away.

Duke Wellington appeared, bowing before her. "Empress, all gifted are on standby, awaiting Lady Vala's arrival."

"Thank you, Duke. She won't be coming for another two days, but I am glad everyone is ready."

The duke nodded. "Yes, Your Majesty." He pulled out a scroll, offering it to her. "Also, this came for you just a moment ago."

"I don't feel like reading any missives tonight. Can you put it aside in my council chambers for the morning?" Ayera looked at her full glass of wine, still deciding if she should even indulge at a time like this, even if it would help calm her nerves.

"Empress, forgive me, but I think you should take a look at it," the Duke pressed. "It's from High Justice Belinda of the Red."

Ayera froze, her face slowly moving to the scroll. Belinda's red wax seal was pressed upon the document.

Reaching out her hand, Ayera carefully took the scroll, then broke the seal delicately. Looking up at Duke Wellington, she nodded. "Thank you. Please leave me."

"Yes, Empress."

He bowed, then exited the chamber, leaving Ayera in silence. For many minutes, the scroll sat in her lap, her hands shaking with nerves. Ayera knew the news wasn't good, but she didn't know how bad it would be.

After taking a deep breath, she gently opened the scroll, reading Belinda's writing:

Dearest Empress Ayera of World Sector Six,

We have received word of the most unsettling news. It has been reported to me that your sister has traveled back in time, and that you have failed to put a stop to your sister's nuisance. Furthermore, you now plan to port all your gifted to another time era, putting a death sentence on all of the gifted in your sector.

High Justice Tyllos has already told you that Ikaria will not impact the future Earth, and still you doubt his visions. And it is said your husband is being held in your dungeons as a prisoner. What in your right mind are you thinking? I demand you release the Emperor at once and put a halt to your plans. If you do so, we might consider sparing your life.

However, if you continue to disobey, and if any of your gifted perish in the past, then we intend to sign your death warrant. The next move you make is imperative to all the world sectors, and it could be your last. You can expect High Inquisitor Rubius of the Red to be in your sector soon to take care of your sister when she returns, as it seems you lack the capacity to do so yourself.

As the God of Light reigns supreme,

High Justice Belinda

Ayera set down the letter gently on the table. According to the High Court, she had already failed. She'd let Ikaria slip through her sector by traveling back in time. But Ayera knew deep down that there was hope in the past to stop her sister. Even if her gifted died doing so, they could get Ikaria. The High Court didn't believe her, but she believed. She had to, otherwise there was no other hope for Earth. Despite what High Justice Tyllos said, Ayera believed Auron's vision.

Another knock, this one much firmer than the duke's, sounded from outside her door.

"Proceed," Ayera called out, rolling up the scroll and throwing it across the table.

"Empress, we have rotated the guards and the gifted between the Emperor and the three gifted in confinement," Lord Nathan said, bowing.

"Very good," Ayera nodded, then eyed Belinda's letter.

"Any word from the High Court regarding the Emperor?" Lord Nathan asked.

Do what is right, and not what people want you to do, Ayera told herself.

Ayera looked away from the scroll, meeting Nathan's eyes. "There has been no word. Continue to rotate the teams."

"Yes, Your Majesty." Lord Nathan bowed, heading toward the door.

"Send word to High Priest Auron," Ayera called out to the man leaving. "I am in much need of prayer tonight."

"As you wish, Empress."

CHAPTER 70

RED

"I'm waiting!" Geeta taunted him, floating in midair above Arcadia. "Never thought you'd be so eager to get your ass handed to you!" Kyle chided back.

Geeta smirked. "Good luck with that."

Blood-red whirlwinds whipped through Kyle's crimson hair. He no longer had white hair; it was completely red, spiked in the same fashion as before. He found it amusing, since when he first met Emerald, she had disguised herself as a redhead. Now he was the redhead. The thought of her sent a fresh surge of determination through him.

Kyle cast another forceful blow toward Geeta, then took a last drag of his smoke and flung it into the sky.

Geeta evaded his forceful blow, then watched the cigarette butt fly past her. Quickly, she whipped her head in his direction, looking annoyed at him for dropping his trash on the city.

"What do you think you are doing?" Geeta narrowed her eyes.

Kyle snorted in amusement. "Do you think one more piece of trash is going to matter in Arcadia? Have you *seen* the filth in the lower levels?"

"You could at least have the decency to disintegrate it," she snapped back. Her purple mohawk stood stiffly on her head as the winds continued to delicately flow around her, waving her clothing and earrings in a gentle purple current.

"Whatever. There's more important shit to worry about than my cigarette butt. Like saving Em."

Just saying her name made Kyle miss her hard, and it took every ounce of his energy not to go insane being separated from her. Every spare moment, he thought of Emerald and the time they had spent together. Time was passing, and he had lived almost a year of his life while Emerald was locked in time. She was tucked away in his every thought, from the moment when he awoke to the moment he passed out. She was there, always with him. In his magic, in his songs, in his mind. She was everywhere.

Taking the opportune moment, Kyle summoned a red maelstrom of lightning to hurl at Geeta. The ruby storm crackled from different directions, each bolt coming together in his hands. At that moment, he felt Geeta's mind attack his, trying to pry and force her way in.

This time, he was determined that she wouldn't get in.

Releasing the crimson lightning toward Geeta, he instantly tapped into his violet abilities, gaining complete control of his consciousness. Deflecting his last spell, Geeta sucked all the lightning into her hands, making it shoot up into the skies where it belonged. Returning her focus to Kyle, Geeta narrowed her glowing eyes. Her forceful magic became harder, squeezing Kyle's mind, trying to take over. Pain erupted within, exploding into thousands of sharp jabs.

The red wind suddenly faded from around him as Geeta continued to work her way into his mind; she was breaking his concentration, and he was slowly losing control of his magic.

Without warning, the winds dissipated, and Kyle was falling toward the ground. Geeta had successfully gotten a hold on him.

Frantically, Kyle called upon his magic. It responded, trying to ward off Geeta as she continued to go deeper within his being. The wind raced against his face, burning his cheeks as he dodged various outcroppings on the buildings and frozen air transports, continuing to plummet to Arcadia's depths.

He was not going to let Geeta win this time. He'd had enough of her games.

It's time to get Emerald, dammit, he told himself.

Kyle felt Geeta make her way further into his mind, but what was about to happen, she did not expect.

All at once, Kyle pulled all of his jealousy and rage from within, letting it flow through his soul. With his emotions burning through his blood and tearing through his mind, he felt Geeta's presence. The violet power from within his life-force surged through her existence, sending her back into her own mind while bringing his own magic and consciousness with her.

This caught Geeta by surprise, because this time, the doors and windows to her soul were wide open with no protection.

Surging his magic within her memories, images and scenes from Geeta's life flooded Kyle's mind, flowing like the strong tides of the ocean.

An image of Geeta faded into Kyle's view. It wasn't what Geeta looked like now but a younger version of her, dressed in ancient garb. Violet, red, and gold colored her robe and loose head scarf. She was adorned with golden jewelry from head to toe, and henna tattoos decorated her skin. Her purple hair was long, thick, and wavy, down to her waist. The only things that were recognizable other than her face were the purple jewel on her forehead, her nose ring, and her bright purple eyes.

Geeta wandered through stone halls and corridors, entering a large room with many shrines. A temple to the gods of the Spectrum, if Kyle were to guess.

There were others there, two men who were bowed in prayer.

A tall lanky man dressed in a yellow robe with a long golden beard and matching hair turned sharply in Geeta's direction as she approached. The gold in his eyes was a startling contrast to his deep-brown skin. Another man with green hair, smaller and shorter, looked up at Geeta slowly from where he was praying.

"Women are not permitted in the temple during their menstruation," the golden man stated sharply, his eyes narrowing at Geeta. The green-haired man cocked his head slightly backward, glancing at Geeta with longing eyes.

What an ass, Kyle thought.

Embarrassed by the golden priest's statement, Geeta flushed a deep red. Her violet eyes lowered to the floor, clearly flustered.

"Husband," Geeta said. "Vihaan, I would never in my heart willingly violate the temple by coming here unclean."

Husband? Geeta? Kyle had always pegged her as someone who was very independent of people. She didn't seem the type who enjoyed anyone's company.

"Then you must leave now," Vihaan said sharply, shooing her away swiftly with a gesture of his hands. Geeta remained standing, and Vihaan returned to his prayers. The green-haired man glanced at Geeta with a concerned look.

I will be all right, Suresh, Geeta told the green-haired man within his mind.

Suresh glanced away, pretending to return to his prayers, but in reality, he was watching the situation unfold out of the corner of his eye.

Geeta didn't move from her spot. She raised her eyes to look at the back of her husband's head. "I had a vision, husband. A vision of the destruction of the world," she said, interrupting the silence once more.

Vihaan began to laugh. His shoulders jerked wildly as his laughter became more uncontrollable. After an uncomfortable, long laugh, Vihaan snapped out of it, stopping himself. He whipped his body to face Geeta, then rose sharply, his silky robes resting at his sides. His golden eyes flared with anger, clearly annoyed that she was not doing as she had been commanded.

Geeta shuddered as he glared at her but did not look away.

"*You* had a vision? *You*, being *violet*? That is impossible."

"It's true, husband. I… felt it in my heart. I think it was a message for a man in the future. I saw him as a ghost man."

Vihaan scoffed. "You defiled the temple just to tell me this?"

Suresh glanced at Geeta, pleading silently. *Don't do this, Geeta,* his mind begged her. *You know how Vihaan gets.*

Suresh, the future of Earth depends on it. The Ghost Man with the gift of the red needs our help. He needs this message.

"You have no power over the magic of prophecy," said Vihaan. "You are being foolish."

Geeta gave him a stern look and continued. "I know this to be true. We must get to this man. He needs our help. The *future* needs our help. Earth needs our help."

"Help?" Vihaan asked incredulously. "You come here, defiling the temple with your impurity, just to tell me of some nonsense dream, and expect me to help? Get out of here and go home!" His golden eyes glared at her venomously.

"No," Geeta stated firmly, raising her voice. "I will not. Many lives depend on us!"

Vihaan shot up quickly and struck her across the face. Geeta flinched but otherwise stood her ground. "You unclean, defiant bitch! Your vision is false! From the gods of the dark side of the spectrum!" Vihaan's angry twisted face yelled into Geeta's, not even an inch away from her. "You know how I know this? I, too, had a vision of this very situation. I, the high priest of prophecy! And what I say is true, not some woman with the gift of the violet," he spat. "If you go chasing your false vision, you are damning the future, not saving it!"

"I will forgive you, this one time, husband. Next time, I will not," Geeta said stiffly, her eyes flaring.

A look of contempt washed over Vihaan's face. "Do not presume to tell me anything, woman." He struck her face again. This time, Kyle heard a loud smack of skin, and Geeta placed one of her hands against the stinging red flesh.

Geeta didn't budge. Instead she narrowed her eyes.

"Go!" Vihaan roared, striking her again.

Suresh stood up, quickly interjecting. "Vihaan, let me take her home."

"You stay out of this, Suresh!" Vihaan ordered, keeping his eyes locked on Geeta.

Kyle watched as Geeta nodded, her hand still resting against her swollen cheek. There was another man entering the temple, with deep-blue hair and eyes. He glanced at Geeta, eyeing her swollen cheek, but remained silent, lighting an incense stick and starting his prayers.

"I am not going home!" Geeta yelled back, flaring her nostrils, the ring in her nose pronounced.

Vihaan whirled around to strike her again but was stopped. Vihaan, Suresh, and the blue-haired priest flew in three different directions, crashing into the back of temple walls with the force of violet magic. Hatred seethed through Geeta's eyes, hatred for her husband. She raised her delicate neck, and the men began to glow their respective colors. Before they cast their spells, Geeta's glowing violet eyes radiated with burning intensity, flashing pale purple. At once, the men's eyes were vacant of expression, and their beings were no more.

She was in control of their minds.

Turning to them, Geeta eyes flared. *Consume your flesh!* Kyle heard Geeta's mind silently order.

Mortified, Kyle watched as the men began gnawing at their flesh, devouring their arms. Glowing blood poured out of their limbs as they tore their skin and muscles away with their teeth. Geeta remained in control, watching in almost sick satisfaction at her husband's demise.

After what seemed like forever to Kyle, Geeta finally relented.

Stop!

The men stood frozen, waiting for her next command.

Geeta walked over to Suresh, frowning. "I am sorry that you had to be mixed up in this, my friend," she whispered to him, bowing her head in shame. She then began to taste the blood on his arms.

After she had consumed some of his blood, she walked over to the blue-haired man, doing the same.

"Please forgive me, Raghu," she whispered to him, patting his arm softly, licking his blood.

Geeta walked over to Vihaan, pausing in front of him. His pupils remained clouded from her control. Absentmindedly, he breathed in with much trouble, as he was losing blood. "As for you, I am *not* sorry, husband," Geeta sneered. She licked the blood off his arms as it pooled out of him.

Then Geeta collapsed to the cold stone floor, writing in pain, screaming. The three men fell to the floor and lay prone in their own pools of blood, their eyes glossed over, as no one was in control of their bodies. Geeta's head turned in the bloodied men's direction, and she began to vomit repeatedly.

What have I done? Kyle heard Geeta's thoughts formulate. *I have violated the laws of the gods!*

Frantically writhing in pain, Geeta called out to the green-haired man. "Suresh, heal yourself and the others! Quickly!"

Geeta pulled out of their minds to let Suresh work his magic. A fog disappeared from Suresh's eyes, allowing him to discover himself and the two others bloodied, with Geeta curled up in a ball. Screams from the other men echoed through the temple. Suresh remained silent while panting with faded gasps of breath, unsure of what to do.

Both stared at each other, waiting for the other to make the first move.

Why. Geeta, why? Suresh cried out within his mind. *You defied the will of the gods by partaking in drinking in the others' gifted blood! You have gone too far with your vision, whether it be true or false!* Suresh's eyes told her of his disappointment and anguish.

Then why aren't you stopping me? You, of all the gifted, could! Geeta argued.

You know why I do not. Suresh's flesh was repairing itself. He laid a hand on his mangled arm. His body burned bright green in a halo of healing light. He slowly got up, then looked over at Vihaan, who was making a poor attempt to heal himself with his analogous color.

"Worthless woman! I demand you come here right now!" Blood spat midair as Vihaan snarled. "You are damned! You hear? Damned and defiled, that's what you are!"

I am sorry, Suresh, Kyle heard Geeta say to Suresh while she continued to writhe in agony.

I am sorry it has to be this way, he replied. *I will pray for your soul.*

Please… come with me! We can do this together!

There was silence. Suresh did not answer her.

Suresh softly laid his hand on Vihaan, basking him in bright-green light. Vihaan's torn flesh slowly restored itself. The healing wasn't complete, but it was enough for Vihaan to move freely, jerking away from Suresh.

Then, Vihaan charged at Geeta.

Still fumbling on the ground in her agony, Geeta summoned a violet, translucent curved shield in front of her.

Vihaan shot out his hand, casting a golden spell, melting away her barrier. Geeta weakly raised her hand, funneling more magic into the barrier. It looked to Kyle that Vihaan's magic was working faster than Geeta's.

"You think that the gods will ever be on your side? I am the high priest, their champion, their voice! You can never win against the gods!" screamed Vihaan. His face contorted as he concentrated more power into melting the barrier. His arm shook while the golden stream continued to flow out of his outstretched palm. "You will destroy everything! You hear me? Everything in this world!" he roared.

A sharp shock pierced through Kyle's mind. The world instantly vanished.

Geeta was fighting back.

His red eyes shot open, and now, instead of him falling to Arcadia's depths, it was Geeta who was falling. Kyle realized with alarm that he still had control over her, as her face was blank, and she was falling like a limp doll toward the earth.

Kyle released his adjacent magic and her mind, calling his power back to him.

Free from his spell, Geeta screamed in anger, flashing in front of him, midair. With a snarl on her face, she pushed with her arms and shot Kyle back with a violent purple force. Her magic was not focused and completely missed Kyle.

Kyle frowned, knowing that he'd hit a soft spot in her. In a way he felt bad, but what else was he to do when she was using her force against him? Shouldn't she be glad that he was finally able to use the full gift of the violet, a color that is not his true gifted color?

Using red and violet magic, Kyle entered her mind to calm her, then gently guided Geeta to a nearby platform with gentle winds, securing her body there. Kyle released the control of her mind, backing out of her memories, but he kept her body locked in place, just to be sure she knew he finally had won.

The violet color in Geeta's pupils returned as her mind was restored to her. With a scowl on her face, she said, "What did you think you were doing?"

"I was doing what I should have been doing," he argued, "fighting back with my mind! You were the one who was trying to take over mine!"

"You weren't supposed to see that!" she shouted. "No one was supposed to see… to see what I did…" she said, her voice trembling. Her eyes began to water, forming a single tear. It trickled down her hard face.

Her words silenced him. Kyle knew that what he had seen had made a huge impact on her life. He didn't even know what to say.

Kyle scratched the back of his neck anxiously. "I'm sorry…"

Ignoring him, Geeta walked off. Violet magic radiated from her, and slowly the image of the staff came into view. She yanked at it angrily, then continued to send violet magic funneling into the staff.

The orb on the staff glowed an intense violet-blue, and suddenly the transparent tint of violet lifted from the world, bringing everything in Arcadia back into color with motion.

The city was alive once again. Time continued to flow.

"You are ready," she called out with her back still toward him.

A moment later, she disappeared.

***

The fierce melody flowed from his lips, while the vibrations of the guitar shook through him.

Tonight, the way Kyle sang Emerald's song was different. Before, the melody strengthened his resolve to train harder. But now that time wasn't frozen, it was a battle cry for what was about to take place.

He would finally see Emerald. God, he missed her like crazy.

The sounds of the city renewed his vigor. Rushing air transports, shouts from the platforms, loud music from the neighbors a few levels below; the energy of the city gave him life. The noises filtered in through his song, bringing more life and more magic.

It had been so long since Kyle had seen Emerald. Would she recognize him? It hadn't been that long in the grand scheme of things, almost a year for him, but still, even Kyle could see the physical changes in himself.

He finished the song, then set the guitar down gently and reached for his cigarettes, lighting one up. The tickle of the smoke triggered a release throughout his body. Taking a drink from his flask, Kyle headed inside, sure that Geeta would be finished with her nightly prayers by now.

As he entered through the patio door, Kyle saw the illumination of Geeta's warm candles casting light against the walls, the incense curling around her. Normally, Kyle would have headed back out to the patio and given Geeta her space. But now he was intrigued.

The spicy incense filled his nostrils as he watched Geeta on her knees, head bowed. The candles flickered, and the shadows of the miniature carvings of her gods danced along the wall.

Her head shifted, aware that he was in the same room as her. Suddenly he was met with her tear-stained face, then she was brushing them away with a hard swipe. Kyle shifted his feet uncomfortably at her stare.

Kyle silently offered his flask to Geeta as he sat down next to her. She held out her hand in rejection as she shook her head. He moved her hand aside, putting the silver bottle in her face.

"You need this."

Geeta hesitantly accepted, then took a drink. She continued to stare off into the distance, not glancing at him. "Now you know."

"Yes, I do," Kyle agreed. "The truth."

"And what truth is that?" Geeta said, her fierce eyes shooting to him, her long dangling earrings swinging over her shoulder.

"That your husband was an asshole."

She lowered her eyes, glancing at the flickering candles.

"Don't let that dick continue to terrorize you. Look at you. You're seriously a kickass woman. You have insanely powerful abilities, one of the purest hearts that I have ever met, second to Emerald, of course, and you trained a sorry ass like me and made me what I am. Stop telling yourself untrue things," Kyle said. "Besides, that asshole had it coming to him."

"I am no different than that wicked sorceress," Geeta said quietly. "I am unclean and will always be."

"Bullshit! I don't believe that for one minute. If that were true, then why did you spend so much time trying to find and train me?"

"You saw it in my mind. I consumed the blood of the other gifted! It is a violation of the laws of the gods, and of nature."

"And? You were just doing what was necessary to find me."

Her face hardened through her flowing tears. "Really? Was it really necessary for me to control those men? Have them consume their flesh because of my hatred for my husband? I let the darkness into my soul and committed an unspeakable act! Drinking another's blood, consuming a foreign power, is completely forbidden, no matter what you believe. It upsets the Spectrum of Magic and can twist one's soul to darkness. That day, instead of being a savior to help you, I gave in to my jealousy, which turned into hatred, making me unclean. And what is worse, I've never felt bad about what I did to my husband. I should feel terrible, but I don't."

"You're right," Kyle said. "What you did was pretty terrible."

Geeta stopped, her eyes wide open, sucking in her breath.

"But you shouldn't feel guilty. He was an asshole and got what was coming to him," Kyle said. "But the question is, what are you going to do about it now? Live in the past and let yourself continue to relive that day and feel guilty? Is there no room for forgiveness? I mean, I'm not religious and all that crap, but doesn't every religion allow humans to make mistakes and be forgiven?"

Geeta blinked, pausing. "You sound like a priest."

"Priest? Me? Now that's fucking funny!" Kyle laughed. "More like a drunk ass blessed by the God of Light by accident!"

Geeta chuckled softly, wiping away her tears. "I just want to be cleansed of my impurity."

"Is there a way?"

"I am hoping your princess can do it when we rescue her."

"I am confident that Em will help you."

Geeta nodded, then took another drink. She turned her head slightly, but Kyle caught it. She had a small, hopeful smile.

CHAPTER 71

RED

Kyle, please! Emerald's voice called out.

A long corridor expanded in front of Kyle, lined with large windows draped with royal-blue satin curtains. The only light source was at the end of the hall—a glowing, soft pale-azure crack of light behind two giant double doors.

More cries echoed in the hall.

He began to run. And run.

Help me...

"Hold on!" Kyle screamed. "I'm coming! I won't let you be taken away again!"

The hall seemed endless and ongoing.

Please... don't, Emerald begged. *Please...*

Kyle made it to the end of the hall, coming upon the oversized doors. The steady blue light continued to shine from the cracks behind them. He yanked the handles, but they were locked. He shook harder, but the doors did not budge.

More cries.

Kicking furiously with his boot, the door broke free, and Kyle burst through the opening.

There was Emerald, completely naked, lying in a bed of blue satin. Her head turned in his direction with empty eyes and no movement from her lips. Her hair flowed around her like a sea of waves flowing gently across the delicate fabrics.

Help me...

A shadow faded into reality. No, not a shadow, but the prince.

The fucker was kissing her neck, guiding his hand over her naked flesh.

Kyle screamed.

Throwing out his arms, the shouts roared through his body, shaking his mind. His body exploded in flames, then engulfed his dream with blood.

Kyle was still screaming when he awoke. He was not on fire, but he was covered in sweat and heaved with rage. He shot up and looked around the room for the staff.

Geeta looked alarmed on the other side of the room, eyes still groggy from sleep interrupted by his screams. "What happened?" she asked. She saw him reach for the staff, then tried to grab it too, only he was quicker. "What are you doing?"

"I'll tell you what I'm doing! I'm going after Emerald! That fucking piece of shit touched my woman, and maybe even..." Kyle let out a loud, frustrated yell, kicking the wall hard. "*FUCK!*"

Geeta faced him, tried to take the staff once more, but he dodged her. "You can't yet! It's not time. The others aren't here yet."

"Fuck time! Fuck those other gifted! Em needs me *now*. I've been dicking around here too long, and it's about fucking time I go after her!" For the first time in a long time, his eyes welled up with tears. "I... I'm already too late," he said, choking on his words.

He headed for the door, staff in hand.

Geeta flashed in front of the door, blocking his way. "You might be able to take on the sorceress, and stave her off for a time, but you have forgotten about the prince having magic too. And they have the princess under their influence, along with that cyborg. You can't take them on all at once!"

"Then fucking come with me, and let's take care of this shit once and for all!"

Geeta frowned. Kyle realized he was being a bit too harsh on her, but he couldn't help it; he was furious.

After a long pause, Geeta sighed. "I am going to regret this."

"Good. Let's get going." Kyle held out his hand, expecting her to take it to have her port them to the palace.

Instead of placing her hand in his, she eyed him for a moment, then closed her eyes. A knife surrounded by violet magic floated to her, hovering above her outstretched hand. Snatching it, Geeta opened her eyes and quickly cut her left wrist. Kyle gasped for a moment, knowing what she was about to offer. A glass floated from a nearby table, appearing below her bleeding wrist, catching the blood droplets.

"You will need this," she said softly, nodding toward the floating glass of blood.

Kyle watched the goblet continue to collect Geeta's trickling blood. "Will I get all of the colors in you, or only violet?"

"I do not know for certain, but I believe that you will get all the colors that I have consumed. Yellow, green, blue, and… mine." Geeta looked at him intensely. "You will have all the colors in the spectrum but one."

"Are you sure?" Kyle paused for a moment, watching the blood pulsate brightly as it continued to flow into the glass.

She nodded. "Yes. I had a vision tonight during my prayers. You used the full power of the Spectrum of Magic. Although this defies all beliefs, for some reason, the gods want you to have this."

"But what about the orange blood?"

"The cyborg," she answered. "He is the key to you completing the spectrum."

Kyle thought about what she was saying. If he had to get the blood from the cyborg, it would be a battle in itself to make that damn robot comply and give up his blood. Somehow, Kyle knew within his life-force that it wasn't a good idea. Not only that, but hadn't Geeta herself said that it was a violation of the gods and nature to consume another gifted's blood? Was this the only way for him to defeat Ikaria?

His thoughts turned back to Emerald. His love, his life. His complement.

Thoughts of Emerald painting flooded his mind, the time when she was mixing her paints together.

So black is all of the colors mixed together? he recalled asking her.

Em's words echoed from his memories. *It is if you are talking about pigments. But if you are referring to light, all of the colors combined makes white.*

"Geeta, do you remember the first time you told me about complements?" Kyle questioned.

Geeta eyed him hesitantly. "Yes. Why do you ask?"

"What was the saying that you said? The one that is taught among your people?"

"The creation of light is through complements, for each color yearns for its other half. The two colors opposite can eradicate all shades of darkness," Geeta recited for him, word for word.

Looking at the glass one last time, Kyle shook his head. "I might regret this later, but I think I understand how to complete the Spectrum of Magic. And it's not with that."

Geeta looked at him in disbelief as the bloodied glass still hovered in the air. "You can't be serious. You must take it! This is the only way!"

Kyle whirled around, glaring. "Really? Because I could have sworn that you just said it defies the law of magic. You said yourself that once you partake in another's blood, you become unclean. I have another plan that the sorceress won't expect."

Geeta stood there, stunned. Her pride evaporated from her face as she tilted her head to one side curiously. He held out his hand once more, expecting her to take him to the palace. Instead, she shook her head.

"What are you waiting for?" he said. "Let's get on with it!"

"No. If you are truly going up against Ikaria, I must warn the future." Geeta paused, taking a deep breath.

"Please don't take too long," Kyle said. "I know I'm the one who wants to kick everyone's ass, but it would be nice if I had a little bit of help."

"I don't plan to. I'll most likely be at the palace before you get there."

"Yeah, probably," Kyle said under his breath, thinking of Emerald. "I'm going to get Em first."

Geeta eyed him, then nodded at his plan. She was sensing his thoughts, and he allowed her in his mind. She understood what he was about to do.

"I will wait for you to get your princess to the royal transport platform, and then we will confront Ikaria," she said, withdrawing from his mind. "I hope you are right about this."

"I know I'm right, because it came from Em." Kyle turned to Geeta, meeting her eyes. "Sorry about the window."

"Window?"

With that, Kyle threw out his hand, causing the window to freeze with his red ice magic. He ran into the glass, shattering it as he broke through. A red swarm of wind spun around him, and he took off flying.

CHAPTER 72

BLUE

Derek awoke early to the sounds of rolling thunder. The dark sky didn't let any light pass through the thick atmosphere and had cast the city in an ominous darkness. It was drizzling outside, and by the looks of it, there were very few transports in operation, as the fog was heavy.

Emerald had slept in his arms the whole night and hadn't moved since she fell asleep. He could feel her naked body inhaling and exhaling softly underneath the sheets. Nothing had felt more satisfying than finally being able to indulge in his desire for her. He had ached for her all these years, and finally he had her.

Derek felt the best he had since he had arrived in Arcadia. No, ever since he'd put the circlet on Emerald's head and married her. His body felt strong, his headaches had disappeared, and he was thinking clearer than he had in the last few weeks. And most importantly, Ikaria was not invading his mind, much to his relief.

Emerald stirred, rolling over to face him. She gave him a small smile, but it wasn't her usual bright smile. Her eyes were devoid of herself.

A sick feeling flared up in the pit of Derek's stomach all over again.

"Good morning, my king," she said.

"Good morning, my beautiful queen." Derek kissed her lips, then pulled her close. The two lay in bed, listening to the rain falling outside the windows.

Emerald sat still, an unusual stillness that made Derek's skin crawl.

"What is it?" Derek asked, continuing to look outside at the dark sky.

"I had a dream."

"Oh? About what?"

"It was about an oddly dressed man in black. He was strange. He smoked cigarettes and rode an outdated motorcycle. I feel like I know him, but I am sure that I would have never met such a man," she said, then turned to him with expressionless green eyes. "It is like my mind is a fog, and I can't remember things," she said calmly with a monotonous voice.

Derek's face grew dark. Somehow, Kyle continued to haunt him, even after Derek had thought it was all over. "It was just a dream," Derek answered as he held her tightly.

"Yes, it was just a dream," she murmured back to him. Then, she paused, making a strange facial expression. "It felt like I knew this man…" Her voice trailed off as she rubbed her temples around where the circlet rested on her head.

"I want you to forget everything about the dream and the man. Everything," Derek said bitterly.

The circlet began to glow, and a violet-black color radiated from it. Emerald's eyes grew emptier than before, looking at him with acknowledgment. With every order he gave her in his thoughts or words, she obeyed.

"Yes, my king."

Derek wondered if the power of the circlet could make her forget about that pathetic loser. There was no better way than for him to try to test it out, just to ensure that he never heard about Kyle ever again.

"My dearest, tell me all about the dream you just had," Derek asked, frowning, afraid of her answer.

"Dream?" Emerald looked at him again, confused. "What dream?"

"You know, the dream you just told me about. The oddly dressed man," he persisted.

"I had a dream?" she asked, expressionless. She put her hand to her head, rubbing it, as if the gentle massage would clear away the fog. "I don't recall a dream, Derek…"

Derek smiled at her. "Perhaps I misunderstood," he said, holding her close to him again. He began to laugh with pleasure inwardly, knowing that the magic worked. Now he had no doubt that her heart would not be swayed by another man, especially not Kyle.

Getting out of bed, Derek stretched, exposing his naked flesh. Grabbing a robe and throwing it on loosely, Derek called out for Silas in the next chamber.

Silas appeared at the door with two cups, saucers, and a small coffee pot. "Your Majesty." He bowed, then set down the cups, pouring hot coffee in each cup.

"Please make haste and gather my outfit for the day. I am to be at the corporation in an hour."

"This early in the morning?"

"Yes." Derek nodded, his gaze moving to Emerald. "And Silas, please call upon the Queen's handmaidens and have them escort her back to her chambers."

"Yes, Your Majesty."

Silas bowed at them both, then made his way into closet, out of Derek's view.

In the corner of his eye, Derek thought he saw the air ripple near the window. Turning his full attention toward it, the cyborg materialized in front of the glass, his eyes glowing with intensity.

The cyborg narrowed his glowing orange eye while the mechanical one focused its lens, making a shifting sound. A shiver ran down Derek's spine, causing Derek's stomach to jitter. Had he been watching them all night?

The cyborg didn't move, instead it gave Derek a snarl. Then with a sudden jolt, the cyborg flickered back to being invisible once again.

It's a good thing I am getting rid of that damn thing.

CHAPTER 73

◆━━━◆

ORANGE

Another storm. Not that Telly minded; she loved the rain.

It was extremely early, even for Telly. She had always been one of those people who got up before sunrise, drinking her coffee and reading the latest science journal on her tablet before anyone else woke up. But today was different. Her nerves had kept her up all night, and she finally decided to get up extra early.

As she walked by her living room window, she noticed how little visibility the rain offered. Telly could have sworn she had seen flashes of red lightning within the storm, but perhaps her mind was playing tricks on her. Her head had been throbbing ever since she got up, and her body ached from the lack of sleep. It was finally catching up to her. Being back in the lab had always made her sleepless. It was worse now that Drew would finally be returning to her today.

Reaching into the refrigerator to get milk for her coffee, the remaining blood samples caught her eye. She didn't know what to do with the remaining ones. She couldn't very well bring the stolen blood back. It had been enough of an effort smuggling them out of the lab in the first place.

Ignoring the samples, Telly closed the refrigerator. She poured her morning coffee, adding milk and sugar to the cup, stirring it hurriedly as she thought of Drew. She slurped down her drink as she hurried to the bathroom, fixing her messy cropped hair and brushing it into place. She put on some simple earrings, then her bifocals, as she knew the prince, no, *King* Derek would be there today, visiting the lab with his royal advisor, Ikaria. She could care less about royal visitors. All she cared about was seeing Drew.

Telly had heard the whispers throughout the lab yesterday. Rumor had it that Derek would be continuing Damaris's order to ready the cyborgs. Telly was a bit surprised hearing that, but none of it concerned her since Drew would be back in the lab under her direct supervision.

I wonder if he's had more memories return to him since I last saw him.

Telly finished getting ready, then left her apartment, locking the door. Walking down the hall, she almost forgot the most important tool to communicate with Drew—her tablet. She hurried back, fidgeting with the door, then bolted back into her apartment, snatching her tablet and shoving it into her bag. Hopefully Gwen wouldn't wake up with all the racket she was making. Or maybe she should make a bunch of noise; that girl constantly overslept and missed her first class more often than not.

Telly walked briskly down the hall, then entered the skyway system. The people in the skyways mimicked the weather; gloom hung over everyone as they made their way to work, schools, or shops. But not Telly. The weather had quite the opposite effect on her. Telly delighted in the rains pouring through the city. Arcadia was mostly sunny all year round. This kind of weather always reminded her of her childhood city, the Twin Kingdoms. There was different weather all year round there, with plenty of rain and snow. Ever since she moved to Arcadia as a young adult, she longed to see any bit of weather that wasn't the usual sunny day.

Telly ran quickly from the mid-level skyway's ending tunnel to the building's main public transport hub, getting wet in the process. The lower levels were probably like rivers right now, flowing with trash and sewage, spilling into the ocean. The drainage in the city was terrible, and heavy rains always caused major damage to the lower levels. It never affected her in the mid-levels, but she did feel sorry for those who were less fortunate.

Soaked, Telly squeezed into the tiny glass shelter along with others waiting for their transport number. The people in the public transport shelter were closer than she would have liked, but there was no room unless she wanted to be out in the rain. She could smell one man's strong cologne, along with another man's sweat, both of them next to her, filling her nostrils with confusion of the clashing smells. She stifled a gag.

Finally, the transport with her number arrived, and she hopped on with a few other passengers. They scanned her ID as she waited to get past the driver. It cleared, allowing her access to the upper levels. After everyone was on board, the transport took off.

While the air transport was en route to the corporation, another peal of roaring thunder, accompanied by red forked lightning, ripped through the skies. A few of the passengers gasped, pointing in the direction of the strange-colored lightning.

It's not just me seeing this.

The transport made its stops, finally arriving at Telly's destination: the corporation employee platform. She exited the transport, then followed the hundreds of other employees arriving for the day. Everyone was entering the building and making their way toward the elevators, escalators, and stairs. Telly moved toward the back elevators, ones that only certain employees had, ones that led underground to her lab.

Using her key card, the elevators opened, and she stepped inside. One of her other coworkers, Michael, entered. Telly eyed him, and his face shifted down as he avoided her gaze.

There was an uncomfortable silence. They had never talked unless they had to, and not all since the day she'd returned to Lab 34. And for good reason.

The elevator made its way down, humming with a low buzz. More uncomfortable silence.

"Was it worth it?" Telly asked, her eyes piercing right at him. Michael continued to look downward, shifting uncomfortably.

"What was I supposed to do?" he said. "You were getting too involved with our assignment."

"You mean, *my* assignment. Drew was donated by *me*. It was *our* research, mixed with the corporation's supplies."

Michael's eyes met hers evenly. "But you forget that *I* was a part of the team that helped Drew get to where he was. I did what I thought was best. You were far too attached to Drew, letting your emotions get the best of you. The directors had to know what was going on. Anyway, it's not like anything big happened. You are back now, are you not?"

"Actually, me getting transferred was big," Telly stated dryly. "Thanks for interfering. I'll always remember it."

Michael lowered his head again. Telly swiped back a few strands of hair that fell in her face, then crossed her arms, gritting her teeth.

Good, at least he knows that I know what he did.

She knew he hadn't reported her to do what was right. He just wanted a damn promotion. He had always envied her. Telly could always see it in his eyes. Regardless, he was in his same position, not promoted, while she'd returned to a position of authority. In fact, upon returning, the directors had urged her to take the elevated position that they had always pushed on her. This time she took it, and now she was the new director of her department, working side by side with Jonathan as his equal.

And now that she had been promoted, she had the freedom to do her desired research while working with the cyborgs in her lab. And she chose to continue to research more ideas and develop possible technology that could recover his memories and rehabilitate him to be as human as possible.

The elevator dinged, stopping at the bottom level, the furthest underground level there was in the building. Michael quickly headed off to his area of the lab. She smiled to herself, walking through the main capsule room that housed most of the cyborgs.

Whenever one showed a bit more promise or more specialized abilities than the others, that cyborg was then relocated to a private lab, just like how Drew had been. Of course, none of them had real magic like Drew; they were only infused with minor capabilities the blood gave them.

The bright lights of the cyborg capsules, along with the computer monitors, lit up the cyborg room, its only light source within the darkness. She passed her coworkers, directors, superiors, and associates—all seemed to be pacing quickly but calmly under pressure as they prepared for King Derek's visit.

It was such a shame that Damaris had suicided. But Telly, including all of Lab 34, liked Derek as their new king, much more than Damaris. Of course, the media was trying to downplay the suicide as much as possible. And why wouldn't they? Emerald was admired and loved, married to an equally loved prince, and now they were king and queen of Arcadia.

Telly made it to her private lab, passing her computer station and the sterile white room with her lab equipment. She peeked into the observation window, wishfully thinking that Drew might have come ahead of the royal party.

His room remained empty.

But he would be there soon. And all would be as it was.

CHAPTER 74

BLACK

Ikaria kept her facial expression still as the royal transport departed, but inside she was screaming with delight. She was inside a *machine*, flying across the expanse of Arcadia, one of the most technological cities of all time. Never had she been so fascinated by anything in her life, including the blond men she so desired. She had to admit that even the magics she'd consumed couldn't compare to the beauty of the machines here, along with the knowledge that she'd drained from them.

Absentmindedly, Ikaria placed one of her hands over the other, wanting to feel the gauntlet's metal. The cool metal felt smooth, and remained invisible to everyone but her. It was intentional, of course, as she didn't want Derek inquiring further about its power, nor did she want the scientists to ask why she had it. Ikaria doubted Derek would care if he found out what it really did, but she didn't feel like dealing with a barrage of questions coming from him. When they returned to the palace, she would make it appear once again.

A thought crossed her mind. What if she simply stayed in the past and ruled Arcadia? The city-kingdom had everything that Ikaria could possibly ever want, and she could reign over the planet, not some patch of sky. She had yet to set foot on the actual earth. Ikaria always thought that she would do it in her time, but what if she did it in this time era? What if she stayed behind, pushed Derek aside, and assumed his throne?

The thought gave her much pleasure. Queen of Arcadia, the kingdom of vast technology. Oh, she liked that. But Ikaria wouldn't have her revenge on the High Court, Auron, and everyone else who was against her if she did so.

That, she couldn't live without. She had to see the high justices' faces when she made an example out of them. Perhaps when the future was settled, with her as the ruling establishment, she could come back to Arcadia.

Ikaria felt the transport jerk, then come to a complete stop. Within a minute of landing, the transport's side door opened, and she exited the vehicle, walking down a small ramp. Derek stayed alongside Ikaria as the two of them exited the platform, heading toward the main entrance of the corporation with a series of guards in front of them. The unique cyborg, Drew, was also in their party, trailing behind, mechanical noises emitting from the joints of his right side with each step. Ikaria didn't understand why Drew wore clothes. Propriety? It was nonsense. After all, he was only *part* human. It didn't give her a chance to take in the beauty of his half-mechanized body.

Derek was usually quiet, but Ikaria knew what he was thinking. He just wanted her gone and to manage the mess that she'd made with Damaris. The new King had feelings of guilt and remorse about taking advantage of Queen Emerald. She could feel it oozing out of him like an annoying, incessant mental sobbing. Ikaria couldn't understand why he was beating himself up over it. Derek needed to live a little, and without her help, he would be sulking all the way back to York.

"Your Majesty," a lab director called out, meeting the group on the platform, then bowing. "Let me introduce myself. Head Director Santiago, Your Majesty. We, including myself, are honored by your visit."

Derek nodded at the director. "Thank you, Head Director. It is good to finally meet you in person."

"You are most welcome, Your Majesty." The director eyed the royal group. "Where is Councilor Zane?" Santiago asked. "He usually he accompanied the late King Damaris on these visits to the corporation."

A group of directors joined the head director, all giving Derek a deep bow, awaiting his orders. Ikaria gracefully emerged in front of Derek, giving the head director a sweet smile. "Oh, the councilor is quite busy and has prior engagements. His Majesty was so kind to ask me to assist him today."

Santiago eyed her curiously with a puzzled look on his face. "Excuse me… Lady…?" he asked, searching for her name.

"Ikaria. There is no need for a formal title. I am an advisor to the King."

"I'm quite charmed," Santiago said, kissing her hand. He turned to

Derek. "I have heard rumors of your new advisor, but no one told me she was so beautiful!"

Ikaria flashed a smile to the director, then turned her head to Derek. "You see, my king," she said in a slight mocking tone. "At least some people appreciate me."

The King let out an annoyed sigh but otherwise chose to ignore her.

The director bowed, then offered his arm to escort her, leading them inside the building. The sound of Drew could be heard, echoing down the large entryway.

As Ikaria and Derek walked the halls of the corporation and into the lab, she touched whatever she could, making it seem like she was doing it absentmindedly, admiring the beauty of the technicians' work. She wanted the knowledge behind each device, each computer, each cyborg... anything to soak up to better her sector. And as she gained that knowledge, she was calculating what magic she could infuse into the machines. Magic she had.

The thought of magical machines sent a warm fuzzy feeling through her spine, then into her lowers. Ikaria's eyes shone as she gazed upon the bodies of the men infused with dark metals, all while daydreaming of their weaponized machinery. A wicked look came over her, and lust for the machines burned inside.

Derek noticed her expression, shooting her a look. "Please keep your fantasies to yourself," he said in a low voice, making sure no one heard them. The head director and technicians were walking in a group with them, guiding them through the lab to show off his newly acquired cyborgs.

"Dear sweet Derek, don't be shy," Ikaria whispered, revealing a half-crooked smile. "I had to endure many days of your fantasies. You can at least allow me the pleasure for a quick moment, can't you?" she said, breathing in at the sights of the cyborgs. "Besides, it's not like you get to see mine. I think you would be rather shocked if you did."

Derek turned red, then lowered his eyes.

"Your Majesty, I was told by the Inner Council that you would be continuing Damaris's orders, that you would like to ready the army," Director Santiago called out.

"Correct," Derek answered. "However, the cyborgs being deployed will not be returning."

"Not be returning?" the head director parroted.

"Yes. My advisor here will be deploying them to York. Don't expect them to return."

Everyone in the group held their breath while Director Santiago's face stilled.

"Your Majesty? Are you sure about this? To put it bluntly, York is far less advanced than these machines. They do not have the technology to maintain them."

It's a good thing they won't be going to York. Won't the High Court be surprised? Ikaria laughed to herself, keeping a straight face to the director.

Ikaria interrupted. "I am sorry Director Santiago, but it is not your place to understand His Majesty's plans."

Derek flashed her an annoyed look.

The director bowed deeply, apologizing. "Your Majesty, I did not mean to be so... forward."

Derek nodded in a silent acceptance, trying to make peace of the situation. "You are fine, Director. Sometimes, my advisor is the one being a bit forward. Please excuse her. One might think she comes off a tad rude, but she means well," Derek said smoothly while giving Ikaria warning glances.

Santiago bowed, leading them further into the lab, to the heart of cyborg operations. Computers glowed, and the capsules emitted a bright blue; it was so beautiful to Ikaria. So many technicians running between capsules while others typed furiously on their keyboards.

"How did Drew work out for you? I had anticipated him being returned to the lab earlier, before the wedding. I know that Ms. Hearly is very interested in getting back to working on him," Santiago called out to Derek. "Hopefully, we can develop more of his kind now that he will be back in the lab."

"Really?" Ikaria raised an eyebrow, staring directly at Derek.

"Yes, really." Derek turned away, ignoring her. "The cyborg was a great help. I needed him as extra protection during the wedding, but he is no longer needed. I think he will be in good hands back here in the corporation with Ms. Hearly. As much as I would love to continue to use him in my service, I believe he will be of much more value here, where his gift can be put to better use. And thank you, Director, regarding Ms. Hearly."

"We were more than pleased to transfer Telly back to the cybernetic division. She is one of the best scientists we have. It was just a misunderstanding, that's all."

"Glad to hear that, Director."

"Ms. Hearly!" Santiago called out, looking around.

"Yes, Head Director?" a woman with mousy blonde cropped hair appeared.

"Assist Andrew back into his capsule. Get him fully hooked up and start a diagnostic scan."

"Yes, Head Director."

Returning the gifted cyborg back to the lab? What was Derek thinking? Obviously he wasn't, because that cyborg was going with Ikaria to the future. She had thought that the cyborg was just accompanying them for an adjustment. At least that was what Derek had made it sound like.

This is what happens when I leave his mind for just a few hours. He goes and screws everything up.

"Well, this is the first I have heard of this, Your Majesty," Ikaria said. "I believe that cyborg was coming with me to York."

Telly paused midstep, her eyes shooting from Ikaria to Derek, casting him a nervous glance. Drew's cybernetic eye made a shifting mechanical sound. This woman… she had the gift. But her gift was defective, just like Cyrus's. Not a true orange.

I see. This woman has an attachment to the cyborg. Well, not for long.

"That is not necessary, Ikaria. This one must continue to stay in Arcadia. You can choose any of the other cyborgs you please, but this one stays," Derek said strongly, flashing his icy-blue eyes at her.

"Your Majesty, he must come with us to York. If you want your plans to succeed, I beg you to reconsider," Ikaria said in a snide tone, choking on the word "beg." She'd never had to beg anyone in her life, even if she was faking it. It was so beneath her.

Derek shook his head. "No. That cyborg is not going with you to York."

Ikaria noticed that the female scientist breathed a small sigh of relief.

Over my dead body. There was no way that woman was going to keep that cyborg. Drew was coming with her.

Ikaria delved into Derek's mind, her force crashing in violently.

Don't make me make *you give the cyborg to me! I have been far too generous and accommodating to you, Ikaria told Derek in his mind while glaring at him. Besides, you have grown on me. I feel like we have gone through so much, you and I. Don't make me out to be the villain.*

Derek snorted in disbelief. He answered her back venomously. *Is this some kind of game to you? A joke? The reason why you are here in the first place, the only reason you obtained the green magic, was because of a promise I made to Ms. Hearly. She risked much to give me the princess's blood. You should be thanking Telly for her generosity!*

It's not my problem how you got the blood. You could have just cut the princess for all I care. But yet you chose to be difficult. I gave you more than enough to make this a trade in your favor. I am not *leaving this time without that cyborg! Now, are you going to comply?*

Derek's piercing blue eyes grew dark, filled with contempt, and his thick black eyelashes lowered. Even the curls on his head told Ikaria that he was angry at being backed into a corner.

Fine. Have it your way, he fiercely told her in his mind. *I just want you out of here as soon as you get your army, and leave me alone!*

Don't worry, I will be gone before you know it. Then you can return to having sex with your little queen doll. Do you have to tell her to moan for you?

Derek whipped around furiously, clenching his hands, turning to the directors. "I think my advisor has a point. Drew will be included with the cyborgs leaving Arcadia," he said.

The woman scientist's mouth dropped open, and her eyes began to well up with tears, but she held them back, standing still in front of the entourage.

Life isn't fair, my dear, Ikaria thought, smirking.

"I want the army readied as soon as possible!" Derek barked furiously. "I want this army on its way to York by this evening."

He stormed out of the lab, his guards hurrying behind him.

CHAPTER 75

ORANGE

After Derek's entourage left the building, Telly ran to her lab, slamming the door behind her, making the walls shudder.

I can't believe him!

Tears flowed down her face, as she began to weep uncontrollably, leaning against the door. She threw back one of her hands and punched the door hard.

He promised me!

Telly replayed the situation in her head over and over again. It had sounded like Derek was going to honor his end of the bargain, but something made him change his mind. After several attempts by his new advisor, he'd caved in, then left in a hurry.

The new advisor was odd. She had unique colorings. Violet hair and strange black eyes. Telly would have normally thought that the advisor's hair would have been dyed, as it was pretty customary for the fashions of Arcadia. And anyone could be born with dark eyes. But there was an overall eeriness to this advisor, and somehow Telly got a feeling that the sorceress's violet hair was far more than natural.

What if this advisor had the same type of powers as Drew, but a different color? Nobody had heard of this woman Ikaria before, even before the wedding. Telly would have thought that if Derek took on a new advisor, it would be all over the news and tabloids. Especially one as pretty as her.

The more Telly thought about Ikaria, the worse she felt.

She would never see Drew again.

Wiping her face, Telly got ahold of herself, fanning herself with her hands, hoping the soft air would evaporate her tears.

A clinking sound came from Drew's old capsule room, the sound of metal scraping metal, along with a heavy thud. Telly slowly walked to the observation window, suddenly a bit frightened, thinking again of the strange advisor. The thought of her in the lab made Telly anxious.

Peering into the glass, Telly saw flickering of orange light, with Drew inside the capsule.

Running as fast as she could, Telly scanned her keycard. The door slid up, and Telly burst through the entrance.

"Drew!" Telly shouted. Realizing she was being too loud, she lowered her voice. "What are you doing here?" she asked, not expecting him to answer. Her eyes glanced at the security camera in the corner. Drew's cybernetic eye glowed orange, then lasered the security camera with magic. Somehow, Telly got the hint that no one could see them on the camera anymore. "You heard the King. You are going with them to York."

"Neg... Negative," he stuttered, twitching.

Telly gasped, breathless at what she had just heard. He had talked!

"My God, Drew, how are you able to talk? Did someone else work on you while you were in the palace?"

"N... n... no. Queen Em... Emerald used h... her power in the f... frequency of 550. Slowly h-h-h-h... healing over time." His body shook as he talked. It was clearly an effort to simply say words. As he spoke, he flashed orange intermittently. "Ob... objective not York."

"Not going to York?" Telly asked breathlessly, then furrowed her eyebrows. "Then where *are* you going to?"

"F... future. No choice b... but to follow orders."

"Orders? Whose orders? *Hers?*" Telly asked, referring to the advisor.

"Affirmative. The master... m-m-m... must not travel." His body jolted mechanically again.

"Master?"

"Master of the gauntlet."

Telly's heart sunk into her stomach. The gauntlet. So they *had* made it without her knowing about it. Years ago, when it was first brought up within the corporation, they had asked her to be a part of the team behind it, since the cyborg creation was the combination of their work. But Telly didn't like the idea of one person being able to completely control of all the cyborgs at once, only those with a certain blood that passed down within the family.

But by the sound of it, the corporation had made it for Damaris anyway. It would only work for him and any offspring that he had, which meant Queen Emerald. After all, if the corporation made it how they originally intended, the gauntlet was most likely infused with the original donor's magical blood. Queen Emerald's blood. Given that her genetic makeup came from Damaris, it should only work for him and the Queen. But how was it that the advisor was able to use the gauntlet now?

"Drew, are you sure that the master is the King's advisor? It is impossible, unless they made some modifications to the project."

Drew shook, the mechanics in his arm twitching while his cybernetic eye adjusted. "The master has all frequencies of the sp-sp-sp-sp… spectrum. Absorbed… Queen Emerald's blood."

"But that shouldn't change the advisor's blood structure… should it?" Telly hesitated, doubting her knowledge. The Queen's blood was magical, after all. And the magic had a way of changing the body if it took to the person. She was living proof of that.

"Her b-b-blood is acceptable to the machines," he said.

His statement made her scared. If the advisor had more magic types than her and Drew, she was not a woman that Telly wanted to mess with. Even King Derek had given in to her.

Telly shook Drew's bicep anxiously. "Drew, what are we going to do? If they find out you are missing from the deployment of cyborgs, that woman will come after us." Telly paced around the capsuled room, formulating plans on how to get them out of the lab. They could use their magic and go invisible, but it wouldn't be long until Ikaria noticed. The way she'd looked at the directors sent chills down Telly's spine.

"Power. In the wavelength of 590 nanometers. P… projected image with group get-t-ting on transport t… to palace. F-f-f… final destination, future. C-c-c… cannot leave Gwen." His mechanical eye focused on Telly's. "Cannot leave you."

"You remember," she whispered. Her eyes locked on to his, and they both stared at each other for a minute. The way he was looking at her… It was like the old Drew was back for just that moment in time.

A single tear fell from her eyes, then she broke their gaze, hugging him tightly. She felt his cold mechanical hand lightly scrape her back, trying to awkwardly hold her, as he'd forgotten how.

But it gave her hope. More and more, he was coming back to her. His memories were being restored.

Drew let her go sharply as he jolted, having no control over his mechanical movements for a few seconds.

"Not much t… time until the master regains control of me. Must get Queen's blood. Now."

"Her blood?" Telly asked, confused. Why would he need her blood? "Drew, you know those samples are on lockdown."

"Need one hundred of them."

Telly's jaw dropped. "One hundred of them? Are you crazy? Do you want to get caught? Even with our magic, security will still detect our bodies. We won't make it out of here alive!"

Drew shook his head. "N… Negative. Not that blood." His cybernetic eye glowed orange, then he gave her a small hint of a smile. Did he really just *smile* at her?

"Then what blood?"

"The b-b-b… blood you stole."

Telly laughed in disbelief, shaking her head. "I only have two samples left! How is that going to equate to one hundred? You haven't even told me why you need it!"

"W… with my power."

"Your power?" she asked. "How is that possible? You can only make illusions."

"Negative. I c-c-c… c-c-c-aaaannnn…" He started to seize, causing Telly to immediately snatch the tablet from her bag and quickly connect a wire to establish a secure connection.

Drew jolted when the plug made contact, but then his body became calm. Telly tapped in some code, ensuring that their conversation was blocked.

"Drew, what were you saying?"

"*I can make transmutations.*"

Transmutations? The very thought would have been exciting to Telly if it weren't for the dilemma at hand.

"*Provide me the location of the samples, and I will do the rest,*" the words on the tablet appeared. "*I will also need supplies.*"

"Then what? You can't bring them back here."

"*No, I will go to the palace.*"

"And do what? You still haven't told me why you need it!"

"*The future. They are depending on me.*"

The future. The whole thing sounded crazy. Could he possibly be seeing other cyborgs' memories and images? Why was he acting out like this? He looked serious. Was that possible, considering he always looked serious as a cyborg?

Deep within her heart, Telly believed him. It defied all reason, but she believed.

Turning to Drew, she whispered, "Do you remember our apartment?"

He nodded.

"The samples are in the refrigerator," she said quietly, hugging him one last time. "Please hurry. I don't want them to notice that you aren't with the others. I would hate to think what would happen if that woman found out."

"*I will.*"

His frozen face cracked a smile, making her heart leap at the sight of his face appearing more human, a human with emotions. A warm orange glow surrounded him, his body disappearing.

"Please, be careful," she whispered under her breath.

Words appeared on her tablet.

"*I will. For you.*"

***

He paused in front of the door to their old apartment. No one had seen him, as he was shielded by his power of invisibility. Why was he hesitating?

Malfunction.

He was acting of his own will, not on the master's orders. This was not a part of the program. But the master had said for him to protect Derek and Emerald until the wedding. He had no new direct orders now that they were married, and somehow the master felt detached from him, leaving his circuits to his own devices.

The dream troubled him, and it would continue to haunt him until he completed his assigned task. The one that the future people were depending on.

Gently guiding one of his mechanical metal fingers to the keyhole, he pressed his fingertip, calling upon the surging power that beat through his veins. Not the power that came from his circuitry but the one that came from deep within.

He faded into view while his fingertip glowed with orange magic. Releasing the coursing magic within, his finger morphed, turning into the shape of a key. Turning the lock with his fingertip, Drew opened the door, stepping inside.

The apartment looked very similar to what was stored in his memories. Same color walls, same furniture, same pictures that decorated the mantle. Even the air felt… familiar.

Familiar?

Malfunction.

He jolted.

Drew set down the backpack that he was carrying, filled with vials and syringes that he had snatched from the corporation. It was needed.

What are you doing? called a voice from within the network.

The master will find out, chanted another.

The master won't find out, because you will not alert her, Drew countered.

That may be true, but what happens if she asks us directly? We must answer the master, cried another voice within the computerized stream.

You had better hope she doesn't become aware of your whereabouts.

Ignoring the voices, Drew stumbled into the kitchen. He spotted the refrigerator, then hurled the door open with his metal hand, swinging it wildly. He batted the flinging door with his mechanical hand, halting it. Condiment bottles and a carton of milk rattled from the motion.

Drew scanned the contents of the refrigerator with his cybernetic eye. The two vials of blood sat on a shelf on their own. They weren't hard to spot since there was hardly any food in there to begin with. What did Telly and Gwen eat?

Malfunction.

Glitching at the thought, Drew snatched the blood with his good hand, setting them on the countertops as delicately as he could. Turning to the cabinets, he ripped them open, looking for something to mix the blood in. Most of the cabinets were also empty, but he did manage to find a pitcher.

He filled it to the brim with water, then emptied one of the blood samples into it. The blood lightly danced within the water, streaming its glowing color through the clear liquid. The visual delighted him.

Delight. Delight.

Cannot process that request.

He jolted.

Malfunction.

Placing one of his good fingers within the pitcher, he thought of his old life. He only had fragments of it, but he tried to recall them as they came. Images of the times he was outside in his former life. It made him feel so alive. The sunlight beating on his face in the heat of the summer. So warm. So human. It filled him with joy. Telly was always with him in his memories, holding Gwen as she cooed. She calmed him with her smiling eyes.

Malfunction.

Her smiling eyes.

Malfunction.

His body shook. He was at the start of an overload, but he continued to focus, struggling against the machine within him.

Her smiling eyes. Her presence. The tenderness of her voice. It filled him with elation.

The swelling energy of joy slowly pumped through his veins, gathering to his finger. Machines didn't feel anything, nor could they. Everything was artificial, like how half his thoughts were. But something had happened when the Queen tried to heal him. His voice wasn't completely restored, but his human side was returning to him at a much faster rate than before. He *felt* more than he ever had. His feelings were *real*. He had retained some aspects of his emotions when he was resurrected, but his calculations told him it was about ten to fifteen percent of a normal human's.

But now, since Queen Emerald had laid her hands on him, his scans told him he was sixty percent more human. If he could be changed by her power, the others of his kind could, in theory, be changed too.

When Drew swelled with as much power as he could contain, he unleashed the joy that radiated from him, and the energy expelled itself into the pitcher.

An orange glow filled the entire pitcher as he began to stir the mixture with his fingertip. The water and blood illuminated an orange color as he stirred. The circular movements of his finger swishing through the mixture, and a small whirlpool within appeared. The liquid slowed its movement, then settled, the orange dissipating into a deep red, still having a slight glow to it. Transmuted blood, exactly the same as Queen Emerald's original blood.

Satisfied with the result, he looked for another pitcher for another batch to mix. There was none, so Drew picked up his pack, grabbing the syringes. One by one, he filled them until there was no more blood in the pitcher. He then began the second batch, repeating the process. After he was done with the second, he distributed the second batch of blood into the rest of the empty syringes.

One hundred vials of blood exactly. It was the perfect amount that was required.

He packed the syringes into his bag, then slung the bag strap across his chest, turning to leave.

A small figure stood in the doorway, blocking his way.

Drew immediately ran a scan. Girl in her teens. Same age and birthday. The information made his circuits run haywire, causing him to shudder.

Gwen.

Shaking, Gwen held a communication device, her eyes wide. "Whoever you are, I am dialing the authorities!"

Drew's good hand snatched the device with precise movement, and Gwen shrieked. The girl took a step back while he placed the communication device in his metal hand, smashing it in his grasp.

"Please, don't hurt me!" the girl cried.

Unsure of what to do, Drew stood there silently, unmoving, watching his daughter. Should he say something?

"Take whatever you want," Gwen continued. "I promise I won't tell anyone that you were here. Just don't kill me." Her eyes stared at his metal hand, terrified.

"N-n-n... never h-h-h... hurt you."

"Then what do you want?"

"Blood."

The teen cried again. "So you *are* here to kill me!"

"No. B-b-b... blood samples."

Gwen blinked at him with bloodshot eyes, breathing a sigh of relief. "Mom's blood samples?" She lowered her voice, leaning in. "Are you one of her experiments?"

Drew nodded.

"I knew it!" Gwen's face lit up, smiling. "Mom would never tell me what she did at work, but I always had an idea." She scrunched up her face. "Why do you look so creepy?"

Drew cocked his head.

"You know, how half your face full of wires and computer parts. Why were you designed like that?"

Drew processed a response, jolting. "Ac-c-c... accident. Years ago. H-h-h... hhhhhalf died. Half lived."

Malfunction.

Drew glitched violently.

The teen looked at him, and her eyes went wide. There was some sort of recognition in her face as she gaped at him, approaching him cautiously.

"You can't be him... can you?"

For the first time, Drew felt frightened. Frightened by his emotions. By the situation.

He stood unusually still.

Malfunction.

Gwen moved closer, circling as she continued to study him. Her hair was the same as Telly's—soft honey blonde. But she had his eyes before the accident. Blue. Light blue. Her jeans were ripped, and she wore a loose graphic T-shirt, her hair pulled back in a ponytail.

"You have to be him. You look just like him in our pictures."

Drew remained unmoving.

Was his heart beating rapidly? Or were his circuits sparking in confusion? Why didn't he say anything?

Gwen looked at him as she curiously inspected his metal arm, running her hands over the metal. Gwen paused, then teared up. "Why didn't Mom ever say anything to me about you?" She let go of his metal arm, her tears falling. "It figures she wouldn't say anything. She never does," she said angrily.

Something in his wires... No, his heart, urged him. Placing a hand on her shoulder, he rested it there. As soon as his hand touched her, Gwen burst out crying, then latched on to him quickly, falling into his arms, hugging him. Her shoulders shook as she sobbed. He placed his other metal hand on her gently, holding her. Holding his daughter.

"I... I thought... thought of y-y-y... you every day when I was r-r-r... restored."

Gwen's blue eyes looked up at him, as she wiped her tears. "Are you back for good now?"

Drew nodded. "Yes, b-b-b… but I m-m-m… must do something first."

Gwen shifted her foot, thinking. "After you're done, will you live with me and Mom?"

"I… I… do not know."

The teen gave him another quick hug. Drew awkwardly returned her affection, but his motions were more mechanical than he intended. Gwen let go, then stepped away, waiting for him to leave.

"Will I at least see you again?"

Drew nodded, giving his daughter an unpracticed smile. "I… I will do w-w-w… whatever I can."

Gwen returned his smile, wiping away her tears. He looked at her, memorizing the moment.

Then Drew summoned his bright-orange power, basking fully in its glow. Slowly, the magic began to fade him away.

Gwen gasped, surprised at the fantastical display of magic. He heard her utter the word "whoa" as he made his way to the door.

CHAPTER 76

RED

Ruby lightning flashed across the skies every few seconds while thunder rumbled loudly. Deep-red clouds formed in the dark morning skies. The storms were groaning outwardly from what he was yearning for inwardly.

His heart yearned for Emerald.

It was like a thousand knives had stabbed him, gutting his insides out. The prince. The damn motherfucking prince. He'd had his way with her. With Emerald. Did she know? Was she stuck inside, watching what was happening to her? Watching what he did to her while her body did nothing she told it to? God, it made him want to *kill* the motherfucker.

No, not want. He was *going* to murder that piece of shit. Murder him until there was nothing left that resembled that coward. But before he did, he had to make sure Emerald was safe. He had wasted too much damn time training with Geeta, and now he'd paid the price. If only he had taken off before Geeta unfroze the world, he could have stopped Derek from…

GOD DAMMIT!

With the staff in hand, Kyle continued to let the crimson winds guide him as he scanned the city below. The morning storm clouds cloaked the city in gray. The brightness of the neon lights glimmered in the falling rains and hazy atmosphere. Where should he even begin to search for Emerald? His best bet was the palace. Kyle turned his attention in the direction of the palace. It glowed with its electric-green glass panels, looming over the city. He would need to find her quickly. And it would be a task in itself to find her in the city's largest structure.

Something in the air unsettled him. Kyle could feel the magic inside of his life-force stirring, warning him about what was about to take place.

Pushing back the unnerving thought, Kyle closed his eyes, taking in a deep breath as he hovered midair. He focused on the thought of Emerald. The complement made for him. His love, his life, his soul. She was all he wanted in life. Forget the damn guitar, motorcycle, being famous—those things were nothing. They couldn't bring the happiness the way she did when she smiled.

Instead of letting his logic try to figure out how to find her, Kyle opened his heart, letting the magic lead him. As his heart pounded with each beat, an overwhelming sensation pulled at him from within. The magic within sought out its other half, the green magic it so needed to be complete. Greater and greater, the need for his complement flowed through his being, until the desire coursed through his blood from all directions, centering within his life-force. The feeling mixed with his red magic, taking over. Kyle closed his eyes and fully submitted to the wind.

He felt his body change course to a new direction.

Opening his eyes, Kyle saw that he was heading straight toward the palace's highest turret. The orb on the staff shifted to an intense, fiery red, burning with his power.

She must be there!

As he neared the palace, Kyle called out for his adjacent color, orange, making him unseen to all the world. Emerald's balcony was in sight, not too far off. The closer he came to it, the more he began to tremble, and his heart raced with anticipation. Another rumble in the skies. A red bolt of lightning flashed. The red rains drenched him, responding to his anguished heart.

In the distance, Emerald appeared on her balcony, viewing the dark morning skies as if she was staring into a dream.

Kyle lost his breath. It had been almost a year since he had seen her. Just the sight of her calmed his heart, causing the rains to cease.

She was more beautiful than he remembered. She was dressed in delicate pale purples and magentas, so much lovelier than the stars that adorned the night sky. Her face shone softly, and her hair flowed like a gentle river at peace. But underneath, deep within her soul, Kyle felt the turmoil in her heart.

The red rushing winds landed him on her balcony, off to the side. From his gust of wind, Emerald's hair flew back softly, then the green waves settled once more at her sides.

Emerald was oblivious to his arrival, as Kyle was still as transparent as the air itself. Or was it that she was too far gone in Ikaria's control to understand what was happening around her?

"Emerald," Kyle said quietly as he began to release his adjacent magic.

She turned slowly at the sound of his voice. "Who's there?" her monotonous voice answered. She continued to glance around until her vacant eyes met his. "*You.* You were the one at my wedding," she said in an unseemly accusing tone. She turned her body fully toward him, the silk fabrics spinning around her.

Kyle wiped the rainwater off his face, then reached out his hand toward her, softening his voice. "It's time you came back to me."

Emerald's eyes flared a menacing, glowing dark green.

Life-draining magic shot out from her hand and into his heart, ebbing away his life-force. Immense pain twisted his flesh on the inside, like a knife spinning and peeling his innards away.

Fighting through the agony, Kyle gripped the staff, calling forth his violet magic. The orb changed its hue from red to red-violet, burning with magic. Within the blink of an eye, Kyle's consciousness was thrown into Emerald's mind, just like how he trained with Geeta.

Kyle's spirit felt an instant disconnection from his body and the new host of Emerald. He peered around her mind, looking for a way to dive further in. It was nothing but a deep-green barren wasteland, no doubt from Ikaria's void magic. No doors, no walls, just one vast plain of pure nothingness. In the center of the wasteland was her consciousness, in the form of a large green gem. An emerald, glowing a bright hot greenish-white color.

Encircling the emerald was a swirling black-violet force of energy. Ikaria's magic.

As Kyle's spirit neared the gem, he could see an image of Emerald's spirit encased within, pounding from the inside.

Help... her mind called out to his spirit.

Seeing her soul in despair inflamed him. His soul roared. He yelled harder and louder than he ever had in his life.

Summoning his magic, Kyle outstretched his hands, continuing to yell in desperation. Red-violet magic surged at the dark magic's barrier in a constant, streaming force.

As Kyle's magic shot itself at the barrier, the dark force field fought back, pulling all of the black from its black-violet magic to the spot where Kyle surged his power, leaving the rest of the barrier violet. Kyle probed the stream of magic. The barrier was reinforcing itself, strengthening the magic that guarded Emerald's spirit. Within the gem, Emerald was mouthing silent screams in between her cries.

Kyle grimaced through his roars as he continued to pour out his magic with all his might. The barren ground started to shake beneath his feet, and he felt the barrier weaken, but it did not break.

He wasn't going to give up until Emerald was free, even if it meant that he had to spend his whole damn life inside her mind.

Pulling everything he had in his life-force, he pushed aside his anger and his joy, fully allowing jealousy and hatred to rush through his being, embracing the raw emotion.

The constant stream of magic from his power turned from red-violet to pure violet. The barrier let out a loud crack in response as he continued to flood his magic at it. The dark-green wasteland world turned black as night, and the barren world groaned in agony, then began quaking violently.

More cracks appeared on the magical barrier, and the sounds from the fracture echoed across the voided land. Kyle grunted but held fast.

Kyle felt Emerald's mind became unstable as the wasteland continued to tremor vigorously. Her spirit and the gem glowed a bright white; Emerald's spirit was emerging.

You are in control! his spirit called out to her.

Waiting until the last second, Kyle shot out the remainder of his magic, all that he had left in his life-force. Upon contact, the barrier shattered like thin glass, striking Emerald's consciousness awake. Calling upon his power once again, he left her mind, jumping his consciousness back into his own body.

Emerald screamed. Her mind was awakened.

Kyle stumbled for a moment, accidentally dropping the staff. He was breathing hard at the expense of his magic and from Emerald's magic preying on his life-force.

Emerald cradled her forehead with both her hands, dropping to the floor, then ripped the crown from her forehead, throwing it to the ground. The circlet skidded across the floor, the dark magic fading away sharply. Her eyes suddenly became clear, and the pupils within her green depths became visible.

"Kyle?" She turned and faced him, a look of recognition appearing on her face. "It's really you!" Tears formed as she ran breathlessly to embrace him.

Kyle held out his arms weakly, still breathing heavily. She fell into his arms, and he gripped her tightly. Her body trembled, then she began to sob.

"Kyle... something happened," her voice jittered through her cries.

"I know." He held her tight in his arms. "It's not your fault, Em," he whispered to her. "You had no control. Absolutely no control."

"Please don't ever leave my side," she whispered through stiff cries.

"Never. I will *never* leave you again. I promise."

Kyle softly caressed her smooth cheek, then brushed away her tears with his fingertips. Emerald looked up at him, then caught her breath. She placed one of her hands on the hand wiping the tears away, then held it there.

She stopped crying, and for a moment, her soul was at peace. Just for a moment.

Emerald leaned in to him, her lips touching his, then she closed her eyes, kissing him deeply. Kyle could feel her love for him, but he could also feel her sorrow and hatred. His heart raced at the slightest movement of her hands, his body trembling at her touch. If only he had been able to stop Derek in time...

After a moment, she pulled away gently, studying him with her intense eyes. "What happened to you? You look... different." She ran a hand through his crimson hair.

"Well, someone has to be the redhead around here," he said.

Emerald smiled softly, then giggled under her breath. He had not meant for it to be a joke, considering the moment, but luckily it distracted Emerald from her heavy heart.

"I like it." She skimmed her right hand across his rugged face, then lightly touched his lips and jaw. "Your face, though... It's... changed somehow. I can't quite tell what it is, though."

"I aged."

"How?"

"Through another person's magic. She froze time while my life continued," Kyle explained. "We had to make sure that I had enough understanding of my power before I came for you. The last time, I got my ass handed to me."

Emerald stared at him, then her eyes watered. "Was it because of me?"

"Well, you and everyone else. Four against one isn't really good odds."

"I'm so sorry," she whispered, lowering her head.

Kyle held her once more, kissing her forehead. "There is no reason to apologize, it's not your fault. Don't ever think otherwise. I won't let any of those assholes have any power over you ever again."

She turned to him with a look of alarm on her face. "We should leave now, before that wicked woman comes back. Or Derek."

Derek. That name infuriated him.

Holding her face gently with both of his hands, Kyle leaned in, his forehead touching hers, whispering, "Em, we have to defeat that bitch-ass Ikaria. But before we do, I need to know if you can summon your other two colors, yellow and blue." He brushed her hair with his silver-ringed fingers.

She looked at him, then thought hard, and finally nodded. "I think so. I have done it before; I am sure I can do it again."

"I believe in you," Kyle said, feeling the flames come alive within his crimson eyes. "When I say so, you need to hold on to the staff and do it."

"I will," Emerald said assuredly.

Kyle held her hands, helping her to her feet. "I will make sure you are as far away from that bitch as possible, but we have to get close enough to focus our magic," he said as he grabbed the staff off the floor.

Emerald nodded.

Kyle looked at her, then turned his thoughts to get to where Geeta told him to meet her. The royal palace platform, wherever that was.

Kyle's stomach became knots all over again. The bad feeling returned.

Ignoring the warning from within, Kyle continued, "Em, we need to get to the royal transport platform. Can you guide us there?"

Emerald smiled, blushing. "I can take us there with my magic."

She held out her hand, and as he took it, he smiled back at her. God, it felt good to be with her. He felt so… complete.

Squeezing his hand, Emerald closed her eyes, concentrating on her analogous powers. Kyle knew she was trying to summon the gift of the blue. Her face contorted as she fought to summon it.

Slowly, a green-blue glow emitted from her, then extended through their hands. As they held each other, the power surged through them, radiating brightly. Then they flashed green-blue, disappearing from Emerald's balcony.

CHAPTER 77

ORANGE

Telly's communication device chimed. Head Director Santiago had messaged the corporation: All remaining cyborgs that were scheduled for York needed to be loaded in the next batch of ships, and the head staff was to report to the docks to assist with the loading process. Immediately.

Drew wasn't back yet. King Derek's advisor would notice. She watched her surroundings, her eyes keen. Hopefully the woman hadn't discovered Drew's illusion on the platform above, or else Telly knew that she would end up dealing with the consequences.

Telly gulped, nervously staring at the director's message. Her heart raced in her chest while she nervously adjusted her glasses.

Come on, Telly, she told herself. *Just get to the docks and don't go near the advisor. That's all you have to do.* It was much easier telling herself the plan than actually doing it.

Taking a deep breath, Telly emerged from another cyborg holding room and walked into one of the main labs, making her way to the elevators. She passed by the other technicians, watching them make their preparations, unplugging the cyborgs from their glowing blue capsules. Some moved much more robotically than Drew, others moved like humans, as each of them were different percentages of human. After all, the corporation had had to replace bad human organs in the subjects as well as enhance them. They needed them to last as long as possible and be in prime condition.

Telly knew that she'd taken too long to wait for Drew down in Lab 34 and that the head director, along with Derek's advisor, was most likely getting impatient. Others were also behind schedule, as she saw some of the cyborgs malfunctioning as they were being unplugged from the mainframe, having to then be replaced with different fully functioning cyborgs to meet Derek's quota.

A vibrating buzz came from within Telly's lab coat pocket.

Great, just what I need, more frantic messages from the head director.

Telly anxiously pulled out her device as she and the other technicians filed into the elevator, every one of them swiping their ID cards. Casually looking down at her device, Telly gasped.

Meet me on the platform across from the palace's royal transport platform. I need your help.

There was no callback number, no contact information, no trace.

Drew. He'd hacked the communication networks.

Quickly deleting the message, Telly stuffed her device back into her pocket, hoping no one had seen it over her shoulder.

How was she going to make it to that platform? Any platform anywhere near the vicinity of the palace was heavily monitored and guarded. Unless…

Sighing, she knew what she had to do. One of these days, she was going to get caught with how much she pushed her luck. She had already been extremely lucky that Derek hadn't had her arrested when she appeared in his transport before. Now this…

The elevator climbed to the heights of the corporation building, then dinged, opening its doors to reveal the loading platform docks. There were several air transports docked on the oversized platform, waiting for the precious cargo to be shipped off to York. Or to the future as Drew believed.

As Telly walked out onto the platform, she saw King Derek and his advisor, Ikaria, waiting outside their transport, surrounded by many of the corporation's directors. The advisor's strange black eyes sparkled with delight, a huge grin on her face. She didn't say anything but stood there proudly, as if she were someone with more authority than the King himself.

Telly lowered her gaze, walking to the other side of the platform, where Director Jonathan was, trying to avoid the advisor noticing her. Jonathan was loading a line of cyborgs into one of the transports.

"Telly, help that transport out over there; they're taking too long getting the cyborgs loaded. Sometimes it amazes me the level of incompetence in individuals of such high IQs," Jonathan said, helping the next cyborg get loaded in line. "You'd think they would have enough common sense to get the job done quickly."

Telly smiled nervously, nodding in response, then made her way over to the transport that Jonathan pointed to. It was closer to the King and his advisor, but luckily the loading door was on the other side of the royal party.

There was already another director helping load the cyborgs when Telly approached. He noticed Telly, nodded silently, and continued to guide the cyborgs inside the ship, leaving Telly outside of the vehicle.

"Is this all five hundred of them?" Telly heard Derek's voice call out from behind the transport she was helping with.

"Yes, Your Majesty," answered Head Director Santiago's voice. "I apologize that we were a bit behind schedule, as there were a few issues with a couple of them."

"Understood. Just get the rest of them loaded, and ready the transports."

Derek came into Telly's view, along with the advisor. Through the corner of Telly's eye, she saw Ikaria strut by one of the cyborgs in line, her hand playfully touching the machine's chest. Briskly walking over to her, Derek slapped her hand away, giving her a dirty look. Ikaria smiled sweetly, almost so sweet it was sarcastic.

"Don't get any sick ideas," the King muttered under his breath.

Ikaria laughed, then said something quietly back to him, but Telly couldn't hear what she said. But what she said made Derek turn red in the face, and he turned away from her.

Pretending that Telly hadn't heard their exchange, she made herself look busy with the other cyborgs, helping them get loaded onto the ships. There was a good number of palace guards helping the directors get the cyborgs loaded, then they boarded the transports themselves. Several of the ships were ready for takeoff, starting their engines.

The other director that was helping Telly load was suddenly called over to another transport, leaving Telly by herself.

Now's my chance!

Turning her head around, she saw that all of the scientists and directors were too busy paying attention to the King or busy loading the remaining cyborgs.

Shaking from her nerves, Telly called forth the unsettling power from within her.

Quickly! she demanded of her magic.

Telly saw her hands disappear along with the remainder of her body with a flash of pale-orange magic. The remaining cyborgs in her line stared in her direction but otherwise made no movement or indication; they simply waited for their orders.

Slipping inside the transport, Telly pushed her way through the standing cyborgs toward the middle, crouching by their feet, then settling there.

"Where's Telly?" she heard Jonathan's voice call outside of the transport door. "Wow, did she really just leave in the middle of loading?" he grumbled to someone she couldn't see. "Get inside," he called out to the remaining cyborgs. Telly heard a shove as the last three of them settled inside, and the door sealed shut.

The noise of the ship's takeoff burned in Telly's ear as they moved into the air.

CHAPTER 78

THE SPECTRUM

Auron walked among the other gifted, all of them traveling through a vast space of galaxies, stars, and magical portals as Vala led the way. Some were excited, talking in exhilarating whispers about traveling through time. Others were nervous, trailing silently behind the group. But how Vala managed to scrounge up more gifted than what Auron initially asked her for was beyond him.

Not only had his niece convinced some of the gifted in her court to aid World Sector Six in their most desperate hour, but she also persuaded several other of the world sectors' gifted as well. Vala had always been keen on conversation, arguments, and persuasion, but this took her skills to a whole new level. In fact, if she were to stand in front of the God of Light himself, Auron was sure she would be able to convince him to grant her the gift of the red, telling him he'd made a simple error in choosing her color.

It was surreal to Auron that he was traveling to another time for others to live and for him to die. It was truly moving that the gifted that surrounded him were willing to give their lives so time could continue and the future Earth could exist, even when they knew the ultimate outcome. The concept left Auron feeling melancholy.

Geeta had returned to Ayera and the court just moments before they left, informing them that they should meet her and the Ghost Man back in the past at a different time than what was first agreed upon. It wasn't by much, but Auron still had a premonition that something was not right, whether it be the new time or what his visions were telling him.

All through the night and into the morning before they departed from their time, the visions continued to hammer at Auron, haunting his every thought. The screams. That was the worst part, the screams. He knew what the visions meant—that all the future gifted would perish in the past. But it was inevitable. His visions always came to pass, and Auron knew deep down he would have only several minutes of life when they exited the space-time continuum.

Auron saw Vala's silhouette against a large brilliant vivid portal that rippled black-violet, pulsating between the two colors.

Ikaria's portal.

She turned back to Auron, then eyed him. "We are here. Are you ready?"

Auron's heart beat quickly. He said a final silent prayer to the God of Light, asking if there was anything that he could do to intervene on the deaths of the future gifted. But as much as he prayed, he knew that it wouldn't change the God of Light's decision. They were all going to die; the God of Light had told him prophetically.

Auron nodded, giving Vala the signal to continue her spell.

Vala hesitated, then closed her eyes, taking a deep breath. A blue glowing magic began to surround the group, enveloping them entirely, like mist from a fog. The blue burned brighter, and the galaxies and the stars started to spin, blurring into the vibrant blue magic. The stream of light swirled faster, until space and stars were replaced with azure light.

Suddenly Auron felt no ground beneath his feet, and his stomach jumped into his throat at the sensation. He was falling. Falling through the endless blue space.

The momentum of his fall increased, and an intense pressure weighed on Auron's chest. His consciousness faded from the pressure, and he could no longer breathe. Through the endless fall into the blue, the bodies of the other gifted began to glow their respective gifted colors.

Then his body burst with his magic, radiating a bright yellow.

***

Leaning against of one of the palace turrets, Geeta waited for the future gifted to arrive. The red rains pattered against her, and every so often she wiped her face with her arm. She was soaked but tried not to think of her discomfort.

What was taking them so long? The future gifted should be here already. Had something gone wrong? She kept scanning her eyes across each of the palace platforms, waiting for any sign of the time portals to appear, but none came. Only then did she notice some odd movement across the royal transport platform. A plant, bumped by an invisible force, shook then stilled. Geeta wondered if it was the gifted she was waiting for, but there was no other indication. Frowning, she continued to scour the area.

Suddenly, the red rains ceased. Geeta smiled inwardly, knowing the reason why.

Something caught her eye far off in the horizon. The sun peeked through the dark clouds, and a bright white flash twinkled for a split second.

As she watched the direction of the flash, black specks appeared. They continued to grow larger, heading in her direction.

A sense of dread came over her. It was Ikaria's power within that mass of black flying in Arcadia's skies. Closer and closer they came. They were no longer black specks, and as they came into view, Geeta saw they were air transports, the largest ones she had ever seen.

Hurry, Auron!

The first of the transports arrived, docking on the platform. Derek and Ikaria emerged from the ships, along with a host of cyborgs.

Those mechanical men… She's taking them to the future!

Ikaria briskly walked past the cyborgs and stopped in the middle of the platform. She extended both of her hands to the skies above as a black glow enveloped her. Dark magical winds came rushing past the cyborgs and gathered to where Ikaria was standing, circling the platform. The black winds funneled into one place, then formed a large portal.

It rippled in front of Ikaria, black with violet sparkles. The sun went behind the morning clouds again, causing the city to fall back into darkness, giving the illuminating portal a more demanding and ominous presence. The palace guards stood amazed, staring at the whirlpool of time, as the black-and-violet glows danced on the platform. They were in awe but not completely fazed by Ikaria's magic.

They have seen magic before, Geeta noted. *Probably from the princess.*

Ikaria extended her right hand, showing the cyborgs what was on it. A metal gauntlet. There was an orb in the middle of the outward part of her hand, glowing with a black intensity.

"All of you are now under my command," she said. "You will travel with me through the portal. Once you are on the other side, you are to wait for me. If anyone engages in a fight with you, you need no longer wait for me. Instead, I want you to obliterate them." She gazed down the rows, eyes glowing an eerie black. "Do not fail me."

The cyborgs began to line up in formation on the platform. Upon more shouts from Ikaria, they began marching toward the black-violet whirlpool of light, basking themselves within the color, and the first of them faded away.

Derek walked up to her briskly, pushing aside his cape.

"Why did you lie to me about that thing on your hand?" Derek demanded.

"I told no lie, sweet King."

"That thing…" he said. "It controls this whole army! Why didn't you say anything to me about that? I have a right to know. I am the king of Arcadia now!"

"What do you care? I specifically remember you telling me that you wanted these cyborgs gone. What does it matter to you how I go about your wishes?" Ikaria shrugged, turning away from Derek.

The sorceress's plan would fail, Geeta thought. The cyborgs would crumble away when they traveled through time. They couldn't withstand it, could they?

That bad feeling returned. Her veins began to burn with a warm feeling, a tingle of yellow magic that came to her every so often.

No vision accompanied the magic, but a sense. A sense that those human-machines *would* survive.

Scared at the thought, Geeta cursed in her mind. *Auron, what are you doing? Ikaria is already starting to send them through the time portal!*

Geeta knew she couldn't wait for them any longer. With or without the future gifted, she had to stop Ikaria from sending the cyborgs, and herself, through time.

Kyle's voice rang in Geeta's head. *You're fucked,* he would say.

Yes, I am, she told herself.

There was no sight of Kyle, either. Everyone was taking too long.

Just when Geeta was about to summon her space-dimensional magic, a bright blue portal appeared on an adjacent platform, streaks of bright ruby light shooting out of it.

Geeta's heart quickened at the sight. It was the gifted from the future, flying through their summoned portal. The red-gifted that shot through first burned brightly with their magic and a trail behind them, like loose fireworks gone awry.

Without waiting a moment longer, Geeta summoned her dimensional traveling magic, bathing herself in an intense violet, then jumped off the turret, disappearing.

It was time to confront Ikaria.

***

Telly felt the transport land, then the rumble of the engines ceased and the transport doors opened. The cyborgs began exiting the vehicle, giving Telly some space, allowing her to stretch from being cramped up inside.

As the last of the cyborgs departed, Telly walked beside one of them, still surrounded in her invisibility. Making haste down the ramp of the transport, Telly froze in place.

A giant black-violet glowing portal swirled at the center of the royal platform. In the distance, she could hear the advisor yelling out orders for the cyborgs.

My God... Telly sucked in her breath. *That's how the units are going to the future!*

The colorful portal suddenly made her very afraid. She had already been frightened by the advisor, but Telly now understood the vast power Ikaria had.

Telly looked around all the surrounding platforms within the area. There were a couple of close ones that Drew could possibly be on, but one in particular was closer than the others. If she had to guess, Drew would probably be on the closest one. But now how to get over there?

Walking as silently as she could, Telly neared the edge of the royal platform where the guardrails were. Overhead, more ships were flying in and landing on the royal platform.

Drew, how am I supposed to get over there? Telly asked herself.

Then there was a bright blue flash where the adjacent platform was, and red streaks came shooting out of it.

Blinded by the brightness, Telly covered her glasses from the radiance. With a sudden force, a body collided with hers, snatching her up. The winds raced against her as the body held her. A mechanical hand rested against her back, holding her tightly as they flew through the air.

"Drew!"

Telly saw the outline of his hand wrapped around her, radiating orange power. The rest of him was still masked with his magic. Was it that her magic made it so that she could detect him?

They landed on the adjacent platform as the newly formed second portal rippled, shooting out reds, oranges, yellows, and blues. Telly looked around wildly, not believing what she was seeing, releasing her magic.

Drew came into focus as his orange magic dissipated. He yanked the bag that was strapped on him, then flopped it open, revealing blood-filled syringes. He grabbed a couple, handing them over to her.

"What am I supposed to do with these?" Telly asked, her head turning to look at the colors streaming out of the portal.

"I-i-i-n-n-n... inject the f-f-f... future gifted," Drew stuttered, his circuits jolting.

"But how are we supposed to get their attention?"

A black force rocked the buildings all around the palace, as if an earthquake rocked the area. Telly and Drew stumbled to the ground for a moment, the syringes falling out of the bag and rattling around the platform.

"I will get t-t-t... them. You inject."

Drew closed his eyes, resting his hands on his forehead, glowing a bright orange. Then he flew up into the sky.

***

Auron's eyes shot open, acutely aware that he was not falling but flying. He felt a strong grip on him. A human hand, and... was it *metal*?

His eyes darted across the strange hand, running his gaze up the arm. The arm had... technology? Was he in the arms of a *machine*? Mixed with a *human*?

The machine noticed that Auron was awake and gripped him tighter.

"Let go of me!" Auron demanded.

A mechanical eye flashed orange. "No," it responded.

Auron pushed within the machine's powerful grip, trying to pry the machine's hands off him. The machine's grip held firm. "Do n-n-n... not force. Need blood."

"What did you say?"

"Y-y-y... you need blood."

Did this *thing* have what the future gifted needed... the green-gifted blood? Was this the answer to his prayers?

The machine looked away, quickly guiding Auron to an aerial platform attached to a tall structure. Was this what the past really looked like? Auron marveled at the architecture, but then reminded himself that all that he saw was to be decimated in the future. All because of their arrogance in technology.

They landed on the platform near a bright blue portal. The future gifted continued to shoot out of the gateway, out of control from the eternal fall from Vala's spell. Auron watched as a few of the red and blue gained control of themselves, then went after the oranges and yellows who couldn't fly or move dimensionally.

A woman wearing strange glass rims around her eyes ran up to the machine, carrying a heavy bag.

"Inject," the machine told the woman, pointing to Auron.

The woman nodded, her eyes wide in wonder. Auron noticed her eyes were pale orange behind her glass mechanism.

"I need your arm. Please roll up your sleeve," instructed the woman.

"Is that... blood of the green gift in that device?" Auron asked, frightened at the sight of the glass vessel holding the blood.

"Yes. Now hold still. It will only take a second to administer. It might help if you take a deep breath when I say when."

The woman held up the blood device as Auron glanced at her curiously. "How did you know that we needed the blood?" he asked, still confused as to what was going on.

The woman looked toward the machine. "He had a dream about it. When."

He forgot to breathe and let out a loud yelp in response, flinching as the sharp needle stuck him.

"I told you to breathe in when I said when," the woman said, shrugging.

Auron turned his attention back to the woman in disbelief. "That machine? He had a dream about the blood? Truly?"

"Yes. He was quite adamant about it. He had an overwhelming feeling that he needed to help the future," the woman said, rolling up Vala's sleeve. "We have enough for a hundred of you."

A machine helping us? Did the God of Light intend that? Machines and technology are inherently evil…

As Vala was given the blood injection, Auron turned to her. "Get the word out to the other gifted as quickly as possible about the blood of the green," Auron ordered. "The machine and the woman have enough for everyone. No one is to be left behind."

"Yes, Uncle." Vala nodded, then vanished into space, reappearing in a blue twinkle across the platform, grabbing on to an orange-gifted midair.

Auron looked around while the woman continued to administer the blood to his people. From across the way, he saw Ikaria, surrounded by machines in the form of men, just like the one that rescued him. She was commanding them, yelling out loud as they entered the portal. Her gauntlet burned a strange black.

I have got to get over to that other platform!

There was a flash before Ikaria.

Geeta.

He clenched his fists. *Now I really have to get over to that platform!*

"Need a lift?" a voice called out from above him.

Auron looked up, his gaze meeting a red-gifted man holding a green-gifted woman in one of his arms while the other held a staff that cast an intense reddish-white light.

His staff.

"Are you the Ghost Man?" Auron asked the man hovering above him.

"That's what they keep calling me for whatever damn reason," the man replied while the green-gifted woman held on to him tighter.

"I see that Geeta gave you my staff. That gives me hope."

The Ghost Man looked at the staff, then shrugged. "This thing? You can have it back once we kick some sorceress ass."

Ghost Man swung the staff hard in the air, leaving a trail of vibrant red light in its path. Bits of dust, dirt, rock, and debris began to assemble midair, bridging the two platforms together. With another solid swipe of the staff, ice formed all over the bridge, solidifying the structure.

"This should hold temporarily, I think. But if I were you, I wouldn't sit my ass down too long on the damn thing. Not sure how much weight it can hold."

"Thank you," Auron said reverently.

Turning behind him, Auron summoned his protective magic, casting barriers on the gifted who started to cross. Auron saw the green-gifted in the Ghost Man's arms shoot out protective barriers as well on those flying by, her barriers being greenish yellow.

Auron gaped. She had the ability to cast magic outside the green capabilities. Had she consumed other gifted's blood too? Or was it truly like what Geeta had told him, that gifted had the ability to cast adjacent powers?

No time to wonder. Auron and the gifted began to charge over the bridge while other gifted flew above past him.

Then the machines swarmed the skies. And they looked angry.

Auron heard a loud booming noise coming from their hands. Some of their hands weren't hands, but long barrels.

Metal barrels.

From the metal barrels, it began raining metal.

***

Damn! I hope we aren't too late.

Kyle flew past the half-assed bridge in his funneled red winds, gripping Emerald tightly and holding the staff.

That shit better hold. He eyed the bridge one last time before turning his focus to the royal platform.

A warm flow of bright green-yellow magic surrounded them both, encasing them in a translucent barrier. It was right on time, as firepower shot through the skies, raining metal not only on them, but also the other gifted on the bridge.

"Oh no!" Emerald cried, gazing in horror at the gunfire. "We have to stop them!"

"We will. I just have to figure out how without killing them all."

The future gifted fought back, sending out firepower of their own, ranging from hurling fireballs and ice storms to jolts of red electrical power. Some of the blue-gifted stopped time on a handful of them, with the bullets freezing midair.

Kyle noticed that magic did not seem to be very effective against the machines, especially against orange illusion magic. The machines were not fooled by illusions, and they were using their calculations to see through the magic, gunning right for the gifted. Several of the cyborgs that had been damaged started to heal themselves, regenerating back to their original state.

Kyle slashed magic toward the cyborgs with the added power of the staff, casting a wave of electric magic, enough to cause them to go into overload. Emerald cast new barriers on the gifted as older spells faded away.

Shit, she won't be able to keep this up for long. Yellow wasn't her main color, so he knew it took her more effort to cast the barriers.

"Try not to kill them," Kyle called out to the gifted below. "They are my people."

"*Your* people are very strange," called out a gifted from the bridge.

Yeah, that's not the first time I've heard that.

Many of the cyborgs fired again, this time unleashing a giant wave of firepower while other cyborgs engaged with the gifted, hacking at them with their built-in weaponry. The magical barriers protected some of the future gifted, while other barriers faded instantly, the bullets and blades breaking through. Many of the gifted fell to the ground while others were flung off the bridge.

Shit!

The rumbling of air transports could be heard nearby. Kyle turned and saw the crappiest transport he had ever seen. He couldn't believe that the scrap of metal was actually flying, and then he caught sight of a familiar face.

"Hey, asshole, you need some help?" Garrett's voice called out from an open window. Behind him, Kyle could see Reila piloting the contraption. Another transport hovered nearby, in just as bad shape as the first one, with Victor and Jared inside.

"Garrett? What the hell are you doing here?" Kyle yelled back, casting another spell at a cyborg coming at him.

"I can't let you have all the fun!" he answered. Garrett armed himself with a grenade launcher, then aimed at the bridge with the cyborgs.

"Are you fucking crazy? You're going to shatter the damn thing!" Kyle roared. "Everyone is gonna fall!"

"Kyle, we can't let them die!" Emerald chimed in.

"Hey, I got this, okay?" Garrett called out above the sounds of the transports, getting into position.

- 612 -

With a sudden force, the launcher boomed, and a metal device shot out, landing on the bridge. It rolled along the bridge, then stopped two feet in front of a cyborg.

Underwhelmed by Garrett's weapon, Kyle turned back to him. "How the hell is that thing supposed to help?"

"Shoot your lightning into it, idiot!"

"And why would I want to do that?"

"Kyle, more cyborgs are coming," Emerald said.

"Just do it, asshole! You'll see!" Garrett called out. He motioned, and both transports vacated the area.

Turning back to see the metal device on the bridge, Kyle swung the staff, aiming at the ball, then sent a large bolt of red lightning at it. Upon the magic's contact, a pulse of energy emitted from the device, sending a shock wave across the bridge. The second the shock wave hit the cyborgs, their technology died, shutting down their power.

The humanized cyborgs started acting in confusion, their machine parts inanimate. It gave the gifted the time they needed to prepare their spells, freezing the stunned machines into place.

"Damn, that was pretty useful," Kyle said.

"Kyle! Down there!" Emerald said, pointing frantically at the injured on a platform below.

"All right! Hold on tight!"

He released the wind from around them. They fell for a short moment, then the wind surrounded them once more, and they made contact with the bridge, breaking their fall.

Emerald rushed over to one of the gifted. The injured gifted was mutilated, bleeding from numerous wounds, most of them resembling puncture wounds from a cyborg's blade. There were two yellow-gifted trying to utilize their newly acquired green skill that had been injected into them, but it wasn't enough. They didn't understand how to fully utilize it. Their attempts could only soothe the injured instead of heal them.

Emerald began vigorously casting her healing magic. As she did so, Kyle looked over toward the royal transport platform where Geeta was. There were so many bodies swarming the morning sky—the colorful gifted casting their magic and the dark machines that hadn't been hit by Garrett's bomb.

He turned to Emerald. "I need to go stop Ikaria before shit gets out of hand. Geeta is up there waiting for us."

"Geeta?"

"My mentor. No time to explain now."

Emerald nodded, quickly kissing him, then started healing the mangled gifted's body. "I will join you after I heal them. I promise." Her eyes told him that she didn't want to part from him for long, but the need to help was too great to ignore.

"Hurry. I'll hold the witch off until you get there."

"Okay." Emerald nodded, giving him a concerned look.

He gave her a smile, then gathered all of his wind power, funneling it around him. He shot into the sky, the staff glowing fiery red in his grasp, a newly formed storm raging around him. Red lightning shot into the staff's orb as thick red clouds swirled around him, gathering all of the air. Some of the gifted stopped in awe at the sight of the intense power.

As Kyle flew toward the platform where Geeta and Ikaria were, a body basked in blue magic appeared right in front of Kyle. The blue magic created a blue-violet force, hurling Kyle out of his path. Within the glowing blue magic, a dark figure emerged with a menacing grin.

Derek had a smug look on his face, narrowing his eyes. "How did I know that you were going to show up? Don't you have anything better to do in the lower levels than stick your nose in Arcadia's business?"

"Em's business is *my* business," Kyle snarled.

"So crass. I can't believe she was actually soft on you." Derek's crystal-blue eyes began to glow. "She's already forgotten everything, especially you."

Kyle scowled. "Yeah, look at the big bad king. You had to fucking control her in order for her to be swayed by you, so fucking classy. More like a piece of shit, is what you are. A cowardly piece of shit!"

Kyle grasped the staff, then shot toward Derek, flames burning from his hands. Just when he was about to make contact with Derek, Kyle released them, hurling a huge fireball toward him. Derek disappeared, then reappeared behind him. Kyle spun around and struck the King firmly, landing a solid blow to the chest. Derek faltered for a second, giving Kyle the opportunity to clock the King in the face.

"Damn you!" Derek snarled, wiping fresh blood from his nose. His body began to slowly radiate blue magic. As he did so, everything around Kyle began slowing down and turning blue as Derek's magic burned brighter by the second. The world was coming to a halt.

Kyle started summoning an ice shard, intending to hurl it at the King, but his movements were coming to a standstill. Kyle's body was locking into place, and his face was slowed to the point that he could see the beauty of the ice crystals forming at a painstakingly sluggish pace, the reflections of the blue magic being cast shining across the smooth icy surface.

Just as Kyle couldn't take watching the torturous slow motion of the spell, he felt speed return to him, and the motion of his ice spell continued at a normal pace. Kyle looked immediately at the prince. Derek sneered, then burned his blue magic brightly, causing Kyle's movement to slow down once more.

As soon as he slowed down, the usual speed of his movements returned, reversing the time spell, and his ice shard continued to form.

Derek yelled in frustration at his time magic being countered, struggling to summon more blue magic once again, but he was unsuccessful. Off in the distance, Kyle saw a gifted woman with a deep skin tone and big reflective jewelry, basking in an immense burning sapphire light, whirling streams of blue magic circling her. Derek saw her too and realized that his magic couldn't counter this woman's power, no matter how much he tried to counter her. But Derek was hellbent on having his way.

With Kyle's ice shard completely formed, he hurled it at the prince. It struck Derek's shoulder, breaking his concentration. Derek snarled in response, grabbing the shard and yanking it out of his shoulder. Part of the tip broke, and a chunk of his tunic tore off.

Derek's eyes burned with hatred as he narrowed them on Kyle. With a flash, Derek appeared right in front of Kyle, his hand glowing blue-violet. He bashed Kyle violently with a force so strong it knocked the wind out of Kyle's lungs, causing Kyle to spin aimlessly through the air.

Kyle lost focus on his red winds, causing him to fall as Derek disappeared, flashing blue into the dark sky. A split second later, Kyle felt another gifted's winds surround him. Looking around, a redheaded woman hovered to the side of him, nodding as her magic flowed around him. Kyle nodded in thanks as the woman flew off toward an aerial cyborg. It was just what he needed to regain focus, and he gathered his winds to find Derek.

Flying back up to where they'd fought, he spotted Derek on the royal platform, giving orders to the guards, intermittently grasping his wounded shoulder.

Kyle gritted his teeth, then charged. Derek spun around, caught off guard. Kyle flashed, becoming invisible, then cast an illusion in his place, sending it toward Derek at the same speed.

Derek disappeared just as Kyle's image was about to make contact. When Derek reappeared, Kyle came from behind, cinching the King in a choke hold.

"Two can play at your disappearing game," Kyle grunted as he reappeared, keeping his arm wrapped around the King's muscular neck. The act of squeezing Derek gave him some satisfaction, especially while thinking of what he did to Emerald. Damn did Derek ever deserve to die.

Derek struggled back and forth under his grasp, grabbing at his arms to get him to release him. Derek was much stronger than Kyle had pegged him, even with his maimed shoulder, but Kyle was not going to let go, whatever the cost. But he had to do something fast, because he was starting to get tired.

Calling upon his red-violet magic, Kyle jumped into Derek's consciousness, hoping to control Derek and get him to stop fighting. An incredibly strong black power met him, a force so overwhelming that it shook him to his core. The power was shielding anyone and anything from getting into the depths of Derek's mind.

This has to be Ikaria's spell.

The darkness of the magic threatened to overwhelm him. The King was under the influence of the witch's spell. Derek was too far gone in the darkness, and there was no way of breaking into his mind.

Reentering his own body, Kyle regained his awareness. He still had Derek in a choke hold, and both men were flopping back and forth. What Kyle hadn't noticed until now was that the staff had been dropped onto the platform, kicked away by their tumble. One of the cyborgs eyed it and picked it up.

Looking over at the staff, Kyle knew he had to let Derek go. He couldn't let the staff get into the wrong hands. Kyle rolled his body toward the staff, kicking it away from the cyborg. But he didn't let Derek go; Derek rolled with Kyle as they neared the staff.

Derek flopped himself over, forcing Kyle onto his back. Then Derek turned to face Kyle and wrapped his hands around his neck.

His air supply cut off, Kyle began to gasp. Through his peripheral vision, he saw delicate hands pick up the staff. Unable to break free, Kyle began to suffocate.

Deep down, Kyle could hear the call of his inner fire.

Flames burst from his body, raging from his wrath. His body began searing Derek's hands and arms with an intense heat.

"Stop, Derek!" screamed Emerald.

Derek whipped his face in her direction, and his flesh began to smoke. He continued his hold on Kyle. "Never! You are mine! I won't stop until he is dead!" screamed Derek. His face poured with sweat from the heat, the flesh of his arms melting, a putrid smell soaking the air.

"She doesn't want you! One way or another, someone is going to die, and it's sure as hell not going to be me!" Kyle roared hoarsely as Derek's grip tightened. Derek's flesh continued to burn in the flames.

"NO!" Derek screamed. Then he turned and looked at Emerald. Her face twisted in disgust, then disappointment. "I can't let you go…" Derek said softly, almost in a light sob.

Emerald stood above them, her soft, wavy locks of hair flowing in the wind. "I will never love you, Derek," she said, her voice strengthened with finality. "Take a look at what you have become! You are not the Derek I once knew!"

Finally, when Kyle thought he was about to take one of his last breaths, Derek loosened his grip. Kyle coughed hard and rolled over, catching his breath. Derek slunk down next to him, his face red with pain and covered in sweat and tears.

A black flash appeared before them, then a strong current forced everyone except Derek back. He lay there cradling his melted flesh.

Through the black swirls, Ikaria glared at Kyle, death on her mind, then she looked back at Derek. She flung her hand toward him, and energy swirled around Derek's flesh, partially healing his melted hand and arm. It wasn't fully restored, but it was enough for Derek to slide away from Kyle and rest his back upon a large planter on the platform. There he remained, breathing heavily.

"What do you think you are doing to His Majesty?" she said in an accusing tone to Kyle, then glanced over at Emerald. "I see you are not wearing your lovely crown. A travesty," she remarked coldly.

"You have no power over me! Never again!" Emerald yelled as she gripped the staff.

Ikaria laughed. "Oh? Is that so, Queen?"

Kyle ran toward Emerald, reaching out to hold the staff with her.

"Now!" Kyle yelled. "Summon your powers, Em!"

Ikaria looked over at him, her black eyes flashing, locking his body in place before he got a chance to touch the staff, her magic weighing him down like a ton of bricks. She cackled as black magic flew around her, whipping her hair wildly. She threw her hands out to both sides, her eyes black.

Emerald tumbled to the ground, her eyes drained of life. Just like when she had the circlet on.

He was too late. Just a fucking second too late to complete the Spectrum of Magic. And seeing Emerald compromised once again made him rage. Rage with hatred for the sorceress.

"You bitch!" Kyle cursed at the sorceress. Angrily, he called forth his own red-violet magic. It ran through him, freeing his mind and allowing his body to move.

The staff was lit with an intense, deep-green light. Emerald sat up and began draining life, sucking away all the life-force from the future gifted. Screams erupted. Some of the gifted crashed into the platforms; others began to plummet to Arcadia's depths.

"You see, you can't have her. She is mine. I was just loaning her to Derek. Pure destruction, this one is." Ikaria laughed. "She's coming with me to the future."

Roaring, Kyle began to cast his flames, creating a fire wall around them, then hurled all of the conjured fire toward the sorceress. Ikaria waved a finger, and the flames died instantly.

"Em!" Kyle yelled.

Emerald didn't respond. Her empty shell continued to rip the life-force of the future gifted, funneling it back into her, Ikaria, and the remaining cyborgs.

Ikaria threw her head back, laughing wickedly. The sound echoed off the turrets and into the sky. "I see you have been recruited by Auron," she said to him nonchalantly, looking at the staff in Emerald's hand. "How pathetic. The fool doesn't know when to stop. It's too bad, really. His own weapon is used against him. It will be his downfall."

Then Geeta appeared in front of Kyle, shielded by the brightest yellow magic he had ever seen. She summoned a vortex, swirling it around the sorceress, compressing Ikaria's body. Tighter and tighter the magic wound, trying to squeeze the sorceress into oblivion. Kyle reached for ice from within his soul, shooting it into the vortex, hoping it to shred Ikaria while the vortex spun around the witch.

Instead, Ikaria kept laughing. Her black eyes sparkled, and the vortex stopped instantly. With a wide sweep of her hands over her head, she called down the storms from the skies, disappearing into them.

Geeta and Kyle looked around quickly, then kept moving, hoping that the sorceress wouldn't be behind them. Through the darkness of the clouds, Kyle saw a bright yellow light with a man at the center of it. It was the same gifted man he'd seen on his makeshift ice bridge at the beginning of the battle. The man's eyes glowed pure gold as he cast a transparent shield, his elegant white robes flowing around him.

Through the storm, black rains whipped around them while the wind and lightning raged. Kyle could no longer see Geeta or the yellow-gifted man, only the storm clouds.

A scream broke through the gusty wind.

Geeta's scream.

Kyle ran toward the sound and found Geeta bleeding on the platform, a blade through her heart.

"Geeta!" Kyle screamed, rushing over to her, falling to his knees.

The blade in Geeta's heart looked like a cyborg blade. She needed healing, healing way beyond her capabilities.

"The gifted cyborg…" she said, gasping for air.

Kyle suddenly felt a sharp jab at his side, and the wound exploded in pain. Grunting, Kyle whirled around, trying to spot the cyborg.

Drew was not hiding. He made himself known, his orange eyes peering out through the storm. Blades grew from his hands, replacing the lost blade that had been stuck in Geeta. His body pulsated bright orange as he began to multiply himself.

In response, Kyle gathered the lightning from the storm clouds, funneling their energy. The lightning turned red, multiplying in intensity. Kyle released it, sending it shooting out to the copies of the cyborg. The images that were touched by lightning faded as others came toward him.

A woman appeared through the storm, her unkempt short hair flying in her face as her hands held on to her glasses steadily. She looked around frantically, searching.

"Drew?" she called out.

The copies continued to come toward him. With each copy, he rolled, dodged, and shot them away by force.

"Drew! What are you doing?"

One of the images noticed the woman's voice, then slowly the images faded away to one cyborg.

The woman ran over, extending her arms to embrace him. As she neared the robot, he methodically reached for her throat, then clutched it tight, holding her off the ground with her heeled shoes dangling in the air.

Right as he was about to squeeze the life out of her, she yelled, "Drew! It's me. Telly!"

He paused, hesitating. Then he squeezed her throat again.

"Please, put me down!" the woman cried, struggling with her words, choking. "I know you can't help it… you can't override the gauntlet. Please… remember me! Remember… Gwen!"

Kyle angrily flung out his hands, gathering every bolt of lightning he could muster between the heavens and his soul, gathering it in the palms of his hands. A massive red ball of energy formed, crackling with lightning.

Shooting out his hands, Kyle released the ball of energy, and it completely enveloped the cyborg. Drew released his grip on the woman and shook violently, jolting over and over, convulsing from the overload. His circuits caught fire and his body smoked.

The woman screamed.

With no time to spare, Kyle bolted from the two of them, searching for Emerald and Ikaria. There was too much damn fog and clouds to see where they'd gone.

Holding out his hands, Kyle calmed the atmosphere until the clouds and fog dissipated. As the fog subsided, Kyle saw Ikaria and Emerald near the portal. It looked like they were about to enter.

Fuck no! Kyle thought. *Not on my life!*

Kyle saw Emerald still casting her draining magic on the future gifted. One by one, more gifted wilted away like dying flower petals.

Closing his eyes, Kyle called upon the full violet force within him, pleading with the magic to shoot him across the platform.

The magic responded with a hurling force, and his body landed in front of Emerald.

"Em!"

The green light of the staff shone on her pale face, her eyes glowing. With an outstretched hand, she began sucking the life-force out of him.

"Em, please, for God's sake, wake up!"

Emerald's magic tore through him, much more powerful than the last time. Her power ripped right into his soul, sending excruciating pain surging through him. Kyle stumbled, snarling to get ahold of himself. But with Emerald using the staff, it made it near impossible.

Fighting hard not to think of the pain, Kyle instead focused on transferring his consciousness into her mind.

As soon as he entered Emerald's mind, he felt Ikaria's consciousness. She had a strong hold on Emerald. The power was too great, just like with Derek, and he exited immediately.

Ikaria shot him a look of contempt as she grunted, reinforcing her power over Emerald. Emerald flung her head back, screaming in pain from the witch's magic.

Pain ruptured in Kyle's head, sending him into shock. Ikaria was in his mind. She'd caught him off guard, and there was no way to protect himself. He didn't have protection magic like Geeta and Emerald.

With Ikaria in his mind and with Emerald draining his life-force, Kyle stumbled to the ground, feeling almost nothing left in his life-force. Emerald's magic continued to surge through his body, ripping away his soul.

He was fading. Fading so fast that he could no longer feel his body.

Green magic swirled around him, showing him pictures of his life. Images flashed before his eyes—images of the wastelands when he was little. Him sitting on a desert rock, looking out into the vast barren lands. Riding his motorcycle as the hot winds blew through his bleached hair. The band members giving him shit while he played his music. And of course, Emerald. Her gentle touch, soft as a warm desert breeze.

Come back to me, Kyle… Come back to me, her voice whispered.

***

All Derek wanted to do was fade away into nothingness. His soul had been ripped from him, torn into pieces and thrown to Ikaria, who took his dignity, and Emerald, who already had his heart.

And now he was nothing.

It was all a lie. Everything Ikaria had told him was a lie. She didn't really care if they got married or not. Ikaria had been planning on taking Emerald to the future this whole time and leaving him behind, alone. She was foul. Cruel. A disgusting human being. And she had made him into someone he wasn't. He hated her.

But he hated himself more.

Derek flopped onto his belly, away from the planter that he'd been resting against, then began crawling with his maimed arms, slithering his way toward the edge of the platform. As he reached the metal railing, he saw the vast ocean of Arcadia's buildings far below, eerily glowing within the morning fog.

It wouldn't be hard to squeeze through the metal bars horizontally, to fling himself into the pits of Arcadia. He more than deserved it.

Derek pressed his face against the railing, breathing in.

He hated to admit that the bastard punk was right. He did deserve to die.

Derek hesitated, staring across the vast city. Looking over his shoulder, he saw the woman who had held his heart hostage.

Emerald.

She had one hand out, casting a dark-green magic at the people from the future, her other hand clutching the staff and funneling more power to her and the sorceress.

And it all came back to Ikaria, controlling everyone and everything.

How had Derek let himself get so out of control? How did this even happen? He knew Ikaria had a deep hold on his mind, but he was the one who'd given in to his fantasies and let Ikaria control him in the first place. He wished he'd never come to Arcadia. Emerald hated him, and he loathed himself. They were married, and the two kingdoms were united, but it was under a darkness that was all his doing.

Derek turned away, looking back at the menacing city below. The colored fog, the falling gifted, and the cyborgs soaring through the skies. They could all go to hell for all he cared. That was where he was going.

He began to squeeze his muscular body through the lowest bar, his arms still badly burned. He let out a grunt while he exerted the last of his energy trying to shove his body through, his head hanging off the platform.

Two worn leather boots shuffled nearby, then stopped next to him. Derek look over to the brown boots but had a hard time seeing who it was with his head hanging over the platform. Squeezing his head back slightly, he cast his glance upward. The area was poorly lit, and all Derek saw was a shadow of a man's face, illuminated by the magic from afar.

The shadowy man laid his hands on Derek, and Derek felt a brush of life through his body, his arms glowing deep green. Through the magic, Derek saw the man's face illuminated with the green power. He had olive skin, forest-green hair, and glowing green eyes. He was another gifted with green magic, just like Emerald.

"If I were asked what you were doing, I would say that you wish to fall off the edge. Am I right?" the man asked in a thick accent. He looked at him with sympathy.

Derek didn't say anything and nodded.

"We need more gifted to help stop this woman. Especially the one who the prophecy called for, the Ghost Man. He needs our help."

With a look of contempt mixed with sadness, Derek turned away. "He doesn't need my help."

"Why is that?"

Derek shot him a look. "You have no idea what I have done. All of this"— Derek waved his healed arm, gesturing toward the battle—"is all because of me."

The man paused. His eyes stopped glowing, revealing glassy deep-green eyes that matched his hair. "I see. Perhaps you need healing on the inside to overcome your broken spirit."

There was hope in the man's voice. Was he saying he could do it?

Derek looked at the man, then lowered his eyes, the overwhelming sadness rotting in the depths of his being. Hesitating, Derek asked, "You… can do that?"

"No, but you can."

The man held out his hand, waiting for Derek to take it. "How? I don't have that kind of power," Derek said.

"You can start by making it right," the green-gifted man replied. The man waited, and Derek finally took his hand. The man helped Derek to his feet.

After he got up, Derek glanced over at Ikaria. She was near the portal, and Emerald was finishing off what gifted were left. Several of the barriers were fading fast. Emerald continued to be possessed by Ikaria's mind, sucking the life out of them. Screams from the gifted echoed through the skies, the smell of their blood coating the air, mixed with the smell of fried circuitry from the cyborgs.

Turning his gaze, Derek saw a few gifted bodies strewn across the platform nearby. Feeling the power of his blue magic, he flashed over to them, inspecting them. One of the bodies was armed with an enchanted dagger, glowing an eerie red-orange color. Derek had noticed that the future gifted used these weapons. Perhaps they were the best defense for a spellcaster. Or maybe it was to break another's casting or concentration.

Derek took the dagger, then looked over to the man. He nodded at Derek with a look of approval.

Derek gathered all his power from deep within his soul. He gathered his sadness, his despair, his emptiness—all that he had left in his heart. He gathered until there was nothing else to give. He'd taken advantage of the woman he loved, used her, enticed by the notion of power.

He was the lowest of human beings.

He was nothing.

Flashing his ice-blue eyes, a light-blue power surrounded him, unlike his usual deep-blue magic. He looked over at Ikaria, who had just dispatched the last of the gifted attacking her. Her violet barrier started to fade.

Quick as lightning, he flashed in front of Ikaria just as the barrier faded completely, leaving her vulnerable for a second. It was more than enough time for him.

Time was on his side.

With a powerful, vengeful thrust, he stabbed her in the heart.

***

Emerald awoke from her dark dream.

Kyle. He was in front of her…

His eyes rolled back in his head as his body slumped over, and the dark-green magic surrounding him faded away.

Emerald shook her head in disbelief, her body trembling.

"Kyle?"

She ran over to his still body, falling to her knees, shaking him violently. "Kyle!"

Her stomach churned and twisted. Her heart skipped beats. He wasn't moving.

"No, no, no. This can't be happening!" Emerald cried, her eyes stinging with tears.

It was all her fault. She'd killed him.

"What have I done?" Emerald shrieked at the top of her lungs, clutching his body.

Emerald squeezed her eyes shut, drawing everything that she had within her. Kyle needed life. Now.

A burning surge of life ran through her veins, swelling in her fingertips, emitting a bright-green glow.

"Come back to me," Emerald cried, laying her hand on his chest. "Please, come back."

Emerald released the tidal waves within her soul, her life-force mixing with rebirth magic, a magic that she had never called upon before. It streamed gently to Kyle's body, encasing him in a green brilliance.

His body glowed green as she cried, waiting for him to return to her. But there was no movement from Kyle, nor any breath from his lungs.

Emerald screamed again, crying, resting her head on his chest. Through the light of her magic, Emerald saw Ikaria narrowing her eyes, grimacing·in pain. The sorceress's hand was pressed over her gushing, bloody chest. With a forceful yank, the enchanted blade was flung to the ground. Healing her deep wound, the sorceress spun around, eyeing Derek. Ikaria shot up a hand, and the enchanted blade hovered, flying toward Derek and plunging into his body. He dropped to the ground, breathing heavily, groaning in agony.

Kyle's heart remained quiet within his chest. Emerald tried reviving him again, filling his body with her life-giving magic. "Kyle, please, you have to come back! Don't leave me, please…" Emerald faltered. Tears continued to flow down her face. Kyle didn't move.

Em… Hey, Em.

Emerald whirled around, checking to see if Kyle had moved. Nothing.

We have to defeat her, Kyle said in her mind. *We need to complete the Spectrum of Magic.*

Confused, Emerald looked down at Kyle's body, but it remained unchanged.

Come on, what are you waiting for? Let's beat this bitch!

He was here with her. His spirit still lingered…

Emerald stood up, gripping the staff and filling it with her magic. She drained herself of all the magic from the corners of her heart and the depths of her soul, channeling it into the device. The staff's orb lit up bright green, sparking with energy. Her magic intensified as it funneled back and forth between her and the staff. Then the magic turned from green to an almost hot-white color.

In one hand, Emerald pointed the staff in Kyle's direction while her healing magic swelled in her other outstretched hand. She released the magic of the staff and her hand, aiming for his body.

Without warning, Emerald felt Ikaria trying to enter her mind. But someone interfered, and Ikaria's consciousness was flung out of her body. A transparent violet barrier surrounded her, getting between the outside of her body to the inside of her mind. Her consciousness was protected.

Ikaria froze in place, then screamed and writhed in agony.

Emerald heard a woman's voice call out from the darkness. "Whatever you need to do, you need to do it now while I have her mind!" she yelled as Ikaria continued to scream. "I can't hold on long!"

Filled with heartbreak, Emerald clenched the staff, closing her eyes.

Remember what I told you, Kyle's comforting voice said.

"I remember…" she whispered under her breath, answering him.

She thought back to the time where Kyle watched her paint, the very same night she gave her love to him. She had been mixing all of her paints, making the color black.

So black is all of the colors mixed together? he'd asked.

It is if you are talking about pigments. But if you are referring to light, all of the colors combined makes white…

That was it. That was how Kyle was planning on completing the Spectrum of Magic. She and Kyle needed to piece together fragments of light by bringing forth all the colors of magic to equal light. White light.

Still sensing Kyle's spirit, Emerald summoned the different magics within her, calling upon the raw emotions that fed those magics. Desperation, sadness, and love filled her entire being.

More blue and yellow… he said, his voice reverberating within her mind, encouraging her.

Emerald reached down within her being, calling forth more of her adjacent colors while thinking of Kyle. He did anything and everything he could for her and was willing to die for her. And she'd killed him with her own magic. The thought made her soul ache. The flow of emotions crystallized into her adjacent magic, flowing into the staff. The wetness of her tears streamed down her cheeks unendingly.

Like a soft breeze in the wind, she felt a touch. It was ever so slight, but it was there.

Opening her eyes, Emerald didn't see anything, but she *felt* a powerful force. It held her like a lover, wrapping its energy around her. Violets, reds, and oranges flowed around an invisible presence, forming the shape of a man. The magic swirled around the airy presence, then passed through her body, wrapping her in its power.

Emerald felt him. She felt Kyle. She had his power and hers combined. Their power together created pure light. Pure white light.

Ikaria screamed as she struggled with the violet magic that opposed her mind. The sorceress threw her hands out, casting a powerful shock wave to a violet-gifted woman. Geeta. It had to be the one who Kyle had mentioned.

Geeta flashed away, then appeared, shooting purple ice at the sorceress. Ikaria struggled, locking the woman into place, then shot black lightning at the woman, throwing Geeta to the ground.

Noticing Emerald's staff and the power radiating from it, Geeta yelled, "Every gifted left, focus your power on that staff! Now!"

Within seconds, the sky filled with color, beaming colored magics into the orb of the staff, intensifying the white light, strengthening the very essence of the Spectrum of Magic in its purest form.

Emerald drained the pure white energy. She glowed a bright white that matched the staff's orb.

She had the power of the Spectrum of Magic within her.

Glancing at Ikaria, Emerald's face burned with anger, vengeance, and retribution for what she had done. Ikaria had wreaked havoc on all of Arcadia. Now it was her turn to pay.

The power within her raged and became too great for Emerald and the staff to handle. She placed her other hand on the staff to steady it as the power shook. No one should have the full power of the Spectrum of Magic. It was intended for the God of Light alone. But for a moment, he was gracing her with his power.

"Auron! Get that orange-gifted cyborg!" Emerald heard Geeta's voice scream from behind her. "Ready your barrier magic for an enchantment!"

Charging toward Ikaria, Emerald jumped, then hurled every ounce of the white light at Ikaria, immersing the sorceress in the light. Light from God himself.

Then the world exploded, and all Emerald saw was white.

White. All was white.

Emerald landed on her feet, then waited in the pure light, wondering if it would ever disappear. It eventually did, but instead of Arcadia, she was in a bedchamber.

The chamber itself was rather large, with mica-flecked white marble floors and crystal-like walls that were transparent, but strangely, Emerald could not see the other side. The light from the window captured the beauty of the crystal walls, reflecting the spectrum of colors onto the floor. Silver lamps hung on the wall, burning a bright white light, surrounded by an orange glow. It was not needed, as it was daytime, and the sun was shining into the room, but it lent an elegance to the quarters. The bed itself was silver with embroidered purple sheets and pillows. In the center of the room was a magical fire pit to keep the room warm.

This room seems familiar…

There were two chairs next to the brightly burning fire, both empty. The chairs themselves were large enough to pass as thrones, with high backing, silver scroll work, and purple leather cushions.

I've been here before! Emerald thought, recognizing the room. *When I accidentally traveled in time!*

Sobs filled the room. Mournful sobs.

Emerald turned her attention to where the sobs were coming from. A beautiful woman lay strewn on the floor, crying. It was Ikaria, Emerald realized. She looked the same as when Emerald saw her before in time, when she appeared in front of the High Court. She even had the same outfit on.

Ikaria's sobs intensified until she was wailing. Her long violet hair flowed all over the ground in different directions, some of it covering her elegant lavender kimono. She lay in the fetal position, her elongated eyes streaming tears. Each teardrop fell silently on the floor, sprinkling the floor like a light rain.

A servant came in, and Ikaria stopped crying, wiping away her tears, looking anxious.

"Well? Did you deliver my message? Is he coming?" Ikaria asked in a shaky voice.

The servant girl shook her head, bowing. "Lord Cyrus sends his regards. He states that he has other prior engagements."

Ikaria whirled around with a look of contempt, wiping away fresh tears angrily. "Is he with my *sister*?"

The servant didn't say anything but looked to the floor.

"*Leave me!*" she screamed. The servant girl scuttled away, closing the door behind her.

As soon as the servant was gone, Ikaria fell back to the floor, crying in waves of gut-wrenching sobs. Emerald felt Ikaria's heart radiating with sorrow, betrayal, and loneliness. Despair washed over Emerald, knowing how Ikaria felt. No one cared for her. Not her father or mother, not her sister, and not her lover. No one. Emerald knew how that felt. A princess living in isolation from happiness.

After what seemed like forever, Ikaria's angry, heartbreaking sobs ceased. There was a moment of silence, then the sorceress let out a loud scream. Violet flames enveloped her, burning her body. She rose from the floor, hovering in midair, still screaming in rage. Her kimono and obi flew wildly around her, her long hair whipping in every direction. She snapped her eyes open, and Emerald saw passion, rage, and sadness within their violet depths.

Ikaria threw out one of her hands as if reaching for something, then clenched her fist tightly. Across the room, Emerald saw that one of the thrones was floating in midair. Ikaria shrieked with rage as she flung her arm hard, her magic throwing the throne. The throne flew across the room quick as lightning, hitting one of the crystal walls and shattering the interior. With loud raging screams, she levitated the other throne, shooting it across the room, shattering the other wall.

Her body softly floated to the floor, leaving her hovering just a couple inches from the ground. Then her magic dissipated, dropping her the last couple inches. She began to cry again. This time, they were soft cries.

Emerald stood over her, feeling the sadness, the jealousy, and the darkness taking hold of Ikaria's heart.

No more, she told the darkness. *You cannot have her.*

The room was enveloped in light, everything basked in pure white energy. Then the white faded away, revealing the current Ikaria.

They were back in Arcadia on the platform.

Ikaria's body radiated pure white, hovering in the air while her hair floated gently in the air. Her eyes were closed. Magic filled Emerald, a similar magic that she felt with her healing, life-giving, and rebirth magic, but this was different. It was a feeling of renewal filling her heart. It flowed within her veins, awaiting orders.

Siphoning the renewal magic into the staff, Emerald released the power, casting the staff in the direction of Ikaria. The power encased the sorceress, seeping into Ikaria's body, making her translucent.

After a moment, the power faded away, eradicating all black magic within the sorceress. Slowly, Ikaria's body floated to the ground, settling on the platform, and she lay there as if in a deep sleep. The gauntlet snapped off the sorceress's wrist and melted into a pool of liquid metal.

She had done it. Emerald had done it.

Ikaria's spirit had been renewed, and her body purified, changed back to its original state with her violet blood.

Feeling Kyle's presence surrounding her, Emerald whirled around and ran to where Kyle's body lay.

CHAPTER 79

GREEN

Within a heartbeat, Emerald felt Kyle no more. He was gone. Her magic couldn't save him.

His spirit returned to her for a moment. Just for a brief moment in time. Then he had left her, leaving to join the other spirits in the lifestream, for that was what spirits did after their bodies died. But even knowing that, it left her with a deep knowing sadness; she was alone once again. All alone in Arcadia.

Looking at Kyle's lifeless face, Emerald buried her face into his neck, her tears falling upon him. She nuzzled her nose against his, feeling the coldness of his flesh, reminding her that he was no more.

Maybe she'd done something wrong with her magic? Or she was too late and was only able to beckon with his spirit to come back. Either way, he was gone. And it was all because she couldn't control her own mind against the sorceress.

She screamed with immense, sorrowful pain, shaking at the thought she would never see him again. How could this happen? Would they never be together? It was fate playing a cruel trick on them both, as if they were destined to be apart forever.

A hand touched her shoulder softly. Through her blurry eyes, Emerald saw Geeta kneeling down beside her.

"Your Majesty… he is gone," she whispered. "I am truly sorry."

"I… couldn't save him with my magic…" Emerald's lip quivered as the salt of her tears stained her face.

Geeta gazed at her with her deep-purple eyes. "We can't save everyone with our magic. Perhaps the gods had other uses for him. Although, he would most likely fight the gods above and rain down fire from the heavens," Geeta said, smiling sadly.

Emerald looked at Geeta as her tears continued to run down her face, then gave a small laugh through her sobs. That would definitely be something Kyle would do. "You know him well," Emerald managed to say.

Geeta nodded. "Well enough. Every thought that crossed his mind, every song he sang, and every spell he cast was all to get you back," she said slowly.

Emerald's eyes filled up with fresh tears from Geeta's statement, her heart filling with anguish.

"He loved you, that I know," Geeta whispered.

Emerald gazed at her, thinking of what she said. Knowing in her heart that Kyle loved her brought her more soul-crushing despair.

"And now I'm alone," Emerald whispered.

"You are not alone. Look around you. There are many gifted here that surround you."

"And then they will leave."

Not arguing, Geeta rubbed her shoulder softly to comfort her, but Emerald knew the woman had no comforting words.

Pausing for a moment, Geeta shuffled her feet, then said, "My Queen, I have been all throughout time on a mission to find the Ghost Man, to stop Ikaria. Now that it is over"—Geeta paused, lowering her eyes—"I am in dire need of your cleansing."

"Cleansing?" Emerald glanced at her, blinking away her tears. "You mean, similar to what I did to the sorceress?" Emerald faltered, lowering her gaze to Kyle's corpse.

"Geeta?" a hesitant voice called out from behind, interrupting them.

Emerald and Geeta turned and saw a green-gifted man with dark-green hair and eyes.

"Geeta! It is you! I didn't recognize you with your… new garb? You look completely different!"

"Suresh? What are you doing here?" Geeta answered, completely surprised. The man ran over to Geeta, hugging her.

"To help you, of course! Well, actually, to help your Ghost Man. It turned out that I was not needed. I arrived late," Suresh said. "But at least I was able to help someone out."

"I can't believe you came... after all that I did at the temple..." Geeta looked down, not meeting his eyes.

Suresh looked at her intently. "Geeta, I knew your heart. Vihaan was a terrible, wicked human being, drunk with power and arrogance. I believed in you, and so I had to help. And I can tell you with certainty that the other priests believed in you too."

"Suresh, what happened to them?"

"After you disappeared, I drank Raghu's blood, knowing I had to come after you. You remember how bad I was with my analogous colors, right?"

Geeta slightly chuckled. "Yes, you were always disastrous when it came to blue-green magic."

"We both were when it came to using blue."

Geeta half smiled at him. "True. I just never liked to admit it."

Suresh gave her a bright smile in return, nodding. "Anyway, after my blood mixed with Raghu's, I healed them, then began searching for you through time. You didn't kill them, but they would have died without my aid."

Geeta let out a sigh of relief, like a weight had been lifted from her. "That truly is good news. I have felt... like a monster these past years. I can't tell you how dark my soul has been." Her voice lowered, turning serious. "Suresh, the more I thought about what happened years ago, the more I mediated and prayed about it. I am convinced that Vihaan was deceived with false prophecies. It is only speculation, nothing I can prove, but I feel the gods telling me so."

Suresh returned her gaze, then lowered his eyes in thought to what Geeta had said. He was about to respond, but his gaze met Kyle's body.

His eyes went wide, and he took a step backward, staring at the lifeless corpse.

"What is it, Suresh?" Geeta asked.

Emerald saw Suresh's face go pale, his eyes locked on Kyle's dead body. After a brief second, he turned away, summoning a greenish-blue time portal.

"Suresh, what is going on?" Geeta stood up, blocking his way in front of the rippling magical gateway.

Suresh's eyes met Emerald's, then he turned away.

"There is something... something that I need to make sure of."

"Well, can you be more specific? Or can I help?"

"I heard you tell her you want to be cleansed, Geeta. You cannot come with me if you are to be cleansed. In fact, you cannot stay here. You must return to our time. Do you want me to summon a portal for you in case you choose the cleansing?"

Geeta paused, unsure. "I do want to be cleansed, but... I don't want to go home." Geeta looked over at Emerald. It was as if her plan had been lit up in flames.

Turning to Suresh, Geeta paused, hesitating. After a moment, she broke the silence. "Don't worry about summoning a portal for me, Suresh. I'll find my way home... eventually. This is where I belong, not some ancient time. The technology and lifestyle here in Arcadia has grown on me." Geeta turned to Emerald. "My queen, could you hold off just for a little bit? I meant what I said, but I would like to stay here in Arcadia for the time being."

"Are you sure?" Emerald asked.

"Yes," Geeta assured her. She turned to Suresh, then gave him a hug. "Goodbye, Suresh. I will see you sometime in the past."

"Hopefully." Suresh gave her a hug back, then bowed to Emerald. "Queen Emerald, I am truly sorry for your loss. I have no words that can bring you solace and comfort. Know that love comes again, in many different forms."

More tears flowed down Emerald's face as she watched Suresh disappear into the swirling portal. Emerald heard other footsteps behind her. Many of them, in fact.

Turning around, she saw the future gifted, all standing behind a yellow-gifted man.

Geeta looked to the other gifted, then stepped aside. "It looks like there are others that are in need of your magic."

"Your Majesty," the yellow-gifted man said, bowing. He was the same man that she and Kyle first saw when he had created the bridge. "Before we return, we need to be cleansed of your blood. We must not return to the future with blood that doesn't belong to us."

"Why? Will it affect you?"

"No, my queen," the man murmured, "but our future is too involved with magic, and it would cause many problems within our society with if we returned infused with your green magic. We don't want another incident like Ikaria to happen ever again. Besides, it is a violation of the law of magic, and of the God of Light. We need our blood to be purified."

"Understood," Emerald said, getting to her feet. She felt tired. So very tired. "I'll stand near the portal as everyone leaves, cleansing them one at a time."

"Thank you, Your Majesty. And please, keep the staff as a token of gratitude for saving our Earth and our future."

Emerald glanced between him and the staff. "Oh, I am so sorry! You should take it, Sir...?"

"Auron. And no, it has served me for many years. I know that somehow, through time, it will come back to me." Auron smiled, his golden eyes flaring.

Emerald saw a portal appear near her, swirling gently as the blue-gifted from the future began to cast their magics into it. An image appeared on the other side of the portal—a woman who looked like Ikaria, but with long black long hair and dark eyes. She bowed to Emerald.

"You also have Empress Ayera's sincerest gratitude," Auron said.

"Give her my regards," Emerald replied, gazing at the Empress in reverence, enthralled by her beauty.

"I will."

Several gifted walked by Auron and Emerald. They pushed a transparent magical barrier in the shape of a box, Ikaria inside of it. The box gleamed with orange, yellow, and violet magic. This had to be the enchantment that Geeta called out for, to create a magical barrier to hold the sorceress.

Ikaria flashed her violet eyes at Emerald, remaining silent. It was a look of understanding. In that moment, despite everything, they bonded through their loneliness, and the sorceress finally felt that someone understood her.

Emerald watched as the gifted led Ikaria's magical box to the portal. For a moment, Ikaria turned back to Emerald. "The dark magic... it takes what you love most and twists your desire into consumption, corrupting one's soul. It was no different with Derek," she said cryptically, not giving any more details. There was a hint of guilt in her voice, and she turned away, not giving Emerald the chance to see her expression.

To anyone else, it seemed sudden that the sorceress would tell her this. But Emerald knew exactly why she did so. Her words cut deep, making Emerald feel sick, sad, angry, and confused, all at once.

Pushing aside her feelings, Emerald angrily wiped fresh tears away, then cleansed the three gifted pushing the box. There was no need to cleanse Ikaria; her body and spirit had already been purified by Emerald's power.

The three gifted disappeared, along with Ikaria, into the portal. The Empress on the other side disappeared as well, but the portal remained open for the others to return to the future.

"Don't worry about Ikaria, Your Majesty. We will ensure that she is contained in our time. She won't be going anywhere, believe me," Auron promised, then bowed.

Emerald returned the favor, bowing back. "Thank you, Auron. I would say that I hope to see you again, but I am sure that our paths won't cross." Emerald felt saddened by the thought that she'd finally met others with the gift, but now she wouldn't be able to live out her time with them. Then her thoughts turned to Kyle, and her heart sunk in her chest.

"I am sure they won't. Good luck to you, Your Majesty," Auron said. "And again, I am truly sorry for your loss."

Emerald lowered her eyes, then nodded.

Auron stood before her, waiting to be cleansed. Holding out the staff, Emerald summoned her renewing power, cleansing Auron's blood. Her green light covered him for a moment, then dissipated. After his blood purification was complete, he walked through the portal, fading away.

When the last of the gifted were cleansed and the portal closed, Emerald saw Geeta alone on one end of the platform. She hugged herself, looking down at the city below.

Walking over to Kyle's lifeless body, Emerald clutched it, holding him in her arms once again, then began to cry. Sending one more burst of magic through herself to him, green magic flowed all around his corpse, encasing his body with an intense green light.

"Don't leave me, Kyle…" she whispered, tears falling upon his face. The glow of the magic faded away, and his body remained lifeless.

"Come back to me…"

CHAPTER 80

Two months later

Telly stepped out of her trailer, zipping up her jacket. The icy morning desert winds were chilly, much more than those in the high levels of Arcadia. Even after two months of living out in the desert, she still was not used to the extreme cold.

"Hey, Telly!" Garrett called out from across the camp. He waved at her, moving quickly toward her trailer.

"What is it?" Telly asked curiously, shoving her hands in her jacket pockets. Any bit of warmth she could get was welcome. Her hands were freezing.

"Reila found another cyborg! She sent communication that she's on her way back now."

Telly smiled. "Looks like there's more work to do."

"Every day, it keeps piling up on us." Garrett chuckled, then ran off.

Telly heard the door behind her creak open, then heavy footsteps. She had been working on it with Drew, his walking and his speech. One day, he would be close to what he was, almost fully human. Him and the other cyborgs. But Telly knew their rehabilitation process would take years.

"They found another one," Telly said out loud, filling Drew in.

Drew moved next to her silently, watching the pink sun slowly rise in the distance. Telly looked over at him, curious at his strange expression.

"What are you thinking about?" Telly asked, seeing the foreign emotion on his face.

"That… that I am happy."

Surprised, Telly raised an eyebrow at his response. "Happy? Out here in this freezing cold?"

He turned to her, his cybernetic eye flashing, his orange human eye watching her. He looked so human in that moment, like his old self. "Happy living with… with you and Gwen." Breaking the moment, he robotically turned back to stare at the sunset.

Stepping into him, Telly put her arms around his waist. "I love you, Drew," she whispered.

Drew never answered her back when she told him she loved him, but he always jolted right after. He was still trying to process his emotions, figuring out what it meant to be human. He would get there one day. Telly was sure of it.

Like Telly predicted, Drew jolted. Telly gave a soft laugh, elbowing him playfully.

Just then, the door behind them opened again, and Gwen popped out of the trailer.

"Hey, Mom. Hey, Dad," the teen said, skipping quickly down the steps and starting to run into the camp.

"Where are you going?" Telly demanded. "You can't just run off without telling anyone."

"But I did. I just told Dad inside before I left," Gwen argued. "I'm going to hang out with Garrett for a while. They found another cyborg, and we're going to run a diagnostic on it!" The teen waited for her, giving Telly big, expectant eyes.

Telly gave Drew the stink eye, and he stared in response, giving her a slightly innocent smile.

"Just because you are only half human doesn't mean you get out of this!" Telly scolded him, trying not to smirk. She turned to Gwen, calling out, "Go, have fun. Tell me what you find."

"Thanks, Mom!" Gwen called out, running off in the direction of Garrett's trailer.

When Gwen was out of sight, Drew put his arm around Telly's waist, holding her close. Surprised, Telly blushed.

The two of them stood staring into the morning sun, watching it rise to a new day.

***

Light flurries of snow filled Arcadia's daytime skies.

Emerald would have never guessed it was day seeing how the dark clouds covered the city. Snow hadn't fallen on Arcadia in over two hundred years, according to the records, and she personally had never seen it before.

As she watched the soft, white magic fill the sky, Emerald realized it was the first time she had felt her spirit uplifted since Kyle's death. The snow tickled her nose and dusted her eyelashes, giving her a sense of peace.

It had been two months since the battle, and she missed him terribly. Since then, her heart had sunk deep within her soul, never to experience joy. The days were dull, and the nights were painted in shades of gray. Nothing brought her happiness. Without him, Emerald felt an emptiness within her spirit, never to be replaced.

Emerald reached out a hand, feeling the light snowflakes as they fell onto the palm of her hand, then melted away. Looking at the city below, she saw Arcadia covered in white, the neon signs trying to light their way through the thick atmosphere. Even most of the public transports had ceased operations, as the city was not prepared for this type of weather.

The patio glass slid open, and Emerald heard footsteps approaching from behind her. Two steps, then the person hesitated.

Derek.

Ever since that day, he'd looked at her with eyes wounded with shame and remorse. Silently, his ice-blue eyes asked for cleansing, to be free of all magic, but Emerald would give him nothing. There was no room in her heart for him. He needed to live with the consequences of what he had done— inviting the sorceress to their time, taking over Arcadia, and putting the world in jeopardy.

And that night. That night would be forever ingrained in the back of her mind, haunting her thoughts. It pained her to remain married to Derek. She had no desire to be anywhere near him, and the thought of him being her husband angered her. But if she were to insist on a divorce, Arcadia would be solely his, as by law, her father had left the kingdom to him, not her. And Arcadia's citizens looked to her as their queen. She was only doing it for the good of the people. It was all she had left to live for—her kingdom and her people. Most of the time, Derek hid from her in council meetings or other busy work. But there were other times he did attempt to talk to her, and every time she was curt and short and spoke to him only if she had to.

"My queen," Derek's unsure voice called out from behind, "I was told you have been out here all day. I am would hate to see you fall into ill health." There was a hint of sadness in his voice, but also concern.

Without looking at him, she continued to stare at Arcadia's snowfall dusting the sky in white. "I am fine. You needn't worry about me," Emerald said matter-of-factly.

She heard him pause, then heard the rustling of his robe, and he bowed. "Yes, my queen." He turned and opened the door.

"Derek," Emerald called out, still staring into the white sky.

She heard him hold his breath. It was the first time she'd said his name in months.

"Yes?" he said quietly.

The snow continued to fall. It was almost like magic. Kyle's magic. Emerald recalled what the sorceress had told her about the power of the dark magic's stronghold. She paused, taking a deep breath, reflecting on the sorceress's words as her thoughts turned again to that fateful night.

"I don't know if I can ever forgive you," Emerald said with a quiet bitterness. "But I do know this: I will *never* forget." She turned to look at him, her eyes filled with snow and tears, her hot breath steaming through the cold air.

For a moment, Emerald thought he was going to say something, but instead he bowed and went inside quietly.

Emerald remained outside, letting the snow fall on her, imagining that Kyle's magic was blessing her, restoring her heart.

EPILOGUE

Don't leave me, Kyle, Emerald's gentle voice whispered. *Come back to me. I'm trying*, he thought. *The tide is too strong.*

The vibrant green lifestream was carrying him further down the flow of time as he fought against the roaring currents and high tides. It held him hostage, holding him under the raging green waters of time.

Two life-forms in the shape of embryos glowed with white light as they passed him by, flowing through the green world. Kyle felt a strong connection to one of them—it had his blood. But as quickly as he saw them, they were gone, disappearing into the rippling green waters that glimmered with glowing white-and-green sparkling orbs.

The bright-green current continued to push him further away from his destination. Emerald. The more he thought of Emerald, leaving her all alone in the world, the more he kept fighting the tide. And the more he fought, the more the stream pushed him. The flow was strong, and his soul couldn't overcome the lifestream's power.

I am lost, he told himself. *Lost in the sea of time.*

Come back to me. Her voice reverberated within his being, echoing in the lifestream. *Don't leave me, Kyle.*

I'm trying, his consciousness cried out to her. *Believe me, I am fucking trying!*

ACKNOWLEDGMENTS

First off, I just wanted to give a big thank-you to the readers who took a chance on a first-time author with a massive story. I'm no Hemingway, but I can tell a decent story, or at least that's what I tell myself so I can sleep at night.

An everlasting thank-you to my husband, who stuck by my side while I wrote this behemoth. There were many Saturdays he devoted to watching the kids while I pored through my manuscript. Without that time that he gave me, I would probably still be in the early stages of this story, and most likely this endeavor would have taken another year. My husband was my biggest inspiration in this story, whether he knows it or not. From the storms of life that we endured together to his love of motorcycles, familiarity of the high desert, and off-the-wall comments, they all made this story what it is today. He is my Kyle and true hero.

A special thank-you to those who have inspired me over the twenty years that this story has been brewing around in my head. To Billy Idol for his *Cyberpunk* album; a world unfolded in my mind every time I listened to that album. All of the songs on that album inspired me in one way or another. And to all of the old Shinder's crew from 1998–1999: Thank you for being there for me when I had no one else to turn to, and for opening my eyes to the whole underground punk scene. I don't need to name names; you all know who you are. You made a huge impact on my life.

I would also like to thank my two editors, Amy from Story Centric Editing for developmental editing and Crystal Watanabe from Pikko's House for copy and line editing. Amy navigated a story that was completely rough and helped me craft it into something special. Crystal completely understood my characters, and I absolutely love how she helped elevate my manuscript to the next level. There were times I sat and laughed at her comments (believe me, they were all good comments) due to her sense of humor. I am thankful to have met both these wonderful women who have strengthened my writing journey. Also, thank you to the two proofreaders from Pikko's House, Sarah and Cheryl, for finding all the little errors throughout the story. I am forever grateful to you both!

A wonderful thank-you to Mansik Yang (Yam) for doing the illustrations for my cover and character portraits. When Yam replied to my email inquiry for the project, I think I didn't sleep for a whole week—that's how excited I was. His level of detail never ceases to amaze me. The first time he sent over a black and white sketch of the novel cover, I cried. It was a special moment to see Yam capture the very essence of my characters. It was like he knew exactly what I was picturing in my head. I am truly blessed and humbled that he was able to contribute to this project.

Thank you to Jenny from Seedlings for laying out a kick ass cover, and to Doug for the awesome maps. You took my silly, nonsensical drawings and made it look freaking sick. You're the best!

I would also like to thank my alpha readers, Heather, Jessica, and my husband. I can't tell you how much incredible feedback I got from these three, who helped develop my story into what it is. Heather helped me make Kyle more loveable and had amazing feedback for almost every single character and plot point. Jessica gave me good insight into the story, especially with Derek's storyline. My husband evaluated the story from a male perspective, telling me what men would and wouldn't do and helped me understand how to ride a motorcycle.

I also want to thank my beta readers and readers who read snippets of my story to give me specific feedback, especially my multiple prologues (I had eight different ones written!). Air V, Devin, Lauren, Katie, and Kenneth. If I am forgetting anyone, please forgive me! I thank you, too!

Sending a quick shout-out to Brian Alvarez for naming Kyle's band.

And finally, a big thank-you to A Bunch of Lunatics and 200 Rogues, two writing groups that have given me so much support, and my friend David, who has supported me on my writing journey.

ABOUT THE AUTHOR

Beth Hodgson was born and raised in Minnesota. During her college years, she worked and went to school in downtown Minneapolis, the city that inspired the kingdom of Arcadia in *Fragments of Light*. She worked as a graphic artist and illustrator for several years, then switched industries to retail management in high fashion.

Currently, she is married and stays at home with her three young children and writes in her spare time. When not writing or hanging out with the family, Beth loves to make costumes, doodle her characters, and play *Skyrim* and *Hearthstone*. Her favorite color is violet, but she has a secret love for green.

Made in the USA
San Bernardino, CA
11 January 2019